ISBN 978-0-276-44453-1

www.readersdigest.co.uk

Published in the United Kingdom by Vivat Direct Limited (t/a Reader's Digest),
157 Edgware Road, London W2 2HR

# of love & life

Three novels selected and condensed
by Reader's Digest

Reader's
Digest

The Reader's Digest Association Inc., London

CONTENTS

To the moon and back

Jill Mansell

Ellie Kendall has never been so happy. She's married to Jamie, the love of her life, the most gorgeous man in the world, and every day with him is a joy.
But life is fickle and accidents happen and Ellie and Jamie's relationship is about to change irrevocably.

Chapter 1

'WHAT WOULD YOU DO without me?'

Fresh from the shower, Ellie took in the alluring view from the bedroom doorway. Seriously, could anything beat the sight of a drop-dead gorgeous 28-year-old male wearing nothing but white boxers while clutching a steam iron in one hand and a black skirt in the other?

And to think he's mine, all mine. She had the marriage certificate to prove it.

'OK, don't answer that, I know what you'd do.' Jamie bent down and unplugged the iron at the wall. 'Go out wearing a crumpled skirt.'

'Possibly.' She fastened the lime-green bath towel round her chest. 'But I don't have to, do I? Because I have you.' Reaching across the ironing board, she planted a kiss on the mouth she never tired of kissing.

'So you're grateful, then?' He gave the edge of the towel a playful tug.

'I am. Very grateful. Thank you, thank you to the moon and back.'

'Because if you feel like repaying the favour, I can probably think of a way you could do that.'

'But we don't have time. I need to get dressed and do my face . . . *wah*, no, stop it, get away from me!' She snatched the skirt and danced out of reach before Jamie could ravish her. Tonight they were going out separately. Along with a crowd of friends from work, she was heading off to a performance of *The Rocky Horror Show,* where dressing up was mandatory. Hence the black skirt, bought in a charity shop last year and cannibalised with garden shears to give it a zigzaggy hemline for a Halloween party. It would be just the thing for a Rocky Horror outing, teamed with mad hair, over-the-top eyeliner and fishnets.

'Right then, which shirt should I wear? Blue? Or white?' Jamie was off to a school reunion in Guildford.

Ellie said, 'How about the pink one?'

'I don't know. I'd rather wear the blue tonight.'

She took the fuchsia-pink shirt out of the wardrobe. 'But this is beautiful! Look at that *colour*. Why wouldn't you want to wear it?'

'Because I don't want everyone saying they didn't know I was gay.'

'Oh, come on! Just because it's pink?'

Jamie pulled a don't-make-me-say-it face. 'It's a very gay pink.'

'I bought it for you for Christmas! You could have taken it back to the shop.' Ellie shook her head in disbelief. 'But you said you loved it!'

'I didn't want to hurt your feelings. Besides,' Jamie ventured, 'I kind of like it to *look* at. Just not to, you know, *wear*.'

'The colour would really suit you.'

'I'll wear it soon, I promise.' He shrugged on the blue shirt.

'Right, that's it, wait until next Christmas. No presents, that'll teach you to turn your nose up at my choice of shirt.'

Jamie grinned. 'Does that mean I don't have to buy you anything?'

'You just wait. You'll be sorry. No, get off me!' Shrieking with laughter, Ellie found herself backed into a corner of the living room. 'I told you, we don't have *time*!'

Jamie snaked his arms round her waist and pulled her against him. 'Sometimes,' he murmured persuasively in her ear, 'you just have to get your priorities right and *make* time.'

DDDRRRINNNGGGGGG went the doorbell and Jamie clutched his heart, staggering backwards as if he'd been shot. 'No, no, not fair . . .'

'Oh, what a shame. Just as I was about to change my mind, too.' Skipping past him, Ellie went to the window and peered down to the pavement below. Todd waved up at her. She waved back.

'And to think he used to be my friend.' Jamie flung open the window and yelled, 'You're early.'

'I know. That's because you told me not to be late.'

Jamie rolled his eyes. 'The first time in twenty years he's been early for *anything*.' Raising his voice he called down, 'Look, we're kind of busy just now. How about doing us a big favour and just going for a ten-minute jog round the block?'

'Get lost!'

'Or that's something else you could do.'

'Not a chance. Stop buggering about and open the door.' Energetically stamping his feet and rubbing his hands together, Todd called up, 'It's arctic out here. I'm freezing my nuts off.'

'Look at you,' Todd marvelled, greeting Ellie with a kiss when she finally teetered out of the bedroom, dressed and ready to go. 'Understated. I like it. Off to church?'

'Ha ha.' She loved Todd, which was just as well, seeing as he was Jamie's best friend. For almost twenty years the two boys had been inseparable. Their personalities complemented each other and their shared sense of humour enabled them to bounce jokes off each other so effortlessly that they never tired of it.

'Right, are we ready?' Jamie was driving tonight; rattling his keys, he ushered them towards the door. 'Let's go. Where are we dropping you?'

Ellie gave her backcombed hair one last blast of glitter spray for luck. 'Just at the tube station. Everyone's meeting at the Frog and Bucket.'

'You're not going on the tube on your own dressed like that,' Jamie said as she headed past them down the stairs. 'We'll give you a lift to the pub.'

'Pleurgh.' Todd smacked his lips together in dismay. 'I've got hairspray in my mouth.'

'Open wide.' Peering in, Ellie said, 'Whoops, there's glitter in there.'

Jamie grinned. 'That's so when he meets up with the girls he used to fancy at school, he'll be able to make sparkling conversation.'

Ellie brushed a speck of glitter from Todd's cheek. 'God help those poor girls.'

By the time Ellie arrived back at their Hammersmith flat it was almost one o'clock. You knew you'd had a good old Rocky Horror night when your throat was sore from singing and the soles of your feet were on fire. Throughout the show they'd jumped up and joined in with the dancing, bellowing out the words to the songs they knew off by heart.

'That's ten pounds fifty, love.'

She paid the taxi driver, clambered out of the cab and looked around to see if Jamie was home yet. No sign of the car, but he might have had to park round the corner. And the windows were in darkness, but that could mean he was crashed out in bed.

Letting herself into the flat, Ellie felt the stillness and knew she was the first one home. OK, that was fine, she was still buzzing with adrenalin. If Jamie came back soon she might seduce him, make up for what they'd missed out on earlier thanks to Todd's untimely arrival. Toddus Interruptus, ha. Their very own living, breathing contraceptive. She smiled to herself and switched on the light in the living room. She'd make a toasted sandwich and put on a DVD. Oh, the light was flashing on the phone. She pressed the button and listened to the message.

'Hey, Jamie, what's going *onnnn*? It's Rodders here, man. What happened to you and Todd, eh? You said you'd be here. Give us a bell, mate. You missed a cracking night.'

The call ended. That was it. Rodders was Rod Johnson, who had organised the school reunion in Guildford. And he had made the call an hour ago, which made no sense at all unless Jamie and Todd had arrived at the event early, decided it looked like rubbish and beaten a stealthy retreat. Because what other explanation could there be?

Ellie fumbled in her bag for her phone, switched off since they'd entered the theatre five hours ago. Seven missed calls. One message. Her heart juddering, Ellie experienced split-screen consciousness. One half of her brain was telling her that this couldn't be happening, there'd been some mistake, and any minute now Jamie would be home.

Yet somehow, simultaneously, the other half of her brain was listening to a calm female voice relaying the message that Jamie Kendall had been involved in a road traffic accident and could she please call this number as soon as possible . . .

And now the ground was tipping and another voice, a male one this time, was advising her to make her way to the Royal Surrey County Hospital in Guildford. Jamie was currently in a critical condition, the voice on the phone explained and he was in the process of being transferred from casualty to the intensive-care unit.

The sound of the heart monitor filled Ellie's ears. As long as it kept on doing it, everything would be all right. With every fibre of her being, she willed the bipping not to stop.

It was four o'clock in the morning but the intensive-care unit was flooded with blue-white light. Most of the nursing staff were busy working on an elderly patient at the other end of the ward. Ellie shut out the noise they were making. She had to concentrate all her attention on the bips. And on Jamie, who was lying on the bed looking like a life-sized waxwork model of himself.

How can this be happening? How can it?

The left side of Jamie's head was swollen and purplish-blue. He was unresponsive, in a deep coma. His skin was warm but when she held his hand he didn't curl his fingers round hers. Saying his name provoked no reaction. For God's sake, he wasn't even able to breathe on his own. A ventilator was doing the job for him. Every function was electronically monitored. It looked like something out of a film but with ultra-realistic special effects. Except it was real.

Time to phone Jamie's dad. Oh God, how was she going to tell him about this? But she had to. On wobbly legs, Ellie made her way outside. The subzero temperatures gripped her and her teeth began to rattle. The ground was slick with frost, the puddles were frozen. How had Jamie felt as the car had begun to skid on the ice? She couldn't bear to think about it, but she couldn't *stop* thinking about it.

OK, just do it, call Tony in LA. Would he be able to come over or would he have filming commitments he couldn't get out of?

Ellie's hands shook as she found the number on her phone. Right, just press Call. Do it. Moments later she heard his familiar voice at the other end of the line. *Do it now.*

'Tony?' Aware that she was about to break his heart, her voice cracked with grief. 'Oh Tony, I'm so sorry. There's been an accident . . .'

Making her way back into the intensive-care unit, Ellie sat in the chair beside Jamie's bed. *Oh Jamie, wake up, please just open your eyes and tell me everything's going to be all right.*

Two new patients arrived, a skeletal yellow-tinged woman and a teenage boy. Relatives sobbed round their beds and looked strangely at Ellie in her jagged short skirt and fishnets. When none of the nurses had been looking she had kissed Jamie's face but it hadn't felt remotely like his face and now he had bits of glitter on his forehead and cheek.

'Sorry about the glitter,' Ellie told the nurse when she came to do his obs.

'It doesn't matter a bit. We'll just wipe it off with some damp cotton wool, shall we, so it doesn't get into his eyes. Now, do you want me to see if we've got some spare clothes you can change into, or can you call a friend to bring something in?'

It still felt like the middle of the night, but the clock on the wall showed it was nine thirty. And it was light outside. With a jolt, Ellie realised she was supposed to be at work.

'Um, I'll call a friend.'

Outside again, she rang work. Paula answered the phone and let out a squeal of mock indignation. 'You lazy bum, I had way more to drink than you last night and *I* managed to get in here on time!'

'Oh Paula, I'm at the hospital and I need you to h-help me . . .'

Hollow-eyed with lack of sleep, Ellie stayed at Jamie's bedside. Doctors came and went. Various medical tests were carried out. Paula arrived in a taxi and floods of horrified tears, with a change of clothes and toiletries. Not allowed into the unit, she clutched Ellie's hands and kept sobbing, 'You poor thing, I can't *believe* it,' and, 'He's going to be all right though, isn't he? I mean, he's not going to die?'

Numbly, Ellie submitted to the hugs. It was a relief when Paula finally left. All she wanted was to get back to Jamie and listen to the bips.

More hours passed, then the nurse came and told her that Todd was outside. This time, in lieu of family and because he was Jamie's oldest and closest friend, the nurses agreed to let him onto the ward.

Ellie's stomach clenched at the sight of Todd as he made his way over to the bed. There were cuts and bruises on his head and hands; kept in overnight for observation, he was limping but otherwise OK. He put his arms round her but she felt herself shrink away. She didn't want to be touched and hugged; her skin was too sensitive. It was like having flu, when it hurt even to brush your hair. How could two people be in the same car, in the same car crash, and one of them escape with scarcely any injuries at all? It was unfair. Fond though she was of Todd, why did it have to be Jamie lying unconscious in the bed?

Sitting back down, Ellie watched him rest a hand on Jamie's bare shoulder. A muscle jumped in his jaw as he gazed at his best friend.

'How did it happen?' Ellie asked.

'I don't know.' A helpless shrug. 'We weren't going too fast. The car just took a bend and went into a skid. It was like slow motion, but kind of speeded up at the same time. I said, "Oh shit," and Jamie said, "Oh fuck."' His knuckles turning white with the effort of holding back the tears, Todd said, 'We didn't even know there was ice on the road until it was too late.' His voice broke. 'And then we just . . . *went.*'

Todd left. More tests were carried out. Night came and so did Jamie's father. Calling the unit, Tony informed them that he had just landed at Heathrow and was on his way to the hospital. The nurse who spoke to him recognised his voice and put two and two together. Within minutes, word had spread that Jamie was the son of Tony Weston . . . you know, *the actor.* Behind the professional exteriors, excitement grew. Watching them, clutching at straws, Ellie wondered if this meant they would somehow make more of an effort to help Jamie recover.

Forty minutes later, Tony appeared. In his mid fifties, tanned and handsome, he was immediately recognisable to the staff as the respected actor who had moved to America and made his name as the quintessential upper-class Englishman, despite having been born and raised on a council estate in Basingstoke. If everyone else on the unit was discreetly thrilled to be seeing him in the flesh, Ellie felt only relief. She no longer had to be the one in charge. Jamie's dad was here and he was a proper grown-up. Tears of exhaustion leaked out of her eyes as he hugged her.

'Oh, sweetheart.' It was all Tony said, all he needed to say. Turning his attention to Jamie, he gazed at him in silence and seemed to vibrate with pain. Finally he murmured, 'Oh, my baby boy,' and his voice cracked with grief.

The consultant materialised within minutes and introduced himself. Ellie watched him carry out the various neurological tests the doctors had been performing at regular intervals since Jamie's arrival in the unit. She studied the expression on the man's face, searching for clues. Finally the consultant turned to face them, and Ellie felt as if her chair had been abruptly pulled away. A great rushing sound filled her ears. Next to her, Tony was shaking his head slightly but the rest of his body had turned to stone.

Don't do this, please don't say it, Jamie might hear you . . .

'I'm so very sorry,' the consultant said, 'but the tests are conclusive. There is no remaining cerebral function.' He paused. 'Do you understand what that means?'

No, no, nooooooo . . .

'You're telling us his brain is dead.' There was a world of agony in Tony's words. 'He's gone. My boy's gone.'

The consultant inclined his head in agreement. 'I'm afraid he has.'

Chapter 2

Fifteen months later

'Look, are you sure you don't fancy the cinema?' It was Friday, it was five o'clock and Paula was clearing the debris from her office desk. 'Because if you want to come along, we'd love to have you with us.'

Ellie was touched; it was thoughtful of Paula to make the offer, but she wouldn't dream of taking her up on it. Paula had only been seeing Dan for three weeks but it was obvious that she was besotted.

'Thanks, but I'm fine. I want to get to B&Q and pick up some wallpaper.' Did that sound boring? Oh well, never mind, dull but true.

Paula paused and gave her the sympathetic look she'd come to know so well. Then she said brightly, 'Well, that'll be nice, won't it? When it's done, I mean. Is this for the living room?'

Ellie nodded. There was black mould growing on the living-room walls. Since scrubbing it off and painting over it hadn't worked, covering the whole lot with wallpaper appeared to be the next logical step.

'Well, look, if you want some help with that tomorrow, me and Dan could come over and give you a hand if you like.'

Grateful for the offer, Ellie gave her a hug. 'I won't be doing any tomorrow. Tony's over for a few days and he's taking me out to lunch.'

'He is? Oh, you lucky thing!' Then she winced and clapped her hand over her mouth. 'God, sorry. I'm so stupid!'

It had happened dozens of times. No matter how often Ellie told her to stop worrying about it and apologising, Paula kept on doing it. At work, everyone did; it was a kind of Pavlovian reaction they couldn't control.

'Anyway, I am lucky. We're meeting at the Ivy.'

'Wow.'

'Meeting at the Ivy, eating at McDonald's.'

Paula's eyes widened. 'Really?'

So sweet, so well-meaning, so easy to tease. 'No, not really.' Ellie relented with a smile. 'We'll probably have lunch at the Ivy too.'

'**B**loody . . . bloody . . . *bloody* useless stuff . . .' By midnight Ellie was ready to murder the wallpaper. Hanging on to the stepladder and jabbing wildly at the top right-hand corner of the length she'd been battling to hang for the last forty minutes, she had no hands free to prevent the adjoining section from unpeeling itself and rolling down the wall.

'Right, that's it, I've had enough of you!' Let it all fall down if that's what it wanted to do. Leave it, just step away from the carnage and get a KitKat out of the fridge instead.

Returning from the kitchen, Ellie turned her back on the desperate scene—it had *all* unpeeled itself now—and threw herself down on the sofa. She unwrapped the KitKat and began flicking through the TV channels. Ooh lovely, *Sleepless in Seattle*, how long had it been on?

Then Jamie came into the living room and joined her on the sofa. He was wearing his old jeans and the pink shirt he'd refused to put on for his school reunion. He wore it a lot these days. Ellie loved to see him in it and she'd been right about the colour, it *was* great on him.

'Great job with the wallpapering.' He grinned at her.

'I know. I'm brilliant.' Ellie took in every detail of his face, the sparkling blue eyes, the sun-streaked blond hair, the golden tan.

'You should turn professional. You know what this is, don't you?' Jamie nodded seriously, indicating the bare walls, the crumpled, fallen-down paper. 'It's post-modern shabby chic.'

'If you'd given me a hand I might have had more luck,' said Ellie.

He smiled sadly. 'Oh sweetheart, I would if I could. You know that.'

Ellie felt the familiar prickle of heat behind her eyes. Of course she knew that. They'd worked so hard together to make this flat their own. And she *wasn't* going to cry. 'OK, that's enough, you can go now. I'm going to watch this film.'

'Is it a slushy girlie film?'

He knew her so well. Ellie nodded. 'Oh yes.'

Jamie held up his hands in horror. 'I'll leave you to it. Bye, gorgeous.'

But the film wasn't able to hold her attention tonight. After ten minutes Ellie switched off the TV. She could get Jamie back, but she wouldn't. It was starting to concern her, just slightly, that it wasn't quite normal to be doing what she'd been doing for the last year. Because Jamie wasn't here any more. And he wasn't a ghost either. All she did was conjure up a mental image of him in her mind, talk to him and have him talk back as if he were real. Imagining that Jamie was still around, she had discovered, was actually a really comforting thing to do. It just made her feel . . . *better*.

She missed Jamie so much she sometimes wondered how she'd managed to carry on, but it had been fifteen months now, and one way or another she had. Maybe she was going a bit batty, conjuring Jamie up and having imaginary conversations with him, but it was her coping mechanism and she wasn't ready to give it up yet.

Ellie always looked forward to her lunches with Jamie's dad when he came over to England. They had each lost the most important person in their lives, and their meetings could so easily have been morbid, but Tony never allowed that to happen. Obviously the grief was still there but, in public at least, it wasn't dwelt on. Instead they talked about Jamie, celebrating his memory and recalling happier times. They laughed a lot, ate well, generally ended up sinking a couple of bottles of wine, and ended up coming away with precious snippets of information they hadn't known before about the boy they'd both loved.

This was the best bit; it was like discovering buried treasure. Today, amid the busy, buzzy atmosphere of the Ivy, Tony had already regaled her with the story of Jamie's sixth birthday party, when one of the young girls had demanded a kiss in return for giving him his present and Jamie, utterly horrified, had promptly handed the gift back.

'He was never that wild about social kissing.' Ellie grinned, the tale triggering a memory of her own. 'The first time he met the girls from work, one of them gave him a kiss on the cheek at the end of the evening and you should have seen the look on his face. You'd think she'd *licked* him.'

'Speaking of which, anything happening in that direction?'

It wasn't the first time Tony had broached the subject. He raised his eyebrows, nodding meaningfully to indicate that he was talking about her. Specifically, had she kissed or been kissed by another man yet?

'No, no. Nothing.' Ellie shook her head.

'It'll happen.' His smile was reassuring. 'Sooner or later.'

Later, then. She wasn't remotely ready for anything like that. Apart from anything else, what if Jamie was watching her from somewhere, like through celestial CCTV? *What if he didn't approve?*

Ellie dipped a tiger prawn in hollandaise. 'I know. But not yet.'

Effortlessly changing the subject, Tony took a sip of white wine and said, 'How's the flat? Did those noisy neighbours of yours move out?'

'Oh yes. Two weeks ago, thank God.' She smiled and didn't elaborate; he didn't need to know that the replacements were shaping up to be a hundred times worse. The last family had played Eminem pretty loudly, quite often. The new lot made them look like rank amateurs. In the last fortnight there had been half a dozen major fights, the police had been round most nights, and the family's dogs barked nonstop. Worst of all, Eminem had been replaced by Celine Dion and Josh Groban.

Zack McLaren had arranged this lunch meeting with the director of an IT company he might soon be doing lucrative business with. Normally he was able to concentrate on the subject in hand with no difficulty, but today was proving to be different. Earlier, as he'd been standing outside the restaurant taking a phone call, a girl in a pink coat had caught his eye as she headed down the street towards him. Her hair was long and dark, her eyes light brown, her cheeks rosy, and the effect she'd had on him was extraordinary; he couldn't stop looking at her. Whoever she was, he wanted to know more. Heavens, what a weird feeling; he'd never experienced anything like this before.

As she passed him, Zack caught a waft of her perfume, something fresh and herby. He turned, watching the back view of her glossy hair, fitted pink coat and long legs in black tights. Incredible legs, actually. His heart, unbelievably, was thudding in his chest. She was heading into the Ivy . . . Hurriedly ending his call, Zack followed her inside. Just in time to see her being warmly greeted by someone he did recognise.

Now, an hour and a half later, he was still struggling to pay attention to what his lunch companion was saying. Across the room sat the girl, now minus her pink coat and wearing a thin wool dress the colour of Parma violets. If she'd been having lunch with a female friend, he would have approached her, introduced himself, said something—God only knows what, he'd never done anything like that before in his life—and asked if he could call her, found out if she would like to have dinner with him.

Except she wasn't with a girlfriend, was she? Instead she was having a lovely entertaining lunch with the actor Tony Weston. They were chatting together, laughing a lot, clearly well acquainted and enjoying each other's company. Which meant any form of approach wasn't likely to be appreciated. Instead, he was stuck over here while the company director sitting opposite him droned on about financial forecasts and—

'So what do you think about that, then?'

Shit. Typical. Zack snapped his attention back to the reason he'd come along to the Ivy today. Well, the original reason.

'I think it's . . . interesting.' He nodded thoughtfully.

'And what's the verdict? Do we have a deal?'

'Ian, I can't come to a decision today.' Chiefly because he hadn't the faintest idea what Ian had been saying for the last hour. 'I need to go over the figures again, have a word with a couple of other people. But I'll get back to you by Monday afternoon, and that's a promise.'

Ian sat back, took a swallow of water and shot him a suspicious look. 'Everything OK? You seem a bit . . . distant today.'

What would Ian say if he were to tell him, if he leaned across the table and said, 'The thing is, there's a girl over there, a complete stranger, but just looking at her is making me feel like I've never felt before in my life'? How would bluff, ruddy-faced Ian react to that?

'I'm fine. Just a touch of jet lag.' He flashed a reassuring smile at Ian.

By the time they left the restaurant it was three-thirty. Out on West Street, Tony flagged down a taxi and Ellie gave him a hug.

'Thanks so much for lunch. It's lovely to see you again.'

He opened the cab door. 'Hop in. I'll drop you home.'

'But it's out of your way. I'm fine, I can get the tube.'

'It's raining. Let me give you a lift.' Indicating that she should climb in ahead of him, he added, 'Please?'

OK, he was right about the rain. It was starting to come down more heavily now too. She gave in gracefully and climbed into the cab. It wasn't until they were on their way to Hammersmith that Tony said, 'Besides, I want to see this wallpapering disaster of yours.'

'Oh no, you can't come in!' The words burst out before she could stop them. Each time she and Tony had met up over the past fifteen months, it had been in restaurants. He hadn't visited the flat for almost two years. Ellie knew he'd be shocked by the state of it now.

'That's not very friendly,' Tony observed mildly.

'I'm sorry, I don't mean it like that.' She shook her head, ashamed. 'It's just . . . you know, messy.'

He smiled. 'You mean there's washing-up in the sink?'

'It's worse than that.' Ellie felt her cheeks flush. 'The whole place is, oh God, it's all just a bit . . . yuck. I'd really rather you didn't come in.'

But Tony Weston hadn't got where he was today by giving up easily. He patted her hand and said, 'I'm not going to judge you, sweetheart. I just want to have a look at this troublesome wallpaper of yours.'

Jesus,' said Tony. 'So this is why you didn't want me here.'

'Yes, well. Now you know.' Mortified and ashamed of herself for having put up with it for so long, Ellie watched him pace round the living room. A year ago, her lovely gentle landlady, Moira, had died, leaving her son to take over the property portfolio. Less than lovely Ron had wasted no time at all filling the flats with dubious characters.

As if to prove it, what sounded like a rugby scrum was currently taking place in the flat upstairs. On bare floorboards, because their putrid carpet was currently occupying the table-sized front garden. Josh Groban was belting out something heartfelt at maximum volume. The two dogs were going mad. The matriarch of the family, a fifty-something woman with a face like a bulldog and a voice like a cement mixer, was roaring, 'If you two fookers don't fookin' stop that, I'll chuck youse through the fookin' window.'

'Is she talking to the dogs?' said Tony.

'Maybe. Or her sons. There are four of them.'

'And get out the way of the TV, ya fookin' junkies!'

'That'll be the two youngest boys,' Ellie explained.

'This is diabolical.' Tony was outraged.

Tony surveyed the bare wall she'd been working on last night. 'If you managed to put wallpaper over that mould it'd fall down again in no time. For crying out loud, this place is a health hazard. Haven't you asked the landlord to get it sorted out?'

Only about a million times. But why would he bother? Ellie knew Ron wanted her out; packing another family in here would allow him to crank the rent right up. She shrugged and said, 'I have asked, but—'

Peering down at the tiny front garden, most of which was taken up with spilled-open bin bags and stained carpet, Tony said in disbelief, 'There are syringes lying in the mud.'

'I know.' Ellie's neck prickled again, as ashamed as if she'd thrown them there herself.

'Ellie, in God's name, why didn't you tell me it was like this?'

She shrugged, unable to explain. On the scale of misery, losing Jamie had been a ten. Compared with that, having to tolerate undesirable neighbours had barely scraped a two. And if that made her sound ridiculous, well, too bad. 'You get used to it. It's just noise.'

'There are used syringes in your front garden. This flat should carry a government health warning. You can't stay here.'

'Fook off, ya gobshite, that's me last can!'

Ellie knew he was right. But this was where she and Jamie had lived together. They had found the flat, moved into it as ridiculously happy newlyweds, loved and laughed and had the best time here for over three years. The rooms were filled with memories and she didn't know if she could bear to leave them behind . . .

'OK, I'm not completely stupid.' Tony's voice softened as her eyes filled with tears. 'This is about Jamie, isn't it?'

Her throat had constricted. 'Yes.'

'So the flat didn't used to be like this. But it is now.'

She nodded.

'If Jamie could see this place now, he'd be horrified.' Tony's manner was gentle but firm. 'He'd want you out of here.'

'Owwwww, ya bastard, I'll fookin' get you for that!' There was a roar, a crash and a shower of glass rained past the window, along with a spraying, somersaulting can of Tennent's Extra.

Three days after their lunch at the Ivy, Ellie found herself standing outside an imposing Victorian end-of-terrace property on Nevis Street, just off Regent's Park Road, in the heart of Primrose Hill village. The outside of the house was painted palest yellow, the sash windows were framed in white gloss and the front garden was small but well tended, without a manky discarded carpet in sight. This was a Seriously Nice Area.

'Well?' Tony stood next to her. 'What do you think?'

'Honestly? I feel sick. I can't believe you're doing this.'

'Listen, I'm not doing it for you. It's a sound financial investment. Every time I come over to the UK, I stay in a hotel. It's a very nice hotel, but it isn't home.' Indicating the building in front of them, he said, 'I need a pied-à-terre, and this looks pretty good to me. But if it's going to be standing empty most of the time, my insurance premiums will shoot up.

And I'll spend all my time worrying about squatters. Whereas if I have someone living in the place, keeping an eye on things, I won't have anything to worry about. Makes sense to me.'

The estate agent arrived and let them in to the first-floor flat. There were two good-sized bedrooms, each with a bathroom en suite. There was also a small third bathroom, a huge airy living room and an ultra-modern kitchen. It was like something out of a glossy magazine.

'No mould,' Tony pointed out. 'No damp. No Celine Dion.'

'Just as she was starting to grow on me,' said Ellie.

'Do you like it?'

'Of course I like it.' She shoved her hands into the pockets of her red jacket to hide the fact that they were trembling.

'Could we have a moment?' Tony waited until the estate agent had left them alone. 'Sweetheart, now listen to me. I can afford it. We'd be doing each other a favour.' He paused. 'James was my only child. What else am I supposed to do with my money?'

Ellie nodded. 'I know, and I'm grateful. But . . . it feels like too much.'

'OK, how about this then? Say I buy the flat anyway. And you don't move in, and squatters take over the place, and they wreck it and cause all kinds of trouble and end up bringing down the whole neighbourhood.' He shrugged. 'If that happens, it'll be all your fault. Everyone in Primrose Hill will hate you.'

She smiled. 'No pressure, then. Um, can I meet you downstairs in a couple of minutes? I'd just like to have another look around on my own.'

Tony followed the estate agent down the stairs. She knew she was being ridiculous, but it was something she just needed to double-check. Ellie closed her eyes, concentrated hard, then opened them again.

'Oh ye of little faith,' said an amused voice behind her.

Turning, she saw Jamie leaning against the closed living-room door.

'Did you seriously think I wouldn't turn up?'

She exhaled with relief. 'I just wanted to make sure.'

'Well, I'm here.' He spread his arms. 'Ta-daaa!'

Ellie searched his face. 'So what do you think?'

'About this place? It's fantastic.'

'Should I say yes, then?'

'I think you'd be stupid to say no,' said Jamie.

Which was cheating really, because the words were coming from her brain. She was making him say them. Oh well. He didn't seem to mind.

'Right then.' She nodded. 'I'm going to do it.'

Jamie winked and gave her the kind of encouraging smile she missed the most. 'Good.'

'God, look at this place, it's like a dream come true, you're so lucky . . . oh no! Sorry!' Paula clapped her hands over her mouth. 'I've done it again, you're not lucky at all. Ow.'

'From now on, every time you say sorry I'm going to have to hit you over the head with a cushion.' Ellie put the grey velvet cushion back on the sofa and gave it a little house-proud pat. Had it only been a month since she'd come along with Tony and seen the flat for the first time? Here she was in her new home, surrounded by packing cases and so far not missing the old Hammersmith flat at all.

Well, it had only been three hours.

'OK, tell me what to do.' Paula made a show of rolling up her sleeves and looking efficient. 'I want to help. Shall we start on these?' Without waiting for an answer, she ripped the tape off one of the boxes and said, 'Just let me know where you want everything to go . . . oh . . . oh no, are these Jamie's?' Appalled, she hurriedly bundled the armful of shirts and sweaters back into the box. 'I'm sorry, I didn't mean it! I didn't know!'

Paula left at five. Between them they had done a fair amount of unpacking, and it had been kind of her to give up her day off to come over and help. Ellie was grateful, but it had also been kind of exhausting. Emotional, softhearted Paula had welled up when she unwrapped a silver photo frame containing a picture of Ellie and Jamie on their honeymoon in Cornwall. She'd wailed, 'Oh God, how can you *bear* it?'

Ellie had found herself, not for the first time, having to comfort Paula. Not even for the hundredth time, come to that.

The next morning Ellie didn't wake up until gone eleven, partly because she was exhausted but chiefly because her alarm clock was still packed away. The good news was that she had three days off work, so it didn't matter. In her white towelling dressing gown, she sipped a mug of tea and stood at the window gazing across the street. The sun was shining, glinting off the polished windows of the houses opposite. Tiny wrought-iron balconies bore pot plants, and well-tended window boxes abounded. Even the air seemed cleaner here in Primrose Hill.

A taxi drew up, an emerald-green front door swung open and a blonde raced out of the house opposite. For a moment Ellie thought it was a skinny boy in a white T-shirt and low-slung combats with his hair bleached silver-white and cut in a super-short, choppy crop. But no, it was a female; when the figure turned, she saw the bright red lipstick, dangling earrings and jewel-encrusted shoulder bag.

As Ellie watched, the girl suddenly screeched to a halt, signalled to the cab driver to wait, let herself back into the house and reappeared twenty seconds later triumphantly waving her mobile phone and slamming the door shut behind her. Then she threw herself into the back of the cab and disappeared off up the road. Leaving something small and glittery swinging from the lock on the front door. Whoops.

Were the residents of Primrose Hill really as relaxed about security as those in village communities in the nineteen fifties?

Just in case they weren't, Ellie left her coffee mug on the windowsill, fastened the tie belt on her dressing gown, ran downstairs to the ground floor and let herself out. Better safe than sorry.

The tarmac was cold beneath her bare feet as she hurried across the road. A passing teenager in a grey hoodie, having also spotted the keyring dangling from the lock, had abandoned his bike on the pavement and was heading for the emerald-green front door.

Ellie sprinted past him and snatched the keys a millisecond before he could reach them. Looked like Primrose Hill wasn't so different from Hammersmith after all. Startled, the boy blurted out, 'I wasn't going to do anything, honest. I'd've taken them to the police station.'

He was pale, spiky haired, radiating guilt.

'Of course you were. But it's OK, you don't need to now.' Flashing him a cool smile, Ellie dropped the keys into her pocket. She turned triumphantly to cross the road. Ha, get her, less than a day in Nevis Street and already a pillar of the community! If she hadn't intervened, the girl over the road could have come home to a furniture-free house.

Ellie let herself back into her own flat. Upstairs, she showered and dressed in black jeans, charcoal sweatshirt and pink flip-flops. Before getting on with the unpacking she wrote a note, searched and failed to find any Sellotape and ended up using the next best thing. Heading once more across the road, she unpeeled the backing off the Elastoplast and stuck the note securely to the doorbell.

Pleased with her own ingenuity, she then returned to her flat.

By three thirty Ellie had a collection of cardboard boxes, emptied and collapsed and ready to go out for recycling. Twenty minutes later, in the middle of a complicated battle to get the cover on her duvet, the doorbell rang. Ellie prepared a cheery smile and went to answer it.

'Hi, you've got my keys?' The voice over the intercom was breathless.

'Oh hello. Yes, I have! I'll just press the buzzer and you can come on up. You'll have to excuse the mess, I only moved in yesterday so it's—'

'Sorry, but I'm in a real rush, could you just chuck them down?'

Oh. Oh. Put out, Ellie took her finger off the buzzer and went over to the living-room sash window. Pushing up the lower half, she leaned out and saw the girl with the cropped white-blond hair waiting impatiently on the pavement. The moment she spotted Ellie, she held out her arms and yelled, 'I'll catch them. Quick!'

The keys were on the coffee table, held together by a multicoloured Swarovski crystal keyring. Ellie threw them down to the girl, who let out a shriek as they scooted into the road, inches from the drain.

When she'd retrieved them, she called out, 'Cheers, you're a star,' before hurrying past the waiting taxi and letting herself into the house.

Never mind thank you. Oh well.

Ellie exhaled and went back to the bedroom to resume her fight with the duvet. Five minutes later the phone rang in the living room. As she answered it she saw the blonde girl emerge from her house once more, now wearing a bright red dress and matching stilettos. She dived into the taxi without so much as a glance up at her window.

That evening the emptiness closed in, and even a visit from Jamie didn't help.

'You've hardly eaten all day,' he pointed out in that maddening way of his. 'Come on, cheer up. Make some pasta or something.'

She looked at him. 'Don't tell me what to do.'

'I'm just making a suggestion. You could do that sauce I used to like.'

Ellie's stomach rumbled. He was nagging her, but he had a point. She made the tomato and red wine sauce, and left it to simmer on the hob. God, there was nothing to watch on television. She felt herself weakening, her eyes drifting over to the box of DVDs pushed up against the wall.

She sorted through the DVDs, found the one she wanted. Was this cathartic or a form of self-torture? Putting the box of tissues within easy reach, she pressed *Play* and sat back to watch Jamie and herself on the beach in Cornwall two years ago. Not imaginary Jamie, *real* Jamie, actually on the TV screen, captured by Todd with his camcorder. Back when life had been normal and happy.

Bbbbbrrrrrrrbbbbb.

The doorbell. At eleven thirty at night. In disbelief, Ellie clambered off the sofa and went over to the intercom. Curtly she said, 'Yes?'

'Are you awake?'

She closed her eyes. 'What?'

'Sorry, I know it's kind of late. I saw your light was still on. You weren't asleep, were you?'

'No.'

'Oh good. Now listen, was I a bit rude earlier?'

Ellie listened to the anxiety in the girl's voice. 'Possibly, yes, a bit.'

'Oh bugger, I knew it! Did I not even say thank you for my keys?'

'Now you come to mention it, no, you didn't.'

'OK, so will you let me tell you why? The thing is, I was so bursting for the loo that I thought my bladder was going to *explode*. I could hardly speak, let alone make it up your stairs. So that's why I forgot to thank you. And I'm really, really sorry if you thought I was rude.'

Ellie smiled and felt herself relax. 'Apology accepted.'

'Hooray!' The girl gave a little whoop of relief. 'I've got something for you, too. OK if I come up?'

'Only if you think your bladder can stand it.'

Having pressed the buzzer, Ellie opened the door and waited for her visitor to appear. Within seconds the girl with the cropped white-blonde hair came clattering up the stairs.

'Hi, I'm Roo! I bought you a little thank-you present. Only from the late-night supermarket, but everywhere else was shut.' Up close, she was tanned and goosepimply in her strappy red dress, bare legs and sky-scraper heels. Bursting into the flat, she said, 'Ooh, smells nice in here,' before dumping her carrier bags on the coffee table and pulling out two bunches of bright orange roses. 'These are for you.'

'Thanks.' Ellie was touched by the gesture. 'You didn't need to.'

'Shut up. Here, this is for you too.' With a flourish she produced a bottle of Chablis followed by a box of chocolate truffles. 'And these.'

Ellie shook her head. 'This is way too much.'

'It isn't, it's to say sorry and thanks.'

There was something weirdly familiar about her voice. Puzzling to work out where she might have heard it before, Ellie picked up the chilled bottle. 'We can open this now if you like.'

'Fab, I love it when people say that!' Eagerly Roo followed her into the kitchen. 'Ooh, pasta sauce. That smells fantastic.'

Her voice was still ringing bells. Now, covertly studying her face, Ellie really felt they'd met before. Probably in her early thirties, slim and toned and with huge dark eyes dominating a heart-shaped face, Roo was strikingly pretty beneath the layers of make-up . . .

'Ah, the cogs are turning.' Roo took the corkscrew from her and began energetically uncorking the bottle. 'Managed to figure it out yet?'

'Oh God, now I'm embarrassed. I *knew* I knew you from somewhere.' Time for a wild stab. 'OK, I work at Brace House Business Centre in Twickenham. Are you one of our clients?'

'Nope.'

Damn. 'Um, let me think . . . have you ever worked in a shop?'

'No, thank God. Way too much like hard work.' Roo sloshed wine into two glasses.

'OK, let me think.' Ellie was floundering. 'Dentist's surgery? Hospital? Hairdresser? Or did we meet at a party? Ooh, ever been to the Frog and Bucket in Fulham?'

'No, and I never want to. Sounds too slimy for words.'

'Sorry, then. You'll have to give me a clue.'

Roo clinked her glass cheerfully against Ellie's. 'OK, picture me with long black hair down to *here*. On TV. Prancing around in a sequinned boob tube,' she added, 'while miming badly into a microphone.'

'Oh my God, I've got it! You're one of the Deevas!' OK, even more embarrassing; they'd never met before, she'd just seen Roo on TV.

'Don't feel bad. I prefer it when people don't recognise me.' Roo tweaked her spiky white-blonde fringe. 'Hence the hair. Anyway, that was way back. We grew up. Well, kind of. And we moved on.'

Crikey, the Three Deevas had been huge seven or eight years ago. Billed as the girl band with claws, they had been sparky, feisty and full of attitude, the natural successors to the Spice Girls. Their songs had been played everywhere. One black girl with blond hair, one white girl with black hair and one Asian girl with super-long eyelashes and no hair at all. Dolly,

Daisy and Mia Deeva, those had been the names they'd gone by. Their first single had been the fantastically successful 'If I Loved You, I'd Remember Your Name'. It had to be bleeped because of the line, 'Men are good for a shag, and a new handbag.'

But eight months later, Dolly Deeva had blotted her copybook when she'd flashed her boobs live on children's TV. Then Mia Deeva had fallen off the stage at a benefit gig and broken both legs. Finally Daisy Deeva had given a tipsy interview to MTV announcing that she couldn't sing in tune, Dolly Deeva wasn't really a vegetarian and their fat git of a manager needed to come out of the closet. After that, the magic formula unravelled. A year after they'd burst on to the scene, it was all over. The Three Deevas broke up and slid back into obscurity.

Fascinated, Ellie said, 'You were Daisy.'

'Just don't ask me to sing.' Roo pulled a face. 'Because I really can't. Anyway, I'd much rather talk about you.'

But first they had to put a pan of spaghetti on the boil, to go with the sauce. As soon as that was done they headed back into the living room. Spotting the azure seas and white sandy beach on the still-frozen TV screen, Roo exclaimed, 'Ooh, what were you watching? *Mamma Mia*?'

Before Ellie could react, she'd seized the remote control and pressed Play. Belatedly, Ellie said, 'No, it's—'

'OK, not *Mamma Mia*.' Gazing intently at the screen, Roo watched as Jamie chased Ellie into the water, pulling her into a jokey Hollywood clinch as a wave broke behind them. Todd, manning the camcorder from a safe distance, called out, 'You two, get a *room*.'

'That's you.' Roo glanced back at Ellie, then at the box of tissues on the arm of the sofa. Realisation dawned. 'Oh no, you were sitting here all on your own, playing home videos and getting emotional. Who's the guy? Don't tell me, let me guess. You're not together any more.'

Momentarily lost for words, Ellie said, 'Um, well, no . . .'

'Ha, knew it! And he's the one who buggered off, that's obvious, because otherwise why would you be watching this stuff? Now look, this isn't doing you any good. OK, so he was pretty.' She turned back to the TV and pressed *Pause*, freezing the screen to capture Jamie mid-leap in a game of beach volleyball. 'But he left you, so don't dwell on the good points. Be *critical*. Ask yourself what kind of bloke wears a T-shirt the colour of baby's poo. And what about those legs? They're too skinny! And I bet he snored!'

Ellie hesitated, her mind racing. It was already too late to tell Roo the truth about Jamie; she would be mortified. What's more, she would stop being irreverent and funny and treating her like a normal person. It happened every time, without fail. As soon as anyone found out she was a widow, their attitude towards her changed in an instant.

Sorry, Jamie. Aloud she said, 'OK, sometimes he snored.'

'I knew it!' Roo clapped her hands. 'Concentrate on the bad points and you'll be over him in no time. Trust me, I've had heaps of practice.'

'You're right, I'm going to do that. Starting now.' Retrieving the remote control, Ellie switched off the DVD player with a flourish. 'There, I'm feeling better already. Come on then, your turn now. Tell me what it's like living in Primrose Hill.'

'**O**h my giddy aunt, did you even listen to a word I *said*?'

In the sunny bathroom, Ellie pulled the flush and washed her hands. When she emerged, Roo was standing in the hallway brandishing the honeymoon photo in the silver frame.

'That was on my bedside table,' said Ellie.

'I know! You and thingy with the skinny legs! Look, it doesn't do any good to keep stuff like this out. You're making things worse for yourself.'

'What were you doing in my bedroom?'

'Having a snoop around. I'm very nosy. It's OK, I don't go through people's drawers, I just wanted to see what you'd done with the room. And it's looking very nice,' said Roo. 'Apart from *this*.'

'That was taken on our honeymoon.'

'You were married? You didn't tell me that.'

'There's something else I didn't tell you. We didn't break up, exactly.' Another quick breath, because it was still a hard thing to say. 'He died.'

Silence. Finally Roo said, 'Oh God. When?'

'January last year.'

'Oh *God*. And I made fun of his legs.'

'Don't feel bad.' Ellie half-smiled. 'I used to make fun of them too.'

Back in the living room, Roo threw herself on to the sofa and grabbed a handful of Twiglets. 'OK, I'm really sorry about everything I said before. But now you have to tell me all about him.'

Had it really only been nine days since she'd met Roo? The first night they had talked for hours. Since then, Roo had taken to popping over the road most days, and now it felt as if they'd known each other for years. The timing had been fortuitous; it probably wouldn't have happened if Roo's best friend Marsha hadn't recently moved to New Zealand, leaving her with a friend-shaped gap in her life. But Ellie was grateful for that: Roo was entertaining company, funny, impulsive and with an outrageous track record when it came to men.

She made tea and spent the next hour talking about Jamie. Roo asked to see more photos and together they pored over an album.

Finally, Roo said emotionally, 'Why didn't you tell me this before?'

'OK, keep your face like that. Don't move a muscle.' Jumping up, Ellie took the bevelled mirror above the mantelpiece off its hook and brought it over to the sofa. 'There, now just take a look at yourself.' She held the mirror in front of Roo. 'That's why.'

Horror, sympathy, pity . . . it was all reflected there in Roo's face. Seeing it for herself, she said, 'Oh. Right. Sorry.'

'It's OK. You get used to it. But it's been nice to be treated normally. Sometimes at work it just feels like everyone's tiptoeing through a minefield when they talk to me.'

Roo said at once, 'I won't do that. It's just not the way I am.'

'Except you've just looked through a whole album of photos,' Ellie pointed out, 'and you haven't once made fun of how we look.'

'Oh well, but that's because it wouldn't be fair. And it might hurt your feelings. I'd feel *awful* if I said something to upset you . . .'

'Sshh. This is what I get all the time.' Ellie finished her second mug of tea. 'I'd rather you were normal.' She tapped her watch. 'And it's seven o'clock. Aren't you supposed to be meeting Niall at eight?'

Roo jumped up. 'It's *what*? But I haven't done anything yet!' Getting ready for a date entailed *hours* of preparation. 'Oh God, I feel terrible leaving you on your own.'

'Sshh.'

'OK, sorry, I'm going.' Roo paused. 'Oh I know, but it's just—'

'I'm not three years old,' said Ellie. 'I can cope. Go and have a fantastic time with Niall and tell me all about it tomorrow.'

She saw Roo take this in. Finally. Thank God.

'*All* about it?' Roo said it with a raised eyebrow and a glint in her eye.

'You can leave out the biological bits.' Ellie relaxed; all she wanted was to be treated normally. 'I've forgotten what any of that mucky stuff's like.'

An email dropped into her inbox at lunchtime the next day. Still at her desk at Brace House Business Centre, Ellie was working her way through a mountain of reports waiting to be typed up. Paula had brought her a coffee and she was eating a sandwich. She clicked onto the email from Michael, her boss, asking if she could put in a couple of extra hours this evening, to help clear a backlog of work.

Damn, how could she wriggle out of this? The last time she'd said no, Michael had launched into an interminable story about how, when his messy divorce had been going through, plenty of overtime had taken his mind off the heartbreak. The next moment, a new email pinged up on the screen and her heart gave a squeeze at the sight of it. The subject was Hi, and the sender was Todd.

Why was Todd contacting her now? The last time had been four months ago, on the anniversary of Jamie's death. He had written her a brief stilted email and she had sent an even more stilted one back.

It was all her own fault and she hated herself for it. Todd and Jamie had been so close. And the three of them together had been a team. That they wouldn't stay friends for life had been unthinkable.

But following Jamie's death, they had both been overwhelmed with guilt and grief. Todd had blamed himself: with a reputation for turning up late wherever he went, it haunted him that on that night he had arrived at the flat early. If they'd left at the right time—the late time—the accident wouldn't have happened. He had told her this before the funeral. Up until then, it hadn't occurred to Ellie that it might have made a difference. But once he'd said it, resentment had begun to grow. His untimely arrival had interrupted her and Jamie. Thanks to Todd, they had missed out on the last sex they would ever have. And he'd been right about the accident not happening if they'd left the house thirty minutes later, because by then—she knew this for a *fact*—the gritting lorry would have been along to make the road safe.

By the time she'd come to her senses and realised that of course Todd wasn't to blame, it was too late. The damage was done, the awkwardness between them had been too much to overcome. Three months after the accident, Todd had moved over to the States and Ellie had been relieved. She still hadn't been able to stop wishing that, out of the two of them, Jamie could have been the one to be saved.

It was shameful, unfair, and she hated herself for thinking it, but that was the way she felt. Basically, she was a horrible person.

She clicked on Todd's name and brought his email up on the screen:

Hi Ellie,

Well, it's been some time, hasn't it? Hope you're doing OK and work is going well.

My news is that I've left my job here in Boston and I'm coming back home next week, going back to work at the London branch. One year was enough. Once I'm back, I wondered if we could meet up. I'd like to see you again, talk about old times. Hope you'd like to see me too. Let me know. Are you still in Hammersmith?

Love,

Todd

PS You have no idea how long it's taken me to write this email. I hope life is as good as possible for you, Ell. I've missed seeing you.

Ellie sat back. There was that familiar feeling of dread in the pit of her stomach, the one signalling that something was going to happen whether you wanted it to or not. But what could she do? Pretend the email had got lost in the ether?

'Hard at work, Ellie?'

Shit, Michael was right behind her. Damn those Hush Puppies of his, enabling him to creep silently round the offices.

'Sorry.' Hurriedly she clicked the email off the screen.

'You know what company policy is, where personal emails are concerned.' Michael had an irritating habit of sucking air in through his lower teeth. Ellie squirmed as he did it now, then squirmed again in response to his hand on her shoulder. 'But under the circumstances, I'll let you off. So, how about a couple of extra hours tonight?'

'Um, the thing is, I'm supposed to be . . . doing something . . .' Oh, it was no good, she was rubbish at lying under pressure. Caving in, Ellie said, 'Well, OK, I'll do an hour.'

'We really need to catch up. Make it two and I'll give you a lift home.'

She glanced out of the window. The rain had been hammering down all day. There were engineering works on the Northern Line. 'OK, deal.'

Michael beamed. 'You're a great girl.' *Squeeeeeeeze*.

The moment he'd left the office, Ellie clicked back onto her emails. Come on, get it over with, then she could put it out of her head.

Hi Todd,

I'm glad you're well. Hope your trip back home goes OK. I'm doing all right. As well as can be expected, I suppose. Keeping very busy. Doing lots of overtime at the moment so not many evenings free. Maybe we could meet up when things are less hectic.

Love,

Ellie

She pressed *Send*. There, done. When Todd received her brittle, stilted reply he'd know she wasn't ready to see him yet.

Todd wasn't stupid; he wouldn't hate her for it. He'd understand.

Chapter 3

AT EIGHT THIRTY, Michael pulled up outside the flat in Nevis Street. The rain, battering down on the roof of the Honda Civic, sounded like a never-ending drum roll. There wasn't another soul in sight.

The lift home was welcome, the conversation less so. As they'd made their way across the city, Michael had talked at length about his loneliness. Quite movingly, in fact. Since the break-up of his marriage he had had to watch his ex-wife remarry and give birth to twin girls.

'See, nobody else knows how I feel.' His face was pale and earnest under the glare of the street light. 'Except you, Ellie. We're in the same boat, you and me. You understand what it's like.'

Ellie unfastened her seat belt. 'I know, but things'll get better. You'll meet someone else. Anyway, thanks for the lift—'

'Don't go!' Michael seized her hand. 'Ellie, you're on your own. So am I. We deserve to be happy, don't we? So how about being happy together?' He was edging closer now. Stunned, Ellie realised his mouth was puckering up, homing in on hers like a heat-seeking missile while his other hand reached out to clasp her by the waist and—

Click. Phew, saved by the seat belt. Out of practice when it came to making romantic advances, Michael had forgotten to take his off.

'Michael, no. Stop it.' His face fell. 'I can't do that.'

'No?'

'Sorry. It's not what I want. But it's kind of you to . . . offer.' Oh God, his chin was starting to wobble, please don't say he was going to cry.

'Fine, I know, I get the message.' Michael sat back, his eyes swimming with tears. 'Loud and clear. I'm not your type.' He heaved a sigh. 'I'm thirty-five years old and nobody's ever fancied me.'

'Oh Michael, that's not true. Your wife must have fancied you.'

He shook his head mournfully. 'She said she only married me because I had a three-bedroomed house.'

'**U**gh, that's so gross.' Roo was paying a flying visit on her way out to a comedy night at O'Reilly's bar in Camden. 'What a creep.'

'He's not a creep, that's the thing. He's just sad and lonely.' Ellie paused. 'It was *slightly* gross.'

'You turned him down. And he's your boss. That's going to make things awkward at work.'

She had a point. Fending off a clumsy, slobbery advance then having to comfort your manager when he sobbed on your shoulder wasn't ideal. It hadn't upset her. But Michael was going to be mortified.

'Maybe it's time to start looking for something else.' Ellie had been vaguely considering this for the last fortnight. She had worked at the business centre for six years now. Since moving to North London, getting to and from Brace House had become more complicated.

'I have to go.' Roo jumped up at the sound of an idling diesel engine outside. 'Are you sure you don't want to come along?'

Ellie shook her head. 'I'm shattered. Being propositioned takes it out of you. I'm having a bath and an early night. But thanks anyway.'

'I hate leaving you on your own. Will you be OK?'

'Now you're sounding like Paula. I'm fine, I promise. Go!'

The little blue and white café among the row of shops along Regent's Park Road was one of Roo's favourite places to spend an hour while she was waiting for inspiration to strike. At least, that was her excuse. The official line was that she was on the hunt for ideas for lyrics while also trying out possible melodies in her head. In reality she just loved the buzzy atmosphere, the people-watching, the mugs of hot chocolate and the cheese and spicy mushrooms on toast.

The sun blazed down out of a cobalt sky and it was hot enough to sit outside in a T-shirt. Roo, giving her new sunglasses their first outing, was comfortably set up at one of the steel tables along the pavement and tapping away on her laptop. Anyone watching would admire her businesslike manner and air of efficiency. They wouldn't suspect that she was actually scrolling through photos of Richard Armitage, and checking out all the latest scurrilous gossip on Popbitch.

'. . . so that's that, it's all decided. We're moving to Albufeira!' The dark-haired woman at the next table was proudly relaying her big news to her friend. Both in their late fifties and frumpily dressed by Primrose Hill standards, they were huddled together over cups of tea and plates of lemon cheesecake. 'Roy's going to play golf all day and I'll be a lady of leisure!'

'Oh, how marvellous, you'll have a wonderful time! I mean, we'll miss you being here.' Her grey-haired friend nodded eagerly. 'So, have you handed in your notice at work?'

'Not yet. Zack's up in Manchester today. I'm going to tell him tomorrow. He'll be devastated to lose me, of course.'

'But he won't have any trouble finding someone else, will he? I mean, he's Zack McLaren. He'll be inundated with offers from girls desperate to work for him!'

'That's not what he wants though, is it? He wants someone capable of doing the job. Not some simpering ninny in a short skirt.'

Roo, currently wearing a very short skirt, idly typed the name into Google Images and watched as a series of photos popped up on the screen. Zack McLaren, it appeared, was an entrepreneur. Bloody hell, the bossy old trout worked for this man? He was a *looker*.

Ten minutes later the woman daintily brushed cheesecake crumbs from round her mouth, finished her tea and rose to leave.

'Well, back to work. Lots to do in the office this afternoon. I tell you something,' she added smugly, 'Zack's going to have his work cut out finding someone who matches up to me.'

Her friend nodded. 'You're right there, Barbara.'

'I'm always right.' Barbara beamed. 'Anyway, I'll be in touch, dear.'

Raising her sunglasses, Roo watched Barbara strut off up the road like a squaddie on a route march. Just before she was due to disappear from view, an idea popped into Roo's head. Hurriedly shutting her laptop, she jumped to her feet and set off in pursuit.

Barbara had turned the corner. By the time Roo got her in her sights again she was halfway down Ancram Street. Then she paused, took a key from her bag and climbed the steps to a white Georgian-style house.

This must be where she worked. Reaching the house, Roo rang the bell. The box next to the glossy cranberry-red door emitted a squawk and an officious, 'Yes?'

'Barbara? I have a message for you.'

'What kind of message?'

'OK, it's more of a proposal,' Roo said. 'Can I come in?'

The door was opened seconds later. Barbara stood in the doorway, her gaze flickering over Roo on the top step. Finally she said, 'You were sitting outside the café just now.'

'I was. Well spotted!' Roo beamed. 'And I couldn't help overhearing what you were saying about having to leave your job.'

'Really.' Barbara didn't invite her in. 'Where's this leading?'

'Well, wouldn't your boss appreciate it if you could present him with a replacement when you tell him you won't be working for him any more? I think he would,' said Roo. 'And I think it was fate that had us both sitting outside that café today.'

Barbara's pale eyes narrowed. 'Well, it's very kind of you to offer, but I don't think you're quite the type we're looking for.' She was gazing at Roo's abbreviated skirt, silver Uggs and turquoise T-shirt with I'VE HAD YOUR DAD emblazoned across the front.

'Oh God, no, it's not *me*. Ha, what a thought!' Roo waved her hands in horror. 'No, no, someone else. She works in a business centre in Twickenham, but this would be so much handier. And she types like lightning. Honestly, you should see her, she'd be perfect for here.'

'How old?'

'Nearly thirty.'

'That's younger than we'd want,' said Barbara.

'I know. But I heard what you were saying earlier about girls wanting to work here. And this one isn't like that. She doesn't wear short skirts. She's efficient and hard-working and she wouldn't go gooey over your boss. I'm telling you,' said Roo, 'you'd be mad not to snap her up.'

'**Y**ou did what?' It hadn't been the easiest of journeys home. Delays on the Circle Line had resulted in far too many commuters being sardined into too few carriages, and Ellie had ended up sandwiched between two men who hadn't been introduced to deodorant.

'I found you a job.' Roo had been waiting for her to get back. Now she was firing up her laptop. 'Well, possibly. But you said it was time for a change, so I got you this.' She pulled a card out of her left bra-cup and waved it. 'All you have to do is call this number and fix up an interview.'

'Where's the job?'

'Right here in Primrose Hill. Ancram Street. Five minutes' walk from here. Take a look at this.' Roo swivelled the laptop round so Ellie could see the screen.

'Who's he?'

'Zack McLaren. The one who needs a new PA. I'd volunteer for the job myself, only you need to be able to do all sorts of nifty typisty stuff. But what about him, eh? Pretty impressive? He's an entrepreneur!'

Ellie studied the photo. There was no denying he was an attractive specimen, what with that glossy dark hair and those film-star cheekbones. Beneath the well-cut suit he clearly had an athletic body. Nice eyes, too. Next to her, Roo was visibly drooling.

'The thing is, I can see that he's good-looking but it's wasted on me. All that stuff's just irrelevant right now. I'm not interested.'

'I know, but he doesn't want someone who's going to be all over him. That's what's so great. Because you wouldn't do that. You'd be *perfect*.'

'Well . . .'

'And if things don't work out between me and Niall, this one can be my first reserve.' Roo lovingly stroked the computer screen. 'He looks like he'd be fantastic in bed.'

Two hours later, Ellie reached across the coffee table and scooped up the business card. As she'd been leaving, Roo had urged her again to think about it, and now she had. The job would be close to home and would be somewhere where her past wouldn't colour people's attitudes towards her because they wouldn't know about it.

She picked up the phone and pressed out the number.

The phone began to ring as Zack let himself into the house. After a long day of meetings all he wanted was a cold beer and an hour of mindless TV before crashing out for the night.

Except that wasn't an option. Instead he had a detailed business plan to put together and several letters to dictate. Peeling off his jacket, he dumped his briefcase on the desk and answered the still-ringing phone.

'Oh hello, is that Mr McLaren?'

It was a female voice he didn't recognise. 'Speaking.'

'Hi there! I'm calling about the job.'

'Job?'

'That's right. My name's Ellie Kendall, and my friend persuaded me to call you. I'm local, hard-working, my typing speeds are brilliant and I—'

'Hang on, sorry, you've lost me here, I don't know what you're talking about,' said Zack.

'Oh!' She sounded taken aback.

'What kind of job are you applying for?'

'Well, working as your PA.'

'I'm afraid there's been some misunderstanding. I already have a PA.'

'Oh right, but . . . no, OK, I'm really sorry. My mistake.' Hurriedly the girl said, 'Sorry to bother you. Bye.'

'Wait—' But it was too late, she had already hung up.

'**S**o there we are. I know this has come as a shock, but rest assured you don't have to worry about a thing. I shan't leave you high and dry.' Barbara's tone was consoling. 'I'm going to devote myself to the task of finding you a worthy replacement.'

Zack looked at the official letter of resignation she had handed him.

'Well, I'll be sorry to lose you, but it'll be exciting for you. And the Algarve's beautiful. You never know, you might take up golf yourself.'

Barbara shuddered. 'I can assure you I won't.'

He smiled slightly. 'And at least this solves one mystery.'

'Oh?'

'I had a phone call last night from someone applying to be my PA.'

Barbara closed her eyes in despair. 'That dreadful pushy girl. I'm so sorry. She *knew* I wasn't telling you until today.'

Mildly diverted, Zack said, 'But you told her yesterday?'

'Of course I didn't tell her! She eavesdropped on a private conversation! Then she followed me here and said her friend could take over my job. She was most persistent. I'm afraid I ended up giving her one of your cards, otherwise I'd never have got rid of her.'

'Well, you could call that enterprising. And the friend sounded very keen on the phone. Maybe I should see her.'

'Oh no no no.' Chins wobbling, Barbara vehemently shook her head. 'No, trust me, absolutely not the type of person you'd want to hire.'

'But . . . hang on, you didn't actually meet the girl's friend.'

'I didn't need to. This girl had hair like a *punk rocker*, all chopped and dyed. And silver boots!' Barbara shuddered. 'The entire outfit was bizarre. Believe me, you wouldn't want to employ anyone who's friendly with a girl like that. No, leave it to me. I'll find you the right lady.'

True to her word, Barbara had drawn up a shortlist of six eminently suitable applicants for the position of replacement PA. Zack had spent an afternoon interviewing them, and it was safe to say it hadn't been the most enthralling three hours of his life.

All the ladies were super-efficient, incredibly organised and vastly experienced. Each of them had been in their mid to late fifties, with sensible hair and minimal make-up. Smart interview outfits. Low-heeled shoes. Basically, Barbara had provided him with half a dozen clones of herself. Zack knew why she'd done it, and in theory he agreed, but the prospect of choosing one of them didn't fill him with joy.

Heading downstairs to the office, he flipped back through the notepad on his desk until he found the page he was looking for.

There was the number he'd scribbled down, the one belonging to the friend of the unsuitable girl who had so alarmed Barbara. Smiling slightly at the memory of her reaction, Zack dialled the number.

It was picked up on the third ring. 'Hello? *Whoops.*' There was a clatter followed by a big thud. 'Sorry about that. Hello.'

'What happened there?'

'I reached over to pick up the phone and rolled off the sofa. Who's that?'

'Zack McLaren.'

'Oh! Look, can I just say I'm so sorry about last week? I really put my foot in it, didn't I! Your poor PA, I hope you weren't cross with her.'

Amused, Zack said, 'I'm never cross. Listen, you sounded pretty enthusiastic before. I just wondered if you'd like to come over for an interview tomorrow morning?'

'Really? Oh, wow, that'd be fantastic! But I can't do tomorrow; I'm catching the first train up to Glasgow.' She sounded genuinely apologetic.

'It's my gran's eightieth birthday and she's having a surprise party and I can't miss it. Could we make it next week instead?'

Damn. 'Sorry, I've already seen all the other applicants. I promised to let them know by tomorrow.'

'Oh.' There was a pause. 'Well, I'm not doing anything right now. Apart from falling off the sofa. How about if I just throw some clothes on and come round?' Another pause. 'Um, that makes it sound as if I'm naked. I'm not naked, I'm wearing pyjamas. Oh God, this is too much information. Shall I see you in thirty minutes, fully clothed?'

'I can't do it,' Zack said. 'I have a business dinner this evening.' He was the main guest speaker, so he couldn't be late. 'Well, we gave it a try, but I guess we'll have to leave it after all. Just a case of bad timing.' Glancing at his watch, he saw that it was eight o'clock. Seeing as his car would be here in ten minutes, he needed to get a serious move on. 'Thanks anyway.'

'OK.' She sounded disappointed. 'Well, thank you too, for thinking of me. It was nice of you to call. It's a shame we couldn't meet up.'

She had an attractive voice, clear and musical, the kind that would be a joy to listen to. *If you had time*. 'I'm sorry too. And good luck with finding another job,' said Zack. 'Bye.'

How's your new woman doing?' Next to Zack in the passenger seat, Louisa checked her lipstick in the mirror. 'Settling in?'

Zack nodded. He'd gone for Christine in the end, out of the six applicants, and she was proving every bit as efficient as Barbara. Christine was in her late fifties and uninterested in fashion; with bushy eyebrows and a penchant for pleated skirts. But she typed so fast her sausage fingers became an actual physical blur. She also brought packed lunches to work and ate egg mayonnaise sandwiches at her desk, swilling them down with weird-smelling herbal tea.

'Still eating the egg sandwiches?'

'Every day.'

'Oh well, maybe she'll move on, give cheese and tomato a try. Can you pull up over here?' Waving her hand at the rank of shops ahead, Louisa said, 'I need a couple of mags for the journey.'

Zack's heart sank a couple of notches. He'd been seeing Louisa for almost three months now and she was confident, glamorous and strikingly attractive. They were heading down the M4 to the wedding of one of

Louisa's friends in Bristol; stopping at the newsagents, he had learned from bitter experience, meant that she would be spending the next couple of hours reading bits of celebrity gossip aloud to him from magazines.

He drew up at the kerb and Louisa jumped out of the Mercedes and disappeared inside the newsagents on Regent's Park Road.

Ellie was queuing to pay for her newspaper and a packet of Rolos when she glanced across at the racks of magazines and saw a cover featuring a large black girl in a gold bikini and a white-blond wig. The caption shrieked, 'Dolly Deeva: Bigger, better and back with a splash!'

Only last night, Roo had been wondering how Dolly was doing these days. Ellie darted out of the queue and reached for the magazine, the last one on the rack. She'd buy it for Roo.

'Whoops, sorry!' Her elbow was jogged by another customer. She smiled apologetically at the elegant redhead in the pink and grey outfit, even though it hadn't been her fault. The redhead graciously accepted the apology with a nod and said, 'Where did you get that mag?'

'Up there.' Ellie pointed to the empty space.

The redhead heaved a sigh of annoyance. 'You mean there aren't any more?'

'I don't know.' Was she seriously expecting her to hand it over? Ellie said pleasantly, 'I'm sure they'll have them in another shop.'

A couple of minutes later, having paid at the counter, she made her way out of the newsagents and flicked through the pages of the magazine. There was the interview, with Dolly insisting that her boob-flashing days were behind her and, what's more, she was now a born-again Christian. Squeezing between a dark grey Mercedes and a sky-blue VW Beetle, Ellie crossed the road and headed up the hill. From what Roo had told her about Dolly Deeva, she'd have a good laugh about that.

'There you are! I thought the car was empty.'

Zack straightened up. 'I was just sorting through the glove compartment. Found some CDs I'd forgotten about.'

Louisa settled herself into the passenger seat. 'I couldn't get the mag I wanted, some girl grabbed the last one. *So* annoying. Anyway, I found some others instead.' She patted the three glossy magazines on her lap. 'These'll keep me going until we get to Bristol.'

'Good.' Zack slotted his long-lost Gogol Bordello CD into the machine, pressed *Play* and started the car. 'Have you heard this before? It's brilliant.'

Less than two minutes later, Louisa reached out and turned it down. 'Ooh, can you believe it? What a liar!' She jabbed her finger at the photograph of a well-preserved former Bond girl. 'She's fifty-five if she's a day, and she says she's never had Botox!'

'Zack, I'm so sorry. I just can't cope any more. I thought I could, but I can't. It's too much.'

'Really?' Zack's first reaction was amazement; his second, relief. It hadn't occurred to him that he was that demanding an employer. On the other hand, *no more egg mayonnaise sandwiches*. Thank God.

'It's my husband.' Christine wavered, her pale eyes beginning to swim. 'He's not . . . himself any more, you see. He goes to a day centre while I'm at work, but it's at night that he's really difficult. I'm just not getting enough sleep and I'm exhausted. So my doctor's told me to give up work. I can't tell you how bad I feel, letting you down like this when you've been so lovely to work for.'

OK, now he felt ashamed. Zack shook his head and said, 'Please, don't feel bad. I'm sorry about your husband. I had no idea. And don't worry about having to work out any notice. I can manage.'

Christine gazed at him and fumbled up her sleeve for a tissue as a tear brimmed over. 'Oh Zack, that's so kind. But I couldn't do that to you. I can't leave you high and dry.'

'Hey, what's more important? A bit of typing and filing, or your health? In fact, why don't you go home now?' Rising to his feet, Zack reached for his keys. 'Come on, I'll give you a lift.'

'OK, this is another long shot.' Zack McLaren's voice echoed down the phone. 'You've probably found another job by now. But just in case you haven't, the lady I took on has had to leave. So I'm looking for someone else, and I thought I'd let you know.'

Zack McLaren. Was this fate? Sitting cross-legged on the sofa, Ellie put down her mug of tea and said, 'She had to leave after a fortnight? Does that mean you're the boss from hell?'

He sounded amused. 'I'm not, I promise.'

'So you're inviting me along for an interview?'

'If you're still interested.'

'Oh yes, I'm definitely interested. When do you want to see me?'

She heard him say, 'As soon as you like. How about now?'

'You're on.' Ellie was already scrambling off the sofa. She might get there and discover she didn't want to work for this man. But some inner instinct told her she would.

*B*loody hell. It was her.

The shock of it jerked Zack back from the upstairs window. The girl currently making her way along Ancram Street was the one he'd seen at the Ivy. She'd made such an impression on him back then—*over two months ago*—that he could still remember every single detail about that lunchtime. He had even skilfully engineered the ending of his own meeting so that they'd exited the restaurant at more or less the same time. Emerging onto the pavement, he had watched her jump into a taxi with Tony Weston and had experienced an almost uncontrollable urge to yank open the door and pull her back out again.

He hadn't of course. He had controlled himself. Instead he had stood there in the rain, watching the taxi disappear off up the road and thinking that Tony Weston was old enough to be her father.

Now she was here, walking towards his house, and the chances were that in less than a minute she would be ringing his doorbell. Because this girl, in her white shirt and on-the-knee blue skirt, was surely dressed for an interview. Which meant she had to be Ellie Kendall.

Zack's mouth was dry. Emotional complications were the last thing, the *very* last thing he needed in his working life. Everyone knew that getting involved with your PA was asking for trouble.

So how was he supposed to deal with a situation like this?

Ellie rang the bell and waited. When the door was opened, she knew from the images on Roo's laptop what to expect, but in real life he was taller than she'd envisaged. And undeniably impressive. No wonder Roo had been so enthusiastic. Great eyes, and there were those killer cheekbones. Hopefully he also had a sense of humour.

'Ellie, hi. I'm Zack.' He hesitated for a split second, then took her hand and shook it. 'Good to meet you at last. Come along in.'

Clutching her shoulder bag, Ellie followed him through to the office on the ground floor. He was wearing jeans and a pale grey T-shirt. Roo would approve of that bum, too. Ellie might be immune to other males herself, but she could still acknowledge their good points.

'I've brought along my CV.' She took it out of her bag and handed it to him. 'There isn't much I don't know about running an office. My typing speeds and computer skills are good. You can test me on them. And I'm really hard-working.'

'Glad to hear it.' Zack smiled briefly. For the next twenty minutes he explained the nature of the work she would be expected to carry out.

He dictated a letter and she transcribed it. He showed her the filing system, which was straightforward. He asked her about Brace House Business Centre and she told him she'd been perfectly happy there for six years but that now she was ready for a change, and it would be nice to work just a few minutes' walk away from her flat.

'Am I allowed to ask what happened to the last PA?'

Zack explained about Christine, then said good-naturedly, 'So if you don't have an invalid husband to look after, that's a bonus.'

This was good practice at being normal. Ellie summoned up a bright smile and said, 'Well, I definitely don't have one of those! I'm not married.'

Then he offered her a coffee and showed her through to the kitchen, which was all sage green and stainless steel and opened out through French windows onto a small garden at the back of the house. They headed up the stairs to the living room, decorated in shades of deep red and dove grey and showing reassuring signs of actually being lived in.

'Have a seat.' Zack indicated the sofa and sat down on one of the chairs opposite. He was being polite, charming even, but there was still a faint but discernible edge of reserve. Ellie wondered if she already had the job in the bag, or had he not made up his mind yet?

'Thanks.' She concentrated on not spilling her coffee.

'So, you live in Nevis Street. Very nice.'

'I know. And being so close would mean I could be flexible.' Selling herself didn't come naturally but she wanted this job.

'Excellent.' After a moment, he said, 'Share with other girls, do you?'

'Um, no.'

'Oh.' He shrugged. 'Just wondering. I mean, there must be a pretty big mortgage on a place like that.'

'I don't have a mortage.' Ellie prevaricated. She'd never been asked these kinds of questions at an interview before.

'Rent, then. The rent would be high. That would still be manageable, would it, on the kind of salary I'm offering?'

'Well, ye-es.' She felt herself begin to flush beneath his scrutiny. Telling him about Tony would only make matters more complicated, but he was gazing at her so intently now, she had to say something. 'The thing is, I'm not really renting the flat either. I'm just . . . you know, living there. Kind of . . . looking after it.' She swallowed. 'For a friend.'

There followed what felt like an awkward silence. She felt her skin heat up by a few more degrees. Zack finally nodded and said, 'Right.'

What had he done? Jesus, what was he *thinking* of? Zack now stood at the window and followed Ellie Kendall's progress as she left the house and made her way back along Ancram Street.

He had gone against everything he'd ever lived by. He'd offered Ellie Kendall the job and she had delightedly accepted it. If Barbara were here now, she would have boxed his ears. But he hadn't been able to help himself, because of the way she'd been in his company. The reason he'd taken to hiring women like Barbara and Christine in the first place was because two previous PAs had developed unreciprocated crushes on him. This time, he appeared to be the one in danger of getting emotionally involved.

What's more, there was a good chance that Ellie was living in a flat paid for by the actor Tony Weston, who was old enough to be her father.

Oh God, this was crazy. He shouldn't have offered her the job. If he felt this way about her, he should just call her, explaining why it wouldn't be sensible to take her on and inviting her out to dinner instead. But he could only call up a girl and ask her out to dinner if there had first been a spark of attraction between them. And this was the precise reason he wouldn't have been able to do it, because on Ellie Kendall's side, there had been no spark of attraction. None whatsoever. Which meant that if he were to call her up and invite her out, the chances were that she would politely but firmly say no. Which would mean he wouldn't have any reason to see her again. Which was just unthinkable. So unthinkable, evidently, that he'd had to offer her a job instead.

'**G**uess what?' Roo demanded two days later when Ellie met her in Café Rouge after work.

'What?' From the look on Roo's face, the news wasn't fantastic.

'When a man sounds too good to be true . . . and *looks* too good to be true . . . the chances are that . . .'

'He's too good to be true?'

'Spot on. Cor-rect.' Roo was drinking red wine and wearing white jeans, which probably wasn't wise given her current state of agitation. 'Then again, why am I even surprised? This is my life we're talking about, after all.'

'Is it to do with work?' She used the term loosely: Roo's work appeared to involve meeting up with fellow songwriters, singing random lines and playing chords to each other for a couple of hours, then deciding that today wasn't a happening kind of day, musically, and going down the pub instead.

'No, it's more to do with finding out that my boyfriend is married.'

'Niall?' Oh Lord. Shocked, Ellie said, 'Are you sure?'

'Pretty sure, yes. Seeing as he's the one who told me.'

'You mean they're separated? Getting a divorce?'

'Nope.' She shook her head. 'They're still together.'

'Oh no, what a bastard.' Ellie's heart went out to her. 'Well, it's his loss. And you're better off without him,' she said consolingly. 'Trust me, you'll find someone a million times nicer. What a slimy git.'

Roo flinched. 'Don't say that.'

'I bloody well will say it! He's a sleazebag and you're well out of it.'

'You haven't met him, though.'

'I'm glad I didn't! Oh, come on. You'll be OK. There are loads of fantastic men out there, just waiting for you to meet them. Lovely men . . .'

'*Sshh.*' Roo jumped as her mobile started to ring. Snatching it up from the table, she pressed it to her ear and whispered, 'Yes? Yes. No. No, I know. Yes, me too. OK. Right. Yes. Bye.'

The furtive look on her face told Ellie who'd been on the other end of the phone. 'That was Niall, wasn't it?'

'Yes.'

'What did he want?'

'Just . . . seeing how I am.' Furtiveness was now mixed with defiance.

'You're still talking to him, then.'

'Looks like it.'

'Still seeing him too?'

'Maybe.' Pause. 'Yes.'

'Oh God.' Ellie shook her head. '*Why?*'

'Don't look at me like that,' Roo wailed. 'I love him!'

So this was why Roo hadn't liked her calling Niall a slimy git. Marvelling at the power he had over her, Ellie said, 'But he's *married*.'

'Not happily, though!' Roo leapt to his defence. 'She trapped him.'

Ellie gave her a long look. 'You mean, like in a big metal man-trap?'

'Worse than that.'

'So you're telling me they have children.'

Two bright spots of colour appeared in Roo's cheeks. 'One child. Look, he's not a bad person,' she pleaded. 'He's just trying to do the right thing. He was about to finish with her when she told him she was pregnant. He stayed for the sake of the baby. But she's just been a complete nightmare. She's made his life a misery—'

'The baby?'

'No! The wife! Yasmin.' Roo's lip curled. 'That's her name. Isn't that just so . . . princessy? And she's a complete bitch, you have no idea.'

'So he's going to leave her?'

'Well, yes, of course he will. But, he can't do it yet, not while the baby's still so young. He has to stick it out until it's a year old.' Roo paused. 'You don't approve, do you? Don't tell me I'm doing the wrong thing. You're not allowed to nag.'

'When it all goes wrong, am I allowed to say I told you so?'

'It's not going to. Please, don't say anything else,' Roo begged. 'When you meet Niall you'll understand. I *love* him. It's not my fault he's married.'

Chapter 4

IF YOU WANTED to make grumpy Londoners talk to you, Ellie had discovered the answer. All you had to do was carry a huge Cellophane-wrapped bouquet home from work.

'Those for me, love?' said the newspaper seller outside Brace House as she left the building on her last day there.

'Cheers, darlin', they're my favourites,' said a transport worker on the underground.

It was like living in Mary Poppins world.

Actually, it made a nice change, having her final commute transformed into such a jolly affair. Reaching Nevis Street, Ellie let herself into the flat. Tony was already here.

'Hello, sweetheart. Are those for me? You didn't need to do that.' Delighted by his own wit, he relieved her of the flowers, then gave her a warm hug. 'You're looking good.'

'You too.' Tony was over for a few days to meet film producers and give a few interviews. It was lovely to see him again.

'All settled in now?'

'Completely. It's brilliant here. And on Monday I start at Zack's.'

'Great. How was your leaving party?'

Ellie began unwrapping the flowers. 'Emotional. Paula cried buckets. Everyone kept reminiscing about the past. They're worried about how I'm going to cope without them. I just felt guilty because it was my decision to leave and I'm really looking forward to the new job. Zack still doesn't know about Jamie, by the way. I'm not going to tell him.'

'That's fine.' Tony nodded. 'Whatever's easiest for you.'

He made coffee while she arranged the flowers in a bowl. Before heading out to meet the film producers, he told her about the project. 'They're pitching it as *Lock Stock* meets *Gavin and Stacey*. They want me to play a lovable gangster who runs a line-dancing club, keeps Chihuahuas and has people shot if they annoy him.'

'I'd watch that,' Ellie said. 'So are you definitely going to do it?'

'Maybe. We'd be on location in London, Cardiff and Reykjavik. We'll see.' He added sugar to his coffee and stirred. 'By the way, I had an email from Todd the other day. He's living back here now.'

She concentrated on the flowers. 'I know. He emailed me too.'

'Have you seen him?'

'No.'

'Why not?'

'Don't know.' Ellie shrugged and snipped another stem. 'Just haven't.'

'Do you hate him?'

'Of course I don't hate him!'

Tony backed off. 'OK, no pressure. Just asking.'

The doorbell went and Ellie felt a rush of relief; no more talk of Todd. 'There you go, that'll be your car.'

At lunchtime on Saturday, Ellie caught the tube to Camden, then headed along Parkway in the sunshine. Before leaving the flat earlier, Tony had said, 'By the way, I've booked us a table at York & Albany. One o'clock.' And when she'd protested that there was no need, she could rustle up something to eat here, he had shaken his head. 'If I was staying in a hotel, we'd be meeting up somewhere decent for lunch, wouldn't we? So let's carry on doing that.'

As Ellie reached the restaurant, her stomach rumbled. She was ten minutes early, but maybe Tony was already here.

He wasn't, yet. She made her way downstairs to the ladies, faffed about with her hair for a bit and redid her lip gloss.

Heading back up the stairs, she saw a new arrival sitting at a table by the window. Her scalp prickled and her mouth went dry. *Oh God, no*. At that moment, alerted by the sound of her heels on the wooden floor, Todd turned to see why the footsteps had so abruptly stopped.

From the expression on his face it was clear he'd had no idea either. He was as shocked as she was. He looked older, more grown up. Gathering herself, Ellie approached him.

'Hello, Todd.' Did she look older too?

'Hi, Ellie.' He rose awkwardly to his feet. 'Fancy meeting you here.'

'Well, I'm guessing this isn't a coincidence. Tony asked me to meet him for lunch.'

'He asked me as well.'

Trust Tony to take matters into his own hands. And he wasn't even here yet. Taking out her phone, Ellie called his number.

'Hi, sweetheart. Is he there?'

'Yes. Are you joining us?'

'Ellie, just have lunch with him. Will you do that for me? And don't worry about the bill.' Tony's voice was soothing. 'All taken care of.'

Ellie hung up and looked at Todd. 'He's not coming. I can't believe he's *done* this.'

Todd eyed her with caution. 'So what happens now?'

'I don't know.' Ellie said, hating the fact that she'd been set up.

'What's that noise?' Todd looked incredulous. 'Is that your stomach?'

Stupid stomach, it was rumbling like a cement mixer. She hadn't had any breakfast. 'I think I'm going to go home,' said Ellie.

'What did Tony say on the phone?'

'He wants me to have lunch with you.'

Todd said steadily, 'Why don't you want to?'

Ellie's toes curled. 'I just . . . ' *Grrrrrowwwllllll*. For crying out loud. 'Fine.' Ellie pressed her hand over her rumbling stomach. 'Let's eat.'

For the first five minutes they concentrated on the menu. Finally, Ellie said with a sigh, 'Sorry.'

'That's OK.' Todd put down his own menu. 'Sorry about what?'

'You know. Everything.' A huge lump grew in her throat. 'Today. The emails. Not wanting to see you. All of it.'

'Do you know why you felt like that?'

'Because I'm a horrible person.'

He shook his head. 'Come on. You're not.'

'I am.' The lump in her throat was expanding and the pretty waitress was coming over to take their order. Pushing back her chair, Ellie said, 'I'll have the duck terrine and the risotto. Just give me a moment . . .'

She clattered downstairs for the second time, locked herself in a toilet cubicle and wept silently until the other female customer left the bathroom and she could let out a series of honking great sobs in peace. It was a noisy, messy, undignified business and it went on for some time. It just had to burn itself out.

God, what a state. Ellie eventually confronted her reflection in the mirror and winced. Puffy eyes and blotchy cheeks, just like old times. Rummaging in her bag, she found her all-in-one compact and trusty lip gloss. OK, still moderately scary, but it would have to do.

'No need to say it,' she told Todd, resuming her seat. 'I know.'

'Sorry.' He looked awkward.

'Don't be. It was just a bit overdue, that's all. Anyway, I'm feeling better now. Did you order?'

Todd nodded.

'Can I tell you why I'm a horrible person?'

'Let me guess. Jamie's gone and I'm still here. If one of us had to die, you wish it could have been me.'

'Yes.' Shamed, she nodded.

'Ell, you think I hadn't worked that out? From day one?'

'Sorry. I tried not to. But I couldn't help it.'

'And there was me, feeling guilty because I was still alive. Because why should I be? It's not a good feeling,' said Todd. 'I knew I wasn't better than

Jamie. I didn't deserve to be the one who was saved. I've asked myself that question a million times. Why me?' His eyes were pain-filled, reflecting his anguish. 'And the thing is, there's no answer. So the guilt never goes away. My best friend isn't here any more and I miss him so much . . . and I still think that if only I'd turned up late instead of early that night the accident wouldn't have happened.'

He'd been torturing himself with that too? Now Ellie was the one overcome with guilt. She reached across the table and took his hand.

'Oh Todd, I miss him too. But it wasn't your fault.' She squeezed his fingers to show she meant it and saw the beginnings of relief on his face. 'It really wasn't. And I'm not going to be a cow any more, I promise.'

Their first course arrived and the atmosphere relaxed. Now that she'd confessed to having wanted him dead and Todd had forgiven her for it, the tension between them miraculously melted away. The food was delicious but they were too busy catching up to do it proper justice. Their wine glasses were refilled.

'Do I look older?' Ellie leaned closer.

'No.' He smiled. 'You're exactly the same. Why?'

'Because you look older. Sorry.' She pulled a face. 'Maybe it's the haircut. You look . . . more like a grown-up.'

'I *am* more like a grown-up. I'm more mature. I've even given up watching *SpongeBob SquarePants*.'

Encouraged by this flash of his old humour, Ellie said playfully, 'So how about the girls in Boston? Meet any good ones? Meet any deranged enough to go out with you?'

'Honestly? More than you'd think.' Todd grimaced. 'More than I was expecting, that's for sure. It's the British accent apparently.'

'So you're telling me you were inundated with offers.'

'With offers.' He nodded, holding back.

'What does that mean?'

'You want the truth? OK, I went out with one girl. For a few weeks. She was . . . fine. Nothing wrong with her. But I just couldn't let myself get involved. Because I felt guilty. It wasn't fair that I could still be doing all that stuff when Jamie couldn't.' Todd shrugged, 'So I didn't.'

'You mean have sex?'

'Spot on.'

'And how did the girl feel about that?'

'She was devastated, thought it was all her fault. Then when I told her about Jamie she thought maybe I was gay.' Todd took a drink. 'So I had to explain that I wasn't. And after that I was a challenge. Girls were falling over themselves to seduce me. Talk about weird.' He shook his head. 'I've never been so popular. Bloody typical that I didn't get to take advantage of it. I bet Jamie was up there laughing his head off.'

How had she kept her distance from Todd for so long? He'd loved Jamie just as much as she had. Ellie said, 'I bet he was too.'

It was Monday afternoon, a balmy summer's day, and all human life was out here on Primrose Hill. Well, not *all* human life. But enough to keep you entertained for hours. Following a morning of press interviews, Tony was enjoying being able to give his voice a rest. From his position on this south-facing bench, possibly the most spectacular view in London was stretched out in front of him. There were dog-walkers out in force, and parents with small children playing games on the grass. Toddlers ate ice lollies and investigated daisies, teenagers played football and a grand-father was gamely attempting to teach his grandson how to fly a kite.

Grandchildren. Tony, who would now never experience that particular joy, was speared with fresh grief. *Don't think about it.*

A rollerblader swooshed past with a Labrador on an extendable lead. On a bench farther down the hill an old man was feeding the birds with a carrier bag of seed. Straight-backed and lost in concentration, a woman sat at an easel, painting the view. Her hair was very short, her skin was coffee-brown and she was wearing a long geranium-red cotton dress that covered a generously curved body. Tony watched as her brush moved confidently across the paper. At one stage she smiled with satisfaction and he found himself smiling too, because the pleasure she was taking in creating the picture was infectious.

Over the hill behind her came a teenager pushing a buggy and attempt-ing to kick a football for the pre-school boy with her. The baby in the buggy was crying, the small boy running ahead.

'Kick it! Kick it to me!' he yelled.

Distracted, the teenage girl managed to get the ball over to the boy and he aimed a wild kick at it, sending it sailing through the air. The boy chased after it . . . and with a thud the ball hit the woman in red squarely in the back.

Oh dear. Even from this distance Tony saw the paintbrush go *splat* against the painting and fly out of the woman's hand. The boy, realising he could be in trouble, abruptly stopped running and looked scared.

But when the woman turned to identify the culprit, she broke into a wonderful smile and bent to retrieve the ball from its position under her folding chair. Beckoning the boy over, she handed the ball back to him then rested a hand lightly on his shoulder as together they discussed the painting. Within seconds the boy was giggling.

As Tony sat and watched them, a grey cloud passed over and the temperature dropped. A couple of minutes later, the first drops of rain began to fall. The teenager called to the boy and he ran back to her with his ball, stopping to wave at the woman in red before they disappeared back over the hill. The woman waved and called out, 'Bye, darling.'

The shower grew heavier as the cloud moved overhead. The woman had already flipped the easel over to protect her painting from the rain. But she wasn't packing up her things or running for cover. Getting to his feet, Tony headed for the shelter of an oak tree. As he passed her, he said, 'Would you like a hand with your things?'

'No thank you, darling, it's fine. This rain isn't going to last long.'

Her voice was beautiful, velvety and lilting.

Tony said, 'You're going to get wet.'

Her smile broadened, lighting up her face. Running her hand over her bare arm, she replied easily, 'No worries, I'm waterproof.'

Within five minutes the rain had stopped and the sun was back out. As soon as the woman in red had tilted her easel back into position and opened the lid on her paint box, Tony made his way over.

Up close, her close-cropped dark hair glittered with water. At a guess, she was in her late forties, but her good Afro-Caribbean bone structure and unlined complexion made it difficult to tell for sure. She was wearing no make-up. Her eyes were an amazing colour, the light golden brown of maple syrup.

Not that she'd actually turned to look at him yet. All her attention was currently concentrated on the painting in front of her. Or, more likely, on the crimson *splat* courtesy of the football landing in the small of her back. The rest of the painting was a joy, executed with verve and style, depicting not just the wider view over London but the individual stories of the various characters spread across the hill. Tony smiled, spotting the jogger and the rollerblader with his excitable Labrador, the pair of them colliding as the dog's extendable lead wrapped itself round one of the ornamental lampposts along the path.

'Did he ruin it?'

'The little boy? Bless him, he was almost in tears.' The woman shook her head. 'I told him it didn't matter a jot, and that it might even make the painting better.' Taking out a pencil, she deftly sketched round the splat for a minute or two. Then she sat back. 'There, see? How about that?'

Tony leaned closer. In the lower left quadrant of the painting, a plump lady had materialised, sitting in front of an easel. She was gazing at her own painting, which now sported the red splodge, while overhead a guilty-looking seagull flew past clutching a tipped-up pot of paint.

'Clever.' There was something about the painting that just pulled you in. Utterly drawn, Tony said, 'Do you sell your work?'

'Sometimes. Why, are you interested?'

'Could be. I like a picture that tells a story. How much?'

'One hundred and fifty pounds.'

Tony nodded. 'I'd like to buy it.'

'Really? That's very sweet of you.' Smiling, she continued adding detail. 'In that case, you don't have to buy it. You may have the painting.'

'What does that mean?' He was taken aback.

'Tell me, have you ever given someone else a present and known for sure that they absolutely loved it?'

'Well . . . yes.' He nodded.

'And doesn't it feel fantastic?'

'There's no other sensation quite like it.'

Turning to look at him, her golden eyes danced. 'Which is why it gives *me* pleasure to give *you* my painting. If you enjoy it enough to pay for it, it's yours. A little gift to you from me. When it's finished, of course.'

There had been no flicker of recognition when she'd looked at him. Years of practice enabled Tony to be able to tell when people were pretending not to know who he was. This woman, with her guileless smile and easy manner, wasn't playing any kind of game.

'That's incredibly generous of you. Thank you. But you're never going to make the shortlist for Businesswoman of the Year.'

'Ah, but I know my painting's going to a good home.' She loaded a fine brush with topaz yellow. 'That's good enough for me.'

'Where do you exhibit your work?'

'Nowhere fancy. Just the occasional art fair. And online.'

'What's your name?'

'Martha Daines. Now, are you local? Could you be here tomorrow afternoon?'

'After two, no problem.' He had an interview at twelve-thirty.

'See you tomorrow, then. I'll bring it with me. And your name is?'

'Tony.' She didn't have a clue.

'Tony. It's been lovely to meet you. Thank you for liking my work.'

It was almost the end of her first day. With all the new information she was absorbing, Ellie felt as if her head was ready to explode. Zack had been in and out of the house, receiving visits from clients and disappearing to meet others. His working life was chaotic and his phone never seemed to stop ringing. She was typing up reports, fielding calls, making travel arrangements for trips to Zurich and Madrid, and familiarising herself with the general workings of the office.

Zack was upstairs taking a conference call when the doorbell went at ten past five. Opening the front door, Ellie found herself face to face with a polished, sheeny-looking redhead in a sage-green linen dress.

'Well, hello. So you're the new girl.' Her mascaraed lashes batted as she carried out a comprehensive up-and-down. 'Alice?'

'Ellie.'

'Right. I'm Louisa, I expect Zack's mentioned me.'

He hadn't, but Ellie diplomatically didn't say so. She recognised Louisa from the newsagents the other week and wasn't at all surprised that Louisa hadn't, in turn, recognised her. She didn't seem like the kind of person who would. And presumably she was Zack's girlfriend.

Then they heard footsteps on the staircase and Zack appeared.

'Darling, hi.' Louisa moved forward to greet him with a kiss that announced, loud and clear, that he belonged to her. Ellie wondered if it would save all sorts of hassle if she just said, 'Look, it's OK, you don't have to worry about me, I'm really not after him.' Instead she said, 'I've booked the flights and the hotels, and the letters are ready for signing.'

'Great, thanks. Come on through.' Leading the way into the kitchen, Zack said, 'It's time for you to meet someone you're going to get to know pretty well.'

'Who?'

He grinned. 'The love of my life.'

Ellie guessed who it was by the way Louisa rolled her eyes. During her interview Zack had asked how she felt about dogs. He'd then gone on to explain about Elmo, but she hadn't seen him yet.

'Geraldine's back from visiting friends in Brighton. She just called to say he's coming over.' Somewhere outside they heard a rhythmic clattering noise. Zack paused then said, 'Five . . . four . . . three . . .'

'He'd better not be muddy,' warned Louisa.

'Two . . . one . . .' Another clatter, this time closer to hand, then the dog flap in the back door swung open and Louisa backed into a corner as a dishevelled-looking dog burst through into the kitchen. Yelping with joy, he danced round Zack for a few ecstatic seconds before launching himself into his arms.

'I'm not scared,' said Louisa. 'It's just these stockings are eight denier.'

So this was Elmo, Zack's true love. A three-year-old wild-haired terrier cross, with attitude, Elmo had button-bright eyes, lopsided ears and a jaunty manner. Not to mention bushy eyebrows and a straggly beard.

'I'll wait upstairs, Zacky,' Louisa announced. 'Don't be long, OK? We're meeting the Drewetts at six fifteen.'

Zacky? Oh good grief, Ellie thought, did she actually call him that?

'I'll be up soon.'

Turning round, Zack pointed and said, 'Elmo, say hello to Ellie.'

It would have been extra impressive if Elmo had actually said hello back. But she was still charmed by the way he snuffled and wagged his tail and gave every sign of being thrilled to meet her. Zack lowered him to the ground and Ellie knelt to greet the little dog properly.

'He's gorgeous! Hello, baby, I'm going to be friends with you! You are *fab*.' She blew kisses as Elmo rested his front paws in her hands. Looking up, she said, 'And he doesn't get confused, living in two houses?'

Because Elmo was a timeshare property. Two years ago, Zack's neighbour Geraldine had said how much she'd love to have a dog, but her bad leg made it impractical. Zack, in turn, had told her that he'd always wanted a dog but the hours he worked and his frequent trips abroad meant it would be unfair on any animal. The next day he had come up with the solution, and a week after that Elmo had entered their lives.

'It works fine. He has the best of both worlds. Geraldine's at home most of the time. We have matching dog flaps into our kitchens.' Nodding out of the window, Zack indicated the specially lowered section of wall separating their gardens. 'Elmo just hops over when he fancies a change of scenery. If I'm working too hard, he'll go and see Geraldine for a bit of company. If he wants a walk, he comes back here. We share vet's fees and make sure we keep track of who's feeding him, otherwise he'd end up the size of a barrel.' His gaze softened like a proud father's as he watched her scratch the dog's ears. 'He likes you.'

'Well, good. I like you too.' Ellie kissed Elmo's whiskery eyebrows and got her chin licked in return. 'You're so . . . huggy!'

'Zack?' Louisa's voice drifted down the stairs. 'Come on, you need to get changed before we leave. We mustn't be late.'

'**S**o, first day at work. How did it go?'

'Pretty good. Busy.' Ellie was in bed; she put down her book and looked at Jamie, lying on his side across the end of the bed with his head supported on one elbow. 'I think I'm going to enjoy it.'

'You're moving on.' Jamie's gaze was intent.

'I don't feel as if I am.' It was hard to explain, but part of her didn't want to move on; the prospect made her feel guilty. 'I still love you. I'm never going to stop. It's a new job, that's all. With people who aren't going to treat me differently because of what happened.'

Jamie said easily, 'Zack sounds all right. What's the girlfriend like?'

'Louisa? Confident on the surface, insecure underneath. Wishes I was thirty years older. It's funny, she doesn't trust me. If only she knew.'

Jamie grinned. 'If only she knew what a sex maniac you are?'

'I meant what a eunuch I am. Zack couldn't be safer with a lesbian nun.'

'I used to know a joke about a lesbian nun.'

Ellie pulled a face. 'I know you did.'

'I can't remember how it went. You'll have to ask Todd.'

'But then he might tell me.'

'Don't be like that. My jokes are hilarious.'

'Todd's coming over at the weekend.'

'Good. I'm glad you two are talking again.'

Of course he was glad. Wasn't that why she'd done it, safe in the knowledge that it was what Jamie would have wanted?

'It was your dad. He was the one who set it up.'

'But you did your bit. You made the effort. I'm proud of you.'

'Don't make me cry.'

'Oh baby. I love you.'

'Me too.' She wiped away the tear from the corner of her eye.

'You're doing OK. Get some sleep now. Night, baby.'

Ellie closed her eyes and felt the aching loneliness well up inside her chest. 'Night.'

He couldn't remember the last time he'd looked forward so much to seeing someone again. It almost felt like a date. He climbed the last section of the hill and there she was, sitting in the same spot as yesterday. Tony stopped to look at her and felt his heart lift. She was wearing a long emerald-green dress today, with some kind of bright pink necklace round her throat. There was something about the way she held herself, the sense of how supremely comfortable she was in her own skin, that was utterly beguiling. Just looking at her made him want to smile.

Martha spotted him as he made his way towards her. She waved her paintbrush in greeting and called out, 'Hooray, you turned up!'

Her voice was warm and velvety and redolent of the Caribbean.

'Did you think I wouldn't?' Up close, he saw that the necklace was composed of huge uneven pebble-shaped beads painted a dazzling shade of fuchsia pink.

'No, I thought you would.' Martha smiled. 'I hoped you would. Otherwise I'd have lugged this thing all the way for nothing.' Leaning to one side, she reached down for a flat canvas bag lying on the grass.

Tony's heart began to beat faster as she slid her smooth brown arm into the oversized bag and drew out the completed painting, professionally double-mounted on ivory bevel-edged board.

'I still can't believe you're doing this. You didn't have to have it mounted.'

'Oh shush, that was no bother at all, I did it myself.' Her eyes sparkled. 'I'm a demon with a Stanley knife. Anyway, it finishes it off nicely. You can choose your own frame. Here, take it. It's yours.'

The added pen and ink detail enhanced the quirky characters she had observed yesterday afternoon. The result was charming and captivating in every way.

'I have no idea how to thank you.' Tony shook his head. 'This means a lot to me. You don't know how much.'

'I'm just happy you like it. And I certainly do know how much it means.' Reaching up to touch the pink necklace, Martha said, 'I felt exactly the same way when my son made me this.'

OK, that explained the lumpy pink pebbles. Tony wondered how old she was. Had she had her son when she was in her early forties?

'Of course, that was a while ago.' Answering the unspoken question, she said, 'He's twenty-eight now, and a criminal lawyer. It embarrasses him no end that I still wear it. Which is always good fun. But every time I touch this necklace, I see him as clear as day, sitting at the kitchen table in his little shorts, rolling up the clay to make the beads then painting them with my brand new bottle of nail varnish.'

Tony nodded, a long-forgotten memory flashing up of the day Jamie had rushed home from school and presented him with a clay pot. Glowing with pride, he'd announced, 'It's a thumb pot, Daddy! We made them with our thumbs! You can keep your cuff links in it!'

What had happened to that funny little blue pot? He had no idea. OK, don't think about Jamie now, don't mention his name, don't announce that you had a son too, but he died. It would only create awkwardness and bring the mood crashing down.

Instead he said, 'It's a great necklace. It has character. I took a look at your website, by the way.'

'And . . .?' She clutched her chest in mock terror. 'I always get nervous when people say that. It's like being back at school and your teacher saying he's read your essay.'

'Well, you get an A plus from me. I'm officially a fan of your work.' Tony paused. 'And I'd like to buy more. But this time you'd have to let me pay.'

'Really?' Martha looked delighted.

'Really.'

'Now I feel like a drug dealer. Giving you the first taste for free, making sure you come back for more.' She searched his face. 'Seriously, so long as you aren't doing it just to be polite.'

Tony said gravely, 'I'm very rarely polite.'

She smiled. 'Which ones would you be interested in?'

'The swimmers in Hampstead Ponds. The one with the fireworks on the Thames. Possibly the wedding party.'

'Oh, sorry. That one's sold. But there are plenty more at home,' Martha said. 'I haven't got round yet to putting them on the website.'

'Right.' He nodded. 'Well . . . I'd be really interested in seeing them.'

'OK, great.' She carried on painting.

What did that mean? Tony said, 'So, will you put them on the website? Or is there some way I could get to see the actual paintings?'

Martha sat back. 'Is that what you'd prefer?'

'Yes.'

'We can go now, if you like. If you have time.'

'I have time.' It was what he wanted, more than anything. 'Are you sure this is OK?'

She smiled. 'If I wasn't sure, I wouldn't say it.'

Together they packed away her things and headed down the hill.

She lived on Lanacre Road in Tufnell Park, in a terraced house with bright hanging baskets either side of the topaz-yellow front door.

'Why doesn't it surprise me that you have a yellow front door?' said Tony.

'Ah, I'm a lady of colour.' Martha opened the door. 'It's one of life's joys. Come along in.'

He inhaled the light summery scent she was wearing as he followed her into the living room. Cleverly, she hadn't overdone the colour. Three walls were white, one was a vivid shade of peacock blue. The sofa was upholstered in bottle green velvet, and there were white rugs on the polished wooden floor. Bookshelves were crammed with books. There were paintings on the walls and bowls of flowers everywhere.

'They're not yours.' He indicated the framed paintings.

'I couldn't hang my work in my own living room. That would be too weird.' Martha smiled. 'Now, I can either cart everything down here or we can go upstairs to see my paintings.'

She genuinely had no idea who he was. Charmed by her manner, by her character . . . OK, by pretty much everything about her, Tony said, 'Let's go up and have a look at them, shall we?'

The front bedroom had been converted into a studio. Here were the paintings, propped up against all four walls, some familiar to him from the website, others not. The sun streamed in through the windows. Another easel was set up in the centre of the room and paint-spattered white sheets covered the carpet.

'They have to be there,' Martha apologised, 'because I'm such a mucky pup. Mind you don't trip on them. Now, let me talk you through the paintings.' Resting her hand on his arm, she said confidingly, 'I tell you what, see if you can guess which one's my favourite.'

From that moment on, Tony was lost. It was almost impossible to concentrate on whatever it was she was saying. All he could think of was how close she was to him, how wonderful she smelled.

'. . . Well?'

OK, he needed to pay attention. 'Well what?'

She surveyed him with amusement. 'Have you been listening at all?'

'That one. That's your favourite.' He pointed to a painting of a picnic on the beach.

'I just asked you what colour your walls were. Where you're going to hang them.'

'Oh sorry. I'm distracted.' Bracing himself, Tony said, 'By you.'

'Me? Why?'

'Because you're such a lovely surprise.' Did that sound completely ridiculous? Well, it was true. Aloud he said, 'You don't know how happy I am to have met you.'

Martha looked away, then back at him. Finally she exhaled. 'Me too. You're a very nice man.'

'It's not just me, feeling it?'

She shook her head and swallowed. 'Not just you.'

'I want you to know that I don't make a habit of doing this.' Reaching for her hand, he stroked the brown fingers. 'But I want to do it now.'

The next moment she was in his arms and he was kissing her, and it was like being twenty again. Martha's soft body pressed against his, her silver bracelets clinking as she ran a hand through his hair. She was trembling with emotion. God, she was *so beautiful* . . .

'Tony?' Breathlessly she pulled away to study his face. 'Are you single?'

He nodded. 'Divorced many years ago. I've been on my own for a long time.'

'Me too.' He felt her sadness. The next moment it was dispelled. 'And I want you to know that I've never done this before either.'

Another kiss, then she led him out of the studio. Her bedroom was smaller, ultra-feminine in shades of cream and gold.

Tony turned her to face him. 'You're sure this is all right?'

There was a world of emotion in her golden eyes. Her voice unsteady, she whispered, 'I've never wanted anything more in my life.'

An hour had passed. Possibly the most incredible hour of his life. When he said, 'OK, there's something I have to tell you,' Tony saw a flash of fear.

Martha had gone very still. 'Tell me.'

'I don't live here in London. My home's in Los Angeles.'

She sank back against the pillows. 'Oh. That's a long way away.'

'But we can sort something out. I want to keep on seeing you. I hope you want to keep seeing me. I can come over every few weeks. I don't know, maybe you could come out and stay.'

'You work over there?' She searched his face. 'What do you do?'

'I'm an actor.'

Her eyebrows went up. 'Really? Any good?'

'Pretty good, yes.'

'Successful?'

'Yes. Yes, I am.'

Martha thought for a moment then said slowly, 'Are you famous?'

He nodded.

She broke into a huge smile. 'Well, that explains it, then! While we were on our way back here, I saw a couple of people looking at you. But more than just a normal look, you know? More *interested*. I thought it was because you were so attractive. But it wasn't, was it? They recognised you. Oh my God, what's your name?'

'Tony Weston.'

'I've heard that name!' Martha clapped a hand over her mouth. 'You *are* famous! You were in that film about the two brothers . . . ooh, what was it called . . . *Mr and Mr Black*!'

'That's right.'

'I heard all about it on the radio! They said you were very good.'

Tony smiled. 'They were right.'

'You must think I'm hopeless. I should have known who you were! Oh God! I just had sex with a film star!'

'Fantastic sex,' Tony corrected.

'Fantastic sex. Absolutely. God, sorry, I've come over all unnecessary now. This is just bizarre.'

'Can I tell you something?' He traced the tips of his fingers along her collarbone. 'It's the most miraculous thing that's happened to me in years.'

Martha nodded, her eyes filling up. She whispered, 'Me too. When do you go back to the States?'

'The day after tomorrow. You could come with me.' But she was already shaking her head.

'I can't. But thank you. Oh my word, is that the time? I didn't realise it was so late.' Pulling on a cotton robe, she said, 'I have to be somewhere by six. And you haven't had a proper look at the other paintings.'

'**O**h wow, look at those. They're so . . . happy!' Home from work, Ellie encountered the four paintings lined up on the sofa. She pointed to the Primrose Hill picture. 'That's the one you told me about last night. Did she give you all of these?'

Tony shook his head. 'I paid for them. We went back to her house and she showed me her work. I bought the other three.' He kept the rest to himself. He was Ellie's father-in-law; there was no way he could tell her what else he'd done this afternoon.

'You should buy paintings more often.' Ellie was smiling at him. 'It suits you.' His soul was singing. If only she knew.

'I might do that.'

The next morning was taken up with meetings, followed by lunch in Soho with an old actor friend he couldn't let down. By two-thirty, as the taxi took him to Tufnell Park, Tony's heart was flick-flacking away in his chest. Fifty-five years old, and he felt like a teenager on a first date.

This was unbelievable. It had never occurred to him that something like this could happen. At his age, too. Love—or something perilously close to it—at first sight. Martha, Martha, just saying her name in his head gave him a thrill.

They reached Lanacre Road and he paid off the cab. He raised his hand and rang the bell. It would be their last time together for weeks; would she let him spend the night here?

The door opened and there was Martha, wearing a violet shift dress and looking . . . completely different. As if seeing him on her doorstep was the very last thing she wanted. Even her head was shaking fractionally from side to side as she said, 'Oh hello, is this about the paintings? I'm afraid it's a bit of an awkward time.'

'Who is it, Martha?' Behind her, another woman came into view. Older, Afro-Caribbean, with grey hair and sensible shoes. Over Martha's shoulder she surveyed him with an unwavering gaze.

'Nobody, just someone interested in my work . . .'

What's going on?

'My name's Tony.' He held out his hand to Martha and shook it, then reached past her and said pleasantly, 'Hello there. Tony Weston.'

Forced to shake his hand, the grey-haired woman nodded briefly.

'Could I come in? I've sent my taxi away now.'

Martha swallowed and said fearfully, 'OK, just for five minutes.' She stepped aside. Tony followed the older woman into the living room.

'I'll bring the pictures down.' Hurrying upstairs, Martha said, 'Eunice, why don't you make Mr Weston a cup of tea?'

Eunice raised an eyebrow. 'Are we a café now?'

'It's fine, don't worry.' Tony smiled. 'I'm a great fan of Mrs Daines's work. Are you a friend of hers?'

'Sister-in-law.'

'Oh.' Did that mean Eunice was the ex-husband's sister? Or was she married to Martha's brother?

In less than thirty seconds Martha was back with an armful of mounted prints. One thing was for sure, she was like a cat on a hot plate. As soon as the paintings were spread out on the table, she said, 'There you are, that's all of them. Which one would you like?'

The tension in the room was palpable, like an overdose of air-freshener. Tony put her out of her misery and pointed. 'I'll have that one.'

'Excellent.' Martha managed a smile. 'Good choice.'

And that was it. Within four minutes of ringing the front doorbell, he found himself being propelled back out onto the pavement. With a painting under his arm and his plans for the rest of the day well and truly scuppered. On his way out he said in desperation, 'Could I have your number, in case I wanted to buy another one?'

Eunice replied crisply, 'She doesn't hand out her telephone number to strangers. Do you, Martha?'

Martha swallowed. 'If you want to contact me about my work, my email address is on my website.'

'Fine, I'll do that then.' Pointedly Tony said, 'I'm going to be out of the country for the next couple of weeks, but I'll be back at the beginning of July.'

'OK. Well, it's been nice to meet you, Mr Weston.' Clearly desperate to close the door, Martha said, 'Enjoy your painting. Goodbye.'

'Or I could give you my number?' It was a last-ditch attempt; he so badly needed to speak to her before he left.

'That won't be necessary,' Eunice coolly intervened. 'Why would she want to phone you?'

Because we spent yesterday afternoon in bed together, you bloody interfering old witch. And I'm in love with her.

But of course Tony didn't say this out loud.

Chapter 5

'CAN YOU GET THAT?' Ellie was busy scrubbing her favourite Havaianas pink flip-flops in the sink when the doorbell went on Saturday morning.

Todd pressed the button on the intercom and waited.

'Hi, it's me.' Roo's voice echoed tinnily through the speaker. 'I'm heading out on an undercover mission. Want to come along?'

'What an offer.' Todd launched into his Sean Connery impression. 'Shall we go in my vintage Aston Martin?'

A split second of silence, then, 'James Bond, is that you?'

'Shweetheart, I'm afraid that's classified information. I could tell you, but then I'd have to seduce you.'

'Let her in.' Ellie rinsed the flip-flops. This was going to be interesting; how would her old friend and her new friend hit it off?

Roo bounded up the stairs and into the flat in a black and white checked shirt, white denim skirt and black Uggs.

'I can guess who you are.' She waggled her fingers at Todd. 'But do you really have an Aston Martin?'

'Sorry.'

'I'm disappointed. And you don't look like Sean Connery either.'

'I'm younger than he is. I'm funnier,' said Todd. 'Plus, I have hair.'

'What's this mission in aid of?' Ellie finished patting the flip-flops dry with kitchen paper and put them on her feet.

'OK, Niall came over last night. And while he was in the loo I happened to find a shopping list in his jacket pocket. Just nappies and baby wipes and stuff. But it was written in girly handwriting on a Post-it note with the name of a beauty salon printed along the top.' Roo narrowed her eyes in sleuthlike fashion. 'Now, Niall refuses to tell me where his wife works. So I rang the salon this morning and asked if Yasmin was in today . . . and she is! And guess what? I've booked an appointment with her for this afternoon! We can go together!'

Ellie pulled a face. How could anyone think this was a good idea?

'Who's Niall?' said Todd.

Roo looked at him. 'My boyfriend.'

'He has a wife?'

'Yes, but she's awful.'

'And there's a baby?'

'That's the only reason he's still with his wife.'

'What are you doing having an affair with a married man?'

'I love him. And he loves me.'

'Where's your self-respect?'

Roo stiffened. 'What's your problem?'

'When I was a kid, my father had an affair with another woman. He walked out on me and my mum. I just happen to think wrecking other people's marriages is a pretty low thing to do.'

Roo said defensively, 'Trust me, Niall's marriage was wrecked long before I came along.'

'So why have you made an appointment at this place?' said Ellie.

'Because I want to see her. I just want to find out for myself what she's like. I'm not going to do anything,' Roo protested. 'She won't know who I am. Oh, please come with me,' she begged. 'It'll be easier to have a conversation with the two of us. And then you'll be able to tell thingy here that I'm not a complete monster.'

Todd was ice-cool. 'Thingy can make up his own mind, thanks.'

Oh dear. Off to a rocky start.

The salon was in Hampstead. From the outside it was all subtle shades of rose-pink and cream. Inside it smelled like heaven.

Roo was nervous. And the woman behind the reception desk with the terrifying ice-queen face could be Niall's wife.

'Twelve thirty . . . let me see . . .' She ran a ferocious crimson nail down the appointments book. 'Yes, there you are. Just take a seat and Yasmin will be with you very shortly.'

They sat and waited and watched one of the other customers have a pedicure. Within two minutes the door to the salon burst open and a woman in her twenties rushed in with a multipack of nappies under one arm and a carrier bag from Lloyds the chemist in the other.

Having stowed them in the back room, she returned. 'Hello, sorry to keep you waiting, just had to dash out to the shops. I'm Yasmin. Gosh, if your hair was different you'd look like that singer from years ago. What's her name . . . thingummy . . . Daisy Deeva.'

'I get that all the time.' Roo pulled a face. 'I saw her once, in Selfridges. She was buying a really horrible hat.'

'Wouldn't mind her money though, eh?' Yasmin didn't seem like a nightmare. She was smiling and friendly, with wavy honey-blonde hair and pretty eyes.

Ellie watched as Roo's hands were painstakingly cleansed and moisturised. Finally Roo said, 'I saw you with the nappies. Does that mean you have a baby?'

Yasmin grinned. 'Yes, we've got a boy, Benjamin. Seven months. He's just adorable.' Her eyes were shining. 'How about you?'

'Kids? Me? No.' Roo shook her head, then clearly realised a child might come in handy. Indicating Ellie, she said, 'She's got one.'

Yasmin turned to her. 'Have you? Aren't they fantastic? Boy or a girl?'

'Girl.' Ellie nodded and prayed they weren't about to start swapping childbirth stories. 'Five months. Her name's Alice.'

'Ah, that's lovely.' Cheerily Yasmin said, 'Hard work, though, aren't they? Does your chap help out much, or is he as useless as mine?'

Ellie said, 'Not much. They're all pretty useless, aren't they?'

'Tell me about it! My husband was supposed to be buying those nappies yesterday, and what happens? He comes home at midnight, says he had to work late, but it's just a big fib. I know exactly where he was!'

Roo swallowed.

'Where was he?' said Ellie.

'Out with his friends, of course! It's that old meet-up-with-your-mates-on-a-Friday-night thing. He just can't give it up.' Yasmin shook her head. 'Still, that's men for you. They can't multitask like us.'

'What's he like with the nappies?'

Smiling, Yasmin said, 'He changed three-quarters of a nappy once. I'm telling you, that was a sight to behold. You'd have thought he was detonating an unexploded bomb. It was hilarious. There now, let's just wrap your hands in warm towels to let the moisturisers sink in.'

'But he must do it sometimes.' Ellie frowned. 'I mean, like today, while you're here working.'

'Oh, he's not looking after him now.' More amused resignation. 'Niall likes his lie-ins on a Saturday morning. I drop Benjamin off at my mum's before I come into work.'

'This is interesting,' Ellie murmured when Yasmin disappeared to attend to another client. Roo must be devastated to discover that her boyfriend's wife was so nice.

'See? I told you she was a nightmare,' Roo whispered. 'She's just a complete control freak.'

Todd was waiting for them in the pub watching tennis on the giant TV screen up on the wall.

'Well? What was she like?' Todd asked.

'Lovely,' said Ellie.

'Oh please, that's not fair.' Roo shook her head. 'She was *pretending* to be lovely because she was at work; I'm her client, of course she's going to put on a good show. But you could tell what she's really like.'

'She was great,' Ellie insisted. 'Cheerful, warm, working her socks off. Do you want my honest opinion?'

'No.' Roo was busy fiddling with her sunglasses.

'Niall sounds like an arse.'

'You're biased. I wish I'd never taken you along with me now.'

'And Yasmin's like a single mother,' Ellie went on. 'She does everything and he does nothing.' *How could Roo not see it?*

'Because when he does try to do anything, she tells him he's doing it all wrong!'

'He told her he was working last night. But he was with you.'

Roo was defensive. 'If he goes home, all she does is nag him.'

'She's probably exhausted looking after the baby on her own!'

Todd, his head swivelling between them, said, 'This is better than the tennis. So come on, are you going to finish with this bloke?'

'Don't be so horrible! I love him!'

He looked exasperated. 'The guy's a liar and a cheat.'

'Everyone tells lies.' Their drinks arrived and Roo took a gulp of hers. 'You should have heard Ellie going on about her baby.'

'What baby?'

Roo spread her arms. 'I rest my case.'

Todd was staring at Ellie. 'Are you *pregnant*?'

Ellie spluttered into her glass of wine. 'No! How could I be pregnant? We just pretended I had a baby so we'd have something in common.' She saw the look of relief on his face. 'It was a white lie, that's all.'

'Speaking of white.' Roo knocked back the rest of her vodka. 'I've got an appointment to get my roots done, so I'm off.' She looked at Todd. 'I'd say it was nice to meet you, but that would be another lie.'

He said pleasantly, 'That's because I'm right and you know it.'

The tennis had evolved into a tense five-set match that had got everyone in the pub cheering. Afterwards Ellie and Todd went out for pizza, before heading off to a club in Camden to see a band.

'That was . . . loud,' said Ellie three hours later as they made their way back through Chalk Farm to Primrose Hill. 'My ears are ringing.'

Todd nodded in agreement. 'They were so loud I couldn't even tell if they were any good. Is this a sign that we're getting old?'

'We are old. Maybe next time we could stand outside on the pavement, just hear it from a distance.'

'Why stand? We could take a couple of deck chairs along. Get comfy, roll up our trouser legs.'

'Wear knotted hankies on our heads,' Ellie said. 'You can't beat a knotted hankie. In fact, why bother with going to see a noisy old band anyway? What's wrong with watching Morris dancers instead?'

'Now you're talking, Ethel. We'll take along a Thermos of tea and a packet of ham sandwiches.' He paused, checking she was OK.

Ellie managed a smile to reassure him she was fine. This had been his and Jamie's thing, taking an idea and running with it.

'God, I miss him,' said Todd.

She nodded, the all-too-familiar hollowness in her stomach expanding like a balloon.

They reached Nevis Street and Ellie fished out her key.

'Thanks. It's been a good day.'

'I've had fun too.'

'You didn't have to walk me home. You've missed the last tube now.'

Todd shrugged easily. 'No problem. I'll get the bus.'

'OK.' She stepped forward and gave him a kiss on the cheek.

'I'll give you a call. If you're free next weekend, we could do it again. Check out what bands are on, stock up on ear-plugs.' He hesitated. 'No pressure. Only if you want to.'

Did she want to? Ellie thought she probably did. She looked at Todd. He was Jamie's oldest friend, and now she'd got over her stupid resentful phase she was comfortable in his company.

'Yes, call me. I'd like to do that.'

Elmo was dancing around like a lunatic, chasing dandelion seeds as they drifted like mini parachutes above his head. Zack stuck his fingers in his mouth and whistled. Like a D-list celeb spotting the paparazzi, Elmo pricked up his ears and came racing back.

Zack reattached Elmo's lead. 'Come on, we need to get home now.'

He and Elmo left the hill and made their way back to Ancram Street. Later on this morning he was flying to Amsterdam to meet a co-investor. He'd be home by eight. Tomorrow he was visiting a shoe factory in Derby. The following day he had back-to-back appointments with prospective partners. But this was how Zack lived his life. Work came first; it always had, and personal relationships came second.

At least they had, until Ellie Kendall had come into his life. The situation he found himself in was crazy, it was just ridiculous. Never before had his mind been occupied during important meetings with thoughts of a female who *wasn't even remotely interested in him.*

His phone began to ring and Louisa's name flashed up on the screen. 'Hello, you.' She was using her consciously sexy telephone voice. 'Listen, how about if I come over this evening?'

Zack knew it was wrong that the suggestion didn't fill him with joy. Their relationship had started out so well; it had taken a while for the realisation to sink in that the Louisa he'd first got to know was something of a front, a beguiling persona created to give a good impression. They were turning out to have less in common than he'd first thought. 'The thing is, I'm going to be shattered when I get back from Amsterdam.' A lie, but a necessary one.

'I know, that's why I'm suggesting it. I'll cook dinner and spoil you rotten. Go on,' Louisa purred in his ear. 'You know you want to.'

He really didn't, not tonight. 'Look, I don't want to mess up your evening. I may have to stay on for a couple of drinks with the Van den Bergs. Who knows what time I'll be back.'

'Oh darling, you're so thoughtful, but I really don't mind.'

'But I do. It's not fair on you. Let's leave it for tonight, OK?'

'Oh right. Well, how about tomorrow then?'

'Tomorrow. Fine.' His voice softened. He knew he should finish with Louisa but he also knew it was going to be hard work. Louisa was so dramatic, she wouldn't leave without kicking up a fuss. It was a daunting enough prospect that it put him off broaching the subject.

Zack ended the call and headed for home. It was ten past nine and Ellie would be there by now. He also knew it was wrong to be seeing Louisa while feeling the way he did about someone else. But Ellie's absolute indifference towards him meant it hardly mattered. It wasn't as if finishing with Louisa would make her suddenly change her mind and fall for him. It just didn't work like that.

Ellie was in the office, smelling gorgeous and with her hair tied back with a grey velvet ribbon to reveal her neck. The post had already been sorted into piles and she was now watering the forest of plants that had taken up residence along the windowsill, courtesy of Barbara.

She was wearing a grey jersey top with a square neck and elbow-length sleeves, and a red skirt. Moving closer, Zack breathed in the fresh, lemony perfume and watched the way her dark hair glinted in the sunlight streaming in through the window.

'There's a message on the phone from someone called . . . Huggy?' She looked bemused. 'Is that right?'

'Huggy Hill. My first ever business partner.'

'How did it happen? Was that when you were still at college?'

He nodded. 'That's right. Huggy was a mate. I was taking a degree in Business Management. He'd set up this tiny company selling mobile phones and he started asking me for advice. After a couple of months I saw the potential of what he was trying to do—this was before mobiles went mega—and I took a stake in the business in exchange for all the work I was doing for him. Chiefly because it was the only way he could afford to pay me. Then things started to take off and I realised I'd far rather be working with Huggy than carrying on with a degree course.'

'So you dropped out of university.'

'I did. We built up the business and sold it two years later for crazy money. By then I'd already begun to diversify. I discovered I had good instincts, I could see why other people's companies were failing and what it would take to bring them back up again. I did some stuff with a computer-support consultancy that turned it round.'

She nodded. 'Then there was the ice-cream business.'

He smiled. 'I loved that one.'

'And the holiday park in Dorset.'

'You've been doing your homework.'

'And the restaurant with the home-delivery service. Did your friend Huggy start investing in other companies too?'

'No, he moved to the Caribbean, spent his days surfing and became a professional beach bum. He's still there now. Having a great life.'

'Do you ever wish you were doing what he's doing?'

'Never. I'm happy here.' Did that make him sound boring? Work-obsessed? *Was he boring and work-obsessed?* He said, 'Would you do it?'

Ellie thought for a moment. 'It would depend on who I was with. Living in the perfect place with the wrong person would be horrible.'

'How about living with the perfect person in a horrible place?'

Something flickered behind her eyes for a second. Then she half-smiled and said, 'If they're the perfect person, it would still be perfect.'

OK, what did that smile mean? Was she thinking of Tony Weston? Was she thinking that she *could* live with him in some dump and be happy about it, but luckily she didn't need to slum it because—hooray!—he'd set her up in a love nest in Primrose Hill instead?

On the few occasions he'd subtly asked questions about her private life she had veered away from the subject. Therefore he wasn't going to push it. He knew that Ellie wasn't remotely interested in him. So he was going to hold back completely. Be charming and as nice as he knew how to be. But without flirting at all. It wouldn't be easy but he was going to do it. He had to. Because this was too important to mess up.

What was going on? Tony had no idea, but he knew he needed to find out. Over the past fortnight he must have sent Martha a dozen emails. All he'd had in return was a single brief message on the first day. In it, she had apologised and said their encounter had been a huge mistake. They mustn't meet again, she was sorry if she'd led him on and could he please respect her privacy and not attempt to contact her in any way.

That was it. Since then, each subsequent email had gone unanswered. Directory enquiries had declined to give out Martha's phone number. Tony, stuck in Hollywood filming, had been counting down the days. Anyway, he was back now. Another day, another taxi. And no way was he capable of respecting her wish for privacy. As they pulled into Lanacre Road, Tony's chest tightened in anticipation.

The taxi driver said, 'Where d'you want me to stop?'

'Farther along. It's the house with the yellow door, up on the left.' As the taxi slowed, Tony said, 'Pull over behind that blue van.'

The next moment the yellow door opened and Disapproving Eunice came out. Followed by Martha.

'Oh God, don't stop.' Tony shrank back from the window and hissed, From the depths of the cab he glimpsed Martha's profile as she turned to lock the door behind them. The taxi trundled on to the end of the road and stopped at the junction.

'Where to now, then?'

'Um . . .' Peering out of the back of the cab, Tony saw that the two women were heading off in the opposite direction. 'Turn round and wait. See if they get into that car.'

'You want me to follow them? Hey, you don't know how long I've waited for someone to say that and actually mean it!' Chuckling, he swung the cab round. 'You're Tony Weston, right?'

'Yes.'

'Am I allowed to ask what's going on here?'

'I'd rather you didn't,' said Tony.

'They're not getting into any car. Looks like they're walking.'

Tony thought fast. 'Let's follow them.'

'Are you serious, mate? They're on foot.'

'You'll just have to go slowly then, won't you?'

Luckily Martha and Eunice didn't look back. The taxi remained at a safe distance behind them, trundling along at the speed of mud. When they reached the busy main road it got trickier, the cab driver having to stop and start and work hard not to get trapped in the bus lane.

Eventually turning off the main road, Martha and Eunice made their way down leafy side streets.

'There you go,' said the cabbie as the two women finally turned into the driveway of a property set well back from the road.

Tony leaned forward. As the taxi drew closer he saw the sign by the gate: Stanshawe House Nursing and Residential Care Home.

'Mystery solved. They're visiting some old granny.'

'Maybe. Maybe not. They could be visiting anyone.'

'Or else they work there,' the cabbie amended. 'Anyway, what now? Are you going in after them?'

'No.' Tony sat back in his seat. 'Take me back to Primrose Hill.'

Ellie was still out at work. Back at the flat, Tony looked up Stanshawe House in the Yellow Pages and copied down the number. Then he forced himself to sit and wait, because the one thing he couldn't do was phone them while Eunice and Martha might still be there.

At five o'clock he made the call.

'Oh hello, I'm calling about one of your residents. By the name of Daines.' It was a shot in the dark, but the only shot he had.

'Sorry, who?' The woman sounded distracted.

'Daines.'

'Could you give me the first name?'

Tony hesitated, he didn't know the first name. 'Um, well . . .'

'Oh, do you mean Henry Daines? Sorry, I'm new here, I've just found him on the list.'

Bingo. 'That's it. Henry.'

'Right. And what is this about? Let me take a message.'

'Oh, no message. I'm just calling to . . . find out how he is.'

'Hang on, I'm just writing this down. Say again?'

God, she was dippy. 'I haven't seen Henry for some time. I heard that he's in your care,' said Tony. 'Could you tell me why he's with you?'

'Ooh no, we're not allowed to do that! Sorry! Why don't you contact his family? They'll be able to give you all the information you need.'

Typical. 'OK then, can you tell me who his family—'

'Oh my goodness, now the red light's started flashing! Sorry, love, I'm going to have to go, just call his family . . . OK, bye!'

At nine o'clock the next morning, Tony rang Martha's bell and heard the sound of footsteps inside the house.

The topaz-yellow door opened and for the first time in a fortnight he came face to face with Martha. It was so wonderful to see her again.

He kept his voice low. 'Are you on your own?'

She nodded. 'Oh Tony, don't do this. You shouldn't have come here.'

'I had to. You can't just tell me to leave you alone and expect me to do it. I thought we *had* something . . .'

'Please, no.' Martha was shaking her head in despair.

'Can I come in?'

'No. I told you, we can't see each other any more. Tony, just go. Do you think this is easy for me? Because it isn't, I can promise you that.'

'I know, I know, but we need to talk.' He paused. 'Who's Henry?'

She froze. 'Who told you?'

'Is he your father-in-law?'

'No.'

'Brother-in-law?'

Martha shook her head.

'So that means he's your ex-husband.' Tony had already guessed as much; he didn't need to look at her to know he was right.

'He's not my ex-husband,' Martha said finally.

'You mean you're still married.'

She pressed her lips together, gave a funny, wobbly nod.

'Why don't I come in?' said Tony. And this time she stood back to allow him into the house.

In the kitchen, Martha said, 'I still don't know how you found out. Was it Eunice?' She shook her head. 'It couldn't have been Eunice.'

Tony said, 'Just tell me about Henry.'

'We've been married for thirty-three years. Very happily.' Her voice began to waver. 'Well, up until six years ago. OK, I'm going to cry now. Don't say anything, just ignore it.' Reaching for the roll of kitchen towel, she tore off a couple of sheets and rested one hip against the kitchen units. 'He has Alzheimer's. It started seven years ago when he was only fifty-five. Just gradually, you know, losing keys and forgetting people's names. We joked about it at first. Until he made a serious mistake at work and it stopped being funny.'

The tears were rolling down her cheeks. 'Then he saw the doctor and we got the diagnosis. We were both devastated and I promised to look after him. Henry was a high-powered accountant. Within a year of giving up work he couldn't put together a shopping list.' Martha paused to wipe her eyes. 'It all happened so quickly.'

She stopped again to gather herself, and it was all Tony could do not to take her in his arms.

'And it carried on going downhill from there,' Martha said quietly. 'I did my best, I swear I did. But it was so much harder than I ever thought it would be. He started having mood swings, then temper tantrums. It wasn't his fault, he was just scared and frustrated. But it was like trying to keep a six-foot toddler under control. He wasn't . . . easy.' Martha's voice broke. 'It's horrible. And I know I'd promised to look after him, but it was just the l-loneliest job in the w-world . . .'

'That's why you told me you'd been on your own for a long time.'

She nodded, struggling to regain control. 'It is. But it wasn't fair for me to say that. I let you think I was divorced. That was so wrong.'

'It was completely understandable.'

'No, it was . . . disgusting. And I've never been so ashamed.'

'I interrupted,' Tony said. 'Carry on with the story.'

'I carried on as long as I could. With help from Eunice,' she amended. 'She's Henry's sister. I owe her a lot. Anyway, a year ago it all got too much for me. I just couldn't cope any more. I sold our big house in Notting Hill and bought this one instead. Thanks to Henry, our finances were in good shape. And how did I repay him?' She sighed. 'By putting him in a nursing home. That was nice of me, wasn't it?'

'He's getting the best care. You visit him, who's to say that isn't *better*?'

Martha gave him an odd look. Tony held up his hands in surrender. 'I'm sorry. I followed you yesterday afternoon. I had to know.'

She nodded. 'It was stupid of me to ignore you and hope you'd disappear. But you do see now, why we can't see each other again?'

'It's a terrible situation.' All he wanted to do was comfort her and make the pain go away. 'How is he now?'

'Confused. Sad, sometimes. But he still recognises me. He knows who I am. He calls me his beautiful wife.' Martha's expression changed.

'When I saw you that day on the hill, you seemed so happy,' Tony said. 'That was what drew me to you.'

'I was happy.' She inclined her head in agreement. 'At first after Henry went into the home, I was relieved. And every time I felt relieved, I felt guilty. I was ashamed of myself. But as time went on, the guilt started to fade. For the last couple of months I've let myself relax and feel OK about my life. And, I was outside on a beautiful summer's day with the sun on my face. My painting was going well. I suddenly realised I felt completely at peace. It was the most amazing experience, like having a great weight lifted off my shoulders. And then you came along, and you were lovely too. It was as if you were part of it.'

So that was why she had wanted to give him the painting. The money aspect had been irrelevant, the fact that he'd loved her work was all that mattered.

'And the next day was a continuation of that,' said Tony.

She nodded. 'I still can't believe I did it. You were just . . . so perfect. It was like taking a holiday from being myself. I felt normal. No I didn't, I felt *wonderful*.' Fresh tears sprang into her eyes. 'It was like the best dream ever. And then it was over, and I woke up.'

'But it wasn't a dream.'

'I know that. I wish it had been. I was unfaithful to my husband and I hate myself. Which is why you have to leave me alone and not contact me. Because it's never going to happen again.'

'I don't think what we did was wrong.'

'That's not true. Of course it's *wrong*.' Martha eyed him sadly. 'You're just trying to justify it. For better, for worse. That's what I said when I made my wedding vows.'

'But that's not—'

'Don't say it.' Martha held up her hands to stop him. 'Would you like to ask Eunice if she thinks there's justification? She lives just across the street, by the way. That afternoon we came back here, I knew she was away visiting friends in Stockport. Then when you turned up the next day, she was here. She'd come back early. And Eunice isn't stupid. Which is why you have to go now.'

This was unbearable. Tony said, 'But I love you.'

She flinched, the words hitting her like arrows. 'Don't say that either. It can't happen. You're a Hollywood actor and I'm an ordinary married woman from Tufnell Park.'

'You're not ordinary.'

Martha pressed her lips together and crossed the kitchen. Out in the hall, she pulled open the front door.

'I can't do this any more. You have your life to live and I have mine.' She sounded as if her heart was breaking, but the look she gave him was resolute. 'If you care about me, you'll leave. Now.'

A nasty riding accident seven years ago had left Dr Geraldine Castle with a broken left hip that had never successfully knitted back together. Now arthritis had set in as well: walking was painful, horse-riding a thing of the past. High heels these days were only for looking at. It didn't stop her buying them, though. Once a shoe queen, always a shoe queen.

The postman, unable to deliver the parcel next door earlier, had left it with Ellie instead. Now back from lunch with an ex-work colleague, Geraldine had arrived to pick it up.

'OK, you have to see these,' she exclaimed. 'They are just to die for!'

Neither her limp nor her carved ebony walking stick detracted from her glamour. At sixty-one, Geraldine coupled innate style with the posture of a model: heads turned when she entered a room. Last year she had retired from a career in medicine, having spent many years in general practice.

In the office, she sat down and unwrapped the parcel.

'Look at you! Aren't you beautiful?' She lifted the shoes out of the box and lovingly stroked the butter-soft lilac leather. 'They're a work of art. They demand adulation!'

She truly loved them. Sometimes she would even wear them, but only while sitting down.

Ellie watched her reverently place the shoes back in the box. 'I prefer flip-flops.'

'That's because you're a heathen. Where's Zack today?'

'Northampton. He'll be back around six.'

'You've been here for almost a month now.' Geraldine's eyes were bright as they searched her face. 'Enjoying it?'

'Definitely. No more getting squashed on the tube,' Ellie said. 'Bliss!'

An eyebrow was raised. 'That's all, is it?'

'And getting to see Elmo every day.'

'Well, that goes without saying.' Geraldine looked amused. 'I was thinking more of Zack. Isn't it a bonus getting to see him too?'

This wasn't the first time Geraldine had attempted to find out if Ellie was secretly harbouring a crush on Zack.

'He's a good person to work for,' Ellie said patiently.

'And don't forget handsome.'

'OK, he's nice to look at. But that's all.' Ellie shrugged. 'Really.'

'You mean it, don't you? This is so disappointing. Zack's so lovely, that's all I'm saying.'

'I'm sure Louisa thinks so too.'

'Oh, *her.*' Geraldine's tone was dismissive. 'He can do better than that. You're far nicer than Louisa.'

'But I still don't have any designs on Zack,' Ellie pointed out. 'And he knows I don't. That's why he employed me.'

'You're absolutely right, darling.' Recognising when she was beaten, Geraldine closed the shoe box and prepared to leave. 'Touché.'

There had been something different about this evening. The realisation had crept up on Ellie gradually. At first she'd thought she was imagining it. But she wasn't. Well, that was pretty obvious now.

Furthermore, she appeared to be having an out-of-body experience. Todd Howard was kissing her and she was mentally standing back, noting her reaction to it. It felt completely bizarre, yet you couldn't call it unpleasant. Breaking contact, she drew back and opened her eyes. Todd was watching her, waiting to gauge her reaction.

'Sorry.' He was breathing quite heavily. 'Are you OK?'

'Yes.' She still felt like an observer. They'd fallen into the habit of spending time together at the weekends. Today had been no different: shopping on Portobello Road, a couple of drinks in the afternoon, then a stop-off at a pizza takeaway on the way home. Once back at the flat, they had relaxed on the sofa, washed the slices of *quattro staggioni* down with white wine and started watching *Ocean's Eleven* on DVD.

Then halfway through the film, Todd had turned to look at her and said, 'Ell? I want to kiss you.'

And she'd been so astounded she'd said, 'Seriously?'

'Yes.'

'Oh.' And more out of politeness than anything else, she had heard herself say bemusedly, 'OK.'

The next moment, Todd's mouth had descended on hers. *And they were kissing.* Half of Ellie had been evaluating the pressure, the wetness, the taste of the kiss. The other half had felt like a mannequin in a shop window. But it was bound to feel weird. It was eighteen months since Jamie had died, eighteen months since her last experience of mouth-to-mouth contact. And this was an unfamiliar mouth.

It was also saying something. Whoops, she'd been so busy assessing how it felt she hadn't been listening. 'Sorry, I missed that.'

'I just asked if you're sure you're all right.'

'I'm all right.' Poor Todd, he was looking so worried. 'I'm fine.'

Todd looked relieved. 'I've been plucking up the courage.'

'Oh?' What else could she say?

'Yes.' He nodded, searching her face for a reaction. 'I like you, Ellie. It never occurred to me to think about it before, when you and Jamie were together. But these past few weeks . . . I don't know, I just really like being with you.' His eyes were bright. 'You're lovely.'

'Am I?' It was bizarre to hear him say it.

'Oh yes.' Gaining confidence, he added, 'Mind you, I can be pretty lovely too, when I put my mind to it.'

Her smile broadened, because that was the kind of banter he and Jamie had engaged in.

'Look,' Todd went on, 'no pressure. I'm going to go now. The ball's in your court, OK? Give me a call whenever you want. I know it must feel a bit strange. But we could give it a try, see how we go. If you want.'

She rose to her feet. 'OK, thanks.' This was weird.

Todd gave her a quick, just-good-friends hug and said, 'I'll wait to hear from you.'

She reciprocated with a polite, just-good-friends kiss on the cheek. 'Right, thanks.' It still felt surreal. She patted his arm. 'Bye.'

Chapter 6

'I'M SORRY, Zack's not here today. Did you have an appointment?'

The couple on the doorstep looked disappointed. The girl, who was petite and dark-haired, said, 'We just called round on the offchance. Oh, what a shame! We read that piece about him in the *Telegraph* the other day and thought he sounded like our kind of person.'

'Not afraid to take a flier occasionally, if he comes across a proposition he likes.' The man with her was tall, thin and slightly beaky looking, but in a good way. His hair was Scandinavian-blond, his manner was enthusiastic and he resembled a scruffily dressed tennis player. Eagerly he said, 'And that's what we think we have for him.'

'OK, well, come in and let's see what we can do.' Ellie ushered them through to the office. Pulling the appointments diary across the desk, she said, 'I tell you what, he's had a cancellation for tomorrow morning. I could put you in for eleven o'clock. How does that sound?'

'We can do that. Brilliant.' They looked at each other and beamed.

'Give me your names.' Ellie picked up a pen.

'Kaye and Joe Kerrigan.'

'And the proposal's in there, is it?' She indicated the padded A4 envelope Joe was clutching. 'Why don't you leave it here, then Zack can have a look through it before he sees you? That'll save some time.'

'Oh, but . . .' Kaye looked worried, then stopped herself. 'The thing is, we kind of wanted to talk him through the whole thing . . .'

Joe put a bony hand on her arm. 'Let her take it. Whatever's easiest for Mr McLaren. We'll see him tomorrow.' He flashed Ellie an apologetic look. 'Sorry. This just means so much to us. You have no idea.'

'It means everything in the world,' Kaye echoed longingly. 'If anyone can make this happen, it's Zack McLaren.' Her eyes were shining. 'You're so lucky. He must be fantastic to work for.'

'He's a nightmare.' Ellie broke into a smile. 'No he isn't, he's great. I'll make sure he gets this. And we'll see you tomorrow.'

Zack arrived back at four. Ellie brought him up to date with everything that had been happening in the office. Then she passed him the folder that had been inside the padded envelope.

Zack flicked through the proposal for all of twenty seconds, then closed the folder and frisbeed it onto the desk.

'You have to read it,' Ellie said.

'Just have.'

'And?'

'It's a film script.'

'I know!'

'They want me to be their backer, to provide the finance to get the film made.' Amused, Zack shook his head. 'It's completely crazy. Not my thing at all. No way.'

'But if it took off . . .'

'It wouldn't. We're talking about the riskiest business on the planet. I wouldn't touch a project like that with a barge pole. It would be madness.'

'You haven't even read the script,' Ellie protested.

'I don't need to. What would be the point?'

'Oh, come on, it might be stupendous. You just don't *know*.'

'OK, OK. You've made your point. You win. I'll read it.'

'Promise?'

'Promise.' His phone burst into life and Zack answered it. 'Robert, thanks for getting back to me, do you have time to run through these figures now? Great, hang on, my notes are upstairs . . .'

Ellie opened the folder and detached the film script from the rest of the paperwork. She fitted them into the photocopier and pressed *Print*. She was going to read the script, even if Zack wasn't.

Well?' Ellie demanded the next morning.

'Well what?'

'Did you read the film script.'

'Oh, that. Yes I did.'

'What was it like?'

'Actually, it was pretty good.'

'And?'

'Still not doing it.'

'Who was the priest?' said Ellie.

'What priest?'

Ha! 'The one in the film script who turned up at the end.'

'Oh, that priest.' Zack narrowed his eyes in concentration, then said innocently, 'Sorry. I don't think I can remember.'

'You promised.'

'I was really busy last night.' He was watching her reaction. 'Anyway, how do you know there's a priest in it?'

'I made a copy, took it home last night and read it.' Meaningfully, she added, 'Unlike some people.'

'So what did you make of the script then?'

'I thought it was brilliant. It *is* brilliant. It's funny, it's moving and it's original. If it was made into a film, I'd go and see it.'

'And would you cry at the sad bits?'

'Maybe. OK,' Ellie conceded, 'probably.'

'Like when Mary finally meets the son she put up for adoption and discovers it's Father Dermot?'

'Oh God, *yes*!' She stared at him.

Zack half-smiled and said, 'It just came back to me in a flash.'

'So you did read the whole thing?'

'I wasn't going to. You shamed me into it.'

'Excellent.' Ellie flushed with pleasure. 'And will you back them?'

'I still can't do that.' He looked regretful. 'It's not my field, the risks are astronomical, I don't have any contacts who'd be prepared to invest in that kind of venture. But I did like the script,' he went on. 'A lot. When they get here, I'll let them down lightly.'

'Right.' Oh well, at least she'd tried.

The doorbell went at two minutes to eleven. Ellie opened the door to the Kerrigans and saw the naked hope in their eyes.

As she showed them into the hall, Kaye whispered excitedly, 'Has he read the script?'

'He has.'

'We didn't sleep a wink last night! And on our way over here this morning we saw two magpies. Two for joy!'

Oh dear. And now Zack was about to dash their dreams. Ellie led them up the staircase and knocked on the living-room door.

They were with him for almost thirty minutes. Ellie, typing away with her ears on elastic, finally heard the door open upstairs. If the meeting had lasted half an hour, could that mean Zack had changed his mind?

Zack put his head round the office door. 'Joe and Kaye would like a quick word before they go, so I'll leave you to show them out.'

'He can't help us,' Joe explained when Zack had disappeared back upstairs. 'But we just wanted to say thanks for fighting our corner.'

'He told us about you nagging him to read the manuscript.' Kaye was being heartbreakingly brave. 'And he said you read it too.'

'I thought it was brilliant.' They were such a lovely couple.

'That means so much.' Kaye smiled at her.

Ellie said, 'Look, I don't know anything about getting films made, but do you have to do all this yourself? How about sending the script out to all the big film companies? Maybe one of them will snap it up!'

'We've already tried that. Every company, every last screen agent. They all turned us down.'

'Oh.' OK, now she felt stupid.

'We have enough rejection letters to paper a whole house. It's just so frustrating.' Kaye *sounded* intensely frustrated. 'Anyway,' she said, 'you need to be getting back to work. But we just wanted to say thank you for being so enthusiastic and for doing your best with Zack.'

'Don't give up,' Ellie said as she showed them out.

'Don't worry.' Joe paused on the doorstep. 'We won't.'

Tony, back from three days in Wales, was watching *Deal Or No Deal* when Ellie arrived home from work.

'I've ordered Indian.' He waved to her from the sofa. 'It'll be here in twenty minutes. How was your weekend, darling?'

Ellie waited until the food had been delivered before telling him what she knew she had to tell him. Tony was flying back to LA tomorrow morning and he deserved to know the truth. That was, if they didn't burst from overeating before she could get the words out.

'Did I order too much?'

'Maybe a bit.' Practically every surface in the kitchen bristled with foil containers and discarded lids.

'I can't help it, I just hate the thought of missing out.' He was helping himself to lamb jalfrezi, peshwari naan, saag aloo, bindi bhajis and mushroom rice. 'Remember the time I ordered *the* tandoori chicken and they thought I'd said *three*?' Chuckling at the memory, Tony said, 'Jamie never could resist a challenge, could he? Ended up eating every last one of them.'

Oh no, and now he'd brought Jamie into the conversation. Her heart sinking, Ellie took a deep breath. 'Tony, do you think Jamie would be OK about it if I started . . . um, maybe seeing someone else?'

'Oh my darling, of course he'd be OK. It's been a year and a half. Haven't I said this before? You *should* be getting out there again. Jamie would be happy for you, I know he would. And I'm happy for you too. So long as it's someone nice, someone who deserves you.' He looked at her sideways. 'Is it someone nice?'

'Yes.' Ellie braced herself. *Just tell him.* 'It's Todd.'

Tony broke into a broad smile and said, 'Really? That's great news. I had no idea.' He seemed genuinely pleased.

'Me neither. I thought we were just friends. And now it seems as if it might be . . . you know, turning into something else.' Hurrying to reassure him, Ellie said, 'It's very early days, though. He only told me on Saturday. Nothing's happened yet.'

'Trust me, Jamie would want you to live your life.'

Hopefully he was right. 'I'm doing my best. But it still feels funny.'

'Bound to. It's just a question of getting used to the idea: So long as the basic attraction's there, you'll be fine.'

Hmm, that was the other thing she wasn't so sure of. *Was* there a basic attraction? How could she even tell when she was this much out of practice? Since Saturday evening she had given it a lot of thought. Like the kiss itself, the prospect of becoming emotionally involved with Todd didn't fill her with abject horror. Whereas if she turned him down, his feelings would be hurt. Consequently she had decided to go along with the idea for the time being.

Their plates were both full. No longer even hungry, Ellie picked hers up and said, 'Shall we go through?'

In the living room, keen to change the subject, she launched into the story of Kaye and Joe Kerrigan's unsuccessful meeting with Zack.

'It's tough.' Tony nodded in agreement. 'You've got more chance of being struck by lightning than you have of getting a film made. In LA,' he went on drily, 'you've got more chance of being struck by lightning than you have of finding someone who hasn't written a film script.'

'This one's really good, though.'

'Thousands of scripts are really good. It's a tough business.'

The next morning Tony was up early, packed and waiting for his car to arrive and deliver him to Heathrow. Carrying his cup of coffee through to the living room, he flicked through the jumble of newspapers and copies of *heat* in the magazine rack in search of something to take with him to read on the plane. Then he came to the screenplay Ellie had been banging on about last night. At one stage she'd even pulled it out of the rack and tried to persuade him to read it himself. He'd retaliated by arguing, 'Is there a part for me in this non-existent movie?' And when her face had fallen and she'd said, 'Well, not really,' he had replied, 'So that would be like asking an alligator to be interested in a dandelion sandwich.'

Ellie had abandoned her campaign after that. Instead they had watched *The Apprentice* on TV, made fun of the contestants and chatted about his weekend in Wales with the cast of his upcoming film.

Now Tony straightened and glanced out of the window. His car had pulled up outside. Fine, he'd pick up a few magazines when he reached Departures, but he could still do with something to pass the time on the way to the airport.

Tony drained his coffee cup, picked the screenplay out of the rack and surveyed the title page: *My Long-Lost Irish Daddy* by Kaye and Joe Kerrigan. With a Godawful title like that, was it any wonder it hadn't been taken seriously by the professionals? Right, he'd take the thing with him and read through it on the way to Heathrow.

Another weekend, another Saturday out with Todd, another awkward moment at the end of it.

And three—three!—kisses this time; one when he'd arrived at the flat, another while they'd been walking through Regent's Park and now this, the goodbye one on her doorstep at the end of the evening.

Ellie did her best to make her muscles go loose. She'd been trying to just let herself relax into it, but it still felt weird. Her whole body was uncomfortable. Worst of all, she was now unable to banish from her mind the idea that Jamie was up there somewhere, looking down at them, watching her and finding her ineptness hilarious.

It was all so off-putting. No wonder she couldn't concentrate.

'I've had a really good time.' Todd stroked the side of her face, smoothing back a stray strand of hair.

'Mm, me too.'

'Sure?' Jamie's voice was in her head, as clear as anything. 'Because you never used to kiss me like that.'

Shut up, shut up, shut up.

'If you've forgotten how to do it,' Jamie added helpfully, 'maybe you should sign up for evening classes.'

For crying out loud, was it any wonder she couldn't relax?

Todd was still smoothing her hair. 'Are you OK?'

Could he stop doing it now? 'Yes, fine. Just a bit tired, that's all.'

'Oh dear, oh dear.' Jamie tutted with amusement. 'Now that's definitely not true.'

'Tired,' echoed Todd, clearly equally unconvinced.

'Sorry.' She could tell from his expression that he knew what she was saying. Basically, if he'd been entertaining hopes of staying over, it wasn't going to happen. Again.

'No problem.' As before, Todd hid his disappointment well. 'You have a good night's sleep. I'll call you tomorrow.'

'What's this? I didn't send you this.' Tony's agent had called by the house in Beverly Hills to get a sheaf of contracts signed. Now, out on the shaded terrace, he homed in on the screenplay lying on the table. 'Where d'ya get this thing, Tone? Jeez, that's the crappiest title I ever heard in my life.'

'I know. But the script's bloody good. In fact it's amazing,' said Tony. 'Don't pick it up.'

'So who wrote it?'

'No one you know. Just leave it. Here, have a drink. Are you hungry?'

Oh, it was so easy to wind Marvin up. Reverse psychology was a wonderful thing. Tony covertly watched as his agent picked up the script and turned to the first page. In all honesty, it wasn't the best first page in the world. Ninety-nine per cent of agents would have given up. Then again, ninety-nine per cent of agents didn't have Tony Weston saying, as if he meant it, 'I'm serious, Marvin, put it down, it's nothing to do with you.' What could be more enticing than that?

Tony got on with signing his way through the contracts. And he waited. When several more minutes had passed, he said, 'Well?'

'Interesting. Different. But, there's no part in it for you.'

'I know. But I have a real feeling about this script. And it never does any harm to be the person who introduces the right script to the right producer. I have a few contacts that—'

'Hello, who has more contacts in this business? You or me?'

'Yes, but—'

'Cor-*rect*.' Marvin pointed a stubby finger at him. 'I do. Who works for one of the biggest talent agencies in the country? Oh wow, would ya believe it, me again. Tone, do the right thing here, wouldja? Just let me take care of this, let me take it back to the agency and show it to Stephen. If anyone can get a buzz going, he can.'

Tony hid a smile. In the space of a few minutes he hadn't done such a bad job on the buzz front himself. But that was this industry for you. Appear desperate and you're dead in the water. Tell someone they can't have something and they'll snap your hand off. Welcome to Hollywood, baby.

'**D**arling, come on, just say yes. You know you want to really.'

OK, the time had come. Zack prepared himself for the imminent fall-out. He hadn't actually planned for this to happen this evening, here in Louisa's flat, but she had forced his hand. Throughout dinner all she'd talked about was holidays. Friends of hers had rented a luxury villa in Tuscany in late August and were keen for Louisa and Zack to join them, but they needed a definite answer by tomorrow.

Louisa was longing to go. 'Think about how fabulous it'll be. And best of all, it's adults only! No ghastly screaming kids to ruin the ambience and fill the pool with inflatables.' Evidently inflatables in a pool were on a par with used condoms. 'Just peace and quiet, wonderful food, grown-up conversation and fine wine. What could *be* more idyllic?'

Right, here we go. Brace, brace. Zack said, 'Honestly? It doesn't sound that idyllic to me. My idea of a great holiday is going home to Cornwall and piling down to the beach with my nephews and nieces. We play volleyball and dig holes in the sand, we eat ice cream, we throw each other into the sea and we make a lot of noise.'

'Oh!' Louisa sat back, startled. 'Oh . . . sorry, I had no idea.' Mentally regrouping, she said hastily, 'But that sounds nice too! Look, maybe we could pop down to see your family before we go to Italy . . .'

'I really don't think you'd like it,' said Zack. 'I think you should go to Tuscany,' he said. 'You'll have a great time.'

The smile faltered. 'You mean . . . on my own?'

'Look, we need to talk.' God, he hated this bit. 'The thing is, I really think you'd be happier with someone else.'

'I'd be happier with someone else,' Louisa echoed, dumbfounded.

'Not just on holiday. In general. In your life.' He was rubbish at this. How did other people do it? Please don't let her start crying.

'You're finishing with me?'

'I just think it would be better if we . . . you know, called it a day.'

'But it wouldn't be better for me. I don't want to call it a day.'

Zack took a deep breath and said steadily, 'Yes, but I do.'

She let out a wail of anguish. 'Zacky, *why*?'

He cringed. She'd just called him *Zacky*. Could he cite this as reason number one? But that would be cruel. He didn't want to be cruel. 'Look, you're great. It's not you, it's me. I work too hard. You deserve to be with someone who'll make you happy.'

'You make me happy.'

'I wouldn't.' Zack shook his head. 'Not in the long term.'

'But I thought we were in it for the long term!'

'I'm sorry.' Zack stood up. 'I should go. You'll be fine . . .'

'Are you seeing someone else?' She searched his face.

Zack kept his expression carefully neutral. 'No, no one.'

'Sure? Because that would make sense. More sense than you just decid-ing out of the blue that we like different holidays so let's break up.'

'I'm not seeing anyone else.'

'Not even what's-her-name? That cute little PA of yours? Ellie?'

'No.' He shook his head.

At least they were in Louisa's flat, meaning he could be the one to leave. In the hallway, she tried to throw herself into his arms. He gave her one last apologetic hug.

'How about Disneyworld?' She mumbled the words damply into his shoulder. 'We could go there if you like.'

He didn't reply.

Louisa pulled away and gazed miserably up at him. 'No?'

'Sorry.' Zack shook his head; it was time to get out of here. 'Bye.'

OK, was this sneaky? He didn't resort to underhand tactics as a rule. But if they helped, why not?

Zack unclipped Elmo's lead and pushed the front door shut behind him. Elmo, tail wagging, trotted down the hallway to greet Ellie.

'Hello, baby! Did you have a lovely walk?'

'Morning.' By the time he reached the office, Elmo was up on her lap. 'On a diet?'

'No.' She looked at him, mystified.

'Good. You can have one of these, then.' Zack opened the lid of the cake box to show her. 'I had to get them. We were walking past the deli and they were in the window.'

'Calling out to you.' Ellie grinned. 'Beckoning and whispering your name. They do that. Especially those naughty strawberry ones.'

He loved the way she instinctively mimed the beckoning and whispering as she said it, without having the remotest idea how irresistible it made her look. He could watch her for ever.

'You like them?'

'Just a bit!'

'I'll get us a couple of plates.'

'Thank you,' said Ellie when he came back from the kitchen. She tipped Elmo off her lap and helped herself to one of the pastries, biting into a glazed strawberry with relish. 'Mm, gorgeous.'

Zack took a cake for himself and pulled out the chair opposite.

'Just so you know, you won't be seeing Louisa round here any more. We broke up.' He said it casually but kept a close eye on her reaction; wouldn't it be fantastic if her face lit up, betraying the feelings she'd worked so hard to keep hidden from him all this time . . .

'Oh no, I'm sorry.' Ellie put down her cake. 'Are you upset?'

So much for hidden feelings. 'No.'

'Was it her decision or yours?' She looked genuinely concerned.

Zack smiled briefly and said, 'Mine.'

'Oh well. In that case, I'm glad. She wasn't right for you.' Picking her cake back up, Ellie licked a swirl of cream. 'And she *definitely* wasn't right for Elmo.'

'I know.'

'She was suspicious of me, too. Like, she didn't trust me working with you. I mean, that was just downright embarrassing.'

OK, you can stop now . . .

Zack pulled the diary towards him. 'I may need to ask you a favour.'

Ellie didn't hesitate. 'No problem. What kind of favour?'

Oh yes, he was brilliant. This could make all the difference. It had only occurred to him this morning that he might be able to use the situation to his advantage . . . maybe socialising with Ellie outside the office environment would enable her to view him in a different light.

'There are evening events I have to attend. Sometimes I need to take along a partner. It's just that everyone else does, so it messes up the numbers if you go on your own . . . they're usually OK, not too boring . . .' *Shut up, listen to yourself, you sound like an idiot.* 'So how about it? Does that seem like something you wouldn't mind helping me out with sometimes?' *Jesus, never mind an idiot, you sound like a complete dick.*

'Why not? Sounds like fun. Yes, that would be great.' Ellie was smiling at him as if he wasn't a dick. But sadly not as if she found him completely irresistible either.

'Great.' *No, she just said great, you don't say great too.* 'Right, well, this is the first one, let me tell you about it.' He tapped the page he'd stopped at. 'It's being held at the Dorchester next Wednesday and—'

'Wednesday?' Ellie's hand flew to her mouth. 'I can't do next Wednesday! Sorry!'

'No problem, I'll manage. So, something nice?'

Ellie hesitated. After a moment, as if debating whether or not to tell him, she said, 'Hope so. It's a party for my boyfriend's mum.' It was her very first invitation to a social event as Todd's girlfriend.

Well. That was a bolt from the blue. Was she coming clean after all this time about her relationship with Tony Weston? Plus, if it was him, how old must his mother be? A hundred and forty?

Aloud he said, 'Well, you can't miss that. Where's the party?'

'In her garden. It's a barbecue. She's sixty.'

Not Tony Weston's mother, then. Zack's heart was hammering against his ribs. 'So what's this boyfriend's name?'

She turned pink. 'Todd.'

'You've never mentioned him before.' It was hard work, keeping his tone casual.

'No. Well, it's all pretty new. We've only been seeing each other for a couple of weeks.'

'Going OK?'

Ellie nodded and said brightly, 'Going great!'

Damn. Damn you, Todd, whoever you are.

'And was there someone else before that?' Was he asking too many personal questions now? Possibly, but he needed to know.

She hesitated. 'What, you mean *ever*?'

'I meant since you've been here in Primrose Hill.'

'No, this is the first for a while.' She looked puzzled. 'Why?'

Zack said, 'It's just that someone happened to mention they thought they'd seen you with Tony Weston.'

Ellie's flush deepened significantly. 'Oh.'

'And then I realised, that time I called you at home a while back, he was the person who answered the phone.'

'Right. Yes, it was.'

'And you did say you were living rent-free in your friend's flat.'

'Oh *God*.' Half laughing, half mortified, Ellie said. 'He's a *friend*. He's not my boyfriend! I can't believe you thought that!'

'Sorry. I'm sorry.' He'd jumped to conclusions and got it oh-so-wrong. Zack said, 'I can't believe I thought it either. Blame it on Michael Douglas and Catherine Zeta-Jones.' Right, so the good news was that Ellie had never been romantically involved with Tony Weston. The bad news was that he appeared to have missed his window of opportunity and she was now ecstatically happy with someone else.

'He's just a friend.' Ellie was still cringing and shaking her head.

'And what a great friend to have.' To change the subject, Zack said, 'How did you come to meet him?'

Ellie swallowed, then gazed out of the window, visibly psyching herself up. On the desk, the phone started to ring. 'Well, er . . .'

'Leave it,' Zack stopped her as she moved to lift the receiver. 'If it's important they'll call back. Carry on with the story.'

The phone stopped ringing. Ellie was still holding on to Elmo for dear life, while Elmo revelled in the attention.

'Tony's my father-in-law. Well,' Ellie said, 'he *was* my father-in-law.'

'So you were married.' The moment the words were out of his mouth, Zack made the connection. *He knew.* Hadn't he Googled Tony Weston that very first day, after seeing the two of them together at the Ivy? Hadn't he read that Tony Weston's real name was Tony Something-else? But back then, the fact that his surname was Kendall hadn't been significant enough to remember, which was why it hadn't rung any bells when Ellie had eventually come into his life. And hadn't he also read about the tragic loss of Tony's only son in a car accident? Oh God.

'I was married. His name was Jamie. He was . . . lovely.' She carried on gently stroking Elmo's head. 'But he died.'

'I'm so sorry. I didn't know.'

She shrugged. 'I'm sorry too. I should have told you. I kind of wanted to start off with a clean slate.'

'Understandable.' Did this explain her lack of reaction towards him, or was he just not her type anyway?

'Can I say something? I don't want you to start being nice to me now.'

'You don't want me to start? Does that mean I've *never* been nice to you?'

'You know what I mean. I'd just like everything to carry on like before.'

'OK.' More than anything Zack hoped everything *wouldn't* always carry on like before. At some stage in the future, please God, their situation would change. 'So, does this father-in-law approve of this new chap of yours?'

'Tony? Oh, he's delighted. You'd think he'd planned it himself. He couldn't be happier.' Ellie's eyes were shining.

'Right. Excellent.' Zack nodded as if he was delighted too. *Damn.*

'Look, you need to get to your meeting.' Bringing the subject to a close, Ellie said, 'But about next Wednesday, I could ask Roo if she's free to come with you to the Dorchester. Would that help you out?'

The mad friend with the risqué past and outrageous taste in T-shirts?

'I don't think so,' Zack said firmly. 'But thanks.'

Phew. Well, that was that cat out of the bag. When Zack had left the office, Ellie heaved a sigh of relief. Hopefully, she and Zack had evolved a strong enough working relationship by this stage that his discovering the truth about her past wouldn't alter the way he treated her.

Abruptly Ellie's eyes stung and she blinked back tears. Sometimes it still happened without warning. Don't cry, don't cry.

Oh Jamie, where are you? Are you still there? Am I doing OK?

Tony slowly massaged his aching temples; this was definitely a side effect of growing older he could do without. Back in the day, half a dozen large Scotches would barely have touched the sides. They definitely wouldn't have given him a hangover of this magnitude.

But his headache was the least of his worries this morning.

What was that invention thingy he'd heard about? Some kind of dexterity test connected to your computer that you had to pass before it would allow you to access the internet. So that if you just happened to down, say, half a dozen large Scotches then be seized by a burning compulsion to send the kind of email you wouldn't dream of sending if you were sober, you wouldn't be able to send it. But since he hadn't had that invention thingy installed, he'd opened his laptop, entered Martha's email address, typed out his message and pressed *Send.*

There, done. As easy as that. And he hadn't been so trolleyed that he couldn't remember what he'd written, either. Lacking in literary excellence his words may have been, but they'd come straight from the heart. His wounded, lonely, desperate and inebriated heart.

Oh Martha,

I know I shouldn't be doing this but I just have to. I miss you. I miss you so much, Martha, all the time. I know I shouldn't, but that only makes it worse. I'm doing my best to get over you. Guess what? It's not going so well. I hope all is well with you. And how is Henry? And are you doing OK? I won't ask if you miss me too.

Right, I'm off to bed now. Will you even read this? Maybe you just delete my mails without looking at them. But don't worry, either way I won't expect a reply.

Sorry. Just needed to say it. I love and miss you, beautiful Martha, more than you'll ever know.

But I do understand. Be happy. All love, T x

Tony watched the computer screen shimmer into life. Then his heart did a flip, because there among the emails that had come in overnight was one from Martha. For the first time in weeks, she'd sent a reply.

His hand shook as he moved the mouse. *Click.*

And there was Martha's email up on the screen. Very short and to the point, she'd written:

I miss you too.

'**O**oh, I've missed you *so much!*'

'I can't breathe.' Niall was grinning at her, his hair slick with rain. 'You're choking me.'

Roo loosened her grip on him; when he'd come through the front door she'd launched herself at him like a monkey. 'I can't help it. I'm excited. Did you have a miserable weekend too?'

'What do you think?' He'd been forced to spend it at a business conference in Southampton. 'I've had sales targets and expansion strategies up to here. God, let's not talk about it now. *You*,' his fingers deftly unfastened her navy satin bra, 'are looking spectacular.'

'Not so bad yourself.' Roo retaliated by sliding off his suit jacket and removing his tie. She wasn't going to ask him how Yasmin and Ben were. She wouldn't even think about them. It was Monday lunchtime, Niall had rushed over from work and they only had forty minutes before he had to race back. They had no time to waste. Hence the fact that she was wearing scarcely any clothes in preparation . . .

Thirty minutes had passed in the most glorious way imaginable. Roo lay on her back in the bed and stretched pleasurably, like a cat. In the bathroom across the landing, Niall had already jumped into the shower. In ten minutes he would be on his way back to work.

De-dee-doo-ding. Roo turned her head. It was a muffled sound, quiet but instantly recognisable, signalling that Niall's mobile had received a text. In all the months she'd known him, it was the first time Niall had left his phone unattended. Roo slithered out of bed and followed the direction the noise had come from.

And there it was, in the pocket of his trousers. She held the phone in her hand and saw that the text had come from a contact listed only as V.

V . . . V . . . Offhand, all she could think of was Vivica, one of his former co-workers. She had left the company a couple of months back; Niall had gone along to her leaving party. He'd also mentioned in passing that she was a bloody good saleswoman, single and hard-working.

Roo stood there, naked and clutching his mobile, her mind in a tizz. Partly because it was the first time she'd been able to clutch his mobile. But also partly because some sixth sense was telling her she really should be opening this text.

Her thumb hovered over the button. If she pressed it, the message would appear. If she pressed it, Niall would know she'd pressed it.

The next moment, in the bathroom, the shower was turned off. If she was going to press the button, she had to press it now.

On the one hand, Niall might hate her for spying on him. He might be furious. On the other hand, she had to know what the message said. *Had to.* Oh please don't let it be bad . . . She pressed it.

OMG, best weekend ever!!! When can we do it again? (And again and again!!!!!) Call me asap. Lots of love, V xxxxx

No, please no. Roo whimpered with fear, her brain struggling to take in the significance of the words. She felt sick . . . She could hear Niall opening the shower door. She couldn't confront him; her head wasn't ready yet. He'd be out of the bathroom in less than forty seconds, there wasn't time for anything now, he had to be back at work . . .

OK, get rid of the message. Breathless and fumbling, Roo pressed and pressed the necessary buttons. Finally the message was deleted, vanished, gone for ever. *Almost as if she'd imagined it, except she knew she hadn't.* Clumsily and in the nick of time she slipped the phone back into Niall's trouser pocket.

Then the bathroom door opened and he reappeared, vigorously towelling himself dry with her favourite lilac towel.

Roo blurted out, 'I need the loo,' and hurried past him.

By the time she re-emerged, he was dressed and ready to rush off.

'I don't want to go.' He planted a perfunctory kiss on her mouth, at the same time patting his pockets. 'But I have to. Shit, where's my phone?'

She stood there and let him find it, saw the momentary look of anxiety change to one of relief as he pulled the mobile out of his trouser pocket and checked the screen. No new messages. Cool. He shot her a confident smile and said, 'Right, I'm off. I'll see you tomorrow, OK?'

'Yes.' Her voice sounded high and strange, but Niall didn't notice. He ruffled her hair then raced downstairs, let himself out of the house and—*woop, click, clunk*—jumped into his car.

Frozen to the spot, Roo listened to the sound of it disappearing off up the road. Less than ten minutes ago, she'd had a boyfriend that she adored. OK, so he had a wife and baby, but other than that he'd been close to perfect. And now, thanks to one little text, her whole world had been turned upside down.

Five minutes later, she'd managed to track down Vivica on Google Images. There were three photos of Vivica Mellon being presented with a trophy for achieving outstanding sales figures last year. She *looked* like a saleswoman too. Her shiny dark hair was cut in an efficient bob, she used red lipstick and lipliner and she was wearing a navy crimplene trouser suit. OK, the crimplene bit probably wasn't true but it made Roo feel better to think it. The look of stop-at-nothing triumph on Vivica's heart-shaped face told her all she needed to know about her character. If she worked in a shop and you wanted a pint of milk, she wouldn't let you out again until you'd bought the fridge.

Was it her? Was she sleeping with Niall?

Shaking, Roo switched off the laptop. She couldn't bear it. All her life she'd fallen for men who started off perfect and morphed into bastards. Time after time, one way or another, they'd let her down and broken her heart.

Meeting Niall, she'd really thought she'd hit the jackpot. This time it would be different. Then, once he'd captured her, he'd told her he was married. Which wasn't great, admittedly, but there were excellent reasons why he was being unfaithful to his wife. Or were there?

And now this. It was looking as if Yasmin wasn't the only one Niall was cheating on. Roo felt panicky and nauseous and horribly alone.

Niall's name came up on the screen and Roo braced herself. This was it. She picked up the phone and pressed *Answer*. 'Hello?'

'Hi, it's me.' His voice was cautious. Which, on its own, pretty much confirmed her worst fears.

'Oh, hi,' Roo kept her own tone cheery. Last night she'd barely slept. Today her stomach was still churning and she hadn't been able to eat a thing. But it was important to sound normal, normal, normal . . .

'Everything OK?'

'Everything's fine! Why wouldn't it be?'

'No reason.' Pause. 'Um, did you look at my phone yesterday?'

'Your phone?'

'It's just that someone sent me a text as a joke, but I didn't get it.'

He'd worked out the timings, hadn't he, found out exactly when it had been sent. Roo waited, then said evenly, 'Would that be someone beginning with V? And ending in kiss kiss kiss?'

His silence told her everything she needed to know.

'It was just a joke,' said Niall. 'One of the guys at the office was messing about, winding me up—'

'Niall, it wasn't a joke. Why don't you just be a man and admit it? You've been sleeping with Vivica Mellon.'

More silence. The final confirmation.

'I suppose some people are just greedy,' Roo went on. 'Why settle for one mistress when you can have two?'

'Look, I swear to God, she's just someone I used to work with.'

'And now you're sleeping with her.'

'Once. One weekend, that's all it was. She made all the running.'

He was still lying. All of a sudden she could tell. It was like a one-way mirror suddenly, magically, becoming two-way, revealing everything. 'Oh my God,' said Roo, 'you are unbelievable.'

'Well, fine then.' Niall abruptly switched gear. 'So that's it, is it? You don't want to see me again. All over.'

Fear and panic engulfed her. And a sense of déjà vu. Of course, that was it, the good old double bluff. It was a ploy she'd encountered before, designed to frighten you into backing down. And she *had* backed down, because the threat of losing something instilled terror and desperation into your very soul . . . But not today. She wasn't going to fall for those tactics again. This time she was going to do the right thing.

'Yes, it's all over.'

'Roo.' His voice softened. 'Babe, you know you don't mean that.'

'Oh, I do.' She was shaking but determined. 'I really do.'

'You want to give up what we have together, all for the sake of a silly . . . blip? That's crazy. I told you, Vivica means nothing to me. Look, I'll come over this evening, then we can talk properly, sort everything out.'

'Don't come over. I don't want to see you again. Or speak to you again. I can't believe I ever trusted you. But that's me, I'm just stupid.'

'Roo, we need to—'

'And I won't be changing my mind either.' She had to get off the phone now, before she lost all control. 'Goodbye, Niall. Tell Vivica her lipliner really doesn't suit her. And tonight, just for a change, why don't you try going home to your wife?'

'**H**ow does it look?' Ellie emerged from the bedroom and did a twirl, showing off her new red dress with spaghetti straps and floaty hem.

She'd bought it specially for tomorrow night. 'Good enough to meet your family?'

'Perfect.' Todd held out his arms and came towards her. *Oh God, here we go again, he's gearing up for another kiss.* She got out of it by puckering her lips and turning it into a jokey one instead.

'Mwah! Right, let me just change out of it now, then we'll be off.'

Escaping his grasp, she headed back to the bedroom. Tonight a group of girls from Brace House were going out to a show. Paula, who had arranged the evening, had insisted she go along with them and stay the night on her sofa to avoid a late journey back across town. Ellie was looking forward to it. And Todd, who had come over to show off his new car, was giving her a lift into the West End.

As Ellie changed into white jeans and a khaki vest, the doorbell went and she called out, 'Can you see who that is?'

Moments later Todd called back, 'It's Roo. She's on her way up. I think she's crying.'

Ellie put down the coat hanger. '*What?*'

Roo was crying. Her bleached white hair looked as fraught as she did and her eyelids were puffy. When she saw that Ellie was dressed up for her night out with the girls, she said, 'Oh, you're going out . . .'

'Here, come and sit down. What's happened?'

'It's Niall.' Roo was clutching a balled-up tissue. 'It's all over.'

Todd raised an eyebrow. 'He finished with you?'

'No, I finished with him. He was seeing someone else.'

Ellie gaped. '*Besides* you and Yasmin?'

'Oh yes. Some girl he used to work with. They spent the weekend together.' She wiped her eyes. 'He's such a bastard.'

'But you already knew that,' Todd announced. 'Good riddance, that's what I say. You're better off without him.'

'I know.'

'So I don't get why you're crying.' He looked genuinely baffled.

'Because I loved him. Because I thought he loved me.' Roo sniffed and said miserably, 'Because it's the story of my stupid, pathetic, useless life so far.'

'Oh Roo . . .' Torn, Ellie checked her watch; they really should be leaving now.

'And he might come over,' Roo went on, 'to try and make me change my mind. I don't want to be there in case he turns up. But you're going out.' She gazed beseechingly at Ellie. 'Could I stay here, just for a couple of hours? Would that be all right?'

Ellie made up her mind. 'Look, I'll cancel. Let me just call Paula and explain, then I can stay here with you.'

'No, no.' Roo shook her head vehemently. 'No way, you're not giving up your night out because of me. That'd just make me feel worse.'

'Well, I'm not leaving you here on your own.'

'Look, I'll stay with her.' Todd turned to Roo. 'OK?'

She blinked, taken aback. '*You?*'

Ellie had always been aware of the slightly tricky atmosphere between them. Todd had made no secret of the fact that he disapproved of Roo's relationship with Niall. Roo, in turn, had reacted by becoming flippant and defensive.

'I don't know if that's a good idea,' said Ellie.

'Come on, it's the only way. I'll drop you on Shaftesbury Avenue then come back and keep her company.'

Roo said warily, 'And give me hassle all night? Because I'm telling you now, I'm not in the mood to be lectured to by Mr Morality.'

'He won't. He'll be nice. *Won't you?*' Ellie pointed a warning finger at Todd. It wouldn't be fair to let Paula down now.

Todd said evenly, 'Of course I'll be nice.'

'And you're not allowed to say you told me so, either.'

Todd didn't reply.

'Oh *God*.' Roo let out a wail of despair. 'What the hell, I deserve to be miserable. Just go ahead and say it. It's all my own fault.'

It was eleven o'clock, and the most bizarre and powerful thing was happening. For the last three hours, Roo and Todd had talked nonstop. He had told her all about growing up with Jamie, their deep friendship, his past girlfriends, his family and his career. In return she had told him about her music, her childhood and her lamentable history with the opposite sex. And somehow, over the course of the evening, her perception of Todd Howard had undergone a complete sea change.

Or . . . or . . . *his* perception of her had altered and the fact that he was now viewing her differently meant she was able to relax and stop being so prickly and defensive. Or something. Either way, out of nowhere, a kind of electricity had sprung up. Each time she looked at Todd she could feel it. And from the way he was looking back at her, gazing unwaveringly into her eyes, he was feeling it too.

'OK.' Todd abruptly broke the silence that had fallen. 'Are you waiting for me to go first?'

'What?' Roo's glass was empty but she picked it up and took a nervous pretend sip anyway. Her teeth clanked against the rim.

'You know what.' He took the glass and placed it on the coffee table. Then he reached for her, cupped her face in his cool hands and said, 'I never thought I'd be doing this, not in a million years. But I have to.'

'What about Ellie?' Roo's voice came out as a croak.

'Oh God, I know. I don't want to hurt her. But . . . it's not right.'

'I know it's not right! We can't do this! I have to leave . . . that's it, I'm going home.' Roo struggled to pull away, scrambling to her feet. But Todd was shaking his head, standing up too, not releasing his grip.

'I didn't mean it like that. It's me and Ellie . . . our relationship's not right. I've tried, but it just isn't working. It's not even a proper . . . *thing*.'

'We still shouldn't be *doing* this.'

'I know.' He pulled her close to him, and just held her tightly. Without moving. For twenty, thirty seconds they stayed like that. The longer Todd didn't kiss her, the more desperately she wanted him to. Her skin was buzzing, her whole body had never felt so alive. Finally, he released her and gazed deep into her eyes. 'Well? Shall we stop now?'

Roo couldn't speak. All she could do was gaze back in wonder and drink in the details of his face, of those features that had seemed so ordinary before yet had become, in the space of just a few hours, *extra*ordinary . . . oh God, she had to back away but she couldn't do it . . .

'No.' Todd smiled, reading her mind. 'Me neither.' He reached for her hand again and led her to the doorway. 'Come on, we can't stay here.'

Together they left the flat and made their way across the road. The tingling skin was still happening. Roo felt as if she were in a dream . . . she was no longer responsible for her actions . . .

Oh, for crying out loud, how utterly pathetic, of course she was responsible. Who else was she hoping to blame it on? She stopped dead on the pavement outside her own house and dug her heels in. 'This is wrong. It's not going to happen.'

'Roo.' Todd took a deep breath. 'Just so you know the truth. I need to explain about me and Ellie.'

She clapped her hands over her face; it was Niall and Yasmin all over again. 'I don't want to hear it.'

'You must. What did I tell you before? Listen to me. It's not a proper relationship. There's no sex,' said Todd. 'There's no intimacy. It's not real, it's not working. I thought it would, but it hasn't. And now I'm trapped. I've got myself into a situation that I can't get out of.'

'So you're telling me you don't want to be with Ellie.' Roo gripped the black wrought-iron railings. 'But she wants to be with you.'

'I don't know. I think so. But I can't honestly tell.' There was genuine pain in his eyes. 'And I was the one who started it, so what can I do? On paper we're perfect for each other. I wanted to make her feel better. And I've tried my best, but it's just not happening.' Todd shrugged helplessly. 'If it was anyone else, I'd finish with them, but how can I do that to Ellie? She's been through so much.'

Talk about a close call. Thank goodness she'd come to her senses in time. Filled with self-loathing, Roo said, 'Of course you can't. Oh God, and look what we almost did to her tonight. I can't bear it.'

'But you did it to Niall's wife.'

Was that how Todd thought of her? As the lowest of the low? 'That's different.' Even if it was still despicable. 'Ellie's my friend.'

'It's not just sex, though. You and me.' He gazed at her with genuine emotion. 'This . . . thing between us . . . it feels *real*.'

'Forget it. None of it's real and nothing's going to happen. You're leaving now, and I'm going to bed.' Awash with shame, Roo said, 'Will you tell Ellie about any of this?'

In disbelief, Todd said, 'Of course not.'

'Right. Bye, then.' Roo watched him turn away. The guilt almost more than she could bear, she didn't tell him that she might.

Chapter 7

'WHAT ARE YOU DOING?' said Todd.

Ellie carried on texting. They were on their way to his mum's barbecue in Wimbledon. 'I've been trying to get through to Roo all day. She's still not answering her phone. I hope she's all right.'

'She'll be fine. You look nice.'

'Hmm?' Her fingers flying over the keys, Ellie finished her message:

Roo, call me back. Are you OK? Worried about you! Love, Ellie xxx

She pressed *Send*, then said absently, 'Oh, this dress? Thanks.' Now why was he looking at her like that? Had she done something wrong?

'Here they are! Oh, will you just look at this?' Maria Howard's excitement knew no bounds as she turned and saw them coming through the French doors that opened onto her back garden. 'My wonderful son and his beautiful girlfriend! Come here, come here . . . oh Ellie, it's so lovely to see you again! And don't you look perfect together!'

'Sorry,' Todd murmured in her ear. 'I did warn you.'

He had, but there was still no escape. Ellie found herself smothered in Maria's Lauder-scented embrace. She was touched by the welcome, even if it did mean she felt a bit of a fraud. Everyone was going to think she and Todd were a proper couple in a normal relationship. Whereas in reality she was feeling more and more like an alien doing her best to pass herself off as a human being.

'You don't know how happy it makes me,' Maria said. 'Seeing the two of you like this. Poor Jamie, we all loved him so much. But he'd want you to move on with your life.'

Ellie nodded and said, 'I know,' a lump springing to her throat. The last time she'd seen Todd's mum had been at Jamie's funeral, and her memories of that day were hazy. Hastily she handed over the card and present she'd brought along and changed the subject. 'Anyway, happy birthday! You're looking fantastic!'

'Am I? Oh, you're so sweet!' Maria gave her another hug. 'Now, come over and let me introduce you to everyone. They've all been longing to meet you. Todd, get Ellie a drink and something to eat . . . Sue, Sue, where's Tanya? Look who's here!'

It was past midnight and Roo's stomach was in knots. Guilt wasn't an emotion that had ever featured largely in her life. Until today, this morning, when it had seized her in its vicelike grip and changed everything. Oh yes, it was making up for lost time now.

And she, Roo Taylor, was going to change as well. Because to date she'd led a charmed, stress-free, *selfish* life. And let's face it, she hadn't always been a nice person. She had drunk too much, taken too many drugs, slept with men she should never have slept with. And if they'd happened to have wives or girlfriends at home . . . well, she'd still gone ahead and done it anyway. Her behaviour had been abysmal, and she should have been thoroughly ashamed of herself. Gazing out of the window at the empty, darkened street, Roo dug her nails into her palms. Well, now she was. And she was determined to make amends. Her old life was behind her and the new one had begun.

Roo stiffened as headlights rounded the corner, lighting up the street. A minicab pulled up opposite, and she held her breath.

Ellie was back. Please let her be on her own. Yes, she was. Throwing open the window, Roo stuck her head out and called, 'Ellie?'

Ellie swung round and looked up as the cab moved off down the road. 'Oh sweetie, I've been so worried about you! Are you all right?'

Her chest tightening with fear, Roo said, 'I'm OK. Look, I'm sorry, I know it's late.' Her voice cracked. 'But can you come over?'

'So that's it. Todd didn't want me to tell you, but I had to. And you mustn't blame him. It was all my fault. But I promise on my life it'll never happen again. And I'm going to make it up to you, if you'll let me. I know you must hate me. I hate myself. But I've changed. I'm a different person. I'm going to make up for every bad thing I've ever done. But I just want you to know I'm so, so sorry.'

Ellie shook her head. She'd listened in silence while the whole confession had come tumbling out. Now she said, 'Thank God.'

'What?'

'This is the best news I've heard in ages.'

Wrong-footed, Roo said, 'How can it be good news?'

'Because it wasn't working for us. It felt all wrong and I kept pretending it didn't, but it *did*. And I couldn't hurt Todd's feelings. I started off thinking it was just because I was out of practice, but it wasn't. Todd and I were never meant to be anything but friends. And now he knows that too. Oh thank God, this is fantastic, you have no idea!'

Roo's face was a picture. 'Are you just saying that?'

'No.'

'You really aren't angry with me?'

'No!'

'But I did a terrible thing.'

'Did I miss something?' said Ellie. 'Did you have sex with him?'

'No!'

'Did you even kiss him?'

'No, but I wanted to! I *nearly* did.'

'Well, now you can. You can do anything you like with him.'

'No.' Roo vehemently shook her head.

'But I *want* you to.'

'Ellie, I told you. I've changed. I made a pact with myself today. First, no more lies. I had to tell you the truth, even if it meant losing you as a friend. Second, if I didn't lose you, I'd make it up to you somehow. And third,' Roo was counting on her fingers, 'either way, nothing's going to happen between me and Todd.'

'But that's stupid. You like him. And he likes you.'

'All the more reason. It's my punishment.'

'You don't have to punish yourself.' Ellie frowned; was she not making herself clear here? 'I'm *glad* it happened.'

'Maybe, but that's irrelevant. The point is, I didn't know you'd be glad, did I? I just went ahead and did it.'

'But you didn't do anything! I'm happy that Todd and I don't have to pretend to be a couple any more. We can just go back to being friends. And I'd love it if you two got together.'

But Roo was already shaking her head, clearly dead set on punishing herself. 'No way. That's not going to happen. I won't let it.'

'**H**ow was the party last night?' Zack, between appointments, came into the office eating a slice of toast.

Well, he was bound to ask. Ellie said, 'It was great! No rain, everyone was lovely, food was fantastic. I ate seven chicken samosas. How did your posh do at the Dorchester go?'

'Probably a lot more boring than your barbecue. And sadly lacking in samosas.' He finished his toast. 'There's another event on Monday evening at Claridge's. Could you make that, do you think?'

Claridge's? Wheeeee!

'Monday? No problem, that's fine.' As Ellie nodded enthusiastically, the doorbell went, signalling the arrival of his next appointment.

'Good. Excellent. I'll get that.' Looking pleased, Zack swung out of the office to let the client in and take him upstairs.

Ellie went back to her typing. She hadn't been able to bring herself to tell him about Todd. It was only last week that she'd mentioned him for the first time, boasting to Zack about how happy they were. What kind of an idiot would she look like if she were to announce, just days later, that it was all over? If she tried to explain that she was delighted, Zack wouldn't believe her. He'd think she'd been heartlessly dumped. Worse, he'd feel sorry for her. She'd be back at square one all over again, the poor widow to be pitied and handled with kid gloves. No, far easier for now to not mention it. There was no reason at all to tell him the truth.

Speaking of the truth, there were still things to sort out with Todd.

Todd came over straight after work. He couldn't have been more penitent. 'I'm so sorry.'

'Oh, don't you start. I told you, this is good news! It wasn't working out. We both knew it. We were just too polite to say so. Now we can relax and stop trying. We don't have to do any more of that yucky kissing stuff!'

Todd visibly relaxed. 'Oh God, wasn't that weird? I had no idea it could be like that. I couldn't figure out why it felt so . . . so . . .'

'Gross,' Ellie supplied helpfully. 'No offence. It wasn't you.'

'It wasn't you either.'

'It was just wrong. Like a Marmite and strawberry sandwich. We're both nice, we just don't go together.'

'Piccalilli and chocolate,' Todd nodded in agreement.

'Liquorice and bacon. OK,' she waved her hands, 'we have to stop now. I'm starting to feel sick.'

'We'll go back to being friends.'

'You know what? I'm feeling so much better already. Thank goodness Roo told me. We could have carried on being all wrong for each other for months.' Ellie fanned herself with relief. 'In fact, you need to get yourself over there now.'

Todd hesitated. 'She said we couldn't see each other.'

'Oh, that was then. She'll be over it by now. Come on, I'll come with you so she knows it's OK.'

'**N**o.'

Ellie tried again. 'Roo, come on, just open the door.'

From the upstairs window, Roo shook her head. 'I will not.' She was refusing even to glance at Todd. 'He isn't coming in. In fact, I'm quite hurt that you think you can get me to give in. This isn't a whim, you know. It's a whole new me. With morals. And scruples.'

'And a messy T-shirt,' said Ellie, because there were grey smudges across her front. 'What have you been *doing* up there?'

'Clearing out. Detoxing my life. Actually, has he got his car here?'

'I can hear you,' Todd pointed out. 'And yes, I do have my car.'

'Right. Wait there.' Roo disappeared from view.

'See?' Ellie said. 'I told you it'd be OK. She's on her way down.'

'No I'm not.' Roo's head popped out again. 'Stand back.'

'What are you going to do?' said Ellie. 'Shoot us?'

Ffflump. Ffflump. Fffflumppp. Three fully loaded bin bags landed on the pavement. One of them, not properly tied, had a pair of leopard-print jeans poking out of the top. 'If you want to make yourself useful,' Roo called down, 'drop these off at the charity shop.'

Ellie bent down and checked the label on the jeans. 'What's going on?

These are your favourites!' Plus they were Vivienne Westwood.

'I know. Now they can be someone else's favourites.'

Her beloved purple suede jacket, the black lacy top with the red velvet trim, the white skirt, the silver leather belt . . . scrabbling through the contents of the bag, Ellie said, 'Oh Roo, this is everything you love best. You can't do this.'

Ffflump, fffffflump-flump. Ellie darted out of the way as the next lot of bags came sailing through the air.

'I can,' Roo retaliated. 'I have to.'

'Oh my God,' Todd muttered. 'Two days ago I fell in love with the girl of my dreams. Tonight I find out she's insane.'

'You fell in *love* with her?' Ellie turned and gaped as Todd realised what he'd just blurted out. He began furiously to back-pedal.

'Look, I didn't mean that, I meant fell *for*, don't read things into—'

'Your subconscious said it. That means your brain knows how you feel.' She clutched his arm. 'Don't be embarrassed, just go with it.'

'Like I said, that was before I found out about the insanity.'

'Roo? Let Todd in now. He's in love with you!'

'He's not coming in. I want him to go.'

Ellie carried on arguing his case but Roo refused to budge. Since there was nothing else he could do, Todd loaded the many bin bags into the car and drove off. When he'd gone, Roo unlocked the front door and said, 'Don't try and make me change my mind, because it's not going to happen. Here, try this.' She aimed the nozzle of the atomiser skywards and squished perfume into the air.

The scent was divine. 'It's your Annick Goutal.'

'If you want it, it's yours. Come up, I've got loads more stuff upstairs.'

The place was full of boxes and half-filled bags. 'You can have all my make-up,' Roo gestured carelessly. 'I won't be needing it any more.'

She was bare-faced, wearing just the dusty old T-shirt and a battered pair of jeans. Ellie said, 'OK, this is getting too much now. You can't give away your make-up.'

'If you don't want it, I'll find someone else who does.'

'Roo, you don't have to do this.'

'I want to. It makes me feel better. And I've got a job.' She beamed. 'I start tomorrow.'

Oh good grief. 'What kind of a job?'

'I'm volunteering at the hospice charity shop on Ormond Road.'

'That means you'll be standing up all day. It'll make your feet hurt.'

'If little old ladies can do it, I'm sure I can too.'

This was debatable: little old ladies who volunteered in charity shops tended to be made of sterner stuff than Roo. She was something of a hot-house flower.

'Have you heard from Niall?'

'No. I've blocked his number.'

'You could be a nicer person and still see Todd, you know.'

'Don't keep on. Not seeing Todd is my punishment for having been bad. I *deserve* to be punished,' said Roo.

As the taxi pulled away down Brook Street, Ellie glimpsed her reflection in the window of Vidal Sassoon opposite Claridge's. She was looking like a better than usual version of herself, and Zack, in his dark suit, was quite literally turning heads.

Zack steered her across the street towards the hotel, and she caught sight of them both in another window.

Yee-ha, look at us, heading towards the entrance to Claridge's like a proper glamorous couple in a Chanel ad, if girls in Chanel ads have ever worn emerald-green shoes from Topshop and jewelled hair combs from Primark. Well, you never know, they might.

'Oh, hello! It's Ellie, isn't it? How funny, I was just admiring your dress and then I recognised you from the salon!'

It was Yasmin Brookes. And she'd never met Niall but Roo had shown her a picture of him. The man with Yasmin was definitely Niall. Heavens, out with his own wife, what was he thinking of?

'Oh yes, hi.' Yasmin was glancing at Zack; hastily Ellie leapt in before she could come to embarrassing conclusions. 'This is my boss; we're off to a business event.'

'At Claridge's, how fab! This is Niall, my husband.'

As Niall nodded affably at them, Yasmin said to him, 'We had a lovely chat in the salon, the three of us. I told you about Ellie's friend. She was the one who looked like that pop singer, Daisy Deeva. Remember from the Three Deevas, years ago? It wasn't her. But she was still nice!'

Niall's expression had frozen; his eyes darted from Yasmin to Ellie, a muscle tensed in his jaw and his neck went blotchy as he realised who she was. Ellie smiled back at him, revelling in his discomfort. Was this Schadenfreude? Excellent!

Aloud she said, 'She is nice,' and saw Niall's Adam's apple bob up and down like a rubber duck in a choppy sea.

'And is she looking after your baby while you're out this evening?'

Yeek, this was Schadenfreude coming back to bite you on the bum. Ellie said quickly, 'Yes, yes she is. So where are you off to tonight?'

'Oh, just meeting up with friends. It's a treat, isn't it, getting out in the evening? Ellie has a girl,' Yasmin explained to Niall. She turned back to Ellie. 'I'm so sorry, I've forgotten her name . . .?'

Oh bugger . . . Ellie couldn't remember, and Zack was now giving her a quizzical look . . . oh for crying out loud, *what was her baby's name*?

'Got it! Alice!' Yasmin mimed relief that didn't begin to compare with Ellie's. 'Honestly, I hate it when that happens. This is what having babies does to us, isn't it? Gives us nappy brain!'

The narrow escape had left Ellie feeling sick. Alice, that was it, thank heavens one of them had remembered. She managed a smile and said gaily, 'Tell me about it. I can't remember my own name sometimes!'

Once inside, Zack said, 'So I take it your friend Roo isn't babysitting.'

'No, she isn't.'

'I hope that doesn't mean you've left Alice home alone.'

'Oh, she'll be all right. As long as she's got a bottle of rum and the TV remote in her hand, she's happy. She's very advanced for her age.' She exhaled and said, 'Thanks for getting me away from them.'

'Don't mention it.' Zack had skilfully intervened, explaining that they were late and needed to get inside. 'Although I have to say, for a few seconds you had me there. I was starting to wonder if this was another family member you hadn't told me about.'

'I don't have a baby. I promise.'

'I gathered that, when you couldn't remember its name.'

'Oh *God*.' Ellie winced. 'Was it obvious?'

'Only to someone who was fairly certain you didn't have a baby. I don't think they noticed.'

'Phew. Anyway, I'm never going to see them again.' She checked her watch. 'Are we late? Shall we go up now?'

'We have a few minutes.'

'You mean you want to hear all about my imaginary child?'

'Want,' said Zack, 'would be an understatement.'

'OK, I'll tell you, but it's not pretty.' Ellie took a deep breath. 'Niall's the married man Roo was having an affair with. She found out where his wife worked and made me go along with her to see if Yasmin was the nightmare Niall said she was. At the time it seemed like a good idea if I had a baby, so we'd have something to talk about. Anyway, you've just met her. Yasmin was lovely. But Roo couldn't bring herself to admit it. Except last week she found out she wasn't the only mistress. So she's dumped Niall and now she's busy turning herself into a nun.'

'And he's one of those men who isn't happy unless he's cheating on his partner. Nice. I hope your chap's not like that.'

'No, he isn't.' Since she still hadn't come clean about Todd, she could hardly tell him about the Todd-and-Roo fiasco.

'He doesn't mind you coming here this evening with me?'

'He really doesn't mind.' This much was true at least.

'Good. Well, we'd better head on up there.' As Zack ushered her towards the lift, his hand brushed against her arm and Ellie's skin tingled. Weird; she'd never noticed that happen before. The next moment, the lift doors glided open and he tilted his head, indicating with a brief smile she should go in ahead of him. For a split second she felt a squiggly response in the pit of her stomach. Oh God, stop it, she was hopelessly out of practice on the man front, and her first attempt at a comeback had been a disaster. Don't say she was about to launch into a desperate rebound-crush on—of all people—her own boss. How embarrassing. How completely, humiliatingly inappropriate.

Right, this wasn't going to happen. She was going to put a stop to it before it could take hold. *Just . . . don't let it start.*

This evening's dinner was more pleasure than business. Bob Nix was a big brash Texan billionaire financier with whom Zack had done deals in the past. Looking to extend his circle of contacts, he had invited a dozen business people plus their partners along for drinks and dinner in the Clarence Room, one of the sixth floor's private suites.

The atmosphere was noisy and relaxed. If you took J. R. Ewing and pumped him full of air with a bicycle pump, you'd end up with Bob. He was as loud and jolly as you'd expect of a Texan billionaire. In his late fifties and six foot five without his Stetson, he towered over his wife Bibi, who was young and super-glamorous in a Dolly Partonish way. But she was as welcoming as Bob. Within minutes of complimenting Ellie on her hair combs she'd discovered they were exactly the same age; in no time they were chatting away about fashion, music, shoes and make-up.

'So are y'all a couple?'

'No, no, I just work for Zack.'

'Hey, you can work together and still be a couple.' Bibi's eyes sparkled. 'That's how I met Bob! I was his personal trainer.'

'Well, that's not going to happen. Zack only hired me because he knew it wouldn't. Plus I have a boyfriend.'

'Oh right. Sorry. Zack's pretty cute though.'

I know he is. Aloud Ellie said, 'So's my boyfriend.'

Bibi laughed. 'Hey, don't mind me, I'm just a hopeless romantic! Bob and I are so happy together I spend all my time trying to fix other couples up.' She caught the glimmer of surprise in Ellie's eyes. 'Ah, see? Y'all thought I was a gold-digger, didn't you! But I'm not. He's the love of my life. And I've signed a pre-nup. If we break up, I walk away with nothing but my pride.'

'Good for you.'

'And the keys to the safe, obviously. Joke!'

Over dinner, the conversation turned to Tuscany, where everyone else appeared to have holidayed. Several of them owned villas there. Bob said, 'How about you, Ellie? Where d'you like to vacation?'

She smiled at him. 'I like Cornwall best.'

'Corn-waaaall?' Mystified, he shook his head. 'Bottom left-hand corner of England, am I right? Can't say I've ever been there.'

'Oh, you should.' Ellie put down her wine glass. 'It's beautiful. My favourite place is Looe, it's just—'

'Loo?' Bibi clapped her hands in delight. 'You mean like the *toilet*?'

'That's exactly how I'd describe it,' Kara, one of the businessmen's wives, drawled. 'The place was full of oiks.'

The fork in Ellie's hand was loaded with seafood in a saffron sauce. The temptation was enormous. 'I go there.'

'So you'll have seen them. Wearing knotted hankies on their heads and drinking cans of lager on the beach. Screaming babies, kids dropping ice creams, souvenir shops . . .' Kara's upper lip did its best to curl.

'Well, I've never been to Italy. But I'm fairly sure they have souvenir shops in Florence. And babies that cry.'

'Oh well, we're all different.' A thin smile of satisfaction stretched itself across Kara's face. 'Some of us are probably just suited to Tuscany more than others.'

Bibi said, 'We tried it once, Bob, didn't we? Bored the backside off us. Give me Disneyworld any day.'

Ellie could have hugged her. Kara looked as if she'd been bitten by a mongoose. Across the table, Zack's mouth was twitching.

At the end of the evening Bibi hugged her goodbye. On impulse Ellie removed the jewelled combs Bibi had admired earlier. 'Here, you said how much you liked them. I want you to have these.'

'Oh God, I can't believe it, that's so kind of you! Hang on . . .' Bibi said, 'let me give you something too.'

Hastily Ellie stopped her. 'No, you can't do that.'

Well, she could, but the item Bibi was struggling to unfasten was a diamond tennis bracelet, which was a slightly embarrassing exchange for a couple of combs from Primark that had cost one pound fifty each.

They left the hotel at eleven fifteen. In the taxi Ellie said, 'Sorry about the thing with Kara. I hope I haven't got you into trouble.'

Zack was finding it almost impossible to tear his gaze away from her. In this light her eyes were huge. Her hair, no longer fastened up in a semi-chignon, now framed her face. Her expression was unrepentant; she was apologising for possibly causing problems in the business sense but not for saying what she'd said.

'Doesn't matter a bit. She's a crashing snob, and I wasn't wild about her husband either. I didn't know you were such a fan of Cornwall.'

'Oh God, I love it. Ever since we started going down there when I was a kid. We used to stay on a caravan site between Looe and Polperro. Then after that it was camping holidays with friends, sometimes on the south coast, sometimes in Newquay.'

'And then you met Jamie.'

'I did. And he loved Cornwall too. It's where we spent our honeymoon, in St Ives. We used to talk about moving down there one day. It was our dream.' She paused for a moment. 'But that didn't happen.'

More than anything, Zack wanted to comfort her. He wondered what she'd do if he kissed her. Jump out of the cab, probably.

Ellie tilted her head. 'So how about you? Ever been to Cornwall?'

'I have. It's where I grew up.'

'Seriously? You never told me that!'

'I didn't know I had to.' Something relaxed inside him: *at last, a connection.* 'My family still live there. I head down whenever I can.'

'Whereabouts?'

'Perranporth.'

'I know Perranporth! Just down from Newquay! Oh my God, I know Perranporth!' Her eyes were shining, her whole face was lit up.

'And I know Newquay. I used to spend weeks at a time on Fistral Beach.'

'Fistral Beach is the best for surfing. Full of oiks, obviously.'

'Oh, I like being an oik,' Zack said, 'Shall I tell you why I finally broke up with Louisa? Because she wanted us to join some friends at a villa in Tuscany for a child-free, fun-free, oik-free fortnight.'

'No!' Ellie burst out laughing. 'Is she related to Kara?'

'It wouldn't surprise me. Anyway, that was my breaking point.'

'I call it a narrow escape. Start going on holidays like that and you'll end up reading books by Salman Rushdie.'

'And discussing them,' said Zack. 'In interminable detail.'

'When you're not talking about wine-tasting and how your favourite Montepulciano has undertones of Marmite and top notes of Weetabix.'

'With just a touch of peanut butter and a dash of deodorant.'

'Will you just listen to us? We are *complete* oiks.'

'Thank God for that.'

'Tell me about your family in Perranporth.'

'My parents still live in the house where we all grew up. It's far too big for them now, but they don't want to move.'

'What are their names? Sorry,' Ellie flapped her hand. 'Being nosy. You don't have to tell me that.'

'Why wouldn't I want to tell you about my family? They're embarrassing, but they're not that embarrassing. My mum's Teresa, but everyone calls her Tizz. My dad's Ken. They ran a landscape-gardening business up until they retired a couple of years ago. And I have three sisters who all live in Cornwall. Claire's in St Ives, she's married with three children. Steph's living with her chap in St Austell and they have twin girls. And Paula's in Helston with her two, a boy and a girl.'

Ellie was suitably impressed. 'Wow. So you're an uncle, big time.'

'Just a bit. Five girls and two boys aged between three and eleven. When we all get together it's not what you'd call peaceful. And there are dogs too. You should see us when the whole family hits the beach.'

'I hope you hand out ear-plugs to all the poor people trying to read their Salman Rushdie books in peace.'

'Nobody reads Salman Rushdie on Fistral Beach, that's the joy of it. We're all oiks together.'

'I could have seen you there.' Ellie was shaking her head, marvelling at the idea. 'We could have been there at the same time. I've got loads of photos at home of us down there. Wouldn't it be incredible if your family was in the background?'

They were almost home now. Zack wasn't feeling remotely casual but thank God it came out that way. 'I don't know what Jamie looked like.'

Ellie smiled. 'He was lovely. I can show you photos.'

'I'd like to see them.' *Casual, relaxed, no pressure.*

'You mean tomorrow? Or tonight? Because you can come back now if you want. I could get the albums out, show him to you.'

'Would that be difficult? I don't want you to feel pressurised.'

'I just invited you, didn't I?' Her face softened. 'I love talking about Jamie. Just because he isn't here any more doesn't mean pressing a delete button and forgetting he was ever here.'

It was the first time he'd visited her flat. Well, Tony Weston's flat. Ellie had already explained that Tony was in LA. Having kicked off her emerald-green stilettos and made coffee, she pointed him towards the sofa and handed him a small grey leather photo album.

'Here you are. No jokes about my hair either.'

Zack turned the pages of the album and took in every detail in the photographs. This had been her life. Ellie and Jamie at someone else's wedding. The two of them dancing at a party. Ellie and Jamie sitting outside a sunny restaurant with Tony Weston, the three of them radiating health and fun and happiness.

Jamie had surfer-blond hair, an open, friendly face and a killer smile.

'He looks pretty cool.' What else could he say? Could he ask her if she liked guys with dark hair too?

'That's because you haven't seen his legs yet.' Ellie tucked her hair behind her ears. 'By the way, I'm allowed to make fun of them. You're not.'

'Wouldn't dream of it. Can I ask one thing, though?'

'Go ahead.' She leaned across the arm of the sofa to see which picture he was pointing to.

'Who's the teenage boy in the skirt?'

'Hey! What did I tell you? No mickey-taking.' Ellie made a grab for the album. 'The hairdresser said having it short would suit me.'

Zack grinned. 'Sorry. It did suit you. I just think having your hair longer suits you more.'

'This is us two years ago,' said Ellie. 'On Fistral Beach.'

Zack looked at the photo. An energetic game of volleyball was in progress. There was Jamie, leaping in midair to knock the ball over the net, above the head of his opponent.

'Who's that?' Zack pointed.

'Todd.'

Todd. The one who had taken Jamie's place. In fairness, he looked perfectly OK. His brown hair was short and tufty, his smile broad.

The final shot, a close-up, captured the look being exchanged between Jamie and Ellie as Jamie lovingly lifted a long strand of wet hair from her cheek. It was a look of pure love, to the extent that Zack realised with a jolt he'd never been in a relationship and shared that depth of feeling. All these years, this was what he'd been missing out on.

'That's it.' Ellie closed the last page. 'You get the gist. That was Jamie. You've seen him now.'

He saw her casually wipe the corner of her eye, where a lone tear had escaped. 'I can see how happy you were.'

She nodded. 'We were happy.'

'Ever argue?'

'Oh God, yes, all the time. And over the silliest things. That's something else I miss. We used to argue about toast. Jamie liked butter on hot toast, I like it on cold so it doesn't melt.' Ellie's voice cracked as she struggled to maintain control. 'I really miss all that stupid stuff.'

'Have you argued with anyone since Jamie died?'

She thought about it. Slowly her expression changed. 'I hadn't realised until now. But I really haven't. Everyone's always too busy being nice to me . . . I haven't had one single argument. God, isn't that weird? It's *abnormal.*'

'Not even with Todd?'

Ellie shook her head in wonder. 'Not even Todd.'

'OK. Well, you need someone to argue with. Have you thought of phoning your local tax office? Or a car-clamping firm? Maybe heading over to the council offices for a good old rant about roadworks?'

She looked thoughtful. 'You mean I should ease myself back into it gradually. Practise on strangers to begin with. Start with a bit of trolley rage, something like that?'

'We could try some bickering in the office if you like.'

'That's very kind. But you'd have to promise not to sack me.'

'I won't sack you.' Zack rose to his feet; he wanted to stay but it was time to leave. 'Thanks for tonight. And for showing me the photos.'

'Thank you for being interested.'

At the door Zack wanted to kiss her but he couldn't do that. He said, 'What happened to those comb things you had in your hair? You didn't lose them, did you?'

'No, I didn't lose them.' She opened the door. 'Bye. See you tomorrow.'

Ellie stood at the window and watched as Zack headed off down the street. Having given away the hair combs on a whim, she was now worrying that it had been a foolish thing to do. They'd been so cheap, Bibi had most likely only said it to be polite. She'd never actually wear them. Oh well, at least Zack didn't know.

Chapter 8

It HAD BEEN a toss-up between Claridge's and the Berkeley, but in the end Tony had gone with the Berkeley. Ellie had no idea he was even over here in the UK. Crazy, of course, to buy a London pied-à-terre then not use it, but with Ellie and Todd's relationship still in its tentative early stages, he didn't want to be in their way.

Those were the altruistic reasons, anyway. The third one was that if all went well on this visit over here, he wouldn't want Ellie to be the one left feeling awkward. This way they all had their privacy.

Downstairs, ten minutes later, Tony's breath caught in his throat as she walked into the lobby, exactly on time. Oh God, and even more beautiful than he remembered. Now he committed every last detail to memory and opened his arms wide.

Martha, wearing a fitted lemon-yellow dress and matching shoes, held his face in her hands and said hesitantly, 'This is wrong. Last time it wasn't planned, but this is premeditated.'

Which sounded promising. Inwardly marvelling that the sensation of her skin touching his skin could create a reaction of such intensity, Tony said, 'It's so good to see you again.'

Good was the understatement of the year. Seeing her made him feel properly alive. He squeezed her hands and saw the maelstrom of emotions in her amber eyes.

'Oh Tony.' Martha's voice was unsteady. 'What have you done to me? I used to think I was a nice person. Honest and decent.'

'You are. All we're doing is meeting for lunch.'

'I know. Just lunch.'

The next three hours flew by. They drank Prosecco, ate wonderful food and talked nonstop. The connection was still there, stronger than ever. When the restaurant closed, they moved through to the Blue Bar and carried on, enclosed in their own private bubble of bliss. Oh, would you look at those eyes. That perfect mouth. The way her dimples flashed every time she smiled. He loved every inch of her, every last glorious caramel curve. And to know that she'd been missing him as desperately as he had missed her . . . it gave him such hope. Somehow, somewhere, surely they could be together in a way that was miraculously guilt-free . . .

'Are you listening to a word I'm saying?'

'Sorry. You're making it hard to concentrate.' He captured her fingers between his own, wondering if he'd be able to kiss her before she left. Would she let him? 'What is it?'

'Oh, hang on, that's mine.' Reaching for her bag, she pulled out the ringing phone and grimaced. 'Oh Lord, it's Eunice. I told her I was meeting a client.'

'Leave it.' Tony already knew she wouldn't.

'I can't. Won't be a second.' She jumped up and made her way out of the Blue Bar. Tony watched her go. Please don't let Eunice be putting pressure on her, playing the guilt card.

'Henry's lost.' She was back, searching agitatedly for her purse. 'He's gone missing on Hampstead Heath . . . I'm sorry, I have to go.'

How could he let her go alone? Outside the Berkeley, the doorman flagged down a black cab and together Tony and Martha jumped in. Ensconced inside the hotel, they hadn't even realised it had begun to rain. Now as they made their way to Hampstead, the taxi's windscreen wipers struggled to cope. Thunder was rumbling, the sky had darkened to slate grey and lightning crackled overhead.

'There's no point in you coming with me.' Martha's face was taut with anxiety. 'You can't look for him. Eunice mustn't see you.'

'I can keep out of her way.' He wanted to hug and reassure her, but it wasn't the time. 'How did it happen, anyway?'

'Eunice took him to the Heath for a walk. It was still sunny when they got there. They sat down on a bench and she dozed off.'

'*Dozed off?*'

'She's exhausted. You can't blame her; she never stops. Anyway, it was only for a couple of minutes. But when she woke up, Henry was gone. And then it started to rain. Oh God, this is my punishment for not going with them. I came to see you instead and now he's lost.'

'Stop it, don't panic, nothing's going to happen to him.' Tony was firm. 'Trust me, he'll be found.'

But when they eventually reached Hampstead, Henry was still missing. The taxi driver stopped at the bottom of Millfield Lane, close to the Highgate Ponds. Martha, on the phone with Eunice, ascertained that she was up by the most northerly of the ponds.

'I'll head on up there. She's distraught. There are park rangers out looking for him.' She opened the door of the cab. 'Please, Eunice mustn't see you. Leave this to me. You go home.'

'OK, I'll do that. Call me as soon as you can.' Any kind of kiss would be hideously inappropriate now. Tony let her go. The moment she was out of sight, he paid the driver and jumped out of the taxi. Where Martha had turned right, he checked that no glimpses of her lemon-yellow dress were visible through the trees and turned left.

The rain was hammering down like gunfire. There wasn't anyone else about and the branches of the trees were being wrenched this way and that, whipped into a frenzy by ferocious gusts of wind. Martha had told him that Henry had gone missing on Parliament Hill, but his favourite section of the heath was where the ponds lay. Getting wetter by the second, Tony headed towards them. At one stage, in the far distance, he saw a tiny figure up on the hill and heard a voice, barely audible, yelling Henry's name.

Ten minutes later it happened. Did he hear a noise? Or was it sheer chance that he turned and looked to one side and saw a bare foot sticking out of the undergrowth ten yards away? Stumbling across the uneven ground, Tony saw the leg attached to the foot, clad in sodden brown trousers. Then a long thin body, long arms, the head . . . yes, it was definitely him . . .

'Hello?' Tony approached with caution. Henry was half-sitting, half-lying beneath a tree with his eyes closed and his mouth slightly open.

Then the eyes opened and Henry was looking at him. 'I'm wet.'

'Henry? Are you OK?'

'Yes, thank you. I'm wet.'

'I can see that. What happened to your shoes?'

Henry gazed in bemusement at his bony bare feet. 'I don't know. I'm sorry. I'm quite wet.'

'Are you able to stand?'

'I'm quite hungry. Is it time for breakfast?'

Henry's voice was gentle, bewildered, educated. Obediently he held out his hands and allowed Tony to help him to his feet.

They stood and gazed at each other for several seconds in the rain. Then Tony watched as Henry searched in his trouser pockets and produced a grey sock. He proceeded to put it on his left hand like a glove. This was Martha's husband; he had been an accountant. God, Alzheimer's was a brutal, disgusting disease.

Tony reached for his mobile. His finger hovered over the phone. 'Henry, who's Martha?'

He saw a flicker of recognition in the silver-rimmed brown eyes. 'Martha? I think she lives next door, doesn't she?'

Tony said gently, 'Martha's your wife.'

'Ah yes. Yes, that's right.'

'Do you love Martha?' Did this make him a truly despicable person? 'Henry, do you love her? Your wife?'

'Oh yes. I love her very much.' He was nodding earnestly now. 'A ham sandwich. That would be nice. I'm quite hungry, you know.'

Tony made the call. 'I've got him, he's fine.'

'Oh thank God!' Martha let out a sob of relief. 'Where are you?'

He told her, adding, 'Don't say anything to Eunice, just get yourself straight down here.'

It took Martha less than five minutes to reach them.

'Hello!' Henry's face lit up at the sight of her heading through the undergrowth towards them.

'What's her name?' said Tony.

'Oh my goodness. Let me think . . . she's my beautiful wife.'

'Oh Henry, we were so worried about you. We didn't know where you were.' Martha clutched his hands, one of them still encased in the grey knitted sock. 'Where are your shoes?'

'Harrods, I think. Or Sainsbury's. I'm wet.'

'I know, darling. It doesn't matter, we're going to get you home now.' She looked at Tony and said, 'Thank you so much. You have to go. But thank you.'

As Tony turned to leave, Martha was already calling Eunice to tell her that everything was OK, Henry was safe.

Henry, carefully examining the sock on his hand, said to no one in particular, 'Or roast chicken would be nice.'

Working in a charity shop might not be glamorous but it was undoubtedly a good thing. People gave away stuff they no longer wanted, and it was bought by people who did want it, and the money raised went to a worthy cause. It was just a shame that sometimes people gave away stuff they no longer wanted without first making sure it was clean.

This was Roo's first morning in the shop and she was discovering that rubber gloves were a necessity. Already, unpacking the mound of plastic bags left outside over night, she had lifted out a pair of jeans with boxer shorts still inside them. Neither of them had been washed. For a good long while. If ever. But it didn't matter, because she was atoning. Making up for a lifetime of hedonism and selfishness. She wasn't going to throw a diva strop and demand to be given something easier and less gross to do.

The phone rang that evening just as Ellie was getting ready for bed.

'Oh, hi! Is that Ellie? Ellie, hi there. Honey, is Tony with you?' It was Tamara, Tony's personal assistant in LA.

'No. He's not here.' Ellie frowned. 'He isn't in Britain. He's in LA.'

'No, honey, he's not here. He's definitely over there with you.'

'He isn't, though. And he would have told me if he was coming over.'

'Well, he asked me to organise it. I booked the plane tickets myself and drove him to the airport. OK, don't worry, I just need to ask him about fitting in an interview but his cell's switched off. No problem, I'll keep trying. Bye, honey, bye!'

OK, this was officially strange. Ellie tried Tony's number. Tamara was right: it was switched off. She left a message asking him to call her and said, 'If you're here, why didn't you tell me?'

Most odd. But he must be all right, surely. There had to be a simple explanation. Ellie yawned, brushed her teeth and went to bed.

He got back to Ellie while she was at work the next day.

'Tony! Are you all right?' She'd actually started to worry when his phone had still been switched off this morning.

'I'm fine, sweetheart.'

'Where are you?'

'At home in LA.'

God, who'd ever trust an actor? He was such a plausible liar. 'No you're not,' said Ellie. 'I spoke to Tamara. You're over here.'

'Oh. Damn. OK, you're right. I knew I should have returned Tamara's calls first.'

'Your phone's been switched off!'

'Battery was flat. I forgot to pack my charger, that's all.'

'Why didn't you come to the flat?'

'I thought you and Todd would appreciate having it to yourselves. I was being discreet, giving you a bit of space. You and Todd don't want me hanging round and—'

'Oh Tony, that's over, it didn't work out. It just wasn't right.' Ellie lowered her voice; Zack was only in the kitchen and she didn't want him to overhear. 'We tried, but we're happier as friends.'

'Oh sweetheart, I'm sorry.'

'Don't be. We're both fine about it. So you can check out of that hotel and get yourself over here. You won't be a gooseberry, it'll just be us.'

'Except I'm heading back tomorrow. It's hardly worth it now.' He sounded . . . sad.

'Are you busy tonight?'

'No, no, nothing planned . . .'

Something definitely wasn't right. 'Come over, then. I'll cook dinner,' Ellie volunteered. 'I've learned how to do Thai green curry.'

'Really?' It was his favourite. 'Is it nice?'

Honesty forced her to prevaricate. 'It *might* be nice.'

'Or it might not?'

'I'm still practising. Come over and let me give it another go. If it all goes horribly wrong, we'll order a takeaway.'

Sounding more cheerful, Tony said, 'Or shall I just order it now?'

Somehow, against all the odds, a tiny miracle had occurred. The Thai green curry had turned out well. The chicken was tender, the jasmine rice fluffy and the spices took the roof off your mouth, but in a good way. Which was just as well, seeing as Tony was desperately in need of cheering up. To begin with he'd asked her about Todd and she'd told him how relieved she was to be free of the fear that she was trapped in a relationship that was all wrong. Tony was sad but sympathetic, and helped himself to another beer.

OK, enough. Ellie said, 'Tony? Are you going to tell me what's wrong?' She waited, watching him pour the beer slowly into his glass. 'Because otherwise I'm going to start worrying that you're ill.'

Tony put the bottle down. His misery was tangible. 'I'm not ill, sweetheart.'

He was an actor. She watched him closely. 'Sure?'

'I'm sure. I promise. It's not that.' He rested his elbows on the table. 'OK, I'll tell you. Remember those paintings I bought, months ago? The ones by the artist I met on Primrose Hill . . .?'

Ellie's throat was on fire, her body was a dead weight and she couldn't stop shivering. It was almost too painful to turn over in bed. It was even an effort to lift her head and peer at the alarm clock. Eight thirty. Oh no, what about work? But there was no way she could go in today; this wasn't a cough or a cold, it was full-blown flu. She'd have to call Zack and let him know.

It took superhuman strength to crawl out of bed. Unbelievably, all she'd felt last night was extra tired and a bit hot. Now it was all she could do to make it to the bathroom for paracetamol, a glass of water and a wee.

Then through to the living room to collect her phone.

Back in bed, breathless and weak with exhaustion, Ellie pressed buttons until Zack's name came up. Then she heard his voice telling her he was busy right now and could she leave a message.

'Zack, it's me. Sorry, um, I've got flu.' Even holding the phone was sapping her energy. 'Can't come into work.' Her throat was burning and she was croaking like a frog. She sounded ridiculous, like the worst kind of malingerer putting on one of those feeble I'm-so-sick voices that didn't fool anyone. She ended the call and hauled herself over onto her side. Her eyes closed, which could only be a good thing. Sleep would take the pain away, wouldn't it?

The next time Ellie woke the phone was ringing. She freed herself from the depths of the duvet and managed to locate the phone.

Dozily she croaked, 'Hello?'

'Did I wake you?' It was Zack's voice. 'I just wanted to make sure you're all right.'

'Oh.' Her throat felt as if it were being squeezed by a giant fist, she could barely swallow. 'Um, I don't think I'll be able to come into work tomorrow . . .' She began to cough feebly. '*Ow*, sorry . . .'

'Don't apologise. Of course you can't work. Have you seen a doctor?'

'No . . .' She hadn't yet got round to registering with a local surgery.

'Is there someone to look after you?'

Another fit of coughing seized her. 'No.'

'Where's Todd?'

'Away at a business conference.'

'Can you get out of bed?'

'Yes . . .'

'Right. I'm coming over.'

'No, no . . . I'll be OK. You don't want to catch this.'

Zack ignored her. 'Is there anything you need?'

I need Jamie. She whispered, 'Painkillers. Strong ones. I've run out.'

'I've got some. I'm on my way.'

Ellie rubbed a hand over her face; had she ever looked worse than this? Oh well, too ill to care, she swallowed with difficulty. 'Thanks.'

The doorbell duly rang fifteen minutes later. She pressed the buzzer to let him in and collapsed back into bed.

Zack entered the flat and heard a voice call out weakly, 'I'm in here.'

The door to her bedroom was open, the curtains drawn across. Huddled under the duvet, Ellie lay shivering and deathly pale. She murmured, 'Don't come any closer.'

'I'm never ill.' Ignoring her, he approached the bed. 'Have you been here on your own all day?'

She nodded fractionally and winced. 'It's only flu.'

'I've brought ibuprofen, paracetamol and Night Nurse.' He placed them on the bedside table and picked up the empty glasses. 'I'll get you some fresh water. Or how about a cup of tea?'

Ellie shook her head. 'Just water.'

Zack wanted to scoop her up and carry her home. Instead he left the bedroom and pushed open the door to the kitchen.

He came back with a glass of water. 'Now let's sort out your pillows.'

Ellie rolled over to the side of the bed and he plumped up the flattened pillows. Then he helped her into a semi-sitting position so she could take two tablets and wash them down with water. It was the most physical contact they'd ever had and it felt incredible. Ellie was ill and he loved being able to help her. She was wearing a dark blue nightdress that was slipping off one shoulder and he wasn't even going to think about the fact that this might be the only item of clothing she had on.

He picked up the tissue box on the bedside table. 'This is almost empty. Do you have any more?'

'No. It's OK, there's loo roll.'

'You can't use that. I'll get you another box. I need to go now but I'll be back in a couple of hours.'

'You don't have to come back.'

'I'm not leaving you on your own like this. You're ill. Get some sleep now.' Zack straightened pillows that didn't need straightening. 'Do you want to give me the key so I don't have to ring the bell?'

She nodded. 'In my handbag in the living room. Could I have a . . ? No, it doesn't matter.'

'Say it. Anything you like.'

A faint smile lifted the corners of her mouth. 'Great, I'll have a red Mercedes and a diamond tiara.'

'Right.' In that moment Zack knew he loved her, *he actually loved her*. 'Well, that might take a couple of days to organise. Anything else in the meantime?'

'A can of Tizer would be fantastic.'

'Now you're just being greedy. But you're the invalid, so OK.'

Another smile. 'Thanks.'

Ellie slept again, waking up two hours later to the sound of Zack letting himself into the flat. So kind. A grateful tear squeezed out of the corner of her eye; when you felt this ill, it was so lovely not to feel alone.

She probably needed a shower but that was impossible; the thought of drops of water pummelling her skin was too agonising to contemplate. Ellie prayed she didn't smell.

But when he came into the bedroom with a can of Tizer and a pink bendy straw so she didn't spill it down her front, Zack didn't appear to be holding his breath. Maybe she was OK.

'It's dark outside.' The Tizer, ice-cold and delicious, soothed her burning throat.

'Ten o'clock. Time for more ibuprofen.' He handed them over before tearing open the new box of Kleenex. 'Can you manage anything to eat?'

Ellie closed her eyes, contemplated food, shook her head. 'No thanks. Not hungry. This Tizer is perfect.'

'Good. Now, do you want to lie on the sofa and watch TV for a bit?'

'I think I'm too tired.'

'OK, you go back to sleep. I've brought my laptop with me. I'm going to do some work for the next couple of hours. If you need anything, just give me a shout.'

'You don't need to stay. I'll be fine.'

'You might be fine. But what if you're not? Look, it's not a problem. It makes no difference to me whether I'm working here or at home. And just so you know, there are plenty more Tizers in the fridge.'

So kind, so thoughtful. Ellie drifted off again, comforted by the knowledge that there was someone else in the flat.

It was four-thirty when she next came to, nudged into semi-consciousness by her bladder. For several seconds she couldn't work out if it was morning or afternoon. Right, still dark outside, that had to mean morning. Blurrily she felt her way out of bed and across the room to the en-suite. That was better. OK, now she was upright, how about a trip to the kitchen for another cold Tizer?

Shuffling along the hallway she saw the living-room door was ajar and prodded it open. Zack was stretched across the sofa, fast asleep.

Fuzzy-headed and weak-limbed though she was, Ellie couldn't stop looking at him; it was literally impossible to tear her gaze away. She'd never seen Zack sleeping before. In the warm glow of the table lamp his face was relaxed, softened. There was stubble on his chin. His breathing was even. Best of all, he wasn't making a sound. A non-snorer. Always nice to know.

OK, stop that. You're ill.

Ellie headed for the kitchen. Feeling fractionally better than before, she opened the fridge and took out a can of Tizer. Zack had also bought yoghurts, strawberry mousses, jellies and various bottles of freshly squeezed juice. She closed the fridge and left the kitchen, unable to resist another peep into the living room on her way back to bed.

But this time Zack's eyes were open, her fridge investigation evidently having woken him up. He said sleepily, 'You were supposed to give me a shout. I'd have got that for you.'

'It's OK, I needed a wee anyway.' *Oh God, I can't believe I just said that.*

'How are you feeling?'

Ellie hung on to the door. 'Embarrassed that I just said *wee* in front of my boss.'

He laughed. 'Don't be. It's what all my sisters say. I'm quite used to it.'

'I thought you'd gone home ages ago.'

'I'm not fussy where I sleep. This is a comfortable sofa. You're looking a bit better.'

'That's hard to believe.' Ellie raked her fingers through her hair. Glancing down, she double-checked that the nightie came down to just above her knees. If she'd realised he was still here, she would have put on a dressing gown.

Zack stretched and sat up. 'Is there anything else you want?'

She hesitated. 'Maybe . . . could you do, um . . . cheese on toast?'

Zack grinned. He rose and pointed to the sofa. 'Here, you sit down. Are you asking me if I know *how* to make cheese on toast?'

She managed a brief smile in return. 'It's OK if you don't. Just a Weetabix would be fine.'

Ellie sat with her feet up on the sofa, her head resting on the same cushions Zack's own head had rested against only minutes before. It was silent outside the flat. Here they were in the middle of the night, and it felt as if they were the only two people awake in Primrose Hill.

Then Zack came back with two plates of cheese on toast, grilled to perfection. He'd cut hers into soldiers to make them easier to eat. He'd also made himself a cup of strong black coffee. Together in the living room they shared a mini picnic in weirdly companionable near-silence. When the toast was finished, Zack brought her a strawberry mousse. Somewhere in the distance a siren wailed. Ellie's eyelids grew heavy and the exhaustion overtook her once more. From what felt like a great distance she was aware of Zack adjusting the sofa cushions to make her more comfortable. Her head was pounding but it didn't matter. She smiled and murmured, 'That feels nice . . . you're so lovely . . .'

She woke again, hours later, with a start. Still on the sofa, alone in the flat and suffering the most hideous of flashbacks.

That feels nice . . . You're so lovely . . . Oh God, had she really said that while she'd been in her enfeebled, almost-asleep state?

Investigating some more, Ellie discovered she was wrapped in her duvet; at some stage Zack must have fetched it from the bedroom and covered her with it. And there on the coffee table, secured by her phone, was a note in his distinctive handwriting:

Morning. How are you feeling? I've gone to take Elmo for his walk and catch up on some paperwork. Back by eleven at the latest. Anything you need, just give me a call.

See you soon,

Z.

The Z ended with a little squiggle that might or might not have been a cross, a cartoon fish or a kiss. Ellie found herself studying it, trying to work out which of these he could have meant it to be. OK, stop it and get a grip, he hadn't written her a love note. It was just a squiggle.

Also on the coffee table was her alarm clock, the packet of ibuprofen, a glass of water and another unopened can of Tizer. He'd thought of everything. After her inane burblings last night it was a wonder there wasn't a straitjacket.

Ellie swallowed the painkillers and drank some water. Everything still hurt, and dozing off again was a tempting option. But it was nine thirty, Zack could be back in an hour and she needed to get clean.

The water hit her skin like bullets, the pain was intense and she hadn't realised standing up in the shower could be such hard work. Even lifting her arms to shampoo her hair was exhausting . . .

Her legs were feeling weak and the heat of the water was making her head muzzy . . . oh, and now there were dots dancing in front of her eyes, this wasn't good, dots getting bigger . . . OK, out of here, sit down before you fall down . . . *oof*.

'**O**h God, how did this happen? What did you do?' Zack was looking at her in horror.

Ellie told herself it could have been worse. She might have been knocked out completely. Zack could have let himself back into the flat and found her lying in a wet naked heap on the bathroom floor. At least she was wearing her dressing gown and had made it back to the sofa.

'I fainted in the shower. Well, half out of the shower.' She pressed the handful of tissues to her temple; the bump had swollen to impressive proportions but the bleeding had almost stopped. 'I hit my head on the edge of the radiator. It's OK, I don't need stitches or anything.'

Zack closely inspected the injury. 'I can't believe you thought having a shower was a good idea. For crying out loud, you've got *flu*.'

'Sorry. I just wanted to feel better.'

'And didn't that work well. You could have cracked your skull open. Right, that's it, I'm not leaving you here on your own again.'

'It's OK, I promise I won't have any more showers.'

Ellie lay back as he disappeared into the kitchen. He returned moments later with a packet of frozen sweetcorn wrapped in a clean tea towel. 'Here, let me do it. You're as white as a sheet.'

'Are you always this bossy?' She closed her eyes as the icy parcel covered the egg-sized lump on her temple.

'Always.'

'But you can't stay here all the time.'

'I know. But you need looking after. That's why you're coming back to Ancram Street with me.'

Zack brought his car round, double-parking it outside the flat and not even allowing her to make her own way down the staircase. Instead he carried her in his arms. Who said flu didn't have its compensations?

'I feel like I'm being kidnapped.' It felt fantastic. Ellie had to keep her eyes averted in case he could tell what was going through her mind.

'Can't have you falling down the stairs and breaking your neck.' Zack's tone was brusque. It was a struggle to keep her head upright. Giving in, Ellie rested it against his shoulder.

'I hope I'm not heavy.'

'You're fine. We're almost there. Mind your feet.' He reached the downstairs hallway and manoeuvred her out through the door.

Two minutes later they arrived at Ancram Street and the process was repeated in reverse. Ellie closed her eyes, remembering the time after their wedding when Jamie had ceremoniously carried her over the threshold of the Hammersmith flat. He'd pretended to buckle under her weight, she'd jabbed him in the ribs and they'd ended up laughing so much he'd almost dropped her.

OK, don't think about it. She didn't have the energy to get emotional now. She was carried up the stairs. Past the living room. Along the corridor and through the door at the end. Zack's spare room was all pale green and white with a summery feel and billowing leaf-green curtains. The queen-sized bed was comfortable.

Twenty minutes later there was a gentle knock at the door, then it was pushed open.

'Only me.' Geraldine came in, leaning on her walking stick. 'Oh my darling, you do look poorly. Zack asked me to come and check you over. That's a pretty impressive bump you have on your head there.'

Ellie was wiped out. She allowed herself to be examined. Her temple throbbed. She said, 'I'm being a real nuisance, aren't I?'

'Not your fault, is it? OK, all done. Nothing sinister. Just rest and keep up the fluids. You'll be feeling better soon.'

'Poor Zack, being landed with me.'

'Some people like having someone to look after. And it's nice to see Zack like this.' Geraldine waggled her eyebrows. 'I always think a good bedside manner is a lovely attribute in a man.'

Zack knocked at the door and said, 'OK to come in?'

Ellie was sitting up in bed, wearing a clean white T-shirt. Her face was pale and there were violet shadows beneath her eyes but to him she still looked lovely.

'Hi. Thanks.' She reached for the mug of tomato soup he'd brought up to her. 'I can't believe I woke up wanting soup.' She smiled and took a sip. 'That tastes fantastic. I must be over the worst.'

Which was good news, of course it was. But a small, selfish part of Zack didn't want her to be over the worst. Until this evening Ellie had been so unwell it had made absolute sense to insist she come to stay. But as soon as she was better, she would return to her own flat. And Todd would be back from his conference in Glasgow. He hadn't said so to Ellie, but he thought Todd could have made more of an effort; his girlfriend was ill and he wasn't exactly inundating her with phone calls. I mean, did he not care how she was? Was he not even bothered? Would it kill him to send her some flowers?

Maybe this was a hint that their relationship might not be going such great guns after all. He said casually, 'Heard from Todd today?'

'Oh yes. He called earlier.' Ellie nodded and looked defensive. 'And he's been texting me.'

Was she embarrassed by the lack of attention he'd been paying her? Excellent. 'And he's OK about you staying here?'

She nodded. 'Absolutely. He's grateful to you for looking after me.'

'No problem. You can repay me when you're better.' Zack smiled briefly. 'I've got another favour to ask you.'

'Oh? Go on then, fire away.'

'I've just had an email from Steph.'

'Your sister, the one who lives in St Austell,' said Ellie. 'Twin girls.'

He felt absurdly touched that she'd remembered.

'That's the one. Well, Steph and Gareth have been together for seven years but they've just decided to get married. In September.'

'*This* September? Wow.'

'That's Steph all over. No patience. Once she decides to do something, that's it. Basically they heard that a wedding had been cancelled at the village church and grabbed the chance while it was there.'

'Like Lastminute.com,' said Ellie. 'Why not?'

'They're having the reception at Mum and Dad's. A hundred guests.'

'Crikey.'

'It'll be fine. Mum's in her element. They had Claire's wedding at home too; it was a triumph.'

Ellie finished her mug of soup. 'So where do I come in? You want me to help in some way? Oh, is it the invitations, d'you need me to—?'

'Not that kind of help. Actually, it's more personal.' Zack sat on the end of the bed. 'The thing is, Steph's asked her friend Mya to be one of her bridesmaids. I used to go out with Mya, years ago. Now, she's nothing like Louisa,' he added hastily. 'Mya's more like a Labrador, all bouncy and enthusiastic. According to Steph, she's already getting overexcited about me being there. If I go on my own I'm just going to be fending her off the whole time. She's a nice girl and I don't want to hurt her feelings.' He hesitated. 'So what would really help would be if I was to take someone else along with me. Then she'd leave me alone.' This was all true. But he was ruthlessly taking advantage of the situation and using it for his own purposes. With a bit of luck. 'So, up to you. I know it's a big ask, but you'd be really helping me out. And it'll be a good do.' Another pause. 'If you think Todd wouldn't mind.'

Zack McLaren, you have a nerve.

Ellie's eyes were bright and a flash of colour had returned to her cheeks. For a couple of seconds she thought it through. Finally she swallowed and said, 'I'll explain it to him. I'm sure he won't mind.'

'OK, good. Thanks.' His heart was actually thumping against his ribs. Ellie had just agreed to come down to Cornwall with him to attend his sister's wedding. *Result.*

Chapter 9

LOVELY THOUGH it had been to be looked after by Zack, Ellie was aware she had imposed for long enough. It was now Sunday, she'd been here for three days and no longer qualified as an invalid. Her appetite was back and the utter exhaustion had receded too. She felt human again, albeit a bit on the fragile side.

'Now, are you sure you'll be OK?' Zack had insisted on driving her the few hundred yards home. 'What time's Todd getting back?'

'Very soon.' Ellie climbed out of the car; it was three o'clock in the afternoon. 'Thanks for looking after me. I'll be back at work as soon as I'm up to it. Wednesday or Thursday.' He'd done so much for her, she didn't know how to express her gratitude. At least being riddled with flu germs meant a polite kiss on the cheek was out of the question. And anyway, he was her boss. She was his employee. It would be wrong.

Instead Ellie said, 'Bye,' and did an awkward little wave before fitting her key into the lock and letting herself into the house.

Why didn't you let me know you were ill? I'd have come straight back! I could have looked after you!'

Oh dear, Roo was offended.

'You were visiting your mum,' Ellie pointed out. 'Anyway, you wouldn't have been so happy if you'd caught my bugs.'

'I'd still have done it. I *owe* you, remember? How am I ever going to make things up to you if you won't let me do stuff?'

'You don't owe me, I've told you a million times. You did me a favour.' Ellie sighed; Roo was still sticking obstinately to her newfound vow of saintliness. No alcohol, no make-up, endless do-goodery and a stubborn refusal to answer Todd's calls and messages. It was getting a bit wearing, to be honest; she wished the old, fun-loving, irreverent Roo would make a comeback.

'Right, let's do a list.' Roo whipped a notebook from her bag. 'Tell me what you need and I'll go out and get it. Anything you want.'

'OK. Thanks.' Ellie watched her perch on the arm of the sofa. 'Apple juice. And some more bread. White, medium sliced.'

Roo wrote it down. 'Got it. Next?'

'Call Todd.'

The pen abruptly stopped. 'And say what?'

'Tell him you'd like to see him. Just put him out of his misery. All you're doing is cutting off your nose to spite your face.'

Roo jutted her chin. 'Maybe my nose deserves to be cut off.'

'You said you'd do anything I want. This is what I want, for you and Todd to get together.'

'Not going to happen.'

'But you're making *me* feel guilty. If it wasn't for me, you'd be a couple by now. So it's all my fault!'

'Nice try,' said Roo. 'But the answer's still no.'

'Thanks, yes, I'll let him know about that. Bye!' Ellie hung up and scribbled the message on the notepad next to the phone. Zack was upstairs conducting a conference call. Her recovery was now complete; it was Thursday and she'd been back at work for a full week.

The doorbell rang just as the office phone went *ting*, indicating that the conference call upstairs had ended.

Ellie opened the front door, her heart sinking slightly at the sight of the Kerrigans on the doorstep. Zack had already said he couldn't do anything. It really wasn't fair of them to turn up again and pester him.

'Hi,' Kaye said eagerly. 'It's us! We're back!'

'Hello.' Ellie's smile was brief. 'Look, I'm afraid Zack's *really* busy—'

'It's OK, we aren't here to see Zack.' Joe Kerrigan took a step towards her and, with a flourish, produced a bunch of enormous yellow orchids. 'These are for you. Because you have been . . . magnificent! And we'll never be able to thank you enough for what you've done.'

'Hold on. What have I done?'

'We've sold our script.' Kaye looked as if she was ready to burst with excitement. 'Our dream director wants to work with us on this and future projects. And it's all thanks to you. You made Tony Weston read our screenplay and you've changed our lives!'

In shock, Ellie hadn't even heard Zack come down the staircase. Appearing beside her, he said, 'I didn't know about any of this.'

'Me neither.' She shook her head. 'I had no idea Tony even looked at the script. I tried my best to make him read it, but he said he wasn't interested if there wasn't a part in it for him.' She tailed off at the sight of Kaye and Joe both grinning and shaking their heads at her.

'Well,' said Zack, 'however it happened, it's fantastic news. And you can't stand out there. Come on in and tell us everything.'

Joe and Kaye relayed the story of how Tony had taken the script with him on the plane, then piqued the interest of his own agent Marvin, who had in turn piqued the interest of Stephen, a leading screen agent. A buzz around the script had duly been created, several studios had been keen to option it and frenzied negotiations had ensued.

'It was unbelievable,' Kaye exclaimed. 'They flew us out there. First class! We had champagne and little slippers and everything!'

'And then we had all these meetings,' Joe took over. 'You can't begin to imagine what that was like. They're talking budgets and ideas and

A-list stars . . . they're telling us our script is totally brilliant—'

'I knew it was brilliant,' Ellie blurted out. 'I knew it!'

Joe still looked like a scruffy tennis player, but today he was a scruffy tennis player who'd just won a Grand Slam tournament and couldn't believe his luck. His eyes crinkling, he rubbed a hand across the golden stubble on his jaw. 'We know you did. So anyhow, the contract's been signed. Our feet have hardly touched the ground, but we're back in London. So now you understand why we had to come and see you.'

Ellie was overwhelmed. 'I'm so glad you did.'

'Ellie?' Kaye said. 'Is it OK if I give you a hug?'

Ellie laughed and got herself enthusiastically hugged.

Meanwhile Joe shook hands with Zack, then Kaye gave Zack a hug too.

'OK,' said Kaye, when they'd finished. 'Well, that's it!' She gave Joe's arm a light tap. 'I'll wait outside.' Turning to Ellie, she added, 'Joe wants a quick word with you. Is that OK?'

Joe in turn glanced at Zack. 'A quick private word, if you wouldn't mind. It's just something about Tony Weston . . . kind of private . . .'

'Of course. No problem.' Zack opened the office door and indicated for Kaye to go ahead of him. 'I'll show Kaye out.'

The door closed behind them.

'I lied,' said Joe. 'This isn't about Tony Weston.'

'No?'

'OK, of course we wanted to thank you. But I also had an ulterior motive for coming here today.' He exhaled. 'Bringing you those flowers is my way of saying I think you're gorgeous and I've fancied you rotten since the first time I saw you.'

Ellie did a double-take. Was he serious? *What?*

'Oh yes. So how about it? Fancy meeting up one evening?' Another pause, then Joe said with an easy smile, 'You look pretty shocked. I'm not that bad, am I?'

Ellie felt herself flush with anger. 'What about Kaye?'

'What about her?'

'You're married!'

'I'm not married! Who would I be married to? *Kaye?* Oh my God, I can't believe you thought that. Kaye's my *sister*.'

'Oops,' said Ellie. 'I got it wrong. Just kind of assumed. You have the same name. You look married.'

Alarm mingled with horror. '*How?*'

'I mean, you aren't anything alike.' It was an understandable mistake, surely. Joe had messy blond hair and green eyes; he was tall, thin and gangly. Kaye was small and dark and neat. She also wore a wedding ring. Together they were the Kerrigans.

'I'm like Mum, Kaye takes after Dad. She's married. No kids. We write together, that's all, I promise. I'm completely single. So shall I ask the question again?'

'Hang on, just let me think this through.' Seeing someone in a whole new light took a bit of adjusting to.

'Just so you know,' said Joe, 'I'm starting to get nervous now.'

'Really?'

'Oh yes, really. The worst thing is, Kaye said you'd turn me down. And I hate it when I'm wrong and she's right.'

'Is she unbearable?'

'Kaye's a gloater. You can't imagine what it's like, having her as a sister. Actually, I've run out of nerve. Can we forget this ever happened? I'd rather back out now than get turned down.'

'How do you know I'm single? I might not be,' said Ellie. 'I could be living with someone.'

'I asked Tony Weston. You're not. You broke up with some guy recently. But you're not heartbroken about it,' said Joe. 'I checked.'

Ellie relaxed. He was funny, unthreatening and good company. The more she thought about it, the more attractive Joe Kerrigan was becoming. The indefinable spark that had so resolutely failed to appear between her and Todd was actually showing discernible signs of life. Best of all, Joe wasn't her boss. And if there was one thing she knew she needed right now, it was an opportunity to get over her embarrassing crush on Zack. What better way of diverting her attention?

'OK,' said Ellie.

Joe looked cautious. 'OK what? You're agreeing I should back out now? Or that you'll come out with me?'

'That one. The second one.'

'Seriously? Wow, fantastic.' His face lit up. 'When would suit you?'

'Any time.' Recklessly, Ellie said, 'I'm free. How about tonight?'

He shook his head in admiration. 'You are my kind of girl. I knew I liked you. Ha, come on, it's my turn to gloat. Wait until I tell Kaye.'

Out in the hallway, Zack and Kaye were talking about dogs. Kaye turned to look at them. 'Well?'

Joe looked proud. 'She said yes.'

'Did she?' Kaye beamed at Ellie. 'Did you? Damn, I said you'd say no!'

'Sorry.' Ellie was aware of Zack's gaze upon her.

'Sorry about what?' said Zack.

'I asked Ellie out on a date,' Joe explained cheerfully. 'Kaye didn't think I stood a chance. Ha, we're going out tonight.'

Zack looked as if he'd been secretly electrocuted. 'Oh.'

And Ellie realised she'd completely forgotten about Todd.

Kaye and Joe left. Zack disappeared into the kitchen to make coffee. When he entered the office minutes later, he said evenly, 'So am I allowed to ask what's going on? Are you building up a collection?'

Ellie stopped typing and felt a prickle of perspiration on the back of her neck. She'd lied to him; no wonder he didn't sound amused.

'Will you be telling Todd, or weren't you planning on him finding out? Not that it's any of my business,' Zack went on. 'I'm just surprised.'

'Look, Todd and I aren't seeing each other any more. It didn't work out. We broke up, but we're still friends. Sorry I didn't mention it. I didn't want to bore you, banging on about my personal life.'

'Right. Well.' He clearly wasn't pleased that she'd neglected to tell him. 'So now you're going out with Joe Kerrigan. Tonight. Are you sure about this?' He frowned. 'I mean, isn't it all a bit sudden?'

OK, he was telling her she was desperate. And maybe she was, but not for the reason he thought. 'Why can't it be sudden? Haven't you ever met someone and felt an instant connection?'

'I'm just—'

'No,' she broke in, 'let me say this. I didn't agree to meet him because I'm desperate for any old date, I did it because I think this could be special. I'm looking forward to it.'

Zack headed upstairs, ostensibly to work on a business proposal ahead of tomorrow's meeting in Milan.

In reality, one word was going round in his head. *Fuck, fuck, fuck . . .*

How had this happened? How *could* it be happening? Why couldn't Ellie have told him before that the thing with Todd was all over? And now it was too late, because she was in the grip of an instant connection and there was nothing he could do about it.

Ellie pressed her hands against the washbasin and leaned forward, gazing at her reflection in the bathroom mirror.

This was it then. She wanted it to happen and it was going to happen. Her mind was made up.

Who'd have thought it? Looking back, it seemed inconceivable that life could alter so drastically. The last seven days had passed in a whirlwind of activity. This time last week she had been just another boyfriendless PA with a hopeless crush on her boss. Then Joe Kerrigan had turned up and changed everything. On their first date he'd taken her out on a boat on the Thames. On their second date they'd gone rollerblading in Hyde Park. The third date had been a picnic in Kensington Gardens, the fourth a trip on the London Eye. Joe was fun, they had a fantastic time together and when he kissed her she enjoyed kissing him back. The chemistry that had been so painfully absent between herself and Todd was here in spades. The prospect of taking things further no longer made her feel panicky and slightly sick. Her libido, after nineteen months in deep-frozen hibernation, was back.

And the time had now come to take things to the next level.

Here, tonight, in just a few minutes' time.

Ellie peered closely at her reflection. Quite often when she looked in this mirror, she would see Jamie in the bathroom behind her. But there was no sign of him tonight and her mind skittered away from the idea of conjuring him up. What for, so she could ask him if it was all right? No, this was her night. It was only fair that Jamie should stay away, leave her alone to get on with it.

Get it over with.

That wasn't fair. It was just a big step. As soon as 'the first time after Jamie' was out of the way, it would be easier.

There was a light knock on the door.

'Hello?' said Joe from the other side. 'Are you still in there? Or have you jumped out of the window?'

Ellie smiled and opened the door. 'I'm still here.'

He wrapped his arms round her. 'Nervous?'

'Kind of.'

'We don't have to do anything if you don't want to.'

'I do want to.'

'Well, that's good. So do I.' Joe kissed the tip of her nose, then rested his forehead against hers. 'Just so you know, I'm a bit nervous too.'

Maybe she shouldn't have told him he'd be the first since Jamie. It was bound to put him under pressure. Ellie led him across the hallway towards the bedroom. 'Come on, let's do this thing.'

Joe grinned. 'Get the first time over and out of the way.'

See? He understood. 'Exactly.'

And then, hopefully, they could do it again.

It was a stunning morning, sunny and warm with a cloudless sky overhead, the kind of morning that made you feel glad to be alive.

Zack, walking Elmo, wasn't feeling glad about anything. The last week surely ranked among the crappest of his life. In between his trip to Milan and another flying visit to Dundee, he had been forced to watch Ellie fall in love with another man. Or in lust. Whichever, it had been a hideous experience. There was a new light in her eyes, she always seemed to be on the brink of smiling and there was an aura about her that definitely hadn't been there before. It was fizzing out of her like an out-of-control Alka-Seltzer.

Elmo danced on the end of his lead, snuffling at a sweet wrapper on the pavement. Zack pulled him away, carried on walking and checked his watch. Half eight.

As a rule, the journey from Primrose Hill to Ancram Street didn't take in Nevis Street. But today, he told himself, he just happened to feel like heading in that direction. Coincidentally he'd felt the same way yesterday. OK, and the day before.

Well, a bit of extra exercise never did any harm, did it? But in the same way that listeners never hear good of themselves, less than two minutes later Zack saw what he really hadn't wanted to see. He and Elmo stood at the upper end of the road and watched as the front door of Ellie's house opened and Joe Kerrigan came out.

Looking as if he'd spent the night having sex.

Zack's jaw tightened. He felt as if he'd been punched in the stomach.

As he watched, Joe turned and gazed up at the first floor. Then he broke into a grin and called out, 'See you later.'

The window was flung open and he heard Ellie say, 'What was that?'

'I'll see you later.' Joe's grin broadened and he blew her a kiss. 'Missing you already.'

OK, he'd heard enough. Zack moved out of sight before Joe had a chance to turn round and recognise him.

Back home now.

Served him right for having come this way in the first place.

Ellie arrived at the house dead on nine o'clock, her hair still damp from the shower. She was wearing a pale pink shift dress, pink and silver sandals and a thin silver bracelet Zack hadn't seen before.

'That's nice.' He indicated the bracelet.

'This? Thanks! Isn't it pretty? Joe gave it to me last night. I love it!'

Another sucker punch. Great. Aloud he said, 'Excellent. Well, I'm off to Monte Carlo on Tuesday, so I need you to book me a flight to Nice.'

'No problem. I'll do that now.' Her eyes were sparkling; she might not have got much sleep last night but she was running on adrenalin.

But by mid-afternoon the lack of sleep was catching up with her. Twice while he was in the office he caught Ellie yawning. Three times her phone chirruped to signal the arrival of a text and she stopped typing in order to read the messages and reply.

The last straw came when Zack attempted to return a call and discovered she'd written down the wrong number.

'Look, I'm sorry if I'm keeping you up, but you need to be paying more attention.' Marching into the office, he found her sending yet another text. 'I'm trying to make an important call here and this isn't the number.' He pushed the piece of paper across the desk.

'OK, let me try. That's definitely the one he gave me.' She reeled off the numbers. 'O-two-six-seven-three . . .'

'No, you've written O-two-O-seven-three.'

'That's a six.' Ellie pointed to it.

Unreasonably annoyed, Zack said, 'It looks like a zero.'

'It might look like one of your zeros,' she retaliated, 'because you don't always bother to close yours. But I do close mine. It's a six.'

Unfairly, the figure was now looking more and more like a six.

Zack was unwilling to concede defeat. 'And you haven't stopped yawning all morning.'

'I might have yawned a couple of times.' Ellie was defensive. 'But it hasn't stopped me working.'

'Maybe not, but all the texting's certainly managing it. I'm just saying, it's not very professional, breaking off from whatever you're doing every few minutes to read a text from your boyfriend, then send one back.'

'Fine. Here you go, help yourself.' She reached over, grabbed his left wrist and slammed her phone into his upturned palm. 'Have a good look, scroll through the texts I've sent today. Read them.'

'No.'

'Yes.'

'I don't want to read your texts.'

'I don't care whether or not you *want* to.' Ellie snatched the phone, pressed a few buttons and shoved it back at him. 'You're going to.'

Which meant Zack was forced to stand there and read each of the texts in turn.

None of them were from Joe Kerrigan. Instead, Ellie had been in contact with the PAs of two of the other business people due at the meeting in Monaco. Thanks to her negotiations, the journey from Nice airport to Monte Carlo would no longer be by car; they were to be whisked there by helicopter instead.

'Oh God. I'm sorry.' Zack handed the phone back.

'That's OK. You've been a bit twitchy today. In a funny mood.'

'I know.'

Ellie was looking at him. 'Is something wrong?'

What could he say? *Yes, something is wrong, and it's all your fault?*

'No. I shouldn't have had a go. I'm not usually like that.'

'I know you aren't. Anyway, thanks.'

'For apologising? That's the least I can do.'

'Not for the apology,' said Ellie. 'For the argument. My first proper one in a long time.'

'Oh.' He began to relax. 'Did you enjoy it?'

'Very much. Especially the bit where I won. In fact . . .'

'In fact what?'

She was eyeing him thoughtfully. 'Was this all part of the plan? You knew I missed having arguments so you decided to start one?' A slow smile was spreading across Ellie's face. 'Oh my God, am I right? Did you do it on purpose?'

Zack briefly considered the alternatives. 'OK,' he said finally, 'I'd love to be able to tell you that was true. But I'm afraid it wasn't. I was just being a bad-tempered old git.'

Ellie's smile broadened. 'The thing is, you say that now. But I'm still not sure I believe you.'

Zack couldn't speak. All he wanted to do was kiss her. And he wasn't allowed to do that either.

The irony of the situation didn't escape Roo. Here she was, lying in a reclining chair allowing her ex-lover's wife to inflict pain on her.

Swiftly, skilfully, Yasmin manipulated the twirled-together threads, whisking out tiny hairs and leaving perfectly sculpted eyebrows in their place. Well, hopefully she was. Roo imagined sitting up at the end, gazing into the mirror and discovering that one eyebrow was arched and the other one flat. Or missing altogether.

'So,' Yasmin said cheerfully, 'how's everything been going with you?'

'Not so bad.' Between the razor-sharp *ting ting ting*s as each hair was tweaked out, Roo updated her with the latest goings-on in the shop. Then said, 'How about you?'

'Me? Oh, I'm getting a divorce.'

'*What?*' Roo's eyes had been closed. Now they snapped open. 'You mean, you and your . . . husband?'

'That's generally how it works.'

'But why?' Was she sounding too shocked? Oh God, this was awful.

'Nothing very original, I'm afraid. Same old story. I found out he's been having an affair.' Yasmin stopped threading and handed Roo a mirror. 'Here you are. Have a look and see what you think.'

Roo gazed at her reflection and saw a selfish, marriage-wrecking harlot with stunning eyebrows. It was hard to look at herself. Roo put the mirror down.

'OK, the skin's a bit red. I'm going to put some aloe vera gel on there to cool it down. You just lie back and relax.'

When the gel had been applied, Roo said, 'Who was it?'

'Who was what?'

'The other woman.'

'Oh, they used to work together. She's a sales rep with another company now.'

'That's awful.' What would be *really* awful was if she were accidentally to mention Vivica's name. 'What happened? How did you find out?'

'Total cliché. Came home unexpectedly and caught them at it.'

Oh God, that could have been me. It couldn't have, because she'd never visited their house, but Roo covered her mouth in horror anyway. Swallowing with difficulty, she said, 'Then what?'

'Actually, I was quite proud of myself. I threw a can of super strength hairspray at him. I'm usually rubbish at throwing, but I got him on the forehead. It was one of those brilliant moments when you wish there'd been someone there to video it. I'd love to have put it on YouTube.'

'So you've kicked him out of the house?'

'No, I didn't want to stay there. Me and Ben are back at my mum's.' Yasmin's dimples deepened again. 'It's lovely.'

'You don't seem that upset.'

'Truthfully? I'm not. Being married to Niall was like being a single mother anyway. He never made any effort. He's selfish. I ended up doing everything. I'll let you into a secret.' Yasmin lowered her voice. 'I'm pretty sure this one wasn't the first. I think he's had other affairs.'

For a terrifying second, Roo felt the backs of her eyes prickle with tears. *Stop it, stop it, don't you dare do that . . .*

'You do?'

'Oh yes. Anyway, never mind. I've only myself to blame. Niall was never what you'd call good husband material. I kidded myself we'd be OK. My friends tried to warn me, but I wouldn't listen. It's funny, isn't it? I was so sure I could change him. I thought loving him would be enough. But it wasn't. And he didn't want to change. Why would he, when he could carry on having his cake and eating it and helping himself to chocolate biscuits too?'

Roo swallowed. She'd been one of the chocolate biscuits.

'So is he still seeing this girl?' she ventured. 'The ex-work colleague?'

'No idea. He says not. But that's the thing with Niall; he says lots of things. There, the redness is fading. Do you want to sit up?'

Roo did as she was told. Was Yasmin putting on a brave front or was she genuinely taking the break-up in her stride? Roo followed Yasmin across to the pay desk and took out her purse.

'Gosh, thanks.' Yasmin's eyes widened as Roo handed her a twenty pound tip. 'Are you sure?'

It was guilt money, pure and simple. But it made her feel better; it was one of her prime reasons for coming here.

'Absolutely,' said Roo.

Zack was in Monte Carlo. Ellie had just received a text from him: 'Helicopter fantastic. The only way to travel. Thanks for thinking of it. All OK at the office? Z.'

Ellie texted back: 'Have sold your company and run off to Barbados with the proceeds. Byeeeee . . .'

She pressed Send, then began a second text: 'OK, maybe I haven't. Knew you'd love helicopter. No need for thanks, I am your brilliant PA. All fine this end. Have fun!'

As she was sending it, the post clattered through the letterbox out in the hall. Ellie went to pick it up. Anything business, she opened and dealt with if necessary. Anything that looked personal, she left for Zack. But among today's delivery was a postcard. On the front was a picture of boxing kangaroos.

On the back of the card was a scrawled message:

Hi Zack, I'm coming home! Lost my phone, so don't have your number. Call me at Mum's any time after the 29th August. Missed you so much and can't wait to see you again. All love, Meg xxxxx

Zack had mentioned Meg when they'd talked about past relationships. He'd been busy building up his business, Meg had worked as a journalist on a glossy magazine and their affair had ebbed and flowed over the course of several months, until Meg had taken off on a round-the-world trip. And that was it, she had gone.

When Zack had told her, Ellie had said, 'Did you miss her terribly?'

And he replied, 'Yes, I kind of did.'

'What would have happened if she'd stayed here?'

Zack had shrugged. 'Who knows.'

Ellie gazed at the postcard and wondered what might happen now that his former girlfriend was on her way back. What was she like? Would Zack say casually, 'Oh, by the way, you don't need to give up your weekend to come down with me to my sister's wedding. I'll be taking Meg instead.'

Just imagining him saying those words made Ellie want to stick her fingers in her ears and go, 'La-la-la-can't-hear-you!' while inside she felt sick with disappointment because, Joe or no Joe, the trip down to Cornwall with Zack was something she'd been looking forward to.

Rrrrrrrrrrrinnnnnnngggggg.

Opening the front door, Ellie came face to face with a dumpy woman in her late fifties. She was wearing a peach crimplene blouse and a turquoise pleated skirt, and it was probably safe to assume this wasn't another of Zack's former girlfriends. At least, she hoped not.

'Hello, dear, is Zack at home?'

'Sorry, he's away. Maybe I can help you.'

'Oh, I do hope so! I'm Christine, dear. I used to be Zack's PA.'

Ellie had heard all about her. Nicknamed Crimplene Christine by Zack, her skirts reacted with the nylon in her tights and petticoat, creating a build-up of static charge each time she moved. Shaking hands with her, Zack had gravely explained, was a positive health hazard.

'Come along inside. I'm Ellie. It's lovely to meet you.'

'Ah, there it is. You still have it, thank heavens for that!' Christine was pointing to a large plant on the window ledge.

'This one?' Ellie moved towards it. 'It's yours?'

'Not the plant. The pot it's in. My bossy sister gave it to me for Christmas,' Christine explained. 'She's coming to London tomorrow to stay for a couple of days. Before she got off the phone this morning she said, "And I hope you're using that lovely plant pot I gave you; it had better not be hidden away in the back of a cupboard." Well, I'm telling you, my poor heart nearly jumped out of my throat. For a couple of seconds I couldn't remember what I'd done with the thing. Then it came back to me. I'd left it here. Now look, I know it's a bit of a cheek, but do you think Zack would mind awfully if I took it home?'

Ellie managed to reassure Christine that Zack wouldn't mind a bit.

Relieved, Christine asked chattily how she was enjoying working for him. Then she started asking how Zack was, and if he was still seeing Louisa. The next thing Ellie knew, Christine had made them both a cup of tea and settled herself down for a nice chat. Christine was gratifyingly pleased to hear that the relationship with Louisa was now over.

'And how are things with you?' Ellie asked. 'Zack told me about your husband not being very well. It must be so much easier for you, not having to work full-time any more.'

'Well, actually, I am working. It was all quite fortuitous really. You see, the daycare place couldn't cope with Eric any more. Now, I love my poor hubby to bits, but the two of us being at home together was too much. Anyway, my doctor suggested respite care and we ended up going to look at a nursing home not far from us. While we were there I happened to see a notice up on the board saying they were looking for part-time staff. Well, I spoke to the lady who runs the place and we reached an agreement. I'm working there three days a week and Eric comes along with me. And once or twice a week he stays overnight so I can go home and have an evening out, or just a rest on my own and get a proper night's sleep. It's working out really well.' Christine smiled bravely. 'It's nice to get to know other people in my situation. And Eric likes it too. It's a good place, Stanshawe House. The staff are wonderful.'

Stanshawe House, Stanshawe House, why did that ring a distant bell? It only took a couple of seconds to make the connection. Should she mention it? Or keep quiet?

'I think a friend of mine knows someone who lives there.' For a moment Ellie couldn't remember the surname . . . Martha Daines, that was it.

Christine took a sip of tea. 'One of the residents? Who is it?'

'Mr Daines.'

'Henry?'

'That's the one.'

'Oh my dear. Didn't your friend tell you? Henry died a few weeks ago.'

Ellie sat back. 'Oh, I didn't know. Well, that's sad. What happened?'

'Nothing dramatic.' Christine shrugged. 'Bless his heart, he was such a dear gentle soul. He just passed away in his sleep, which isn't the worst way to go. Do you think your friend knows he's dead?'

Ellie shook her head. 'I don't think he does.'

'Oh my goodness, I hope I haven't spoken out of turn.' Looking worried, Christine said, 'Maybe he should speak to Henry's wife, Martha. Poor darling, she took it very hard.'

'It must be a terrible time for her.' Ellie nodded in agreement. 'I'm sure he'll do that. I'll let him know.'

They chatted for a while longer about Zack, then Ellie lifted the plant in its blue pot and carried it outside to Christine's little car.

'Bye then, dear. Thanks so much for the plant. And I'm glad you've settled in here. Give Zack my regards.' With an unexpected twinkle, Christine said, 'You can give him a kiss from me, if you like.'

Which was slightly alarming, and ironic, to think that Zack had hired Christine in order to be safe, when it was becoming scarily apparent that she'd had a crush on him all along. It just went to show, no matter how unprepossessing the exterior, a flirty soul could still lie beneath.

Chapter 10

ELLIE SAT DOWN on the sofa and switched on her laptop. Sending an email to Tony about Henry was off the agenda. Telling him his lover's husband had died would be just so wrong. If Martha had wanted him to know, she would have contacted him herself. And she hadn't. Of course she wouldn't. Her guilt would be as all-consuming as her grief.

Ellie typed Martha Daines into Google and up came the link to her website. There was the home page. There was the gallery of paintings. There was the email address. She wrote the email straight from the heart, without stopping once.

Dearest Martha,

I have just heard, via someone who works at Stanshawe House, about the death of your husband, Henry. I'm so very sorry, please accept my deepest condolences. My father-in-law Tony is a great admirer of your work. I haven't told him about Henry. I was married to his son Jamie, however, and do know how it feels to lose a husband, so I understand some of what you're going through. If you ever feel you'd like to email or speak to me, please do so at any time . . .

Ellie gave her phone number and home address and the link to an online forum for widows that she had found helpful last year when the grief had been at its most overwhelming. She concluded with:

Love, Ellie Kendall

PS I mean it about contacting me. You don't have to if you don't want to, but it does help to talk.

'Your boyfriend's waiting outside.'

Was there a particular reason for Zack looking ever so slightly pissed off about it? Ellie checked her watch: three minutes to five.

'It's OK if he meets me here, isn't it?' She heard herself sounding defensive; Zack hadn't been in the sunniest of moods recently. 'Is there anything else you need me to do, or can I go?'

He shot her a look of impatience mixed with a hint of an eye roll. In retaliation Ellie shut down her computer and pushed back her chair.

'Right, well, I'll be off then. See you tomorrow. Have a nice night!' She flashed him an extra-bright smile to cover up for the fact that having to sidle past him in order to reach the door was having its habitual heart-galloping effect.

Evidently bored now, Zack turned his attention to the calendar on the wall as she left. 'You too.'

Outside, Joe held out his arms and gave Ellie a huge hug.

'I've been waiting for ages.'

'I know. Zack said you were out here.'

'I saw him at the window. Thought he might have invited me in.'

Overhead the sky was leaden and it was spitting with rain.

'Sorry, he's been a bit funny lately.'

'Speaking of funny. There's something I have to tell you.'

'Oh God, is it my hair?' She knew she shouldn't have cut her fringe last night. Ellie's hands went up to tug at the ends. 'Is it crooked?'

Joe shook his head. 'It's not your hair. Listen, this is pretty major.'

He gazed at her in his intense way. It was raining properly now. They were standing on the pavement outside Zack's house, getting wet.

'Come on, let's get home.' Ellie began to walk up the road. 'Tell me on the way.'

'OK.' Joe loped alongside her, his arm round her shoulders. 'Here goes. I've just had a call from Stephen in LA.' Stephen was their agent.

'And?'

'Mac Zeller's been in touch.'

'Right,' said Ellie. Mac Zeller was the producer-director who had bought his and Kaye's film script.

'He wants us to work exclusively with him on a new screenplay . . .'

'Wow, fantastic!'

' . . . and he's also produced a sitcom that's breaking all records in its very first series in the States. *The Afternooners*. It's set to be bigger and better than *Friends*.' The words were tumbling out now. 'And Mac wants us to join the writing team. Me and Kaye! It's just unbelievable. I could hardly breathe when Stephen told me . . . ' Joe stopped walking and gripped her hands, his silver-rimmed glasses speckled with rain.

'That's great.' Ellie reached up and wiped them clean, so he could see. 'It'll mean going back out there for a bit.'

'More than that. It means going out there for a while. Six months, minimum. A couple of years, preferably. It's just not something we can do from over here. We have to move to LA.' His hands were trembling. 'Ellie, he's made us an offer we can't refuse. It's the chance of a lifetime. There's no way we can turn it down.'

He was searching her face for a reaction. Ellie hugged him. 'Of course you can't! It's amazing. And you deserve it.'

Joe pulled back, his own expression unreadable. 'Seriously?'

'God, yes!' Why wouldn't she mean it?

'OK, here's the thing. I was kind of hoping you might be a bit more upset, so that I could say, "And I want you to come with me."'

'Oh.'

His crooked smile flickered like a light bulb struggling not to go out. 'Well? How would you feel about that?'

Fifty yards away, in his first-floor living room, Zack watched from the window as Ellie and Joe stood and faced each other, oblivious to the increasing rain. He'd have a better view if he flung the window wide open and leaned out. But that wasn't really on. Ellie had just hugged Joe and he was now stroking her cheek. She was smiling up at him. Zack turned away, slightly despising himself. As he did so, his phone rang in his pocket. Taking it out, he saw the caller's name. Meg.

Back at Nevis Street, Ellie took off her wet jacket and put the kettle on, prevaricating while she worked out what to say.

But Joe wasn't stupid. He already knew. 'So you're not tempted?'

She turned to look at him. 'I can't, sorry, no.'

'That's a real shame. I have to go,' said Joe. 'You do understand that, don't you?'

Ellie nodded. 'I do.'

'I'll really miss you.'

'I'll miss you too.'

'But not as much. Otherwise you'd come along.'

'Joe, can we be honest with each other? Marks out of ten for how you feel about me.' Ellie held up her hands. 'And don't say ten. You have to be *completely* honest.'

Joe raked his fingers through his damp hair. 'Nine. OK, not nine. Eight and a half. But that's good, that's really good.'

'Thank you. Now it's my turn.' Ellie had been going to say eight. To be kind she said, 'You're an eight and a half too.'

'They sound like pretty high marks to me.'

'They are. But not high enough. If you're planning to live with someone, it has to be tens all the way.'

His eyebrows went up. 'You told me not to say ten.'

'Because it wouldn't have been true.' Ellie reached for his hands. 'But you've given me my confidence back, and that's the best present in the world. Thanks to you, I know I can feel normal again, do all the stuff that normal people do, have sex and enjoy it.'

Joe said gravely, 'It's a special talent of mine. I've always been excellent at sex.'

Everything was going to be OK. She felt herself relax. 'You're great in bed. And out of it.'

'In an eight and a half out of ten kind of way.'

Ellie broke into a grin. 'When you meet your perfect ten out of ten woman, I want you to phone me up and say, "Now I get it, now I understand. Ellie, I'm sorry. You were right and I was wrong."'

'Come here, you.' Joe pulled her into a hug. 'It's OK, I already know you're right. I'm just going to miss you, that's all. We've had a good time, haven't we?'

'The best.' She planted a kiss on his mouth. 'Thank you.'

His face softened. 'Trust me, it's been a pleasure.'

'For me too.' It had stopped raining. Ellie said, 'Come on, we have to go out and celebrate. My treat. You're going to Hollywood!'

'You're feeling normal again.'

'We've had a fantastic fling,' she agreed happily.

'And some fantastic sex,' Joe modestly reminded her.

Ellie smiled and kissed him again. It had been good. Inside her own head, though, it hadn't always been Joe she'd been having the fantastic sex with. But she wouldn't tell him that.

Yasmin finished cleaning the old polish off Roo's toenails and began massaging her feet with exfoliating scrub. 'Go on then, tell me more!'

Roo smiled: Yasmin loved hearing about the bizarre goings-on in the charity shop. 'OK, yesterday this girl came in. Early twenties. Skinny, huge boobs, blond extensions, big blue eyes. She gave us two huge bags of clothes. Really good stuff, all size eight.'

Yasmin looked up expectantly. 'And?'

'So first thing this morning she came back. Except this time she wasn't smiling. Mad as a box of maggots. She said, "Has that bitch been in here?" Then she saw one of her dresses and went berserk, started screaming and swearing and trying to rip it off the mannequin . . .'

'Why?' Yasmin sat back, mystified.

'Yesterday morning she had a massive fight with her sister,' said Roo. 'Her identical twin sister.'

'Yaz?' Jackie, one of the other beauticians, was peering out of the window. 'Sorry to interrupt, but he's back again. He's on his way over.'

Roo's blood ran cold. It couldn't be him, surely not . . . and if it was, what could she do?

'He's got flowers!' Jackie hastily backed away from the window. 'OK, here he comes . . .'

Roo heard the door swing open behind her. Yasmin scrambled to her feet. Oh God, oh God, this was a nightmare, Roo felt sick . . .

Then everything went dark and she felt the soft folds of the towel being patted into place over her face and head, for all the world as if she'd just had a nice relaxing steam facial. Which she hadn't.

Which kind of implied . . . Except how could it?

'Niall, this is silly.' Still winding the ends of the towel behind Roo's head, ensuring that none of her hair was visible, Yasmin said, 'I've told you before, you can't just turn up here. I'm busy.'

The galloping in Roo's chest was so thunderous it felt as if horses were about to burst out. She was lying back in a reclining chair with her feet slathered in gritty gunk and her whole head wrapped in a dark blue towel. Less than six feet away from Niall. She could smell his aftershave. Sense his desperation. Hear the tremor in his voice.

' . . . but you won't let me into your mother's house and you refuse to come home, so what else can I do? Yaz, I'm sorry.' He was gabbling now. 'I've told you a thousand times. I made a mistake and I'm going to spend the rest of my life regretting it. But you're the one I love. You and Ben. We're a family and we should be together . . . here, at least take these, they're your favourite.'

'Just leave them on the desk, Niall,' Yasmin said. 'I'm not going to let you do this in front of my client. It's unprofessional. Plus, you're making an idiot of yourself.'

'Yaz, don't you understand? I don't care! I want you to forgive me.' Niall's voice cracked with emotion. 'I want to win you back, and I don't think anyone would begrudge me a couple of minutes to try.' A hand came to rest on her shoulder and Roo, aghast, pressed herself back into the reclining chair so hard the plastic covering squeaked. 'Would you?'

Rational thought was still a struggle but she was stingingly aware that this was Yasmin's situation. *And she was the one who had covered Roo's face with a towel.* Did this mean . . . oh God . . . That she *knew*?

Either way it wasn't her place to sit up and reveal her identity by whisking the towel off her face, Scooby Doo style.

Instead Roo shook her head and heard herself adopt a kind of strangled Cockney growl. 'Nah, s'alright.' Heavens, she sounded like Dot Cotton with bronchitis.

'Look, we're a family.' The hand left her shoulder; Niall was addressing Yasmin again. 'I miss you so much. I miss Ben. I'll do anything you want.' He was pleading now. 'I'm never going to see Vivica again and I swear that's the truth. Baby, it was one mistake, that's all. Just give me another chance, *please*.'

'OK, three things.' Yasmin remained calm. 'I don't like it when you call me Baby. I never have.'

Ouch. Niall sounded as if he was shaking his head. 'Sorry, sorry.'

'Plus, I don't want to give you another chance.'

'But—'

'And the third thing is,' Yasmin continued as if he hadn't interrupted, 'you're still lying to me now. One mistake, you said. But that's just not true, is it? Vivica isn't the only woman you've had an affair with.'

Ohmygod. This was why Yasmin had covered her face with a towel, so that she could be the one to perform the triumphant unveiling. All they needed now was a drum roll . . .

'I swear there hasn't been anyone else.' Niall was adamant.

'Yes there has, Niall. You know there has.'

'Baby—um, Yaz, honest to God, I'm telling the truth!'

OK, here it comes, here it comes. Roo's nails dug into her palms.

'Are you? OK, fine, have it your way. But our marriage is still over,' said

Yasmin. 'And I have work to do here. So now that you've had your little say, could you go and leave us in peace?'

Hey? What? What about me?

There was a long silence. Finally, Roo heard Niall's footsteps as he made his way out of the salon. The door opened, then closed.

Everyone waited.

At last Jackie announced, 'He's back in his car. Driving off. Gone.'

And the towel was lifted away from Roo's face.

Yasmin gazed down at her. 'Oops.'

Roo's mouth was as dry as the Sahara. 'How did you know?'

'OK,' Jackie broke in. 'For a start, you're Daisy Deeva.'

'What? You mean *all* of you know about this?'

'Of course we do.' Jackie's tone was cool. She glanced out of the window again. 'Yaz, Mrs Simpson's here for her appointment. She's just paying the taxi.'

'Right.' Yasmin indicated Roo's unpainted toes. 'Shall we clean you up and give these a miss for today? After this next appointment it's my lunch break. How about if you wait in the café up the road and I'll join you in twenty minutes?'

Roo swallowed and said, 'Right.' What other choice did she have?

It wasn't twenty minutes. More like forty. It felt like forty hours. Roo couldn't stop shaking. How could Yasmin possibly have known?

Finally the door opened and Yasmin came in. She ordered herself a latte then made her way over to the table where Roo was sitting.

'I'm so sorry,' Roo blurted out. 'Really I am. I hate myself. And I know it should never have happened in the first place, but it's all over now, I promise.'

'I know it is,' said Yasmin.

'How did you find out?'

'OK, from the beginning? Over the years I've got to know my husband pretty well. And I know he's a good liar. Apart from one thing: he can't control his neck.' Yasmin patted her own neck. 'Maybe you noticed it yourself. It goes kind of blotchy. Dead giveaway. Anyhow, the first time you came into the salon we thought you were Daisy Deeva but you said you weren't. So that night I was telling Niall about you and the weirdest thing happened. His neck went blotchy!'

For heaven's sake, was she serious? 'That was it? Just his neck?'

'Well, I wasn't sure. But you'd lied,' Yasmin pointed out. 'So that made two things to be suspicious about. Then there was the evening we were out and we bumped into your friend Ellie. It did seem slightly strange that she couldn't remember the name of her own child.'

'So then you knew.'

'Well, the neck thing happened again. Worse this time. It was pretty obvious that Niall was wondering what the hell was going on!'

'It was all over by then. I'd finished with him.'

'OK.' Yasmin nodded. 'So was he also seeing Vivica then?'

'Yes.'

'And that's why you stopped seeing him?'

Roo flushed and nodded, awash with shame.

'Out of interest, did Niall tell you where I worked?'

'No. I found a list of things you'd asked him to buy. Written on salon headed paper.'

'Ah. That makes more sense.' Yasmin took a sip of her latte.

'Why didn't you tell me you knew?'

'Honestly? I've no idea. I was just so curious. You kept coming back to the salon. And you seemed really nice, which was confusing. I had no idea what you were up to. But I didn't want to confront you, because then you'd disappear.' The corners of Yasmin's mouth lifted. 'And this might sound mercenary, but you're the best tipper I ever had.'

'You must hate me so much.'

'You'd think so, wouldn't you? That's the weird thing, though. I don't. I never have.'

'The first time we came, it was to find out what you were like.'

'To see if I was as awful as Niall said I was, you mean? Nagging, moaning, bad-tempered and always shattered? I can imagine what he told you. And sometimes it was true.' Wryly, Yasmin went on, 'Having to work and look after a baby and run a household while your husband does bugger all can have that effect.'

'I'm sorry. I should have chucked him the moment I found out he was married. I'm a bad person.' Roo's eyes filled with tears. 'I'm doing my best to make up for it, I promise.'

'Oh God, please don't cry! I didn't mean to upset you.' Yasmin hastily shoved a paper napkin at her. 'Listen, you heard me when Niall came in today. I don't want him back! I'm better off without him. If he's still seeing

Vivica now, you can bet he'll be chasing some other piece of skirt by Christmas. I don't think one woman will ever be enough. He'll always be on the hunt for the next adrenalin rush.'

Roo blotted the tears and willed herself to get a grip. 'I think you're right. But I'm still sorry. And I'll never *ever* do it again.'

'How did you find out about Vivica?'

'I read a text from her on his phone while he was in the bathroom.'

Yasmin shook her head and tut-tutted. 'Basic schoolboy error. He won't be doing that again in a hurry.'

'I thought you were going to whisk the towel off my face when he was in the salon.'

'It did occur to me. But then Niall would just blame you for wrecking his marriage. No,' Yasmin smiled briefly. 'I prefer it this way. It's like a bit of one-upmanship on my part. And I want you to carry on coming to the salon.' She checked her watch. 'In fact, we could head back there if you want. I can give you that pedicure.'

Roo checked her watch. One fifteen. 'I can't. My shift's at two.'

'This is what we haven't been able to work out.' Yasmin looked puzzled. 'You're Daisy Deeva. Why are you working in a charity shop?'

'I told you. I'm trying to become a better person. I'm making up for all the bad things I've done.'

'Crikey.' Yasmin looked suitably impressed. 'All because of Niall.'

'Not all. There was something else too. I nearly kissed Ellie's boyfriend.' There, she'd said it. Now Yasmin knew everything.

Yasmin's eyes widened. 'Does she know?'

Roo nodded wearily. 'Oh yes. I told her.'

'Did she go crazy?'

'No, she was relieved.' Oh God, the tears were back. 'She'd been wondering how to break up with him. But that's beside the point; I didn't know that at the time. And I still nearly did it.'

'OK, don't be offended by this.' Ready to leave now, Yasmin reached for her pale blue leather bag. 'But when I do eventually find myself another man, I probably won't introduce him to you.'

Yet another wave of shame engulfed Roo. 'I wouldn't do anything, I swear I wouldn't. This is what I'm trying to say.' She was desperate to explain. 'I'll do anything, *anything* I can to make it up to you—'

'Roo.' Yasmin stopped her. 'Calm down. It was meant to be a joke.'

Little Venice. The sun was blazing down out of a cloudless blue sky, glittering on the surface of the water and making Ellie wish she hadn't sat on her sunglasses last night.

She'd walked from Camden Lock along the Regent's Canal. Now here she was at last, at the intersection where it met the Grand Union Canal and Paddington Basin. It was a beautiful afternoon and the towpaths were busy with tourists and locals enjoying the unexpectedly good weather. Ellie surveyed the scene and scanned the opposite bank.

There she was, wearing a flowing emerald-green dress and with her easel set up on the towpath. Ellie headed across the blue iron bridge.

No one had been more surprised than Ellie when Martha had replied to her impulsively sent message. To the point, she had thanked her for the email and insisted that she most definitely *didn't* want Tony to be told about the death of her husband. That had been all.

Until two days later when, out of the blue, another mail had arrived in Ellie's inbox:

Dear Ellie,

Was I rude before? A bit abrupt? If so, I'm sorry. Many thanks for your kind offer. I don't feel it would be appropriate to come to your flat, but I shall be painting in Little Venice on Sunday afternoon.

If you happened to be free and in the area, it would be nice to meet you.

Best wishes,

Martha

At close quarters, Ellie saw that the easel might be up but no painting was getting done. Martha was sitting on her stool holding a piece of charcoal but only the most basic outlines were in place. Tony had described her as voluptuous and glowing. Well, that wasn't currently the case. Attractive she might be, but her face was drawn and there were dark circles beneath her eyes. But when she turned and saw Ellie watching her, she broke into a smile that made a difference.

'Hello. Is it you?'

'It's me,' Ellie agreed.

'Thought so. Hello, darling, nice to meet you.' Martha sighed and gestured at the few lines sketched on the artist's pad in front of her. 'I think I'll give up on this. Shall we go and have a cup of tea?'

'Can't we stay here?'

'But there's nowhere for you to sit . . .' There was a moment of hostess panic. 'Oh dear, I didn't think this through.'

'Hello? Are you suggesting I'm ancient and decrepit?' Ellie was wearing old jeans and a white shirt with the sleeves rolled up. She sat down cross-legged, just to the right of Martha. 'I'm fine like this.'

'Only if you're sure. Let me know when your bottom goes numb. I keep trying to paint,' said Martha. 'But I can't seem to do it any more.' She looked stricken. 'I might never paint again.'

'How are you feeling? You can tell me. And I mean properly tell me,' said Ellie. 'That's why I'm here.'

'Darling, I know. And bless you for coming. Truthfully?' Martha paused. 'I feel like a rabbit that's been hit by a car and left in a ditch to die. I feel guilty and alone and sometimes I wonder if Henry's in a better place now, and then I hate myself for thinking that . . . actually, I hate myself pretty much all the time. And I miss him, I miss him so desperately I could rip out my own heart because it couldn't hurt as much as this. How does that sound?'

'Truthfully?' echoed Ellie. 'It sounds familiar.'

'You know about me and Tony? You must do.'

'Yes. He told me.'

'And while you were married to Jamie, did you have an affair with another man?'

'No.' Ellie shook her head. 'I didn't.'

'Well then. You didn't have that to feel guilty about.'

'I know. But the guilt still gets you, one way or another. I blamed myself for not forcing Jamie to take the train instead of the car.'

'That's just part of the grieving process, though.' Martha sat back. 'I've read the leaflets. But I do actually have a valid reason to hate myself.'

'Your husband wasn't himself.'

'That's not good enough.'

'Look, there's nothing I can say that'll make you feel better.' Ellie watched a pair of swans glide past. 'But it's only been a few weeks. Things will get easier in time.'

'That's what everyone tells me. I can't imagine it happening.'

'It will. Look at me. I couldn't ever imagine getting involved with someone else. But I did,' said Ellie.

'Oh yes. Tony told me.' A smile flickered across her face. 'He was so pleased for you. Jamie's best friend. I heard all about it. That's lovely.'

Oh dear. 'Actually, that didn't work out. But then someone else came along,' said Ellie, 'and it was great. I felt normal again.'

Martha looked interested. 'And are you still seeing him?'

'Well, no . . .'

'Why, what happened?'

'He's moving to America. He asked me to go with him. But I didn't want to.'

'Why not?'

'Because he was nearly right,' said Ellie. 'Just not exactly right.'

Martha said, 'You know what being an artist means? It means noticing every last detail. The kind of tiny details other people might miss.' She paused. 'So what I'm interested in finding out is, why did you start blinking really fast just then?'

Ellie swallowed. 'You mean when I looked at the water and the sun made my eyes sting?'

'No. Come on, what aren't you telling me? And that big gulpy swallow you just did? I saw that too.'

For heaven's sake, what was she, some kind of witch?

Oh well, they were here to be honest with each other. Ellie pushed her fringe out of her eyes and said, 'You could get burned at the stake for doing that, you know. But OK, just between us, there's someone else. But it's embarrassing and nothing's ever going to come of it.'

'Why not? Is he married?'

'No! It's just . . . he's my boss.' There, it was out. She'd said it.

'Well, that's been known to happen. It's fine. Oh,' said Martha as something else occurred to her. 'Unless he's gay?'

Ellie smiled; it would almost be easier if he was. 'He isn't gay.'

'Well then, what's stopping you?'

'He's not interested. And the last thing he wants is that kind of complication. He only hired me in the first place because I made it clear nothing like that would ever happen. Because at the time,' Ellie said evenly, 'it was true. I didn't feel anything at all.'

'Oh sweetheart, but you've changed your mind. Isn't that a good thing?' Martha looked hopeful. 'Maybe he's changed his mind too.'

'Believe me, he hasn't. And he's never going to know how I feel. If he did, I'd have to leave.' Ellie shook her head. 'Which would be awful, because he's a fantastic boss. And I love my job. Apart from the pathetic yearny crush bit, obviously. What are you doing?' Oh God, Martha was on her feet, packing everything in her bag. Had she upset her?

'You're cheering me up. And I'm not going to get any work done today. I'm not a great drinker,' said Martha, 'but I think I'm in the mood for one now. Come on, it's so lovely to meet you. Will you let me buy you a glass of champagne?'

You're late.' Roo pulled open the front door. 'I said to be here by six. It's six thirty.'

'I know. I'm sorry.'

'Where have you been?' Roo's nostrils quivered. 'Are you drunk?'

'No, I've just had a lovely afternoon,' Ellie protested.

'Drinking! I can smell the fumes!'

Roo's new-found teetotalism had its drawbacks; she was in danger of turning into the no-fun alcohol police.

'It was only going to be a glass each. But it was cheaper to buy a bottle. We sat outside a bistro in Little Venice and just talked and talked for ages. I didn't notice the time.'

'Who were you with?'

There was no need for Roo to know about her meeting with Martha. It had been a perfect one-off, not to be repeated. She had promised never to tell Tony about Henry's death and Martha had promised to keep the story of the Embarrassing Hopeless Crush to herself.

'Dinner smells fantastic,' she said. 'Have you done Yorkshire puddings?'

'I did, but they look a bit burnt.' In the kitchen, Roo peered through the smoked-glass front of the oven. 'It's your fault for being late.'

'Sorry.' Ellie gazed at the pans bubbling away on the hob. There were carrots and broad beans. Next to them on the granite worktop sat bowls of roast potatoes and balsamic braised onions.

Ellie hid a smile; with her blue-and-white stripy apron and her hair spiked up in all directions, Roo was half domestic goddess, half frazzled chicken.

'And why won't you tell me who you've been with?' As she spoke, Roo picked up a whisk and began vigorously stirring the gravy.

Ellie thought for a moment. Todd had always been mad about gravy;

he and Jamie had once knocked a pint of it back in one go for a bet. She said, 'I was with Todd.'

'Oh right. Don't tell me.' Roo's voice was brittle. 'He's still going on about how he wants me to stop being stubborn so we can get together.'

The great thing about alcohol was, it had a talent for rearranging your mental processes and making you think about things in a way you might not have thought about them before.

'He didn't say that. Actually, he didn't mention you once. Between you and me, I'm pretty sure you can relax now. He's over it.'

Splitt went the gravy. Just a tiny bit. Roo said casually, 'Oh?'

'He's met someone else,' said Ellie. This was great; like a magician pulling ribbons from his mouth, little white lies were tumbling out. 'That's what we were talking about. He couldn't stop. Her name's Lisa.'

'Oh. Well, good for him. That's . . . great.' Roo flashed a bright, couldn't-be-happier smile.

'And he says she's really pretty! He's completely smitten.'

'Can you pass me the gravy jug? It's in the cupboard behind you.'

'She's a maths teacher. Isn't that amazing? Did you ever have pretty maths teachers when you were at school? Because we definitely didn't.'

'OK, nearly ready now.' Bustling around the kitchen like a hyperactive rabbit, Roo said, 'Why don't you go and wait in the living room? I'll bring everything through in a minute.'

'Guess how they met,' said Ellie.

'I don't know. Here, take my glass of water.'

'Her car broke down in Fulham. She was waiting at the traffic lights and they went green and her car just died on her. Everyone was tooting their horns and getting really annoyed. And it was raining too. Anyway, nobody was helping her. But Todd had just come out of the Tesco Metro and he saw what was going on. He put down his carrier bags and pushed the car round the corner out of the way—'

'Right, is that enough roast beef? Do you want mustard with it?'

'So then he went back to pick up his shopping and guess what? Someone had run off with it! But the funny thing is, they ended up doing him the most massive favour, because when he told Lisa, it broke the ice. He waited with her until the breakdown people arrived, and then Lisa said seeing as it was her fault someone had run off with his food, the least she could do was buy him dinner. So that's what happened, and it's all gone on from there! Isn't that just incredibly romantic?'

'Yes it is. Now can we change the subject?' Roo practically shooed her out of the kitchen. 'I'm really not interested.'

It was a wonder her nose hadn't telescoped forward and crashed against the opposite wall. Satisfied, Ellie carried the water through to the other room. Leave it now, don't say another word. Job done.

Ellie was on the internet putting together a complicated travel schedule for Zack's upcoming trips to Copenhagen and South Africa. So far, the chief problem seemed to be that there were two meetings already arranged, leaving him with roughly twenty minutes to fly from Cape Town to Johannesburg. Basically, it wasn't a plane he'd be needing, more like a Tardis.

Zack came into the office. 'Have you seen the email from Bob Nix?'

'No, but we need to do something about this. Come and have a look.' She tapped the list of times and dates on the writing pad next to the PC. 'You organised this meeting and they organised that one. Shall I see if I can shift Cape Town back?'

'Ah, I see what you mean.' One hand resting on the desk, Zack leaned over her shoulder in order to study the schedule. 'Yes, give Anika a call and ask if we can meet first thing in the morning. Do it in a minute,' he went on. 'There's something else I want to show you.' Speedily he went to his email account and clicked on the message that had come in just a few minutes earlier.

Ellie focused her attention on the screen. Being so physically close to Zack was causing all kinds of inner havoc. She should be used to it by now but, if anything, it was getting worse.

'Hey Zack, Great job with the SpencerInc deal last week—heard about that from Ted. Impressed. Bibi asked me to send you the attached photo. She says hi, and can you show Ellie? Sure hope she's still working for you! Bob.'

'Go on then.' Ellie nodded.

A page from a magazine filled the screen. Bob and Bibi had been photographed at a glitzy charity ball in Dallas. Their teeth were dazzling white. Bob looked like a huge jovial bear in a dinner suit. Bibi was wearing a silver lamé dress that showed off her spectacular bosom and tiny waist. Her turquoise eyes sparkled. Her hair, piled up in an explosion of curls and ringlets, was fastened in place with silver jewelled combs.

Across the bottom of the photo, Bibi had scribbled: 'Ellie! I've never had so many compliments!'

Ellie smiled. Behind her, she was intensely aware of Zack's warm breath on the back of her neck.

'Those hair things.' He sounded puzzled. 'They look like the ones you wore that night we met them.'

'They do a bit.'

'They're exactly the same.' He looked round at Ellie. 'Are they yours?'

'Yes.'

'You gave them to Bibi?'

Ellie flushed; was he cross with her? Embarrassed that she'd given the wife of a billionaire such cheap combs? 'She said she liked them. I didn't think she'd actually wear the things.' She indicated the photo on the screen. 'Especially not to something like that.'

'Hey, I'm not complaining.' Zack straightened. Searching her face, he said, 'Did you think I was?'

'I don't know.' Ellie felt herself getting flustered; when Zack was looking at her like this it was hard to concentrate. 'After I got home I thought I shouldn't have done it.' *Really* hard to concentrate. 'I mean, you wouldn't believe how cheap they were . . . I just hope no one lets on to Bibi . . . people might laugh at her for wearing them and then she'll be mortified.'

'Bibi's a smart lady who knows her own mind. She wears whatever she wants to wear and I wouldn't want to be the one who tried to laugh at her. It was a nice thing to do. Bob and Bibi liked you very much.'

'I liked them.' Ellie shifted in her swivel chair; had the atmosphere changed? For the past few weeks Zack had been distant and businesslike. But now he was leaning against the desk, his leg inches from hers, and it was as if all the tension had melted away. There was a return to the laid-back, relaxed Zack who had cared for her and been such easy company while she'd been ill with the flu.

In fact, maybe even more than that. Was it her imagination or was he looking at her almost as if there was something he wanted to say but didn't know quite how to say it? Or did she just wish there was?

Zack picked up the diary and idly flipped through the pages. She saw him check his appointments for September. There at the end of the month was the weekend of his sister's wedding. He flicked on past without saying anything. Had he forgotten about inviting her? Had he made arrangements to take someone else? *Was this why he was in a better mood?* Ellie's stomach clenched with anxiety. Just because Zack hadn't talked to her about it didn't mean it wasn't happening. *Right, ask him.*

'Er . . .' Bugger, her throat had gone funny and her mouth was dry. Pushing back her chair, she said, 'Cup of tea?' It would be easier to ask the question when he wasn't so close.

'Thanks.' But when she went into the kitchen, he followed her. Right, just get it over with. Ellie threw tea bags into two mugs. 'So what's happening with your sister's wedding?'

'Utter chaos.' Zack visibly relaxed. 'A million things to do and not nearly enough time to do it in. The twins are refusing to be bridesmaids unless they can wear trainers that light up. Steph's tearing her hair out. But it'll all get sorted out in the end.'

The tea bags fizzed and filled with air as Ellie poured boiling water onto them. 'Look, if you don't need me for that any more, it's fine.'

'Why?' Zack stiffened. 'Don't you want to come?'

'No . . . I mean yes . . .'

'Is it Joe?'

'No, I just thought you might have someone else you'd rather take.'

'Someone else like who?'

She may as well say it. 'OK, I saw the postcard that arrived for you the other week. From Australia. I wasn't being nosy,' Ellie went on hurriedly, 'I just couldn't help seeing what it said.'

'The one from Meg.' She caught a glimmer of a smile. 'What makes you think I'd want to take her along to Steph's wedding?'

'Well, she used to be your girlfriend. And she seemed pretty keen to see you again.' OK, she sounded *so* nosy. 'Look, sorry, but it makes things easier if I know what's going on.'

'Nothing's going on.' Zack took the milk out of the fridge and passed it to her. 'You're right, Meg was pretty keen. I met up with her for a drink the other evening. It was nice to catch up with her news, but that's as far as it goes. There's no way we'll be getting back together.'

'Oh. Right.'

'And I definitely won't be inviting her to come to Steph's wedding.'

Milk. Slosh. Milk. Bigger slosh. Whoops. Flustered, Ellie said, 'So you still want me?' *Oh God, did I really just say that?*

After a moment, Zack replied evenly, 'Yes. If you still want to go.'

Oo-er. Was it her or was it getting hot in here?

'I do want to. I'm looking forward to it.' The way he was watching her was having a strange effect on her knees. 'Meeting your family.'

'It'll be good fun. You may need ear-plugs,' said Zack, 'but you will like them. You'll get on really well together.'

And now he was looking at her mouth. Was this how it felt to be hypnotised? Barely able to think straight, Ellie murmured, 'They sound great,' and wondered if she'd said it right or if her lips had gone all rubbery and completely lost control of themselves. And still he was gazing at her in such a way that it was almost as if—

'Woof! Woof-woof!'

Chapter 11

ELLIE LEAPT a foot in the air as the dog flap clattered and Elmo erupted into the kitchen. She heard Zack exhale with what could have been frustration. Or was that just more wishful thinking on her part?

'It's not time to go out,' Zack told Elmo, who was still barking and leaping around like a landed salmon. He shook his head at the dog, then gave in and said, 'Oh, what the hell, come on then.' He reached for the red lead, hanging on a hook by the back door. As Zack bent down to clip it on his collar, Elmo scuttled into reverse, did a speedy three-point turn and hurtled back out through the dog flap.

'What's he playing at?' Zack frowned and hung the lead back up.

Ellie went to the window. Elmo was dancing around in the garden, jumping up onto the wall then down again. The next moment, still yapping noisily, he launched himself back into the kitchen. Ellie picked up the phone and called Geraldine next door.

'No reply.' She looked at Zack. 'Did she say she was going out?'

He shook his head. 'No.'

'Where's the spare key?'

'She asked to borrow it last week when her sister came to stay. Hasn't given it back yet.'

'Let's see if she's there.' Ellie opened the kitchen door. The three of them jumped over the low wall. There was nothing to see through Geraldine's kitchen window but Elmo was still yelping in a state of full-on agitation. Yelling Geraldine's name provoked no response.

'OK, I'll give it a go.' Ellie slid her arms out of her pink cotton cardigan, handed it to Zack and eyed the dog flap in Geraldine's back door.

'Can you get through?' Zack was looking doubtful; it was a flap designed for a medium-sized dog.

'Thanks for that vote of confidence.' She took a swipe at him. 'If I get stuck, it's your fault for buying so many doughnuts. And no videoing this and putting it on YouTube. Right.' She kicked off her shoes.

Was this wise? If she did get stuck, would the fire brigade have to be called and the entire door dismantled?

'You'd better not be laughing at me.' Ellie went through arms first and began wiggling her shoulders through the tight bit.

Above her, Zack said, 'Wouldn't dream of it.'

He was definitely laughing. She prayed her skirt hadn't ridden up. OK, halfway through now. Hips and bottom next. It was going to be a tight squeeze. Ellie said, 'And if I can't manage this, don't go calling the fire brigade. Just leave me here until I've lost enough weight.'

But she eventually got through. Just. As she scrambled to her feet, it occurred to her that they may have overreacted. Geraldine had probably gone out to visit a friend. Either that or she was upstairs having a bath or an afternoon nap, and Elmo had been doing his Superdog-to-the-rescue impression for a laugh.

'Geraldine?' She raised her voice as Elmo dived in through the dog flap behind her. 'Hello? GERALDINE?'

And then she heard Geraldine, very faintly, calling out, 'Ellie? Thank God. I'm up here.'

Ellie turned, unlocked and unbolted the kitchen door and opened it to let Zack in. 'She's upstairs.'

They followed Elmo up to the top floor. Geraldine was lying in the doorway to the bedroom, a curled-up copy of *World Medicine* magazine to the right of her and her walking stick to the left.

'The cavalry's arrived.' She managed a faint smile at the sight of them. 'Don't touch me. I've fractured my right femur.'

Zack was already calling an ambulance. Elmo licked Geraldine's hand and she fondled his ears with gratitude. 'Clever boy. Did you bark at them in Morse code?'

'Put it this way, forcing him to watch all those Lassie DVDs really paid off.' Ellie knelt on the carpet beside her. 'How did it happen?'

'There was a massive spider up on the wall and I tried to splat it with my rolled-up magazine. But it scuttled off to one side. So I went to whack it again. That's when I lost my balance and came crashing down.'

'That's karma for you,' said Ellie.

'You're telling me. I've been lying here for the last twenty minutes and it's been smirking down at me the whole time.'

Ellie followed the line of Geraldine's gaze and let out a squeak: the spider was indeed up there, malevolent-looking and measuring a good three inches in diameter.

Zack ended the call. 'Right, ambulance is on its way.'

'Thanks for coming to the rescue. Oh Lord,' Geraldine sighed. 'They're going to cart me off to hospital.' She looked at Ellie. 'Could you be an angel and help me get a bag packed?'

'No problem. Zack, kill the spider, would you?'

'What, and end up like Geraldine? Let him live. I'll go down and keep an eye out for the ambulance.'

When he'd left them, Geraldine murmured with amusement, 'Just like my late husband. Scared of them but would die rather than admit it.'

Rising from her kneeling position, Ellie said, 'Tell me where your overnight bag is and what you want me to pack.'

Zack accompanied Geraldine to University College Hospital and waited with her until she'd been seen in A&E, then admitted onto a ward. Surgery to pin and stabilise the intracapsular fracture was scheduled to be carried out first thing tomorrow, and the pain was under control. As he made his way home, a text came through from Ellie:

> Travel schedule sorted, meetings rearranged. Taking Elmo for a run, back by six. Give Geraldine our love xx

The kisses, needless to say, were for Geraldine, not for him. But that hadn't stopped him looking at the text three times already. On a whim, as the taxi reached Primrose Hill and Regent's Park Road, Zack told the cab driver to stop. The hill itself was bathed in sunshine and there were still plenty of people about. Heading up to the top, he kept a look out for Ellie. This afternoon he could have sworn her attitude towards him had changed; just thinking about the incredible longing he'd experienced brought it all back. He'd so badly wanted to kiss her, had been right on the verge of doing it, right up to the moment when Elmo had come crashing through the dog flap.

And then he saw her. Having reached the brow of the hill, Zack saw a flash of pink. There they were, Ellie with her long dark hair flying and Elmo's tail wagging in joyful anticipation as she hurled his red ball into the air and he launched himself after it. She had no idea he was there. Zack didn't want to move. He could stand here and watch her for ever; her complete lack of self-consciousness was irresistible.

Gripped by a surge of longing, he made up his mind. After the events of today, surely he had the perfect excuse to invite her back to the house for dinner. They could discuss the care of Elmo in the weeks ahead, maybe recapture the moment that had felt as if it might have been about to happen before bloody Elmo had interrupted them. When he'd checked with Ellie earlier that she could look after Elmo if he was held up at the hospital, she had said it was fine, she wasn't seeing Joe tonight. Which could only be good news. Wherever Joe might be this evening without her, it served him right.

'**H**ey!' Spotting the figure heading her way, Ellie waved. When they reached each other she said, 'I can't believe you're making me do this.'

'Don't be like that. It'll be great.'

'It won't be great! You've already told me it's going to be horrendous. You just want me there to share the agony.'

But Ellie was smiling; she couldn't help herself. Roo had called her twenty minutes ago, desperate for support. Brian, in his late forties and terminally dandruffy, was a fellow volunteer at the charity shop.

'OK, it's true,' Roo admitted. 'But he doesn't have any friends. He joined this amateur dramatics society to try and make some, and it didn't work. What could I say?'

It was the opening night of Brian's first play, being held in a church hall in Crouch End. This afternoon he'd proudly presented Roo with two tickets for the performance. 'They're his friends and family tickets,' Roo had explained during her begging phone call, 'and there's no one else he can invite. Please, *please*, say you'll come with me.'

Vowing to become a good person was all very admirable, but Roo wasn't above taking other people down with her. 'Because if it's just me,' she'd pointed out, 'Brian might get it into his head that it's some kind of date. And he'll insist on walking me home afterwards.'

Ellie shielded her eyes from the sun, watching as Elmo wrestled playfully with a pair of terriers for control of his ball and ended up rolling down the grassy slope. 'What time do we have to be there?'

'Eight o'clock, curtain up.' Roo was tilting her head to one side. 'Now is this who I think it is?'

Ellie followed the direction of her gaze and felt her stomach give a little squeeze. Seeing Zack unexpectedly had that effect on her.

She nodded. 'That's Zack.'

'I guessed. And that's what I call a body.' Roo raised a mischievous eyebrow. 'Don't look so shocked. I'm not going to do anything.' She grinned. 'Just pointing it out, in case you hadn't noticed.'

In case she hadn't noticed. Oh God, wouldn't *that* have made life easier. 'Hi!' said Ellie over-brightly as Zack approached. 'How's Geraldine?'

'Pretty good, all things considered.' He nodded at Roo. 'You're Roo? We meet at last. I've heard all about you.'

'Same.' Roo perched her sunglasses on the top of her head and beamed at Zack. The next moment Elmo came racing up.

'You said you were bringing him for a walk,' said Zack, 'so I thought I'd meet you here.'

'And am I glad you did,' Roo exclaimed. 'If you hadn't made it back in time, Ellie might have said she had to stay at home and look after your dog. But you're here, so it's OK, we can go out tonight!'

'So much for my get-out clause.' Ellie looked at Zack. 'Thanks.'

There was the tiniest of pauses. Then Zack said, 'Where are you going?'

'To the theatre. To see a play. It's going to be awful.'

'We don't know that for sure,' said Roo.

'We kind of do.' Ellie shook her head. 'You said Brian was playing the part of a singing Spanish juggler. You also told me he's pale blue, tone deaf and can't juggle.'

'Well, we're going and that's that.' Roo put her dark glasses back on.

Taking Elmo's lead from Ellie, she handed it to Zack. 'We need to go home and get changed first, too. Bye then.' She flashed him another smile. 'See you again sometime.'

'I bet you're jealous.' Ellie rolled her eyes at Zack. 'If we'd had a spare ticket you could have joined us, but apparently they're *very* in demand.'

'It's a sell-out.' Roo called over her shoulder as she headed down the hill. Ellie ruffled Elmo's ears. 'Bye, sweetie, see you tomorrow.'

And another plan hits the rocks.

'Bye,' said Zack.

'**W**e've been trying to think of ways to raise money for St Mark's Hospice,' said Yasmin. 'They looked after my auntie before she died last year. It's the most amazing place, but they're desperate for more cash. If they can't reach their target by Christmas they might have to close.'

Roo said, 'That's terrible. *Ow.*' Yasmin was good at leg waxes but not that good. It still hurt.

'Sorry! So anyway, we've decided to have a raffle here at the salon. And seeing as you're one of our celebrity clients, we wondered if you'd donate a prize.'

More pain. Roo flinched. 'Of course I will, but I'm not a celebrity.'

'I know, but you used to be. Maybe you could give us a signed photo or something. Or one of your old stage outfits. Anything really.'

Roo felt bad. She didn't have any stage outfits she could donate. Wasn't there any other way she could help? *Ow.*

'Who else are you asking?'

'Gosh, pretty much everyone! We're offering prizes of sessions here at the salon, obviously. And quite a few of the clients have offered to bring in boxes of chocolates, homemade cakes, that kind of thing. Everyone's being great,' said Yasmin. 'They all want to chip in.'

Which was all very lovely but it wasn't going to save a hospice on the brink of closure. Roo said, 'Who are your other celebrity clients?'

'Well . . . we're not really the kind of salon that gets celebrities.'

Jackie, ever the optimist, said, 'Gary Barlow walked past our window the other week.'

'That doesn't really count though,' said Yasmin.

Jackie thought for a moment. 'But we've got Ceecee Milton!'

Another blast from the past. Roo had met Ceecee Milton a couple of times, back in the day when they had both been experiencing success. Like herself, Ceecee had briefly risen and enjoyed her moment in the celebrity spotlight before fading back again into obscurity. This had largely been down to the fact that her husband, a sleazy operator who doubled as her manager, had managed to alienate most of the big guns in the business. And so her career had bitten the dust.

'Who else is there?' said Roo.

'Um, that's it, really.' Yasmin looked apologetic.

'Just me and Ceecee?' Oh dear. Talk about scraping the bottom of the celebrity barrel. 'A couple of old has-beens.'

'She's really nice. She'll definitely give us something good for the raffle.'

'I'll give you something too. I just don't know what yet.' *Ow.* 'Is she still married?'

'Not to that awful one. She dumped him a while back. Got herself a lovely new husband now.' Yasmin broke into a smile. 'See? It can happen. There's hope for us all.'

The rain was hammering down as Roo emerged from the tube station. Within seconds her hair was plastered to her head but Roo didn't care, her brain was fizzy with excitement. It was ten to nine in the morning, she'd had no sleep whatsoever and this was something she had never experienced before.

'Oh my goodness.' Yasmin, arriving to open up the salon, discovered her waiting in the doorway. 'What's happened? Are you OK?'

'I'm great.' Roo followed her inside. 'I've been up all night. Writing.'

Yasmin passed her a towel. 'Here, dry yourself off. I didn't know you were doing that now. What is it, an autobiography?'

'Not that kind of writing. I've done a song. It's really good.' Roo tried again. 'Actually it's not, it's better than that. It's brilliant.'

'Ooh, how fab! Sing it to me, then!'

At the best of times Roo's singing voice resembled a cat in a vet's waiting room. 'I can't. I need Ceecee to do it. Can you give me her number?'

Yasmin was clearly puzzled. 'Ceecee Milton? Why?'

'Because this is the best song I've ever written. I can't quite believe I've done it, but I have. And I want us to put it out as a charity single,' said Roo. 'For your hospice. If we do this properly, we can make it happen. In a big way.'

'Really? Seriously? Oh my God, how?'

'Blag. Beg. Use every contact we have.' Roo's head was positively bursting with possibilities. 'And get a buzz going.'

'How do we do that?'

'Well, I think mainly we want to use a mixture of rumour and gossip and technology. And some massive porkie pies.'

Ellie had never seen anything like it. It was eight in the evening by the time she arrived, summoned to a town house in St John's Wood. The huge extension at the back of the house had been turned into a recording studio, there were technical types doing technical things at the mixing desks, and the buzz in the air was tangible.

Roo was there at the centre of things, running on Diet Coke and adrenalin. Having pulled every string she could conceivably lay her hands on, she had brought together a team of experts to weave their magic. Musicians, music producers and backing singers were milling around the studio. And there was Yasmin with her baby son on her hip, chatting to statuesque Ceecee Milton, who was black and beautiful and balancing her own baby daughter on hers.

'Hello!' Spotting her and beckoning Ellie over, Yasmin said, 'Can you believe all this is happening? This is Ceecee, by the way.'

'Hi there. You must be the one with the invisible baby.'

'Sorry about that.' Ellie glanced at Yasmin. 'The good thing is, the nappies are invisible too.' She paused to listen as the opening bars of music filled the room. 'This is just amazing.'

'Wait till you hear the whole thing.' The music stopped. 'Ceecee's voice is fantastic. And the track itself . . .'

Someone raised their hand for silence, the music began again and everyone listened intently. Within thirty seconds Ellie knew just how special it was. Ceecee's heartbreaking vocals were making the little hairs on her arms stand on end. As the song continued, the backing singers joined in and Ceecee's own voice began to soar. 'You're the light in my life . . . you're everything . . . when it's dark you're my light, you're my world, all I believe in . . .'

Oh God, there was such emotion in the words, Ellie had to turn away. She was going to cry; how embarrassing. Fumbling in her bag, she surreptitiously pulled out a mini pack of Kleenex. The next moment

Yasmin was in need of a tissue as well. Gazing around, Ellie saw they weren't the only ones. The music, haunting and powerful and emotive, was impossible to resist. It gripped you by the throat and it didn't let go. Grown men were standing there with tears in their eyes. The skinny man with the goatee who had been at the recording desk put his arm round Roo's shoulders and gave her a squeeze as the song reached its crescendo . . .

Ellie knew that such an extreme reaction to a song you were hearing for the first time was a rare thing. When the final notes had died away, there was absolute silence for a couple of seconds. Then Ceecee dabbed her eyes and said huskily, 'Damn, I'm good,' and the studio erupted with whoops and cheers and wild applause.

In a daze, Roo said, 'We've done it. Have we? I think we've done it.' She sank down onto a conker-brown leather sofa and buried her face in her hands.

All round her, people continued to celebrate. Within thirty seconds Roo was fast asleep.

By eleven o'clock the video had been completed. It hadn't taken long at all. Quite simply, someone was despatched to the local Chinese take-away for a pile of brown paper bags. A camcorder then recorded the process of the track being laid down while everyone wore bags over their heads with just eye holes cut in them to avert unfortunate accidents. Ceecee and the backing singers wore them too. Every last member of the team would be anonymous.

By midnight the video had been edited together and posted on YouTube. Next, the whispering campaign began. Everyone posted links on websites, Twitter, MySpace and Facebook, dropping hints as to who might be involved: Bono, Jay-Z, Elton John, Beyoncé . . . Next, they called in favours from journalists, TV people, other music contacts, anyone they could possibly think of. Each person contacted was asked to listen to the song just once, then spread the word that it was a) for charity, and b) the track of the year.

By one o'clock the word was already spreading like wildfire, the YouTube clip had been viewed almost half a million times and speculation as to who could be behind it was rife. Goatee man contacted Bono, Jay-Z, Elton and Beyoncé and asked them to remain enigmatic, neither confirming nor denying involvement in order to promote the cause.

Had it only been ten days? Roo was incredulous; was it actually possible that it could all have happened so fast? Eleven days ago the song hadn't existed, yet now it was known to millions, maybe even billions of people all over the world. Talk about surreal.

Roo was in the green room waiting to be called out on set. Live TV was always scary. Well, it hadn't been when she was a Deeva because she'd generally been off her head and it had all been a laugh, but doing it sober now was in another league altogether. How could you ever be completely sure what might come out of your mouth next?

'Everything OK?' One of the friendly runners came up to her. 'Are you sure you wouldn't like a glass of wine?'

'No thanks.' This was an enormous lie, obviously; she'd love a glass of wine. She just wasn't going to have one. Especially since she'd already broken one vow: trying to explain earlier to the bewildered make-up girl that she didn't wear make-up had been a waste of breath.

'Oh no, you have to let me do your face! This is TV!' The girl had stood firm. 'You don't want to look like something that's just been dug up, do you? We can't let you do that—you'd scare the viewers!'

Vanity had vied with exhaustion. Aware that she was promoting a worthy cause and should be making a good impression, Roo had caved in. Just this once wouldn't hurt, would it?

Ceecee, in her crimson velvet dress, was looking glorious. Batting her shimmering gold eyelids and extravagant false eyelashes at Roo, she did a show-off twirl and said, 'Look at us. For a couple of old rejects, I think we've scrubbed up pretty good.'

'Well, I have,' said Roo. 'You're still looking a bit ropey, if you ask me.'

'Girl, will you look at these eyelashes? I'm smoking hot and you know it!' Blissfully happy in her second marriage, Ceecee shimmied her generous hips. 'I'm telling you, my Nathan isn't going to know what's hit him when I get home tonight.'

In five minutes they were due on. Tomorrow they were booked, along with Yasmin, to do a series of newspaper and magazine interviews. So much for the idea that everyone involved would remain anonymous; that had lasted all of four days. But that length of time had been enough to serve its purpose, piquing the interest of millions and instigating a torrent of speculation. By the time they'd been unmasked—OK, debagged—their work had been done. 'The Light In My Life' had shot to the top of the download chart. The YouTube clip had been viewed seven million times. When it became apparent that it hadn't been written and performed by superstars, the general public decided they loved it all the more. This week it was at number one, outselling all other singles many times over.

Already Roo and Ceecee were under pressure to fly to the US to appear over there on the major chat shows. The last few days had been a complete whirlwind. Roo had no idea what would happen next; all she knew was that when the news of her involvement had broken, nobody had been able to get in or out of the charity shop on account of the vast number of paparazzi milling around outside. Nor had the situation improved when the staff discovered she was raising money for a rival charity. The manageress had lost her temper. This level of disruption simply couldn't be tolerated. And that was it, she was ordered to collect her things and leave. Sacked on the spot. From a charity shop. That was the thanks you got for trying to be a good person.

As always, despite her best efforts, Roo found her thoughts drawn back to Todd. What was he doing? Who was he with? Were he and Lisa curled up together on a sofa right now, watching the TV? OK, block that, don't think about it now. On the TV screens, the first interview was in the process of being wrapped up and an assistant was making her way across the green room towards her. Time to go.

Ellie had been shopping in Oxford Street searching for something she could wear to Zack's sister's wedding. In a hurry to get back to watch the show, she'd ended up buying three outfits without trying them on. The plan had been to buy something peacock blue, to go with her newest shoes, so of course she'd come home with a crimson wrap dress, a pale grey top and skirt with silver lace overlay, and a bottle-green dress and matching swirly jacket with a fuchsia-pink lining.

Having switched on the TV, she stripped down to her bra and knickers and tried the wrap dress first. As expected, it was OK but a bit safe. No. Back in the bag. Silver lacy outfit next. Oh crikey, how was it that you could see something in a shop and think it would look great on, when in reality it made you look like Peggy Mitchell from *EastEnders*?

Ellie peeled off the top and skirt and put them back in the second carrier. Right. She picked up the third and final outfit and prayed it would do. Bugger, the dress had the kind of zip at the back that you needed to be double-jointed to do up.

And there, just when you didn't want him, was Jamie, stretched out across the sofa with an arm behind his head.

'Taking a lot of trouble over this,' he observed.

'It's a wedding. I want to look nice.' Having stepped into the dress, she got the zip up as far as she could. Oh, for heaven's sake. She was a size twelve. If this was a size twelve, she was a pencil.

Jamie pulled a face. 'Maybe it'll be better with the jacket.'

As if. She put the jacket on and gazed at herself in the mirror above the fireplace.

'You look like one of those Slimmers of the Year,' he said helpfully, 'wearing your old clothes to show how much weight you've lost.'

'Disaster,' said Ellie. 'I'll have to take the whole lot back.' It was so frustrating. 'What am I going to *wear*?'

'How about my favourite? The one we bought on our honeymoon.'

'I've worn it before. When we went to Claridge's.'

'Did we? I don't remember that.' Jamie's eyes were sparkling with mischief; he was doing it on purpose.

'When I went with Zack.'

'And does that mean you can't wear it again?'

'No. I'd just like to wear something different.'

He looked mystified. 'Why?'

'Because we don't all want to go around in the same clothes all the time, wearing them until they disintegrate.' To make her point, she eyed his frayed jeans.

'It might be that.' Jamie conceded the point with a grin. 'Or it could be because you don't want to wear your honeymoon dress while you're having a weekend away with another man.'

Was he right? Was that the real reason? Ellie collected up the carrier bags of clothes and marched past him. Dumping them in the hallway, she went into the bedroom and returned wearing a sweatshirt and shorts. On the TV, the ad break was over and the second half of the chat show was about to start.

' . . . From has-beens to heroes!' Vince Torrance, who prided himself on his cheeky chappie persona and liberal use of irony, was making his introduction. 'From lucked-out losers to record-smashing sensations!

From the gutter to the stars . . . and now right here in this studio . . . ladies and gentlemen, please welcome Ceecee Milton and Daisy Deeva!'

Reaching across the sofa for her phone, Ellie pressed the call button. When it was answered, she said, 'Are you watching?'

He knew it was on. She'd texted him earlier. 'No,' said Todd.

'Put it on.'

'What am I, a complete masochist?' But the next moment she heard the sound of the TV echoing down the line.

'Doesn't she look fantastic?'

'Yes she does. Just explain something. How is this supposed to make me feel better?'

'Sshh, I can't hear what they're saying.' Ellie returned her attention to the TV, where Vince was making jokey comments about Roo's time working in the charity shop.

'. . . and this outfit you're wearing tonight.' He jokingly indicated Roo's charcoal jacket and skinny white trousers. 'I'm assuming that's where you picked these things up.'

Roo nodded. 'Yes, I did.'

'Ah! OK.' Wrong-footed, he laughed. 'Well, that's admirable. So forgive me, but this is quite a transformation for you. In the old days you were a pretty wild child, I think it's safe to say.'

'Oh, I was.'

'And what's brought this change about?'

'I didn't like myself very much,' said Roo. 'I decided it was time to become a nicer person.'

'And do you think you are nicer?' Vince looked genuinely interested.

Roo shrugged. 'I hope so. I think I am, yes.'

'And you've written this phenomenal song, with all the proceeds going to St Mark's Hospice. That's something to be incredibly proud of. You must be over the moon, surely.'

Clearly embarrassed, Roo shifted in her chair. 'Well, yes, we're thrilled with the way it's taken off.'

'So is this the happiest time of your life?' Vince was watching her closely, pushing. 'It has to be! You must be unbelievably happy!'

For a moment Roo's huge brown eyes swam with tears; she tilted her head back, gazed up at the ceiling then back again at Vince. 'The hospice was going to have to close down. Now that isn't going to happen. It wasn't just me, it was Ceecee and everyone else involved in the campaign. And it worked: we've got everything we wanted and more.' Her smile was bright but anyone who really knew her could see that it wasn't quite reaching her eyes. 'Of course I'm happy,' said Roo.

In exasperated unison into their respective phones, Ellie and Todd shouted at the TV screen, 'Liar!'

The car rounded the corner into Nevis Street and pulled up outside Roo's house. It was ten thirty, a crescent moon hung in the sky at the end of the road and the stars were out tonight in force. Roo climbed out onto the pavement, thanked the driver and watched him leave.

Was Ellie at home? Was she awake? Her living-room lights were on but Roo had sent her a text twenty minutes ago saying she was on her way home and hadn't received a reply.

Roo took out her phone again, ready to ring Ellie, then stopped as she saw movement at the window. The curtain was pulled back and Ellie appeared. She waved, flung the window open and leaned out.

'Hey, I know you! You're that songwriter person I was watching on telly earlier.'

Roo felt herself relax. How could she have got through the last couple of months without Ellie? Then again, if it hadn't been for Ellie, she would never have got to know Todd either. OK, never mind that now. *Don't think about Todd.*

Roo shielded her eyes from the glare of the street lamp. 'Was I OK?'

'You were great. But there was one thing.' Ellie rested her elbows on the windowsill. 'Why isn't this the happiest time of your life?'

'What?'

'You heard. Except we both know the answer. It's because you're still crazy about Todd.'

Roo's stomach scrunched itself into a tight knot. This wasn't fair; she wasn't up to another lecture, not now, not tonight.

'Don't look at me like that.' Ellie's voice softened when Roo didn't say anything. 'Oh Roo, haven't you punished yourself enough now?'

Roo's eyes began to prickle. She bit her lip.

'Listen, you did some bad things,' Ellie went on. 'But now you've done good. More than enough good. I *promise.*'

A single tear slid down Roo's cheek and dripped off her chin. *More than enough good*; had she actually redressed the balance at last? She gazed up at Ellie and said hopefully, 'Do you really think I have?'

'Yes,' Ellie nodded. 'I do.'

For the first time Roo found herself able to acknowledge that maybe, just maybe, Ellie was right. But there was still the matter of Todd's teacher girlfriend.

'OK, this is crazy, why am I stood out here like a lemon?' She continued across the street. 'Open the door, I'm coming up.'

'No, you can't.' Ellie's voice stopped her in her tracks. 'Sorry, but I'm so shattered, and Zack's making me go in extra-early tomorrow. I just have to go to bed.'

'Oh.' Stung, Roo said, 'OK.' *Five minutes wouldn't hurt, surely?*

'Hang on, though.' Ellie straightened up. 'I've got something for you.'

'What is it?'

'Wait a sec.' She disappeared from view. A few seconds later, Ellie's front door opened.

And there was Todd. Standing there, watching her. With something like determination in his eyes.

Oh God . . .

Roo was unable to move. She was having trouble staying upright. Now he was closing the short distance between them and she was mouthing helplessly like a goldfish, which probably wasn't attractive.

'Sshh.' Todd shook his head. 'Don't say anything. Stop it,' he warned as a kind of strangled croak found its way out. 'Not a word.'

But Roo managed it. She had to. 'Wh-where's Lisa?'

'Lisa.' Another shake. 'Don't worry. She's gone.'

Gone, yes, thank you . . .

The next moment Todd reached her and seamlessly drew her into his arms. His face, the face she hadn't been able to put out of her mind for so long, was now inches from hers. In the glow from the street lamp she could see the amber flecks in his grey eyes, the way his eyelashes curled at the corners, the tiny scar below his left eyebrow. And then there was his mouth . . . oh God, would it really be all right?

'Come here,' Todd murmured, sliding one hand behind her neck. And then she *was* there. Their mouths met at last and she gave a tiny shiver, because this . . . *this* was the kiss she'd spent so long waiting for. Except now she was messing it up, making a complete hash of it, because the emotion was too much and she was about to burst into tears, and if there were two things you really couldn't do simultaneously, it was kiss and cry . . .

Roo drew back in the nick of time as a great braying sob broke out. Anyone listening would think there was a donkey loose in the street.

'Hey, hey.' Half-laughing, Todd held on to her. 'I'm not that bad.'

'S-sorry. I'm just so h-h-happy.' Weeks of pent-up tension had to escape somehow. She clung to him, overwhelmed and overcome with emotion. 'I can't believe you're here . . .'

'Me neither. This wasn't planned, you know. Ellie called and invited me over. You weren't supposed to find out I was upstairs.'

Roo smiled and kissed him again. It was OK, the explosive crying jag had passed. She turned to look up at the window. It was closed now, Ellie having beaten a diplomatic retreat.

'I love that girl,' she said.

Todd grinned. 'So do I.'

'What happened with Lisa?' Roo held her breath.

'She disappeared,' Todd went on seriously. 'Back inside Ellie's head.'

It took a couple of moments for this to sink in.

'You mean it wasn't true?' Roo searched his face.

'None of it was true. Ellie made her up. She invented the whole thing,' said Todd, 'I'm never going to believe a word she says again.'

'Nor me.'

'But she was right about you not being happy. She saw it on the TV. Well, we both did.'

Roo ran her fingers wonderingly through his hair. 'And she made me realise I'd done enough. At last. So she's quite clever really.'

'I love you.'

'Me too.' She leaned into him. Their noses were practically touching.

'I'm so proud of you.' Todd's expression softened. 'You're amazing.'

'I made some horrible mistakes.' She could feel the heat emanating from his body.

'Everyone makes mistakes. But you stopped and did something about it. Most people don't bother.'

Together they turned and made their way across the street to her house. Roo linked her fingers through his and gave them a squeeze. She could hardly wait.

Chapter 12

IT WAS the last week in September and Ellie had that squiggly going-on-holiday feeling in her stomach. There wasn't a cloud in the luminous blue sky, and she and Zack were on their way to Perranporth. If Zack had any idea how much she'd been looking forward to this . . . well, it would scare the living daylights out of him.

Ellie gave a little wriggle in her seat and sat back, enjoying the feel of the sun on her face and watching the scenery whoosh by as they sped down the M4. Elmo was asleep in the back of the car. Geraldine, out of hospital now and recuperating nicely, had gone to stay with her sister in Exeter. Roo and Todd were so besotted they could barely tear their hands off each other.

Ellie took a packet of wine gums out of her bag and offered them to Zack. 'Want one?'

'Thanks. Can you find me a green one?'

'Green? What, seriously?' She winced. 'Are you sure?'

'Yes. Why?'

'Nobody likes green! They're the ones you only eat when everything else is gone. You have to be desperate.'

'Green's my favourite,' said Zack.

'Well, that makes you officially weird. But also kind of useful to have around.' Ellie found one and passed it over.

He glanced across at her. 'Which are Joe's favourites?'

'No idea. I've never offered him a wine gum.'

'I haven't asked for a while how things are going with you two.'

'Fine.' Ellie helped herself to a red one. They were the best by a mile.

'Did you see him last night?'

She nodded, glad of the sweet in her mouth. 'Mmm.'

'OK. That's clever. Because on Twitter this morning he posted a photo of himself taken last night at a party at the Beverly Hills Hotel.'

Ellie stopped chewing. Bugger. Zack added helpfully, 'Which is in Beverly Hills.'

'I thought you weren't on Twitter.'

'I'm not. Joe sent me an email yesterday. Just a friendly catch-up letting me know how things are going for him in LA. So I was pretty curious.' He said drily, 'You don't need to be on Twitter to look someone up.'

She heaved a sigh and fiddled with the clasp on her bag. It had only been a little white lie, but she always seemed destined to be found out.

'Handy hint,' said Zack. 'In future, probably better to keep the other person in the loop so they know what they should or shouldn't say.'

'I'll make sure I do that.'

'You could have told me, you know. Why didn't you?'

Because I'm crazy about you and I don't want to make a complete fool of myself. Because it's easier if you think I'm seeing someone else.

Aloud, Ellie said, 'It was just . . . embarrassing. You never really seemed to approve of me and Joe in the first place.'

'I didn't dislike Joe. He was a good guy.' Zack inclined his head. 'He still is. But I could see he wasn't your type.'

'Oh.' She was instantly on the defensive. 'He didn't dump me, you know. He asked me to move with him to LA.'

'So what stopped you?'

'Well, there's this guy I work for. Pretty hopeless character. God knows how he'd manage without me to organise him.' That was better, she'd made him smile. 'Honestly? It was never going to happen.' Would he understand if she said it? Ellie gave it a go. 'He was an eight. You can't move to another continent with someone who isn't a ten.'

Another sidelong glance, another eyebrow raised. 'And what does somebody have to do to be a ten?'

She raised her chin; he was teasing her now. 'They don't have to do anything. Just be themselves, and be right. Go on then, how about you?' Time to turn the tables. 'What makes a girl perfect?'

The corners of Zack's mouth began to twitch. 'It helps a lot if she doesn't call me Zacky.'

'**O**K, brace yourself.' It was five in the afternoon; they were approaching Perranporth. Zack said, 'Sometimes my family can be a bit overwhelming. If my mother asks any impertinent questions, ignore her.'

Ellie's stomach was in knots; she'd thought his family knew she was just a friend. It wasn't until they'd left the M5 behind them that Zack had explained how it had been easier to tell them they were a new couple. 'It just made sense. I don't know why it didn't occur to me before. My family can't keep a secret to save their lives; someone would be bound to tell Mya. Whereas this way, only we know the truth.'

Fear-filled adrenalin was now zinging like sherbet through Ellie's veins. The old have-to-pretend-we're-a-couple ploy was one she'd seen in romantic films, but only ever at the beginning of the film when the couple genuinely couldn't stand the sight of each other. Having to do it when you had a Kilimanjaro-sized crush on your boss and he really didn't have a crush on you in return was going to be a whole lot trickier to pull off.

Minutes later they turned a corner and there it was, set back from the road at the end of a curving driveway. A long Georgian farmhouse built of pale grey stone and smothered in ivy, with a silvery slate roof. The gardens surrounding it were spectacular but not off-puttingly formal. The front door was painted emerald green. Almost all the sash windows downstairs were open. Behind the house a pink and white marquee was visible. The overall effect was incredibly welcoming.

'Look at those windows flung open,' said Zack. 'Bet you any money my mother's been burning cakes again.'

He brought the car to a halt. Elmo, on Ellie's lap, gave a bark of recognition and began scrabbling his paws against the passenger window. The next moment the bright green front door opened and a horde of people and dogs began spilling out.

'Welcome to my family.' Zack's tone was dry. 'Well? Do you think we can do this?'

Ellie grinned at him. 'Zacky, don't panic, it'll be fine.'

'Darling, how lovely, it's been too long!' Teresa McLaren gave her son an enthusiastic hug, then turned to Ellie. 'And you must be Ellie. It's even lovelier to meet you!'

Zack said, 'Mum, call her Piglet. Everyone does.'

'No they don't.' Ellie shook her head at Teresa. 'Ignore him, he just made that up.'

'He's a shocker. But everybody does call me Tizz, so you must too.' Tizz was beaming. In her mid sixties, she had flyaway brown hair escaping from a hastily assembled bun, Zack's dark eyes and a streak of flour across her forehead. She was wearing a stripy blue and white shirt over crumpled jeans and had a rangy, boyish figure. 'We've been so looking forward to this. Now, let's introduce you to everyone . . .'

'Mum, why are all the windows open?' said Zack.

'You know exactly why, darling. Too much going on, too much chatter and I forgot to set the timer on the oven.' Tizz was unrepentant. 'I burnt the bloody shortbread.'

By eight o'clock Ellie felt as if she'd known Zack's family for years. Zack's father Ken, returning from a trip to the shops for unburnt shortbread and extra supplies of Bombay Sapphire gin, was tall and suntanned with a loud booming laugh, twinkling faded grey eyes and a big bumpy nose that Zack hadn't inherited.

Zack's sisters were equally welcoming, each of them possessing a recognisable mix of their parents' genes and a raucous sense of humour. Claire was the blondest, Paula the one with the wickedest, loudest laugh. And Steph, due to be married less than forty-eight hours from now, was the most laid-back future bride you could imagine, especially seeing as her twin daughters Joss and Lily were still dead set on wearing trainers with their bridesmaid dresses.

OK, Joss and Lily, identical twins, tick. Gareth, Steph's about-to-be husband, tick. Paula's children were Tom and Zaylie, tick, tick. Claire and her husband Paul—no, *Phil*—had two girls and one boy, Suki and Belle and . . . hang on a sec, Lewis, that was it. Tick, tick, tick.

As for the dogs, they were a boisterous mix of Labradors, mongrels and terriers and Ellie wasn't even going to attempt to work out which of them belonged to which branch of the family. It was enough for now that Elmo was having the time of his life.

So far they'd all been down to the beach to give the dogs a run before sundown, before calling in at the best takeaway in Perranporth. Then, back at the house, they'd sat outside on the lit-up terrace eating fish and chips, drinking gin and discussing the plans for the wedding.

After a while the conversation turned to Zack when he was young.

'He made me jump over a wall,' Claire relayed with relish, 'and there were ten million stinging nettles on the other side.'

Zack narrowed his eyes. 'Only to pay you back for tipping live crabs into my Wellington boots.'

'But you deserved it,' Paula chimed in. 'You'd hidden whitebait in her school bag.'

'I'd forgotten about the whitebait.' Claire was outraged. 'They stank!'

The children were shrieking with laughter. Joss squealed, 'I'm going to do the crab thing tomorrow to everyone in my class!'

'You mustn't.' Zack pointed a chip at her. 'Because it's not funny and it's not clever.'

'Is Ellie your girlfriend?' Zaylie asked.

'Yes she is, she's my new girlfriend.'

Ellie's breath caught in her throat. *If only.*

'Has she seen you with no clothes on?'

Oh crikey, just the thought of it. 'No, I have not.' Above the laughter, Ellie said with horror, 'Yuk, no *way.*'

'I know where there's a picture of Uncle Zack and he's sitting in a paddling pool *naked.*' Zaylie's face was triumphant. 'It's in a book of photographs in Grandma's room. She was showing us the other day. Do you want me to get it and show you?'

'Mum, I thought I told you to throw that away.' Zack looked pained.

'Oh darling, how could I? You were so adorable.'

Ellie kept a straight face. 'Was it taken very recently?'

'Very funny. I was two. And you don't want to see it,' said Zack.

Sometimes an opportunity came along that was simply too good to pass up. And she was supposed to be his girlfriend, wasn't she? 'Actually,' Ellie's gaze was innocent, 'I think you'll find I do.'

'Goodnight, Ellie, sleep well. It's so lovely having you here.' Tizz gave her a fond hug and a kiss on the cheek. Claire and Paula had left with their respective families earlier. Steph and Gareth, who were staying until the wedding, had put the twins to bed hours ago. Now it was gone midnight and everyone was heading upstairs.

'Thanks for everything. Night.' Through the open window, they could hear Zack and Gareth outside, giving the dogs a last run around the garden before turning in for the night.

If this had been a film, Zack's mum would at this point have said merrily, 'Now, no spare rooms left so I've put you in together! That won't be a problem, will it?' As a result of which, all manner of embarrassing and comical situations would inevitably have ensued.

But this was a big house, a six-bedroomed one, and Tizz had said earlier, 'Now then, I did ask Zack if you'd be sharing but he said separate rooms. So yours is here.' Bending her head closer to Ellie's, her tone conspiratorial, she'd added, 'Good move, by the way. Well done, you!'

Meaning she thought Ellie was playing hard to get, treating her new boyfriend mean in order to keep him keen.

Zack was coming up the staircase five minutes later as she emerged from the bathroom.

'You're doing a great job.' He was keeping his voice low. 'Apart from the bit with the naked photo.'

He smelt of aftershave, cognac and the seaside. Ellie committed the delicious smell to memory. 'The kids thought it was hysterical.'

Having finished settling the dogs into their baskets in the kitchen, Gareth was now on his way upstairs. Ellie's heart began to gallop as Zack moved closer, for all the world as if they were a proper couple on the verge of exchanging a goodnight kiss. For a moment she thought it was actually going to happen. Then, as if noticing Gareth's presence, he pulled back and called out, 'Night.'

'Night, you two.' Gareth ambled past, raised a hand and disappeared into the room at the end of the landing. Leaving them alone once more.

OK, this was crazy, she was standing here waiting, *like someone expecting to be kissed*. Dragging herself out of her dopey trance, Ellie took a deliberate step back and said, 'Right, see you tomorrow.'

Zack gazed at her for a long moment before moving away. 'Yes, tomorrow. Sleep well.'

It was Friday afternoon, sunny and breezy, and the good weather had brought people flocking to the beach. The Atlantic Ocean was glittering, breakers were rolling in and the surfers were out in force.

Zack smiled at the sight of two surfers in particular. Joss in her little wetsuit was struggling with a crisis of confidence. Ellie had been helping her for the last thirty minutes, showing her how to stay balanced on her board, yelling encouragement alongside her each time she attempted a new wave then catching her when she came tumbling off.

Last-minute wedding preparations were occupying his parents back at the house. They had encouraged Zack and Ellie to escape down to the beach with Steph, Gareth and the twins for a couple of hours. Tizz had taken Zack aside this morning and murmured not so subtly, 'This one's worth hanging on to, you know. She's fab.'

And he had felt torn on so many levels, because on the one hand he hated deceiving his mother, but on the other hand she was the world's most incurable blabbermouth.

Plus, she was right. He knew only too well that Ellie was worth hanging on to. But he was also terrified of making his feelings known and ruining their amicable working relationship. Being scared wasn't an emotion Zack was familiar with, but it had him in its grip now. Last night he had wanted so badly to kiss her, he'd been on the brink of giving in to temptation. Only imagining the awkwardness at the wedding if she rejected him had stopped him from just doing it.

And here they came now, racing up the beach together with their boards under their arms and the others following behind.

'I'm f-f-freezing.' Joss, her teeth chattering violently, collapsed onto the rug and unzipped her suit.

'Wasn't she brilliant?' Ellie grabbed a turquoise towel and began energetically towelling her dry.

'She was.' Zack loved Ellie's enthusiasm, the light in her grey eyes, the way her skin glowed and the tip of her nose had turned shiny and pink with cold. 'Here, you get yourself warm, I'll help Joss.'

'Ellie, look at me! I'm not cold!' Lily, who loved nothing more than a bit of sibling one-upmanship, came dancing up to them. 'Can we play volleyball next? Volleyball's my favourite!'

'In a minute, sweetie.' Ellie was now vigorously towelling her own hair; when she'd got herself looking like a scarecrow she pulled a comical cross-eyed face at the two girls.

'Zack, I'm good at volleyball, aren't I?' Joss turned to him, bristling with indignation. 'I'm better at throwing than Lily is.'

'Oh!' Lily pointed over Zack's shoulder.

'What?' Zack started to turn, to see what was happening behind him. And that was when everything went black.

So this was Mya. Ellie had seen her making her way across the sand towards them, holding a playful finger to her lips. Dark haired, curvily attractive, she was sporting a white lace shirt, tight black jeans, lots of silver jewellery and a good half-bottle of Chanel No. 5.

Well, it was either Mya or Nancy Dell'Olio's much younger sister.

'Surprise! Hi! I just dropped in on your mum and she said you were all here, so I thought I'd come on down.' She took her hands away from Zack's eyes and gave him an enthusiastic just-good-friends kiss and a hug before greeting the rest of them with a smile. 'Hey, kids, excited about tomorrow?'

'Ellie, this is Mya.' Zack performed the introductions. 'Mya, my girl-friend Ellie.'

'Hi, Steph said you were coming to the wedding. Nice to meet you.'

Mya was friendly and cheerful, but Ellie knew she was being given a thorough once-over. Oh well, couldn't be helped. She combed her fingers through her Worzel Gummidge hair and said, 'You too,' smiling back in a Yes-I'm-his-girlfriend-aren't-I-lucky kind of way.

'Come on!' Lily was scrambling impatiently to her feet, sending up a spray of sand. 'Let's play volleyball! Mya, you can play too.'

To her credit, Mya was a good sport and she did join in. Bracelets and necklaces clanking like a jailer's keys, hair rock-steady thanks to the impenetrable coating of Elnett super-strength, she threw herself into the game with enthusiasm and on several occasions accidentally-on-purpose threw herself into Zack's path. Ellie couldn't help liking her; when Zack had described Mya as a Labrador puppy he'd been spot on.

Two pairs of trainers flash-flash-flashed, changing colour with each step taken as Lily and Joss trooped up the aisle behind their mother. They'd won, but so cleverly that no one begrudged them their moment of victory.

Ellie, standing beside Zack in one of the front pews, smiled at the memory. She had been making coffee in the kitchen earlier while the girls gazed dispiritedly at the lilac satin shoes on their feet. At length Joss had said, 'Mummy, why did you choose to wear that dress for your wedding?'

Steph, fabulous in slinky oyster satin, had replied, 'Because this was the one I liked best, sweetie.'

Prompting Joss to say in a sad voice, 'Oh. I liked my flashing trainers best.'

Ellie and Steph had exchanged a look across the kitchen. And that was the moment Steph gave in. After all, she explained to the rest of the family, the whole point of getting married in the first place was for the sake of the kids.

And now they were. Getting married. In a beautiful fourteenth-century church, surrounded by friends and family. The service was being conducted by a jolly vicar who had known Steph since she was seven.

The atmosphere during the service was relaxed and celebratory. When the vows had been exchanged and the vicar declared that Gareth may kiss the bride, Lily said in a despairing voice, 'They're always doing that,' prompting much laughter and a round of applause when Gareth announced that he was about to do it again.

Zack smiled at Ellie. He reached for her hand and gave it a squeeze.

After the service everyone spilled outside into the sunshine. Ellie's high heel skidded on one of the steps and she almost went flying. Grabbing her in the nick of time, Zack held her up.

'Are you OK?' His arm was round her waist. *It felt gorgeous.*

'I'm fine. That was a real slip, by the way. Not a Mya-type one.' She didn't want him to think she'd done it on purpose.

'I know that.'

'Oh my goodness, look at me.' Tizz was dabbing at her eyes with a tissue. 'Crying like a baby, how ridiculous. I'm not used to this make-up malarkey.' She presented her face to Ellie for inspection. 'Have I smudged anything? Do I look like a panda?'

Since neither of them had a mirror, Ellie took control of the tissue and carefully wiped away the mascara spillage. 'There, all done.'

'You're a star.' Tizz leaned in and murmured not very discreetly, 'You never know, it could be you and Zack next!'

'Mum,' said Zack.

'What? I'm just saying it could be!'

'The photographer wants you.' Zack pointed to where a rotund man garlanded with cameras was attempting to corral the main players into a neat group.

'He'll be wanting all of us. Come on.'

OK, embarrassing. Ellie tried to hang back. 'It's a family shot. You don't want me in it.'

'Don't be silly, of course we do.' Zack was being dragged over by some of the children. As soon as he was out of earshot, Tizz clutched Ellie's elbow and said, 'I have such a good feeling about you. I'm serious, darling. High hopes. We've been waiting so long for Zack to meet the right girl and I really think it's happened at last.'

This was awful. Ellie hated having to lie. 'But it's early days . . .'

'Maybe so, but I see the way he looks at you.' They were approaching the photographer now. 'And let me tell you, Zack's pretty smitten. I'm his mother.' Tizz's eyes were sparkling. 'Trust me, I can tell.'

Then she was seized by the photographer and ushered to her allotted position. Zack murmured in Ellie's ear, 'What's she been saying now?'

His mouth accidentally brushed the top of her ear as he said it, causing a fresh attack of the zingers. When they'd died down, Ellie whispered back, 'Your mum's convinced you like me. She says she can tell.' Ellie marvelled at her ability to sound amused. 'I'm impressed; I didn't know you were such a good actor.'

By three o'clock they were back at the house and the wedding party was in full flow. A gypsy punk band from St Austell was playing catchy Russian-style music, violins and balalaikas duelling with the hypnotic beat of the drums. There was wild dancing, there was singing, even the dogs joined in. Then it was time to sit down and eat.

The tables were covered in white swagged tablecloths strewn with flowers and silver confetti. The wine had been flowing for the last hour and everyone was nicely relaxed. As the hired caterers began serving the first course, Zack introduced Ellie to the other guests on their table: two long-standing neighbours of the McLarens, three old schoolfriends of Steph's and a well-dressed man in his early sixties who explained that he was Gareth's godfather.

'So are you going to be next on the list?' The woman who had lived next door to Zack for many years gave him a jokey nudge.

'Who knows? It could be a possibility.' Ellie found herself on the receiving end of the kind of smile from Zack that would have anyone believing him. God, he was brilliant at this.

By the time the plates were removed, Zack had got talking to Gareth's godfather, whose name was Paul. Moments later, Elmo arrived to pay them a visit, scrabbling to be allowed onto Zack's lap.

'Sorry about this. *No*, Elmo. Get down.'

'Oh, let him join us, I don't mind. I love dogs.' Paul gave Elmo's ears a friendly scratch. 'But if your name's McLaren, why does it say Castle on the identity tag?' He looked at Ellie. 'Or is that you?'

Ellie shook her head. 'He's a timeshare dog. Zack and his neighbour have dual custody. Neither of them can manage a full-time commitment. Zack takes Elmo for most of the walks while he's at home. Then when he's away, Elmo goes to live with Geraldine.'

Paul nodded. 'Makes sense. Good plan.' Then he smiled and rubbed Elmo's head. 'Geraldine Castle, that takes me back. I used to know some-one by that name years ago.'

'If you met our Geraldine, you'd never forget her. She's a character,' said Zack.

'So was the one I knew. Quite a girl. She once danced with a skeleton at our May Ball.'

Ellie and Zack exchanged a look. Ellie said, 'Our Geraldine's a doctor.'

Switching from fond reminiscence to dawning realisation, Paul put down his wine glass. 'So am I.'

There was a tiny pause. Could it really be the same Geraldine? Ellie said, 'Where did you study medicine?'

'Edinburgh.'

'That's it,' Ellie nodded. 'Edinburgh's where she trained. She told me once about a crowd of them having a wheelbarrow race down Princes Street. In real wheelbarrows.'

'Did she mention she was wearing a bikini top and hula skirt while she was doing it?' Paul was shaking his head in disbelief. 'This is amazing. I was there. We'd been to a fancy-dress party. It was midnight, there were roadworks going on and the wheelbarrows had been left out, so we decided to put them to good use . . .'

'You and Geraldine! Oh wow! Were you two a couple?'

'No, no, nothing like that. I had a girlfriend. Geraldine had a boyfriend. Although I must admit, I did have a secret crush on her. She was a stun-ning-looking girl back then.'

Ellie couldn't tear her eyes off him; his hair might be streaked with silver now, his eyes crinkled and his jaw line less than chiselled, but she wouldn't mind betting that in his day he'd been a bit of a looker.

Hastily Paul added, 'Don't tell her I said that!'

'We have to call her,' said Ellie. 'This is brilliant.'

'No . . .' He looked panicked.

But Zack already had his phone out. 'We must.' He pressed a few buttons and waited. 'Hi, Geraldine? Yes, Elmo's fine. No, nothing's wrong, it's all good. Listen, about the time you got yourself carted along Princes Street in a wheelbarrow.' He hit the hands-free button just in time to catch Geraldine's parrot-like squawk of recognition.

'Oh my God, how did you find out about that? I don't believe it!'

'And what was it you were wearing? Not very much, by all accounts.'

'A lei, a red bikini and a grass skirt. Which in Edinburgh, let me tell you, is pretty intrepid. I can't imagine how you've got to hear about it.'

'We're here with someone who knew you back then.' Zack's dark eyes glittered with amusement. 'His name's Paul.'

'Paul Fletcher.' Mortified, Paul clearly didn't expect her to remember him by his first name alone.

'Oh my giddy aunt, Paul *Fletcher*? Are you serious? He never knew this, but I had such a crush on that boy! We used to call him the Greek God,' Geraldine exclaimed. 'He was just *beautiful*.'

They all watched a sixty-something doctor blush deeply. Zack switched off hands-free and carried on listening. Finally he said, 'No, no, of course I won't tell him you said that. Hang on, let me just go and find him, I'll pass you over and the two of you can have a chat.'

He covered the phone. Everyone round the table was agog. Paul was visibly trembling. 'I can't do this. She thinks I'm a Greek God.'

'It isn't Skype.' Ellie gave his arm a comforting pat. 'She can't see you. Anyway, you're still quite handsome.' *Ach, wrong thing to say.*

'Thanks.' Paul's smile was wry.

'And Geraldine's wheelbarrow-racing days are long gone,' Zack chimed in. 'She's currently getting over a fractured hip.' He uncovered the phone and handed it over. 'Here you go.'

Paul took it and pushed back his chair. 'I can't talk to her with you lot listening. You have no idea what this is doing to me. It's like asking me to talk to Barbra Streisand.'

He left them, weaving his way between the tables and heading out into the garden before raising the phone to his ear.

Twenty minutes later, Paul's main course had grown cold on his plate and everyone else had demolished theirs. Strawberry pavlovas arrived. The talk round the table was lively and punctuated with laughter.

Finally, over forty minutes later and just as the speeches were about to start, he reappeared. Trying hard not to look like the cat that got the cream, the prawns and the Loch Fyne salmon.

'Well.' He shook his head and sat down.

'Couldn't think of anything to say?' Zack offered him a top-up of wine.

'No thanks, I mean, yes.' In a daze, Paul covered his glass. 'No wine. That was amazing. What a woman . . . yes, thanks, take it away.' He waved at his untouched plate and flashed a distracted smile at the waitress. 'Sorry, I'm sure it was delicious. Wow, who'd have thought something like this could happen out of nowhere? We couldn't *stop* talking. No, not for me.' Now the waitress was attempting to refill his wine glass. 'Just water, thanks. She's staying in Exeter, did you know that?'

'Yes,' Ellie said. 'Her sister has a bungalow not far from the university.'

'It's only seventy miles from here. Geraldine's invited me to stay.' He was checking his watch. 'I can be there in an hour.'

'You're leaving *now*?'

'I'm fine to drive. I've only had half a glass of wine. Gareth won't mind if I leave early. God, just hearing her voice again was incredible.' His hand went up to smooth his silver-streaked hair. 'Do I look OK?'

He was dazed, happy, as besotted as a teenager.

'You look great.' Ellie smiled.

At the top table, the best man rose to his feet and dinged a glass with a spoon to attract everyone's attention.

'Speeches,' said Paul. 'I'll wait until they're over.' He sounded as if he'd like them to be over in the next five minutes. 'Then I'll head off.'

He was as good as his word. Half an hour later, when the speeches had been concluded and the dancing was about to begin again in earnest, he made his excuses to Gareth and Steph. Finally, he shook Zack's hand and kissed Ellie on the cheek.

'Am I glad they put me on your table!'

'Drive carefully.' She hugged him in return. How amazing that he was doing this.

'I will.'

When he'd left the marquee, one of Steph's friends on the other side of the table said, 'Wow, old people don't hang about, do they!'

Tara, next to her, said, 'They can't afford to. Why waste time when you might be about to die?' She turned to Zack. 'You'll have to tell us what happens. We need to know if there's a happy ending.'

'We will.' Zack rested his arm across the back of Ellie's chair and tilted his head. 'Well? Are we getting out onto that dance floor now?'

'Oh yes, we definitely are.' But Ellie needed the loo. She pushed back her chair and said, 'Just give me two minutes.'

Outside the marquee, the trees glittered with fairy lights and the air was fresh and cool. Ellie made her way across to the house. The downstairs cloakroom was occupied so she waited in the hallway for it to become free. There were people chatting in the kitchen. Idly half-listening, she recognised Mya's voice, then realised they were discussing her.

'I mean, she's nice. I really like her. But the twins told me they're sleeping in separate rooms! Now, is it just me or is that weird?'

'Her husband died, though.' Ellie didn't recognise the second voice and the door was only slightly ajar; another of Steph's girlfriends, presumably. 'Maybe it's something to do with that.'

'Yes, except I've been watching them. They *look* like they're crazy about each other,' said Mya, 'but he hasn't actually kissed her. Not once, not on the lips. And you have to admit, that is *seriously* weird.'

The cloakroom door was unlocked and Gareth's mother emerged. She smiled at Ellie.

A minute later, Ellie pulled the flush and washed her hands. It was a beautiful cloakroom, spacious and decorated in silver and white, with a Venetian mirror above the sink.

And Jamie, reflected in the mirror, wearing his pale grey polo shirt and pink board shorts.

Ellie wasn't surprised to see him. She'd made him appear. Jamie was her conjured-up creation, from his messy sea-salted hair all the way down to the skinny legs and the dusting of sand on his tanned bare feet.

'Now listen, what do you think? Should I kiss Zack or shouldn't I?'

'Do you want to?' he asked.

'Of course I want to! I'm just worried I might not be able to stop! What if it turns into a cartoon and my mouth won't let go and he has to wrench me off his face like a sink plunger?'

Jamie looked thoughtful. 'Do you want me to come with you?'

'No!' She definitely wasn't having that.

'So what's brought this on, all of a sudden?'

Ellie exhaled. 'Paul and Geraldine. He isn't wasting time because they're in their sixties and who knows how long they have left? But look at us.' She could feel her heart thudding away like a bass speaker. 'How long do any of us have left? I could die tomorrow. So that's it, I'm just going to go ahead. If it all goes horribly wrong, you can have a good laugh about it later.'

'Hey, remember how we met?'

He was giving her a playful look. Of course Ellie remembered; how could she forget? They'd each been with their own group of friends at a club in Piccadilly. Having spotted her looking at Jamie, her friend Lisa had given her a nudge and said, 'Dare you to go over there and kiss him without saying a word. If he tries to talk to you, pretend not to speak any English.' So she had.

The kiss had been amazing. Afterwards, she had talked gobbledegook. 'Ke, mi andzengo. Vamejski.'

'Vamejskiola!' Without missing a beat, Jamie had broken into a grin and lightly touched her cheek. 'Laksadi ja, pelodria. Tibo!'

And that had been it; in those few miraculous seconds they'd both known this was it; they were in it for the long haul. It had been that instantaneous. *Till death us do part.*

But that was then. She was a different person these days.

'Sweetheart, go for it.' Jamie was remembering that night too; she could tell by the smile on his face. 'It worked wonders for me.'

Ellie wished she could reach out and touch him. 'I know we don't do this as much as we used to. But I do still miss you.'

'Hey, no need to feel guilty. I'll always be here if you need me.' His expression softened. 'Five, ten, twenty years from now . . . it doesn't matter. Well, except for one thing.'

'Which is?'

The irreverent grin was back. Jamie said, 'You're going to get old and wrinkly, sweetheart. But I'm always going to look this good.'

Plans, however, didn't always work out. By the time Ellie returned to the marquee, another female had taken advantage of her absence and dragged Zack onto the dance floor. So much for the sisterhood.

She sat down and poured herself more wine. Then she watched as Zack laughed and joked with her rival. And her heart did that crumpled little squeeze of love because really, was there anything more irresistible than a man not caring that he was making a complete fool of himself in front of everyone, because it was making his current dance partner happy and that was all that mattered?

Zack and Lily were giving it everything they had, dancing like maniacs to 'All the Single Ladies'. Joss barrelled across the dance floor and joined in. There was Beyoncé-style foot-stamping, hip-wiggling, hand-clapping and head-shaking. Attitude was the key. Then the song ended, everyone applauded and Zack scooped up a twin in each arm. He pretended to stagger with exhaustion. The DJ, taking pity on him, began to play something slow. And Zack, looking across the room to see if she was back from the loo, saw her at the table and broke into a smile.

Oh heavens, and now here he was, standing in front of her, holding out a hand. 'Our turn now. Sorry about that. I was kidnapped.'

'I noticed. Don't worry, we filmed it. You'll be on YouTube by midnight.'

They reached the dance floor and Zack drew her into his arms. *Heaven.* They began to move slowly along with the music. *More heaven.* Ellie took a breath and said, 'There's something we're going to have to do.'

'What's that?'

She loved him. Everything she was feeling now, this was it, this was love. 'I overheard Mya in the kitchen. She's suspicious.'

'Why?' His eyes. The way he looked down at her. His hands, one resting on her waist, the other in the small of her back.

'She's been watching us. Paying attention. We haven't kissed.' *There, I said it.* Ellie gazed steadily up at him. 'I think we need to.'

'You do?' His expression was unreadable but she felt the tension in his shoulders. Oh God, was he horribly shocked?

'Nothing too major. Just . . . you know, a little one.' She no longer trusted herself; any more than a peck might be too much to handle.

'A little one. You mean . . . right here, right now?'

'Might be best. So we get it over and done with.' Her heart felt as if it were about to explode out of her chest; no way was she backing down now. 'Sorry, but we should. Look, Steph and Gareth are doing it.'

'I don't know . . .' He was prevaricating, about to say no.

'Don't be such a baby. It's only a kiss, it'll be over in two seconds.' Ellie reached up a hand and curled it round the back of his head. Detecting resistance, she murmured, 'Just *pretend*, OK?' and lifted herself up on tiptoe, her face tilted up to his. Her mouth brushed his mouth, a shot of electricity zipped through her body and her lips parted . . .

Oh God, was this what heaven felt like? Their mouths were a perfect fit, too much adrenalin was making her dizzy and what she'd feared might happen was indeed happening, because now she'd started, there was no way in the world she could stop. But somehow it no longer seemed to matter, because Zack didn't appear to want it to end either. He'd evidently decided not to put up a fight and was going along with the game instead. His left hand was in her hair, his right hand in the small of her back and their bodies were pressed together . . . oh wow, this was everything she'd dreamed of happening and more . . . except they were still standing in the middle of the dance floor.

'OK, we're on show.' Tearing himself away, practically causing her to let out a whimper of desolation, Zack seized her hand and propelled her towards the exit. Were people looking at them? Yes they were. Was she managing to walk more or less normally? Well, kind of. Was Mya there? Yes she was, on the far edge of the dance floor, watching them with a glimmer of disappointment . . .

Once they were outside he led her round to the back of the house until they were out of sight of everyone. And then they were kissing again . . . and Ellie was so on fire with longing for more she couldn't even begin to imagine what it meant. Except, unbelievably, Zack appeared to be feeling it as intensely as she was. His breathing was uneven, his hands were cupping her face—oh heavens, he was a sensational kisser—and it was carrying on and on, even though there were no longer any suspicious ex-girlfriends around to see them.

Which *might* mean . . . No, she couldn't let herself think it.

Zack drew back at last and surveyed her. It was dark, but not so dark she couldn't see his face.

'Well?' he said. 'How was that?'

Talk about a loaded question. Was she panting? 'It was . . . good.'

'I suppose that's better than bad.'

She could barely swallow. 'I don't know what to say.'

'Why not?' There was a glint in his eye, a definite hint of a smile. 'You started it.'

'I wasn't expecting you to join in.'

'Was it just for Mya's benefit?'

'Slightly. She wasn't the whole reason.' OK, just plunge in. 'I wanted to do it.' Ellie paused, still struggling to catch her breath. 'Am I going to get sacked now, for impertinence and sexual harassment?'

'You have no idea,' Zack shook his head, '*no* idea how long I've wanted this to happen.'

Was he serious? 'You haven't.'

'Oh yes I have.'

'Really? You can't have.'

'Why not?'

'Because you wanted a PA who *wasn't* going to get all doofy over you. A proper professional working partnership. No shenanigans.'

'True, that is what I wanted.' Zack conceded this point. 'Until you came along and completely got to me.' He paused. '*Doofy?*'

'It just came out. Sometimes only a made-up word will do.'

Her brain had been attacked by egg beaters; it was a wonder she could speak at all. She clung to him in disbelief. 'Did I really? Get to you?'

'Oh yes. And that was before you ever saw me. The time you met Tony for lunch at the Ivy, remember?' Zack's dark eyes glittered in the dim light. 'You passed me in the street in your pink coat and I just felt something here.' He pressed his hand to his chest. 'Nothing else like it has ever happened to me before. But that day it did.'

Ellie was trembling. 'You never said. You never gave any kind of hint.'

'You weren't ready.' He touched her face. 'Not for anyone. Which was fine, I was prepared to wait. Then the Todd thing happened. And that took some coming to terms with. Then you and Todd broke up—'

'But I was too ashamed to tell you. I felt such a failure.'

'And then along came Joe.' One eyebrow lifted. 'I couldn't *believe* I'd missed my chance again.'

'And all this time I've been desperately trying to hide how *I* was feeling. I thought you'd be horrified.'

'I haven't been able to stop thinking about you. One way or another you were always out of reach.' He pulled her closer and she felt the heat from his chest. 'I think I'm in love with you.'

Was this a dream? 'Really?'

'Actually no, that's not true. I know I am.'

Ellie's head was in a spin. She'd tried her hardest but things hadn't been remotely right between her and Todd. Then Joe had come along and they'd been better, although nowhere near good enough. And now this. You could never know for sure, but this just might be . . . perfect.

Ellie gave herself up to yet another sublime kiss. Zack really was very good at it. The next moment they belatedly sprang apart at the sound of footsteps on the flagstoned path.

'Whoops, sorry . . .' Having left the house, Tizz was making her way back to the marquee. She stopped and beamed at them. 'Well now, don't you two look happy!'

Zack looked at Ellie. Ellie looked at Zack, struggling to keep a straight face. The silence lengthened. Mystified, Tizz said, 'Come on then, spill the beans! What's up?'

'OK, let me tell her. I told you a bit of a white lie before. Ellie and I weren't actually together before today.' Zack's arm slid round Ellie's waist. 'But we are now.'

'You weren't? You are? Well, that's marvellous news! But you should have asked me if you were perfect for each other.' His mother's eyes danced. 'I could have told you that.' A thought occurred to her. 'Ha, so *that's* why you asked for separate rooms!'

'Sorry.' Ellie grinned. 'And you thought I was playing hard to get.'

'Oh my darling girl, don't apologise, that just makes me love you more. Come along then, let's get back to this party!'

That was it then, so much for sloping off. There was to be no early escape. Tizz was insistent and, as it turned out, it didn't matter a bit. If anything, it only served to heighten the delicious anticipation. For the next three hours Ellie and Zack danced and celebrated and socialised with friends and family, all the while enjoying the sizzle of sexual tension that had existed between them for so long but which had only now, at long last, been acknowledged.

Finally, just as she was beginning to wonder how much longer she could hold out, Zack murmured in her ear, 'OK, we have to go now. This has been great, but I'm only human.'

Hooray!

Hand in hand, they slipped discreetly away, out of the marquee and back to the house. In through the creaking back door, across the deserted hall and up the curved staircase.

'People are going to wonder where we've got to.' Ellie pushed open the door to her bedroom.

'They won't notice we're gone,' said Zack as the thud-thud-thud of the music continued to reverberate round them. 'They're having fun without us.'

'I think we might have more fun without them.' Whether or not this worked out, Ellie knew she would never regret it. Sometimes you just had to take the risk. Maybe it would be a brief but wonderful romance, maybe it would last a lifetime. She reached for Zack and kicked the door shut behind her. At that moment the music faded out and they heard the DJ say, 'OK, Eminem next, the clean version. Now this one was requested by

Ellie and I can't see her on the dance floor. Come on, Ellie, get yourself over here, where are you?'

'Oops.' Ellie pulled a face. 'I forgot about that. Should we go back?'

Through the loudspeakers the DJ bellowed, 'And Zack? No sign of you either. Give us a shout, mate—we're all waiting for you!'

'Oh God.' Zack tightened his hold on her and smiled ruefully. 'We're not going.'

'Good,' said Ellie.

Over in the marquee, meanwhile, the realisation that they had both vanished from the party was giving rise to laughter and bawdy cheers.

'No? No sign of either of 'em? Honestly, this is a shocking state of affairs,' said the DJ. 'Sloping off for an early night, what's wrong with these people? Right then, if they're not here to appreciate my efforts, I'm not playing Eminem. We'll have more Status Quo instead!'

Epilogue

Eleven months later

Ellie leaned out of the second-floor window and watched the goings-on below. There was Todd, playing football with an apple, dribbling it past Zack's nephews as he zigzagged across the manicured lawn and through the croquet hoops. There were Tizz and Ken, chatting with Paul and Geraldine while they admired the flowers in the borders. And over there was Steph, kneeling to retie the bows on Lily's shoes. No flashing trainers this time. Lily had chosen them herself. These were bright green with sequinned butterflies on them; she was currently going through a sparkly stage that had Joss curling her lip in disbelief.

To think that it had been almost a year since Steph and Gareth's wedding. And now she was having her own. How life had changed in the past eleven months.

Her mobile phone rang and Ellie glanced at it before answering. 'You're five minutes away? Great. Yes, everything's fine. See you soon.'

It had been Zack's idea to hold the wedding here, at Colworth Manor Hotel where they had spent such an idyllic weekend last November. That had been shortly after he'd sought suggestions for a romantic proposal from Roo, and she had excitedly exclaimed that he must drop the diamond engagement ring into a glass of champagne. She'd seen it done in a film and it had been so romantic she'd cried buckets.

Ellie's eyes danced at the memory. Zack had nearly cried too, when she'd taken a big swig and almost swallowed the ring.

But the sentiment had been there. It was the thought that counted, and the three dazzling diamonds had glittered proudly on her finger ever since. She knew without a doubt that Zack was the right man for her; in fact, more than that, he was perfect. They were as besotted with each other now as they had been on that first night. These days they laughed, loved and argued with each other and every day together was a joy. The desolate pain she'd experienced following Jamie's death had lessened and shrunk more than she'd ever imagined possible.

Nor did she see so much of Jamie now, either. The need was no longer there. Occasionally Ellie conjured him up for a couple of seconds, just to touch base and say hi, but their long conversations were now a thing of the past. It was enough to know that Jamie approved of Zack and the next step she was about to take.

Ellie gazed at herself in the elaborate full-length mirror. Oh my word, would you look at that, she was like an actual proper bride! Her hair was up, but in a tousled rather than a superglued way. Her dress was ivory silk, bias cut and full length. All in all, if she did say so herself, she was looking pretty good.

'Just as well,' said Jamie, appearing in the mirror behind her. 'Otherwise Zack might run a mile, and that would just be embarrassing.'

Ellie smiled. It seemed only fair to have him drop by, today of all days.

'So?' She held up her hands, did a pose. 'Will I do?'

'You look fantastic. I'm so proud of you.'

'Thanks.' She wasn't going to cry, not today. 'I do still love you.' She needed to say it, to make sure he understood. 'Just because I'm getting married again doesn't mean I'll ever forget you.'

'I know. But you've got Zack now.' He looked thoughtful. 'The only thing I'm not too happy about is his legs. They're not as skinny as mine.'

'I know. But his knees are knobbly. So that makes you even.'

'Glad to hear it. OK, I'm going to go now. Be happy, sweetheart.'

OK, maybe just the one tear. 'Thanks. Bye.'

Ellie carefully blotted her eyes with a tissue. When she looked up again, Jamie had gone.

Moments later there was a knock at the door. She called out, 'Come in,' and Tony appeared.

They hugged each other, hard.

Tony drew back finally and surveyed her with pride. 'Oh sweetheart. I miss my boy so much. And I never thought I'd be saying this, but today is going to be a very good day. It's going to be . . . splendid.'

Moved, Ellie straightened his pale grey tie. Tony was smartly dressed, but the last year had taken its toll on him. There was a lot more silver in his hair now. The lines on his face were more pronounced. He put on a brave front but she knew he'd been working hard on various projects in order to take his mind off the emptiness in his own life. He'd kept the Nevis Street flat on after she'd moved in with Zack, but these days it was a seldom-used pied-à-terre with most of his work concentrated in the States. Ellie was fairly certain she knew why. He had learned of Henry's death through the internet but had respected Martha's wishes not to resume contact. No one knew better than Tony the power of grief.

'It will be.' She brushed a fleck of lint from the shoulder of his morning suit. 'You're looking very handsome.'

'Flatterer.' Ever the actor, he was adept at hiding his loneliness beneath that ready, charismatic smile. Glancing out of the window, he said, 'By the way, should pregnant women run around like lunatics?'

He was referring to Roo, her topaz-yellow dress plastered to her impressive seven-month bump as she raced barefoot across the lawn with Lily, Joss and Elmo in hot pursuit. With her shoes in one hand and Elmo's favourite new squeaky toy in the other, she was squeaking it wildly, sending Elmo into a frenzy of excitement.

'Roo's fine. It's good exercise.' She turned away from the window to face Tony again. 'Now listen, can you do me a huge favour?'

His expression softened. 'Anything.'

'Everyone here knows pretty much everyone else. But I've invited a friend along who doesn't know anyone at all.' Ellie pulled a face. 'Which means she's going to feel a bit on her own. I was hoping you could kind of look after her. Would that be OK?'

'Oh God, do I have to?' Evidently not enthralled, Tony hesitated for only a split second before good manners took over. 'Sorry, that's fine, of course I will. Is it someone you used to work with?'

Ellie checked her watch. 'Come on, she'll be waiting downstairs. Let's go and find her, and I'll introduce you.'

Together they made their way down the impressive staircase. In twenty minutes the wedding was scheduled to begin. Tony would escort her into the drawing room where the ceremony was being held, and give her away. But before that happened, there was one other small thing she had to do. One other small *exciting* thing, hopefully.

She led Tony through the door on the left, and there was Martha waiting for them, thinner but still beautiful, wearing a flowing purple dress and jacket and nervously clutching a tray-sized gift bag.

Tony stopped dead when he saw her. Ellie let go of his arm and moved discreetly to one side. Martha did her level best to smile over at her but her attention was being dragged towards Tony.

'Martha . . . my God, you're *here*.'

'Ellie invited me. We've been talking things through.' The lilt and the warmth in her voice was unchanged. 'She made me see that it was OK. I couldn't have done it before. Now I can. It's been a nightmare year.' Martha paused, her smile hesitant. 'But I'm on the mend.'

Tony took a step towards her. 'I can't believe this is happening.'

'She was worried you might have moved on,' Ellie put in helpfully. 'Met someone else.'

'No. Never.' He shook his head. 'I'm so sorry about Henry.'

'Thank you.'

'And Eunice? Is she well?'

'Very well. She's living in Carlisle now, close to her daughter.' The twinkle in her eye signalled that whether Eunice's daughter was thrilled with this development was debatable. The next moment, remembering the gift bag in her hand, Martha held it out to Ellie and said, 'Sorry, this is for you.'

'That's so kind. You didn't have to.' They exchanged a hug.

'Oh darling, I'm just glad I was able to.'

'Right, I'll leave you in peace for five minutes.' Ellie pointed to Tony. 'Then you have a bride to give away.'

The expression on his face told Ellie she'd done the right thing. 'Thank you.'

'You're sure you don't mind looking after her?'

Tony squeezed her hand. 'I'll give it my very best shot.'

Ellie closed the door behind her. Out in the hallway, she lifted the painting out of the gift bag. There it was, a sunny summer's day in Little Venice. Martha had returned to the exact spot where they'd first met, in order to demonstrate that her ability to paint had returned. Along with her enthusiasm for life.

The next moment another door opened and she heard Zack's voice a split second before he emerged from the drawing room.

'Close your eyes,' Ellie blurted out.

Zack appeared, dark hair slicked back. His eyes were closed.

'It's unlucky to see the bride before the wedding,' Ellie reminded him.

'So move away,' said Zack. 'You'll have to, I can't see where I'm going.'

Well, sometimes a situation arose that was just too good to pass up. Crossing the hallway, Ellie planted a kiss on his unsuspecting mouth.

'How do I know it's you?' He kept his eyes closed. 'It could be anyone.'

'It's me.'

'I'm not sure I believe you.' The beautiful mouth was twitching.

'Put it this way.' She pinched his bottom. 'It had better be me.'

Zack touched her face, exploring the various curves and angles, before kissing her again. 'OK, it's you. I recognise you now.' He broke into a slow smile. 'Ellie Kendall, you have no idea how much I love you. Will you marry me?'

Was it possible to feel happier than this? 'Play your cards right,' she ran a playful finger down the front of his waistcoat, 'and I just might.'

Jill Mansell

How did the idea for *To the Moon and Back* develop?

I was drawn to the idea of someone who is dead appearing as a character in the book. Like Patrick Swayze in the film *Ghost*, except I didn't feel I could suddenly write a ghost story after so many 'non-ghostly' novels—readers might have found that hard to cope with. So Jamie isn't a ghost, he's just mentally conjured up by Ellie when she needs to talk to him. And he talks back. He's actually one of my all-time favourite characters.

And how did you come up with the title for the novel?

My son thought of it! When he was younger we used to say, 'I love you to the moon and back,' to each other. Now that he's a teenager it no longer happens, obviously, but when I was desperate for title ideas he said he thought it would make a great title for a book and he was absolutely right.

Elmo is adorable. Where did the idea for a time-share dog come from?

A friend of mine had one. She worked long hours and couldn't have a dog of her own, so she shared one with another friend. The dog loved having two mums and got the best of both worlds out of the deal. I'd quite like a time-share dog myself, but I'm so easily distracted when I'm meant to be writing that I can see me not getting any work done at all if I have a dog to entertain me.

Did you model Zack on anyone? How do you get inside the male brain?

That's one of those questions I don't know how to answer, because getting into my characters' heads isn't something I ever try to do. It just happens.

Zack falls instantly for Ellie. Do you believe in love at first sight?

Yes, I really do. Whether or not it lasts is another matter, but instant reactions are pretty powerful. It's happened to so many people and I love it when it does.

And lost loves? Do you think you can rekindle the flame after many years, as Geraldine and Paul do?

Again, definitely. Look at all the relationships that have been renewed on Facebook. And there's nothing I love more than newspaper stories about people separated during World War Two, who find each other and fall in love all over again sixty years later.

So you are a true romantic. What's the most romantic thing that has ever happened to you?

Ha-ha-ha, I can't think of an answer to this one, although when I was in hospital after having given birth to my children, the hospital food was pretty dire, so my partner, Cino, used to cook my favourite meals and bring them in for me. That was lovely!

Do you still write while watching daytime television?

Of course!

What's your favourite programme?

This Morning with Phillip Schofield and Holly Willoughby. I love it. And it gives me ideas for my books.

Do you still write in longhand or have you moved to computer/iPad?

I still write my books in longhand, but I do now have an iPad.

What do you use your iPad for?

Emails and Twitter mostly.

Favourite Apps?

iBooks and iPlayer. Google Earth with Street View. Ooh, and Art Authority, which is amazing, like carrying the world's biggest art gallery around in your handbag.

You're a big Twitterer. Describe yourself in a Tweet.

Snacks a lot, wears too much glittery stuff, owns far too many lipsticks.

What's been your most recent indulgent purchase?

A new car, but only because the gearbox was about to explode on the old one!

And the best piece of advice you've ever been given?

'You know what, Jill? You should think about trying to write a book . . .'

Do you have any burning ambitions that you still have to fulfil?

I'd love one of my books to be made into a film. But a really good film, not a rubbish one. A romantic comedy classic—that would be nice.

Daughters-in-Law
Joanna Trollope

Rachel has always loved being at the centre of her large family. She has devoted herself to her three sons all their lives, and continues to do so even now they are grown up.

But when the three of them marry, Rachel discovers that her daughters-in-law want to establish their own family traditions and to do things their own way, and so, to her grief, do her sons . . .

CHAPTER ONE

FROM THE FRONT PEW, Anthony had an uninterrupted view of the back of the girl who was about to become his third daughter-in-law. The church had a wide aisle, and a broad carpeted space below the shallow chancel steps, where the four little bridesmaids had plopped themselves down in the pink silk nests of their skirts during the address, so that there was a clear line of sight between Anthony and the bridal pair.

The bride, tightly swathed in ivory satin, seemed to Anthony to have the seductively imprisoned air of a landlocked mermaid. Her dress fitted closely—very closely—from below her shoulders to her knees and then fanned out into soft folds, and a fluid little train, which spilled carelessly down the chancel steps behind her. Anthony's gaze travelled slowly from the crown of her pale, cropped head, veiled in gauze and scattered with flowers, down to her invisible feet, and then back up again to rest on the unquestionably satisfactory curves of her waist and hips. She has, Anthony thought, a gorgeous figure, even if it is improper for her almost-father-in-law to think such a thing. *Gorgeous*.

He swallowed, and transferred his gaze sternly to his son. Luke, exuding that raw and possessive male pride that gives wedding days such an edge, was half turned towards his bride. There had been a touching moment five minutes before, when Charlotte's widowed mother had reached up to fold her daughter's veil back from her face and the two had regarded each other for several seconds with an intensity of understanding that excluded everyone else around them. Anthony had glanced down at Rachel beside him and wondered whether her composure hid some instinctive yearning she would never give voice to, and how her primitive and unavoidable reaction to yielding a third son to another woman would manifest itself in the coming months and years.

'OK?' he said softly.

Rachel took no notice. He couldn't even tell if she was actually looking at Charlotte, or whether it was Luke she was concentrating on, admiring the breadth of his shoulders and the clearness of his skin, and asking herself, at some deep level, if Charlotte really, *really* knew what an extravagantly fortunate girl she was. Instead of a conventional hat, Rachel had pinned a small explosion of green feathers to her hair, and the trembling of the feathers, like dragonflies on wires, seemed to Anthony the only indication that Rachel's inner self was not as unruffled as her outer one.

Anthony looked up at the roof. How lovely it would have been if Luke could have been married, as his elder brother Ralph had been, in the church at home, and not in this cosily domesticated bit of Buckinghamshire with no marshes, no wading birds or reed beds or vast, cloud-piled skies. How lovely it would be if they were all in Suffolk, *now*.

The church at home would, of course, have been perfect. Anthony had no orthodox faith, but he liked the look and feel of churches, the dignities and absurdities of ritual, the shy belonging of English Anglican congregations. He had known his own village church all his life; it was wide and light and welcoming, with clear-glass windows and a marvellous, small, modern bronze sculpture of Noah releasing the dove, to commemorate the first performance there of Benjamin Britten's church opera, *Noye's Fludde*. That had been in 1958, when Anthony was eleven. He had heard all the church operas there, sitting through them dressed in his school grey-flannel shorts and a tie. It was where he had first heard *Curlew River*, which remained his favourite, long before he had dared to put drawing at the heart of his life, long before birds became a passion.

They had all been christened there, Edward and Ralph and Luke. Anthony might have preferred some simple humanist naming ceremony, but Rachel had wanted them christened in the church.

'They don't have to stay Christian,' she'd said to Anthony, 'but at least they have the option. It's what you had, after all.'

The christenings had been lovely, of course, and moving, and Anthony's sense of profound association with the church building had grown deeper with each one. In fact, so intense was his assumption that that was where the boys would marry—when, if, they married—that he was startled when his eldest, Edward, appeared with an elegant and determined young Swede, and announced that they were to be married, and, naturally, from her home, not his.

His fiancée, a laboratory researcher into the analysis of materials for museums and galleries, had been well briefed. She drew Anthony aside, and fixed her astonishing, light blue gaze on him.

'You needn't worry,' Sigrid had said in her perfect English, 'it will be a humanist ceremony. You will feel quite at home.'

The wedding of Edward and Sigrid had taken place at her parents' summer house, on some little low, anonymous island in the archipelago outside Stockholm, and they had eaten crayfish afterwards, wearing huge paper bibs, mountains and mountains of crayfish, and aquavit had flowed like a fatal river, and it never got dark.

The morning after the wedding Sigrid had appeared, packet-fresh in white and grey, with her smooth hair in a ponytail, and taken Ed away in a boat, not to return. Anthony and Rachel were left marooned among Sigrid's family and friends under a cloudless sky and entirely surrounded by water.

On the flight home Rachel had said, looking away from him out of the window, 'Some situations are just too foreign to react to, aren't they?'

And a bit later when Anthony said, 'Do you think they are actually married?' she'd stared right at him and said, 'I have no idea.'

Well, that was over eleven years ago now, almost twelve. And there, on the carpet below the chancel steps, sat Mariella, Edward and Sigrid's eight-year-old daughter. She was sitting very still and upright, her ballet-slippered feet tucked under her pink skirts, her hair held off her face by an Alice band of rosebuds. Anthony tried to catch her eye. His only granddaughter. His grave, self-possessed granddaughter. Who spoke English and Swedish and played the cello. By the merest movement of her head, Mariella indicated that she was aware of him, but she wouldn't look his way. Her job that day, her mother had said, was to set a good example to the other little bridesmaids, all Charlotte's nieces, and Mariella's life was largely dedicated to securing her mother's good opinion.

'I'm delighted to announce,' the priest said, removing the stole that he'd wrapped around Luke's and Charlotte's linked, newly ringed hands, 'that Luke and Charlotte are now husband and wife!'

Luke leaned to kiss his wife on the cheek, and she put her arms around his neck, and then he flung his own arms around her and kissed her with fervour, and the church erupted into applause. Mariella got to her feet and shook out her skirts, glancing at her mother for the next cue.

'In pairs,' Anthony saw Sigrid mouth to the little girls. 'Two by two.'

Charlotte was laughing. Luke was laughing. Some of Luke's friends, further down the church, were whooping.

Anthony took Rachel's hand. 'Another daughter-in-law—'

'I know.'

'Well,' Anthony said, 'if she's only half as good as Petra—'

Rachel sighed. 'If.'

The reception was held in a marquee in the garden of Charlotte's childhood home. It was a dry day, but overcast, and the marquee was filled with a queer, greenish light that made everyone look ill. Through an opening at the lower end of the marquee, the immediate bridal party could be seen picturesquely on the edge of a large pond, being ordered about by a photographer.

Oh God, water, Petra thought. Barney, who was still not walking, was safely strapped into his pushchair with the distraction of a miniature box of raisins, but Kit, at three, was mobile and had been irresistibly drawn to water all his life. Neither child, in the unfamiliarity of a hotel room the previous night, had slept more than fitfully, so neither Petra nor Ralph had slept either. Ralph had finally got up at five in the morning and gone for a long walk. And now, uncharacteristically, he had joined a roaring group of Luke's friends, and he was drinking champagne, and smoking, despite the fact that he had given up cigarettes when Petra was pregnant with Kit and, as far as she knew, hadn't smoked since then.

Kit was whining. He was exhausted and hungry and intractable. Keeping up a low, uneven grizzle, he wound himself round and round in Petra's skirt, shoving against her thighs, dishevelled and beyond being reasoned with. He had started the day in the white linen shirt and dark-blue trousers that Charlotte had requested, even though she considered him too young to be a page, but both had become so filthy and crumpled in church that he was back in the Spider-Man T-shirt he insisted on wearing whenever it wasn't actually in the washing machine. She put a hand on his head. He felt hot and damp and unhappy. Intensely aggravating though he was being, he was to be pitied. He was her sweet, sensitive, imaginative little boy, and he had been plucked out of the familiarity that he relied upon, on an entirely and exclusively adult whim, and dumped down in an artificial and alien environment.

'Petra,' Anthony said.

Petra turned with relief. 'Oh, Ant—'

Anthony gave her shoulder a pat, and then squatted down beside Kit. 'Poor old boy.'

Kit adored his grandfather, but he couldn't give up his misery all of a sudden. He thrust his lower lip out.

Anthony said, 'Might you manage a strawberry?'

Kit shook his head and plunged his face between Petra's legs.

'Where's Ralph?'

'Somewhere,' Petra said.

Anthony regarded her. 'It's not much fun for you, all this. It is—'

'Well,' Petra said, 'weddings aren't meant for people of three, or for people with people of three to look after.'

'Yours was.'

She glanced down at Kit. He was still now, breathing hotly into her skin through the fabric of her skirt. 'Ours was lovely.'

'It was.'

'Perfect day, walking back from the church to your garden, all the roses out, everybody's dogs and children—'

Anthony smiled at her. Then he said casually to Kit, 'Crisps?'

Kit stopped breathing.

'Maybe,' Anthony said, 'even Coca-Cola?'

'With a straw!' Kit shouted into Petra's skirt.

'If you like.'

'Thank you,' Petra said. 'Really, thank you.'

'I am sitting next to Charlotte's mother at whatever meal this is. Marnie's a noted plantswoman and amateur botanical artist so we are put together at all occasions. I shall fortify myself by feeding Kit the wrong things first.' He looked down. 'If you don't come with me, Kit, I shall choose your straw colour for you and I might choose yellow.'

'No!' Kit shouted. He flung himself away from his mother.

'You're a lifeline,' Petra said.

Anthony winked at her. 'You know what *you* are.'

She watched them walk away together, hand in hand. She looked down at the pushchair. Barney had finished the raisins and torn the box open so that he could lick traces of residual sweetness from the inside. He had brown smudges across his fat cheeks and on the end of his nose.

'Where,' Petra said to him, 'would we be without Granny and Gramps?'

It was amazing, Charlotte thought giddily, to be so violently happy. It was better than waterskiing, or dancing, or driving too fast, or even the moment just before someone you were dying to kiss you actually kissed you. It was amazing to feel so beautiful, and so wanted, and so full of hope, and so pleased to see everyone and so awed and triumphant to have someone like Luke as your husband. Husband! What an astonishing, grown-up, glamorous word. Hello, this is Mrs Brinkley speaking, Mrs Luke Brinkley. She looked down at her hand. Her wedding ring was brilliant with newness. The diamonds in her engagement ring were dazzling. The stones had come from an old brooch belonging to Luke's grand-mother, and they had designed the ring together. Luke had actually done most of the designing because he was the artistic one, coming as he did from an artistic family. Charlotte's mother was an artist too, of course, but of a very controlled kind. The table where she worked at her meticulous drawings of catkins and berries was completely orderly. It wasn't like Anthony's studio. Not at all.

Charlotte loved Anthony's studio. She thought, in time, that she might rather come to love Anthony himself—oh, and Rachel, of course—but at the moment, with her own father dead only two years, it seemed a bit disloyal to think of loving anyone else in the father category. But Anthony's studio, in that amazing, messy, colourful house, was a perfectly safe thing to love, with all its painting paraphernalia, and sketches and pictures pinned up all anyhow everywhere, and the photographs of birds and models of birds and sculptures of birds and skeletons of birds on every surface and hanging from the beams of the ceiling in a kind of birdy fly-past. She'd been there once when Anthony and Rachel were looking after their little grandson, Kit, the one who was so shy and difficult to engage with, and Anthony had taken down the skeleton of a godwit's wing from a dusty shelf, and drawn out the frail fan of bones so that Kit could see how beautifully it worked. Kit had been quite absorbed. So had Charlotte.

When she mentioned, at work, that she had met someone called

Anthony Brinkley, a boy looked up from the next desk in the newsroom and said, 'The Anthony Brinkley? The bird painter? My dad's mad on birds, he's got all his books.' And now here he was, her father-in-law. How amazing to have parents-in-law, and brothers- and sisters-in-law, and to be going to live with Luke in the flat he had found two minutes from Shoreditch High Street. How cool was that? How cool was it to be married, well before she was thirty, to someone like Luke, and to be so happy that she just wanted the day to go on for ever?

She caught Luke's eye across the heads of a group of people and he blew her a lingering kiss.

Quite soon, Charlotte thought, I'll be back in bed with him.

'**D**on't sit there,' Edward said to Sigrid, 'disapproving of English weddings.'

'I'm not disapproving—'

'Well,' Edward said, 'you look like someone enduring something that you know you could do much better.'

'I don't think,' Sigrid said, 'that we're being made to feel very welcome. Do you? This is all about the bride's family. If we were in Sweden, the groom's family would be made to feel part of the wedding. Remember ours.'

'Oh, I do—'

'Your parents were made to feel really welcome. My parents made a real fuss of them. So did their friends.'

Edward looked round. 'Where's Mariella?'

'Organising the little girls. She had them in an imaginary schoolroom just now, having a lesson on the weather. She has just done weather at school, you see.'

Edward was looking at a group of Luke's friends. 'Luke is only six years younger than I am, but that lot feels like a different generation.'

'They are single, mostly. Not married, anyway.'

Edward took a swallow of his champagne. It was warm now, and faintly sour. He said, casually, 'Do you like being married?'

'Mostly,' Sigrid said again.

'Your famous candour. I remember saying in my wedding speech that you were one of the most honest people I had ever met.'

'And?'

'And now I sometimes wish you would temper it slightly, even while I know I wouldn't believe you if you did.'

'I think,' Sigrid said, 'that our new sister-in-law looks quite stunning, but that she is very young for her age. How old is she? Twenty-six? Twenty-seven?'

'About that. She's certainly a looker. D'you know, Ralph's in that gang over there. What's he doing? He hates all that heavy lad-stuff.'

'Weddings make people behave very strangely.'

'You mean,' Edward said, 'English weddings.'

'I didn't say so.'

'But you liked Ralph's wedding—'

'That was charming,' Sigrid said. 'So simple. In your parents' garden and Petra taking her shoes off. Where is Petra?'

'Probably chasing her children.'

Sigrid stood up. 'I shall go and find her.'

'What shall I do?'

'Find your parents,' Sigrid said. 'See if your daughter has instructed those children properly about the effect of El Niño. Find out where we're sitting for the meal.'

'Salmon,' Edward said, 'and strawberries. Pink food. Wedding food.' He stood up, too. 'Dad's down there, by that pond thing. Kit's paddling.' He paused. 'Naked from the waist down.'

Rachel had her eye on Ralph. He looked awful. Well, not ugly; Ralph couldn't look actually ugly, but gaunt and tired with shadows round his eyes and his thick dark hair in tufts, as if he'd had a seriously bad haircut. Which he probably had, being, of all her boys, the least vain, the least worldly, the least concerned with appearances. He had never been easy to pigeonhole, never been orthodox, that was a great deal of his charm, but it was to be hoped—very much to be hoped—that he wasn't leading Petra too much of a dance by being too inaccessible and uncooperative.

When Ralph and Petra had told them that they would like to get married, she and Anthony had been overcome with relief as well as happiness. Petra was exactly what Ralph needed, they told each other; Petra would give Ralph the stability and purpose that he seemed to find so hard to achieve, while needing it so badly. And now, when Ralph looked as he did today, and left Petra to cope with the children on an occasion that plainly called for two parents, not one, Rachel felt clutches of the old intermingled anxiety and protectiveness that she'd felt since

Ralph emerged into the world and arched away from her when she first tried to put him up against her shoulder.

He shouldn't, Rachel told herself, be in that crowd. Luke's friends were quite different from his brothers' friends: heartier, simpler, more conventional. And was that a cigarette in his hand? Rachel had been so thankful when he'd given up smoking. Ralph was the only child she'd really worried over when it came to drink and drugs; he was the only one inclined to see the possibility of addiction as a challenge rather than a threat.

Perhaps, Rachel thought, she should go and talk to Petra. She stood up and smoothed down her skirt, green linen bought in a sale in a dress shop in Aldeburgh and, as it happened, a good contrast to Charlotte's mother's old-rose lace. Such an odd woman, Charlotte's mother, and anally tidy. Well, at least Charlotte wasn't that.

As she moved to start her search for Petra, Ralph materialised beside her. He was holding a bottle of lager and he smelled of cigarettes.

'You OK, Ma?'

She looked at him. He was her adored son, but she had Petra to think of now, too. 'I'm fine,' she said. 'What about you? Is everything OK?'

'Of course,' he said. He tilted the beer bottle, as if toasting her. 'Of course everything's OK. Why wouldn't it be?'

When Anthony was a boy, the building that was now his studio had been a decayed barn, used for storing the lawnmower, and various defunct pieces of semi-agricultural machinery. It had been a dim and dusty place, with barn owls nesting precariously on the beams and colonies of bats and swifts swooping wildly about in the summer dusks. It was known to Anthony's parents as the Dump, and every year it settled itself more deeply and crookedly into the earth.

It was Rachel who had thought of rescuing it, and making it into a studio, Rachel who had come from the Welsh hills and who had such profound misgivings about the flatness of Suffolk and—even more— about moving into the house where her fiancé had grown up.

'God,' she'd said to her sister, 'you should see it. I mean, it's a lovely house but they've lived there since the dawn of time. *Everything's* sacred, everything. Anthony thinks it's all perfect.'

Rachel's sister, married to a dedicated inner-city teacher and struggling in a council flat with a splintered front door where someone had kicked it in, didn't much want to hear about huge, if decrepit, Suffolk houses that you were being given—*given*—however much ancestral baggage was inconveniently attached.

'I think you're bloody lucky, Rach.'

'Well, yes. It's lucky not to have to *buy* anything. But it isn't lucky to inherit an old heap you're expected to *revere*, rather than restore.'

'Of course you can restore it. It's your home, isn't it? Give Anthony his bit and make it plain that you've got as much right to the rest of it as his mother had or his granny or his great-granny or whoever.'

'What d'you mean, his bit?'

Rachel's sister sighed. She tried not to notice that the aquamarine on Rachel's engagement finger was the size of a Fruit Gum.

'Oh, you know. The shed thing. The place where men go and mess about making things that don't work so that they have to unmake them again. Doesn't Anthony draw?'

'Actually,' Rachel had said proudly, 'rather well.'

'There you are then,' her sister said.

'It could be a studio,' Rachel had said, some days later, to Anthony.

'What could?'

'The Dump.'

'But it's always been the Dump.'

'Well,' Rachel said, squinting up at the enormous East Anglian sky, 'it isn't going to be any more. It would make a wonderful studio. It even has a big north wall, for a window. You could paint in there and draw, and make models of birds the size of aeroplanes. There's enough room in there to *build* an aeroplane, even.'

Anthony had sold a piece of his parents' old and unproductive orchard to the neighbours, for the price of turning the Dump into a studio. He put in windows and skylights, and a wood-burning stove, and laid old bricks on the floor and tongue-and-groove panelling against the walls. He brought in old kitchen tables, and battered armchairs, and rugs that had worn down to the canvas after a lifetime on stone-flagged floors. He put up his easels, and lines of shelves, and old saddle brackets on which to hang frames. He added books, and the decoy birds carved out of wood. And then, in pride of place, he had hung a reproduction of Joseph Crawhall's *The Pigeon*, painted in 1894 by one of the Glasgow School, which he had taken Rachel all the way to see, in the Burrell Collection.

Rachel had gazed at the pigeon, its white plumage flecked with grey, its pale coral beak and feet, its hard, wild, small eye. 'It's wonderful,' she said. 'Why is it so wonderful?'

'Because,' Anthony said, 'because you feel the inner life of the bird.' He took her hand. 'Crawhall painted from memory, as he had been taught as a boy. I've taught myself. I'd rather there was life and truth in a painting, than romance. I want an emotional charge.'

'Yes,' she had said, respectfully.

The studio, even separated as it was from the main house by a stretch of weedy gravel, became as significant to their lives as Rachel's kitchen. All three boys had their babyhood daytime sleeps in there, tucked into the huge, old, coach-built pram that had once been Anthony's, and then, as time went on, brought their homework in, to sit at one of the cluttered tables, and complain about fractions and French vocab.

It was years, though, until the studio, and what Anthony produced in it, made any money. During those years, Rachel cooked for local people's parties and held small, informal cooking courses in the kitchen she had made by knocking a warren of little rooms into a single space. Her efforts were supplemented by Anthony's part-time job teaching at a big art college fifteen miles away, a job he kept, out of habit and affection, even after his work began to be exhibited, and widely sold, and he was made a Royal Academician. It was a job that had led to his encountering Petra.

He had noticed her, at first, because she never said anything. She sat at the back of the class, dressed in the whimsical and bohemian rags that most of Anthony's students affected, and took notes. When he looked over her shoulder as he strolled, talking, up and down the aisles between the students, he saw that she was writing in pencil, with a strong and characterful script. Her hair was twisted up in a bit of rough, blue muslin patterned with gold spots, and her hands were shrouded in torn, black-lace mittens. She went on writing as he paused beside her, and he could see that she was writing exactly what he was saying.

'Correctness can become a terrible inhibition. You see, there's the truth of what we observe, and then there's the truth of how we *interpret* what we've observed. When you're painting a bird, say, you want to give the sense that you were there, that you are responding to that moment in the life of a living bird.'

Petra had underscored 'terrible' and 'interpret' and 'there', following his vocal emphases. And later, when he had made them loosen up their drawing arms by sweeping charcoal across great sheets of drawing paper, he saw that she was either a natural, or had been very well taught already, and that she was far, far better than anyone else in the class. But she would not look at him, and she did not speak.

'There's a girl at college,' he said to Rachel. 'Odd girl. I should think she's nineteen or twenty. Never speaks. But she draws like an angel. It's years since I've had anyone who draws like her.'

Rachel was grinding pine nuts for a pesto. 'What's her name?'

'Petra something.'

'Petra?'

'That's what it says on my class list. I've never heard her say it. I've never heard her say anything. She's completely mute.'

Rachel began to drip olive oil into the green sludge of basil leaves and pine nuts. 'Ask her here. I miss all the boys' friends coming round. I used to love that, when the kitchen was full of them and they were all always so starving.'

'I can't ask her anything,' Anthony said, 'until she speaks.'

Rachel put a finger into the sauce to taste it. 'Perhaps she'll do for Ralph. He doesn't speak much, either.'

'He wouldn't accept any choice of ours—'

'Probably not. Is she pretty?'

Anthony thought. 'Well, she's not Sigrid kind of pretty.'

'OK,' Rachel said, spooning the pesto into a dish they had brought back from a birdwatching holiday in Sicily. 'When she speaks and you like how she sounds, ask her here anyway. I could do with more young.'

A month later, Petra spoke. Anthony had been talking to the class about the importance of never having an eraser—'Keep going, as fast as the bird moves. Soft pencils, 4B to 6B, pencil sharpener vital but no eraser. Never'—and Petra had looked up and said in a hoarse voice, presumably from lack of use, 'Is the angle of the bird's body more important than its outline?'

The whole class had turned to look at her.

'We thought you was mental,' a boy next to her said, not unkindly.

Petra went on looking at Anthony for an answer.

'Yes,' Anthony said.

Petra glanced at the boy. Then she looked back at Anthony. 'That's what I thought,' she said, and went back to her drawing.

Two weeks later, Anthony said to the class, 'I wonder if you would all like to come and see my studio?'

They came on the local bus, as exotic-looking as a troupe of travelling players. Petra was wearing small, studious-looking, steel-framed spectacles and her hair hung down her back, almost to her waist, over a paisley shawl and purple Turkish trousers gathered at the ankle.

'I'm not going to ask your names,' Rachel said, 'because I won't remember any of them. But I'm Rachel and those are scones I've just made, and that's a chocolate cake. Obviously.'

The food released them. They ate with the focused concentration of babies, and then they began to talk. Anthony let them into the studio, and they all gasped and began to chatter and point things out to one another and Rachel said to Petra, 'Do you go birdwatching?'

Petra took her spectacles off. Her eyes were greenish, with a definite dark rim to the iris. 'Not really—'

'Well, you should,' Rachel said. 'Anthony thinks very highly of your drawing, but you need to observe, like he does.'

Petra nodded.

'What about your family? Does anyone in your family draw?'

Petra cleared her throat. 'I don't really have a family—'

'Oh,' Rachel said. She waited a moment, and then she said, 'Meaning?'

'My mother died and my father went, ages ago. And now my grandmother's gone to Canada.'

'Leaving you all alone?' Rachel demanded.

'It's OK,' Petra said. 'We weren't close. I've got somewhere to live.'

Rachel looked at her. 'What are you doing in Anthony's art class?'

'It's what I want,' Petra said. 'I work in a football-club bar weekends, and a coffee place weekdays except my college day.'

'How old are you?'

'Twenty,' Petra said. She put her spectacles back on. 'It's OK. I'm OK. I'm used to fending for myself.'

Later that evening, Rachel said to Anthony, 'I think we should help her. I'll teach her to cook. You take her birdwatching, to Minsmere.'

'Rach, I can't go round rescuing students. You know I can't. Especially girls. You're regarded as an old perv if you even look at a girl student while you're talking to her.'

Rachel sighed. 'I'll ask her. I liked her. She's not ordinary. And then, after a bit, you can take her birdwatching.'

Petra, it turned out, could cook. She'd never made bread, or a white sauce, but she knew what to do with chillies and lemon grass and fish sauce. She had several ingenious ways of turning a tin of baked beans into something interesting and surprising. And she was a quick learner. Rachel liked having her in the kitchen.

'Who's this Petra person?' Edward said to his father on the telephone. 'Mum keeps talking about her.'

'Actually,' Anthony said, 'she's one of my students. A seriously good draughtsman. Mum has rather taken to her.'

'And you?'

'I don't want to be thought weird—'

'Dad!'

'But I think she's great. She's a bit peculiar and very talented and she's only twenty and she's great.'

'Are you grooming her for Ralph, by any chance?'

'It has crossed our minds,' Anthony said, 'that they might have something in common. Yes.'

'So you're sort of keeping her on ice?'

'I'm taking her birdwatching,' Anthony said, slightly stiffly.

'Ah,' Edward said affectionately, from his office in London with its view of another office. 'The East Hide at Minsmere. The Garden of Eden.'

'Exactly,' Anthony said, and smiled into the telephone. 'Exactly.'

He had driven Petra, on one of the rare weekend days she allowed herself off, down the long, wooded entry to the nature reserve. She was, as usual, silent, looking about her at the spreading oak trees, the pairs and groups of quiet, earnest bird people, the view out across the marshes to the white dome of Sizewell, like some exotic temple on the skyline.

Anthony had hired her a pair of binoculars, and taken her out among the whispering reed beds, past wooden seats dedicated to the memories of ardent birdwatchers—'He loved all living things'—to the East Hide to see, he said, because it was summer, the avocets in their precise black-and-white plumage, stalking about on their long, grey legs with their shiny, upturned black bills questing for worms and insects.

'Avocets,' Anthony said, 'and, over time, sandpipers and spotted red-shanks and black-tailed godwits. All we have to do is wait, and watch.'

It was the first visit of many to the East Hide. Sometimes, Anthony left Petra there alone, and took himself off to the bittern hide, to wait for a rare glimpse of the big, striped birds stealing through the reed beds and uttering their peculiar booming call. And when he came back to find her, the pages of her sketchbook would be filled with the rapid, energetic drawings that gave him such satisfaction.

'Would it,' Rachel said, 'have felt like this, if we'd had a daughter?'

'No.'

'Why d'you say no?'

'Because it wouldn't have felt so friendly. There'd have been baggage. There always is.'

CHAPTER TWO

THEN RALPH CAME HOME. Ralph had been abroad. Ralph had been sent, by the American bank that had, to his parents' surprise, hired him, to Singapore. He had not fitted in. He had said he would stick it for three years, until he had made enough money to come home and buy a cottage in Suffolk and start up some business of his own, one that didn't mean wearing a tie. He had given no hint of what was going on in his personal life, and slid past all Rachel's questions with the ease of practice.

'He'll come back,' Rachel had said, 'married. Or not married. But with a Malay girl or an Indonesian girl. And a baby. There's bound to be a baby. And she'll hate Suffolk and be miserable and cold and then she'll want to leave him and go home.'

'Probably.'

'Don't you care?'

'Desperately,' Anthony said, 'but what can we do? What have we ever been able to do, about Ralph?'

Rachel had looked at him quickly, and then looked away, but not before he had seen tears spring to her eyes. Rachel had never been tearful, had never resorted to weeping when upset or frustrated—except where Ralph was concerned. Ever since his babyhood, ever since his complex and elusive childhood, Ralph had presented Rachel with a conundrum she could neither solve nor relinquish, an Achilles heel that she could only bear if she kept him close to her, supervising, involved, worrying. Sometimes Anthony had tried to say that it was perhaps not a good idea to indulge Ralph in his persistent oddness, but Rachel would fly to his defence. He was so clever, she'd say, so talented, so unusual, it was really unimaginative, as well as depressingly orthodox and limited, to expect Ralph to conform to mere convention.

But then Ralph came home, alone. He had resigned from the bank. They had begged him to stay, but he had persisted in his resignation. His manager had asked, with some force, if the money he was being offered wasn't enough.

'I don't get it,' he had said. 'I simply don't get people like you.'

'No,' Ralph said, 'you wouldn't,' and then he had taken his tie off, and dropped it in a corporate waste bin.

He looked, Rachel thought, very well. The bank had required that he have regular and conventional haircuts, and weekends of hiking and snorkelling had honed him and tanned him. His eyes were clear and his teeth, courtesy of some skilful Singaporean cosmetic dentistry which he had agreed to, because the bank had paid for it, were a marked improvement on the slightly ramshackle mouthful of his adolescence. He settled back into his old bedroom with complete nonchalance, bundling his business suits onto wire hangers at the back of his wardrobe, and emerging, as he had done all his life, at random times of the day and night in search of cornflakes or coffee or the sports section of the newspaper.

'Do you have any kind of plan?' Anthony said.

Ralph was hunched over a Sudoku, nursing a mug of soup. He glanced up briefly, but didn't speak.

'Well,' Anthony continued, 'I don't want to play the heavy father. Or even the especially conventional one. But you are not far off thirty, and have had a thriving, if brief, career, and sitting about in your mother's kitchen in a sweater you have had since school doesn't appear to me to be a very satisfactory way to live.'

Ralph regarded his father. 'I've bought a cottage.'

'What!'

'I've bought a cottage.'

'When—'

'The other day.'

'Ralph—'

'It was easy,' Ralph said. 'I heard about it, I saw it, I liked it, I bought it.'

'Where is it—'

'Shingle Street. It's cool. It's in a little terrace. Right on the shingle.'

'But what will you do, in Shingle Street? How will you earn a living, away from everything?'

There was a pause. Ralph took a noisy swallow of soup and looked back at his puzzle. 'Leave that to me,' he said, 'why don't you.'

When Petra next came, Ralph was out at his cottage, which he had so far declined to let his parents see.

'Why not?'

'I'm painting it.'

'Are you? Inside or outside?'

'Inside.'

'Oh, lovely. What colours?'

'White,' Ralph said.

'Would you like some help? Would you like curtains and things? Why don't you make a list of furniture you need—'

'No, Mum,' Ralph said. 'No. Thank you.'

Neither Rachel nor Anthony had mentioned to Petra that Ralph had come home. Petra made a lasagne with Rachel, and then she went across to the studio and watched Anthony experimenting with a brush drawing using black watercolour. He was drawing vultures, angrily squaring up to each other, wings up, heads jutting. Petra sat beside him, like a pianist's page turner, and watched his brush intently. Occasionally he said things like, 'Sometimes directional lines are useful,' or, 'D'you think that's better because it's more a diagram than a drawing?' but mostly they sat in silence, broken only by the faint hiss and crackle of the wood-burning stove.

When Anthony finally said, 'Tea?' Petra said, 'Oh, yes,' and then they left the studio and crossed the gravel to the house and there was Ralph in the kitchen, with white splashes of paint on his hands and clothes. Anthony did not catch Rachel's eye.

Rachel said, 'Petra. This is our middle son. This is Ralph.'

Petra looked slightly past Ralph. 'Hi.'

'Hi,' Ralph said. He waited a few seconds. Then he said, 'Why are you called Petra?'

'After the ancient city in Jordan?' Anthony said, too heartily.

'No,' Petra said. 'After the dog on *Blue Peter*.'

'Dad says you draw. You draw birds.'

'A bit.'

'I made a gingerbread,' Rachel said. 'Tea and gingerbread.'

'When I was away,' Ralph said to Petra, 'in Singapore, the birds were quite different. Utterly different. Very brightly coloured. And raucous.'

'Mugs or cups?' Rachel said.

Ralph pulled a chair out from the table and gestured at the seat. 'Have a chair. Petra.'

She sat down wordlessly.

'Well, mugs, then,' Rachel said. 'They hold more tea and it stays hotter.'

Ralph took the chair beside Petra's. He had, Anthony noticed, paint in his hair as well as on his hands, and a splash above one eyebrow.

'Were you born in Suffolk?' Ralph said to Petra.

'Yes, Ipswich.'

'I missed Suffolk. When I was away. I thought I wanted to get away but I was so relieved to come back.'

Petra accepted a mug of tea. 'I've never been away.'

'D'you want to?'

'What—'

'Go away.'

She looked at him properly for the first time. Rachel risked a lightning glance at Anthony. Surely, surely Petra would be struck by Ralph's looks, only enhanced by old clothes and whitewash?

'No,' Petra said. 'No, I don't. I think—I think I'd pine.'

'Gingerbread? It's got dates in it—'

'I've bought a cottage,' Ralph said to Petra. 'It's right on the sea, practically in it. Just down the coast from here.'

'Really?'

'It's so bleak, it's thrilling—'

'I—like bleak,' Petra said nonchalantly.

'We haven't been allowed—' Anthony began.

Quiet, Rachel signalled, cutting more cake, quiet.

Ralph put another wedge of gingerbread into his mouth. Round it, he said, 'Like to see it?'

Petra put her mug down. 'Yes.'

'C'mon then,' Ralph said, getting up, still chewing.

'But it's getting dark!' Anthony said. 'You won't see anything!'

Petra rose too. 'There'll be light enough, off the sea.'

Ralph smiled down at her. 'I know.'

Petra half turned. She said to Rachel, 'Thank you. Thank you for tea.'

Rachel nodded. Then Ralph almost pushed Petra through the kitchen door and out into the stone-flagged passage beyond. Anthony and Rachel heard the outer door slam, and then the sound of Ralph's car starting up, and the crunch of gravel.

Anthony looked at Rachel. They were both smiling.

Rachel held up both hands, her first and second fingers twisted together. 'Fingers crossed!'

Luke took Charlotte to Venice for their honeymoon. The man who had preceded Luke in Charlotte's life had worked in the City, and his taste in holidays ran to Thailand and the Maldives, just as his leisure tastes had included cross-dressing and cocaine. His cocaine habit had in fact, and finally, put Charlotte right off both him and drugs. She regarded herself as perfectly free-thinking in all sorts of social areas, but she was very clear about drugs.

When Luke first asked her on a date she had said no, with a vehemence that took him aback.

'What d'you mean, no? Why d'you have to say no like that?'

'Because I saw you,' Charlotte had said, 'I saw you last week, at Julia's dinner party. I don't want to have anything to do with, again, anyone who has their dinner off a mirror.'

'It was just a line—'

'People who do coke,' Charlotte said, interrupting, 'are boring. Really, really dull. They're either jittery because they've just had a fix, or jittery because they want one. Gus was unbelievably boring. I thought I could put up with it for the Club Class flights to Sri Lanka, but I couldn't. So, until you clean up your pathetic little act, you'll have to look for dates anywhere but me.'

Luke had been fired up by this speech. He knew Gus, the City trader, slightly, and he knew that Gus made the kind of money that bore no resemblance to the money that anyone in Luke's family had ever, or would ever, make; even Ralph in Singapore. And Gus was not only wealthy, but personable, and athletic, with a flat in Clerkenwell and a brother in a rock band. But if he couldn't keep Charlotte, if Charlotte wasn't prepared to tolerate or join in a habit that was significant in Gus's life, then Charlotte acquired, in Luke's eyes, a particular lustre that went way beyond her looks and her energy and her undoubted popularity.

He began to make real efforts. He started going to the gym more often and he stopped using cocaine, even when nursing a Coke Zero in a room full of insanely, irresponsibly hyped-up people made him feel as if he'd landed on another planet. After a while, he even stopped going to parties where he knew what the menu would include, and instead started taking Charlotte's flatmate, Nora, out for coffee and pizzas so that Nora could relay to Charlotte what an impressively changed character he was.

And then Gus began to try to win Charlotte back again, and Luke heard unnerving rumours of promises of private planes to Paris and a chartered yacht in the Caribbean, and he lost his head and hard-won self-discipline, and rushed over the river on impulse to the Clapham basement that Charlotte shared with Nora, and found Charlotte on the sofa, in a vest-top and pyjama bottoms, with her shorn, fair head unwashed, eating toast and jam and watching *Big Brother* on the television. He had stood there, unable to proceed further in any way, and burst into tears, and Charlotte had got up off the sofa, and leaned against him and he had smelled her hair and a sweet whiff of jam, and had thought he would simply like to die, then and there, of sheer happiness and relief.

Anthony and Rachel gave Luke some money for the honeymoon. With his parents' contribution, he could afford a hotel just behind the Accademia Gallery, with polished-black-marble bathrooms and electric window blinds and wide, pale beds heaped with pillows. They could have breakfast in their room and glasses of Prosecco on a little roof terrace among the seagulls from the lagoon, and walk out one way to the sunlit waterfront of Zattere, or the other over the Accademia bridge to the *campi* and *calli* that would finally lose them in a labyrinth of bridges and blind alleys and decayed, romantic beauty.

Charlotte was bowled over. She had never been to Venice before. She had never been in an art gallery where pictures painted hundreds of years before showed scenes that she could walk through. She had never eaten tiny, soft-shelled crabs out of a paper cone in a fish market, or ridden a water bus, or sat in a hot, dim, late-afternoon church, and thought about the Virgin Mary as anything more than a sort of sacred cipher that belonged to the Catholic girls at school. She had never, either, imagined that she might be married to someone who she not only loved, but who knew so much more than she did.

'I don't, you know,' Luke said. 'I just know about different things.'

'But they're important. I mean, Titian, and Carpaccio, and the Venetian Empire and things. They're important.'

'The Doges would be so chuffed to hear you say that.'

'Are you patronising me?'

'Only,' Luke said, 'a little bit.'

'I don't mind,' Charlotte said, 'I really don't. One day I might, but I love it now, it just makes me feel—' She stopped.

'What?'

'That I can do no wrong,' Charlotte said, and laughed.

Luke smiled at her. 'You can't,' he said.

They had a pact that, in order to preserve the extraordinary and magical bubble in which they were briefly living, they would only turn on their mobile phones once a day, in case there was an emergency. There was never an emergency. There were texts hoping they were happy—cheerfully, rudely expressed from most friends—and a few from Luke's partner, Jed, in the little graphic design studio they shared in Shoreditch.

It was only on the last day but one, chugging back across the lagoon from a slow and languorous day on Murano, that Luke held his telephone out to Charlotte and said, 'What d'you think?'

There was a short text on the screen. It read, 'Bro. Things tricky. Need to talk. Ring? R.'

'Ralph?' Charlotte said.

'Mmm.'

Charlotte squinted at the hazy blue outline of Venice advancing towards them across the glittering water.

'I don't,' she said, 'know them very well. Your brothers, and sisters-in-law. It didn't occur to me, it didn't seem to matter—'

'It doesn't matter.'

She transferred her gaze to look at him. 'It kind of does, now. It's not just a you thing, it's an us thing. Your brother sends a text like that, and you begin to look all preoccupied and distant and I'm your wife now, so I'm in the loop, too.'

Luke put his phone in his trouser pocket. He leaned forward, pinning Charlotte against the rail of the vaporetto, and put his chin into the angle of her neck and shoulder. 'I'll ring him later. When I don't want to thump him for being so thoughtless.'

'Is he thoughtless?'

'By normal standards, yes. But Ralph isn't normal. He's brilliant and he's impossible. I missed him like anything when he was away, but it was so peaceful at the same time.'

Later, while Charlotte was showering with the window open to the warm, bell-haunted sounds of early evening Venice, Luke rang Ralph. Charlotte knew he was ringing, so she had the shower turned on full, and she sang as well, for good measure, in order to indicate to Luke that she was in no way going to influence or pre-empt any reaction Luke might be having. When she had finished, she wrapped herself in a large, white towel and went through to the bedroom. Luke was lying on the bed with his shoes off. His phone was some distance away, on Charlotte's side of the bed, as if he had just chucked it there.

Charlotte sat down beside him. She waited for him to ruffle her hair, or untuck her towel, or slide his hand underneath it. But he lay there frowning, looking ahead at the cabinet that housed the television.

'Is he OK?'

Luke went on staring ahead. He said shortly, 'He's losing his business.'

'*What?*'

'The bank won't either extend his credit or lend him any more, despite him offering their home as collateral, so he'll lose the business.'

'Oh my God,' Charlotte said.

Luke took her hand. 'He said he suspected it would be that bad, at our wedding. He said he was sorry he was a bit weird, but he couldn't help thinking about it.'

'Was he weird?'

Luke sighed. 'He got plastered. He was smoking. Mum and Dad were furious with him.'

'Do—do they know?'

Luke took Charlotte's hand and raised it to his mouth, looking at her over it. 'No. They don't. Nobody does, except Ed, and now me. He hasn't told anyone. He hasn't told Petra.'

Charlotte felt a clutch of panic. She wanted to say, 'You'd tell me, wouldn't you? You'd always tell me everything. Wouldn't you?' but sensed that if she did she might not get any answer that reassured her. So instead she said, 'So, even if he'd offered their house to the bank and they'd, say, accepted, Petra wouldn't have known anything about it?'

Luke regarded her solemnly. 'Yes.'

'But that's awful—'

'Not telling Petra is protecting her. So's not to worry her.'

Charlotte took her hand out of Luke's. 'That's not right—'

'Petra's got no family,' Luke said. 'We've all sort of become her family, so there's this unspoken thing about looking after her. She's only twenty-four, or something.'

'But,' Charlotte said, 'she's his *wife*. They've got *children*. It's a thing you do *together*, bad times.'

Luke sighed. He twisted himself round, and lay so that his head was in Charlotte's lap. Then he reached up to untuck the towel across her breasts. Charlotte put her hand on his.

'Don't—'

'Why not?'

'The mood's not right—'

'Bloody Ralph.'

'It's not Ralph,' Charlotte said, 'not really. It's Petra. It's this Brinkley thing of treating Petra like a child.'

'Well, she is in a way—'

'Only if you all make her like that. She was managing OK on her own, I gather, before she met Ralph—'

'Just.'

Charlotte looked away. She said, 'It's like Ralph found her under a hedge or something, like an abandoned kitten.'

'She was in Dad's art class. He said she never spoke but she was brilliant. She is brilliant. At drawing, I mean.'

Charlotte looked down at Luke. She began to stroke his thick hair back from his forehead. 'And then Ralph fell in love with her—'

'Well,' Luke said, gazing upward and thinking how amazing Charlotte looked, from every angle, even when foreshortened from underneath, as she was now, 'I suppose he did. I mean, he liked her, he really liked her, but I'm not sure getting married was ever top of Ralph's to-do list.'

'Did she ask him, then?'

'Oh, no,' Luke said. 'She got pregnant.'

'Wow,' Charlotte said. 'So he felt he had to marry her.'

'Well, not really. And I don't think Petra would have expected him to, either. She wasn't conventional, any more than he was. She'd probably just have shrugged and got on with it, taking the baby to art classes in a basket, that sort of thing. It was Mum and Dad that wanted the wedding. They wanted them married.'

'To be respectable?'

'Not really,' Luke said. He heaved himself upright and ran his hand through Charlotte's damp hair. 'They don't mind about how things look, how conformist things are. It was more that they didn't want to let Petra go. They'd kind of adopted her. So they couldn't lose her after all they'd invested, all they'd got used to. At least, that's what I think.'

Charlotte was very still.

Luke peered into her face, his eyes inches from hers. 'What is it?'

'It's a bit silly—'

'What is?'

'How I feel,' Charlotte said. 'I mean, I've got my own family, who are lovely, and your parents who've been really sweet to me, but when you describe how they feel about Petra, I—well, I feel a bit—' She stopped.

'What?'

'Jealous,' Charlotte said.

Luke took his face away a little. 'You are one idiot of an adorable girl.'

Charlotte bent her head. She said, 'There's Sigi, you see, all groomed and professional and clever and detached, and she's been in your family for ever, and then there's Petra who everyone treats like a daughter, like a little sister, and it's a bit much to have to compete with all that, especially when you've been competing with sisters all your life and you're not academic or talented or anything—'

'Shush,' Luke said loudly.

Charlotte didn't look up. Luke put his hand under her chin, and tilted it until her gaze was level with his. 'It's only what *I* think that matters,'

Luke said. 'And you know what I think. And when the family know you better they'll think it too.'

He leaned forward, and kissed her, without hurry, on the mouth. Then he said, 'Never mind Ralph and his problems. We've got far more important things to concern ourselves with.' He smiled at her and, with a single, deft movement, he took her towel away.

The flat Luke had found for them in London was at the very top of a tall and elaborate nineteenth-century brick building in Arnold Circus, a stone's throw, as Charlotte excitedly told Nora, and all her other friends, from Columbia Road flower market, from Brick Lane, from—oh my God—*Hoxton*. The flat had two rooms, with a kitchen under the eaves and a bathroom with a huge window from which you could see, giddily, far below, the decayed strip of low buildings, which now housed a series of artisan workshops, including Luke and Jed's studio. You could even pick out the very skylight of the studio, and she imagined how, in the winter dark, she could look down there and see, with lovely, wifely exasperation, that the lights were on in the studio, which meant that Luke was still down there working, when he should have been up in the flat eating the kind of delicious, nourishing supper she was going to practise cooking until she was as good a cook as Luke's mother was. She vowed she would not nag. And she vowed that she would never give him cause to feel that she had to be protected from hard times, like Petra.

Charlotte had no idea what Ralph's business was, except that it was some kind of online financial thing, investment advice or something, and she had no inclination to ask further since the whole situation around Ralph and Petra and the little boys and Anthony and Rachel made her feel strangely unsettled, however many times Luke told her that no one mattered to him like she did. She wished she hadn't told Luke she felt jealous. She wished she'd just navigated the whole topic with the kind of grown-up poise that indicated that she was naturally concerned by Ralph's news, but not in the least personally ruffled by it.

And so, to make amends to herself for an adolescent moment of vulnerability, she said to Luke, when they returned to the flat from Venice, 'Do ask Ralph here, if you want to talk, or anything. He can christen the sofa bed.'

And she'd been rewarded by Luke putting his arms round her and saying, his mouth against her ear, 'You are a complete doll.'

So here she was, getting wedding-present sheets out of their packaging, and pulling a new duvet out of its box, in order to have them ready, later that day, to make the sofa up for Ralph to sleep on. It was seven in the morning, the sun was out, Luke was showering in the bathroom, and Charlotte, in a denim miniskirt, striped vest-top and shrunken military jacket with huge brass buttons, was all ready to leave for her job in a local radio station located on Marylebone High Street.

She banged on the bathroom door. 'I'm off, babe!'

There was a pause while taps were turned off, and then he opened the door. He was naked, and wet. 'Don't go to work, angel—'

She giggled. 'I've got to. I'm on the eight o'clock shift, which means being there at seven forty-five. You know that.'

'I'll be thinking about you all day. All day.'

She blew him a kiss. 'Me too. When's Ralph getting here?'

Luke stepped forward and enfolded her in a wet embrace. 'When he gets here. Miss me. Miss me all day.'

'Promise,' Charlotte said.

Luke's studio was approached along a broad, asphalted path behind the Arnold Circus buildings. It was in a long, low line of what might once have been mews, or garages, brick-built with sizeable sections of metal-framed windows, broken where the studios behind them were unoccupied. The ground-floor walls were punctuated by battered, black-painted doors which, when you pushed them open, gave onto steep, narrow staircases that led up to small landings illuminated by dirty windows, floor to ceiling. In Luke's case, one of the two doors on such a landing had been newly painted, in dark grey matte paint, with a brushed-steel plate fixed slightly to one side of the centre eyeline, which read, in black, lower-case lettering, 'Graphtech Design Consultants'.

Ralph had only been to Luke's studio once before, when Luke and Jed were in the process of moving in, and long before Luke met Charlotte. They'd borrowed the money for the initial payment on the lease and down payments on their computers from Jed's father. Luke, who had always been good with his hands, had been building drawing boards and installing overhead lighting while Jed sanded the floorboards. It had made Ralph think, with some emotion, of how he intended his Suffolk cottage to be, a private space in which to live and to work without the distraction of obligation to anyone else. It was going to be him, and the white walls, and the uncompromising coastal light, and the sea, and the shingle, and the development of his idea to extend the ease and intimacy of internet banking into the limitless world of the small investor.

But, of course, it hadn't turned out like that. He had been in the cottage a few months, four or five maybe, with Petra undemandingly there, now and then, drawing gulls on the beach and doing remarkable things with tins of baked beans and sharing his bed with the same absence of claim, or right, that she brought to most things, when she said, quite baldly, that she thought she was probably pregnant. He had been stunned, then rather overwhelmed and almost tearful, and then asked her, clumsily, what she would like him to do about it.

She had stared at him. 'Nothing.'

'I mean, d'you want to live here? D'you want to come and live here with me?'

'I might.'

He'd held her. He thought that if this was love he liked it. He imagined a baby in his bare sitting room, Petra holding a baby, him holding a baby and showing it the sea, out of the window. But then, impelled by something he could not explain or really remember, they had gone to tell Anthony and Rachel, to *tell* them, not to ask them anything, and from then on everything changed.

The cottage had gone, replaced by a little terraced place in Aldeburgh, with a small garden but no view of the sea. Ralph had a good room to work in, but it looked out over sheds and other people's gardens, and a random parking space, not shingle and sea and sky. Rachel made sure it was comfortable for him and pointed out how much better the internet connection was than it had been at the cottage, and then there was a wedding—which he'd liked, he'd liked a lot—and there they were, living in a little house, in a little town, and the baby turned out to be Kit, two months after they were married. None of it, Ralph thought, now standing outside Luke's studio on a summer evening in Shoreditch, was remotely, *remotely*, what had been in his head or his imagining when he had last stood there. And that had been no more than four years ago.

Not only had the studio changed, but Luke and Jed had, too. The studio looked very together, very monochrome and modern with sophisticated track lighting and computer screens set at angles, like drawing boards. Luke and Jed were wearing a similar, nonchalant kind of non-uniform: black T-shirts, combat trousers, carefully designed trainers, and Luke had a wedding ring now, a flat band of white gold that made his left hand look weirdly grown-up. He gave Ralph a rough hug, and Jed high-fived him and said he'd got to go, good to see him, take care, man, and had hooked a black leather jacket over one shoulder, and loped out of the studio and down the stairs, whistling. And then Luke said, 'You don't look too hot, bro.'

Ralph perched on one of the black stools by the computers. 'How's Charlotte?'

'Great.'

'And Venezia?'

'A-mazing.'

Ralph took a pack of cigarettes out of his jacket pocket and held them out to Luke. 'Smoke?'

'No thanks,' Luke said, 'not any more. No drugs but alcohol. And not in here.'

Ralph shrugged. He dropped the pack back in his pocket.

'Tell me,' Luke said.

'What, now? At once?'

'I don't want you boring Charlotte later. I don't want Charlotte thinking my brothers are tedious and problematic.'

'OK then,' Ralph said. He stuck his hands in his jacket pockets and stared at the ceiling and the skylight. 'I've had my small-business account closed.'

'Ouch—'

'Sometimes I have to wait up to six months for commission on something I do. It can be even longer. That means I need a good overdraft facility, it's important. No, it's crucial. And four months ago, the bank raised the interest rate. Bang. Just like that. Five per cent to 9.9 per cent, take it or leave it. And—' He stopped. He looked at Luke.

'What?'

'There was my personal overdraft rate. It was bad enough, anyway. It was 9.9 per cent. And they upped it, no arguing, to 19.9 per cent, even though I'd never exceeded the limit. And when I objected, they said I'd only get a better rate when there was more money going in. So I pointed out that more money was hardly likely to go in if I was being caned for my necessary, and *agreed*, business account, and they said tough. I have no assets they seem interested in, so it's the end of the story. Except that my investors, the friends from Singapore who helped me set this up, aren't happy. You can imagine the emails I'm getting.'

Luke jammed his fists into his trouser pockets. He felt terrible about Ralph, but he wanted to be up in the flat before Charlotte got home. He said, scuffing at the black floorboards with the rubber toecap of his boot, 'What are you going to do?'

CHAPTER THREE

EVERY WEEKDAY MORNING, Sigrid bought coffee from an Italian who ran a tiny stall opening out onto the pavement not far from the laboratory where she worked. The Italian, Marco, a voluble man from Naples whose English had hardly improved in thirty years, preferred blondes, and every so often he insisted on either giving Sigrid her coffee for nothing, or adding a café-style biscotto as a present. Sigrid liked all this. It was one of the bonuses—the many bonuses—of living in London. In Stockholm, where she had grown up, true blondes were two a penny.

Sigrid's laboratory, independently funded but loosely affiliated to London University, was tucked into the basement of a building in Bloomsbury, behind the School of Hygiene and Tropical Medicine. In the mornings, when it wasn't her turn to drive a carload of small girls to school, Sigrid tidied the house, then walked to catch a Victoria Line train to Warren Street. Then, via Marco and his coffee stall, she walked down Gower Street, to work.

Sigrid's father was an engineer, and her mother a doctor; Sigrid had one brother, Bengt, who had become an avant-garde composer and wrote scores for cult movies, largely made in Berlin, where he now lived. Sigrid herself had taken a Master's degree in computational science at the

University of Uppsala, followed by research at the faculty of engineering at the University of Loughborough, which was where she had met Edward, who'd gone there to celebrate an old schoolfriend's birthday. What a weekend that had been! Even twelve, nearly thirteen years later, Sigrid couldn't recall that weekend without smiling.

And now here she was, thirty-eight years old, Edward's wife, Mariella's mother, and in command of her own particle accelerator which could analyse materials without destroying them and was thus invaluable to museums and art collectors alike. In her lab coat, with her hair tied back and her spectacles on, she was not the blonde in knee-high boots whom Marco wanted to give free coffee to. As far as her professional life was concerned, it was the lab-coat Sigrid who prevailed.

Walking into the building off Gower Street, holding her coffee and her briefcase, Sigrid thought gratefully of the prospect of her lab coat. The head of the laboratory was away at a conference in Helsinki, and whenever he was away the assumption was that Sigrid was in charge, an assumption that nobody in the laboratory seemed to question except for a clever, ginger-haired boy called Philip, who craved Sigrid's attention and believed that challenging her authority was a successful way of getting it. Yet, this Monday morning, even the prospect of batting Philip's tediousness away was attractive; better anyhow than spending the weekend listening to Edward on the telephone to his parents, or his brothers, or his parents again, in an endless cycle of anxiety and suggestion and counter-suggestion and exasperation, which had finally driven her to take Mariella, and her three best friends for that week, to eat immense, pastel-coloured cupcakes at an American bakery.

In the evening, after Mariella was in bed, Sigrid had laid out their customary Sunday-night supper of matjes herring, black bread and pickled-cucumber salad, and then taken a glass of New Zealand Sauvignon Blanc to the small room off the kitchen where a big plasma television screen had been fitted into a wall of bookcases. Edward followed her. Sigrid sat down on the sofa opposite the screen and aimed the remote control at it. Edward leaned forward and took the remote out of her hand, then sat down close to her.

'I need to talk to you.'

'You've been talking all weekend—'

'Yes,' Edward said, 'but not to you. I've been talking, as you well know, to my maddening family and I need to talk to someone with some sense.'

Sigrid sighed. She put her wine glass down on the nearest pile of magazines and turned to face him.

'OK.'

'*Please* don't say it like that.'

'Well,' Sigrid said, 'I know your family. And I know how you all operate. So I can't feel very hopeful, now, can I?'

Edward reached across Sigrid for her wine glass, and took a swallow from it before replacing it.

He said, 'I cannot believe the fuss they are making—'

'Can't you?'

'No,' Edward said. 'I mean, Ralph has lost his company, which is very sad, but not really surprising when you look at the high-handed way he's behaved to his bank all along, and they're all reacting as if one of the children had been run over. I kept saying to Mum it's only a job, Mum, and she said oh, he'll never find another one in this climate and what about the mortgage, they can't afford that and Dad and I can't help them at the moment and Petra is distraught—'

'Is she?' Sigrid said.

'Is she what?'

'Is Petra distraught?'

'Well,' Ed said, shrugging, 'she sounded as if she was doing the usual Petra thing of being all vague and unconcerned till everything had blown over and someone else had thought of a solution.'

'Well then.'

Edward put his hand out again for Sigrid's glass. She moved it deftly out of his reach.

'Have you spoken to Luke?'

'Yes.'

'And?'

'He's still on honeymoon. In his head, anyway. He says it's rotten for Ralph and scandalous of the bank, but Ralph's got to deal with it.'

'He has,' Sigrid said.

'I'm the eldest, Sigi. I really feel that I have to prop up the parents and help the brothers.'

'Only up to a point. You can't live their lives for them, and you can't stop your parents having the priorities they have.'

Edward took Sigrid's hand. 'The geography doesn't help. All of them living so close and being so involved with each other. I said something so stupid to Mum—'

'What?'

'I said,' Ed said unhappily, 'I said, because she said she was really wound up about it all and wasn't sleeping and stuff, I said just leave it to me and I'll think of something and ring you tomorrow, and she said oh thank you, darling, thank you, in a way she never does normally, and now I can't think how on earth I'm going to come up with anything constructive by tomorrow.'

Sigrid let a silence fall, but she didn't take her hand away. Instead, she let her gaze travel along the lines of family photographs in their glass-and-chrome frames, which sat on the front edges of some of the bookshelves: her parents on their boat, her brother in a leather coat and dark glasses on a Berlin street, Mariella in a tutu, Anthony and Rachel on Ed and Sigrid's wedding day, Ralph and Petra's little boys posed on a hearthrug with some coloured wooden bricks. Then she looked back at Edward.

'I can think of one thing. One thing you could do.'

He sighed again. He said, despondently, 'What?'

'Well, Ralph is clever, isn't he. He was successful in Singapore—'

'Yes—'

'Well,' she said, 'why don't *you* offer him a job?'

It was only much later, Sigrid thought now, pulling off her boots and sliding her feet into the ergonomic, moulded clogs in which she worked, that Ed had confessed that he thought Ralph—even if work could be found for him—would be very difficult to work with. It was at that point that Sigrid had lost her temper. She said that she, too, would find working with her own brother difficult, but if she decided to do it she would just *do it*, and not go complaining on, as all the Brinkleys did, and all the time, about everything; that *everything* was a drama with them, and then she had gone into the bathroom and locked the door and, staring at herself in the mirror, told herself that tomorrow she would be in her laboratory, with interesting, impersonal work to do and there would be no Brinkleys, and nobody asking for advice in order to ignore it.

And here she was now, hair tied back, ready. In a sealed box, wrapped in acid-free paper, by her accelerator and microscopes, lay a fragment of medieval textile, sent from a church in Florence. She opened the door to the lab, anticipating a day ahead free of all the clinging tendrils of family preoccupations, and saw at her bench, actually sitting on her particular stool and peering into one of her microscopes, ginger-haired Philip.

Mariella liked her rare journeys to school with her father. She liked being able to talk to him when she had his individual attention.

'Daddy,' she said, buckling herself into the front seat of the car, 'are Ralph and Petra going to have absolutely no money at all, not even enough money for cornflakes?'

'*Uncle* Ralph,' Edward said automatically. '*Aunt* Petra.'

'Petra said to call her Petra. What do you do if you have absolutely no money, not even enough to buy a tiny little piece of cheese that would be too small even for a mouse to live on?'

'They aren't like that,' Edward said. 'They have plenty of money for cheese and cornflakes.'

'You go jabbering on,' Mariella said, 'all weekend, and then you say there's nothing to worry about.' She paused, and then continued, 'D'you think we should spend next weekend making food and driving to Suffolk to give it to Ralph and Petra?'

'That's a very nice idea.'

Mariella glanced at her father. 'If you and Mummy run out of money, Daddy, you're to tell me. OK? At once.'

'Really? Why? Suppose we want to protect you?'

Mariella snorted. 'If I don't *know*, then I can't do anything about it, can I?' She kicked at the rubber mat that protected the carpet in the floorwell under her feet. 'That's not protection. That's just daft.'

Edward rang Sigrid at lunchtime. He told her about his conversation with Mariella and said he hoped she was having a good day untroubled by human provocation, and that he was going to talk to his managing director about Ralph because even though the bank wasn't much in a hiring mood, there were still some opportunities in the analysis team.

Sigrid told him about Philip.

'And he'd brought me flowers.'

'What? *Flowers*?'

'I was so cross,' Sigrid said. 'I was so cross that he tried to disarm me with flowers. I've put them in a mug in the little place where I eat lunch sometimes. I hope he gets the message.'

'As long as you don't like them—'

'Oh, I like *them*,' Sigrid said, 'I just don't like being given them.'

Edward said, 'Mariella wants us to bake muffins and stuff for Ralph and co.'

'At least she's practical,' Sigrid said.

'I'm trying to be, too. Just one thing—'

'What?'

'I quite understand,' Edward said, 'why you said a lot of what you said, last night, and you were right about most of it. But it's much easier to be detached and grown-up about your family, if said family is safely in another country. That's all.'

'Is that a judgement?'

'No,' he said, 'it's an observation.'

'Then you said it in the wrong tone of voice.'

'Sigi—'

'I would like,' Sigrid said, 'to see more of my family than I do. I would like the chance to get as exasperated with them as you do with yours.'

There was a brief pause and then Edward said shortly, 'See you later,' and put the phone down.

Sigrid's colleagues—three girls, a quiet and competent middle-aged man, and Philip—were either eating various forms of lunch in the cubbyhole adorned with the mug of cornflowers, or out. Sigrid wrote a note to deter any interference during her absence—'Please do not touch under any circumstances'—weighted it under a stapler on her bench, and then went out of the lab to have half an hour in a café to settle her thoughts and her temper.

Walking briskly, she made for Charlotte Street, and the lounge of a hotel where she could be sure of the peace of anonymity granted by a public space. The hotel was unaggressively hip, with most life in it being concentrated in its brasserie, so Sigrid found an armchair in a corner, ordered a smoked-salmon sandwich and, opening a book to deter interruption, applied herself to straightening her thoughts.

It was not, she told herself firmly, that she did not like Edward's family. She had always liked them, from that first visit to Suffolk, and now she was used to them. She had grown up in a first-floor flat in a good part of

Stockholm, furnished with pared-down modern furniture, and the colour and sprawl of Anthony and Rachel's house on the flat, Suffolk coast had been a great surprise to her. But she was accustomed to it now, as she was to Rachel's robust cooking, and Anthony's energetic emotions, and the expectation that anyone who came in from the outside would acknowledge, as a matter of course, that they would be subsumed into the Brinkley way of thinking, the Brinkley way of doing things, because the Brinkley way was—well, the best way.

Her sandwich arrived, on a square white plate, garnished with frond-like pea shoots. She regarded it. Smoked fish. Her parents probably ate smoked fish at some point every day. If they—she and Edward and Mariella—lived in Stockholm, would there be a quiet but determined pressure on them to eat smoked fish, too, on a daily basis? Would her parents, unshowily preoccupied with their own lives and professions as they were, be insistent that Sigrid and her family lived their lives by the same rules and expectations as they did themselves? Was Edward right? Had she somehow idealised her parents because they were tidily in Sweden, and not messily right here? She bit into the sandwich.

She leaned back in her chair, chewing, and closed her eyes. I have been here in England, she told herself, for fourteen years. I have been in London for twelve years. I like it here, I like London, I like England, I don't want to go back to Stockholm. But I am still a foreigner to my parents-in-law. To them I am Our Swedish Daughter-in-Law. And nothing can ever change that, because I was born in Sweden, and however good my English is—and it is good—I speak with a slight sing-song accent, as Swedes do, and so every time I open my mouth I remind them.

And then there is Petra. I don't mind Petra. I am quite fond of Petra, in fact. But she is treated differently from me. Nothing is said, but it is in the *attitude*. Petra is English, Petra is an artist, Petra has no family to support her or look after her. So Petra is something they can own, and shape, and make think like they do. And what they don't remember, Sigrid thought suddenly, angrily, is that every time they pull Petra a little closer, they make a little more distance between them and me and, because I don't have my family in this country, I feel that distance, and when I feel it I am sometimes cold to Edward, to punish them through him, and then I am sorry, and angry with myself, and with them, and end up crying in hotel lobbies and not eating my expensive sandwich.

She opened her eyes, sniffing, and sat upright, pulling a pack of tissues out of her bag. She blew her nose decisively. This was ridiculous. She was a grown woman, a scientist, a wife and mother. She had a lovely house and enough money and a husband and daughter who thought the world of her. Her job was to support Edward through family crises, especially when he felt, as the eldest son, that everyone was turning to him in the hope of a solution, and he could not think what that solution could be. It was not her job to isolate him, and refuse to help him, or listen to him, and then shriek at him when he touched a raw nerve in her, which he never did out of malice, but only because he was a man and therefore sometimes clumsy.

She picked up her sandwich again. There was something else now, too, to add to the mix. There was Charlotte. How would Rachel and Anthony be with Charlotte? Would Luke stand up to them, in her defence, if she wanted him to? How was Luke going to manage, balancing the expectations of the Brinkleys? And how would Charlotte relate to Petra, and to the place Petra had at the heart of the Brinkley family? Sigrid swallowed her mouthful. Somehow, the thought of Charlotte made her feel better, less excluded. She blew her nose again, smoothed her hair back and took out her mobile phone to call Charlotte.

Mariella was sitting on the stairs. She had been about to go into the kitchen, but had been deterred by discovering both her parents in there already, with their arms around each other.

Although she was relieved to see them behaving in a way that meant they probably weren't going to get divorced, thank goodness, she found she wished they'd just get it over with, and be like normal, because it was a bit embarrassing, really, and made her feel weird. So she had retreated to the stairs with the cat's cradle someone at school had shown her how to do, made out of a length of purple wool, and she was singing to herself when the telephone on the hall table rang.

She scrambled off her step and down to the hall to seize the telephone. She was supposed to say, 'The Brinkleys' house,' but she always said, 'Hello?' on a rising note instead, because that's what her parents did.

'Mariella?'

'Yes—'

'Mariella, it's Charlotte. Your new aunt, Charlotte.'

'Oh!' Mariella said, beaming. 'Oh, *hi*.'

'You were such a cute bridesmaid,' Charlotte said. 'You looked so great. Everyone said so. What will you do with your dress?'

'Mummy says she has no idea,' Mariella said truthfully. 'You can't exactly go rollerblading in pink silk, can you?'

'Did she say that?'

'Oh yes,' Mariella said.

'Oh.'

Mariella took the phone back to her seat on the stairs. She said confidingly, 'Everyone's really worried now about Ralph and Petra.'

'Yes,' Charlotte said uncertainly.

'Daddy says they've got enough money for little things, like cereal, but not the big stuff. We're going to make a huge load of food and take it to them at the weekend. Are you coming?'

'No,' Charlotte said. 'We're going to see my mother. She's doing a big lunch for me and Luke and my big sister Fiona and her husband and my other big sister Sarah and her husband, and all the little girls you were bridesmaid with.'

Mariella settled herself more comfortably. 'So it's going to be a party?'

'Yes,' Charlotte said. 'My family is big on parties. We have parties whenever we can. When you come to our next party, you can wear your bridesmaid's dress, can't you?'

'OK,' Mariella said.

'Could you give Mummy a message?'

'OK.'

'Could you tell her that we'd love to meet up, as she suggested, sometime. Love to. But at the moment, we just haven't a minute, we're flat out, hardly even time to brush our teeth—'

She sounded, Mariella thought, a bit overexcited. 'I'll tell her.'

'Thank you,' Charlotte said, 'thank you. Give them my love. No, give them *our* love. Byeee!'

Mariella clicked the phone off, and sat looking at it for a while. Then she lifted her head and called out to the kitchen, 'Mum! Charlotte's too busy to see you at the moment, but she'll see you sometime!' and then she untangled the cat's cradle from her fingers and went slowly up the stairs to her bedroom, singing a cheeky song they'd made up at school, about some of the teachers, and was supposed to be a complete and utter secret.

When Ralph was in a mood, Petra had learned, it was better not to be in the house. She thought of his moods like fog, or dark smoke, drifting silently under the closed doors of his office and seeping into all the corners of the house, so that every room was invaded, and affected, and even Barney, who was the epitome of straightforward good cheer, looked at her with anxious eyes and an unsteady lower lip. On such occasions, she had discovered, the best thing was to bundle Barney up into his buggy, and collect all the paraphernalia necessary to nourish and change both little boys, and just leave quietly: no notes, no door-banging, just a swift, undramatic, unremarkable exit.

In the winter, she usually turned towards the high street because Kit loved the shop windows. She hardly ever bought anything, but she liked grazing along the windows at Kit's pace, past the ceramic curlew in the little gallery, which was priced at a fantastical—to Petra—£200, and the dentist with a plaque of a buxom mermaid coyly brandishing a toothbrush while reclining carelessly on a row of teeth, to the amber shop where Kit yearned for the tiny seals and elephants carved out of amber the colour of barley sugar. And then, for Barney's especial delight, they would trail slowly down the other side of the high street, and stop outside the sweet shop, which had huge, foil-wrapped sweets in the window, through which you could see pretty jars on white shelves, and more sweets than you could dream of. Barney never made a sound outside the sweet shop. He simply craned forwards, his arms and fat little hands held out towards the window in rapture.

But in summer, as it now was, their walks went the other way. They would turn out of their scrap of front garden and go past the primary school where they would always stop for Kit to admire the bas-relief of a ship at sea on the gable end, and the fence made of giant coloured pencils that divided the playground, and then they would proceed, very slowly, on account of all the things that needed to be examined on the way, down the footpath to Petra's allotment.

Kit approved of the allotment. He liked Petra's little shed, where she kept her tools, and the elder and lilac bushes that hung over it, and the special wicket gate you went through, from the path. He kept some toys—a plastic digger, a dumper truck, a tractor—in the shed, and he would get these out with a workmanlike air while Petra settled Barney and found a hoe and straightened bean canes. Kit was, Petra often reflected and sometimes pointed out to Ralph—even if it was hard to tell how much it registered with him—very contented when he was in her allotment, and seemed to be free of most of the cares and apprehensions that stalked his waking hours.

'Perhaps,' she said to Ralph, 'he likes being in a sheltered space. He likes knowing where the edges are.'

Ralph gave a little bark of laughter. 'Then he's not like me—'

But nobody, Petra reflected, peering under the stiff, abrasive leaves for new courgettes, was much like Ralph. That was what she had liked about him, apart from his looks, when she first met him; she'd liked his difference, the way he came from quite a posh background, but you'd never know it from the way he talked, or dressed, or thought. He'd been a banker once, after all, in a suit and tie, and even, he told her, had manicured nails, because his Singapore office required you to have that done.

Well, everything about Ralph was a bit ragged now. He needed a haircut, he shaved in a haphazard way that made him look worse than if he hadn't shaved at all, and he wore the same T-shirt every day unless Petra actually picked it up off the floor and put it in the washing machine. Petra didn't mind Ralph looking untidy—heavens, untidy was a natural and proper state to her way of thinking—but grubby and neglected was another matter. And even if Ralph had been the kind of person you could tell off, or try to change, it wasn't in Petra's nature to do either, even if it occurred to her, now and then, that Ralph was the least susceptible-to-change human being that she had ever met.

Rachel had often tried to talk to her about this aspect of living with Ralph. She was sympathetic, and anxious to help and even to ameliorate some of the exigencies imposed by sharing your life with someone who could take imperviousness to extraordinary levels. But Petra, who had never experienced the smallest element of emotional possessiveness until she had children, saw no need to oblige Rachel by minding the way Ralph was, more than she did. She didn't want to interfere with the way Ralph lived or made money for them to live on. She didn't want to change him any more than she wanted him to change her.

Except—well, now she *had* changed. Having Kit and Barney had changed her. Things that would never have crossed her mind as worrying were now troubling her: mundane things like security and fatigue, and the sharing of anxious, fragile burdens like Kit's propensity for unhappiness.

She didn't know if she felt like this because of hormones and motherhood, or because Rachel and Anthony's concern for her had infected her. She just knew, with a heavy heart, as she laid a shiny row of courgettes on the grass strip that edged her allotment, that Ralph's current money and employment worries, and his family's urgent and vocal concern, were getting to her in a way that nothing had ever got to her before.

And Ralph would not talk to her. He was the same as he always was with the children, affectionate and even interested in his intermittent way, but he would not discuss any of his business troubles with her. Petra, who had never even had a bank account before she met the Brinkleys, knew that the bank had refused Ralph something he could not operate without, which was presumably a loan, but she did not know why this refusal spelled disaster, or what degree of disaster it meant. When she thought about having, perhaps, to leave their house, she only felt fear that Kit and Barney would lose the familiarity of their shared bedroom, but when she had tried to voice this alarm to Ralph he had simply said, hardly looking at her, 'You can always go to Mum's, can't you? Take the boys to live with Mum and Dad.'

She straightened up and looked across the allotment. Kit, squatting beside his truck, was filling it with pebbles, which he was piling in carefully, one by one. Barney, under the dappled shade of the lilac bush, was asleep, his hands clasped comfortably on his belly like a caricature alderman. It was perfect, yet she could only see how frail it was, how temporary, how susceptible to being destroyed by the prospect of going home to Ralph's silent fury with himself for having let them all down.

She went and crouched down by Kit. 'What are those for?'

Kit didn't look at her. 'To make a wall.'

'What kind of wall?'

Kit went on piling. 'So the bad guys don't get in.'

'There aren't any bad guys,' Petra said. She leaned forward. 'There aren't any. And if there were, I'd look after you. I wouldn't let them come.'

Kit gave her a quick glance and went on with his pebbles.

'I'm sorry,' Petra said, 'but we've got to go now. We've got to go home—'

Kit got up abruptly. He drew his right foot back and then kicked his truck hard so that the pebbles sprayed out across Petra's strawberry bed, among the canes that held up her sweet peas.

'NO!' he yelled.

Rachel was in their kitchen when they got home. Ralph was there too, in his half-beard and usual T-shirt, and he had made Rachel a mug of tea, and was holding one himself with the air of doing something strictly for politeness' sake. On the kitchen table, which still bore the remains of the children's breakfast, was moussaka in a pottery dish, a plastic box of nectarines and a chocolate cake dotted with Smarties.

'Boys!' Rachel said. She put her tea mug down and darted round the table, kissing Kit and swooping Barney out of his buggy. She held Barney so that he could see the cake.

'Look!' she said. 'Look! Look what Granny's brought you!'

'That's kind,' Petra said. 'I mean, the food—'

'We aren't actually short of food,' Ralph said.

'Well,' Rachel said, jiggling Barney, 'you won't be, after this weekend. Mariella's baking for you. She rang to tell me. She's having a bakeathon, and they're bringing it all up on Sunday.'

'Mariella's coming?' Kit said.

Ralph moved to take Barney out of Rachel's arms.

'Mum, we aren't refugees, you know—'

Barney flipped himself round so as not to lose sight of the cake.

'No, of course not. But food never goes amiss. Does it, Barney?'

'Who's coming?' Ralph said. 'Are they all coming?'

'Well,' Rachel said, with a slightly dangerous emphasis, 'Ed and Sigi and Mariella are. But not Luke and Charlotte.'

'Why not?' Ralph said sarcastically. 'Why aren't they all coming, bringing cast-off clothes and blankets and unwanted toys?'

'Don't be difficult,' Rachel said.

Kit stood on tiptoe, holding the edge of the table, and deliberately, quietly and slowly pushed his forefinger into the chocolate cake until stopped by his knuckle.

'Kit!'

He did nothing, but merely stood there with his finger in the cake. Rachel seized him and pulled him back. Petra gave a little scream, half a sob, and fled from the room. Rachel looked at Ralph over Kit's head.

'It's all too much for her—'

'Of course it is,' Ralph said savagely, 'if you all behave as if it's the end of the world.'

Rachel said nothing. With a knowledge of the kitchen that caused

Ralph to exclaim under his breath, she opened a kitchen drawer, took out a long-bladed knife and said to Kit, 'Let's cut it properly, shall we? Let's cut it and then you and Barney can both have some.'

Ralph pulled out a kitchen chair and sat down, confining Barney with one arm. Rachel said, 'Shouldn't you go and see if Petra's OK?'

'She's OK. Being by herself is what she does when she needs to.'

Rachel put two slices of cake onto plates. 'Are you sure?'

'Yes, Mum!' Ralph shouted.

Kit jumped. He shot his father a fleeting, terrified look. Rachel lifted him onto another chair and put the cake in front of him.

'Don't shout,' she said to Ralph.

'Don't make me shout.'

'There, Barney, there. No hurry, Kit darling, try to eat slowly.' She looked at Ralph. 'I actually had a purpose in coming.'

Ralph broke off a piece of Barney's cake and ate it.

'I bet you did.'

'It's about Petra,' Rachel said. 'When did she last do any drawing?'

'I don't know,' Ralph said. 'Ages ago, months, before Barney maybe—'

'That's what we thought. We thought that what she needs while everything is up in the air is the chance to do some drawing. To have a bird day.'

'It's not up in the air,' Ralph said.

Rachel ignored him. She fetched a cloth from the sink and began to dab at the chocolate smeared on her grandsons' faces.

'We thought we'd take the boys next week, for a day or so, and then you and Petra can have some time together, or Petra can go off and draw.'

'OK,' Ralph said. 'Great. Fine. You can do it on the Wednesday.'

'Why Wednesday?'

'Because,' Ralph said, 'I have an interview next Wednesday.'

'Darling!' Rachel said. 'Fantastic! What amazing news.'

'It's an interview, Mum. Not a job. An interview.'

Rachel came round the table and put her hands on his shoulders. 'Where is it? Where is this interview?'

Ralph looked across the table at Kit.

Kit had picked the Smarties off his piece of cake and was arranging them on the rim of his plate. He glanced up at his father, as if to check that there would be no more shouting.

'London,' Ralph said.

When Petra had first gone to Rachel and Anthony's house, as a student in a group of students, it had struck her as being a wonderful place. She had been bowled over by Anthony's studio, by Rachel's kitchen, by the easy authority they both exercised in their particular spheres. But back then, of course, on subsequent visits and until Ralph came home, she had been alone with Rachel and Anthony, the only child, as it were, and she was lapped about with the privilege of being the only young thing. Nowadays, however, what with her own family, with Ralph's brothers and their families, with so many diverse claims upon the house and its chief occupants, going there no longer had the luxury of the past, or the sense of individual significance. Sometimes going there now, being there, she even forgot to speak, she forgot to claim the right to be spoken to, and included. Sometimes, too, Ralph said to her on the way home, 'Are you sulking?'

It had been like that today. The house had felt as if it was roaring with people. Mariella, a lock of her long hair carefully wound with coloured threads, had dumped a huge baker's basket on the floor of the sitting room, and proceeded to give a kind of performance of benefaction, producing biscuits and buns and cake out of it to the exclamations and applause of everyone. Except Petra. Petra was very fond of Mariella, and very touched by the fact that this baking bounty had been entirely her idea, and partly her achievement, but she found she simply could not speak because she felt she in no way belonged to what was going on. It was too *much*. And Ralph looked mutinous.

Lunch was, if anything, even worse. Rachel had cooked superbly, as usual, and lavishly, as usual, and the usually picky Kit had eaten three roast potatoes, with gravy, and asked for a fourth, and Rachel had been delighted. The conversation had turned to Ralph, and the prospective interview, which was apparently at Edward's bank, by Edward's connivance, and everyone was extremely pleased with him for engineering it.

'What if you get the job?' Anthony said.

'What do you mean, what if I get it?'

'Well,' Anthony said, 'it's City-based, isn't it. You can't commute from the Suffolk coast to the City every day. Can you?'

'Of course I can.'

'No, you can't,' Rachel said. 'You'll be exhausted. You'll never see the children.'

And then Ralph had said calmly, not looking at his parents, not looking at Petra, 'We'll have to relocate then, won't we?' and then, as an answering hubbub rose around the table, he had lifted both his hands in the air and shouted, 'No more speculation! No more discussion! Stop!' and Petra had a distinct sensation that, if she just gradually pushed her chair back to the wall, she could melt into it somehow, and vanish, and escape through it into the air and freedom the other side, and nobody—except Kit—would even notice that she was no longer there.

'Are you sulking?' Ralph said on the way home.

'No.'

'What is it then?'

'I'm stunned,' Petra said.

'What by? That I've got an interview?'

Petra glanced over her shoulder. Both boys were asleep in their car seats. Barney's mouth was open.

'No. Of course not.'

'What then?'

'You said,' Petra said, 'you said that we might have to leave Suffolk.'

'No,' Ralph said, 'I didn't. I simply said that if I couldn't manage the commute, we might have to relocate.'

'I can't do it.'

'I'm not asking you to leave Suffolk. Maybe we just move nearer Ipswich.'

'No.'

'You used to live in Ipswich. You know Ipswich.'

'That was before,' Petra said.

'Before what?'

'Before you. And the boys. And being by the sea, and everything.'

Ralph said nothing for a mile or two. Then he said, 'Nothing's happened yet. Why are we crossing bridges we haven't even got to?'

Petra stared out of the car window. 'There're always new bridges. I liked it at Shingle Street. I've got used to it in Aldeburgh. I don't want to get used to something else.'

Ralph turned the car into their little street. He said, 'You may have to.'

Petra said nothing.

Ralph said again, louder, putting the brake on decisively, 'You may have to.'

'No,' Petra said.

Later, Petra let herself out of the house, and turned towards the footpath. It was a calm, sweet evening, with an apricot light from the sinking sun, and a little, sharp breath of air coming up from the sea. She went along the road past the school, and then crossed to take the path down towards the allotments, remembering that she had forgotten to bring something to put any strawberries in, and wondering if she could balance them in a courgette leaf, or make a pouch out of the hem of her sweatshirt.

She squinted up at the sky. A few geese were crossing the far horizon, faintly honking, and there were swallows diving in the soft air. She would see, she told herself, what happened after Wednesday, and at least Ralph knew now what she couldn't do, what she wouldn't do.

In her allotment, Kit's dumper truck still lay where he had kicked it. Petra got down on her hands and knees and gathered up the pebbles, and mounded them up neatly because Kit would need them next time he came. Then she dusted out the truck with a dock leaf, and began to pick the strawberries, one by one, carefully, laying them in rows in the truck with their green stalks all facing the same way, as she knew Kit would like her to do. Then she stood up and looked down at the truck.

It was the most satisfactory and healing sight of the day.

CHAPTER FOUR

CHARLOTTE WAS, AS USUAL, home before Luke. Her shifts at the radio station were long, but they were regular, and when they were done they were done, and someone else came in to take over the things Charlotte did, like greeting and shepherding guests, and fetching cups of coffee and glasses of water. She liked it that a lot of the guests, especially the regular, male ones, either asked for her specifically or made a flattering fuss if it wasn't her shift. Sometimes, of course, the guests went too far and demanded Charlotte in a frankly sexist way, like the well-known actor who'd said loudly that day, 'Where's Miss Well-Stacked and Wonderful?'

'You are well stacked, of course,' the female producer of the afternoon show had said, not looking at Charlotte, but at the computer printout in her hand. 'And it's a great pity that, as far as he's concerned, you can't return the compliment, and point out his pitiful inadequacy.'

'Oh, I wouldn't do that—'

'I know,' said the producer, looking up, 'you wouldn't. If you weren't so good-natured we'd be obliged to detest you.'

Now, standing in the bathroom in the flat, Charlotte opened her shirt, and surveyed her bosom. She'd had quite big breasts ever since she was thirteen, but were they now even bigger? And were they, when she unhooked her bra, and pressed the sides tentatively, slightly tender, in the way they sometimes were just before she got her period? But, as it happened, she hadn't had a period for—she paused and ticked off the dates on her fingers—nearly eight weeks. Which she hadn't made too much of, in her own mind, because her periods had been so irregular since she stopped taking the Pill, as the doctor had warned her they might be.

It was Luke who had said she should stop taking the Pill. She'd swallowed it, almost without thinking, ever since she was in the sixth form at school, and Luke had said to her one evening, very seriously, that he thought, now that her future was with him, she should give her body every natural chance and stop putting chemicals into it. He said he was very happy to take contraceptive responsibility, so could she please give her amazing body the chance to do its own wonderful thing.

Charlotte had been enchanted by this speech. It was thrilling to have Luke be so mature, and so masterful, and to see her body as something that needed respecting, and taking care of. When she had thrown away the pills she felt unbelievably womanly and fertile and powerful, and this had been very satisfactory for both of them to the point where Charlotte supposed that, if you were quite simply happy enough, you didn't really need to sleep. Nor did you need to think too urgently about the precise and efficient use of contraception if your husband had told you, in his alluringly commanding way, to leave it all to him.

So she had. And now she was standing in her bathroom, with her shirt unbuttoned, and her bra loosened, just wondering. She found she was holding her breath. And then she realised, with a sudden, joyful rush, that if she *was* pregnant it didn't matter, however much they had planned to give themselves two years of freedom before they even considered a baby. If she *was* pregnant, it would be something to celebrate.

She pulled her bra back into place, and fastened the only two buttons on her shirt she considered necessary. Then she went across the sitting room to the kitchen, and the bag she had left on the worktop containing the ingredients—chicken pieces and a pot of hot salsa—for supper. She would put the pieces of chicken to marinate in oil and lemon juice, as her mother did, and wash the salad leaves and measure out the couscous she'd decided on to accompany the chicken, and only when that was done, and the table was laid, would she ring Luke in his studio and ask him—without telling him her simmering suspicions—when he thought he'd be up for supper.

Luke had some new graphics software. It enabled him not just to view things three-dimensionally, but to design in three dimensions too, and the afternoon had been extremely absorbing in consequence. He had a new commission, to design the logo and publicity material for a small chain of spa gyms in Essex and East London, and the software was enabling him to come up with, even at this early stage, some amazing ideas. So when his phone rang, and he knew it would be Charlotte, he picked it up and said, 'Swing down here, babe, I've got something to show you,' even before Rachel had time to say, 'Darling?'

'Mum,' Luke said, in quite another tone of voice.

Rachel said, 'I won't keep you. It was just that you hadn't rung since the weekend, and as we didn't see you I wondered how things were?'

Luke kept his eyes on his screen and his hands on his mouse and keyboard. 'Great, thank you.'

'Did—did you have a nice weekend?'

'Fab,' Luke said. 'Five-star lunch, played tennis—we won—with my new brothers-in-law and Char's sister, Sarah, who has a momentous backhand. Terrific.'

'Oh, good,' Rachel said without enthusiasm.

'Everyone OK?' Luke said.

'Who exactly do you mean—'

'Well,' Luke said, 'you and Dad, Ed and Sigi and Mariella, Ralph and Petra and—oh, what about Ralph and Petra?'

'Ralph has an interview Ed got for him. Ed's been wonderful. And

Mariella baked the little boys a basket of biscuits and things. We had a wonderful day all together.'

'Good,' Luke said.

'We missed you.'

Luke shut his eyes for a second. He removed the phone from his neck, put it against his other ear and said, 'What a relief about Ralph.'

'Why don't you ring him? To wish him luck—'

'Mum,' Luke said, 'I'll make my own decisions about who I call—'

'It would have been supportive if you'd come at the weekend.'

Luke closed his eyes again. He thought of saying to his mother that he had another family in his life now, but he contented himself with saying good-humouredly, 'Cut it out, Mum,' and then adding straight afterwards, 'We'll be up in Suffolk soon, I promise. Char's longing to show you the wedding pictures.'

'Lovely,' Rachel said, flatly.

'I'll ring Ed, and Ralph, and now I must go and find Charlotte.'

'Give her my love—'

'Sure will. Love to Dad.'

'Love to you, darling,' Rachel said. 'Love to you.'

Luke pressed the end button. The phone rang again at once.

'You were engaged,' Charlotte said reproachfully.

'It was Mum rabbiting on about last weekend—'

'What about last weekend?'

'We didn't go to Suffolk—'

'Of course not,' Charlotte said, 'We had a lovely day at home.'

'We did have a lovely day. Babe, I miss you.'

Charlotte giggled faintly. 'Come on up, then.'

'You come down here. I've got something to show you.'

'Will I like it?'

'You will,' Luke said, 'be very impressed by it.'

'So will you.'

'I'm impressed already—'

'No,' Charlotte said, laughing. 'No. Not about that, whatever it is, but about me. About something I've got to tell you.'

'Tell me now—'

'No,' Charlotte said. 'It's the kind of thing you have to tell in person.'

'Then you get your person down here!'

Luke was awake. Wide awake. It was two forty in the morning and Charlotte was asleep beside him, her pale head on his bare shoulder. What she had told him that evening in his studio had been even more momentous than when she'd agreed to marry him, because it was such a surprise and such a responsibility and such a joy.

He hadn't really taken much notice when Sigi was pregnant. He'd been on his gap year, in South America, when Ed and Sigi were married, and although there'd been a huge amount of communication about the wedding and offers of airfares, Ed had telephoned Luke, when Luke was by Lake Titicaca, and said look, we're fine about you not coming back for the wedding, it's only Mum and Dad fussing really; you stay in Bolivia and we'll get together after you're back. So Luke had remained, and when he finally got home, he discovered that Ralph hadn't turned up for the wedding, either, and that Ed and Sigi were living in a flat in Canonbury in conditions, it seemed to him, of impressively grown-up settledness.

Sigrid had got a new job by then, in a laboratory attached to a police forensic unit. She did that job for a few years before announcing, in her steady, undramatic way, that she was pregnant, and by then Luke was deep in life at uni. Petra, of course, had made more of an impact, because she was not conventional like Sigrid, and nor had Ralph ever been, and the responsibility for their future, and their baby's, became a Brinkley family project, which sucked them all in, however often Luke said to Ralph, 'You don't have to do this, bro. You don't *have* to get married if you don't want to.'

But Ralph had been like a sleepwalker. Ralph, who had always been perverse and wilful and recalcitrant, seemed almost paralysed by the thought of this baby, but happy-paralysed, as if he wanted to do whatever would be best for this baby who was going to be, he said in marvelling and uncharacteristic tones to Luke, someone of his *own*. And when Luke had talked to his parents, he discovered that they didn't want a marriage in order to be socially acceptable, but because they thought Petra was the only person who could understand Ralph's singularity, and who would be prepared to support him in it, and that—although this was never expressed openly—they had invested too much in this child who had softened the blow of their own children leaving home to want to let her go.

Luke looked down at Charlotte's sleeping face, at the thick fans of her eyelashes resting on her cheeks. There'd been so much agitation around

Ralph and Petra and their wedding that poor Kit's arrival had been almost incidental, brushed over like the final scene of some uncomfortable drama. Luke had driven up to Ipswich to the hospital, to see Petra and Kit, who had been parcelled up like a solid, white grub in a Perspex cradle, red-faced, with an explosion of dark hair. Luke remembered bending over him and thinking, funny little tyke. Looks like Ralph already, but he hadn't thought, oh wow, this is a new life, this is a real person that Petra and Ralph have made between them, this is the future.

Which is what he was thinking now. His hand was resting on Charlotte's warm leg. Just a few inches above where his hand lay, something now—probably—stirred, some as-yet small collection of cells that would evolve to become a baby, with ears and fingers and toes and, above all, a mind of its own. Tears began to fill Luke's eyes, brimming up and spilling over, and running unchecked down the sides of his face into his ears. Please let it be true, Luke said silently into his dim bedroom, please let it be true. Please let there be a baby.

The doctor had confirmed that Charlotte was, indeed, pregnant. About nine weeks pregnant. She'd looked at Charlotte over the top of her reading glasses, and said that Charlotte's age was an excellent age to have a first baby. She made it sound as if Charlotte had done something especially clever, and she smiled broadly and said well, looking at the two of them, this was going to be a lovely child, and then she stood up, and shook their hands warmly, and they went out in the street in a glow of self-congratulation and apprehensive excitement, to celebrate in a coffee shop which was the limit of the stimulation that either of them were going to allow into Charlotte's system from now on.

In the course of drinking their flat whites—decaffeinated in Charlotte's case—they discussed the advice the doctor had given them about waiting to tell their families until the three-month mark of pregnancy was passed, and Luke had said, 'Well, while you ring your mum, I can ring my parents, can't I,' and Charlotte had spooned some of her coffee into her mouth and said, 'No, after.'

'What d'you mean, after?'

'I mean,' Charlotte said, 'that I'll ring my mother and my sisters first, and when I've done that you can ring your family.'

Luke had put his coffee cup down. 'Why not at the same time?'

'Because,' Charlotte said, as if what she was saying was perfectly obvious, 'the mother's mother is always the first to know. The mother's family comes first.'

'*What?*' Luke said.

'The mother's mother,' Charlotte said, 'is the first grandmother. That's how it works.'

Luke had leaned forward. 'But this baby is half me, half mine. It's as much Mum and Dad's grandchild as it's your mother's.'

Charlotte had looked at him, her gaze clear and confident. 'No, it isn't.'

'But it'll be called Brinkley—'

'Don't be so old-fashioned,' Charlotte said. 'It's not about names. It's about—about the natural order.'

'Could you—could you consider defying this natural-order whatsit and doing our own thing and ringing our parents together? For me?'

Charlotte took a swallow of coffee. 'No,' she said firmly, and she didn't add, 'Sorry.'

Luke had been strangely unsettled by this exchange. He was besotted with Charlotte, and thought her family terrific, and refreshingly different from his own, with their sporty, clean-limbed approach to life. But however exasperating and demanding his family members were, they were as deep-rooted in him as Charlotte's family were in her, and when he thought how his parents might feel if they ever knew that the accepted grandparental pecking order put them firmly in second place, his heart simply smote him.

Luke knew without a shadow of doubt, and had known it all his life, that his parents were on his side, as they were on Edward's side, on Ralph's. At school, and later at uni, he'd seen friends who were not unreservedly loved and supported as he and his brothers were, and if he ever reflected on his childhood he recalled a period of unquestioned security, even if not, both inevitably and properly, of improbable, unalloyed happiness. He also thought, now that he came to consider it, that his parents were pretty good grandparents, indeed wonderful grandparents to Kit and Barney, and as wonderful to Mariella as distance and differing ways of life permitted.

Although it was almost impossible to imagine getting angry with Charlotte herself, it was very easy indeed to get angry about the stupidity of a social class or habit that had allowed such thinking to harden into an apparently perfectly acceptable custom.

It was at the end of a long day churning these thoughts about in his mind that Rachel rang again.

'I just wondered,' she said, 'if we could make a plan for you to come up to Suffolk?'

'Oh, sure—'

'We're sitting at the kitchen table,' Rachel said, 'with the diary, and it looks as if the next three weekends are free, give or take the odd minor thing, so pick any—or indeed all—of them, why don't you?'

Luke said guardedly, his eye on Jed, absorbed in his screen across the studio, 'Can I call you a bit later?'

'Why not now?'

'Well, I'm working, and I'd also like to consult with Charlotte.'

There was a fractional silence at the other end of the line. In it, Luke heard his father say, 'Leave it, Rach,' and then his mother said to Luke, 'Let me just pencil something in—'

Jed raised his head and shot Luke a swift glance.

Luke said, 'OK. Pencil in two weekends from now. I'll call you later.'

He put the phone down. Jed said, his eyes back on the screen, 'You should have stayed single, mate.'

'Oh, no, I shouldn't. Nobody in their right mind would have passed on Charlotte—'

'True. But there's all the baggage. All those mummies and daddies and competition.'

'There's no competition,' Luke said. 'I won't let there be.'

Jed smiled at the screen.

'Good luck, dude.'

Up in the flat, pouring out water for Charlotte and Coke Zero for himself, Luke told her he'd agreed that they'd go up to Suffolk for the weekend in a fortnight's time. Charlotte was on the sofa, with her feet on the coffee table, looking as relaxed as some African wild cat lounging nonchalantly along a branch. She accepted her water to which Luke had added ice cubes and a slice of lime.

She said, 'It'd be more fun to have them here.'

Luke settled himself beside her and laid an arm along the sofa back behind her shoulders. 'You're sweet. But they want us there to feed us, and have an ooh-and-aah session with the wedding photos.'

Charlotte took a big swallow of water. She said sweetly, 'But I don't want that, angel.'

Luke put the back of his hand against her nearest cheek. 'I thought you liked going to Suffolk.'

'I do. I love it. I especially like your dad's studio.'

'Well, then.'

Charlotte turned her face slightly towards him. She said, 'I want the first time we see them when we're married to be here.'

'Why?'

'I want to be here, in charge of it—'

'What do you mean?'

'I want them to see that I can do it. That I can make a home for you. I want your mother to see that I can cook.'

Luke took his hand away. He said cautiously, 'That might be difficult.'

'Why?'

'Well, we didn't go there that last weekend, and we've been married five weeks, and there's been all the Ralph stuff. And I think Mum wants to welcome you there as her definite daughter-in-law and spoil you a bit and all that. I think, in her way, she wants to make a fuss of you.'

'She hasn't done much of that yet—'

'No, but now you're *married* to me, you're a done deed. It'll be different, you'll see. It's only fair to give her the chance, babe, especially as we went back to yours. We've got to be fair.'

Charlotte moved fractionally away from him. She said, 'My mother doesn't ask.'

Luke gave an ill-judged hoot of derisive laughter.

'Oh, come on, babe! She doesn't ask outright like Mum does, but she implies and hints all the time—'

'Shut up!' Charlotte said sharply.

There was a sudden and alarming silence. Luke took Charlotte's hand, the one not holding her water glass. She snatched it back. He waited a few seconds and then he said in a low voice, 'Sorry.'

Charlotte said nothing.

'Sorry,' Luke said, 'sorry. That was completely uncalled for.'

'Yes,' Charlotte said with emphasis.

'We can't fight about this. We mustn't. We mustn't let this family competitive thing get in the way of you and me—'

'No,' Charlotte said, her voice still distinctly unfriendly, 'we mustn't. Which is why I am not going to Suffolk before your parents have come to London to see where and how we live, and celebrate us being married and in charge of our own lives.'

Luke said unhappily, 'Dad hates London.'

'Well, he'll have to get used to it. Doesn't he ever go to Ed's house?'

'Not often,' Luke said. 'Usually Ed and Sigi go to Suffolk.'

Charlotte turned slightly so that she could look directly at Luke. She said, 'We're going to be different.'

'I hope so—'

'We're going to do things *our* way. We're going to establish *our* lives.'

Luke said cautiously, 'Does that apply to your family, too?'

Charlotte took a deep breath. She leaned forward and put her tumbler down on the coffee table. Then she turned to look at Luke again.

'I don't think you get it. My family wouldn't ask me to behave in a way I didn't feel was right for me. They just wouldn't.'

'Oh.'

'I expect it's being all girls,' Charlotte said. 'Daddy always said we belonged to him and Mummy only until we belonged to someone else.'

'Are you implying something? About my parents?'

'I'm just saying,' Charlotte said, 'that now we're married we don't belong to our parents the way we did before we were married. And I want to establish that by having your parents here, and cooking them a lovely lunch and showing them the photographs.'

Luke slumped against the sofa back. 'I don't know why that doesn't make me feel better—'

Charlotte stood up. 'It's what's happening.'

Luke looked up at her. She looked astonishing, seen from his position on the sofa, tall and powerful and more than a little terrifying. He had got out of the habit of being terrified by Charlotte, since those seemingly long-ago, cocaine-argument days, and he was horrified at the thought of going back to it.

A clutch of panic seized him and he said, not wanting to sound appeasing but conscious that he did, 'Why don't we just do one weekend in Suffolk to satisfy them, and then we'll do it our way from then on.'

'No,' Charlotte said. She folded her arms.

'But we went to your mother's—'

Charlotte almost shouted, 'I *told* you why! I *told* you that it's different for the girl's family! We aren't going to keep going there any more than we're going anywhere, but I am not going to Suffolk until your parents have seen us in our own home and that's *final*.'

She unfolded her arms and put her hands to her face and Luke realised that she was crying. He leapt to his feet and pulled her into his arms.

'Don't, angel, don't, don't cry, please don't cry—'

Charlotte said something indistinct.

'What? What, tell me—'

'She thinks I'm such an airhead—'

'Who does? Who thinks anything like that?'

'Your mother.' Charlotte pushed her damp face into his shoulder.

'She doesn't, she couldn't—'

Charlotte said unfairly, 'Don't make me go there—'

Luke kissed the side of her head. 'We've got to, sometime—'

'I know. Just not this time.'

'OK.'

'Please ring them. Ring them and ask them here. Say it would mean so much to us.'

'OK.'

Charlotte took her face away from Luke's shoulder and looked at him. She gave him an uncertain smile. 'If you ask them in three weeks' time,' she said, 'I'll have had my twelve-week scan and we can tell them about the baby.'

'I can't ask them to wait three weeks—'

Charlotte paused a moment and then said, 'Why not?'

'It'll be two *months* since the wedding!'

'Yes,' Charlotte said, and then she paused again.

Luke's arms loosened around her. He looked past her for a while and then he let his eyes travel back to her face. He attempted a smile.

'OK,' he said.

In his studio, Anthony was drawing with a 4B pencil. He had passed a cottage near Woodbridge a few days earlier, and had seen a dozen bantams pecking about in a patch of worn grass outside it, and had stopped the car and gone to knock at the door and ask if he could watch and sketch the hens for a while. There'd been an elderly couple in the house, looking after a toddler grandson, and they had said yes, yes, of course, in a harried way. So Anthony had climbed over a battered wire fence, and crouched down beside the bantams with his sketchbook.

Anthony only taught a day a week now, but he was reluctant to give it up and face the end of the teaching chapter of his life. And it had struck him, often, that domesticated birds were perfect models for new students to use when learning to draw birds, because their outlines were so solid and their movements were much easier to follow than something that was balanced in such a variety of extraordinary ways, like a godwit. And now he was back in his studio, working up a series of sketches.

Anyway, hens were soothing. They weren't romantic and wild and free-spirited like his beloved waders, but they were comforting and familiar, and comfort was what Anthony sought this particular afternoon after a miserable lunchtime conversation with Rachel. It had literally been lunchtime, not lunch, because, although Rachel had made one of her magnificent salads, scattered with seeds and nasturtium flowers, Anthony had not, on account of their altercation, felt like eating it, and the rejection of prepared food had been, of course, the last straw.

The heart of the trouble had been Anthony's standing up for Charlotte. Rachel had been full of indignation at the idea that a whole weekend in Suffolk was to be rejected in favour of an exhausting, unwanted and unnecessary drive to London to have lunch, amateurishly cooked, in a poky flat, and then to be required to admire the trendily insalubrious area in which Luke and Charlotte had incomprehensibly elected to live. And Anthony had then said mildly, 'I think we should go.'

'What?'

'I think we should accept with enthusiasm and go with a good grace.'

'You are so perverse—'

'No,' Anthony said. He looked at the salad in front of him, decorative and colourful in its pottery bowl, and thought that it suddenly looked impossible to eat. 'They want to show the flat off to us, they want us to see the flat—'

'I've seen the flat,' Rachel said crossly, interrupting. 'I saw it when Luke first found it—'

'They want,' Anthony said, 'to be seen to be married. They want to be taken seriously now they are married.'

'You mean *she* does—'

'Possibly. More than possibly, as far as you're concerned.'

'Meaning?' Rachel said dangerously.

'Meaning,' Anthony said, not caring now, 'that you don't think Charlotte has the first idea how lucky she is.'

Rachel took a breath. Then she sat down at the table opposite Anthony, and said, glaring at the salad rather than at him, 'You are an old *fool*. Just because she is pretty.'

Anthony had pushed his chair back then, and stood up. Rachel said, 'And don't imagine I went to the trouble of making this lunch for *fun*.' Anthony waited a second or two, to see if any helpful riposte came to him, but nothing did, so he had gone out of the kitchen and the house, and across the gravel to his studio, to the solace of a 4B pencil and the prospect of hens. Rachel did not follow him.

She would still be in the kitchen, feeling awful. She was no good—never had been—at subduing fierce, primitive impulses and converting their natural energy into something more measured and constructive. She had been a tiger mother when the boys were young, not necessarily overprotective but savagely partisan if they came up against the smallest hint of injustice or disloyalty. It had been evident from Edward's birth onwards that Rachel could not help but feel that being the mother of sons conferred upon her a peculiar and visceral consequence. She loved it, and had striven to be, as she saw it, worthy of it, by not insisting on an exaggerated femininity or caprice, by being supremely welcoming to all their friends, by continuing to support them through all the changeableness and experimentation of their adolescence. But girls—the boys' girls—were another matter. Girls demanded her boys' loyalty, just as she had expected—and got—Anthony's. Sigrid and Petra had, for completely different reasons, somehow managed to sidestep any confrontation about who belonged to whom, but Charlotte was not going to be as easy. Anthony sighed and added a small beady eye to the nesting hen he was drawing. Charlotte was used to having her own way with family, and Luke was top of her family list just now.

The door to the outside opened. It was a warm day, and usually Anthony would have left it ajar, but the altercation with Rachel had led him, instinctively, to close it.

'I've just been talking to Petra,' Rachel said from the doorway.

Anthony didn't turn. 'Oh?'

'She'll bring the boys about half nine tomorrow.' Rachel came quietly across the brick floor, and stood looking at Anthony's drawings. 'Those are great.'

Anthony drew a hen running, her legs splayed out sideways.

'I'm just—worried at the moment about Ralph—'

'I know,' Anthony said.

'And you think I'm taking it out on Charlotte—'

'Mmm.'

'She isn't very bright—'

'You don't know that.'

Rachel sighed. 'I know she's got Luke so's he can't think straight.'

Anthony drew on.

'Well,' Rachel said. She touched his arm quickly and lightly. 'It's the little boys tomorrow, and Ralph's interview, and a day off for Petra. Thank God for Petra.'

Anthony shaded in some neck feathers.

'Yes,' he said. 'Amen to that.'

Petra didn't think she had been to Minsmere since before Kit was born. When she thought about drawing she visualised it as belonging to that other Petra, the Petra who had worked in the football-club bar and the coffee place in order to pay for her rent and her drawing classes. She had not been brought up to regard art as vocational, as central to anyone's existence. So when art got overlaid in her life by babies and keeping house and adapting to the arbitrary demands of living with Ralph, she had accepted it.

But now, suddenly, and because of this interview of Ralph's, which seemed to her to be as full of things to dread as to hope for, she had a day to herself, a day she was to spend, it had been firmly indicated, sketching. The boys had been dropped off and she was heading north, in the second-hand car Anthony and Rachel had given them to replace Ralph's unsafe, old one. Her sketchbooks were in a canvas bag on the passenger seat. Anthony had slipped a couple of pencils into her pocket and Rachel had produced a picnic, in a cloth bag printed with ecological slogans, and they had waved her off with a vigorous enthusiasm that made her feel guilty. There was a strong temptation not to go anywhere near Minsmere, but simply to wander off down an unmarked lane and find a gateway big enough to park the car, and then just go and lie in a field somewhere, and stare at the sky and let all the fretting about Ralph and Kit and money and expectations seep out of her mind and into the air, where it would dissolve of its own accord.

But Minsmere had to be done. The boys were being looked after on the unspoken but firm understanding that Petra would be drawing, all day, with an absorption that would energise and revitalise her. She had no option but to leave the car in Minsmere's sloping car park above the visitor centre, hire binoculars for £2.50 and set out into the marshes and the sighing reed beds to the East Hide, where she might—just might—find consolation and distraction in watching the avocets picking their fastidious way around the Scrape.

The reserve was busy. It was summer, and the school holidays were in full swing, and there were children scuffing along the sandy paths towards the sea. Petra thought that, if she were them, and used to the restless drama of computer games, a day out in a bird sanctuary where shouting and racing about were forbidden, and all adults were weirdly distracted and slow-moving, would be very bewildering. Even frustrating. In fact, she thought, pausing by the ingeniously secluded entrance to the East Hide, I'm not sure I can do it today. Maybe I'd better walk a bit, and get rid of some of this restlessness. Maybe I'll go down to the sea, too, and sit in the dunes and look at the sky and empty my head a bit.

It was calming, down by the sea. Petra crossed the soft, deeply sandy path that ran parallel to the shore, and climbed up the sliding sides of the shallow dunes until the water was visible, shifting and blue-grey under a cloud-streaked sky. There were a few people scattered about, their binoculars trained upwards, and over to one side a young man in an RSPB sweatshirt was rolling up lengths of netting that had evidently been stretched along an area of the beach. Petra sat down to watch him. He moved slowly and steadily, unhurried, bending down to add stakes to a pile, straightening up to pull the netting towards him.

She lay back in the sand. It was warm on the surface, but cool if you dug your fingers in deeper. The sky above her was divertingly striped with tatters of pale cloud and there were the steady, unchanging, insistent sounds of the sea and the wind and the gulls, although the air was still down there, flat on the dunes. Petra wriggled her shoulders to make comfortable dips for them in the sand, and breathed deeply, in and out, in and out. Then she relaxed down into the hollows she had made, closed her eyes and slept.

Steve Hadley finished rolling up the nets and stacked them in a loose pile that he would collect later, after the punters had gone, and the reserve was empty. The nets had fenced off a few areas of the beach, during the early summer, to stop visitors accidentally treading on the little terns' nests, which was particularly heartbreaking when it happened, as the little terns often only laid two eggs in the first place. And the terns themselves were so tiny too, with their black-tipped yellow bills and sleek, black heads in the winter. Steve loved them. But then, he loved most birds, otherwise why would he be here, working with them in all weathers, instead of joining his father and brother in the thriving family opticians' business in Birmingham?

He paused to take a gum packet out of his pocket. He'd been all over the beach to check the nests were clear, that every healthy egg had been hatched, and now he was going back to get a coffee and something to eat before he went off to check the handrail on one of the tower hides on the canopy walk.

On his way up the dunes to the path, Steve passed a girl asleep in the sand. She was deeply asleep by the looks of her, her hands entirely relaxed. She was wearing the usual birdwatching gear of T-shirt and pocketed drill shorts and trainers, and she had RSPB binoculars slung round her neck, and a canvas satchel beside her with the corner of a sketchbook sticking out, but there was something about her that struck him, something more than the little swallow tattooed on the side of her neck or the jumble of coloured ribbons tied round one wrist. It wasn't really, he thought, her appearance, it was more her attitude. She looked utterly comfortable, lying there in the sand, completely at home, entirely natural. She looked as if she had come to Minsmere with the express purpose of falling asleep there, in the dunes, above the sea.

He thought he really ought to wake her. She wasn't being a nuisance or anything, and she certainly wasn't disturbing the birds, but this was a nature reserve, not a place of recreational relaxation, and the visitors were supposed to be here for birdwatching, not slumbering. He bent down, intending to put a gentle hand on her shoulder and wake her, and found that he couldn't do it. She wouldn't, after all, be sleeping like that if she didn't need to. She looked as if this was the best and most restorative sleep she'd had in ages. Steve straightened up again.

'Sleep well,' he mouthed down at her silently, and tramped on through the dunes to the path.

Petra bought a cup of tea from the café, and took it out to one of the picnic tables. She unwrapped the foil packets Rachel had given her and found egg-mayonnaise sandwiches and cucumber batons and flapjacks and dried apricots. She spread these out on the table and looked at them. Very delicious. The reward for a long morning's sketching. Except that she hadn't sketched a thing; she hadn't even taken one of Anthony's pencils out of her pocket, and she had not done anything except sleep in the warm sand until she was woken by two children stamping past and inadvertently spraying sand in her face. It had been a wonderful sleep.

She yawned. She must have slept for two hours or more, in broad daylight. She felt much lighter and clearer as a result, almost happy. She certainly felt—there were hours of daylight yet—that she could draw, after she'd eaten, she could draw enough to demonstrate to Rachel and Anthony that she had fulfilled the terms of the unspoken bargain, and earned her day off. She took her phone out of her pocket and looked at it. There was no signal. A small feeling of relief stole over her.

She finished the sandwiches and cucumber, and her tea, and wrapped the foil round the remainder. Barney would be pleased later to see the dried apricots, and thrilled to see the flapjacks. Kit would whimper over his supper as he did over most meals, put off by any food that was new, or bright, or natural in shape. But she didn't need to think about that just yet, nor, even, about Ralph's interview. She didn't need to think about anything except a few slow, quiet hours in the East Hide with her binoculars to her eyes, and her sketchbook open on the wide shelf below the window.

In the hide, Petra settled herself at the very end of the bench, to give herself a good view to the left as well as straight ahead. There was an absorbed man with a camera on a tripod, and a few people with note-books, but apart from them the other visitors slipped in and out of the hide with all the respectful lack of obviousness of people visiting churches and cathedrals. In any case, Petra soon forgot even to notice the bodies that briefly sat on the bench next to hers. It only took her half an hour of sitting and watching and breathing with increasingly slow, deep breaths before she had a pencil in her hand, and she was drawing.

She was drawing a redshank, marvelling at its brilliant orange legs, when a voice behind her said, 'Sorry to interrupt, dear, but it's five to five.'

Petra looked up, startled. An elderly man with an enamel avocet pin on his pocketed gilet, and thick glasses, stood beside her, notebook in hand.

He said, 'I've been watching you. My wife, too. We come here every week when the weather's good, we love it. And we're very impressed.' He indicated Petra's sketchbook.

'Oh—'

'But maybe you've forgotten that it closes at five? I said to Beryl, was I being an old fusspot, telling you, and she said better have me tell you than one of the staff, and anyway then I could tell you how good we think your drawings are.'

Petra looked down at the page. Her male redshank was in flight, showing the white edges to his wings. 'Thank you—'

'That's all right, dear. There's nothing like birds, is there, nothing. We've found them such a comfort since our daughter died.'

Petra stared at him. 'Oh, I'm so sorry—'

'It's something to do with wings, I expect. Birds and angels. Beryl says it doesn't do to make too many links like that, but I find it helps.'

Petra began to gather up her drawing things, shovelling them into her canvas satchel. 'Thank you for telling me. About the time, I mean. Thank you.' And then she pushed past him, through the door into the reed-lined corridor that led back to the pathway, and fled.

In the car park, she couldn't find her car keys. She turned the satchel out, and her pockets and the picnic bag, and there were no keys. They must have slipped out while she lay sleeping in the sand, she realised, their chinking obscured by the sound of the gulls and the sea.

She put the canvas bag down beside the car and then, on second thoughts, pushed it underneath, with the picnic bag. The car park was almost empty now, with only the cars belonging to the few paid staff still standing close to the entrance to the visitor centre. Petra set off at a run, thinking she would ask at the centre, to see if anyone had handed in her keys, but the centre and the café were shut.

Petra ran on, her mind jerked out of the serenity of the afternoon and scrabbling to find a solution to the problem of a locked car and a useless telephone and two little boys needing collecting half an hour away. When she reached the dunes, she found the spot where she had slept, and fell to her knees, raking through the sand with her fingers, hoping and hoping for a glint of metal.

Then someone called. It was not a shout, but more the sound of someone trying to attract her attention in as discreet a way as possible. She looked up. Away down on the edge of the beach, a quad bike with a trailer was parked, and the trailer was piled with rolls of netting, and the young man Petra had seen earlier was gesticulating with his hand.

Petra scrambled to her feet. She began to run towards him, and he was moving too, so that when he was only twenty feet or so away she could hear that what he was saying was, 'I've got them, I've got them.'

He held the keys out to her. She was breathless, and beaming. She said, gasping, 'Oh, thank you, thank you, you can't imagine, I thought I'd lost them, I can't phone, I didn't know what I'd do—'

He said, 'I saw them when I came down on the bike. They were just lying on the sand.' His voice was easy, with a Midlands accent. 'I thought they must be yours.' He smiled at her. 'I saw you asleep earlier.'

Petra nodded. She held the keys hard against her. She said, 'I don't know how to thank you—'

He shrugged. He said, 'Glad to help. Just luck, really.'

Petra looked past him, at the water. She said, 'I love the sea.'

'Me, too. And seabirds.'

There was a small silence. 'What can I do, to say thank you?'

'Well,' he said, putting his hands in his pockets, 'you could make a donation, I suppose.'

'Yes,' Petra said, 'yes. I'd like to do that. Who shall I say helped me?'

He said, 'I'm Steve.'

She nodded. She said, 'I'm Petra.'

'Unusual name—'

'I live in Aldeburgh,' she said, 'and I've got two little boys.' She held the keys up. 'Who I've got to collect now.' She took a step or two back, towards the path behind the dunes. 'Where d'*you* live?'

He looked up at the sky for a moment. Then he looked briefly at Petra.

'Shingle Street,' he said.

CHAPTER FIVE

RALPH, EDWARD GATHERED, had done well in his interview. Which was a relief. In fact, it was an enormous relief since Edward, having arranged the interview, had had severe subsequent apprehensions about the way Ralph might put himself across, and simultaneous pangs of guilt for his disloyalty in fearing that his brother might let him down. Ralph could not, in truth, be relied upon to be orthodox, or even, on occasion, particularly polite. He might turn up unshaven and unironed, in sneakers, and behave as if he was auditioning for an edgy indie band rather than the analysis team of a small, Swiss-owned bank.

But Ralph had worn a suit, and a tie, and the clarity and speed of his thinking had distracted Aidan Bennett, who was his principal interviewer, from the fact that his hair was over his collar and oddly rough, and his shirt cuffs seemed to have neither buttons nor links. Ralph had also, Aidan indicated to Edward, been extremely candid about his past history, explaining that he had put most of the money he had made in Singapore into his internet business, and had lost it, partly, he said frankly, because of the downturn and his bank's behaviour but also partly, he thought, because his skills were intellectual and catalytic, rather than managerial. He had admitted that he liked problems, he liked unravelling difficulties and discovering the reasons for their having happened. Problems, mental problems, suited him, he said.

'I liked him,' Aidan said to Edward. 'He'd fit in well with the South East Asia analysis team, especially in relationship to business in the US.' He glanced at Edward. 'It would be long hours, of course. Not really possible to do daily from the east coast unless you're a travel junkie.'

'I don't expect,' Edward said untruthfully, 'that that'll be a problem—'

'He's not at all like you.'

Edward said, faintly nettled, 'What's that supposed to mean?'

'Only that he wasn't what I was expecting.'

'Is that a compliment? To me, I mean?'

Aidan surveyed him for a second or two. 'Not really,' he said.

Edward found Ralph in the wine bar next to the bank, with two junior members of the analysis team. They were drinking Peroni beer out of the bottle, and Ralph looked as easy with them as if they'd been working together for years.

'How'd it go?'

'Ade liked him,' one of the juniors said. 'He didn't bother with the charm. That's Ade all over. Only charming when he's about to give you the hairdryer treatment.'

Edward nodded. He said to Ralph, 'Well, I don't think you should count yourself in just yet—'

'I don't, bro. Want a drink?'

'Actually,' Edward said, 'I was thinking of heading home. Are you coming back for the night? I think Sigi's expecting you.'

'I think,' Ralph said, 'I'll just stay put for a while. Thank you, though, and all that.'

Edward hesitated. He wanted to ask Ralph if he didn't want to tell him, in some detail, about how the interview had gone. He also wanted to say don't you want to see your sister-in-law, and your niece, but felt too exposed, especially in front of two men who were both in Aidan Bennett's team, and also very much junior to him. He looked hard at Ralph.

'Sure?'

Ralph smiled at him. He seemed like someone who had come through a considerable crisis and been rewarded by the assurance of an unexpectedly good future. 'Quite sure. Thanks, bro.'

Edward took a step back. Were the thanks for the interview, or for the supper invitation—or for neither? Was Ralph, in fact, telling him to leave him alone? A small spurt of fury at his brother's lack of grace flared inside him. 'I'll leave you,' he said, glaring, 'to your new friends.'

The minute I was outside,' Edward said to Sigrid, an hour later, 'I wished I'd pushed him. I wished I'd made him come home with me.'

Sigrid was laying the table. On weekdays, in term time, Sigrid tried to insist that Edward was home by seven thirty so that Mariella could eat supper with them and they could ask her about her day. Not that she wanted to tell them much. For Mariella, school was still something that you just had to do, every day, like brushing your teeth, or feeding your goldfish, but not something that constituted your real life, which was waiting for you outside school hours. And in the holidays, as it now was, Mariella spent the days with her friend, Indira, whose mother also worked full-time, being looked after by a student earning some vacation money, and devising the kind of elaborate and inconsequential games with Indira which did not, definitely, stand up to parental examination over supper.

Sigrid said, placing the candles which were an integral part of her table-laying, 'I hadn't really expected him—'

'I just rather hoped, you know. After I'd got him the interview. Is that Mariella practising her cello?'

'Arpeggios,' Sigrid said briefly.

'Maybe he was just relishing not being around at home for tea, bath, bed. Time off.'

Sigrid put clean, cotton napkins beside their three plates. 'He had the same upbringing as you. But he is not the same.'

'Not conventional—'

'Not connected,' Sigrid said. 'A little bit autistic, I would say.'

Edward opened the fridge door and took out a half-empty wine bottle. He held it up enquiringly.

'Please,' Sigrid said.

'If Mum rings,' Edward said, opening a cupboard door in search of glasses, 'I'll simply say that she'll have to ask him how today went.'

'Or not answer the phone—'

Edward turned to look at her.

'You've done enough. You got him an interview for the right kind of job, and he seems to have done quite well, but he has not thanked you and he has not wanted to talk to you about it. He would rather drink with two strangers.'

'Are you cross?'

'With him, yes,' Sigrid said. 'With your family, sometimes. With your mother more than with your father.'

'Because of—?'

'Maybe.'

'Sigi,' Edward said, 'that was such a long time ago. And we never told them. Not properly, anyway. You can't blame them for not knowing something they were never told.'

Edward took his wine to the glass doors at the back of the kitchen that led out onto a deck above the small paved garden where Mariella had a netball hoop screwed to the wall that backed onto the house behind them. When she was a baby, they had discussed the possibility of moving further out to a bigger house in a suburb, where there would be a lawn for Mariella to play on. But Edward had soon seen that such a project would never be more than a topic to play with, that Sigrid was, in a way, humouring him, trying to be normal, trying to persuade him—and herself—that she hadn't spent the first year of Mariella's life battling with the most profound and frightening of depressions, but had managed instead to take every change easily in her stride, as she would have wished.

The glass doors stood open to the deck. There were a couple of wooden armchairs on the deck, but Edward stayed in the doorway, leaning one shoulder against the frame, the hand that wasn't holding his wine glass in his trouser pocket, restlessly sifting his change. He took a swallow. That had been a terrible year. Well, more than a year, really, if you took into account the end of a difficult pregnancy and the slow, unhappy settling of Sigrid's hormones, and her insistence, her absolute insistence, that Rachel and Anthony should not know what was the matter, should not know what a bungled and appallingly prolonged birth Mariella's had been, ending in an emergency Caesarean operation because the heart monitor showed—had shown for far too long, in Edward's view—that the baby was becoming acutely distressed.

'Never again,' Sigrid had said. She had been lying on her side in the hospital bed, turned away from him.

'No—'

'I may be a coward, but I cannot do that again, I *cannot*—'

The obstetrician had told Edward that a complicated first birth seldom affected subsequent births. But this, Edward felt, was no moment for pointing this out. Sigrid was weeping. She did not seem to want to try to feed Mariella. She wept and wept and told Edward that she was a bad mother, she knew it, she was bad through and through, and a bad mother was the worst kind of badness there was, and there was nothing she could do about it, nothing, and please don't give her the baby, don't, because it just made her feel worse, just made her realise how bad, bad, bad she was.

Sigrid's mother, the doctor, had arrived from Stockholm. Edward had been thankful to see her. She had been very kind to Edward, and steady, and very firm with the hospital, and she had put Sigrid and Mariella on a plane, and taken them both back to Stockholm, where they had stayed for three months. Edward had flown out most weekends to hold his daughter and feed her and change her and to have Sigrid tell him that he must not come near her, and that she was a bad mother.

'Never again,' she had said, over and over.

And all the time, all during those alarming months, Edward was faced with protecting Sigrid from his parents knowing what was the matter, and with protecting his parents from knowing that they were being excluded from what was the matter.

'It's that mother of hers,' Rachel had said. 'Chilly woman. She was chilly at the wedding, remember?'

'It's hard to have a baby in another language, especially a first baby—'

'She has us,' Rachel had said. She looked at Edward. 'She has you.'

'I hope,' Anthony said, 'she'll come home soon. We can look after her here. We'd love to look after her here. We'd love to have the baby.'

'I expect she's jealous,' Rachel said. 'I expect she resents Sigi marrying an Englishman and having an English family. Not that Sigi seems to want an English family much. She seems to insist on being so Swedish when she's with us—'

'She is Swedish,' Edward had said. He had thought gratefully, and with simultaneous regret, of the ordered calm of the flat in Stockholm, of the long windows and the pale floors and furniture, and the quiet, decided way that Sigrid's mother spoke to her daughter. He longed for Sigrid to be home, yet he dreaded her leaving Stockholm.

'He thinks we don't know,' Rachel had said to Anthony later.

'Well, we don't know—'

'I know,' Rachel had said. 'We're forbidden to go to the hospital, Sigrid gets carried off to Stockholm, Edward looks like a ghost and plainly wants to tell us things he's been forbidden to mention. What on earth could that be, unless Sigrid had an awful time and now has severe baby blues?'

Anthony had got up from where he was sitting, and came over to Rachel and planted his hands on her shoulders. 'Rach—'

'What?'

'Rachel, if Sigrid and Edward make it plain that they don't want us to know, we don't know it. D'you hear me? We *don't* know a thing.'

Rachel had sat very still.

'We do not know,' Anthony repeated.

'OK,' Rachel had said, reluctantly. And then, 'Even if Edward obviously wants us to know?'

'He doesn't,' Anthony said.

'I don't,' Edward had said a week later, when his mother had finally confronted him.

'It's nothing to be ashamed of,' Rachel said. 'More women feel like that than don't, after babies. It's absolutely normal. It's hormones. It shouldn't be called depression.'

Edward had looked away from her. He was consumed by a violent need to protect Sigrid and a dual fury with himself for letting his anxiety show, and his mother for not keeping her mouth shut.

'There's nothing the matter,' he said. 'She just wanted her mother there after Mariella was born, and now she wants to be with her a bit longer. It's what Dad said, about having your first baby in another language.'

Rachel had given a small smile. 'I don't believe you,' she said and Edward, goaded out of self-control by her astuteness and her refusal to restrain it, had yelled, 'Mind your own bloody business!'

It might have been all right, Edward reflected now, drinking his wine and jingling his change, if the matter had been left there, if Rachel had been content with her definite, if unacknowledged, victory. But she had been unable to restrain herself, unable not to make it plain to Sigrid, after she and the baby were back from Sweden, that Sigrid's parents were not the only grandparents, and furthermore that Mariella, being the first grandchild on either side, was of particular importance and significance. Then she had gone on to offer help, and support, and babysitting, and Sigrid, adamant with fury, had told Edward that if his mother didn't leave the house instantly, and possibly for ever, she would go straight back to Stockholm, taking Mariella with her. And then, after Rachel had finally gone, Sigrid had turned on Edward and accused him of disloyalty, and of telling his mother things he had promised her he would never tell anyone, and of being more attached to his family than he was to his wife and child.

So he hadn't confessed. He hadn't told her, then, that he had been so frightened by her suffering, so desperate not to add to it or be the cause of its ever happening again, that he had, when Mariella was ten weeks old, booked himself a vasectomy and handed over his £300 with a determined conviction of doing the right thing for the right reasons in the right way. The procedure had taken ten minutes.

After six months, he had still not told Sigrid. He had, in truth, no need to, because she came to bed in uncompromising pyjamas and made it unequivocally plain that she did not want to be touched. He bore it until Mariella was almost one, and then he told her in a rush, blurted it all out, told her his sperm count was nil and that he was going mad.

She had cried. She'd cried so much since Mariella was born that at first Edward thought exhaustedly, distractedly, that this was just more of the same. But she was smiling. Or at least, she was trying to smile, and she said a whole lot of stuff to him in Swedish, and then she said, in English, that he was wonderful, that she so appreciated what he'd done, but at that moment she had all the libido of a floorcloth. He could do what he liked, Sigrid had said, laughing, sobbing, but he'd have to put up with her just lying there, a fish on a slab, a fish with a scar across its belly.

He finished his wine. God, it had taken ages. Years, probably. Years of patience and frustration and knowing that seeking sex elsewhere would provide the brief, heady release that comes with, say, losing your temper completely, only to be followed by a long, grey drag of remorse and regret and self-disappointment. He'd tried not to remember the Sigrid he'd met at that wild party at the University of Loughborough, the Sigrid who'd caused him to say, happily amazed, 'Is it normal—I mean, is it OK—to have as much sex as this?' He'd tried to concentrate on love, on loving her, on adoring Mariella, on being a man who was not, as someone once said of persistent sexual desire, chained to a lunatic.

And now, here they all were. Mariella was eight and practising the cello. Sigrid was the number two in a serious and highly regarded laboratory. He was well paid, professionally well thought of, and their marriage, if not what it had initially promised to be, was something he could not visualise being without. Maybe that was habit. Or maybe it was just—marriage.

Edward turned back to the kitchen. Sigrid was by the sink, washing lettuce, and Mariella was leaning up against her from behind, as if to make sure that she couldn't go anywhere. He felt, abruptly, rather unsteady, and that if he said anything his voice might come out choked, and a bit ragged, so he just stood there, holding his empty wine glass, and thinking that if all you really needed was love then that was actually a very demanding and complicated recipe for human survival.

Mariella summoned him to say goodnight to her. She was going through a phase of nagging for a dog, and had bought a dog-training whistle with some of her pocket money, which she had attached to a glitter shoelace and hung from one of the knobs of her bedhead, and when she was ready for a goodnight kiss she blew it peremptorily.

She was sitting up in bed in spotted pyjamas with her hair brushed into a smooth, fair curtain. Her bed was full of plush animals and a revolving night light was casting starry shapes on the walls and ceiling.

'Daddy,' Mariella said.

Edward sat down on her bed.

'This dog—'

'Darling, we've explained. Over and over. It wouldn't be fair on a dog, with all of us out all day. Dogs hate it, being without company.'

'OK then,' Mariella said, clasping her hands together, 'we'd better think of something that'll make you stay at home. Let's have a baby.'

'Darling—'

'Look,' Mariella said, 'I know what you have to do. I'll go for a sleepover at Indira's and you can just do it, you and Mummy. I really, *really* want a baby.'

'Darling, it isn't as simple as that—'

'Mummy said she didn't have any more baby eggs—'

'That's about it.'

'What if I don't like being an only child?'

'Then,' Edward said unfairly, 'I would be very sad indeed.'

Mariella sighed. She lifted her hands and interlaced them in front of her face. 'When I'm big I'll have babies and dogs and probably a monkey.'

'Will I want to come and stay with you?'

Mariella raised her chin for a kiss.

'You'll have to. To babysit everything while I go to work.'

Edward paused in the downward movement to kiss her. '*Work?* Are you going to *work?*'

Mariella closed her eyes briefly, as if he was too tiresome to be borne. 'Of course I am,' she said.

In the kitchen, Sigrid was standing with the telephone in her hand.

Edward said, 'Mariella is bent upon a career and we're going to look after her monkey while she does it.'

'I'd be glad to,' Sigrid said. She dropped the telephone back into its charger. 'That was Charlotte. She wants us to go to lunch. When your parents are there, the weekend after next.'

'Goodness. Not what we're used to—

'She sounded very excited.'

'What, about having us all to lunch?'

'Well,' Sigrid said, 'about something. I don't know what. It can't have been about Ralph.'

'Why Ralph?'

Sigrid began to clear plates from the table.

'Ralph was there.'

'With Charlotte and Luke?'

'Yes.' She glanced at him. 'I think he was a little bit drunk.'

Edward put his fists up against his forehead. 'Give me strength—'

'Charlotte said they would make him a bed on the sofa. She seemed to think it was funny.'

'I wish I did—'

The telephone rang again. Edward moved to pick it up, but Sigrid darted ahead of him, laying a hand on his arm as she passed.

'Yes?' she said into the receiver and then, in a carefully neutral voice, 'Oh. Rachel.'

Edward put his hand out automatically for the telephone. Sigrid smiled at him, and turned her back.

'I'm afraid I don't know,' Sigrid said to her mother-in-law. 'No, Edward is at a business dinner and Mariella is in bed—'

There was a brief pause and then Sigrid said, 'Edward worked so very hard to get Ralph this interview. It was not easy, in this climate.'

Edward came up behind Sigrid, and slid his arms round her waist. To his relief, after a moment or two, she relaxed against him. He could hear his mother's brisk tones from the telephone, as if he was listening to her through a wall, or from under bedclothes.

'I'm not aware,' Sigrid said, 'that he has thanked Edward. I'm not aware that he knows the favour he has been done.'

Edward put his face into the angle of Sigrid's neck and shoulder.

'I can't help you, I'm afraid,' Sigrid said. 'I'm sorry Petra is in the dark, too. I'm sure he'll turn up. Maybe he is celebrating. Yes, yes, of course. I will tell Mariella. Love to you, love to Anthony.' She clicked the phone off.

'You saved me,' Edward said into her neck. 'Why didn't you suggest she ring Luke?'

Sigrid turned round in his arms. 'Because,' she said, 'I didn't feel like it.'

On the way to London, Rachel said she would drive. Anthony agreed, as she had known he would, so that he could sit silently beside her, half listening to Classic FM, gazing out of the window at the clouds and the passing landscape, while she could drive and think.

She needed to think. She had tried to think for days, either alone, or out loud to Anthony, but Anthony had not wanted to participate in her thinking, and had evaded her. He had never liked analysis, anyway. All their lives together, whenever there was a problem involving relationships, Anthony had worn the hunted expression of a dog required to walk on its hind legs: a bemused, slightly oppressed expression, and made for his studio. The most he would ever say, if Rachel pursued him with her need to dissect and ferret out an explanation, was, 'Can't we just see what happens? Can't we just wait?'

Rachel knew she was bad at waiting. All her life, ever since the first self-awareness of childhood, she knew that the flip side of her marvellous energy was her impatience. Problems had the effect of firing her up like a rocket, impelling her to chase about in her mind, mentally darting hither and thither, to seek a solution that invariably involved her own zealous participation. When she was thwarted of the opportunity to offer instant resolution, she found herself utterly devastated by her own helplessness. It was then, even after almost forty years of disappointed experience, that she turned to Anthony, and he, as usual, would make it abundantly plain that he couldn't help her.

It was always worse when the trouble was Ralph. Edward's comparative orthodoxy and Luke's relative youth and optimism made them both less of an anxiety to Rachel than Ralph. But Ralph was designed to cause anxiety, and was also designed to be completely oblivious to his capacity for being a constant, small, nagging worry to her, like an emotional toothache; bearable much of the time but with a propensity to flare up without notice, and cause agony.

Rachel had tried to talk to Petra. Petra had been, to say the least, detached about the job interview in the first place. She had stood in her kitchen, making tea for Rachel with maddening abstraction, while Barney crawled peaceably about the floor putting unsuitable bits of detritus into his mouth and swallowing them.

'I don't mind about the money,' Petra said. 'I've never minded about money. I'm used to not having money.'

Rachel had taken a deep breath and averted her eyes from Barney on the floor.

'That was then,' she said to Petra. 'You were a student, and only had yourself to think about. You have children now. You have a house. You have responsibilities. You aren't free to indulge yourself by saying you don't care about money.'

Petra didn't reply. She put Rachel's tea down in front of her, and then bent to extricate a plastic bottle cap from Barney's mouth, but without hurry. Her whole posture, her every movement, indicated to Rachel that she was not going to pursue this conversation, any more than she had engaged in the one about possibly having to move nearer a station, to enable Ralph to commute more easily.

'I can't leave the sea,' Petra said. 'Once I could've, when I hadn't lived by it, but I can't now. The best place I ever lived was Shingle Street. It was the best place for Ralph, too. We were really happy at Shingle Street. The sea was almost *in* the sitting room.'

Rachel had felt her whole body clench with tension. She had so much to say, so much to point out about practicality and common sense and responsibility and maturity and there was no point in uttering a single syllable of it. She had drunk her tea, and gone to find Kit sitting staring and rapt in front of the television, in order to kiss him goodbye, and had then driven home in an advanced state of agitation, to find Anthony determined not to engage with her either.

'We are talking about your *son*!' Rachel had shouted. 'Your son and your daughter-in-law who are declining—no, *refusing*—to face the practicalities and consequences of how their life will be!'

Anthony was in his studio, drawing a dead mole he had successfully trapped as it flung up its chain of miniature mountains across the lawn. It lay on a piece of yellowish paper, quite unmarked, its purposeful front paws half curled, as if still in the act of digging.

'It's their life,' Anthony said, drawing on.

'But they have *children*, they can't ignore that, and if they don't move Ralph will never get home at night and then—'

'Stop it,' Anthony said.

'I can't believe you don't care—'

'I care. I care quite as much as you do. But caring confers no right to interfere.'

'How dare—'

'I am not,' Anthony said, 'discussing this further. Not now, not tomorrow, and certainly not in the car going up to London when I am trapped beside you.'

So, here they were, in the car together, with the radio on to neutralise the atmosphere, and Rachel at the wheel, driving in a way she knew Anthony would both observe and decline to comment on. She had decided not to speak, being well aware after all these decades of living with herself that fear only made her sound angry and, if she added the anger caused by her anxiety over Ralph and Petra to the resentment she felt at being forced to have Sunday lunch in Shoreditch rather than at her own large and familiar kitchen table, she knew she couldn't trust herself to say anything of which she could subsequently be remotely proud. So she drove furiously, and beside her Anthony sat striving to distract himself from her violent silence, and his own inner turmoil at the storms threatening his family life, by examining the cloudscapes and wondering how Constable or Turner or Whistler might have painted them.

Luke had made a table large enough to accommodate seven people for lunch by overlaying their small, black dining table with a piece of MDF left over from his office conversion. Charlotte had wanted there to be eleven people, not seven, but Luke had grown tired, after Ralph's second night on their sofa in a reek of alcohol, of pursuing Ralph and Petra for a sensible answer to their invitation, and had said that they'd just go ahead without them.

'But I want the children,' Charlotte said.

'No, you don't. Barney will wreck the flat at floor level and Kit will whine and make a fuss about eating.'

'I don't mind—'

'I do,' Luke said.

There was a short pause, and then Charlotte said accurately, 'You're worried about your mother coming.'

'I have never,' Luke said, 'had my parents to a meal. Not ever. In my whole life. We always went home. We went home to eat. That's what we did. Always.'

'That's why it's worth making an effort—'

'I *am* making an effort!'

Charlotte waited a few seconds, and then she said, 'Don't take it out on me, babe.'

Luke looked at her. He gave a little bleat of exasperation, and flung his hands out. 'It's—well, it's just all this stuff recently. Ralph, and us not going to Suffolk and not telling Mum and Dad about the baby—'

'We'll tell them today. They'll know today.'

Luke said sadly, 'You told your mother last weekend.'

'I saw her,' Charlotte said. 'I wanted to tell her in person, and I saw her.'

'Three weekends running, seeing your mother—'

'Are you counting?'

'No,' said Luke, 'but Mum will be.'

Charlotte unfolded a white double sheet, and billowed it out over the table. She said, 'Did you get Coke or something, for Mariella?'

'Are you changing the subject?'

Charlotte bent across the table to smooth the sheet out. She was wearing a short, grey, gauze smock over white-lace shorts. Her legs were absolutely amazing. Luke had a sudden vision of those legs stalking past his father and his brother. He said, 'Is that what you're planning to wear?'

Charlotte straightened up. She had smoothed her hair close to her head and added enormous pearl earrings.

'Of course. It's new.'

Luke sighed unhappily. 'It's gorgeous. You look gorgeous. It's just—'

Charlotte began to giggle. She came round the table and put her arms round Luke's neck. 'It's to distract them all from how disgusting lunch is going to be. D'you think it'll work?'

If there are no babies at lunch,' Mariella said, 'I will have completely nothing to do.'

'Bring a game,' Sigrid said, 'or a book.'

She was standing in her bathroom, putting her make-up on, and

Mariella was sitting, fully dressed, in the empty bath beside her, on a stool she had brought in for the purpose.

'Why can't we have a baby?' Mariella said.

Sigrid applied eyelash curlers to one eye, and squeezed. She said, 'I'm afraid I'm not very good at it.'

'You are,' Mariella said. 'You had me.'

Sigrid opened the curlers for her other eye.

'I did. But not easily. Some women have babies easily and are very good at it. Their bodies are very good at it. We are all designed a bit differently, you see.'

'Which bit of you didn't work?'

Sigrid put the curlers down and picked up her mascara.

'My head, darling.'

'You don't have babies in your head.'

'But you have,' Sigrid said, 'thoughts and feelings in your head. Especially when you are growing a baby. You are never just a body, you are a head, too. After all, you have thoughts all the time, don't you? And you have to remember that some people have difficult thoughts and feelings, which you might not have yourself, and you have to be sympathetic to them, all the same.'

Mariella stood up, and climbed out of the bath. She said quite casually, 'Like Granny?'

Sigrid stopped applying mascara. She turned round. 'What?'

Mariella bent to pick up the stool. She said, 'Well, Granny had three babies so she must have thought it was easy.'

'I think she did.'

Mariella put the stool on the bathroom floor. Then she climbed on it, so she was taller than her mother. She looked down at Sigrid, smiling at her own superior position. 'So,' she said, 'Granny forgets sometimes to be sympathetic to someone like you. Doesn't she?'

Well,' Charlotte said, 'we've got something to tell you.'

She was slightly flushed. Lunch had been pretty successful, considering, and even though Rachel had hardly commented on it she had eaten everything on her plate and even said, 'Oh, chervil!' in a tone of pleased surprise when she saw the garnish on the potato salad. Mariella had been adorable and funny, and Anthony had drawn cartoons of them all as birds—Charlotte was an extremely pretty ostrich with false eyelashes and fishnet stockings—and everybody had exclaimed at the flat and the wedding pictures and Charlotte had caught Luke's eye and felt him acknowledge that she had been right to insist on hosting lunch, right to demonstrate to his parents that successful family occasions could happen away from the familiar base in Suffolk. So she tapped a stray spoon against her water glass and said in a slight rush, 'Well. We've got something to tell you—'

Rachel, who was sitting next to Luke, put a hand out to touch his forearm. She said, too fast, 'Oh, darling. A work breakthrough—'

Luke was staring at Charlotte. He looked slightly pent up, as if he was holding something in which would be a relief to release.

Charlotte, in turn, stared at Rachel. 'No,' she said decidedly.

Rachel turned to regard Charlotte. 'Not—'

'Not what?' Charlotte said, dangerously.

'Please—' Anthony said to Rachel across the table.

'Not a baby,' Rachel said recklessly.

'Rachel!' Anthony shouted.

Charlotte stood up. She had lost her temper in an instant.

'Yes,' she yelled. 'A *baby*! We're having a baby! What's wrong with having a baby?'

Rachel said unflinchingly, 'You've only been married ten minutes. Couldn't you have waited?'

The noise erupted. Luke got up, overturning his chair in his haste to get round the table to Charlotte, but Sigrid was there before him, her arms round Charlotte. Edward and Anthony turned on Rachel.

'How *could* you?'

'What are you *thinking* of? Have you lost your *mind*?'

'What business is it of yours—'

'God, you are a liability—'

Mariella was watching. She stayed in her chair across the table from her grandmother, and watched. She saw her mother and her uncle Luke with their arms round Charlotte and, even though she could only see Charlotte's hair and Charlotte's legs, she knew she was crying in there, in all those arms, and she was crying because Granny had said something that she shouldn't have said, and Granny was now sitting there, staring at her lap, while her father and her grandfather shouted at her in angry whispers. Mariella remembered that Charlotte had started all this by saying she and Luke were going to have a baby, and a surge of delight lifted Mariella clean off her chair to stand on it, so that she was taller than anyone else there.

She clapped her hands. 'Shut up, shut up!' she shouted. She looked down at her father. He had stopped ranting at Granny, and was sitting with his head in his hands. Mariella took a deep breath, then she yelled, 'There's going to be a *baby*!'

Anthony said he would drive home. He had taken the car keys from Rachel's bag, and then he held the passenger door open for her, and she had climbed in wordlessly, and buckled her seat belt, and not looked at him as he settled himself into the driving seat and adjusted the mirrors. She asked if he would like to be directed towards the A12, and he said thank you, but there were perfectly adequate road signs, and then he turned on the radio, quite loud, and they drove in wretched silence, all the way back to Suffolk.

It took two and a half hours. For most of the journey, Rachel lay back against the headrest, with her eyes closed, and her face turned away from Anthony. She could not think how to initiate conversation and Anthony looked as if such an idea was the last thing he would have welcomed. She had seldom seen him so angry. She tried to tell herself that what she had said today was no more than the common sense that everyone else was thinking, and dared not say, and failed. She tried to tell herself that Anthony's reaction was exaggerated and unjust and coloured by his tragic male infatuation with Charlotte's looks, and failed. She told herself that, whatever she had done, and whatever Anthony's reaction had been, she would not cry in front of him, and succeeded. And so, through mile after mile of the long road out to East Anglia in the tired sunlight of a summer Sunday afternoon, Rachel sat with her face averted, her eyes closed and her thoughts teeming behind them like a scuttling plague of vermin.

In the drive at home, Anthony waited for her to get out before he put the car into the small barn that served as a garage.

'Actually,' Rachel said, 'I'm taking the car.'

'Where?'

'To Aldeburgh,' Rachel said.

Anthony said, staring ahead through the windscreen, 'Do you imagine you will get a more sympathetic hearing there?'

Rachel said, slightly desperately, 'I need to talk to someone. I need to talk. And I can't talk to you.'

Anthony opened the driver's door, and got out. He said, 'No. You certainly can't do that.'

Rachel slid inelegantly across the gear shift and into the driver's seat. It was still warm from Anthony's body, and the warmth abruptly made her want to cry, more than any of the thoughts she'd had on the way home. When she inched forward she realised that the seat was too far back, and the mirrors were at the wrong angles, so she had to stop a yard from where Anthony had halted the car, and adjust everything, with him standing there watching her, his expression inscrutable but not in any way encouraging. She crept forward over the gravel and out of the drive's gates to the road, and only when she was out of sight of the house and Anthony's still and silent figure did she give way to tears.

The footpath ran along a dyke between flat land to the left of the path, and the River Alde to the right. It was a walk Anthony had known all his life, starting by the quay with its quiet stretches of sheltered water, and spits of low land, and clusters of small sailing boats, moored and clinking in the soft wind. From the quay, the path ran on past wooden sheds selling fresh fish on weekdays and a neat little tea room with a veranda, and the small white cube of the sailing club—all familiar, all timeless, as timeless as, further on, the outline, if he looked inland, of the church and the castle among the trees and hedgerows. The boys had all loved the castle when they were younger. Ralph had chosen it for a school project. Luke had moved on to Second World War stories, and was keenly envious of the excitement Anthony had known as a boy of the dismantling of beach defences, the removal of mines, and unexploded bombs. Edward, now so urban, so cosmopolitan, had been the one who was interested in the natural history of the place, the collector of samphire and sea pinks, the one who would crouch for hours in those flat fields waiting for brown hares to engage in the remarkable boxing matches of the spring mating rituals.

Well, Anthony thought now, descending the steep inland side of the dyke and turning to look at the white blade of a sail serenely passing on the far side of it, there was nothing to be gained by comparing those days with these. Those days involved three boys under twelve. These days involved three boys almost all over thirty. Little children: little problems; big children: big problems. He felt disgusted by the day, by the drama of it, by the wearisome drives, by Luke and Charlotte's contraceptive carelessness, by Ralph's selfish self-involvement, by Rachel's inability to control her thoughts and her tongue and her conduct. He felt dirtied by it all, soured and sullied.

From the wheat about a yard away came the sudden, sharp, drawn-out fall of a bird call. Anthony stopped and stood motionless. There, on a wheat ear, rather than the reedtop of its usual choice, sat a reed bunting, smaller than Anthony's hand, with its boldly striped and speckled body and its coal-black head, garnished with a white collar and a comedy moustache. Anthony waited. The bird had surely seen him. It would have a nest near by, close to the ground and cup-shaped, with maybe half-a-dozen eggs in it, which would hatch into brown babies with black-and-white moustaches above their tiny beaks. The bird and the man were quite still together in the summer evening for what seemed like a miraculous number of seconds, and then the bird uttered its curious little cry again, and took off without hurry towards the reed beds beyond the dyke. Anthony watched it go. He took a breath.

'Thank you,' he said, to the empty air.

Rachel did not return until after dark. Anthony had poured himself a tumbler of whisky and water, and had carried it across to his studio, intending to immerse himself there, in his usual way. He found that he couldn't do it, so he had returned to the kitchen and spread the Sunday newspapers out and tried to read them, and not look at his watch too often, and not pour a second whisky.

Rachel threw the car keys onto the kitchen counter with a clatter. She said, not looking at Anthony, 'I am very sorry.'

He stared at the newspapers. He said, 'So am I.'

'I don't really want to talk about it—'

'I thought you did—'

'I did want to,' Rachel said, 'but it kind of died out of me. Standing in their kitchen, I was just tired of it, tired of myself, tired—oh, tired of behaving like that. Which was just as well.'

Anthony looked up. Rachel was standing where she had halted when

she came in. She looked exhausted and rumpled, and her hair was
sticking up here and there as if she'd slept on it while it was damp.

'What d'you mean?'

'I got there just as bath time started. Ralph was doing bath time.
So I helped with this and that and then I read to Kit and then I went
downstairs, and Petra was drawing at the kitchen table and Ralph was in
his office. And I told Petra about the baby and she didn't look up, she just
said, "That was quick." And I said stupidly, "So were you," and she just
went on drawing and then Ralph came down and said thanks for coming,
Mum, and I realised I was being—I was sort of being *dismissed*.'

Anthony got up slowly from the table. 'So where have you been?'

'Down by the sea—'

'Where—'

'Parked,' Rachel said, 'at Shingle Street. Where Petra said she and Ralph
were so happy.'

Anthony came and stood beside her. It occurred to him to say, 'You have
to let it go,' but then he thought that they were both too tired for what
would inevitably follow, and maybe Rachel knew that anyway, and didn't
want to face it, or couldn't face it at the end of such a day.

After a while she said, 'Did anybody ring?'

'The boys? No.'

'I thought Luke might.'

'No.'

'Or Edward.'

'Stop it,' Anthony said. 'I'm drinking whisky. D'you want some?'

Rachel shook her head. She glanced round the kitchen, at the colours,
at the accumulation of objects, the rows of mugs on the wooden pegs, the
great pottery fruit bowl, the scarred chopping boards.

'This all looks pretty dated, doesn't it—'

'Rachel, don't start. It's too late. We're too tired—'

She gave him a quick look, and he caught a sudden glimpse of the girl
to whom he'd given the aquamarine ring that had once belonged to his
grandmother, the girl who'd known what to do with him, with the Dump,
with his parents' quietly collapsing house.

'Bed,' Anthony said. He put a hand on her shoulder. 'There's nothing
more to be done about today but end it.'

'OK,' she said.

CHAPTER SIX

WHILE PETRA WAS OUT at her allotment with the boys, Ralph got all his old suits out from the back of the cupboard in their bedroom. Dark blue and dark grey, bearing the labels of Singapore tailors, they did not look good, his poor suits, creased and neglected, with grubby linings and stuff in the trouser pockets and cuff buttons missing. Ralph dropped his jeans to the floor, and picked up the top pair of fine wool, grey, chalk-striped trousers. He stepped into them, pulling them up over his elderly boxer shorts and thin, market-stall socks. He fastened the waist and zipped the fly. They fitted perfectly, flat across his belly, skimming his thighs, roomy enough to put his hands in his pockets where he found half a boarding pass for Singapore Airlines and a crumpled Singapore $50 bill. He looked at the note in his hand, remembering. He thought about his flat, in an immense block on Orchard Road, with a vast, shining atrium floored in polished stone and a lift in a glass column that rose silently up among the brilliant green trees of an indoor jungle. He thought about the dealing room at the bank, where they had all screamed into headphones for ten hours a day. He thought about the beaches at the weekends, where he had sat alone on the sand, watching the sun go down, suddenly, into the Straits of Singapore, thinking that, out there, across the indigo sea, lay the first of the immeasurable islands of Indonesia. He closed his eyes. A sudden yearning for freedom struck him so forcibly that it almost took his breath away.

He found the jacket belonging to the suit trousers and put it on, too. Even with a T-shirt, and the crumpled condition of the jacket, the suit was impressive. He straightened his shoulders. The suit gave him definition and authority. He breathed in. He wondered if he still had any shirts—and shoes. He had sworn he would never wear a tie again but there was something ties did for a shirt, a sort of finishing something. Like cufflinks. Were people wearing cufflinks? Did he still own any?

In his socks and his suit, Ralph padded down to the kitchen. He filled the kettle. He wasn't exactly hungry, or thirsty, but he felt a definite stirring of recollection, of remembering something which was—had been—not without excitement, and stimulating, which ought to be celebrated with, at least, coffee. He thought about how carefree it had been in Singapore, how easy it was to exercise his talents but not to be responsible for doing anything more than exploiting what he was naturally good at, and then to be turned loose, in the evenings, at the weekends, and allowed to run free. He recalled dropping his tie—he thought it might even have been an Hermès tie, acquired at Changi airport—into a company wastepaper bin, and marvelled at his lunacy. What could he have been thinking?

The kitchen door to the outside opened. Kit, in his Spider-Man T-shirt, came in holding an earthy carrot and a stick. He held out the carrot.

'I pulled it,' Kit said.

'Well done. Will you eat it now?'

Kit dropped the carrot on the floor. 'No.'

'Wow,' Petra said from the doorway. 'Look at you—'

Ralph struck an attitude. 'What do you think?'

Petra was holding Barney. She bent to deposit him on the floor. He made straight for Kit's dropped carrot.

'Not really my kind of gear,' Petra said. 'But cool.'

'Can you iron it or something?'

'OK—'

'I don't have any shirts—'

Petra went back outside and reappeared with a trug of vegetables.

'Very impressive.'

'I like it,' said Petra.

'The allotment?'

'Growing things.'

Ralph went back to the kettle. 'Maybe we'll find a house with a garden. A garden big enough to grow stuff in it.'

'I like the allotment,' Petra said.

Barney was eating Kit's earthy carrot. Kit was standing by the table, his stick between his legs, like a hobby horse, wedging pieces of Lego into a toast rack. The table had Petra's sketchbook on it, too, and several newspapers and jars, and a carton of milk and a hammer and some bowls left over from breakfast with cereal dried to their sides. Petra put the trug down on her sketchbook. She said, 'This house is OK.'

Ralph tipped coffee out of a foil packet into a cafetière. He added boiling water from the kettle, and replaced the plunger on the cafetière. Then he pushed it down, slowly and carefully, before he said, 'I'll be earning at least sixty grand. Just for starters. More after a three-month trial.'

'I can't think about that much.'

'Well,' Ralph said, 'you should.'

Petra bent down, took the carrot out of Barney's grip, wiped off most of the earth on her T-shirt hem, and gave it back to him.

'It doesn't matter.'

'What doesn't?' Ralph said.

Petra rubbed her hands against the front of her T-shirt. 'The money,' she said.

Ralph left the coffee and came across the kitchen so that he was standing close to her. He said, 'We need the money, hon.'

'Only a bit—'

Ralph put out his arms and turned her to face him. 'Petra. Lesson one. If you don't have money you don't have somewhere to live, you don't eat, you don't have clothes. Lesson two, if you don't have work, you don't have the money for the above. OK?'

Petra didn't look at him. She nodded.

He said, 'You're not working—'

'I could. I did.'

'Yes. But you're not working now. You haven't worked since Kit. I don't mind. I don't mind if you don't work. But one of us has to. I was, and I'm going to again.'

'Yes.'

'And I can't work from this house any more.'

Petra said nothing. Ralph bent down to look in her face. He said, 'I've got to go *out* to work now. I've got to go to *London*.'

Petra took a step back, out of his grasp. She said to Kit, 'Would you like eggy toast for supper?'

Kit was focusing on his Lego, breathing heavily. He took no notice.

Ralph said to Petra, 'It's just going to happen.'

Petra climbed over Barney to get to the fridge and opened it. She said, without heat, 'Why do we go on liking things that hurt us?'

Ralph went very still. 'D'you mean me?'

Petra didn't reply.

'D'you mean,' Ralph said, 'that I'm trying to hurt you?'

Petra straightened up, a carton of eggs in her hand. 'Not trying. But it's happening.'

Ralph said tensely, 'How else do you suggest I support you all?'

'There'll be something—'

'But not something I want to do.'

Petra found a bag of sliced bread under the newspapers on the table.

'D'you want to do this, then?'

'Yes,' Ralph said.

She looked at him. She wore an expression of complete bafflement. 'You *want* to wear a suit and go to London on a train and work all day in an office and never see daylight in winter?'

'Yes,' Ralph said.

'You want it to be like it was in Singapore?'

'I've been given another chance to do something I'm good at doing.'

'We had money before—'

'But I couldn't manage myself,' Ralph said. 'I thought I could, but I couldn't. I'm creative when I don't have to be in charge. I'll be a bloody nuisance, but I'll get results. I'll get results if I'm free.'

'Free—'

'Yes.'

Petra pulled slices of bread out of the bag. 'You'd better *be* free, then.'

'Thank you.' He held up the mug he had just filled. 'Coffee?'

Steve Hadley had got to know Aldeburgh quite well. Ever since Petra's card had arrived at the centre—a card on which she'd painted a male lapwing with its spiky crest, and in which she'd enclosed £10—he'd spent a lot of his spare time in Aldeburgh, looking out for her. She'd said she had two little boys, and although he saw quite a number of smallish young women with children, not many of them seemed to have only boys. But Steve was in no hurry; he'd got all summer to patrol the coast through Aldeburgh.

Without the card, and the trouble she'd taken to do it, Steve doubted he'd have bothered to try and find her. But the painting and the memory of her sleeping in the sand combined to lodge her in his mind in a way that was pleasantly intriguing. So, after work, and on his days off, Steve ambled about Aldeburgh and ate fish and chips sitting on the shingle, and waited.

He finally saw her just as he was about to go home, one afternoon of a day off, and he was standing looking at the primary school, admiring the little, bright boat modelled onto the white wall, when she came past, with a buggy containing a big baby and a little boy beside her, who was dragging a bit on the buggy and emitting that kind of low-grade, steady whine that Steve recognised from his brother's children.

He stepped off the pavement into the road in front of her. 'Hi.'

Petra looked uncomprehendingly, and then her expression cleared. She smiled at him. She was wearing an Indian embroidered tunic over jeans, and sneakers, and her hair was tied over one shoulder in a long ponytail.

'Hi—'

He put his hand out. 'I'm Steve. From Minsmere. Remember?'

She nodded. She said to the little boy, 'I went to sleep in the sand and my car keys fell out of my pocket. This man found them.'

Kit paused in his whine. He looked uncertainly at Steve. Steve squatted down in the road in front of him. 'I've got nephews your age—'

'I'm three,' Kit said guardedly. 'I've got a digger.'

Steve stood up. 'Lucky man.'

Petra said, 'Why are you in Aldeburgh?'

He smiled at her. 'Looking for you.' He pulled the card with her little painting out of his pocket. 'Been carrying that around for weeks—'

'I don't want you stalking me,' Petra said.

'No,' he said, 'I was just waiting. Hoping a bit. You know.' He looked back at Kit. 'What's your name?'

'Kit.'

'And his?'

'Barney,' Kit said and then, 'He's always eating.'

Steve laughed.

Petra was studying him. She said, as if she had suddenly decided something, 'We're going to my allotment.'

Steve nodded. He said hesitantly, 'Can I come along?'

'OK—'

He motioned to Barney's buggy. 'Shall I push him?'

Petra moved sideways. 'OK,' she said again and then, 'I'm married.'

'I thought you would be.'

Petra took Kit's hand. 'Four years—'

'It's not a problem.'

'A problem?'

Steve began to push Barney towards the footpath to the allotments. 'I mean, I like you anyway. I like you for going to sleep in the sand and painting the lapwing. You're different.'

'It's not a help,' Petra said, 'being different. Kit's different, too. Aren't you, Kit?'

Kit looked across his mother at Steve pushing the buggy. He thought that he couldn't usually hold her hand because of the buggy, and he liked holding her hand and he liked it that there was nothing in her other hand, either. He regarded Steve with approval.

'Yes,' he said to his mother.

'I don't want to talk about liking,' Petra said to Steve. 'I don't want anything like that. I'm not in a good place right now. I was just going to the allotment because I feel better there, it settles me.'

'Fine by me,' Steve said.

Barney twisted round in his pushchair and noticed that his mother had been replaced by this stranger. He began to roar.

Petra bent sideways. Kit could see where her free hand was going. She said helplessly, 'Oh, Barn—'

'Come on,' Steve said suddenly. 'Race you!'

He set off at a surprisingly fast run down the path, neatly skimming and swerving the buggy to avoid the bumps. Barney's roars almost immediately subsided into squeals and then shouts of delight.

'Come on!' Kit cried to Petra. 'Come on, come on!'

And he began to run forward, tugging her, and she came stumbling behind him, and he knew she could feel his excitement because she was laughing too—in his charge, and laughing.

Steve was very helpful in the allotment. He mended the bolt on the gate, and dismantled the canes supporting the sweet peas that had died from lack of water, and dug a root or two of early potatoes, and stopped Barney from eating some woodlice and made Kit a track for his digger with a line of old bricks he found on someone else's allotment which they plainly didn't want, he said, because the whole thing was so overgrown and gone to seed. When they left at last, Barney without protest allowed him to strap him into the buggy and steer him out through the gate, and Kit waited until Petra was through before he slid the mended bolt into place, and took her hand again, and this time her free one held a bunch of sweet williams, which was fine, because they were only flowers.

And when they got to the school, Steve stopped pushing, and said, 'Well, I'll say goodbye now.'

'D'you want a coffee?' Petra said.

He shook his head. 'I'll be on my way, thanks.'

She held out the flowers. He shook his head again.

'Thanks for your help.'

'Thanks for your company.'

Steve looked down at Kit. 'See you, digger man.'

Kit said, 'Are you coming to my house?'

'No, mate. I'm not.'

'Yes!' Kit said.

'Tell you what,' Steve said, still looking at Kit and Petra, 'you could come to mine, though. You could come to my house.'

'Yes!' Kit shouted.

'There're enough stones at my house,' Steve said, 'to fill a million diggers.' He glanced at Petra. 'How about it?'

She lifted one sneakered foot and kicked off the brake on the pushchair. 'OK,' she said.

Rachel sent Ralph the particulars of a house in Ipswich, by email. It was semi-detached and unremarkable, but it had three bedrooms, a hundred-foot garden, and was seven minutes from the station. She attached, also, a train timetable of services from Ipswich. In her accompanying email, Rachel said that she and Anthony could probably find a way to help with any shortfall in buying a house more expensive than the one they were selling. And she'd researched schools and there was a good Church of England primary half a mile away, and two pre-schools near by with vacancies for the autumn term. The garden had plenty of space for Petra to grow vegetables. Should she go and view it, on his and Petra's behalf?

'Do. Thanks,' Ralph replied laconically, and clicked 'Send'. Having been so hard, and painful and frustrating, life suddenly seemed to be smoothing out, rolling away in front of him in a manner it hadn't done for ages. He didn't actually want to live in a semi-detached house in a featureless street near Ipswich station, but that prospect, at the moment, seemed merely dimmed by the brightness of all the other things on offer.

He put Rachel's email printout down in front of Petra. 'What do you think?'

Petra peered at it. 'It's OK—'

'It's seven minutes' walk from the station.'

Petra nodded. She stopped looking at the house particulars and picked up her trug. There were new potatoes in it, whitish yellow and the size of walnuts.

'There's a hundred-foot garden,' Ralph said. 'For a football goal. And veg. South-facing.'

Petra tipped the potatoes into the sink and ran the water. 'Nice,' she said, and rumbled the potatoes to rinse off the earth. She pulled out the plug, then picked up a tea towel draped across the back of a chair. She said, looking at the email printout on the table, 'It's no good.'

'What isn't?'

'I'm not living there.'

Ralph gave her a wide smile. 'It's pretty ordinary, I know. I'm sure we can find something else—'

Petra dried her hands. Then she draped the tea towel back over the chair. 'I can't,' she said. 'I can't leave it. I can't leave the sea.'

Charlotte's mother, Marnie, could still look back on Charlotte's wedding day with complete satisfaction, just as she could look back on the months that preceded it with the pleased certainty that the house had come alive again, that the children and their children were constantly there, that the tradition of Webster-Smith hospitality—Gregory had been famous as a host—was as vigorous and welcoming as ever. It had been a wonderful summer. The spare beds hardly seemed to have had time to cool between occupants. Guiltily, Marnie wondered if she had ever been so happy.

But now this. Now Charlotte—who it transpired had already been pregnant before her wedding day—was sobbing in Marnie's arms about how unkind Rachel had been to her. In Marnie's experience, mothers of sons were, broadly speaking, either excessively feminine or forthright and capable. Rachel had seemed to fall into the latter category, and although Marnie had never seen her house, she knew Charlotte was impressed by its bohemian ease and colour and the way life revolved around cooking and painting.

Rachel, Charlotte said angrily, had asked her if they couldn't wait to start a family.

'She didn't say it in a nice voice,' Charlotte said. 'She said it as if she was furious. As if she was—*disgusted* with us. She thinks we're careless. She sounded as if we'd kind of insulted her, let her down.'

'I expect,' Marnie said carefully, 'that it wasn't what she'd planned for you—'

They were together on the big sofa in the sitting room, Charlotte half lying against her mother.

'She had no business to make plans for us!' Charlotte cried. She blew her nose, and pressed her face against her mother's arm. 'It's not her life! It's ours! And—she sounded so horrible. Her voice was horrible.'

'Oh, dear,' Marnie said, as lightly as she could.

Charlotte took her face away from her mother's arm and stared at her. 'Aren't you angry with her? Don't you hate her for speaking to me like that?'

Marnie was conscious of a warm glow, induced by being the parent who was behaving well, the parent who was seen as the ally, not the enemy. 'I'm trying not to, darling.'

'Why? Why aren't you angry? Don't you believe me?'

'The thing is, she feels about Luke as I do about you. Luke is her son—'

'Luke is *mine*,' Charlotte said, blowing her nose again. 'Luke is my husband. He's not her little boy any more.'

Marnie waited a moment. She pulled a clean tissue from the box and expertly wiped mascara from where it had smudged below Charlotte's eyes. She said, 'Of course he knows you're here.'

Charlotte looked past her mother at the wall behind the sofa. 'No, actually—'

'Luke doesn't know? Where does he think you are?'

'Work.'

'And where does work think you are?'

'In bed. With a tummy bug.'

'Oh, Charlotte,' Marnie said.

Charlotte looked back at her. Her lower lip was very slightly pushed out. She said, 'Why d'you say it like that?'

Marnie hesitated. The truth would have been to say, 'Because that's the first lie of marriage that you've told Luke. And it'll be followed by years of half-truths. Years,' but Charlotte did not look as if she could either hear or accept that. So she said instead, 'It doesn't make muddles better if you muddle them further,' and Charlotte said loudly, 'I didn't *start* this.'

'I know you didn't—'

'Rachel did, Rachel ruined my lunch party, Rachel's the one treating us as if we were stupid little kids. Luke and I are *married*.'

'Marriage doesn't change how you feel about your children,' Marnie said. 'Maybe it does, in time, in your head. But not in your heart, really. You go on feeling just the same, and maybe some of those feelings are not as reasonable as they might be.'

Charlotte sniffed. She said, 'Did Daddy feel like that?'

Marnie laughed. She had a fleeting image of how Gregory would have reacted to Charlotte's story, storming out of the house to get the Mercedes out of the garage, and roaring off to Suffolk.

'Daddy, darling, would have been ten times worse.'

Marnie reflected, with more relief than guilt, that Gregory would have been no help in a situation like this. He would have shouted, 'I told you so!' when he heard of the unintended pregnancy, and then he would have got very sentimental over Charlotte and unhelpfully defensive of her outrage at being spoken to without the customary admiration and approval.

Charlotte had been a wilful little girl. Fiona and Sarah had been nine and seven when she was born, and she had been pretty from her first breath, her little round head thatched with thick, primrose-coloured down. Probably we spoiled her, Marnie thought, probably all four of us did, and she thrived on being spoiled so that she can't take anything other than praise, and she can't deal with opinion that doesn't coincide with what she wants to do.

Marnie suggested she go straight home and tell Luke where she had been. Charlotte stood in the doorway, jingling her car keys, and said, 'Well, I'll try. But she made us quarrel! Can you believe it? She actually made us have a row!'

'Then don't let her.'

Charlotte glanced at her mother. 'D'you really feel that calm? D'you really feel it's OK for her to talk to me like that?'

'Actually,' Marnie said, smiling, 'I want to kill her,' and Charlotte laughed. She'd laughed all the way across the drive to her car, and then she'd got in and turned on the ignition, and music suddenly belted out of the speakers, and Charlotte drove away in a whirl of noise.

The thing was, with parenting grown children, you had to learn to hold your tongue. If you wanted them to tell you anything, that is.

'It's Luke,' Luke said into the intercom.

'Luke!' Sigrid said, surprised.

She was in the kitchen, ironing. Mariella was in bed, and Edward had gone out to meet Ralph, who had suddenly appeared at his office that afternoon, and said that he needed help.

'What about now?' Sigrid had demanded.

'I don't know. He wouldn't say till we met later. I'll buy him a beer and a steak and put him on a train back to Suffolk.'

'Your family—'

'I won't be late. Kiss Mariella for me. And count your blessings.'

'What blessings?'

'The loving-family-in-another-country one—'

Sigrid pressed the door-release buzzer. She heard the door slam behind Luke, and then his usual, rapid footsteps on the stairs down to the basement kitchen.

'Hi,' he said, coming over at the same speed to kiss her cheek.

'Where's Charlotte?'

'At a girl movie. With mates. Is Ed here?'

'He's with Ralph,' Sigrid said. 'Didn't you know?'

'I don't know anything,' Luke said, 'except that since that Sunday, Char can't seem to calm down and I'm going mental.'

Sigrid motioned to a chair. 'Have a seat. Coffee?'

'Better not,' Luke said, 'I've drunk too much today, I'm twitching. I'd love a beer.'

Sigrid crossed to the fridge. She said, 'So you wanted to see Edward?'

'Well, sort of. Either of you. Both of you. I just need a bit of help—'

Sigrid handed a bottle to Luke. 'That's what Ralph said to Edward—'

'Can we not think about Ralph?'

Sigrid took a chair on the other side of the table. Luke looked very young and very tired and she noticed that his nails were bitten. She didn't think she'd ever noticed before. She said, 'Is it the baby? Are you worried about having a baby?'

Luke closed his eyes briefly.

'I am absolutely ecstatic about the baby. I don't care that we've only been married a couple of months. I'm thrilled. It's not that. It's—well, it's Mum and Charlotte, of course, and Charlotte thinks Mum despises her because she's pregnant so soon and because she isn't Petra, and she doesn't live in Suffolk and can't draw. And now—' He stopped.

'Now,' Sigrid said.

'Now,' Luke said wearily, 'she wants Mum to apologise.'

Sigrid laughed. 'That's not going to happen!'

Luke sighed. 'I think Mum was well out of order, but it's kind of time to forgive and forget, now.'

Sigrid said, 'Not so easy—' and stopped.

Luke looked at her. He said, 'You haven't had a run-in with Mum, have you?'

'It was a long time ago—'

'I didn't know—'

'And you won't know now,' Sigrid said. 'Maybe we just say that sometimes your mother is careless, a little.'

'Are you angry with her still?'

Sigrid hesitated.

'Wow,' Luke said, and then, after a moment, 'Aren't you going to have a drink, too?'

'Maybe some tea,' Sigrid said, moving towards the kettle.

'Charlotte's got a bit fixated on this Petra thing now, too. It's not just Mum, saying what she said, but also how can anyone compare to Petra.'

'Yes,' Sigrid said.

She took a mug and a packet of valerian tea bags out of a cupboard. Luke said, '*You* don't feel that, do you?'

'Yes,' Sigrid said. She turned round to look at Luke. 'It's a problem.'

'But Petra's like—like a kid, like a kind of half-sister—'

'She had the seal of approval,' Sigrid said.

'But she was pregnant when they married.'

'Logic isn't a part of this. And your Charlotte isn't used to family difficulties, she isn't used to being anything except the centre of the family.'

'She's the centre to *me*,' Luke said.

'Tell her that.'

'I do. I do, but she says I can't mean it if I go on defending Mum.'

Sigrid came back to the table. 'Do you defend her?'

Luke glanced at her unhappily and then looked away. 'I can't—attack her. Can I? Does—does Edward?'

'There is something between the two,' Sigrid said, sitting down again. 'Not defending, not attacking, but not leaving your wife to feel alone, either.'

There was a pause. Then Luke said, half appalled, 'Do *you* feel alone?'

Sigrid looked at him. He seemed suddenly too young to be anyone's husband, sitting there with his clear complexion, and his bitten nails.

'Sometimes,' she said.

When he had seen Ralph off in the direction of the station, Edward went back into the pub where they had had supper and, on impulse, ordered a brandy and soda. He carried it across the room to a small table in a corner with a single chair next to it.

In some ways, Ralph had been quite restrained. He'd drunk a single pint of beer, eaten his steak with salad and without chips, and he'd worn a suit and a shirt, which must have been new since Edward could see the sharp horizontal creases where it had been folded round its packaging. He also made Edward quite a civilised speech of gratitude about helping him to obtain this new job. He said he was feeling really fired up about starting employed work again, and that he knew he was bloody lucky. He then put his knife and fork down and said that there was a problem.

'I was waiting, actually,' Edward said.

'It's Petra. I can't talk to her. She says that the money means nothing to her and that she can't, now, live anywhere except by the sea.'

Edward sighed. 'Oh God—'

'I've explained how life and money works. I mean, she knows that, she's not a fool, but, when things get rough, or she doesn't like something, she goes into inert mode, sort of eludes facing the problem, till it's over. But this one won't be over until she looks at it.'

'Have you told the parents? Wouldn't Petra listen to them?'

'I've let Mum in too far already. She's beavering away finding houses and schools and stuff. I shouldn't have allowed it. I think it's put Petra's back up, although she won't say so. She won't say anything much.'

'Or,' Edward said, 'she's genuinely withdrawn. She's always done that. Dad said she never spoke at all, the first year he knew her. She's probably pretty miserable.'

'She doesn't have the option to be miserable.'

'Hey, steady on—'

'She hasn't contributed anything much since the boys were born. The sale of the odd painting, maybe, but nothing significant. If she wants to go on playing with the boys and growing vegetables, then she has to accept some compromises in return for that freedom.'

Edward leaned forward. 'Ralph, she's never known you in a suit. She's never known you commuting, with a regular payslip and long working days. You've been a superannuated hippy ever since she's known you. You can't blame her for being a bit thrown by the change.'

'It's exciting—'

'Exciting can also be frightening. Can't you just battle with a long commute for a few months until she gets used to the zoot in a suit?'

There was a pause. Then Ralph said, 'No. Not really. I want to do this properly. With all my energy.'

'So you want to move into Ipswich—'

'Hell, that's a compromise!' Ralph said. 'I don't want to live in a suburban street either, but I'm prepared to do it, so that I can walk to the bloody station!'

'And if Petra won't budge?'

Ralph leaned back in his chair. He looked directly at Edward. He said, 'That's why I'm here. I thought maybe you'd have the answer.'

Edward had stared down at his plate. He had a sudden mental image of Petra on her wedding day, taking her shoes off, and running across the gravel of his parents' drive in bare feet, as easily as if she were running on a carpet.

'Well,' he had said slowly, not looking up, 'I suppose you could just not live together for a while. Leave Petra and the boys where they are, and rent a room here for the week? Go home at weekends. For now, anyway. Till things settle?'

Now, Edward drank several satisfying mouthfuls of his brandy and soda. It might be mental in its way, Edward thought, but Petra was only being true to herself, however inconvenient and weirdly adamant that self was. He was delighted to see Ralph's enthusiasm for this new job, and relieved to see what looked like a real determination to make something of it. But he felt deeply, deeply uneasy that he had suggested that they live temporarily apart. The moment the words were out of his mouth, and Ralph was eagerly, energetically seizing upon the idea, Edward had felt his heart sinking. 'Just an idea,' he had said hastily. 'Only a notion. Think about it—'

But it was too late. Ralph had said he must get his train, but his eyes had been bright and, when they stood up from the table, he had put his arms round his brother in a way he hadn't done in years, and hugged him hard.

Edward had said, trying to temper his enthusiasm, 'I'm not trying to split you up, mate,' and Ralph had laughed and said that wasn't a problem, they both knew what to do with freedom, no worries there, and had gone swinging out onto the pavement and into a taxi, leaving Edward feeling that he had, inadvertently, put something intrinsically fragile even further into jeopardy.

Luke prayed that it would not be his mother who answered the telephone. He was dreading the call in any case, but it was also imperative that he speak to his father alone, and in private, and as his father only used his mobile phone intermittently, and in art-college term time, Luke's only choice was to try the home landline at a time when he thought his mother might be out, or in the garden, and his father alone in his studio.

'Hello?' Anthony said.

'Dad—'

'Luke,' Anthony said, his voice full of warmth. 'Great to hear you.'

'How are you?'

'Good,' Anthony said heartily. 'Good. Drawing some sparrows. The Royal Mail might be doing a series of bird stamps. I love drawing sparrows, so sociable. And how are things with you two? I loved your flat.'

'That's why I've rung. Things with us. It's a bit difficult—'

Anthony's tone altered to deep concern. 'Oh, no—'

'I mean,' Luke said hastily, 'we aren't difficult, we're fine. It's just that there's a problem. I'm trying to sort it, for—Charlotte, well, for us, really. Which is why I'm ringing.'

'Tell me,' Anthony said.

Luke paused. He was alone in the studio, Jed being out looking at a new project. It was just as well he was alone, because he'd been so jangled up all day after Charlotte had told him, when they woke up, that she hadn't been to work the day before, but instead had been to see her mother, that Jed would have been bound to notice something. And anyway, he could never have told Jed how horrified he'd been to realise that Charlotte had told him a lie, and that he'd believed her. The horror had deepened because Charlotte didn't seem to think she'd done anything very awful; she was far more concerned, still, with Rachel's awfulness, which she seemed to think justified all aberrant conduct on her part. And he was now appalled to find that his father's voice, sympathetic and encouraging, made him feel distinctly unsteady.

'I don't know how to say it, Dad. It's—well, it's about the other Sunday.'

'Yes.'

'The thing is, Dad, that Charlotte is still really upset. I expect it's pregnancy and hormones and all that, but she doesn't seem to be getting over it.'

'Give it time,' Anthony said. 'It's only ten days or so. I know Mum felt terrible afterwards. I'm not saying she didn't need to feel terrible, but I know she did. They've both got to let it just bed down, and become not such a big deal.'

'Oh God,' Luke said, 'I don't know how to say this, so I'll just say it. Charlotte wants Mum to apologise to her. Could you—could you ever ask her to do that? For—for Charlotte? For me?'

Anthony said less warmly, 'No, lad. No, I couldn't do that.'

'Couldn't you?' Luke said, aware his voice was shaking.

'No,' Anthony said, 'no, she was very much in the wrong, she knows that, I know that, you know that. And she's paying for it internally, if you know what I mean. But I'm not asking her to make an apology, I wouldn't ask her to do that.' He stopped and then he said firmly, 'She's my wife.'

CHAPTER SEVEN

STEVE HADLEY'S COTTAGE at Shingle Street was sunk deeply into the beach. It was brilliantly whitewashed—Steve's landlord made sure to repaint the exterior every spring, after the winter storms—and stood with its narrow gable end facing the sea. From a distance it looked almost as if it was plunging through the shingle towards the shore, but when you got nearer you could see that a concrete gully ran round the house, wide enough for a water butt and a dustbin, and for entry by the only door Steve and his fellow tenant ever used, facing inland, away from the east wind.

Steve shared the house with a man who worked in a fish smokehouse near Woodbridge. They had met online, both seeking short, cheap lets on the coast, and although the landlord of the cottage could have leased it profitably as a holiday rental, he was a man opposed to holidaymakers, a man who preferred to let his few properties to people who worked in Suffolk and were therefore likely to contribute to its economy. So he was pleased to find Steve, and Terry from the smokehouse, who were not only locally employed, but who also would not mind the antiquated hot-water system or primitive kitchen. There were two small bedrooms, a shabby sitting room with a leatherette sofa and chairs, and a television of similar antiquity, and a bathroom where towels never dried and the walls were always sweating.

But there was the beach. Crunching across it, with Barney heavily on her back and Kit slipping and sliding and squealing by her side, Petra wondered how she could ever have borne to be away. The shingle itself— so much of it, so clean and smooth—the flatness, throwing the immense blue dome of the sky into even greater relief, the symmetrical mounds of blue-green sea kale, the creeping skeins of sea pea with its bright purple flowers, the air, the space, the wind, it was all exhilarating, and at the same time profoundly consoling. I'm home, Petra thought, I'm back. This is the place.

'What d'you think?' she called to Kit. 'What d'you think of it?'

He was scrambling through the stones, pink with exertion. 'Windy!' he shouted happily. 'Windy!'

'Do you like it?'

He nodded furiously, bending down to seize handfuls of pebbles and throw them, clattering, down again. Petra laughed. Kit glanced at her, and laughed too, hurling pebbles about.

'Look!' Kit shouted, pointing.

Petra looked. Steve, having seen them approaching, was coming across the shingle to meet them.

'Look!' Kit shouted again to Steve, chucking pebbles. 'Look!'

'Hi there,' Steve said to Petra.

She stopped walking. 'Hi—'

Steve indicated Barney. 'Shall I take him?'

'Yes,' Petra said gratefully. 'He weighs a ton—'

'I'm throwing!' Kit shouted to Steve. 'I'm throwing!'

'I can see you,' Steve said, deftly taking Barney. 'I'm watching—'

'I'll have to watch,' Petra said. 'He's a shocker for water, Kit.'

Barney looked at Steve calmly, without dismay. Steve said to him, 'Hello there, big boy. The sea's not like other water.'

'It's bigger,' Petra said.

'You have to handle it differently,' Steve said. 'I'll take him down to the sea. I'll show him the sea. I'll explain.' He smiled at Kit.

Petra glanced at him. Barney was lolling back in Steve's arms now, like a pasha, and Kit approached to stagger round his knees with handfuls of stones, chattering and chirruping. She said, 'You're a natural with kids.'

'I like them—'

'Have you—'

'No,' Steve said, 'but my brother has. And there's all the schools who come to the reserve. I like the primary schools a lot. I like it when they still want to please you. They're a nightmare when they start wanting to impress each other.'

Petra nodded. Steve said, 'Shall we go down to the water?'

'OK—'

Steve looked down at Kit, still chanting and stamping round him in the pebbles. 'Come and meet the North Sea,' he said to Kit, and he set off through the shingle, carrying Barney, with Kit tagging along beside him, still clutching his stones.

Petra watched the three of them for a moment, standing where they had left her. The day was bright and clear, so she put up her hand to shade her eyes a little as she followed their uneven progress towards the sea. Barney flung his head back in Steve's arms, and closed his eyes in rapture against the sun and air, and then Kit, stumbling, put a hand out and grasped at the nearest leg of Steve's jeans, and Petra saw Steve detach his own hand briefly from supporting Barney, and touch Kit's head with it, and something inside her, something knotted and strangulated that had been there for weeks now, slipped and smoothed and untied itself. She took an immense involuntary breath of relief, and released it out into the huge, blue space above the sea.

Later, Steve made toast for the boys, and tea for himself and Petra. He spread the toast with brilliantly red jam of a kind Petra thought Rachel would never have countenanced—'Chemicals and colourings and synthetic pips; a complete *travesty* of jam'—and cut it into strips without Petra assisting him, or even suggesting it. The boys were entranced.

'*White* bread,' Kit said reverently.

He picked up strips of toast in each hand. Barney was cramming toast into his mouth with his fist.

'Steady,' Petra said to him, but not as if she meant it. Steve had put a mug of tea down in front of her, and a bag of sugar with a spoon stuck in it, and then he held out more toast and red jam enquiringly towards her and Barney lunged at it, grunting urgently through his packed mouthful, and they all began laughing. It was then that Steve said to Petra quietly, under the laughing, 'Who knows you're here?' and Petra said, intending only to be factual, 'There's no one to know.'

'You sure?'

'Ralph's in London for the day. He's at—at an induction meeting, he said. Whatever that is.'

'I wouldn't want any sneaking,' Steve said. 'But I wouldn't want you not to come. Either.'

Petra wanted to say something of what the afternoon had been like, how it had made her feel, how the gritty, abrasive things that had been inside her recently, like little balls of pumice, maybe, had dissolved out there on the stones by the sea. But she couldn't think how to put it, so she just reached across Kit to remove a fragment of toast glued by its jam to Barney's thigh and said, for all three of them, 'We've had a great time. Haven't we?'

Steve didn't say anything in response, but he was smiling. He collected up the mugs and the mess on the table, and put it all in the chipped Belfast sink by the window and then he produced a flannel and ran it under the tap, and squeezed it out, and attacked the boys' hands and faces with it, and they loved it, and shrieked, and squirmed to get away and then thrust themselves back at him for more.

He was not, Petra thought, surveying him, good-looking. He wasn't tall enough, or well formed enough, as he was too stocky and his eyes were too small and his ears were too big, but he was pleasing to look at all the same, because he inhabited himself so comfortably, he moved so quickly and nimbly, and he had an air of flexible practicality. He turned from a deliberately exaggerated swipe of the cloth across Kit's face, and caught Petra's eye. He smiled again easily. Petra smiled back. Then he threw the cloth towards the sink, and came round the table to where Petra was sitting and, without making any kind of drama out of it, leaned down and kissed her lightly on the mouth.

Charlotte's sister, Sarah, had agreed to come up to London and meet Charlotte in a French café in Marylebone High Street. Charlotte, gorgeous in a small white skirt and a black smock top, with bell sleeves and a plunging neckline, came flying into the café, and embraced Sarah with a fervour that suggested that they hadn't seen each other for a year.

'Sarah, I am so pleased to see you, you can't think what it's been like and I am absolutely starving. I'm absolutely starving *all* the time.'

Sarah, although joining in much of the family adoration of Charlotte in the past, took a more objective view of her younger sister these days. Charlotte, it seemed to her, had a propensity to go on trading on her small-child charms to an unacceptable degree, and it was time Charlotte realised that twenty-six wasn't, actually, very young any more, and that marriage wasn't just a continuation of a pink-glitter wedding day, but a serious undertaking involving adult conduct and compromise. She surveyed Charlotte across the table. Not only was her cleavage much on display, but she was wearing a large, jewelled cross on a long chain round her neck, which only drew attention to it.

'You might thank me,' Sarah said, 'for coming to London all of a sudden, to suit you.'

Charlotte looked up from the menu. Her eyes were huge. 'Please don't tick me off—'

'I'm not ticking you off, I'm just saying—'

'I know I've been a bit one-track-minded,' Charlotte said, 'but it really got to me, it really did. And when people can't be supportive, I just kind of crack up. That's why I rang you. I rang you because of Luke. After—after, well, after he called me a nut-nut diva.'

Sarah stared at her. 'He *didn't*—'

Charlotte paused. She looked down at the table.

'Charlotte,' Sarah said warningly.

'He didn't—disagree—'

'He didn't disagree with what?'

Charlotte put her hands on either side of her face, and stared hard at the table. 'Well, I was really upset, really crying after Luke told me that his father refused to ask his mother to apologise, and I lost my cool a bit, and I said to Luke that they were all ganging up on me—which is what it feels like, Sarah—and treating me as if I was a nut-nut diva, and he didn't contradict me. I mean, he said they weren't ganging up, but he didn't say I wasn't a diva. He just went down to his studio.'

'Char,' Sarah said. 'You are being a diva.'

Charlotte cried, 'But you weren't there, you don't know what she said, how she sounded—'

Sarah leaned forward. 'Look, Char. I don't know the woman, but she's a mother-in-law. Nobody will ever be good enough for her boy. She's really tactless but she was just doing what people like her do. Remember our wedding? Chris's mother wouldn't even come, because it wasn't in a church, and she insisted I'd bullied him out of a church wedding. I'd have been fine in a church, it was Chris who wouldn't have it. He said he'd had enough of church in his childhood and he didn't believe in God anyway. But he wouldn't stand up to her, he let me do that. So I was the witch. It's what happens. It's what it's like for lots of daughters-in-law.'

Charlotte leaned to meet her sister and said in a loud whisper, 'I didn't mean to get pregnant.'

Sarah waited a second and then she said, 'I know.'

Charlotte's eyes filled with tears.

'Don't cry,' Sarah said. 'It's not perfect. But it's got some pluses. Two babies before you're thirty, family done and dusted, get on with your life.'

Charlotte said, leaning back a little, 'I don't think Luke feels the same way about me—'

'What do you mean?'

'Well,' Charlotte said, looking back down at the table, 'I sort of could do no wrong in his eyes. I mean, I held him off till he sorted the coke thing and he had to wait till I was finished with Gus, and everything. And now I haven't got that—power any more. He looks at me as if I'd disappointed him, as if he'd opened a Christmas present and found something that wasn't what he'd been hoping for.'

Tempting though it was to say 'Nonsense' in a brisk sort of voice, Sarah found herself softened. She said, 'He loves you, you know. Really loves you. This baby's probably a bit of a bombshell for him, too.'

'He hasn't got to have it—'

Sarah looked at her sister. She said, I was just beginning to feel sorry for you. Don't spoil it.'

Charlotte smiled weakly. She said, 'I'm a right mess, aren't I?'

'We're all thrilled you married Luke, we think he's lovely and the wedding was wonderful. But marriage isn't just more of the same. And most of all, marriage doesn't happen in *public*. You've got to sort it, together. You have no idea about my relationship with Chris, have you? It's never entered your head. Well, it's not a picnic, but we manage. And you'll have to manage. You've got a nice guy and a nice place to live and you're not on the breadline. Deal with it.'

Charlotte sighed. 'OK,' she said.

'And now,' Sarah said, picking up the menu, 'let's order lunch.'

Ralph had found a room to rent. Someone who was about to be a colleague had a flat off Finsbury Square that he wanted to himself at weekends when his girlfriend came over from Dublin, but which had a small second bedroom that he was happy to let out during the week. He said that if Ralph just had showers, and only used the microwave, he thought fifty quid in cash, for four nights a week, would be fine, utility bills and council tax thrown in, no paperwork, no questions asked, how about it? Ralph looked at the room, decorated and furnished to be as impersonal and modern as a hotel, and thought it all looked more than acceptable. He lay down on the bed, and looked up at the ceiling with its tiny, brilliant, recessed lights, and felt a little thrill of excitement at the prospect of liberty. He had no intention of misusing it, he had reassured Edward on the telephone, no stupid bad-lad behaviour just because he was off the lead, but there'd be films, and a gym membership, and going to see his brothers and all that good stuff, wouldn't there? Edward, at the other end of the line, had not sounded convinced or reassured.

On the train back to Suffolk, Ralph thought about the room off Finsbury Square. Fifty quid a week was an amazing bargain, especially for a power shower and a ten-minute walk to work. He thought about Kit and Barney, and how odd it would be without them, and how wonderful it would be to see them at weekends, and how he would make up for his week-night absences by getting them up, so that Petra could have a lie-in, and taking them out to do things that he never seemed to do at the moment, because every day was just an ordinary day, and one day was really indistinguishable from another. He marvelled at how his energy and optimism had returned and how, instead of floundering through life like a half-dead zombie, he was now alert and eager for what lay ahead.

At Ipswich station, he bought packets of chocolate buttons for the boys and looked for flowers to buy Petra. There were none. Never mind, he told himself, she grows flowers anyway, I'll stop on the way home and buy a nice bottle of wine. We'll have wine tonight and I'll cook for her. In fact, I'll cook at weekends from now on, and we'll have a whole new regime and outlook, and the money to pay for it. It'll be like starting again.

Petra was in the bathroom when he got back, kneeling by the bath in order to soap Kit, who was sitting in four inches of water playing with a wind-up plastic frog. Barney, swaddled in an endearing hooded towel with ears, was sitting beside Petra on the bathmat, absorbed in a cloth book whose pages squeaked when he pressed certain places. Ralph heard their voices as he came up the stairs, and he could tell they were happy from the sound of them.

When he went in, and they all looked up and saw him, and the boys squealed, he felt an elating rush of certainty that life was going to stop being a trudge across a plateau, and transform itself instead into a gallop across a plain towards a mountain range of sheer promise.

He bent, holding his tie back with one hand, to kiss Petra and Kit, and then he picked Barney up from the floor, and sat down with him on his knee on the closed lid of the lavatory.

'Good day?' Petra said.

'Very. And you?'

'We went to the sea!' Kit said, scrambling to the end of the bath to be near to his father. He spread his arms. 'It was this big! And full of stones!'

Ralph laughed. He said to Barney, 'What about you, fat Buddha?'

Barney offered him his book. Ralph accepted it and began to press the pages obediently.

'Lots to tell you,' he said to Petra.

'Great. When the boys are in bed—'

'Read to me!' Kit commanded. He dropped the frog and began to scramble out of the bath. 'Read to me, Daddy, read to me, read to me. My digger book—'

'Could we have a change, maybe, from the digger book?'

Petra wound Kit into a towel. 'Give Daddy a break. Give him a break from the digger book, hey?'

'No!'

'Nah!' said Barney delightedly. He gazed up at his father. 'Nah!'

Ralph looked down at him. He looked completely winning, beaming up at his father, displaying his tiny, perfect teeth from under his pointed towelling hood. Ralph felt a rush of love for him, for all of them, for his whole little family, gathered safely round him in their shabby bathroom. He dropped a kiss on Barney's head.

'Of course I'll read the digger book,' he said.

Later, in the kitchen, he unwrapped the wine from its cocoon of paper.

'Wow,' Petra said. 'What are we celebrating?'

'Lots of things,' Ralph said. 'And I'm cooking.'

'I've done it—'

'Done it?'

'Almost. Just a risotto.'

'I love risotto,' Ralph said. 'I love your risotto. Of course, I'd have cooked, but really, I like your cooking.'

Petra put two wine glasses on the table. 'So the meeting was OK?'

'It was more than OK. I met all the analysis team, all good, all seemed fine, and one of them offered me a room. Fifty quid a week! Ten minutes from the office. Perfect.'

Petra stopped moving. She was tipping mushrooms onto a board from a paper bag, and she stopped, the bag in her hand with most of the mushrooms still in it. 'A room?'

Ralph looked up from inserting the screw of the corkscrew into the top of the wine bottle. 'Yes. A room. Like we agreed.'

'Did we?'

Ralph began to turn the corkscrew. 'You know. You said I'd better have my freedom—'

'Yes.'

'Well, you meant it, didn't you?'

'Yes,' Petra said.

'So I'm taking a room on the edge of the City during the week and I'll be back at weekends, and you can stay here with the boys, like you wanted.'

He pulled the cork out and straightened up, smiling at her. 'So we can work this thing out, and you can have what you wanted, can't you?'

Petra tipped out the rest of the mushrooms and picked up a knife.

Ralph said, 'Are you with me?'

She said, not looking up, 'I—suppose so. I'm—just a bit surprised about the room—'

'What did you think would happen? How did you think we'd work it?'

'I didn't,' Petra said truthfully. 'I just thought I'd wait till you decided something, and then I'd see what to do.'

'Well, I have decided. I've got a room.'

Petra looked at him. She smiled. 'Good,' she said.

'And you can go on with your life here. Doing what you like doing. Like going to the sea, like you did today. Wasn't the beach crowded?'

'We didn't go there—'

Ralph began to pour the wine. 'Where'd you go then?'

'Shingle Street,' Petra said, slicing mushrooms.

'Shingle Street? How did you get there?'

'Taxi—'

Ralph stopped pouring. 'A taxi? Both ways?'

'No,' Petra said calmly. 'My friend brought us home.'

'What friend?'

'He works at the bird reserve.'

'*He?*'

Petra looked at him. 'Yes.'

Ralph said, 'How do you have a friend, a *man* friend, from the bird reserve?'

Petra put her knife down. 'He found my car keys when I lost them the day I went drawing there, when you had your interview, when your parents had the boys.'

'And now he's a friend.'

Petra said, 'He lives at Shingle Street. It was amazing to be back there. Amazing. The boys loved it.'

There was a silence. Ralph looked at the wine in the glasses, then he looked at Petra. He said, 'You took the boys—'

'Of course. What else would I do?'

'Is—is that why you're so happy? Is that why the atmosphere here's so good tonight? It's not that you've come round to my point of view, my point about the future, is it, it's because you've had an afternoon—'

'It was the beach,' Petra said.

'An afternoon,' Ralph said, rushing on, taking no notice, 'with some guy who you let be with my children and God knows what else you let happen, it's that, isn't it, it's that—'

He stopped suddenly. He tried to gauge, looking at Petra, what she was thinking. She was standing on the other side of the table, one hand lightly on the pile of sliced mushrooms, the other lying on her knife, quite still and alarmingly composed. She was looking back at him, and although her gaze was veiled, she didn't look as she usually looked when things got difficult and she was trying to evade being involved in a resolution. She looked more as if she'd decided something and then pulled back into herself, decision made.

'Petra, are you happy, not because of me but because you've had a good afternoon with this guy?'

She gave him a faint smile and picked up her knife again.

'Yes,' she said.

Sigrid put down the telephone. She had meant—had wanted—to tell her mother about all the Brinkley family upsets, but when it came to it, she discovered that she felt, oddly, that she ought to protect them. She ought not to expose their inadequacies, even—or maybe, especially—to her mother. So they had an affectionate and anodyne call instead, so anodyne that Sigrid could sense her mother was only just managing to refrain from asking her if anything was the matter.

Sigrid picked up the mug of green tea she had made to accompany the phone call, and looked at it. It was cold now, with a layer of brown sediment at the bottom, and looked as appetising as a mug of pond water. She went over to the sink, and poured it away, and then refilled the kettle. Coffee was the answer. Coffee, in her upbringing, had always been the answer. Green tea was no substitute. Just as, Mariella frequently pointed out, water was no substitute for juice. Or a smoothie. Mariella had been promised some vanilla smoothie—her favourite—when she could not only spell out loud all the words on her summer-holiday spelling list ending in 'ough', but could write them down, too. She had been shut in her room for hours, so she had probably abandoned spelling for playing, and her bedroom floor would be covered with the families of tiny, anthropomorphised toy woodland animals whom she would be putting to bed, in nests of paper tissues, in all her shoes. Sigrid was not going to interrupt her. Absorbed playing with miniature mice and badgers had to feed the inner life more richly, surely, than learning why 'cough' and 'rough' and 'bough' all looked the same but didn't sound it. English! What a language.

Edward's key scraped in the front-door lock, followed by a bang as he swung the door shut behind him. He came rapidly down the stairs to the kitchen, as was his wont, and kissed her—rather absently, she thought—and went straight to the fridge.

'A bit desperate, aren't you?' Sigrid said.

'Water,' Edward said shortly. He took out the filter jug Sigrid kept in the door of the fridge, and poured out a large glass, which he then drank, straight off. Sigrid watched him.

'Is something the matter?'

Edward went on drinking.

'Please,' Sigrid said. 'No dramas. Have you had a bad day?'

Edward put the glass down, and refilled it. 'Yes.'

'Is it your family?'

Edward stopped swallowing long enough to say, 'Why should it be them?'

'It usually is.'

'Whereas—'

'No,' Sigrid said, interrupting. 'No, not in comparison to mine, if you must know. I have just had a very inadequate talk to my mother.'

'Inadequate?'

'I talked to her in a completely pointless way. As if I didn't really know her—'

'Why?' Edward said.

Sigrid let a small silence fall and then she said evasively, 'I don't know. Maybe I was tired.'

Edward sat down heavily on a chair, with his third glass of water.

'I *am* tired.'

Sigrid waited. Edward said, 'I am especially tired of Ralph. At least, poor bugger, I'm not tired of *him*, but I'm pretty tired of the complications he seems to attract.'

Sigrid took a chair across the table from Edward. She said cautiously, 'What now?'

Edward sighed. He said, looking at the tabletop rather than at Sigrid, 'It's Petra. He rang today. He said he'd been sitting on something for about a week, and he had to tell someone. It seems that Petra has—well, I don't know how far it's gone, I mean, I don't know if they're sleeping together or anything, but Petra's got another man.'

Sigrid gasped. '*Petra?*'

'Yes,' Edward said. He got up. 'I'm going to get something stronger. You want a drink?'

'Sit down,' Sigrid said. 'Sit down. We'll get a drink later. Sit down and tell me. Who *is* this man?'

Edward leaned against the table. He said dully, 'He works at the nature reserve. He's a kind of—maintenance man, I suppose. I couldn't really tell. He looks after the fences and steps and handrails, that sort of thing. Petra met him there.'

Sigrid put her head in her hands. 'Oh my God—'

'He's got a place at Shingle Street,' Edward said. 'Where they used to live. Petra takes the kids there, they love it, they—well, Kit anyway—want to tell Ralph about it, they want to take him there.'

'Don't—'

'Ralph said that she doesn't seem to get what she's doing. She just doesn't. They agreed he could live in London in the week, so that she and the boys didn't have to leave Aldeburgh, and she seems to think that gives him a freedom that she's entitled to, too, so she's got this bloke.'

Sigrid said, 'I think I'd like that drink. *Petra.* I can't believe it—'

Edward turned towards the fridge. 'Ralph said he can't talk to her. He simply can't. She won't discuss it. She just looks at him, and smiles, and says she's OK now, so she's fine with him doing this job in London. She doesn't seem to understand that working in London to support your family doesn't exactly equate to unbounded freedom for Ralph. And it *certainly* doesn't give her permission to embark on an affair.'

'*Has* she?'

Edward opened the fridge and took out a wine bottle. 'I don't know. Ralph doesn't know. She just says it's the sea, it's the sea, which is plainly utter rubbish. How can it be the *sea*, for God's sake? There's sea all over the place in Aldeburgh!'

Sigrid got up to fetch two glasses. She said, 'It's always been—a bit funny, that relationship—'

'All relationships look funny from the outside.'

'Goodness, Ed, that's very philosophical, for you—'

Edward put the wine down on the table, and picked it up again. 'I told him to tell the parents. He said he couldn't face it. He asked if I would.'

'Will you?'

Edward began to pour. 'When I know more. When I know what I'm telling them.' He pushed a glass towards Sigrid. 'Stupid, bloody girl.'

Sigrid said nothing. Edward sat down again. He took a swallow of wine. He said, suddenly angry, 'I know Ralph is a pain, I know he isn't the easiest person to live with, but he's doing this for his family and, however stupid and pig-headed he is, he isn't a player, he doesn't play around with other women, he doesn't drink or gamble, he's just Ralph, like he always was. And Petra isn't exactly a picnic, is she, drifting about, refusing to grow up, all daffy and artistic. *Honestly*.' He raised his voice and said in almost a shout, 'Stupid, bloody woman!'

'Who is?' Mariella said from the doorway.

Charlotte lay in bed on her back. Luke was asleep beside her, his right arm across her thighs, where she had moved it, from being across her belly. She had been assured by everyone—her mother, sisters, friends—that if she felt sick it would be in the morning and would be enormously helped if Luke brought her tea in bed, and a plain biscuit or something, before she even put a toe out. But the mornings were fine. It was the evenings that Charlotte dreaded. In the evenings, she was beginning to find that not only could she not face food, she couldn't even face the *thought* of food, let alone the smell, and she daren't even think about coffee or brown bread, for example, without having to race for the bathroom. Luke had been so sweet. He'd had something to eat, the last week or so, in the studio before he came upstairs, and he'd brushed his teeth, too. She'd really appreciated that, and she really appreciated that he wanted to sleep with his arms round her. It was just that she couldn't bear the weight of his finger, let alone his arm, across her belly. So she had, the last few nights, just pushed his arm down her body a little, and that seemed to content him, while she lay waiting for either sleep or sickness to gain the upper hand.

Of course, tonight there was another reason to stay awake, a reason beyond that of simply wondering whether she was going to throw up, or just feel that she might. Luke had come up from the studio, redolent of toothpaste over pizza, and said that Ralph had rung him to tell him that Petra was seeing someone else. Luke didn't seem very clear about any of it, but he was in a stumbling sort of rage on his brother's behalf who, he said to Charlotte, was, he knew, not the easiest bastard to be married to, but hell, he was doing his best with a new job and all that and anyway, Petra hadn't exactly pulled her weight the last few years, and he now saw why she, Charlotte, had always had a bit of a down on Petra, and he should have taken her opinion on Petra more seriously, because she'd been proved spot-on, hadn't she?

Charlotte had wanted to feel the glow of satisfaction at having been so right, and had failed to. When she questioned Luke further about exactly what Petra had *done*, he said he didn't know details and for God's sake didn't *want* to, but that Ralph had been most upset about the fact that Petra was perfectly happy for him to go to London and earn money to keep them all, now that she'd found someone to amuse herself with, who was also prepared to play with the boys.

'That's what really gets him,' Luke said, standing over her as she lay on the sofa, his thumbs hooked in the belt loops of his jeans. 'The kids really like him. Kit talks about him a lot, like Ralph's supposed to join in all this. It's gutting him.' He gave an enormous sigh, and then he said, 'I'd better ring Ed.'

Then he had bent down, with the grace and ease Charlotte appreciated so much when she wasn't feeling so grim, and kissed her, and said he wouldn't be long. He was half an hour in their bedroom. At first, she tried to hear what Luke was saying, but he was not quite audible, and the sounds from the street, even if far below, muffled his voice even further. So, Charlotte had rolled cautiously onto her side, holding a cushion against her, and attempted again to feel the satisfaction of having been justified in her reaction to Petra in the past. It wouldn't come, any more than would even a shred of understanding of Ralph and Petra's relationship, which seemed to Charlotte as weird and unsatisfactory as an apparently grown-up relationship could be.

When Luke came back to the sitting room, he sat down on the edge of the sofa next to Charlotte.

'You OK, angel?'

'Ish,' Charlotte said.

Luke took one of Charlotte's hands. 'I'd feel sick *for* you, if I could—'

'I know,' Charlotte said. She looked at him. 'How was your phone call?'

Luke said, 'Ed feels like I do. We just went round the houses. You know, like you do when there's not enough to put your finger on.'

'What if Ralph stays in Aldeburgh?'

'Char, he can't. He's got to work—'

'But your parents would help, they're always helping them anyway.'

Luke put Charlotte's hand between both of his. 'Ed asked me if I'd go with him, actually.'

'Go where?'

'To Suffolk,' Luke said. 'To tell them.'

Charlotte sat up slowly. She said, 'The two of you, driving all the way to Suffolk? Why can't you tell them on the phone? Why can't Ralph tell them?'

'He can't,' Luke said unhappily. 'He asked Ed and Ed asked me. It's—it's not something you can say on the phone, because, well, because of—'

'Petra?'

'Sort of,' Luke said.

Charlotte swung her legs round and put the cushion in her lap. 'Aren't you all making a big deal out of this?'

'Well, what if it was one of your sisters? What if Sarah suddenly said she was playing around because she didn't like Chris's flying lessons? Wouldn't you want to tell your mother in person?'

Charlotte gave a tiny shrug. 'Maybe—'

Luke pressed her hand between his. 'I know you're fed up with Mum. And Dad. I know you feel let down and everything. I know what you think of Petra. But—they're my family. They just are. And the parents are going to be devastated.'

Charlotte was silent for a moment, staring at her hand sandwiched between Luke's. Then she said lightly, 'Oh, they'll forgive Petra—'

Luke looked across the room. Then he looked back at her intently, and he said, 'I'm not so sure,' and suddenly something shifted in Charlotte's mind and heart.

'I'll come with you,' Charlotte said. 'I'll come to Suffolk with you, at the weekend. With you and Ed. Of course I will.'

He'd given a little exclamation and put his arms round her, holding her hard against him. He said, 'You are a star, a complete star, but suppose Ed and I kind of have to do it alone?' and she'd said, into his shoulder, 'It's fine. I'll be fine. I'd just like to be there, to support you,' and then there'd been a few moments when she'd wondered if he was crying.

He kept thanking her. He'd thanked her so much while they were moseying round each other, getting to bed, that Charlotte had had to—laughing—tell him to stop, because what kind of gratitude would he have left for the really big stuff? And he'd said solemnly, 'That is big stuff. For me,' and she'd felt a mingled rush of remorse and relief; remorse at how she'd behaved recently, and relief that she was back where she'd been, on the pedestal of She Who Can Do No Wrong, to the extent where she was overtaken suddenly by a flood of inappropriate gratitude towards Ralph and Petra, which was as disconcerting as it was powerful.

Now, lying in the dim glow of a city night, with the nausea gradually subsiding, Charlotte considered the journey to Suffolk. Luke had said that Sigrid and Mariella wouldn't be coming, so that left her alone with Edward and Luke. She thought she would offer to do the driving. She liked driving, she was a good driver, and she could tell the boys she'd feel sick if she wasn't driving and that way, when she'd dropped them off at Anthony and Rachel's, she'd be free to do as she chose.

I should paint those,' Anthony said.

He was standing by the kitchen table, which was covered with late-summer vegetables: runner beans and courgettes and a basket of spinach and a great heap of carrots, trailing their feathery green tops over the edge of the table, like hair.

Rachel had been in the garden all afternoon, since it was the day the gardener came, and now she was making tea. She cast a glance at the green pile on the table. She said, 'Can't think why I bother.'

Anthony said nothing. His instinct was to say something soothing like, 'Oh, but I love spinach,' but experience had taught him that this would not have a mollifying effect and, in any case, Rachel had sounded more sad than cross. He regarded her back view, switching on the kettle, stretching up to the cupboards for tea bags and mugs. She was as trim in outline as she had been when he first saw her; in fact sometimes, now, catching a glimpse of her digging in the garden, heaving something out of the car, bending to pick a towel off the bathroom floor, he couldn't believe she was any older, any different from the girl he'd met on a walking holiday in North Wales. She'd had hair almost to her waist then, and a slight Welsh accent. She hadn't got the accent any more, and her hair was cut to her jawline, but there was still a great deal of her that was the same— exaggerated maybe here and there, but the same.

She turned round and put two mugs of tea on the table. She said, not looking at Anthony, 'Please don't behave as if I'll fly off the handle.'

Anthony said reasonably, 'Well, you might.'

Rachel opened a drawer to find a teaspoon. 'I'm more likely to cry.'

'You hardly ever cry—'

'Lately,' Rachel said, 'I've done rather a lot of crying. It happened this afternoon again, pulling those bloody carrots.'

Anthony said cautiously, 'Why were you crying?'

Rachel said, 'Once I couldn't grow enough vegetables. Once we had sackloads of the things at the back of the garage, and it was a triumph if the potatoes lasted till after Christmas. We were pretty well self-sufficient, weren't we, and it *all* got eaten, all of it.'

She stopped, and dredged out the second tea bag.

Anthony said, 'That was ages ago. Years. You're thinking of the boys' schooldays. As far as Ed's concerned, that's about twenty years ago.'

Rachel took a big plastic carton of milk out of the fridge, and splashed some into the tea. 'It wasn't really then that I was thinking about, it was now, it was what's happening now—' She stopped.

Anthony went round the table and put his arms round her. She didn't respond, but she didn't resist him, either. She said, into the dark blue drill of his shirt, 'Nobody's been here, all summer.'

Anthony bent a little. 'What?'

Rachel raised her face slightly and said more distinctly, 'The family. No one's been here, all summer.'

'Yes, they have, we saw the little boys—'

'Weeks ago,' Rachel said. 'Not long after the wedding—'

'And the day everyone came to lunch, when Mariella had done all that baking—'

'One Sunday,' Rachel said. She put up her hand, and blotted her eyes with the back of it. 'Other summers, they've all been in and out, all the time. Last year Mariella stayed for a week, by herself. And the little boys were here all the time, we got the old pram out, you remember, for Barney. And Luke was here, a lot, he went sailing, didn't he, he brought

Jed down and they went sailing, and then he brought Charlotte to introduce her. But not now. Nobody's been, now. I mean, I expect them to have their own lives, of course I do, I just don't expect them to stop seeing us, so completely, so suddenly.'

Anthony took one arm away and reached across to rip a piece of kitchen paper from the roll on the wall. 'Here. Blow.'

He looked down on the top of her head as she blew her nose. He said, 'It's been a worrying summer for Ralph. And then the wedding. It's probably just a one-off, you know.'

Rachel sighed. She pulled herself out of his arms and looked up at him. Then she patted his chest. 'You don't believe that any more than I do. This is *change*. This is a different dynamic altogether, and I don't like it.' She blew her nose again. 'It frightens me.'

'Why?'

'Because nobody wants me to do something I'm good at any more.'

'I do—'

She smiled weakly. 'Ant, you aren't enough people. And you've got painting and the college still.'

'Go back to your cookery courses, then—'

She sighed. 'I'm not sure I've got the heart—'

'Shall we start by turfing over the veg garden, so that you aren't oppressed by all this produce with no one to eat it?'

The telephone began to ring. Rachel said, crossing the kitchen to answer it, 'I'd rather find a solution that didn't look as if I was giving in,' and then she picked up the phone and said, 'Hello?' into it, as she always did, and then Anthony saw her face lighten into a wide smile and she said, 'Luke!' with emphasis.

He walked past her, carrying his tea, saying, 'Send him my love,' in a way that made him feel ashamed of his mild cowardice, after his last conversation with Luke, and then crossed the gravel to his studio. Anthony stood in front of his easel, drinking his tea. On it was propped the beginnings of a drawing of a crane, a European crane, startled into sudden take-off with its big, grey wings and long legs awkwardly splayed, its head just turned enough to show the red patch on the back of it. He'd been lucky to see it, because they were so rare in England, preferring Scandinavia and Central Europe and liking great stretches of marsh and bog in which to make their precarious nests. He thought that, beyond the central crane, he might add some more, in flight, wings spread, to suggest the dance for which they were so famous. He put down his tea and picked up his pencil.

The door to the drive opened. 'Guess what!' Rachel said from the doorway. 'Luke and Ed are coming on Sunday. For lunch. Isn't that lovely?'

CHAPTER EIGHT

WHEN LUKE ASKED CHARLOTTE how she would spend the time while he and Edward were with their parents, she'd said airily that she thought she'd just go and be by the sea.

'Probably sleep,' she said. 'Eat an ice cream. Time off everything.' She'd leaned sideways to kiss him. 'Don't fret, babe. I'll be fine.'

Luke was reluctant to get out of the car. 'This feels really weird, you driving us up here and not coming in. Leave your phone on. All the time.'

Edward, climbing out of the back seat of the car, squeezed her shoulder. 'You're a heroine, Charlotte.'

Then they had trooped away together, towards their parents' house, and Charlotte had thought how young they both looked suddenly, unformed, more boys than men, and she had put the car in gear and driven off, without looking in the rearview mirror to see if Luke was still watching.

She left the car in a back street outside a shuttered house that looked as if its residents were not there to object, and walked down to the sea. It was a cool, fair day, and the beach was dotted with families, and plastic windbreaks, and the immense blue-grey sea was heaving and sucking at the pebbles with a relentless rhythm that might, Charlotte thought, drive you nuts if you weren't a sea person. She wondered if she was hungry, and decided that she was too strung up by what she was about to do to be hungry, so she turned inland to the high street, where she thought she would stop someone who looked local and ask them how she could find Ralph and Petra's house.

Ralph, holding the door open wide enough to see out but not wide enough to admit her, looked as if he could hardly remember who she was.

'Oops,' Charlotte said, 'did I wake you?'

Ralph passed his hand over his chin, as if to check the time by whether he had shaved or not. He was wearing cut-offs and a sagging T-shirt. Charlotte, in a short summer dress and wedge-heeled espadrilles, thought he looked terrible.

'No,' Ralph said. 'No. I—it's just, I wasn't expecting you—'

'I didn't say I was coming,' Charlotte said, 'so you couldn't.' She smiled at him. 'I dropped Ed and Luke off at your parents'. Then I thought I'd come.'

Ralph didn't open the door any wider. He looked past Charlotte rather than at her. 'I'm afraid this—this isn't a very good time—'

'I know,' Charlotte said. 'That's why I'm here.'

Ralph sighed. He said, 'I don't want to be rude to you, but I can't talk to you, really. I don't know you—well enough—'

'No,' Charlotte said. 'Actually, I came to see Petra.'

Ralph said wearily, 'They aren't here.'

Charlotte felt a little clutch of excited panic. Where were they, then? Were they with *him*?

'They're at the allotment,' Ralph said. 'You'll find them there.'

He plainly, Charlotte thought, couldn't say Petra's name. She said, 'Can you show me?'

Ralph lifted an arm. He pointed vaguely to the right. He said, 'Down there, and then right past the school, then left to the footpath.'

'Has Petra got her phone?'

Ralph looked at her with sudden focus. He said crisply, 'I have no idea.'

'Sorry,' Charlotte said, 'I'm sorry. I'm sorry about all of it,' and before the words were fully out of her mouth, Ralph said emphatically, 'Me, too,' and slammed the door shut in her face.

Petra and Kit were kneeling on the ground together, examining something in the earth. They had their backs to the gate. Opposite them, strapped into his buggy, with a carrot in either fist, was Barney. He gave an energetic wriggle when he saw Charlotte, and gestured vigorously with his carrots.

'Gah!' Barney said loudly.

Petra lifted her head. 'What, Barn—'

'Gah,' Barney said again. He looked over his mother's head at

Charlotte, standing by the gate, her hand on the latch. Petra turned.

'Oh!' Petra said, scrambling to her feet.

Charlotte opened the gate. 'Surprise!' she said. She bent forward slightly, as if to kiss Petra. Petra stepped back.

'I didn't expect—' Petra said.

'I know. That's why I didn't tell you. I thought if you knew you wouldn't see me.'

Kit got up from where he had been kneeling, holding a snail. 'It's gone in again,' he said to Charlotte. 'It came out, then it went in again.'

'Yes—'

'It doesn't like noise,' Kit said sternly.

Charlotte crouched down beside him. 'I'll try to be quiet.'

Kit nodded. Petra moved to stand beside Barney's buggy. She said in a neutral voice, 'I know where Ralph's brothers are today. They told him.'

Charlotte glanced up from Kit's snail. 'How'd you know that?'

'Rachel rang,' Petra said in the same neutral tone. She stooped and released Barney, heaving him into her arms. From behind him she said, 'She asked us to go over. Because the others were coming. But we couldn't go.' She paused and then she added, 'So I knew you'd be there.'

Charlotte stood up slowly. 'I didn't go in. They don't know I came. I just drove the boys down, and left them there.' She stopped, and then she said with much less assurance, 'They were—going to tell them—'

'Yes,' Petra said, 'that's why we couldn't go.'

'Look!' Kit shouted excitedly. 'Look! He's done his horns out!'

Charlotte looked down. The snail withdrew sharply.

Kit said, 'Don't look at him!'

Petra sat down on the strip of turf between the vegetable beds, holding Barney on her lap. She said into Barney's hair, 'What d'you think will happen?' Charlotte sat down too, on the other side of a bed of big, fierce marrow leaves. She tucked her legs to one side, looking down at the grass, and leaned on one hand, ripping up single blades with the other.

She said cautiously, 'What is happening?'

'What?' Petra said.

'With—with you. With you and this man—'

'He's great,' Petra said. 'He's easy. He just lets things be. He's called Steve.'

'Have—' Charlotte said, and stopped.

'Have what?'

'Have you slept with him.'

Petra brushed something off the top of Barney's head. 'Not yet.'

Charlotte's head snapped up. 'But, you're *planning* to?'

Petra shrugged. 'It might happen—'

'But you're *married*!'

Petra looked entirely unoffended. She said, glancing at Charlotte over the marrow leaves, 'He said he had to be free.'

'Who did?'

There was a beat, and then Petra said, her voice suddenly catching, 'Ralph did.'

Charlotte got up and went round the marrow bed, Kit following. She sat on the grass by Petra. To her delight and surprise, Kit lowered himself onto her knees, still holding his snail. Charlotte said with feeling, 'Oh, Petra—'

Petra said, her voice shaking, 'He said he had to be free, for all of us. So I let him! I couldn't stop him anyway, so I let him. And I thought that if he was free then I was free, too. Not from the boys, not ever, but from him, kind of, if that's what he wanted. Because—because, whatever I think of him, whatever I want from him, he—well, he doesn't really want me to *be* anything, he just doesn't want me to stop him. So I haven't.'

Charlotte said nothing. She put her arms round Kit, and held him, and he leaned back against her, peering into the snail shell, warm and solid and unspeakably reassuring.

'And there's the sea,' Petra said. 'I know everyone thinks I'm a flake about the sea, but it matters. It matters to me, and it matters that Ralph gets it, and he used to get it, and now he doesn't. Now he wants to be like he was before he met me. He got all his suits out again. Nobody gets what I'm doing, nobody thinks I have any right to live like I need to. They never have. I thought Ralph did, but he doesn't. Not even Ralph. He wants me to be like he wants me to be. Like everyone does.'

'Not me,' Charlotte said.

Petra sighed. She said, 'You don't really know them yet.'

'I know enough—'

'Not to stand up to them—'

Charlotte said, 'That's why I've come.' She held Kit a little tighter. He was really relaxed against her now, almost sleepily, and although her knees hurt from being bent under his weight, she would not have dreamt of moving. 'I don't know what'll happen today,' she said. 'I don't know how they'll react but all I can say is that so far the boys are sticking together. Brother stuff. So—so I don't know how they'll, well, put it. I don't know how they'll tell the story—'

'It won't be good,' Petra said.

'No. I don't expect it will.' Charlotte paused, and considered bringing Rachel, and her own abiding grievance into the equation, and then, buoyed up by the sense of maturity she was experiencing in this whole escapade, told herself not to. Instead, she said, 'I just came to say that not everybody doesn't get it. I do. I might not understand about the sea, and I don't know Steve, but I'm kind of here, if you need me.'

Petra said, 'I'm not in love with him. Or anything.'

'Then why—'

'Because he helps me,' Petra said. 'He knows what I know. About the sea and stuff. He likes what I like. He likes the kids.' She glanced at Kit. 'He's asleep.'

Charlotte looked down. 'What a compliment—'

'He likes women,' Petra said.

'Does—does Kit like his grandmother?'

There was a tiny, significant pause, and then Petra said, 'Yes. He does,' and then she said almost inaudibly, 'She's not going to like me, though. Not now.'

Charlotte smiled at her. She said, 'She doesn't like me, either,' and Petra looked at her, straight at her, and smiled back.

Anthony said, for the fiftieth time, 'I cannot believe it.'

Rachel was lying back in one of the sagging old armchairs in the studio, with her eyes closed. They had been in the studio for hours now, ever since the boys had gone, driving away with Charlotte at the wheel— Charlotte, who they hadn't even known had come to Aldeburgh, and who didn't get out of the car to greet them, but just sat there, smiling, with the window down, the engine still humming.

'Come in,' Rachel had said, stooping to speak to her. 'Come in, at least, and have some tea, before you go back.'

Charlotte hadn't even taken her sunglasses off. She had given Rachel her wide, white smile and said thanks, but they really had to get back, work tomorrow and all that, and Ed and Luke had got in beside her docilely, as if somehow suddenly obedient to her rather than to their parents, and Charlotte had put the car in gear, and driven off, waving and smiling, and they had watched it go, desolate and disorientated, and then turned, as if by unspoken mutual consent, and retreated to the studio.

Anthony was standing by the easel. His drawing of cranes was still on it, unfinished, and out of habit he had picked up a piece of charcoal and smudged at the paper with it, but he couldn't focus, he couldn't recognise his own capacity. He just stood there holding the charcoal, and saying that he couldn't believe it, he simply couldn't. Petra of all people. *Petra.*

Rachel had been quite silent. She had flopped into the nearest armchair and stayed there, head back, eyes either closed or directed at the ceiling. She had given the boys lobster at lunchtime, which she knew they both loved, and that pudding of crushed meringues and strawberries that had always been Luke's favourite. But nobody had eaten anything much. They'd said, 'Great, Mum, thanks,' sounding as they did when they were adolescents, and then they'd exchanged glances as if about to confess to a cricket ball through the greenhouse roof, and then Edward had cleared his throat and said well, actually, there was a reason for their coming, and it wasn't, unfortunately, a very happy reason, and then he started, and Rachel could see, almost from his first words, that Anthony wasn't grasping it, that Anthony couldn't take in what he was being told. And then he did understand, suddenly, and he went grey and put down his spoon, and Rachel had felt such fury on his behalf, such protective rage at his betrayed trust, that she had almost leaped out of her chair.

She was calmer now. She was calmer, and exhausted as, she knew, you can only be when you have been flooded with anger. And she had been. She had said a great many things about Petra that came straight out of her volcano of outrage, outrage that Ralph's efforts to support his family should be rewarded in such a way, outrage at Petra's conduct, outrage that Anthony's faith in her, real love for her, should be repaid so carelessly.

'She's wicked,' Anthony had said, bewildered and distressed, red in the face, his table napkin crumpled into the lobster. *'Wicked.'*

But Rachel knew Petra wasn't wicked. She had, in that first panic of knowing, said terrible things about Petra, but she knew she wasn't wicked. She knew, if she thought about it, if she forced herself right through her violent, primitive, maternal loyalty to Ralph to the other side, that Petra had come up against something in her marriage that was like hurling oneself against a steel door. It wasn't that Petra had encountered something in her life and in her husband that she could not deal with that got to Rachel; oh no, so much of Ralph, and living with Ralph was so profoundly intractable. What got to Rachel, what Rachel could neither understand nor forgive was that, in her trouble, Petra had not come to her and Anthony for help, but had, instead, chosen an alternative solution which was, frankly, disastrous for everybody.

Edward and Luke had described this new man of Petra's as minimally as they could, indicating their distaste for the whole business. Rachel liked their loyalty, but she was equally unnerved by how mild this Steve person sounded, how peacefully attractive his work and his interests, how much—this was the worst—the boys seemed to enjoy being with him. Edward had reported that Ralph was as bemused as he was hurt.

'He says Steve's got nothing, really. Rented, shared cottage, clapped-out Toyota. But he doesn't mind and Petra doesn't mind. It's all birds and sea and throwing stones on the beach with them. That seems to be all. That seems to be enough.'

'Has she been to bed with him?' Anthony had demanded.

Luke made a sick noise.

Edward said woodenly, 'I wouldn't know.'

'It won't last,' Anthony said. 'Flash in the pan. I'll go and talk to her—'

'No!' Rachel had said, loudly and suddenly.

They had all looked at her.

Anthony said, 'But we always talk to her—'

'Not now,' Rachel said. '*Not* now.'

They had gazed at her, astonished. She could see that they were all thinking what's got into Mum, Mum's always rushing in to sort things out, Mum always thinks she's got the answer.

For the first time in decades, Rachel did not know what to do. All that energetic bustling about to try and fix a house in Ipswich for Ralph and Petra now seemed ludicrous, a kind of mad displacement activity for some profound anxiety that she did not care to give a name to. Well, now she knew what that anxiety had been; an anxiety about Ralph's work difficulties causing his strange, opaque, elusive relationship with Petra to dissolve still further, to an extent that no amount of dictatorial, external management could shore it up. Petra was Petra. Always had been, slipping in and out of manageableness like a fish in a wet grasp. But really, Rachel thought now, if she thinks she can get away with treating Anthony like this, after all he's done for her, all his patience and help and affection, well, then she's got another think coming, and a gigantic think at that.

She opened her eyes now and looked at Anthony standing by his easel, staring, unseeing, at the cranes. He seemed much older than he had seemed even that morning; his shoulders slightly stooped, his whole demeanour giving off sadness like a dark vapour.

'Ant?' Rachel said.

He turned slightly, and gave her a half-hearted smile. 'What do we do? What do we do, for Ralph?'

Rachel struggled to sit upright.

'We'll ring him. Later. When we've got our heads a bit more together.'

'Yes,' Anthony said. 'Yes. Poor bloody boy.' He raised his arm and added something to a crane's wing. Then he said with some force, 'You're right. I'm not ringing *her*. I'm not ringing her, Rachel, ever again.'

Luke and Charlotte dropped Edward off at home. He discovered, from a note on the kitchen table, that Sigrid and Mariella had gone to Indira's house, and would not be back until later. He poured himself a glass of water from the jug in the fridge and took it out onto the deck outside the kitchen. Their little patio garden, always tidied to Sigrid's exacting standards, looked tired and spent. Such flowers as were left in the wooden planters that Sigrid had had specially commissioned looked as if it was simply too much trouble, now, to stay vibrant.

There had been nothing left, really, to say in the car. Charlotte had been to the sea, she said, and she'd obviously liked it because she seemed quite animated, and chattered away about the beach in Aldeburgh, and when Luke asked her if she'd been to see Ralph she'd given a short laugh, and said, '*Not* a good idea!'

'So you went?' Luke said.

'I did. I rang the bell, and he answered, but he didn't ask me in. He said it wasn't a good time. He wanted me to go away.'

Edward said, 'Did you see Petra and the kids?'

Charlotte's sunglasses had turned slightly upwards to meet Edward's eyes in the driving mirror. She said, 'They weren't there.'

'Oh God,' Edward said. 'Don't say—'

'Don't think about it,' Luke said. 'We've all had enough today. More than enough. And you,' he said, looking fondly at Charlotte, 'have done all the driving.'

She'd smiled. She said breezily, 'I'd rather drive than throw up,' and Edward had had a sudden stab of something like envy at the simplicity of Luke's situation, at his shiny new marriage to this pretty, good-natured, pregnant girl; such a breath of fresh air after an exhausting day of Brinkley dramas.

He turned the water glass now in his hands, studying the distorted view of his feet visible through the bottom. He felt that he had done the right thing that day, and doing it had been strangely unsatisfactory, because no solution had emerged. It was right to feel that his brother was being wronged, that his parents were being treated with extraordinary ingratitude, he was sure it was. But something unsettled him all the same, something that always unsettled him about going back to Suffolk, where the unalteredness of his parents' lives was, weirdly, more of an uneasy disquiet than a consolation.

He was relieved to hear the front door slam. Mariella came skittering down the basement steps, calling out for him.

'Here!' he shouted. 'I'm out here!'

She came flying through the kitchen and crashed into him, flinging her arms round him and holding up her face. Her eyebrows were traced with tiny studs of blue glitter.

'I'm an avatar,' Mariella said.

Edward bent to reciprocate her embrace. 'So you are. Where's Mummy?'

'Getting stuff out of the car—'

'Did you have a nice time with Indira?'

Mariella pulled free, raced indoors, and began to hop round the kitchen table. 'We played airports. For when I go to Sweden.'

'Oh,' Edward said, not comprehending. 'Ready for next time?'

'Yes,' Mariella said, still hopping. 'Mummy got tickets on the computer before we went to Indira's. She said we'd get the last of the Swedish summer. Before I go back to school.'

'I see,' Edward said. He felt abruptly slightly sick. The front door on the floor above them opened and closed, and Sigrid's footsteps went across the hall over their heads.

Edward looked at Mariella. 'Am—am I coming? Did Mummy get three plane tickets?'

'Oh, no,' she said. 'Mummy said you couldn't. She said you'd have to stay here, and look after your brothers.'

There were plenty of reasons why Rachel should find herself in Aldeburgh. There was the bookshop, after all, and the delicatessen, and the need to buy a birthday present for her sister. So it was not at all extraordinary that Rachel should be there, walking slowly and watchfully along the high street, with her gaze sharpening every time she saw a young woman with a buggy and a small child.

She walked and shopped for over an hour. She bought a monograph by Kenneth Clark about the Alde river from the bookshop, and a variety of different olives from the deli, and a striped cotton dressing gown, cut like a kimono, for her sister, plus a pair of kippers and a loaf of sourdough bread, and stowed them all in the boot of the car. Then, she went back to the high street, and bought a sandwich and a bottle of water, and had a restless picnic, sitting on the pebbly beach on her spread-out fleece jacket, watching the few late-summer families who were left, and willing one of the small boys she could see to turn out to be Kit.

She had decided, wrestling with herself as she made the bed or chopped an onion or tied up the toppling stands of Michaelmas daisies in the border, that her entirely justifiable anger would get her nowhere. Anthony was miserably wounded, but yelling at Petra in defence of Anthony would do nothing to influence one or comfort the other. But she could not accept that she could do nothing. She would not shout, or scold, or even reprimand Petra, but she did have to see her and ask her simply *why*?

Rachel got to her feet, and shook the sandwich crumbs off her jacket. She would walk, she decided, up and down the high street one more time, but she would not knock on Petra's front door, and she would not go down to the allotment. The time might come to insist upon a meeting, rather than just hope for it, but that time had not yet arrived. And if she failed to see Petra, she would never need to confess to Anthony that she had gone to Aldeburgh in the hope of encountering her, and there would be an honesty in that, at least.

She walked briskly down the high street, crossed it, and walked equally purposefully back up the other pavement. No Petra. No girls with buggies at all, in fact, they all being, presumably, still involved with toddler lunchtime and toddler naptime. Rachel turned back towards the sea, and the little square where she had left her car, and there was Petra coming towards her, with no buggy, and no children, and her arms weighed down with shopping.

Petra halted, stock still. She was wearing a kind of gypsy skirt, familiar to Rachel, and her old denim jacket, and her hair was in a rough pigtail, pulled over one shoulder, and tied at the end with a collection of brightly coloured woollen bobbles.

'Hi,' she said to Rachel. Her voice sounded perfectly normal.

Rachel was hurled into a sudden fluster. It would have been natural, instinctive even, to have kissed Petra, but under the current circumstances that wasn't possible. Her voice, when she managed to say hello, sounded unnatural.

Petra was saying nothing, just standing in front of Rachel with her woven grocery bags. Rachel opened her mouth a few times, and made an involuntary gesture or two, trying to indicate a query about where the buggy was, where the boys were. Petra didn't help her.

'How—are you?' Rachel said at last.

'Fine—'

'And—and the boys?'

'Fine,' Petra said.

Rachel got a grip of herself. 'Where are they?' she said. 'I don't think I've ever seen you without the boys—'

'They're with Steve,' Petra said.

'With—with—'

'Yes,' Petra said. She sounded as if what she was saying was so ordinary as to be almost boring. 'Steve's taken them swimming. They love swimming, so he's taken them.' She let a little pause fall, and then she said, 'Because I can't swim. Remember?'

And then she smiled at Rachel, politely and remotely, and stepped into the road to walk past her with the shopping bags.

That evening, Rachel rang Edward to describe her encounter with Petra, and to ask if he thought she should tell Anthony.

'Whyever not?' Edward said irritably.

'Well, he's hurt enough already. And I don't want him picturing his grandsons swimming with this man of Petra's.'

'Well, don't tell him then.'

'But you said—'

'Mum,' Edward said, 'Mum. I don't feel like this conversation. I don't want to discuss this. Or think about it. OK?'

Rachel said sympathetically, 'I expect you're missing Sigrid and Mariella.'

Edward shut his eyes tightly. He thought he wouldn't reply.

'Are they having a lovely time?' Rachel asked.

Edward didn't open his eyes. Sigrid had been away for four days and he had rung once. There was no phone signal on the island where her parents' summer house was.

'Think so,' Edward said.

'Would you like to come up here? The weekend will be grim without them. Come on Friday.'

Edward opened his eyes. 'No, thank you, Mum.'

'Why not?'

'Because,' Edward said, 'I want to stay here.'

There was a silence. In it, the message signal on Edward's mobile phone beeped. Then Rachel said crisply, 'Fine. I'll leave you to be disagreeable in peace. Bye, darling.'

The line went dead. Edward scrolled to his message box.

'In Stockholm for 3 nights. Back Sunday. X'

He dialled Sigrid's number. There was a wait while the signal sorted itself out between London and Stockholm, and then her voicemail message, 'This is Sigrid's phone. Please leave me a message and I'll call you back. Thank you.'

Edward opened his mouth to say, 'Call me,' and thought better of it. He threw his phone down on the sofa beside him. She had left, barely kissing him goodbye, declining to account for excluding him from this last-minute holiday, not even offering an explanation for her impulse, withdrawing into a homing Swedishness which seemed to make her impervious to any consequence of her behaviour and certainly to any reaction or emotion of his.

'Will you miss me?' he'd said to Mariella in Sigrid's hearing, despising himself. Mariella had hugged him as if he were a dear old teddy bear, with no human feelings. 'A bit,' she said. And then they'd left, with a case full of shorts and plimsolls, Sigrid wearing a baseball cap and looking about sixteen, and had gone straight to the island in the archipelago where, Mariella said, they were going to have breakfast in their pyjamas and go sailing and make camp fires on the beach.

'We're going to sleep together,' Mariella said, 'in the big bed. Just me and Mummy.'

He opened the fridge and took out a bottle of beer, slamming it down on the table. Whatever was the matter, whatever Sigrid was up to, he'd just have to bear it. And to crown it all, Ralph was coming to stay for the first few days of his new employment, until his room off Finsbury Square was available.

Edward flipped the top off the beer bottle and took a deep swallow. Sigrid would be back four nights from now, full of air and sunshine and happy Swedishness and, despite all his hurt at her treatment of him, he did not want her to walk back in to a long-faced husband as well as an unexpected-guest brother-in-law. He took another mouthful of beer. No more wallowing, he told himself. No more plaguing myself with imaginings. At least—at least, she's coming home.

Sigrid had intended to stay on the island for a week. She had planned on four or five days alone with Mariella, doing all the simple, peaceful, water-orientated things that she had done on the island when she was Mariella's age, and then she had asked her parents to come and join them for the weekend, expecting a gratified agreement since her parents loved the island, and had not seen Mariella, their only grandchild, for seven months. But Sigrid's mother had said that she was so sorry but her father had an important business function in Stockholm on the Saturday night, and so they would be staying in the city.

'Well, *you* come,' Sigrid said.

'No, I can't,' her mother said. 'I'm going with your father. The invitation is for both of us.'

'Rather than see Mariella and me?'

'Sigi,' her mother had said calmly, 'you have sprung this trip on us. It is last minute. We had plans in place.'

'But I wanted to see you. For you to see Mariella—'

'Then come to Stockholm.'

'But I wanted to be on the island—'

'I must go,' Sigrid's mother had said. 'I leave the decision to you.'

Even with the irritation of her parents not changing their plans, Sigrid anticipated loving being on the island. She longed for the familiar, faintly rough texture of the blue-and-white bedlinen in the cottage, and the mornings, nursing a mug of tea, still in her pyjamas, and watching the sun come up, and the evenings, on the beach, showing Mariella how to gut a fish as her father had shown her and Bengt, and then spearing it on a twig before grilling it. But Mariella did not much like fish, anyway, and certainly didn't want to touch the gluey loops of its innards, and at night, instead of sleeping peacefully and thereby allowing Sigrid to rise, rested and refreshed, to watch the sunrise, she kicked and swivelled in her slumber, seizing the duvet and muttering to such an extent that Sigrid took herself off to her narrow childhood bed in a separate bedroom, where her feet hit the board at the foot of the bed and some plumbing pipes cleared their throats at intervals in the wall behind her head, all night long.

The weather was beautiful, but the days on the island were long—long and, frankly, boring. The sailing classes in which Sigrid had hoped to enrol Mariella were finished for the summer, and after a first nostalgic scramble round the rocks, walks were limited. Because Swedish schools returned weeks before English ones, all the families had gone. Mariella knew not to say outright that she was bored but she did say, now and then, that it was odd to be without a television. It was odd. The whole place felt odd, as if Sigrid's recollection of her childhood there had been conjured out of fantasy rather than out of fact.

On the fourth day, watching Mariella building a little cairn of pebbles with one hand, as if she wasn't sufficiently interested to use both, Sigrid suggested that they return to Stockholm. Mariella scrambled to her feet.

'Oh, yes!'

Sigrid smiled at her. 'Is it so very boring here?'

'Well,' Mariella said, 'it would have been better, really, if Daddy had been here, too.'

Ralph had laid all his suits for London out on the double bed. He couldn't think of it, any more, as 'our' bed, even though they still shared it, turned away from each other, and lined up along the edges in case a stray foot or knee should touch by mistake. Ralph had considered moving out, to sleep with Kit, or on the sofa downstairs, but anger kept him in his own bed, just as anger was revving him up to leave for London as soon as he possibly could. Edward, sensing this rage, had agreed that he could occupy their small guest room—it doubled as Sigrid's study—in order to get away from Aldeburgh as soon as possible. 'I'm going crazy,' Ralph had said to Edward, 'living here. Crazy. And every time I try and talk to her, I get crazier.'

The problem was, really, that Petra was hiding nothing.

'Are you still seeing him?'

'Yes.'

'Are you'—pause—'sleeping with him?'

'No.'

'Are you'—shouting—'going to?'

'Maybe,' Petra said.

'What d'you mean, maybe?'

Petra was at the kitchen table, drawing, her hair hanging, her face mostly hidden. 'I don't fancy him much,' Petra said to her sketchbook, 'but maybe. I dunno.'

Ralph placed his hands flat on the table and lowered his shoulders in order to see her face. 'Look at me!'

Slowly, Petra looked up.

'Why,' Ralph said, trying to control himself, 'do you have to see him at *all*?'

Petra waited a moment, and then she said, 'I got lonely.'

'Why didn't you tell me that?'

'You couldn't hear me,' Petra said.

'Why didn't you tell Mum and Dad?'

Petra bent her head again. 'They'd have wanted to do something. They'd have wanted *me* to do something—'

'But'—shouting again—'you *have* done something!'

'But I chose it,' Petra said to her drawing.

Ralph sat down heavily in a chair opposite Petra. He said, 'What d'you feel about me?'

'What I have always done.'

'Which is?'

'I like you,' Petra said. 'You're cool. But you've changed. You want things I don't want now. I can't change, just to suit you.'

Ralph said wearily, 'I haven't changed, but if we're going to live and eat there has to be money, and I've been given a chance to earn some. How are you going to look after the boys without money, for God's sake? And, as you have no job, it has to be me. I cannot believe how—how *obtuse* you are.'

'I don't need to live in this kind of place. I don't need a car. It's nice to have, but I'd manage. I like things small. I always have.'

Ralph said sarcastically, 'Oh, so my parents' generosity was repulsive to you, was it?'

Petra said sharply, 'They wanted to do what they've done.'

'Meaning?'

'I'm not a complete fool. They've been lovely to me, but I've suited them.'

'You ungrateful little *cow*.'

Petra stood up, holding her sketchbook. 'It's not worth it,' she said.

'What isn't?'

'It's not worth people being kind to you. They always want so much back.'

'But not,' Ralph said, 'lover boy.'

Petra turned. 'He's easy.'

'Then why don't you bloody go and live with him!'

Petra began to move towards the doorway to the hall. 'I don't want to. I might, in time, but I don't want to right now. It's just that he's on my side, he doesn't tell me what to do, he just talks to the kids and digs the spuds and I don't have to—' She stopped.

'Don't have to what?'

'*Earn* my existence all the time,' and then she'd gone out, and he could hear her going slowly up the stairs and into their bedroom, and then a couple of thuds as she took off her shoes, and dropped them on the floor.

When he had finally gone upstairs that night, Petra was not in their bed. He found her instead in Kit's bed, and Kit had flung an arm across her in his sleep, and they were lying facing each other, almost nose to nose. Across the room, Barney was snuffling in his cot, stout legs and arms spreadeagled, his thick lashes astonishing on his cheeks.

Ralph had stood in the dark bedroom between his sleeping family, and felt something so close to the panic of despair that the only solution he could think of was to force it down with a big hit of anger. It was Petra he was angry with, of course it was, Petra who refused to compromise, refused to understand, refused to grow up. It was Petra who had made Kit such a fragile child, it was Petra who had taken all the Brinkleys' open-handed generosity until, on a whim, it didn't suit her to see it as generosity any more, but only as oppression and control and obligation. It was Petra who couldn't support or admire what he was doing, to look after them all. Hell, she couldn't even iron a bloody *shirt* properly. It was Petra—

He had to stop himself. He was shaking, and his fists had clenched. He could not go on being so furious, it was exhausting him, diverting his vital energies, obsessing him. He couldn't understand Petra any more than she claimed not to be able to understand him, so maybe it was better that they were apart, and the sooner the better.

He went out of the boys' bedroom, and closed the door behind him. Edward had said he could come up to London on Saturday, but he thought he would ring in the morning and say he needed to come now, *now*, and if Edward couldn't have him, then he'd find a hotel.

He took down their only big suitcase from the dusty top of the wardrobe. He put it on the bed and opened it, and began to make rapid, methodical piles of shirts and socks and boxer shorts, emptying drawers with speed, to purge himself of all animation other than that which was constructive and forward-looking. And then he got into the half of the bed that wasn't occupied by the suitcase and lay there, panting slightly, and listening to his heart racing away under his ribcage, as if it was just a useful, purposeful muscle, and not the seat, really, of any emotion at all.

CHAPTER NINE

SIGRID TUCKED MARIELLA up in the bed that had been hers when she was a child. The bed was now in her mother's study, and used as a daybed, piled with cushions covered in modern graphic designs, but it still had its old wooden headboard with its row of cut-out hearts. Such papers as were on her mother's desk were in a black lacquered tray, her pens were in a matching pot, the books and files on her shelves upright and orderly.

Mariella was leaning back against crisp, striped pillows, holding a puzzle made of plastic tubes that her engineer grandfather had made for her. The tubes were linked in such a way that there was only one sequence of separation that could part them, and Sigrid's father had declined even to give Mariella a clue as to how to achieve it. Morfar always set her challenges, just as Mormor always made her an apple cake, and rising to these challenges was something Mariella liked to do.

She bent and kissed Mariella. 'Sleep tight. I'll send Mormor to kiss you.'

Mariella went on twisting. 'In ten minutes.'

'Why ten minutes?'

'I'll have done this by then.'

Sigrid left the study door ajar, and walked down the central corridor of the apartment to the sitting room. It was flooded with soft evening sunlight through the long, floor-length windows, and her mother was sitting by one of those windows, in an armchair upholstered in grey linen, reading the *Aftonbladet* newspaper. She looked up when Sigrid came in and said, 'May I go and say goodnight?'

'In ten minutes. She wants to solve Morfar's puzzle.'

Sigrid sat down in the chair opposite her mother's. She looked out of the window into the soft dazzle of late sunlight. Her mother looked at her. After a minute or two her mother said, 'Were you thinking of coming back to Sweden?'

Sigrid gave a little jump. 'Whatever made you say that?'

'I just wondered,' her mother said. 'This impulsive trip. Your restlessness. Something—unsettled about you.'

Sigrid said abruptly, 'I can't breathe for those Brinkleys—'

'Ah,' her mother said.

'They are like Morfar's puzzle,' Sigrid said. 'Except that there isn't a way to unlink them.'

Her mother put the newspaper down and took off her reading glasses. 'So you were thinking that you could escape them by coming back to Sweden.'

Sigrid looked away. 'Only sort of—'

'Well,' her mother said kindly, 'don't. Listen. You've been away too long. It isn't the country you grew up in. All the people you grew up with have changed with the country, and although you have changed with England you haven't moved on here. You haven't been here.'

Sigrid made a little gesture. 'I could catch up—'

'And there's another thing,' her mother said, 'a bigger thing. Which I suspect you haven't thought of.'

'Which is?'

Sigrid's mother leaned back in her chair. 'Me.'

'You!'

'Yes,' her mother said. 'Me. Think of my situation.'

Sigrid looked round the room, laughing a little. 'It looks a very comfortable situation indeed—'

'Really?' her mother said. 'Really? You think it's so comfortable to have two children, both of whom have chosen to live in other countries?'

'But you don't mind—'

'Who says I don't mind?'

'But—'

'Of course, I am happy you married Edward,' Sigrid's mother said. 'I adore Mariella. I love your brother dearly, but he will never give me a Mariella. I like his partner, I love your Edward, I am pleased and proud of what my children have achieved, but I don't know their lives. Not as my friends know their children's lives. How can I? You live in different cultures as well as countries.'

'Goodness,' Sigrid said.

'I have had to adjust,' her mother said. 'And one of the ways I've adjusted to having both my children living in other countries is to throw myself into my work. I work all the time now, as your father does. It suits us. We like it. And when we retire, we will start travelling, and we'll come often to London and we will see more of you, and more of Mariella. But if—' She paused, and leaned forward, fixing her gaze on Sigrid. 'If you come back to Sweden now, I couldn't just dump all my patients and become a full-time mother and grandmother.'

'Why are you talking to me like this? Why are you angry?'

'I'm not angry,' her mother said, 'but as a mother yourself, I expected that you might have a little more imagination.'

Sigrid looked at her lap.

'And,' her mother added, 'for your mother-in-law, too. Didn't she bring up the man you married?'

Sigrid put her hands to her face.

'No crying,' her mother said more gently. 'We are both too old for that. A bit of frankness between women shouldn't make you cry.'

Sigrid's mother stood up. She bent forward and gave her daughter's shoulder a squeeze. 'I'm going to say goodnight to Mariella. Why don't you get us a glass of wine. Friday night, after all.'

'Mamma—I'm not trying to—run away—'

Her mother paused, passing her chair. She said, 'It never works, Sigi. You just take it all with you, anyway. You can change your situation, but it will be the same one if you don't change yourself. I say this to my patients, over and over. I should have it painted on my surgery wall.'

Charlotte's evening sickness was improving. As it diminished, her stomach swelled slightly, but definitely, and her bosom was magnificent. She told her boss at work, who was dramatically unsurprised. The early feelings of anxiety, almost fear, that she had felt at being pregnant, finding herself in a tunnel from which only she could exit, had been considerably subdued by knowing how thrilled Luke was about the baby.

Since the visit to Petra's allotment, Charlotte had kept in touch with her by text. Petra didn't do Facebook, or Twitter, or even answer her mobile, but she responded sometimes to texts, writing cryptic little messages, often mysterious in meaning, but always signed off with a kiss. Charlotte had half a dozen of these little communications in her phone's memory, and they gave her both the glow and the mild kick of being in some kind of conspiracy.

And so when Luke said, one evening, after Edward had rung: 'Ralph's in London. He's actually done it. Maybe that'll bring Petra to her senses,' Charlotte said quite forcefully, 'Why doesn't anyone in your family consider Petra's point of view?'

They had been clearing up after supper, jostling round each other in the tiny kitchen. Luke had a tumbler in each hand, and a tea towel over one shoulder. He stopped on his way to the shelf where they kept their glasses and said, 'What?'

Charlotte was tipping the remains of a chicken korma into a plastic box. She said again, with emphasis, 'Why don't any of you think of what it's like for Petra? Why does she get all the blame?'

'She doesn't,' Luke said.

'She does. You all go on and on about her ingratitude and not having a grip on real life and wanting everything her own way—'

'Well, she does,' Luke said. He put the glasses on their shelf.

'You don't know what she feels. How she's been treated—'

'Treated?'

'Yes.'

'By whom?'

'By you,' Charlotte said, snapping the box shut. 'By all of you.'

Luke picked up a handful of cutlery to dry it. He said, frowning down at the forks in his hand, 'Are we that mean?'

'She didn't say anyone was mean. She just said Ralph didn't understand.'

Luke looked up. '*Said*? When?'

Charlotte stood up straight so that she could look directly at Luke. 'When I went to see her.'

Luke dumped the forks back on the draining board. 'Oh, Char—'

'I saw her while you were at your parents'. When you went with Edward. I drove to Aldeburgh and I went to their house, but Ralph didn't want to let me in, so I went to find Petra on her allotment.'

'Are you sure,' Luke said, 'that you're not just getting even with my mother, somehow?'

'No,' Charlotte said, too quickly. 'Petra needs someone to be on her side. Don't you think?' She paused, and then she said, 'Anyway, we didn't even mention your mother's name.'

Luke sighed. He said, 'I don't expect you needed to. What did you— exactly say to her?'

'I said,' Charlotte said, feeling a sudden and disconcerting diminution in her own certainty, 'that even if I didn't share everything that's important to her, I understood the importance, and I was, well, I was there for her.'

'Shagging the bloke?'

'She isn't shagging him. Why does it always have to be about sex? Why can't she be with someone who isn't always telling her to do things she doesn't want to do?'

'Like what?'

'Like,' Charlotte said, gaining confidence again, 'like saying he had to be free to go to London, but she wasn't free to see anyone else—'

'He's in London,' Luke said, 'to earn money to keep her, and the kids.'

'That's not how she sees it. It isn't what she wants. She just wants to be left, living by the sea, but not by the standards of—of—' She stopped.

'My parents,' Luke said.

Charlotte nodded. Luke put the tea towel down in a damp lump beside the forks. He looked out of the window above the sink, his hands in his pockets. Charlotte waited, watching him, uncertain of how she would defend herself, now that she had been found out. Luke didn't turn.

'It always comes back to that,' Luke said. 'Doesn't it? It always comes back to the fact that you've decided to hate my mother.'

Anthony was sorting canvases. He'd been drawing—a Sandwich tern in flight—but he wasn't concentrating properly, so he left his easel and the bunch of pencils he kept in an old stoneware mustard jar, and climbed a stepladder to haul down, from their unsteady stacks on the rafters, piles of old boards and canvases, to see which of them might be used again, and which could be taken into the college for his students.

He had brought down two piles, blown the worst of the dust off them, and sorted through the endless drawings and paintings, years and years of owls and ducks, of storks and swans and geese. He'd paused over a painting of a group of kittiwakes plunging and splashing together in a lake, and thought that it was actually good enough, arresting enough, to do something with rather than leave to moulder on the rafters, and he was standing with the painting in one hand and some sketches of herons drawn on thick, rough, handmade paper in the other when there was a sudden flurry of gravel outside the studio, as if someone was running unsteadily, and the door was flung open, and Kit appeared, panting.

'Gramps!'

Anthony let both pictures fall to the floor. He knelt, and held his arms out. 'Kit!'

Kit ran to him. He was laughing. He put his arms round Anthony's neck, and held on, chattering in his ear. Then the gravel crunched again and Petra appeared, carrying Barney. She walked through the door, and then halted just inside, looking at Anthony. She didn't speak.

Anthony detached Kit's arms, and got to his feet. Kit clung to his trouser legs, still chirruping. Barney observed his grandfather and leaned forward in Petra's arms, smiling.

Anthony said, 'What are you doing here?'

Petra shifted Barney slightly in her arms. She was wearing jeans, and a loose smock made of green Indian gauze, embroidered with mirrors. Her bare feet were thrust into sneakers, whose toecaps were worn into holes. 'I wanted to see you,' Petra said. She deposited Barney on the floor.

'I'm not sure,' Anthony said, 'that I have anything to say to you.'

'I didn't think you would,' Petra said.

'Then why have you come?'

Petra reached forward to take some nameless, small object out of Barney's hand. 'You've been good to me. Always. I wanted you to know that.'

'I do know it. That's why—what you are doing is so hard to understand—Ralph is my son. He's hurt. I'm hurt.'

Petra sat back on her heels. 'I get that.'

'So maybe you will also get that I don't want to see you.'

Petra stood up, unfolding from the floor in a single movement. She said, 'We'll go—'

Anthony spread his arms and hands in a sudden gesture of helplessness. 'Did you see Rachel?'

'I came to see you—'

'Look,' Anthony said, 'look, I can imagine how wretched this has been for you. I know how tricky Ralph can be. I know you don't want to live in Ipswich or London or wherever, but what—whatever *possessed* you to think another man would be the answer?'

Kit began to roam round the studio, investigating things. Barney had found a walnut on the floor that he was trying to insert into a hole in the side of one of the armchairs. Petra watched them both for a while and then she said, 'He's not—an answer. He's just getting me through.'

'But there's *us*! There's always been us! We've always been here to help, you only had to ask, you only had to whisper—'

Petra said quietly, 'I can't always do what you want. You—forget.'

'Forget what?'

'That not everybody wants what you want. Some people want *less*.'

'If breaking up something like a marriage is wanting something less—'

'I didn't break it. Not at the beginning.'

Anthony looked at her for the first time since she had arrived. 'What do you mean?'

Petra shrugged and said, 'It suited us how we were. It suited us best, at the start, with just the cottage and the beach. Then it changed. But I haven't. I want what I've always wanted. I knew it when I first saw the cottage.'

'But this *man*—'

Petra bent to heave Barney into her arms again. 'You're all fixated on this man. You don't get it, do you?'

'No.'

'Well,' Petra said, 'that's up to you.' She looked about for Kit, dawdling round the table on which Anthony's drawing materials lay. 'But I wanted to come and tell you that, whatever happens, I know how good you've been to me, and I'm grateful.'

Anthony said hoarsely, 'Will you see Rachel?'

Petra shook her head, holding her free hand out to Kit.

Anthony looked at her standing there in her holey sneakers with Barney in her arms, and Kit jigging at her side. He said awkwardly, 'I don't know why I should thank you for coming, but thank you for coming.'

'I thought you wouldn't see me,' Petra said.

Anthony looked at Kit, and then at Barney. He felt weighed down by unhappiness. 'So did I,' he said.

Long time no see!' Marco, the coffee vendor, said to Sigrid.

'One week—'

'*Bella ragazza*,' Marco said on cue, smiling, handing Sigrid her coffee and a small paper bag containing a biscotto.

She walked down Gower Street holding her coffee. It was a grey day, but the sky was light and high, and there was just a little sharp edge to the air, presaging the end of days when she could walk to work in just a sweater, or a jacket, with bare feet inside her shoes. She had been away only a week, but it had, in its unexpected way, been an intense week, a week that had not turned out in any way as she had planned it, and from which she had returned feeling strangely disorientated.

Perhaps work would be reassuring. Maybe the lab, and those fragments of wood and cloth and glass that awaited her, would root her again, restore her to the equilibrium that, earlier in the summer, she was sure she had reliably found. Part of her, on the flight home, had felt a twitch of excitement that that equilibrium might be waiting peacefully at home for her with Edward, but when she got home Ralph was there too, gaunt and overanimated, insisting that he wasn't nervous about his first Monday in a new job, but only eager to begin, and there was no opportunity to do more than be a welcoming sister-in-law, and find him a clean bath towel. Edward had asked, in a slightly forced way, if they had had a good time and Mariella had said, truffling the fridge in search of homecoming favourites, 'You know, Daddy, the island was so, so weird, it was like everyone had just *died*,' and Edward had laughed with what Sigrid recognised as undisguised relief.

At her station at the bench in the lab, everything looked as she had left it, but with the unmistakable air of having been occupied by someone else who had been careful to restore everything to Sigrid's exacting pattern. Everybody said good morning, and asked politely about Sweden, and the head of the laboratory said he was glad to see her back, as a very interesting specimen had just come in from southern Germany which he knew was squarely in her field.

Ginger-haired Philip was blessedly absent for two quiet, serious, concentrating hours until he appeared at Sigrid's elbow, and said that there was someone outside to see her.

'It's eleven o'clock,' Sigrid said, 'I'm working.'

'He says he's your brother-in-law. Said his name was Luke?'

She glanced at him. 'Thank you.'

Luke was waiting in the uncompromising reception area of the laboratory building. He turned round as Sigrid came in.

'Is anything the matter?' she asked.

'No one's ill,' Luke said, 'nothing like that. I just didn't want to come round to your house because I'd quite like this to be private—'

Sigrid motioned him to sit down. 'Are you in trouble?'

'No,' Luke said. 'Yes. Well, sort of. It's—about Charlotte—'

'Charlotte!'

'She's fine,' Luke said, 'she's really well. It's—it's just her—and my mother.' He stopped. He and Sigrid regarded each other in silence for some time. Then Sigrid sighed.

'Oh,' she said. 'That.'

Marnie did not often go to London these days. Today, however, was different. She drove steadily and peacefully to the station. There was plenty of time. Her senior rail card secured her a first-class seat at a very reasonable rate, and she bought a newspaper and a copy of *Country Life*. At Marylebone, Marnie took the Underground. Gregory—had he still been there—would have insisted she take a taxi, but one of her new freedoms was only sheltering herself when she felt she really wanted to.

At Liverpool Street, Marnie left the train and climbed up to Bishopsgate. The train had been full of refreshingly different people from the kind of people Marnie usually saw, which only contributed to her sense of adventure. It was a mild, soft, early September day, warmer in London than it had been in Buckinghamshire. Marnie took off her jacket and folded it over her arm, and then, feeling that this was no way to conduct herself in East London, unfolded it and slung it over her shoulders, pausing in front of the window of a vast bank to admire the effect. It looked suitably nonchalant. She set off northwards towards Shoreditch High Street, and the intriguingly named Arnold Circus, where Charlotte had told her that she and Luke lived, in a flat the size of a shoebox, five floors above the street.

Jed went down the short flight of stairs from the studio to answer the bell. He found himself face to face with a good-looking woman of about his mother's age who looked like Jed's idea of the female half of a Tory Party conference. He wasn't quite sure what to say to her, so he said nothing, just stood there and gawped.

'Is Luke here?' Marnie said.

Jed scratched his head. 'Um—he might be. You from some charity?'

'No,' Marnie said, 'I am his mother-in-law, and you are Jed, and you came to his wedding.'

Jed felt a dark, hot blush surging up his neck. 'Oh, Jesus—'

'Don't worry,' Marnie said kindly, 'it's hard to spot people out of context. And you weren't expecting me.'

'No—'

'And nor was Luke. Is he there?'

Jed held the door a little wider. He couldn't quite look at her. He had a dim recollection of a big hat who someone said was Charlotte's mother, but the hat had had no face that he could recall.

'Scoot up,' Jed said. 'He's up there. Sorry.'

Marnie gave him a smile and squeezed past him. Jed went outside, letting the door crash behind him. He leaned on the wall, and felt for the packet of gum in his pocket. Charlotte's mother! What was she doing here?

Marnie!' Luke said. He was genuinely absolutely amazed.

Marnie said, 'I thought that if I rang you you'd have to tell Charlotte, and I want this to be a complete surprise.'

'Is—is it urgent?'

Marnie smiled at him. 'Well, anything to do with Charlotte is important, isn't it? You and I are in complete agreement about that, aren't we?'

'Of course—'

'We could go up to your flat? Charlotte said I couldn't see it until you'd got some curtains. I don't mind about the curtains, of course I don't, but she wanted it to be perfect for me to see, bless her.'

'OK,' he said. 'We'll go up'.

The flat, Marnie thought privately, was charming but impossibly small. While Luke made coffee, Marnie washed her hands in the midget bathroom—no bath, only a shower, and the shower curtain missing half its rings—and noticed, fondly, that the only shelf was crowded with Charlotte's hair and beauty products.

Luke had laid out coffee mugs, and a milk jug, and a cafetière on the low table in front of the sofa. Marnie looked at him with approval. Young men of his generation saw nothing dangerous in being domesticated, just as her older sons-in-law were such hands-on fathers, to the point where she had sometimes wanted to urge Sarah and Fiona to remember that those children were their mothers' responsibility, too. She sat down on the sofa and looked about her.

'Lovely, light room.'

'It's a great location.'

Marnie thought of her walk to Arnold Circus. It had not been through anything that her own upbringing could have described as a great location.

She accepted a mug of coffee. It smelled wonderful. She smiled at Luke.

'Thank you, dear.'

He sat down on a square, upholstered cube opposite her. 'Now,' he said. He looked perfectly friendly, but also slightly worried.

Marnie said, 'It's about Charlotte and the baby.'

Luke took a swallow of coffee. 'Tell me.'

Marnie had rehearsed this bit. 'I don't want to worry Charlotte, and we all know that she hasn't the best financial brain in the world, but—will you be all right for money?'

Luke drank some more coffee. He said, switching his gaze from Marnie to his mug, 'A bit strapped. But fine,' and then he added, as an afterthought, 'thank you.'

'Well,' Marnie said, her head slightly on one side, 'I have a little plan.'

Luke didn't look up.

She leaned forward. 'The thing is, dear Luke, that Charlotte has always been rather sheltered. Her sisters would call it spoiled, but it's what happens, often, to the baby of the family, especially if that baby is as pretty as Charlotte. And, although I know she is in one way thrilled about this baby, I know that part of her is quite nervous, too, scared even, and I thought I could do something to help that, and help you at the same time. I want, you see, to give you a maternity nurse, to help with the baby after the birth, and reassure Charlotte that she is going to be a wonderful mother. But—' She held up a hand to prevent Luke saying what he was plainly agitating to say. 'But you can't possibly fit a nanny in here. You can't, actually, fit a baby in here. So I am going to help you pay for a bigger flat, and I shall go on helping you until you are both in a position to help yourselves. I don't want any thanks, or any argument. It is absolutely my pleasure to do this for you and my Charlotte.'

She stopped and picked up her coffee and smiled into it, in the sanguine expectation of Luke's relief and gratitude. There was a silence. The silence was, she supposed, because Luke was slightly stunned at the imagination and scope of her offer, but then the silence went on, and she was forced to look up from her coffee to find Luke scowling into his.

'Luke?'

He gave a little jerk, as if he was trying to shake himself into order.

'What do you say, dear?'

Luke looked out of the window. Then he looked at the ceiling. Then he looked at a point slightly to one side of Marnie and said with an effort, 'I'm afraid—not.'

'Not! What *do* you mean?'

Luke managed to drag his gaze onto his mother-in-law. 'I mean, Marnie, that it's really kind of you, but we'll manage.'

'Luke, you can't. Charlotte can't—'

'She'll have to learn,' Luke said. 'Just like me. We'll both have to learn. Like our friends have who've got babies. Like everyone does.'

'Let me help you!'

'No!' Luke said loudly.

There was another, sharper silence. Marnie said with dignity, 'Did you just shout at me?'

'I didn't mean to,' Luke said. 'It's kind of you, but we can't accept—'

'Charlotte might accept—'

'You won't tell Charlotte,' Luke said firmly. 'You won't go behind my back.' He leaned forward a little. 'You *won't*.'

Marnie turned slightly to stare out of the window. 'It seems to me that you are just being obstinate. Showing male pride. I know all about male pride. I lived with it for almost forty years. You don't want to accept help for the mother of your child because you want to be the only provider.'

Luke said, slightly dangerously, 'I am not the same kind of man as Charlotte's father was. I don't want to—can't accept your offer, for all our sakes. Charlotte and I will never grow up unless we learn how. And we can't be beholden. We have the right to learn to be independent that you all had. Frankly, Marnie, we can't be *patronised* this way.'

Marnie swallowed. She said tightly, 'I can only hope you are thinking of Charlotte.'

Luke stood up. He had the distinct, and faintly alarming, air of someone bringing an interview to a brisk conclusion. He said, looking down at Marnie, where she sat on the sofa, 'It's precisely because I'm thinking of Charlotte that I'm declining your offer.'

And then he moved across to the door to the hall, and held it open.

Why didn't you tell me?' Rachel said.

She was standing in the kitchen, fresh from the garden, with earthy knees to her jeans and her hair held off her face by a spotted handkerchief that Anthony recognised as his own.

'I was going to. I always intended to. I was just waiting until I had marshalled my own thoughts about it—'

Rachel went over to the sink, and jammed the kettle roughly under the tap to fill it. 'So I imagine she didn't ask to see me.'

'No, she didn't.'

'What about the boys?' Rachel said, banging the kettle down on its base and switching it on. 'How were the boys?'

'Lovely,' Anthony said. 'Sweet. They looked fine.'

Rachel moved to stand by the sink again, gripping its edge, and staring out of the window above it into the garden. 'Why do you suppose she came?'

Anthony went to stand beside her. 'Because,' he said, 'she isn't without gratitude.' He put a hand on Rachel's. 'Don't focus on her not asking to see you. Don't take it personally all the time—'

'But I'm *hurt!*' Rachel cried.

'Yes.'

'I'm—I'm really fond of her. I've been fond of her for years—'

'You love her,' Anthony said.

Rachel nodded furiously. She took her hand out from under Anthony's and brushed it across her eyes. She said, 'And I was so grateful to her. For taking on Ralph. And letting Ralph be Ralph—'

'Until,' Anthony said, 'he was too much Ralph.'

The kettle clicked itself off.

'Is she going to live with this man?'

'I don't know. She said he was just getting her through. She didn't sound like someone in love to me, but maybe I just didn't hear that because I didn't want to.'

Rachel got two mugs out of the cupboard above the kettle. She said, more calmly, 'What exactly did Ralph do?'

Anthony sighed. 'What he always does. What suited Ralph. Not listening. Not listening, ever.'

'I don't listen,' Rachel said. 'I should start with myself. I should hear myself sometimes.' She dropped tea bags into the mugs. 'She really didn't want to see me—'

'I think she was afraid to.'

'In case I barked. I might well have barked. I've always barked when I'm frightened.'

Anthony waited a moment, then he said, '*Are* you frightened?'

Rachel poured boiling water into the mugs, and stirred the tea bags round with a spoon. She said lightly, 'Yup.'

'Of—what exactly?'

Rachel flipped the tea bags out into the sink. 'Of losing my usefulness.'

'*What?*'

Rachel walked briskly past him to the fridge and took out the milk. She said, 'What am I for, now, exactly?'

'Rachel!'

'Look,' she said, not looking at him. 'Look. I've run a house and garden, I've brought up three boys. They've all married. They've produced three children. One to come. And they are doing just what I did, what I wanted to do, which is what I started doing when I came here and married you. Which is to live my own life, start my own family, make my own world. And it's been my world. And now it isn't—'

In his studio that afternoon, Anthony had been listening to a radio interview with the Dalai Lama. The Dalai Lama had said, in his light, benevolent way, that as far as he could see most of the public trouble in the world was made by men, and most of the domestic trouble was made by women. Anthony visualised the Dalai Lama, in his spectacles and his maroon-and-ochre robes, sitting at their kitchen table and listening to Rachel describing how her life had outrun its purpose.

'Are you listening?' Rachel said.

'Very much—'

'This huge house,' Rachel said, 'an acre and a half of garden. You and me. At least you've still got the studio.'

Anthony said, 'You *could* run cookery courses again.'

'I'm too sad,' Rachel replied. 'And too fidgety. I've got to get used to being good at something no one needs me to be good at any more.' She looked at Anthony. 'I love being a grandmother.'

'I know.'

'Suppose she takes the children to live with this man—'

'Suppose,' Anthony said, 'she doesn't.' He picked up one of the mugs of tea, and took it to the chair he always sat in, with its blue-checked cushion and view right across the room. He said, 'You say you're frightened. Don't you suppose Petra is frightened too?'

Rachel sighed. 'I expect she is—'

Anthony took a gulp of tea. 'Well then,' he said.

Charlotte was charmed when Sigrid rang to ask if they could have lunch together. Or coffee, Sigrid said, if she was busy. But she'd love it if they could meet. She gave Charlotte the feeling that this was evidence of how sophisticated a relationship between sisters-in-law could be, when the bond caused by marrying brothers served, in the end, as no more than a beginning to something that had a life of its own.

'Lunch, please,' Charlotte said, 'I'm always so hungry at the moment. It's such a relief not feeling sick any more. I'm eating breakfast and elevenses and lunch and tea and supper. So lunch would be lovely.'

Sigrid laughed. She said something about how nice it was to hear someone sounding so healthy about being pregnant, and then she suggested that they meet somewhere halfway between their places of work, and why not the first-floor café of that distinguished architectural institute on Portland Place?

So here Charlotte was, slightly early for once, studying the menu with considerable interest, and wondering whether to confide to Sigrid that she had been to see Petra, and had offered her support. She thought that, on balance, she probably would tell Sigrid because Sigrid, after all, had also suffered from not being the favourite, from not quite ever toeing the Brinkley line. Charlotte didn't know Sigrid very well, and was slightly daunted by what appeared to Charlotte an impressive degree of maturity and togetherness on her part, but then, Sigrid had been the one to suggest lunch, which must mean at least the beginnings of a wish to do a little sisterly bonding. When she saw Sigrid coming up the wide, central stairs to the café, she got up, feeling suddenly rather shy, and stood there, waiting to be noticed.

'You look wonderful,' Sigrid said. 'Being pregnant really suits you. I think the word is "blooming", isn't it?'

'I'm going to be like a whale,' Charlotte said. 'I'm eating like one, too. Did you get huge?'

Sigrid took off her jacket and hung it over the back of her chair. 'I was no good at being pregnant.'

Charlotte waited. Some instinct kept her from bouncing back at once.

Sigrid continued, picking up the menu, her voice almost detached, 'It nearly killed me, having Mariella.'

'Oh!' Charlotte said, horrified.

'But we aren't going to talk about that. It was nine years ago, and she is wonderful, and Edward was a saint.' She looked up at Charlotte and smiled. 'And you are going to do it beautifully.'

'God,' Charlotte said, 'I hope so. I mean, we never meant this to happen, and if you don't you kind of have to get it more right than if you do. Don't you?'

Sigrid laughed. 'Let's order you a big plate of food. Pasta and salad?'

'Perfect.'

Sigrid looked up and made a neat little summoning gesture with her menu towards a waitress. Charlotte watched her ordering, with admiration. She looked so in charge of the situation, just as she looked in charge of her appearance, her hair smoothed back into a low ponytail, her white shirt not climbing irrepressibly out of the waistband of her skirt, her lightly tanned hand with its single modern ring holding the menu.

'There,' Sigrid said, 'food for two adults and almost half a baby. Exciting.'

Charlotte buttered a piece of bread lavishly, and told Sigrid how she now felt about the baby, and how she *had* felt, and how sick she'd been, and how great Luke had been and how seriously he was taking the whole baby and fatherhood thing. Then the pasta and salad arrived, and Charlotte asked Sigrid if she'd had a good time in Sweden, and Sigrid said it was lovely to see her parents, and Charlotte said well, talking of parents, she knew Sigrid would understand why she had done it, but she'd actually, without telling Edward or Luke in advance, gone to see Petra, because it must be so awful to be suddenly flung out of the family, like Petra had been, and so Charlotte wanted to offer her some support because, oh my God, she needed it.

'And Rachel,' Charlotte said, spearing rocket leaves on the end of a forkful of tagliatelle, 'can be so fierce. I should know.' She gave a little laugh. 'I mean, I'm not sure I'm quite over it yet, and it was ages ago.'

Sigrid took a sip of water. 'It was very difficult with Rachel when Mariella was born.'

Charlotte gazed at her, another forkful suspended. She said eagerly, 'Was it?'

'I had bad depression. So bad. And I didn't want her to know. I didn't want anyone to know. And Rachel was very angry.'

Charlotte put her mouthful in. Round it, she said, 'She's good at angry.'

Sigrid didn't reply. She sat looking down at her plate, not eating.

Charlotte said energetically, 'None of us will ever be good enough for her precious boys, will we?'

Sigrid looked up. She said, 'I had such a strange conversation with my mother in Stockholm. It made me think.'

'Oh?' Charlotte said. She would have liked to stay on the topic of Rachel, and stoke it up a bit, but there was something that held her back. She said, 'About what?' and ate another mouthful.

'These mothers,' Sigrid said, 'these mothers of ours. They were our age once. They went through a lot of the things we are going through.'

Charlotte gave a snort. She said, 'Well, Rachel's forgotten half of it—'

Sigrid said slowly, 'She's not a witch, you know.'

Charlotte stopped eating. She said, 'She doesn't like me, she doesn't much like you—'

'Oh, I think she does,' Sigrid said, 'and if she hasn't in the past, she will now. She only is as she is because no one ever opposed her, no one ever challenged her position as the only woman in a circle of men. Petra certainly didn't. But now she is having to learn something new, and she must learn to hold her tongue, and that comes hard with her.'

Charlotte put her fork down. 'Wow—'

'Think about it,' Sigrid said. 'Ralph is very difficult; I don't think anyone could have brought up Ralph any differently, but even he is a good father. And the others, our husbands; Rachel brought up good men for us. She did that, you know.'

Charlotte pushed her plate away. She looked down at the table, and the crumbs and smears she had left on it.

'We can't gang up on her,' Sigrid said. 'It's lonely for her now. My mother said she had coped with her own loneliness by working. She's a doctor. Rachel isn't a doctor, she's never worked properly, she is a home-maker, and now—well, I don't know what she is. I expect she is terrified she will lose her grandchildren.'

'But—'

'I think that's why she's angry,' Sigrid said. 'She is a very tactless person, and now she is angry, too. But I don't think she doesn't like us. And I don't think she would want her sons back, even if we offered them to her. I think she has new ways to learn, and she is angry with herself for that, too.' She smiled at Charlotte. 'Think now. If Rachel was a bad woman, wouldn't Luke be bad too?'

Charlotte said, 'What, exactly, are you telling me?'

'Oh,' Sigrid said, 'I wouldn't tell you anything. I would only describe how I see it now.'

'But you were so lovely to me that day in our flat, about the baby—'

'Of course,' Sigrid said, 'it was an unprovoked attack. Rachel was in the wrong, everybody saw that. I expect she saw that, too, even if she could never say so. But after this Petra thing, we have all moved round in the dance a little, we are all in a slightly different place. So is Rachel.'

Charlotte picked up her fork again, and pulled her plate back towards her. She opened her mouth to protest the continuing validity of her own grievance, and found she hadn't got the heart for it.

She looked at Sigrid. 'OK,' Charlotte said with a reasonableness that quite surprised her. 'OK. Point taken.'

Steve Hadley was not a man given to restlessness. All his life he had gone steadily from activity to activity, every waking hour, moving without hurry from one practical task to another, to a point where he was almost unable to think unless his hands were busy with something. He had asked himself, moving steadily round the endless tasks of repair and renewal at the nature reserve, why he went on with Petra. She plainly liked him, liked his company, had done nothing to discourage him, but was not so much refusing to sleep with him as seeming to be oblivious to the idea in the first place.

She wasn't the best-looking, or the liveliest, or the most enticing hard-to-get girl he'd ever pursued, but she had something that chimed with something in him, this profound appreciation of the sea and shore and bird life. She was unusual too, and he revered her artistic talent to a point way beyond mere admiration. And he liked her kids. All in all, there was, definitely, something in Petra that made him disinclined to give up.

He was blithely confident, too, about Petra's marital situation. There was this husband in the background, but Steve had never seen Petra other than alone, and she almost never mentioned her husband, only saying, once, that he had gone to London, in a way that suggested that he had gone for good. Petra was a kind of orphan, it appeared, with no immediate family left alive in England, and this aroused in Steve a protectiveness that was all the stronger for being unfamiliar to him. To be abandoned by both your family and your husband, but not to seem to resent either, seemed to Steve evidence of a remarkable nature. It was just how to get such a remarkable nature to focus on him as someone who might be an all-round answer that was Steve's current preoccupation.

And then an opportunity arose at work. In the internal email bulletins that went round the organisation, a job vacancy caught Steve's eye: a vacancy on an island off the north-west coast of Scotland, an island famous in the bird world for its corncrakes. The job required several practical skills as well as knowledge of bird conservation, and the terms included a tied cottage at the southern end of the island. There was only a small community on the island itself, but on the sister island, merely a short, tidal causeway away, there was a school. Steve was not someone given to romantic fantasies of any kind, but this possibility seemed, all of a sudden, to offer a potential solution to the intriguing and thwarting problem of what to do about Petra.

Jed was alone in the studio. Luke had gone out to buy a new component for their digital camera, and Jed was idly tinkering with something they were both working on when the key turned in the lock.

Jed said, 'You were quick,' to be answered by Charlotte saying, 'It's Char.'

Jed jumped off his stool. 'Hi there, pregnant lady!'

'I wanted to see Luke about something.'

Jed jammed his fists in his pocket. 'He's gone to get a whatsit.'

Charlotte looked round vaguely, as if Luke might really still be in the room. 'Doesn't matter. Will he be long?'

'Shouldn't think so,' Jed said. 'Want a coffee?'

'I'm not drinking coffee—'

'Will caffeine stunt its growth?'

'I'm not taking any risks,' Charlotte said. 'And Luke—'

'Don't tell me about Luke,' Jed said. 'Impending fatherhood has made a right old woman of Luke. And talking of old women—I mean, not *old* but older—I made a complete prat of myself the other day, with yours.'

Charlotte was unwinding a scarf from round her neck. 'My what?'

'Your mother.'

Charlotte stared at Jed. 'My mother? Where on earth—'

'She came here,' Jed said airily. 'To see Luke. And I—I did not,' Jed continued, spacing the words out for emphasis, 'I did not recognise her.'

'Why did she want to see Luke?' Charlotte said.

'Search *moi*. I was too busy feeling a prize idiot to worry. She was very cool about it.'

Charlotte looked distracted. 'Did they talk?'

'They went up to your flat,' Jed said. 'They were gone for most of an hour. Didn't Luke say?'

Why didn't you say?' Charlotte said later, slicing tomatoes.

'You weren't supposed to know. I forgot to shut Jed's mouth—'

'Why wasn't I?'

Luke leaned against the kitchen door frame. He folded his arms, and looked at the floor. 'Because I said no.'

Charlotte stopped slicing. She said, 'No to what?'

Luke said steadily, still looking at the floor, 'To an idea—an offer—your mother made.'

Charlotte put the knife down. She ran her hands under the tap, and dried them off. Then she came and stood right in front of him, almost touching him. 'What offer?'

Luke raised his head slowly. 'It doesn't matter now. It's over. She meant well, but it wouldn't work. It doesn't matter.'

'It does!' Charlotte said sharply.

'I don't want it to turn into a big deal—'

'It'll only be a big deal,' Charlotte said, 'if you won't tell me! I shall go and ring my mother otherwise, whom I suppose you've sworn to silence?'

Luke put out a hand and gripped Charlotte's wrist. 'OK, OK. But don't scream at me—'

'Would I?'

'Yes,' Luke said.

He turned, still holding Charlotte's wrist, and towed her to the sofa. Luke sat down beside her, and dropped her wrist in order to take one of her hands in both his. He said, 'You'll hear me through to the end?'

'Yes.'

'Your mother,' Luke said, 'wanted to surprise you. Her plan was to organise and pay for some nanny, or something, for six weeks after the baby's born, and to pay, also, the difference in rent between this place and somewhere bigger, because she thinks this place is too small for two people, let alone three, and she thinks we'll never manage the stairs. And I said—well, I said thank you, of course—but I said no.'

Charlotte opened her mouth. Luke took one hand away in order to hold it up in a silencing gesture. 'One minute, babe. One minute. I said no because I don't want help. I don't want to be treated like some half-adult who can't manage now his wife's pregnant. I also said no because we've got to be grown-up about this: it's our baby, our marriage. I said no because we can't be beholden to your mother, and because she's got to realise that you're mine now, not hers, and you've got to realise that, too, especially with a baby coming. And I said no because—'

'Stop,' Charlotte said. 'I've heard enough.'

'Well, think about what I said, think about what it means if—we go on being dependent, letting our parents—'

'I *have* thought,' Charlotte said. 'And even though I expect Mummy was pretty hurt after she'd been so generous, I think you were right.'

'You *what*?'

Charlotte smiled at Luke. 'You heard me. I think you were right.'

For Ralph, the first two weeks of work had been, quite frankly, surreal. Waking in his strange, impersonal room by six at the latest was novelty enough, but being at his desk an hour later, showered, shaved, dressed and equipped with a takeaway coffee and a muffin, was almost the stuff of film or fantasy. Seven o'clock was the hour when companies published the announcements that served as the basis for the analyses that Ralph was required to make on behalf of his clients, and if seven o'clock in the past had meant the first reluctant awareness that Kit and Barney were suddenly and completely awake, now it meant a bank pretty well full of its employees, all at their desks, all focused on the first adrenalin rush of the day. The first three days, Ralph had been so knackered by lunchtime that he wondered how any of them made it, full tilt, till early evening, but then an infectious collective acceleration caught him up, and carried him through, as if he'd been riding a giant wave.

The wave then, of course, dropped him with a thud. He had planned all manner of exciting, if only vaguely visualised, ways that he might spend the evenings, but the reality was that he was simultaneously too wired and too tired to focus on anything constructive. He had fallen asleep in the cinema and at Sigrid and Edward's kitchen table, he had drunk too much with work colleagues, and he had subsisted on ready-meals in polystyrene trays banged into the microwave in the flat's small kitchen.

And then there was Petra. He had told Kit, in Petra's hearing, that he would telephone every night at six. Some nights, he did indeed ring at six, but most nights, whatever was going on at his desk meant that he rang at half past, almost seven, when Kit was querulous with tiredness, and cried on the phone and said where was he, where was he, and why wasn't he there in Kit's house?

After these calls, Ralph felt as miserable as he had ever felt about anything but, because of the extreme and involving oddity of his days, was unable to stoke up quite the pure flame of rage and resentment against Petra that he had felt before he left Aldeburgh. He missed that fury: it had made everything so simple and straightforward, almost clean. It had seemed to him, in the white-hot cauldron of anger, that he would apply himself to this enticing, but fundamentally uncongenial job with a ferocious energy driven by his central purpose of gaining custody and control of his children, whom he would then bear into some as yet undefined but decent and structured future.

But the reality was not so clear-cut. The reality was that working like this—if, indeed, this was how one had to work, to make visible money—was too disorientating, too detached from the world of simply trying to be alive at the end of the day, and too, even if disconcertingly, beguiling to imagine how one could possibly incorporate into it responsibility for two very small boys, one of whom could barely as yet walk.

He was thankful to be away from the dreamy muddles of Petra's life, her propensity to stop halfway through cooking a meal to draw a giraffe for Kit. He missed nothing, *nothing* about his life in Aldeburgh except his children, and he was going to prove to everyone that he had lost not one iota of the sureness of touch that led to his being implored to stay in that position in Singapore.

Edward closed the door on Mariella after their goodnight conversation. Mariella said she did not want to be read to, and she did not want to read, she just wanted her father to talk to her. Edward was delighted to talk to her, but discovered that what she really wanted was to talk to him. She wanted to tell him about Sweden and how she felt about being back at school, and whether she and Indira would still be best, *best* friends, and now that she *had* given up the idea of having a dog, could she have tap-dancing lessons or a hamster? Or a rabbit?

Edward sat on the edge of her bed and watched her. While she talked, she played with the ingenious puzzle her Swedish grandfather had made her, so that Edward could regard her uninterruptedly, and think what an extraordinary joy she had been to him since she came home, and how painfully flattering it had been to hear her say that Sweden would have been so much better if he had been there. When she said that he could go now, because she needed to think about hamster/rabbit/tap-dancing priorities, he had bent down to kiss her, and she'd put her arms round his neck and pulled him down until her cheek was against his. She'd held him there silently for a while, and then she said that actually his cheek was a bit prickly, and released him abruptly.

Sigrid was watching the news on television, her feet up on the low table in front of the sofa. She picked up the remote, and turned the volume down. She said, 'Did you hear the phone?'

'No,' Edward said.

'It was your mother—'

'Oh God. What's happened now—'

'Nothing,' Sigrid said.

'That *can't* be true—'

Sigrid patted the sofa cushion beside her. 'Sit down. I think—that's why she rang. Because nothing's happened.'

Edward sat. 'So—so you felt like talking to her this time?'

'I did,' Sigrid said. 'We spoke for ten minutes. I think she is very sad.'

'About Petra?'

'Well, yes. But really because she is now out of touch with everyone. Of the six of us, only one is left in Suffolk, and they are not speaking. She sounded—well, she sounded lost.'

Edward glanced at Sigrid. 'You sound almost—*sorry* for her.'

'I am,' Sigrid said.

Edward waited a moment, and then he took Sigrid's hand. He said hesitantly, 'May—I ask what's brought this on?'

'She doesn't work,' Sigrid said. 'She never has, not really. My mother said to me that when both her children left Sweden her work saved her. She didn't put it quite that way, but that is what she meant. I have been thinking about what she said ever since I came home.'

Edward said nothing. He interlaced his fingers with Sigrid's, and squeezed her hand.

'My mother said also a bit later that although she knew our children are lent to us, that they do not belong to us, she still found it very difficult to let go. She said we would find it so with Mariella, and that we must make sure we have interesting work and—and enough between us, enough relationship so that we are not begging Mariella for the time and attention she should give to her own life. She said—' Sigrid stopped.

She did not take her hand away from Edward's, but she put her free hand up to her eyes briefly, and then she said, not quite steadily, 'My mother said you were a good man.'

Edward made a little self-deprecating noise in his throat. It was, in a way, wonderful when Sigrid was in one of her serious, almost melancholy Scandinavian moods, but it was also awkward to know quite how to respond to them without sounding embarrassingly theatrical, so he sat there beside her holding her hand and feeling at once both pleased and foolish, and then abruptly she leaned sideways, kissed him full on the mouth, and said with fervour, 'And you *are*.'

CHAPTER TEN

Petra sat on the floor by Kit's bed with her arms round her knees. Kit was asleep, flung across his pillow with his arms above his head. Across the room, peering at her through the bars of the heavy, old-fashioned cot that Ralph and his brothers had once slept in, Barney lay on his side, not moving, his eyes round with the effort of keeping them open.

Both boys had been very quiet at bath time, sitting docilely in the water without fighting or splashing and then making no fuss when it was time to get out; Barney even lying peacefully on the bathmat while Petra put his nappy on, without squirming over and onto all fours, so that he could crawl rapidly away out of the door and down the landing. And when Ralph had rung, quite close, this time, to six o'clock, Kit hadn't cried, or shouted for him to come home, but had simply sat there, holding Petra's phone against his ear and nodding, but not saying anything, not responding.

She hoped they hadn't frightened them, she and Steve, when they had their argument. It hadn't been the kind of argument she had with Ralph, when Ralph shouted, or banged out of the house, slamming doors, but the atmosphere had been strained enough for someone like Kit to pick it up, and react to it, and for that reaction to be passed on to Barney, who could not be distracted by another slice of toast and jam, but who crawled to her feet, whimpering, and pulled himself up to lean against her knees, staring up into her face with eyes enormous with distress. He was still staring now, as if he feared that if he closed his eyes she might not be there when he opened them again, as had happened with Ralph.

She was appalled at herself. Why had it not struck her, all those dozy, hazy weeks of avoiding facing the inevitable, that she might have been alarming her children—and herself—into the bargain? Why hadn't she thought of that? Why hadn't she seen something like Steve's proposal coming? Why hadn't she broken out of her own stupid head for just long enough to see that, whatever all this was about, it wasn't just about how *she* felt at this moment, in these precise circumstances; it was about something much broader, and with a future. And what had struck her that afternoon, sitting on the windy shingle while Steve told her his plans, and told her what he wanted, and told her that they could really make a go of things, was that she was no longer in the place in her own heart and mind where she could just say oh wow, cool idea, let's all go and conserve corncrakes on an island.

She couldn't do that any more. Clutched now by a kind of horror at her dangerously sleepwalking state these past weeks, she wondered if, in fact, she ever could have. She took a breath and held it, to fight a rising panic.

Then, to give herself time to calm down, she'd let him talk. She'd let him describe this new job, this new idea, she'd let him go on, about what they had in common, about how he felt about the boys, and she'd looked round her, at the great sweeps of tawny pebbles and the quietly heaving expanses of the sea, and she had waited to feel what she always felt there, the sense of belonging, the sense of reassurance and homecoming. She gazed and gazed—and nothing came. And then her gaze had travelled to rest on the little boys: Kit scrambling on a slope above the sea, Barney sitting in a hollow he had made, throwing stones tiny distances with ecstatic, jerky movements, and it was all she could do to stay still, listening to Steve, and not race to pick up her children and stumble away with them, away from this alarming prospect of embarking on a new life in an unknown place with someone, she realised, that she hardly knew.

She had taken some deliberately deep breaths. Then she said, as emphatically as she could, 'I'm married.'

Steve had glanced at her. 'When did that stop you seeing me?'

Petra looked down. 'You've been really good to me,' she said. 'Really good. I should have told you.'

'Told me what?'

Petra picked up a pebble. She could not say that she had, all along, been watching, hoping for Ralph to look her way again, that she would have given anything, anything right then to have heard the crunch of approaching footsteps behind her, and turned to see that it was Ralph coming to collect them all, and take them home. So she said instead, mustering her courage, 'I should have told you that I wouldn't leave him.'

'I thought he'd left you.'

'That's different,' Petra said. 'Ralph's different. He does things differently. He's got a temper.'

Steve had looked out to sea. He said, 'You're lucky I haven't.'

'I am.' She looked at him. 'I haven't been playing with you.'

'OK,' he said. He got to his feet. He called to the boys, 'Teatime.'

Petra had thought, slightly dazedly, that that was that, that she had survived the bomb blast going off under her feet, and that there would be no repercussions. But once they were in Steve's kitchen, and the business of settling the boys and giving them toast was done, Steve had started on Petra.

He didn't raise his voice. He didn't yell or shout or slam round the kitchen. He simply told her, in a low, steady, furious monotone, what he thought of her, what he thought of her morals, and her cowardice, and her conduct, and her selfishness, and her immaturity. He had told her she had allowed him to believe all kinds of things that could never happen, and presented herself as a rejected outcast, not some right little cow who wanted to have her cake and eat it. He called her all sorts of names, and all the time he was talking she sat by the table, motionless, until Barney came miserably to her knee and roused her as if from a trance. She'd bent down to pick him up, and then she'd stood up, and Kit had scrambled off his chair to be close to her, and she had looked directly at Steve.

'You can call me all the names you like,' Petra said. 'But it takes two to tango, and you know it. And now I'm going home.'

'You'll have to walk,' Steve said. 'I'm not driving you another yard.'

'We'll walk, then,' Petra said. She'd taken Kit's hand. She hoped he wouldn't speak, she hoped he wouldn't make a move towards Steve. Barney had his arms round her neck, and his face buried in her hair. His face was hot through her hair, and he was breathing heavily. She let go of Kit long enough to sling her bag over her shoulder, and then she walked past Steve, out of the kitchen.

In the little, rough parking space by the entrance to the beach, an elderly couple were urging their spaniel into the back of their car. Petra paused beside them.

'Excuse me—'

They looked up at her, standing there in her gypsy skirt with tousled hair, a child in her arms and another beside her.

'Could you please do me a favour?' Petra said. 'Could you drive us, some of the way at least, back towards Aldeburgh?'

The lunchtime bar was full. Luke, holding two pint glasses unsteadily above his head, made his way through the hubbub to where Ralph had managed to corner a couple of galvanised bar stools next to a long shelf.

Ralph had taken his jacket off, and loosened his tie. He looked exhausted, and thin, but he'd had a haircut, Luke noticed, and even if his nails were bitten he had links in his shirt cuffs and his shoes were polished. Despite Ralph's clothes, and despite Luke only being in his work uniform of black combat trousers, black T-shirt and baseball boots, Luke felt very much in charge of the occasion, and very much, he was surprised to find, older than his older brother.

He put the glasses down on the shelf in front of Ralph, who ducked his head, and slurped the first mouthful of beer without touching his glass. Then he lifted his head and wiped his mouth with the back of his hand.

'Magic.'

'You look right manky,' Luke said.

'I'm OK—'

Luke grunted. He picked up his glass and took a long swallow.

'So,' he said. 'How's it going?'

'Good,' Ralph said, 'I'm good. Got given two new clients this week. I'll be in line for a bonus.'

Luke watched him drink. Then he said, 'And what'll you spend it on?'

Ralph put his glass down and stared into it. After a pause, he said, 'A house for the boys and me. And legal fees.'

'Don't be daft,' Luke said.

Ralph glanced at him. 'What's daft—'

'That kind of talk. What are you playing at? Are you going to take your children away from their mother and bring them up on your own?'

Ralph didn't look at him. He said to his drink, 'That's the idea, yes.'

Luke said calmly, 'You are insane.'

Ralph was silent.

'You couldn't do it,' Luke said. 'You don't have a case. No court is going to take two little children away from a perfectly OK mother just because you don't want to admit that this is as much your fault as Petra's.'

Ralph said angrily, 'She's the one who—'

'She hasn't,' Luke said. 'She hasn't had an affair. It's a funny old relationship, but it's not sex. She told Charlotte.'

Ralph said, 'You don't have to have sex for it to be disloyal—'

'And,' Luke said, interrupting, 'you don't have to throw your wife downstairs to be an abusive husband.'

'I'm not abusive!' Ralph yelled.

A group of drinkers near by looked round, and there was a sudden pool of silence in their corner.

'I'm not abusive,' Ralph said again quietly.

'Depends on how you define abuse—'

Ralph said, leaning forward to hiss his words at Luke, 'I am here doing this sodding job, to *keep* them all.'

Luke looked back at him. He waited a moment, and then he said, 'So you are. Heroically battling to pay the bills. Having previously buggered up your online work and kept Petra in the dark about it, and then just telling her what you were going to do next, never asking her, or including her, just frightening her with your sudden plans and turning her whole life upside down. That's all.'

There was an astonished pause, and then Ralph said, 'You've changed your tune!'

'I've had time to think,' Luke said. 'Stuff's happened. You've just let Mum and Dad shove you around all the time and then, when things go wrong, you take it out on Petra. It's not her fault. It's not her fault that she does what everyone wants until she just can't any more, and does some stupid bloody thing, like this bloke, and we all go apeshit.'

Ralph picked up his beer glass and put it down again. He said, 'Well, there *is* this guy. And I don't know what's going on except he sees my kids and I don't like it.'

'Well,' Luke said. '*You're* not seeing them.'

'I told you. I *told* you. I'm working my arse off because—'

'Bullshit,' Luke said.

Ralph made a little jerky movement as if he was going to scoop up his jacket, slip off his stool, and fight his way through the crowd without another word to Luke. But he hesitated. He took his hand off his jacket.

'You like doing this job,' Luke said. 'You like being good at it. Fair enough. But don't pretend it's to put bread into the mouths of your starving children; don't give me all that noble, self-sacrificing *crap*. Just don't. And don't make a complete and utter idiot of yourself, talking about fighting for the custody of your children.'

Ralph turned away slightly, and hunched himself over his beer glass.

He was silent for a minute or two, and then he said grumpily, not looking at Luke, 'So what d'you think I should do?'

Luke picked up his drink and drained it, then set it down on the shelf with a bang. 'Go home,' he said.

Petra decided to travel by bus. It would, apart from all other considerations, be cheaper than a train, and the thought of driving in London, even with her renewed spirit of enterprise, made her heart fail a little. Ralph had sent her a cheque but she didn't feel she could use it. She had a few notes put away in a teapot they never used. She took it down from the shelf where it had been since they moved in, and blew the dust off it. She took the lid off and tipped it upside down over the table.

'Money!' Kit said appreciatively. He was in his Spider-Man T-shirt, ready for the journey, his digger in his Bob the Builder rucksack.

Petra counted the money. 'Sixty-five quid,' she said to Kit. 'Plenty. Plenty for what we're after.'

'Are we going in a rocket?' Kit said hopefully.

'No. In a bus. But a high-up bus, with steps.'

Kit considered this. He said, 'Where are we going?'

Petra looked at him. He had never been a rosy-cheeked child, but the last week or so he had grown especially wan, and now, with his hair still unbrushed from the night before, and a smear of something or other from breakfast around his mouth, he looked pathetic indeed. She said, with enough energy to make it sound like an adventure, 'London!'

Kit said nothing. He picked up a wooden spoon lying in front of him and began to bang it rhythmically against the nearest table leg. He had done that the day before, too, when Steve had turned up and tried to say sorry.

When the door closed behind Steve, and his footsteps had retreated down the cement path, away from the house, Petra put a hand on the spoon. 'Enough, hey?'

Kit held on to the spoon, glaring at Petra.

'Listen,' Petra said. She bent towards Kit. 'Who lives in London?'

Kit thought. He pressed the spoon into one cheek, pushing his mouth sideways.

'Spider-Man?' he suggested.

Petra smiled at him. 'Mariella,' she said.

Mariella had been amazed. She was not allowed to open the front door to anyone, but she was allowed to drag one of the hall chairs across to the door, in order to stand on it and be able to see, through the fish-eye spyhole at adult height, who was standing on the step outside. This time she'd started shrieking, 'Mummy, come, Mummy, *come*, it's them, it's them, it's *them*!' and Sigrid had come running up the stairs from the kitchen, where she'd been starting to get supper, and she'd peered through the fish-eye too, and gasped, and then the door was flung open and there was a great confusion of arms, and bags, and crying, and Kit wanting her to look at his digger as if she hadn't seen it a million times before, and Barney refusing to let go of Petra for an instant and Sigrid saying, 'There, there,' and, 'Don't worry, don't worry,' and then they were all downstairs in the kitchen, and the boys were beginning to laugh, and shout a bit, and then Edward came home and all the confusion started again. It was, Mariella made a note to tell Indira on Monday, just *crazy*.

But it was happy, too. Everything got noisy and sticky very quickly but it felt right, Mariella thought, it felt really OK to have everyone there, and spilt yoghurt on the table, and Petra sitting on the floor as if she knew the house really well, instead of being practically a stranger in it, and Edward giving her a glass of wine and ringing Luke and Charlotte to come over too, and Charlotte arriving with a bag of pick-and-mix sweets which weren't healthy at all, being all sugar and chemicals, but which were so yummy all the same, and Charlotte sat on the floor, too, and Sigrid started cooking pasta for everyone, and it suddenly felt like a party and it just got better and better until Edward said above the racket, really loudly, 'I'm ringing Ralph,' and it was like someone had shut a door or popped a balloon—and everything stopped.

'Please,' Petra said from the floor.

Edward looked at her. He was standing, holding a wine glass. She was below him, holding Barney. 'Please no, or please yes?' he said.

'Please yes,' Petra said.

'Good,' he said. 'Good.' He looked quite stern. 'I wouldn't have accepted please no.'

Mariella glanced at her mother. Sigrid was looking at Edward. Luke looked up from fitting chestnuts out of Sigrid's nut bowl into the bucket of Kit's digger and said, 'I'll go and get him.'

'But—' Edward began.

Luke stood up. 'Much the easiest. I'll call him and say I'm picking him up from work for a beer. And if he's already out having one, I'll go and find him.'

Edward said, 'Are you sure?'

'I'm sure,' Luke said, 'I'm doing it.' He bent and aimed a kiss at the top of Charlotte's head. 'I'm gone.'

Mariella looked at her father. He looked dazed, then he shook himself slightly and glanced at Sigrid. She was smiling. She held out her wine glass.

'More, please,' she said.

I'm fagged out,' Ralph said to Luke.

He had gone down to the deserted reception area to let Luke into the building, through all the security systems, past all the empty desks where people were free to go home because their work didn't depend on the American market, which still had four or five hours' life left in it yet.

'It's Friday, man. Friday night is downtime night. Sigrid's cooking.'

'I don't want any lecturing—'

'Bro,' Luke said, 'stop whingeing and come. You need time off and feeding. It's an impulse-supper at Ed's and we want you there.'

'We?' Ralph said suspiciously.

'We. Char and me. Ed and Sigi. Put your jacket on.'

In Luke's car, driving up to Islington, Ralph told Luke about his week. It was a boring story, particularly as he'd heard most of it earlier that day, but it kept Ralph's mind occupied. Luke thought that he couldn't actually relax until he'd got Ed's front door shut behind him, with Ralph safely inside.

Edward plainly had the same thought. He opened the door to them, and then he stationed himself on Ralph's other side, almost as if he and Luke were a personal police escort, and they went down the stairs in that formation, Edward leading, Ralph in the middle, Luke bringing up the rear, and halfway down you could hear the little boys' voices suddenly, and Ralph stopped and said loudly, 'What is this, what is—' and Edward turned back, and took his arm and led him on down until they were there in the kitchen, and only Sigrid was looking their way because everyone else, wired on sugar and wine, was burying Charlotte with cushions from the sofa and screaming.

Ralph halted. Luke waited for him to turn round and accuse him of betrayal and kidnap. But he didn't. He just stood there and stared at his children, at Petra stopping Barney from crawling ecstatically and heedlessly across Charlotte's face.

Edward gave Ralph a little push.

'Go on,' he said. 'Go on. Go on in and join them.'

Once or twice, during supper, Edward had managed to catch Sigrid's eye. He had wanted to convey to her his surprise and satisfaction at having, for the first time, both his brothers and both their wives round his and Sigrid's kitchen table, with all three children safely asleep in Mariella's bedroom, and a weekend ahead. But Sigrid, although she had smiled at him, although she was plainly enjoying herself, enjoying being the provider, the one who could produce extra pillows, and supper, and a bath toy for Barney as if she did such things every day of the week, was not going to allow Edward to point out, or emphasise, what a rarity this evening was. She was behaving as if it was all perfectly normal, as if Petra often came up to London on the bus as a matter of course, as if there had been no estrangement between Ralph and Petra, no complicity between Charlotte and Petra, no break in the step of her and Edward's married march together. And she is right, Edward thought, she is right not to make a big deal of it, because even if it's a first it's only a beginning.

For a start, Ralph and Petra were at opposite ends of the table from one another. They had not touched all evening; they had scarcely spoken directly to one another and Ralph had announced quite early in the evening that he was going back to his room at the end of it. Petra hadn't flinched. She appeared, Edward thought, remarkably composed and able to look at Ralph in a way he couldn't—yet, anyway—look at her. Charlotte and Luke were flirting across the table, monopolising the noise and the energy, and Edward observed that Petra was watching them with every sign of ease and pleasure, almost indulgently. Funny girl, he thought, odd girl, but we shouldn't underestimate her. Just because someone doesn't know exactly what you know doesn't mean that what they do *know* isn't as important. Or even more important. She's got where she's got all by herself, we shouldn't forget that. He had a lump in his throat. He picked up his wine glass to take a swallow in order to dislodge it. God, he was getting as sentimental as his father.

His father! He raised his hand to his head and smacked his forehead with his palm. The parents! They should tell them, they ought—no, *he* ought—to ring Anthony and Rachel and say that everyone was here together, and fine. He hadn't given them a second thought. That was awful, really awful. He half rose. He'd go and do it in the study, right now.

'Where are you going, man?' Luke said.

Edward's face assumed the faintly careworn expression familiar to Sigrid. 'I just remembered. I ought to ring the parents—'

'No,' Sigrid said. 'Sit down—'

'I'll ring Mum and Dad,' Luke said. 'in the morning. Not now. I'll ring them tomorrow and tell them we were all together.' He squeezed Ralph's shoulder. 'OK, bro?'

'OK,' Ralph said.

Sigrid was leaning back in her chair. 'There,' she said to Edward, 'there. Luke will do it. No need for you to do anything.'

She was smiling at him. He didn't know when he'd seen her so relaxed. He smiled back, and lowered himself into his chair again. He picked up the nearest wine bottle and held it against the light. Empty.

'I'll get another,' Ralph said, taking the bottle out of his hand.

Edward looked round the table. He said, 'What's happening?'

Sigrid was laughing now, and so were Petra and Charlotte. Luke folded his arms on the table, and leaned towards Edward.

'All change,' Luke said. He gave Edward the thumbs-up sign.

The light was fading fast. Every year, Anthony was increasingly taken by surprise at how, once summer was over, the evenings drew in so rapidly. In the past, the winter had been his time of dissection and observation, reconstructing bird skeletons with meticulous reference to diagrams, and wiring them up as if these ghostly creatures were still stepping or pecking or turning in flight. The studio shelves were crammed with skeletons as well as those wired to the roof beams, mostly fractured now, a broken ossuary of past life, past movement.

Every autumn, Anthony surveyed his skeleton collection, vowed to do something to at least rationalise it, and did nothing. Rachel said, annually, that it was most unfair on the boys never to attempt to clear out some of the deep litter of the studio, but just to slide round such a monumental task knowing it would inevitably fall to them, once Anthony was dead.

'They can chuck it all,' Anthony said. 'All of it. It won't mean to them what it means to me. And I won't be there to mind, will I?'

'But it'll be such a depressing task for them. Bags and bags of bones. Why subject them to anything so gloomy?'

But they're not gloomy, Anthony thought now, standing surveying the shelves as the early dusk thickened the light in the studio. Not gloomy at all. They are interesting, every one, and valid. They represented a journey for me, my journey. I never thought I could make a life and a livelihood out of being an artist, nor did my parents. But I did. I have. I've kept it all going, and brought up three boys, and educated them, because not only can I see, but I can, with this hand and this brain, translate what I see in such a way that other people can see it, too. I can make birds live on paper. He raised his right arm involuntarily, his fingers holding an imaginary pencil, and sketched something in the air. There you are, he told himself. There. The power of the unconscious mind. I've drawn a lapwing taking off, and I didn't even have to think what to do before I did it. I *knew*. I knew, because there's a lapwing up there, somewhere, on those shelves, and I expect its head has fallen off and it's missing a wing rib or two, but once I knew every bone in its body and that knowledge is now as deep in me as my DNA. The boys won't mind clearing off these shelves. They'll get it. They'll know that, if their mother's kitchen was always the engine room of the house, of family life, this place was the lookout. It was in here, Anthony said, almost out loud, where we didn't just focus on what had to be done—very necessary, admit that—but what *might* be done. And even if she'd rather die than admit it, I think Rachel knows that too, in her heart of hearts, and is afraid of it in her way, because it's something she can't control.

Like Ralph. Had they ever been able, really, to control Ralph? If he had conformed, as a boy, it was because he wanted to, or it suited him, never because he felt the smallest necessity to be obliging. And because of this innate perversity, Ralph had always exercised a peculiar fascination for his mother. She didn't—Anthony was sure of this—love him any more than she loved Luke or Edward, but she was, in a way, spellbound by him, always had been. So that when he did seem more pliable these last few years, when he had submitted to her brisk, practical organising of his life—the marriage to Petra, the move to the house in Aldeburgh—there was bound to be a price to pay in the end. They, the parents, were no longer at the hub of things. They were now, Luke had made it plain when he had telephoned yesterday morning, to be informed of everything that was going on, but they weren't any longer central to the discussion of what should happen next.

'We're all here,' Luke had said cheerfully. 'We're all spending the day together, all nine of us. Everyone's fine. You're not to worry. Everyone's happy. Barney even walked four steps this morning. He's a riot.'

It was Anthony who had picked up the phone when Luke rang. He was alone in the kitchen. He had stood there, staring out of the window above the sink, while Luke described the evening before and how Ralph had had no idea that he would find Petra and his children at Ed's house, how Petra has clearly come to her senses and done the sensible thing and just got on a bus, with boys and baggage.

When she heard, Rachel wanted to ring, at once, for confirmation. She had her phone in her hand, lifting it to her ear, when Anthony took it from her by force.

'No. Leave them!' Anthony had flung her phone across the kitchen. It had hit the far wall and fallen behind a chair, clattering to the floor.

He had waited for her to scream at him, but she didn't. She said, as if wrestling with tears, 'I need to know if they're OK.'

'You'll know when they choose to tell us. Not before.'

'Whose side are you on?' Rachel demanded.

'No one's,' Anthony said untruthfully.

Rachel had stood there for a minute or two, not making any attempt to move. And then she said with an effort, 'If no one has rung by tomorrow night, by Sunday night, can I ring then?'

But Ralph came. They were clearing up a desultory lunch when they heard wheels on the gravel outside. Rachel had flung down the tea towel she was holding and made as if to dart for the door.

'Wait,' Anthony said.

She paused, almost quivering, like a dog thwarted of chasing after something unimaginably tempting.

'Whoever it is,' Anthony said, 'we can see them here.'

It was Ralph. He was thinner than when they had last seen him and he had dark circles under his eyes, but he had an air of energy they hadn't seen in him in ages. Beside him, Anthony could feel Rachel collect herself. She reached up to kiss Ralph's cheek.

'My goodness, darling,' she said in an entirely normal voice, 'a haircut.'

Ralph grinned. He lifted one foot towards her.

'And a shoe-shine—'

Anthony said, not smiling, just looking straight at Ralph, 'Where are the children?'

'At home.'

'In Aldeburgh?'

'Of course,' Ralph said. 'Where else?'

'And—and Petra?'

'With them. Where else would *she* be?'

Rachel turned towards the table. 'Sit down, and I'll make some coffee.'

'Not for me, thanks,' Ralph said, 'I'm rather pushed for time. I'm going back to London tonight. I'll be down next weekend. And the weekend after. Until we let the house.'

Rachel lowered herself carefully into a chair as if she had a bad back. She said faintly, 'Let the house?'

Ralph took a chair opposite. 'Yes.'

Anthony leaned on the table. 'Could you explain—'

Ralph smiled at him. He seemed in a sunnier mood than Anthony could ever remember. He said, 'Why else d'you think I'm here?'

'We don't know,' Rachel said. She sounded close to tears again. 'We don't know anything—'

'You do,' Ralph said. 'You do know. Luke rang you. Didn't he?'

'But we don't know *enough*—'

There was a small silence. Then Ralph said, 'I'll tell you.'

Anthony straightened up and moved round the table to sit next to Rachel. He had an instinct to take her hand, and a conflicting one to show no reaction whatsoever. So he sat there, his own hands clasped loosely on the table in front of him. 'Tell us.'

'We're going to let the house for the winter,' Ralph said. 'I'm going to be in London in the week, and back at weekends, till we've let it. Petra is going to see the agent in the morning. Then we'll go to London for the winter. We'll find somewhere near Luke and Charlotte, playgroups for the boys, Petra can work a bit in the cafés and places round Columbia Road. Then we'll come back to Suffolk for the summer.'

Rachel said, 'You're—leaving Suffolk?'

'For the winter, Mum. It's called a compromise.'

'So you and Petra—'

'None of your business, Mum,' Ralph said pleasantly.

'But when will we see the boys?'

'When you come to London.'

'London,' Rachel said disgustedly.

'You'll have to learn to like it,' Ralph said. 'You both will. We'll all be there.'

Anthony said slowly, 'But Petra—in London?'

Ralph looked directly at his father. 'She suggested it.'

'And—'

'And,' Ralph said, 'Sigi suggested you stay with them. Regularly. You'll want to, anyway, when the baby comes, won't you?'

'Of course,' Anthony said. He glanced at Rachel. She was looking fixedly at the far end of the table, the place where Anthony always sat when the table was full, full of food and noise and activity.

She said, with just an edge of sarcasm in her voice, 'And Charlotte? Did she have a message for me as to how I might live my life in the future?'

'She sent her love,' Ralph said. 'She sent it twice, actually.' He stood up and said, looking down at his parents, 'Petra would send hers, too, if she did that kind of thing. But she doesn't. You know she doesn't. She never has. But it doesn't mean she doesn't feel it. She feels a lot, in fact, she's more honest than all of us in what she feels. True to herself.' He paused, and then he said, 'We've got to learn to do things differently, both of us.' Then his gaze sharpened, and he said with emphasis, looking straight at his father, 'Just as you and Mum have got to do. Differently. OK?'

They had sat there for a long time after he had gone, side by side at the table in the quiet kitchen. Various little village cries and calls filtered in from the outside, and a car or two went by, but inside the house it was like being under a bell jar, suspended out of time and the turning of the world. Anthony was startled when Rachel said abruptly, 'Well, I suppose I could revive the bed and breakfast idea.'

He had stared at her. '*What?*'

'You know,' Rachel said. 'Ages ago. I thought I'd do bed and breakfast in the summer. It would mean tarting up upstairs a bit. The bathrooms are the complete reverse of state-of-the-art, whatever that means.'

'Could—could you face it?'

She turned to look at him. 'Oh, yes. If I have to. And now, maybe I do?'

He had leaned sideways, and kissed her cheek. 'Good girl.'

'Don't patronise me.'

'I'm admiring you—'

'Well,' Rachel said, getting up, 'go and admire me in the studio. I'm going to spread the stuff out on the table, and think. I'm going to think how to do whatever it is the boys want us to do.'

'Just like that?'

'No,' she had said. She gave a little smiling grimace. 'With difficulty.' And then she said, 'And you can do a difficult thing, too. You can get rid of those bird bones.'

But I can't, Anthony thought now. I can't and I shouldn't. Getting rid of them has nothing to do with changing this stage of fatherhood, it has to do with something essential in me, something that makes me who I am. Ralph said Petra was true to herself. I don't know if that means merely unaffected, or something deeper. But I am a painter of birds, in my true heart, and I need my bones.

It was full dusk now. He went slowly across the gravel to the house. A huge yellow September moon had hoisted itself among the trees behind the roof, and there was a little edge to the air, a little bite, that was as invigorating as brushing one's teeth. The kitchen window was a warm, golden square, and through it he could see Rachel bending over a sea of brochures and folders on the kitchen table. He stood and watched her for a while, his wife, the woman he had married, yet not that woman, as he was not that long-ago man.

He opened the back door. A surge of warmth came out to greet him.

'Anthony?' Rachel called, not turning.

He closed the door behind him.

'Who else?' he said.

Joanna Trollope

Where do you live and write?

I live in West London, which is wonderful, and, for the first time in my life, I actually have a study, having written most previous novels on kitchen tables here and there. It's on the second floor, faces west—and manages to be a room I'm always pleased to go into.

When and why did you start writing and what inspires you?

I started writing stories as a child—but you have to remember that I grew up before universal television. I think I was always fascinated by other people, and as far as that goes, nothing has changed!

Do you do a lot of research?

Lots. And lots. It's a habit left over from writing historical fiction, and as I want to get contemporary life as accurate as I can, it has to go on—and anyway it is never, ever dull, and I learn so much, every time.

How do you create your characters?

The characters are made up, rather like patchwork quilts, out of elements that I have noticed in the behaviour or mannerisms of real people. So they are 'real', if you like, but never wholesale real—my imagination puts various component parts together.

You have two daughters and two stepsons. What prompted you to write a novel about daughters-in-law and their complex relationship with their husbands' mothers?

I was thinking, one day, that most women either *are* a daughter-in-law, in some sense, or *have* one. So it's a topic that resonates with a huge numbers of readers. And any situation that involves two women and a man is fertile ground for fiction!

You are a mother-in-law yourself. Have you found it a difficult role to play?

I'm afraid not! I have two sons-in-law who I've known for ages—one since he was eighteen and he's now forty—whom I'm devoted to, and two stepdaughters-in-law that I am really fond of. But I'm not very possessive by nature, which might help.

Do you think mothers ever truly let go of their children?

I think most children would be horrified to be let go of completely! You want your parent there, always, but at a respectful distance. I think the old adage which reminds us that our children are only lent to us, is salutary—the relationship can always be there, but it has to change as time goes on, if it's going to last.

Do you believe in marriage as an institution?

Obviously marriage is a very solid building block for society to operate from, and when it works—and huge numbers of people try so hard to make it work—it's wonderful. But I don't think it's the only mechanism by which we can achieve a stable society or happy children. Its convenience should not be allowed to obscure its capacity for the exercising of destructive controls by some individuals over other people.

Did you spend many hours at the RSPB reserve at Minsmere? Do you enjoy birdwatching?

I spent most of a weekend at Minsmere and I know a lot more about wading birds than I did two years ago. But I'm not a natural twitcher or birder, I'm afraid—I'm too eager for a narrative in everything for that.

Both artists and authors are great observers of life. Have you ever taken art classes? If not, would you like to?

I cannot draw or paint. A great pity, as my mother is an artist, and two of her siblings are brilliant draughtsmen. The artistic gene just ignored me. But, I have to say, much as I adore looking at paintings, I don't feel a great yearning to create them too. I am so happy just to admire what others can do!

What do you love most about being a grandmother?

Watching them be, and become, their very own selves, almost from the word go.

What do you think would surprise your readers most about you?

Maybe some of the things I've done in the name of research over the years: travelled to Mandalay, been clubbing (house music), spent a day on military exercise, worked in a refuge for victims of domestic violence, walked most of the Boer War battlefields, had breakfast with the Chelsea football team (I'm a passionate Chelsea supporter), been in milking parlours and courtrooms and prison cells, and on shrimp boats in South Carolina . . . shall I go on?

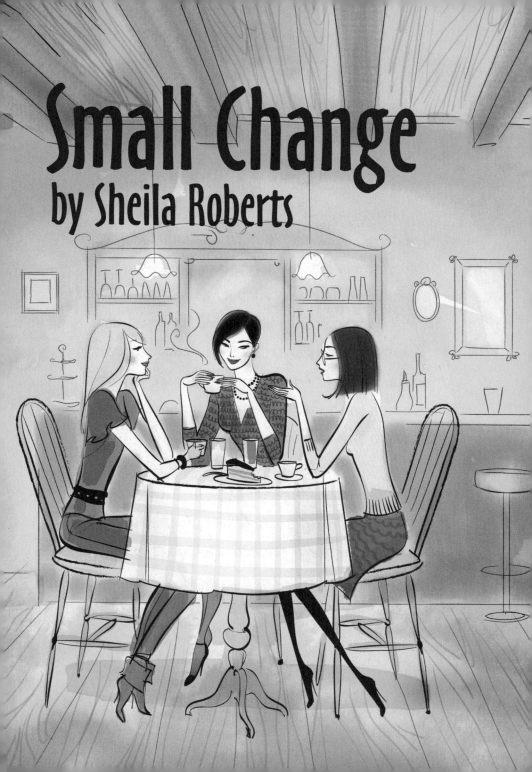

Small Change
by Sheila Roberts

Rachel, Jessica and Tiffany have money problems—major money problems. Rachel is a strapped-for-cash divorcee; Jessica's husband has lost his job, and Tiffany has whipped out the plastic one too many times.

Together they start a financial support group called 'The Small Change Club', challenging each other to bring balance back to their bank accounts and to their lives. Even though living frugally is harder than they ever imagined, the three women soon learn that small changes in their spending habits make a world of difference . . . and that some things, like good friends, are priceless.

Now is the Summer of Our Discontent

1

THERE IT SAT, a Cloud Nine queen-sized luxury gold comforter with red ribbon appliqué and metallic embroidery. Forty per cent off. It was the last one left. Tiffany Turner had seen it, and so had the other woman.

The woman caught Tiffany looking at it, and her eyes narrowed. Tiffany narrowed hers right back. Her competitor was in her fifties, dressed for comfort in jeans and a sweater, her feet shod in tennis shoes for quick movement—obviously a sale veteran, but Tiffany wasn't intimidated. She was younger. She had the determination.

It only took one second to start the race. The other woman strode towards the comforter with the confidence that comes with age, her hand stretched towards the prize.

Tiffany chose that moment to look over her competitor's shoulder. Her eyes went wide, and she gasped. 'Oh, my gosh.' Her hands flew to her face in horror.

The other woman turned to see the calamity happening behind her. And that was her undoing. In a superhuman leap, Tiffany bagged the comforter just as her competitor turned back. *Score.*

Boy, if looks could kill.

It would be rude to gloat. Tiffany gave an apologetic shrug and murmured, 'Sorry.'

The woman paid her homage with a reluctant nod. 'You're good.'

Yes, I am. 'Thanks,' Tiffany murmured, and left the field of battle for the customer service counter.

OK, now she'd gloat.

She was still gloating as she drove home from the mall an hour later.

She'd not only scored on the comforter, she'd got two sets of towels (buy one, get one free), a great top for work, a cute little jacket, a new shirt for Brian, and a pair of patent metallic purple shoes with three-inch heels that were so hot she'd burn the pavement when she walked. With the new dress she'd snagged at fifty per cent off, she'd be a walking inferno. Brian would melt when he saw her.

Her husband would also melt if he saw how much she'd spent today, so she had to beat him home. That was the downside of hitting the mall after work. She always had to hurry home to hide her treasures before Brian walked in the door. But she could do it.

Tiffany followed the Abracadabra shopping method: get the bargain and then make it disappear for a while so you could later insist that said bargain had been sitting around the house for ages. Two years before, she had successfully used the Guessing Game method: bring home the bargains, and lull husband into acceptance by having him guess how incredibly little you'd paid for each one.

Tiffany was a world-class bargain hunter, and she could smell a sale a mile away. Great as she was at ferreting out a bargain, she wasn't good with credit cards. It hadn't taken her long to snarl her finances to the point where she and Brian had to use their small, start-a-family savings and Brian's car fund to bail her out.

She'd felt awful about that, not only because she suspected they'd never need that family fund anyway (that suspicion was what led to her first shopping binge), but because Brian had suffered from the fallout of her mismanagement. He'd had his eye on some rusty old beater on the other side of the lake and had been talking about buying and restoring it. The car wound up rusting at someone else's house, thanks to her.

'Tiffy, you should have told me,' Brian said the day the awful truth came out and they sat on the couch, her crying in his arms.

She would have, except she kept thinking she could get control of her runaway credit-card bills. 'I thought I could handle it.'

It was a reasonable assumption since they both worked. There was just one problem: their income had never quite managed to keep up with the demands of their life. It still didn't.

She sighed. Brian so didn't understand. All he did was pay the mortgage, utilities and the car payments. He had no idea how much it really cost to live. First of all, they had to eat. Did he have any idea how much wine cost? Or meat? And they had to have clothes. She couldn't show up at Salon H to do nails in sweats, for heaven's sake. Food and clothes were the tip of the expense iceberg. Friends and family had birthdays. And she had to buy Christmas presents. And decorations. And hostess gifts.

After the great credit-card cleanup, the Guessing Game method lost its effectiveness and she'd had to retire it. Hiding her purchases worked better anyway.

Her bargains weren't the only things she was hiding. In the last year she'd got two new credit cards, and they were both well used. Brian might panic if he knew, but there was no need for panic. She'd be OK this time. She'd learned her lesson. In fact, she was going to make a big payment on one of them this week.

She checked the clock on the dash: 4:50. Brian got off at five. He worked at the Heart Lake Department of Planning and Community Development. It took him exactly six minutes to get from his office to their cul-de-sac in Heart Lake Estates and another fifty-five seconds to park his car and get to the front door. That gave her seventeen minutes and five seconds to beat him home.

A little voice at the back of her mind whispered, 'You wouldn't have to worry about beating your husband home if you were honest with him.'

She ignored it and applied more pressure to the gas pedal. She could feel her heart rate picking up as two voices began to echo in the back of her head.

BRIAN: *That's a lot of shopping bags. Were you at the mall?*
TIFFANY: *Yes, but I didn't spend much. This was all on sale.*
BRIAN: *You had that much cash on you?*
TIFFANY:

Here the dialogue stopped because she didn't know what script to follow. She wasn't supposed to be charging anything. She'd promised. But she didn't have enough money to take advantage of the sales. And if she didn't take advantage of the sales, how could she save money? It was a terrible, vicious circle.

Her best bet was to get home before Brian. She could make it. She wouldn't buy anything more all month, and she'd take back the shoes. But the dress—fifty per cent off, for heaven's sake.

Just get home and ditch the stuff. Then you can decide what to do. She roared off the exit ramp, then turned right onto Cedar Springs Road. Ten more minutes and she'd be in Heart Lake Estates.

Oh, no. What was this behind her? Her stomach fell at the sight of the flashing lights. Noooo. This was so unfair. Yes, she was going fifteen miles over the speed limit, but she had an emergency brewing here. She could not, COULD NOT, get a speeding ticket. They couldn't afford it.

Heart thudding, she watched as the policeman got out of his patrol car. He was big and burly. Big men loved sweet, little blondes with blue eyes. That had to work in her favour. She saw the wedding ring on his finger. Darn. It would have worked more in her favour if he'd been single.

She let down her window and showed him a pitiful expression. 'I know I was speeding, but pleeease don't give me a ticket. I promise I won't speed again. Ever. If I come home with a speeding ticket . . .' And a trunk full of shopping bags. She couldn't even think about it.

The officer regarded her. 'Lady, you were going twenty miles over the limit. I can't not give you a ticket.'

What? What was this? 'Oh, please. My husband will kill me.'

'Don't worry,' said the officer. 'They take MasterCard at the courthouse. May I have your driver's licence and registration?'

She fished them out of the glove compartment and handed them over. This was sick and wrong and unfair. That cop had no heart.

She looked at the clock on her dash and ground her teeth. This was a nightmare. She was going to have to return the shoes, the top, the jacket and the shirt. The dress, too.

'Aren't you forgetting something?' prompted a little voice.

The towels?

'What else?'

Nooooo. And the comforter.

Brian's old mail Jeep was already parked in the driveway when Tiffany got home. She stuffed the speeding ticket in her bag and left her purchases in the trunk. As she hurried up the front walk, she tried to come up with a reason she was late getting home so that she didn't have to use the *S* word. Brian still didn't need to know about the shopping, especially since she was going to have to take everything back so she could pay for that stupid ticket.

She began to script her arrival.

BRIAN: *What took you so long? I thought you were done at four.*
TIFFANY: *Something came up.*
BRIAN: *Yeah? What?*
TIFFANY:

Oh boy. What could she say next? A client, of course—she'd say someone had come into Salon H with a nail emergency just as she was leaving. Brian would buy that. It happened.

She hated lying to him, though. She never lied to him, except about money. Somewhere along their happily-ever-after road, her spending habits had become top secret.

She sighed as she slipped in the front door.

Tiffany found Brian already on the back deck. He'd changed into his jeans and was firing up the barbecue to grill hamburgers. 'You beat me home,' she said, and gave him a kiss. 'I figured you would. You wouldn't believe the day I had.' So far, so good.

'Busy, huh? That's good.' Brian sounded distracted.

That was normal lately; he had a lot on his mind. But it wasn't sex. The shoes really had been a waste. After two miscarriages, she supposed she couldn't blame him. What was the point?

Love was the point, of course, but sometimes, late at night, after Brian was dead to the world, she wrote a very dark script:

TIFFANY: *Brian, do you still love me?*
BRIAN: *I don't know. You can't manage money, and you can't stay*
           pregnant. What good are you?

That was always where the script ended because she still hadn't come up with an answer that satisfied her.

'How was your day?' she asked now.

He shrugged. He used to have plenty to say about work. There was always a contractor who was hounding him, a property owner trying to pass off plans for a garage as plans for a shed, someone unhappy over how long it was taking to get the permit for the addition on her house. But the local building slump was slowing things down at work and spreading insecurity through the office. It seemed like for the last month, he'd been walking under a dark cloud.

'Is everything OK?' Tiffany asked.

'I don't know,' he said, his voice heavy.

He went inside the house. She followed him in and watched as he pulled minced beef out of the fridge and began pounding the meat into patties. She washed her hands, then went to the fridge and pulled out onions, lettuce and a tomato and set them on the counter.

'It's a good thing all the credit cards are paid off,' he said.

Meanwhile, back at the fridge, Tiffany almost dropped a jar of pickles. 'Is there something you're not telling me?'

'Things are really getting bad at work, Tiffy.' Brian gave a piece of meat an extra hard smack. 'Two people got laid off today.'

'Laid off?' she squeaked.

He put the meat patties on a plate. 'That's why I'm glad we at least don't have a lot of credit-card debt any more.'

She nodded agreement. What was she going to do?

Brian must have read the panic in her eyes, because he immediately looked regretful. 'Hey.' He started to hug her, then looked at his meat-greased hands. He washed them, saying over his shoulder, 'I didn't mean to scare you.'

'I'm not scared,' she lied.

Brian dried his hands, then hugged her, and she pressed in close.

'It's OK,' he said, and kissed her forehead. 'We can make it through this. We just have to be careful. You understand?'

She felt her cheeks burning, but she managed to nod.

'You need to know what we're up against. It could get ugly.'

It could get ugly if he found out about those charge cards. 'I thought you said you didn't want to scare me.'

'I don't. I just want you to understand that this is serious.'

'I do.' It was more serious than he knew.

Rachel Green left her principal's office minus her smile. This was a rotten way to end the school day, not to mention the year. She marched to her empty classroom, mentally chanting, 'Why me?' with each step. The answer to that was simple: some gremlin had pasted a Kick Me sign on her backside.

First divorce, now no job—a kick for each cheek.

She'd known teaching fifth grade at Heart Lake Elementary wasn't a permanent position when she'd stepped in to take Ambika Sinj's class after Ambika had gone on maternity leave. But Rachel had hoped that once

Ambika had her baby she would opt for full-time motherhood. She hadn't.

This school was a great one with an excellent principal and good kids. Rachel didn't blame Ambika for wanting to come back to work. She blamed the gremlin. Inside her classroom she shook a fist and growled, 'You're messing with the wrong woman.'

'Steve Martin in drag. Now, that is scary,' said a voice from the classroom doorway. 'Are you auditioning for a remake of *Planes, Trains and Automobiles?*'

Rachel turned to see Elsa Wilson, a wiry fifty-year-old who taught third grade, regarding her with eyebrows raised. 'Don't get too close to me. I'm a bad luck lightning rod,' Rachel said.

'Let me guess. Ambika's coming back, and you're out of work?'

Rachel nodded. She wanted to cry. Instead, she began erasing the whiteboard. 'Oh well. I'll go back to subbing.'

Elsa joined her and picked up the other eraser. 'Not a bad plan. Between us and the middle school, we'll keep you busy.'

But could they keep her busy enough? 'I know. It's just . . .' She didn't finish the sentence. She didn't need to. Elsa understood. It was much easier to come into the same classroom every day and work with the same students. Most important, a permanent teaching position meant benefits and a regular salary. Money was tight even when Rachel was working full-time. Once she was reduced to substitute teaching, she'd be vacuum-sealed in debt. 'I'll be fine.'

'Of course you will,' said Elsa. 'You're a survivor.'

It was a far cry from being a princess, which was what her parents had raised her to be. When she met Aaron Green the dentist, she thought she'd found her prince. First he told her she had a beautiful smile. Then he told her she had a beautiful body. Then, after two kids, two cars, a mortgage and her fortieth birthday, he'd found another woman and told her goodbye. But not until he'd made sure that much of his money did a disappearing act. Just one of the universe's cosmic jokes. Almost as funny as finding herself with no employment and a student loan to pay off. Now she had a master's degree in education and no job.

Aaron was as lousy an ex as he once was a husband—always late with his child support payments, but still managing to come up with money for presents for the kids and frequent trips to Pizza Heaven to ensure his status as the favourite parent. She'd been coping with all that, pretty much, but now she'd been set adrift in a leaky raft on a stormy financial sea. *Was* she a survivor?

'You bet I am,' she said as much to herself as to Elsa.

Elsa gave her an encouraging hug and left. Rachel finished up in the classroom. Then she went to pick up the kids from Aaron's office, where they were getting their semiannual checkups. The sun was shining, and the lake was looking especially idyllic, ringed with evergreens and cosy houses. It didn't look like the end of the world.

She frowned, listening to the minivan's stumbling motor. It would have to go to the car doctor while she still had a hope of paying for repairs.

She stopped by the Safeway to pick up a take-and-bake pizza for dinner. Of course, she didn't get by with only purchasing what she'd come in for. By the time she was done, her grocery bill had sneaked up an extra forty dollars. Oh well, she thought, they had to eat.

Dan the checker had just finished ringing up her purchases when her friend and next-door neighbour, Jessica Sharp, pulled her trolley up behind Rachel. Jess was in her early forties. She had short, dark hair, the kind of face that turned heads, and a great, curvy body. She drove a red Volkswagen convertible, bought fresh flowers every week, and got her hair and nails done regularly. She didn't work, and she didn't worry about money.

At least she never used to. Now, with the troubles at her husband's bank, which had got bought out by a bigger bank, her husband's job was in jeopardy, and Jess was about to join the end-of-the-world club.

'Any news on Michael's job?' asked Rachel.

Jess shook her head. 'Waiting is killing us.'

'Waiting only starts the dying process,' Rachel said glumly. She pointed to the wine bottle in Jess's shopping trolley. 'If that's for craft night on Friday, you'd better get more. After this week I'll probably inhale an entire bottle single-handed.'

'I hear you,' said Jess. 'And don't worry. I've got something special in mind for Friday. I'll stock up on chocolate, too.'

It would take an entire vat of chocolate to raise her endorphin level, Rachel thought as she left the store. She turned onto Deerwood Avenue, where Aaron had his dental office. Before he moved in with Misty the lingerie model, he brought the kids home after their checkups, but that changed in a hurry. Misty didn't like Aaron coming by the house without her. Misty was smarter than she looked . . . or at least had good instincts.

The children were in the waiting room when Rachel arrived.

'Hi, Mom,' ten-year-old David greeted her. He was a cute boy, with Rachel's long legs. Once he grew into his feet, he'd probably tower over both her and Aaron. The basketball court was already second home to him. Right now he was smiling and clutching a new game for the Wii Aaron had recently given the kids. 'Look what Dad gave me.' He rushed to show her.

Rachel smiled round gritted teeth. 'That was nice of him.'

'Can I go over to his house and play it?'

Of course, Aaron had opted to keep the Wii console at his place even though David and Claire were only over there every other weekend. 'I'll bet you have homework,' Rachel said.

David's smile evaporated.

Thank you, Aaron, for making me the meany. 'I tell you what,' she said. 'You get your homework done, then I'll run you over to Dad's. He can take you to school in the morning.'

Now David was beaming. 'Thanks, Mom. You're the best.'

Yes, she was. Aaron was the faux best.

Twelve-year-old Claire sat slumped in a chair and had yet to surface from behind a copy of *People*. She had the same dark colouring as Rachel and big, brown eyes, and she'd inherited Rachel's full lips. But, much to Claire's dismay, she had inherited her father's nose. It was a little long, but it wasn't a bad nose, really. Still, it wasn't a Miley Cyrus nose, which, for Claire, meant it was ugly. Rachel knew her daughter would grow up to be striking, and she assured Claire of that practically on a daily basis, but motherly assurance was a very small shield to carry against peer-driven standards of beauty.

'What did Daddy give you?' Rachel asked her.

Her face still buried behind *People*, Claire produced a gift certificate to The Coffee Stop from her hoodie pocket and held it up.

Something had put Claire in a funk, and Rachel could guess what it was. The threat of braces, which had been looming on the horizon, had finally materialised. 'It looks like several vanilla chai smoothies for you,' she said. She stepped up to the reception window where Aaron's young receptionist Liz sat, smiling politely.

She smiled back. 'Hi, Liz. Can you tell Aaron I'm here?'

'He's finishing with a patient. I'll tell him.'

Rachel nodded and sat down next to her daughter. She gave Claire a playful shoulder nudge. 'So, are you reading about me?'

Claire rolled her eyes. 'Lame, Mom.'

Ah, the love. If she hadn't been twelve herself once, she'd have been offended. 'How did your checkup go?'

'I don't want braces.' The words came out, powered by misery. A hand went to Claire's eyes to swipe at fast-forming tears.

'Oh, baby,' said Rachel, putting an arm round her. 'I know.'

'Tell Daddy I don't want them. My teeth aren't that bad.'

'I'll talk to him,' Rachel promised, more to make her daughter feel better than because she thought it would do any good. Braces were, after all, the American way.

Claire nodded and wiped away more tears.

Out of the corner of her eye, Rachel could see Aaron approaching. He was forty-four, tall and broad-shouldered, with wavy dark hair salted with a hint of grey to make him look both distinguished and trustworthy. He was walking proof that looks were deceiving.

'How about you two go wait in the car?' she suggested to the children. 'I'll be there in a minute.'

'OK. Bye, Dad,' called David, bouncing out of the room, completely clueless to the unfolding family drama. Claire stalked out after him without a word to her father.

'We really need to get her into braces,' he said. 'I can set up a consultation for you with Rencher for next week if you like.'

Rachel was aware of Liz, sitting a few feet away from them, pretending to work. 'Let's talk.' She took Aaron's arm and pulled him out of the door onto the second-floor landing.

'This is not good timing for me,' Rachel said.

He frowned. 'Rachel. This is our daughter.'

She felt a sudden need to kick him in the shin. 'I'm glad you used the word *our*. Does that mean you're going to take care of this expense?'

His frown deepened. 'Of course I'll pay my share.'

'Your share always seems to be smaller than mine.'

Now he stiffened and looked down his nose at her. 'Is that so? Need I remind you who got the house?'

'And all the bills to go with it,' she retorted sweetly.

'Between what you make and the hefty amount I give you—'

'Hefty?' she said with a snort. 'Oh, please.'

'Rachel, can we stick to the subject?' he suggested in a pained voice.

'I am sticking to the subject. I can't afford braces. I'm not getting hired back next year.'

'Oh. I'm sorry.'

For a moment he almost had her convinced that he was sorry for her, but then she remembered whom she was dealing with. Aaron was only sorry because he suspected her problems meant he'd be asked to step up to the plate and help more.

'We'll work something out,' he assured her. 'I'll talk to Rencher about setting up a payment plan. Look, I've got to get back inside. My patient's probably numb by now.'

Rachel caught him by his sleeve. 'One more thing. You saw how upset she is. What about clear braces? Can I promise her that?'

He shook his head sadly. 'Don't get her hopes up on that. Those aren't as effective for children.' He gave her arm a pat before disengaging himself. 'You'll handle it.'

Sure. No problem.

Back in the car, David was bouncing his basketball off the car ceiling and Claire was plugged in to her iPod and glowering. 'Did you talk to Daddy?' she asked.

'Yes. I'm afraid braces have to happen.'

'It's not fair,' Claire turned her face and was now pretending to stare out of the window. A hand crept up to wipe the corner of her eyes with her sweatshirt.

'Braces aren't so bad anymore,' Rachel said gently. 'You can get them in all kinds of cool colours. Sweetie, practically everybody wears braces.'

'No, they don't,' Claire growled. 'I don't want braces. I'm already ugly.'

'You are not ugly,' Rachel said firmly.

'Aidan thinks you're cute,' David offered.

Learning she had the admiration of a ten-year-old's best friend in no way consoled Claire. 'No one's talking to you,' she snapped.

David shrugged and fell silent.

'Aidan may be the wrong age, but he knows beauty when he sees it,' Rachel said.

Claire rolled her eyes and looked out of the window.

Rachel gave up. For the time being, anyway.

2

IN HER FORTY-FOUR YEARS on the planet, Jessica Sharp had learned several important truths: chocolate is good medicine, housework is highly over-rated, girlfriends make the best shrinks, and—her latest lesson—job security is an oxymoron, especially if you happened to work for a bank, which her husband did.

'I still have a job,' Michael informed her when he came home from work.

Jess was in the kitchen, putting the chicken salad she'd picked up at Safeway into a bowl. She'd had a bottle of wine standing ready in case they needed to console themselves. Now they'd use it to celebrate. 'Thank God,' she said with a sigh of relief. They could take their wine out on the deck and enjoy the early June evening and congratulate themselves on how they'd dodged the bullet.

Or not. Michael was not looking thankful.

'There's one small catch,' he said. 'It's in Ohio.'

'O-what?'

'That's where the corporate offices are.'

Jess felt suddenly sick. 'Open that wine quick.' She plopped down on a stool at the kitchen island. 'Damn that Washington Federal Loan anyway,' she growled as he uncorked the bottle. 'They turned our stock to junk and our retirement to peanuts. Do they have to shuttle us across the country, too?'

'At my level, they do. That's the tradeoff.' Michael poured a glass of wine and handed it to her.

It was all she could do not to bang her head on the granite counter-top, which she'd put in only last year. She took a sip of wine, but it tasted bitter. She set down her glass with a sigh.

Michael wasn't drinking either. 'I'm sorry, Jess.'

She rubbed his arm. 'It's not your fault. I just hate to move.'

She hated the idea of her husband being unemployed even more. She got a sudden image of herself as a bag lady, pushing a shopping trolley full of dirty clothes down Lake Way.

That was enough to make her pick up her wineglass again. She had a new thought. 'What about Mikey?' Their son had left the nest, but after losing his first job, the baby bird had returned, and once more they had another mouth to feed. And that particular mouth gobbled up a lot of food. Jess's grocery bill had doubled since Mikey moved back home.

'He can probably move in with Erica.'

'Somehow I can't picture him wanting to live with his older sister.' Their daughter had got married in February (an event that had cost an arm and two legs) and lived north of them in a suburb.

'He can come with us if he wants,' Michael said.

Jess suspected their son would be about as thrilled with moving as she was. 'Oh boy,' she muttered.

'There is one other possibility.'

Hope blossomed in Jess's heart. 'Oh?'

'I dropped by Puget Sound National, and they might be interested in hiring me.'

He'd still be commuting to Seattle to work. Nothing would change. Perfect! 'Well, call 'em.' Now she could enjoy that wine.

'There's one drawback. The position would be less money.'

'How much less?'

'We'd be looking at about a twenty per cent pay cut.'

'Twenty?' Jess stammered. Suddenly Ohio didn't look quite so bad.

'We could do it,' Michael said. 'We'd have to tighten our belts.'

'Those belts are already on their last notch.'

He shrugged. 'Or else find a way to bring in more income.'

As in her? What marketable skills did she have?

None. Jess had majored in music in college (with a strong minor in boys and Frisbee), and after three years she'd met Michael and bagged the BA, going instead for a Mrs degree. Other than singing in a band on weekends—when she was young and hot and still looked like Pat Benatar—and selling craft creations at holiday bazaars, she'd never worked outside the home. She'd never needed to. But now she needed to. There had to be something she could do to make up that twenty per cent. Nothing came to mind, except panic.

Michael looked at her in concern. 'Jess? Are you OK?'

'I could get a job,' she blurted. *Doing what?*

Relief flitted across her husband's face, but he valiantly said, 'You don't have to. We can make it on less.'

'I'm sure I can get something,' she said. 'If you want to stay here. You do want to stay here, don't you?'

'Of course I do,' he said. 'Heart Lake is our home.'

'Well, then, we'll make it work. See if you can snag that position at Puget Sound National. And I'll . . .' *Oh boy.*

'Find something,' he supplied. 'It doesn't have to be full-time. We can save a lot of money just by not going out to eat so much.'

She nodded and downed the rest of her wine. She had a feeling that what she saved on eating out she'd be spending on booze.

'Don't worry,' Michael said, and gave her a kiss. 'We'll be fine.' The captain of the *Titanic* had probably said those very same words.

The next morning, Jess decided to make a list of possible jobs. She poured herself a cup of coffee, then grabbed a piece of paper and a pen and leaned over the counter, ready to write furiously. The blank page stared at her.

'There has to be something you can do,' she told herself.

Maybe she should start by writing down her strengths. What was she good at? She still played a mean keyboard.

Like that did any good. Even if she lost twenty pounds in two weeks and got Botox, where would she find a band that would have her? As a band chick she was over the hill and out of the loop.

What else? Crafts. She had a closet full of things she could sell. Except there would be no craft bazaar opportunities until the Fourth of July. Selling crafts was too iffy, anyway—hardly profitable enough to earn that extra twenty per cent every month.

So, what did that leave? A temp agency, she decided. That would be perfect. She could earn income, but she wouldn't be locked into anything full-time. She got on the computer and looked up temp agencies in Seattle. She could handle part-time office work, and if she worked in the city, she and Michael could commute together.

The first company she found was A-Plus Office Services. *That's me, A-Plus*, she thought, reaching for the phone.

As it turned out, Ms A-Plus could fit her in for an interview at one. Could she come in?

Why not? She was going to come through for Michael, even if it meant chaining herself to a desk somewhere in the city. Millions of women did it every day.

She encountered a challenge in her closet. Denim jackets, hot-pink tops, and various articles of clothing dotted with sequins greeted her. Hmm. Here was a black knit dress. But black wasn't exactly summery. That decided it. She'd leave for the city right now and detour by Nordstrom's before going on to her interview.

At Nordstrom's she managed to find a cream-coloured linen suit jacket and trousers that fitted well but bored her to tears. The price made her want to cry, too. She couldn't believe how much she was paying for boring. Well, you had to spend money to make money.

A-Plus Office Services was in one of the many tall Seattle buildings that looked down on the city's waterfront. Jess had grown up in this city. She'd attended the University of Washington, and met Michael at the Blue Moon Tavern. He'd looked like Andy Gibb and danced like John Travolta. Within a year, they'd managed to fall in love, elope, get pregnant, and celebrate Michael's graduation. Michael had gone on to become a lawyer, and she'd worked on turning herself into Mother of the Year—a far more noble occupation than band chick.

Although they'd left the city for the 'burbs, they still drove in regularly to take his mom to dinner. Visiting the city was great, but Jess wasn't sure how she felt about working there. Seattle had grown far beyond the little big town it had been when she was a girl. And, at an hour each way by freeway, it wasn't exactly a short commute.

She rode the elevator to the twentieth floor and found the A-Plus office. The reception area was small, with a love seat and matching chair, a blocky coffee table, and, on one side of the wall, a bank of computers. On the other side, at the reception window, sat a twenty-something babe wearing an outfit that looked even more expensive than Jess's. The girl looked Jess over. 'May I help you?'

Jess stepped up to the window. 'I have an appointment with Caroline Withers.'

The girl nodded. 'Have a seat.'

Jess perched on the couch. She looked over at the computers and felt her pulse rate start to rise. You have a computer, she told herself. *You can type. Email counts.* In spite of her positive self-talk, her pulse scooted up another notch.

'Jessica?'

Jess looked up to see a thin woman with shoulder-length grey hair, expensively cut, and stylish glasses looking down at her. The woman was dressed entirely in black. Jess thought of all the money she'd spent to avoid wearing black and sighed inwardly.

The woman was studying her, too, her smile polite. 'I'm Caroline Withers. Why don't you come into my office, and we'll talk.'

Talking was good. Jess followed Caroline through a small conference room and into her office. Caroline settled behind a massive desk. 'I'm happy you thought of us first,' she said, pulling together a pile of forms. 'Did you bring a résumé?'

Jess's palms were suddenly damp. 'Actually, no.'

'Well, you can email it to me later,' Caroline said amiably. 'What kind of work are you hoping for?'

'What kind?' *The kind that pays?*

'Secretarial, accounting . . .'

'Receptionist,' Jess said firmly. 'I have great phone skills.'

Caroline nodded. 'All right. Let's have you fill out some forms.' She clipped the papers on a clipboard and handed them to Jess; then she ushered her back to the conference room. 'You can fill these out, and then we'll get you started on the computer.'

The top form was terrifying. A-Plus wanted to know everything about her: educational background, work background, last employer. Jess was pretty sure Bennie at Bennie's Tavern, where her band had played, wouldn't be the right kind of business reference.

Twenty minutes later Caroline found her still at the table, hunched over a form. 'Is there a problem?' Caroline asked.

'One small one,' said Jess. 'I'm afraid I can't give you the kind of references you want.'

'I see,' said Caroline slowly.

'But I can type,' Jess said quickly. 'And I can certainly file and take messages.'

'All right, let's put you on a computer and test you.'

The computer hated her. She knew it five minutes after she sat down.

Excel was a mystery, and the typing was a nightmare. It was the sweaty palm thing. Her fingers kept slipping to the wrong key. She did well on the spelling and grammar test though. That should count for something.

'Well,' said Caroline when they met again in her office after the computer torture session, 'you can type a little.'

Types a little. There was a glowing recommendation. 'I think I'd be great with phones,' said Jess.

'I think you would, too,' Caroline agreed. 'You could do nicely as a receptionist. Let's have you fill out this card, and I'll put together a folder for you, with a booklet that will tell you about our policies, and a time card, which you'll fill out and submit to us at the end of every work week.'

That sounded official. 'Great. Thanks.'

'It can be hard to re-enter the work force. This is a good way to ease back in. Often companies wind up hiring temps full-time.'

'Full-time. Really?' echoed Jess, trying to convince both Caroline and herself that she was interested. *Goodbye to staying up late watching TV and sleeping in the next morning. Goodbye to driving north for lunch with Erica. Goodbye to Friday morning tennis with the girls. Goodbye to volunteering at the food bank.*

It beats saying, 'Goodbye, Heart Lake,' she reminded herself sternly. And really, it was about time she got a job.

She took her folder and left A-Plus Office Services ready to face a brave new world.

It's always good to go into the weekend with something to celebrate. This was another important truth Jessica had learned in her forty-four years on the planet. Celebrating over her possibly successful foray into the job market beat discussing what lay ahead on Michael's job horizon.

He had been more than willing to celebrate her afternoon's success. 'Way to go,' he said after she'd told him, and gave her a big, smacking kiss. 'You're already out there fishing for something. I'm impressed.'

'I don't exactly have a fish on the line yet,' she reminded him as she ladled canned sauce on their spaghetti.

'But you've baited the hook.'

She frowned. 'You wouldn't believe how much bait costs.'

Both his eyebrows went up.

'I had to buy something I could wear to a job interview. I never realised how noncorporate my wardrobe was.'

Michael smiled at that. 'You've got a point there.' She put her salad-in-a-bag into a bowl, and he took it to the kitchen table.

She joined him with French bread. 'I gave myself permission since I'm investing in my future.'

'You are. You have to dress for success,' he agreed.

'I just hope that investment pays off,' she said.

'You'll get something,' Michael said easily. 'Try another agency next week.'

'Another?'

'The more temp agencies you have your name with, the better.'

'Oh.' That made sense, of course.

She thought of having to face that one-hour work commute on a regular basis and shuddered. *Grow up*, she told herself sternly. *Millions of people go to jobs they hate every day.*

Except her husband. He loved his work. So did Rachel Green. So did Tiffany Turner, her other neighbour and craft buddy. Jess sighed.

'Don't worry,' Michael said as they settled down with their meal. 'I bet you'll have more work than you can handle.'

She nodded and managed a smile. Who knew? She might decide she liked office work. She would definitely like a pay cheque.

'Where's our son?' Michael asked.

'He went over to the Sticks and Balls to shoot pool with Danny.'

Michael frowned. 'I hope he spent time job-hunting first.'

'I'm sure he did,' Jess said quickly. Mikey was asleep when she left for the city, but he'd been gone by the time she got home.

'I don't want him sitting around playing games on his computer all day,' Michael said. 'Our son needs to be looking for a job.'

'He will,' Jess assured Michael. Mikey had a business degree. He shouldn't have trouble finding something. If he looked.

She suddenly understood why her son had been dragging his feet on the job-hunting for the last month. It was hard going out there and putting your ego and your future on the line, hoping you'd impress some stranger enough to want to take a chance on you. She really didn't want to do that again, herself.

After dinner Michael went to his computer to check out some business networking sites, and Jess drifted to the old baby grand piano she kept in a corner of the living room and vented, pounding the ivories. But hard as she banged, she couldn't stop thinking about the pounding she and Michael were about to take.

Tiffany stopped at Safeway on her way home to pick up a little something to bring to Friday craft night. Jess was hosting it this month, and while she always had plenty of goodies, Tiffany never liked to come empty-handed. She found some fresh strawberries that she was sure would be wonderful.

There. That took care of the girls. What about dinner? She decided to pick up some odds and ends from the deli. It was a great way to save time.

But not money. Tiffany checked in her wallet. She was two dollars short. The woman behind the counter had already put everything in little cartons so Tiffany couldn't very well say, 'Put it back.' She'd have to use her charge card.

By the time she got home, Brian was already there, sitting out on the deck. She opened the sliding glass door. 'Sorry I'm late. I had to stop at Safeway. Dinner'll be ready in a sec.'

'I'm not hungry.'

There was something very unsettling about Brian's tone of voice. With a sick feeling, she sat down opposite him.

He was a hottie, with that beefcake chin and those dimples. Except they only showed when he was smiling, and right now he wasn't smiling. 'Tiff, have you been charging things?'

Her heart began to thump wildly. 'Why would you ask that?'

'Because I found an unopened package of sheets under the bed.'

Abracadabra sheets. She'd meant to transfer them to the linen closet and forgot. 'What were you doing looking under the bed?'

'I was looking for my old running shoes,' he said. He looked at her warily. 'You haven't got another charge card, have you?'

She could feel her cheeks sizzling under his gaze. 'I . . .'

'Oh God,' Brian said faintly. 'Tell me you haven't.'

She bit her lip.

His lips pressed into a thin, angry line, and he left the deck.

'Brian, wait.' She followed him through the kitchen. 'I can explain. It's not much.'

He grabbed his car keys from the little table by the front door. 'I can't talk to you right now, Tiff. I need to go cool down. OK?'

No, it wasn't OK. 'Brian, don't leave. Please.'

She turned on the tears to no avail. Her husband shook his head and went out of the door.

Tiffany shut the door and flopped on the living-room couch, where she indulged herself in a good cry.

You'd better do something, cried her conscience.

And right now there was only one something to do. More bargains had to return to the mall. She hauled her unhappy self into the bedroom and took the sheets out from under the bed. She found the receipt for them in her underwear drawer, where she hid all her charge receipts. She also grabbed the receipt for the body butter she'd stocked up on and fetched one of the two jars from under her bathroom vanity. She could part with one.

After much soul-searching, she also parted with a pair of shoes and a serving platter she'd got on sale. Her returns assembled, she put the deli dinner in the fridge, and left for the mall. As she got closer with her returns, she began to cry again. Life sucked.

You're doing the right thing, said her conscience.

'Oh, shut up,' she snarled.

Jess shooed Michael out of the door to go play poker with his pals down the street and got busy setting out the refreshments for craft night. She and her friends were making wineglass charms, and Jess had planned her menu accordingly. She had picked up a couple of bottles of raspberry dessert wine from Bere Vino and truffles from the Chocolate Bar. Wine and chocolate, perfect.

Rachel was the first to arrive. She was tall and willowy, and Jess heartily envied her great legs. If she had legs like that, she'd never waste them on pathetically unshort shorts like the ones Rachel was wearing tonight. Rachel also had on a turquoise-coloured spring sweater set that was lovely with her dark colouring. Lovely, but not hugely sexy. Rachel had never dressed provocatively, but it seemed to Jess that since her divorce the girl had been sinking into schoolmarm mode. Her face was a little too long to call her beautiful, but her big, brown eyes were striking, and she had a gorgeous smile.

When she had something to smile about. From the look on her face as she walked through the door, Jess could tell that she wasn't going into the weekend with any reason to smile.

'You look like you need chocolate therapy,' Jess said as she led the way to the worktable she'd set up in the family room.

'I need therapy, period,' said Rachel.

'Aaron troubles?' Jess guessed. The goodies were laid out on the nearby coffee table. She picked up the plate of truffles and handed it to Rachel.

Rachel popped a truffle in her mouth. 'I don't have a job any more.'

Jess sat down on the nearest chair. 'Oh, no.'

'Oh, yes. But that's not all. Claire needs braces, and the Prince of Darkness is being his usual rotten self.' She took another truffle, then set the plate back on the coffee table.

'What are you going to do?'

'Go back to subbing. I should be able to pick up enough work. It's just—' She shook her head. 'I wanted something to go right. I swear, the day I met Aaron my life became cursed. I feel like everywhere I look I see bills to pay. I just . . .' Her voice broke.

Jess put the plate of chocolates in her lap and a glass of wine in her hand. 'I'm so sorry.'

Rachel went for her third chocolate and rinsed it down with a healthy slug of wine. 'It's OK. I'll be fine. My mom always says God never closes a door without opening a window.'

Jess nodded. 'That's a good thought to keep in mind.'

'I need a window to open really soon,' Rachel said.

'I hear you,' Jess said with a sigh.

'What's going on with you? Does Michael have a job?'

'If we want to move to Ohio, he does.'

Rachel's face lost its colour. 'Oh, Jess. Please tell me you're not moving.'

'We're not,' Jess assured her. 'Michael is looking for something around here. And I'm going to get a job.'

'A job?' Rachel looked at her with new interest. 'Doing what?'

'I'm going to see if I can get work as a temp.'

Rachel gave a thoughtful nod. 'I hear they can keep you busy doing that. I never thought of you as the office type, though.' She took in Jess's tight jeans, pink tank top, and pink sequinned flip-flops. 'I can hardly wait to see what you wear to the office.'

'I can do office boring if I have to,' Jess said, and plucked a chocolate from the plate. They were disappearing fast. If Tiffany didn't hurry up and get there, she'd miss out. Jess checked her watch. It was now a quarter after seven. Well, Tiffany tended to run late.

By a quarter to eight the chocolate was gone and half of the wine, and there was still no sign of her. Jess went to the living room and looked out of the window. She could see Tiffany's Craftsman-style house, which sat diagonally and across the street of their cul-de-sac. Like all the houses in Heart Lake Estates, it was big, too big for two people really, but Tiffany and Brian had planned to fill it up with babies. Tiffany's car wasn't in the driveway. Neither was Brian's Jeep.

'That is so weird,' Jess said, returning to the family room. 'Nobody's home. Maybe I'd better call her and see if she's OK.'

'She probably found a sale, which means we won't see her until after the mall closes. I don't know where she finds the money for all these bargains,' Rachel muttered as Jess went for the phone.

'She got another charge card. Didn't she tell you?'

Rachel's eyes got big. 'No. She knew I'd ream her out.'

Jess called Tiffany's cellphone, but only got her voicemail. 'Hey, where are you? We're ready to start.'

'I *am* starting,' Rachel said. She seated herself at the worktable and began sorting through the tiny charms, which they would then string onto little wire hoops to loop around wineglasses.

Jess joined her. They finished their creations, and still there was no sign of Tiffany. Jess went to the living room and looked out of the window again. The cars were back in the driveway now, and a light was on inside. 'She's home now.'

As she spoke, Tiffany's front door opened and out dashed a petite blonde with a heart-shaped face, wearing designer jeans, a silky pink top, and sky-kissing heels that screamed, *Designer label.*

'Here she comes,' Jess announced.

A moment later Tiffany was at the door.

'Where have you been?' Jess asked, letting her in. 'We were worried.' Then she realised Tiff's eyes were red. 'What's wrong?'

'Brian found out about the charge cards.' Tiffany fell onto the love seat. 'It was terrible,' she said, and burst into tears.

Jess sat down and put an arm round her. 'What happened?'

'He, he, he . . .'

'Oh my God, he's leaving you!' Rachel cried.

'Noooo,' Tiffany wailed. 'He took my credit cards. Even after I returned everything.'

Rachel stopped looking sympathetic. 'Tiff, you should be glad Brian took those credit cards. Think of the mess you could have got into with them.'

'Easy for you to say,' Tiffany snapped. 'You have credit cards.'

Rachel's eyes narrowed. 'Well, let's trade. You can have my charge cards, and I'll take your husband.'

This was not good. Jess had two emotional women in her living room going at it and no chocolate left. 'Come on, you two,' she pleaded. 'This isn't like either of you.'

Rachel sighed. 'Sorry. I'm a little cranky tonight,' she muttered.

Tiffany nodded, but she still looked hurt. An awkward moment passed before she said, 'You're right to lecture me. It's just that somehow it was easier to cope when I could go in the store and buy something on sale. Getting a bargain was like doing a good thing for our family.'

She didn't need to explain what she was coping with. Jess had had a miscarriage herself. It was a grief most people didn't understand. She suspected shopping was Tiffany's way of trying to fill the emptiness.

'We're a mess,' Rachel said. She went to the family room and returned a moment later with the near-empty bottle of wine. She filled a quarter of a glass and handed it to Tiffany. 'Sorry. This is all that's left. We've been consoling ourselves.'

Jess filled her in on Rachel's lost job and the crisis looming on the horizon for her and Michael.

'Rachel's right,' Tiffany said miserably. 'We are a mess.'

'Things could always be worse,' said Jess. 'So we're not rich. Most people aren't. But we've got lots of good things in our lives.'

'Mine all went back to the store,' Tiffany grumbled.

'Yes, but you've still got your husband,' Jess reminded her, 'and he loves you. That's huge. Rachel has her kids, I have my family, and we have each other. I'll admit, we have some challenges right now, but we're not starving.'

'Yet,' said Tiffany. 'They laid off two people in Brian's department this week. If he gets laid off, I don't know how we'll make it.'

'I'm scared, too,' Rachel confessed in a small voice.

But you had to think positive. That was something else Jess had learned in her forty-four years on the planet. 'We can't let a little thing like money problems defeat us,' she insisted.

'Maybe we should take a money-management course,' Rachel suggested. 'We could probably all stand improvement in that area.'

'Except now I don't have any way to pay for one,' grumbled Tiffany.

Rachel frowned. 'Good point. Without a job, I can't afford some big, expensive course.'

'Me, either,' said Jess.

'There has to be something we can do,' said Rachel.

They all sat there, the only sound in the room Tiffany's nails clicking against her wineglass as she thought.

'Wait a minute,' said Rachel suddenly. 'Where's the one place in town where learning is free?'

Jess's face lit with understanding. 'Of course! You're a genius.'

Tiffany looked from one to the other, confused. 'I don't get it.'

'The library,' Rachel explained. 'I'll bet we can find dozens of books on managing money.'

'Why not? Let's go tomorrow morning,' Jess suggested.

Tiffany looked pained. 'I can't go. I have three clients coming in to get their nails done tomorrow morning.'

'We'll find something for you,' Rachel promised.

'It had better be something on how to get through credit-card withdrawal,' muttered Tiffany.

3

THE LIBRARY PROVED to be a treasure trove of free information. The shelves in the finance section offered a wide selection of books, and Rachel and Jess loaded up.

'It looks like you two are going to be busy,' observed Lucy the librarian as she checked out their books. She picked up one. '*Budgets for Babes*. This looks good.'

'Well, good for us, anyway,' said Jess. 'We're babes,' she added with a wink, making Lucy smile.

'While we're here, let's check out the Friends of the Library book sale,' suggested Rachel.

So after they'd stowed their borrowed books in Jess's car, they went to the lower level of the small building, where two rooms had been set aside for the library's popular monthly fundraiser. It seemed half of Heart Lake had decided to check out the sale.

'We're going to die from lack of oxygen,' moaned Rachel as she and Jess swam through the crowd towards the finance corner.

'But we'll die with a book in our hands,' Jess said as she squeezed between two walls of people.

Rachel pulled a hardback off a top shelf. 'Here's a good one.'

Jess read over her shoulder. '*Your Magic Money Make-over*.'

Rachel opened the book and began reading the chapter titles. '"Making Debt Disappear: The Trick to Budgeting".'

Jess read over her shoulder, '"Pulling Extra Money Out of Your Sleeve". Oh, I need that one.'

Rachel pulled another book off the shelf titled *Diva on a Dime*. 'Here's the perfect one for Tiffany,' she said.

Jess gave a snort. 'She'll love it.'

'Let's go show her,' said Rachel.

Salon H was a small salon, with only three chairs and Tiffany's manicure station. Like all the business establishments in town, hearts were the theme. The mirrors had been specially made to look like artsy hearts, and several glass-blown red, orange and purple hearts made by a local artist hung in the window. There were always women chatting in the reception area, drinking espresso that Jody the receptionist had made for them.

Tiffany was in the middle of painting Maude Schuller's nails cotton-candy pink when Jess and Rachel walked in with their finds.

'It's important to learn to manage your money,' said Maude, assuming she was part of the conversation. 'The problem with your generation is that you girls don't know the value of a dollar.'

Tiffany rolled her eyes. 'Yeah, we do, Maude. It doesn't have any value.'

'A dollar still has value when you know how to stretch it,' Maude insisted. 'I was always careful with my money. If you're not careful when you're young, you wind up sorry when you're old. I have friends who have to get their food from the food bank because they were foolish when they were younger.'

'I'm going to live with my children anyway,' said Rachel with a grin. 'Payback.'

Maude waggled a pink-tipped finger at Rachel. 'You joke now, but when you're there, it's not funny.'

Rachel suddenly didn't look amused.

'Let's see those books,' said Tiffany weakly.

'We got one specially with you in mind,' Rachel told her, and dug the book out of her plastic bag.

Tiffany read the cover. '*Diva on a Dime*? I like the diva part.'

'We knew you would,' said Rachel. 'So start reading. You can give us a book report next month when we meet at my place.'

'We never did decide what we want to make,' said Jess.

'Something cheap,' said Rachel.

'Nothing is cheap,' said Tiffany with a sigh.

'You girls,' Maude said in disgust. 'When I was young, we made all kinds of things on the cheap: bath salts, friendship tea, Amish friendship bread. I have recipes for all those things. I'll give them to you if you like.'

'Uh, sure. Thanks,' said Tiffany, looking anything but thankful.

'People don't know how to be self-sufficient any more,' Maude said. 'We made our cakes and casseroles from scratch. And we made syrups and jams. There's nothing like homemade huckleberry jam. If you girls like, I'll give you some of my rhubarb to plant. You can make all kinds of things from rhubarb.'

'Free food? We'll take it,' said Rachel. 'Maybe I'll do an Internet search and find a bunch of recipes we can make out of all this free food we're going to scrounge.'

'You girls,' Maude began, shaking her faux blonde head.

'Had better be going,' Jess said, edging away.

'See you later,' Rachel added, following her.

Once they were outside, Jess turned to Rachel. 'That woman is like the ghost of Finance Future, all gloom and doom.'

'She did paint a grim picture,' Rachel agreed.

'Well, we still have time to get our act together,' Jess said.

'I'm not wasting any,' said Rachel. 'I'm going to start reading my book tonight. With the kids at Aaron's, I don't have anything else to do anyway.'

'You need a man,' Jess told her.

'No thanks. I'll stick with my book and a glass of wine.'

Jess didn't push it. She couldn't blame Rachel for being in no hurry to add a new man to her life. Maybe someday she'd be willing to risk her heart again, but probably not anytime soon. Jess couldn't imagine being in Rachel's shoes and having to do it all alone. Except she wasn't alone. She had her friends. They'd get through this somehow. Together.

Tiffany had fifteen minutes before her next client, so she began to thumb through her new book.

If you're reading this book, let me congratulate you on your excellent taste, wrote the author. *You are obviously a woman who is creative, and creativity is all you really need to live a fabulous life.*

That and a credit card, thought Tiffany.

I'll give you all kinds of tips for squeezing every bit of fun and glamour out of a dollar that you possibly can. I am living proof that any woman can live like a diva on a dime.

Tiffany was up for that. She flipped through the pages to the chapter titled 'Looking Great for Next to Nothing'. *Consignment stores are the way to go. Did you know that you can outfit yourself in designer clothes for second-hand prices?*

What did this diva chick look like? Tiffany turned to the back of the book and checked out the author photo. OK, the woman looked pretty glam. She flipped back to the chapter and read on. *Everything I'm wearing in my photo I got at consignment stores.*

Shut up. Tiffany studied the picture again. You wouldn't find anything like that around Heart Lake.

Tiffany read further. She saw the heading 'The Truth About Tiaras'. That got her attention.

Most jewellery stores have a huge markup. It can run as high as one hundred per cent. You'll save a bundle if you buy your jewellery from wholesalers who don't have the high overhead.

Tiffany probably wasn't going to be able to afford any new bling until she was ninety-nine, but this was good information all the same. OK, maybe there was something to this diva-on-a-dime stuff.

On Saturday night Rachel got comfy in her sweats and T-shirt. Then she dipped into her hidden stash of Hershey's Kisses, and settled on the couch with her secret guilty pleasure: a romance novel. Reading about love and happy endings was good for the soul and gave a girl hope. She popped a chocolate in her mouth and opened the book.

Destiny Vane knew she had found her soul mate when she first saw Auguste Baiser. He was darkly handsome with sensual lips, a chiselled chin, and powerful arms, and he was helping an old woman across the dirty streets of Paris.

Rachel snuggled down deeper among the sofa cushions. After many ups and downs, Destiny and Auguste would, of course, walk off into the sunset hand in hand. In the book, this would take months. At the rate Rachel read, it would take until Sunday afternoon.

Which it did. She gobbled the story down like candy. She was done and ready to return to the real world by the time the children came through the door from spending the weekend with their father and Misty. Rachel was slipping peanut butter cookies onto a cooling rack when the door opened and voices echoed through the house.

David bounded into the kitchen first. 'Cookies!' He scooped up two, juggling the hot goodies in his hand.

Rachel smiled. She couldn't run out and buy her son the latest Wii game, but cookies worked almost as well. 'Did you have fun with your father?' she asked, keeping her voice conversational.

David stuffed a cookie into his mouth. 'Yeah,' he said, spitting crumbs. 'Except Misty can't cook.'

Her son, who was basically a support system for a stomach, always said this when he came home, and she always kept the same thought to herself: Aaron didn't marry Misty for her cooking skills.

Now Claire was in the kitchen, too. She was smiling, which meant Misty had done something cool with her, something where money was no object. It only took a second to guess what. Claire was wearing a new necklace and earrings.

'You look like you had fun. What did you do?' asked Rachel, working hard to sound like a good sport. *Let me guess. Does it start with an S?*

'We went to the mall,' said Claire.

Big surprise. Clothes were Misty's life. How nice to have money to spend on clothes, not only for yourself but to use to buy the affections of someone else's daughter as well.

'Guess what,' said Claire, still smiling. 'Misty had braces when she was my age.'

'And look how she turned out,' Rachel said, finishing her daughter's thought. She'd had braces, too, and had told Claire that. But then Rachel wasn't a model.

'I still wish I didn't have to get them, but I guess it will be OK,' said Claire, helping herself to a cookie.

All right. Rachel still hated Misty, but she could at least be glad that Claire had come home feeling better about her fate. 'It will be OK,' Rachel said, and gave Claire a one-armed hug. 'It always is. Isn't it?' she added, rumpling David's hair.

'Yep,' he said, and took two more cookies.

'That is enough cookies for you,' she told him. 'You'll spoil your appetite for dinner.'

'I'm not hungry,' said Claire. 'We went to Pizza Heaven.'

Oh well, Rachel told herself. Misty couldn't bake. So there.

The next morning Rachel woke up determined to be optimistic. She had a steady pay cheque for a little while longer. If she couldn't find a full-time teaching position for fall, she'd sub. Or she'd sneak over to Aaron's, steal Misty's lingerie, and sell them on eBay. Snort.

'What are you laughing about?'

Rachel turned from where she stood toasting bagels to find her daughter looking at her like she was crazy.

'Nothing. I just thought of something funny, that's all.'

Claire shrugged. She helped herself to a bagel. 'Can I hang out downtown after school with Bethany?'

'I guess, for a couple of hours,' Rachel said.

'Ummm, can I have some money?'

'You spent all your allowance?'

'Pleeease?' Claire begged, dodging the question.

Rachel noticed her daughter was wearing the new necklace and earrings she'd got at the mall with Misty. The woman poured money on Claire like it was water, and Rachel was bickering over a few dollars? 'I have a ten in my wallet. You can have that.'

'Thank you, Mommy! You're the best mom in the world.' All smiles, Claire gave Rachel a kiss and bounded out of the kitchen.

Ten dollars was a small price to pay for being the best mom in the world. Or was it? What was she teaching her daughter about money? Her head suddenly hurt.

Jess had called in to A-Plus Office Services first thing in the morning and learned that they had nothing for her. So, back to the city she went and signed up with Solutions, Inc.

'You don't have a lot of experience,' said Ms Solutions, Inc., offering an empathetic expression to soften the harsh reality.

'You're right; I don't,' Jess agreed.

'It would help if you knew Excel. But we'll keep a watch and call you when something comes up that we think is a good fit for you.'

Jess nodded and left the office with a strong suspicion that she wouldn't be hearing from Solutions, Inc. *You need a Plan B.*

On her way home, she passed Heart Lake High, and catching sight of the school tennis courts suddenly inspired her. Now there was something she could do: teach tennis. She played doubles every Friday. She knew her way round a racket.

As soon as she got in the house, she called her friend Mary Lou, the head of the Heart Lake Park and Recreation sports department and offered her services for the upcoming summer programme.

'I wish you'd called about a week earlier,' said Mary Lou. 'I hired my last instructor on Friday. But we just lost a kinder gym teacher. I could use some help there.'

'Like gymnastics? I can't even do a somersault,' Jess confessed.

'They call them forward rolls,' Mary Lou corrected. 'Trust me. You don't have to be a gymnast to teach kinder gym. I'll train you myself. OK? Come in and help me with my morning classes this week. That way you could start teaching when the new session begins.'

As in she'd be hired? Just like that?

'OK,' Jess decided. It beat hoping to hear from temp agencies.

'Great! You'll love this,' Mary Lou enthused.

You can do this, Jess told herself as she hung up. How hard could it be to teach little preschoolers to hop around on a mat?

Not that hard, she decided the next day, watching Mary Lou in action at the old junior high gym. All the kinder gym pupils were really young, so it was mostly fun and games and an introduction to the basics of gymnastics with lots of stretching at the beginning. 'Stand on your tippy-toes,' Mary Lou said. 'Reach for the ceiling.'

All the little gymnasts (mostly girls in pink leotards) stood on tiptoe on cute, little baby fat legs. Jess fitted right in with her hot-pink tee. She stood, too, on legs that also had fat, the grown-up variety.

Mary Lou made it all look easy. 'See?' she said later as they waved good-bye to the last parents and children. 'You can do this.'

'What if somebody asks me to demonstrate?' Jess worried.

'I'll work with you this week and teach you the basics, like how to do a forward roll and mount the beam—'

'Wait a minute,' Jess interrupted, 'as in balance beam? They learn that in kinder gym?'

'We have a grade school class we need you to help with, too. But you'll only be an assistant. Gene the gymnastics coach will be the instructor. You'll be fine,' Mary Lou assured her.

Jess thought of the office assignments she wasn't getting. 'OK. Teach me a forward roll.'

Mary Lou beamed. 'All right. You do it exactly like we tell the kids: tuck and roll.' She turned herself into a ball and rolled across the mat, then bounced back up. 'See? Nothing to it.'

Right. Jess squatted on the mat and tried to turn herself into a ball. All the blood rushed to her head as she bent over.

Mary Lou was next to her now, coaching her. 'Tuck more.'

Jess made a superhuman effort to fold into something that would roll. The sound of ripping fabric echoed through the gym.

'Please tell me that wasn't my trousers,' Jess groaned.

'Never mind. They're already split, so you may as well keep going,' said Mary Lou, and proceeded to turn Jess into a pretzel.

Now Jess could barely breathe. 'Hey, I'm not made of elastic.'

'Stretch more, and you will be. Come on now, roll.'

Jess let gravity take over and started forward. She was doing great until her nose made contact with something hard. Her knee, of course. She saw stars and rolled over onto her side, landing like a beached whale. 'Oooh, my dose.' It was bleeding. Great.

Mary Lou handed her a tissue. 'Are you OK? Maybe you really aren't cut out for this.'

She'd be darned if she'd flunk forward rolls. 'Let's try again.'

Half an hour later she limped to her car while all the muscles in her body cried, 'Pain, pain, pain.'

'Oh, shut up,' she told them. 'No pain, no gain.'

And she had gained something. She was now a park department employee. She wasn't going to make a fortune, but at least she'd be making something. And something was better than nothing.

Tiffany had driven straight home from work on Saturday. No bargain-hunting detours. Not only had she spent no money, she'd acquired a free book on how to live great on next to nothing. She could already hear the conversation with her husband.

> BRIAN: *You didn't so much as stop at the grocery store? That's amazing. And what's this, a book on saving money?*
> TIFFANY: *I didn't pay anything for it. I'm going to save us so much money from now on, you won't believe it.*
> BRIAN: *I'm proud of you, Tiffy.*

But the conversation did not go as planned.

'*Diva on a Dime*, huh?' he said, stopping work on the Jeep and wiping his hands on a rag. 'You really think you can do that?'

'I'm going to try,' she said.

'The diva part won't be a problem,' he said, frowning at the book. 'You already work that pretty good.'

'What's that supposed to mean?'

'I mean, we don't need half the stuff you bring home. This book looks like one more way to get you to spend money.' He flipped through the pages, landing on the chapter that dealt with how to save on jewellery. He began reading, growing a frown in the process.

'Those are good tips,' Tiffany insisted.

'Yeah, well, an even better tip is don't buy the stuff in the first place,' he said, handing over the book.

'I wasn't going to,' she said. 'I'm trying, Brian. Jess and Rachel found me this book at the library, so it didn't cost us a thing.'

Of course, he hugged her and said he was sorry, but things were a little strained after that. They spent the evening with friends. Then they came home and went to bed, and he kissed her good night.

And that was all. There it was, proof that everything wasn't all right. It hadn't been so long ago that on a Saturday night Brian would have been all over her. Deep down, she knew he was losing interest. How could he not be? She was a malfunctioning baby machine, and he wanted kids. They both did. Or maybe he still hadn't forgiven her for getting those credit cards.

On Sunday, Brian watched a baseball game on TV, and she read her book. It was all very cosy on the surface. The only thing missing was the cosy feeling. On Monday, life went back to the weekday routine with one exception: things were not right between them.

On Tuesday, she got him to watch a chick flick on TV with her, but it didn't inspire him to do anything more than kiss her good night, and by Wednesday, the emptiness deep inside her that had opened up after her second miscarriage was back. She'd managed over the last few months to fill it with all her bargains, keeping herself happy with shots of shopping vaccine, but there was no vaccine now.

On Wednesday, she attempted to nurse her marriage back to health by pulling out candles and her best Victoria's Secret bargain and making margaritas. She managed to lure Brian into sex, but it didn't lead to any real intimacy, no whispering in her ear how much he loved her.

Instead, he wandered off for a shower.

When he came out, she asked, 'Can we do something together tonight? It doesn't have to cost a lot of money.'

'Like what?' He began pulling his clothes back on.

'I don't know. Something romantic.'

He looked at her with a perplexed smile. 'We just did.'

'Something more,' she said. 'I know! Let's go to The Family Inn and see what we can get for five dollars.'

He frowned. 'Five dollars, ten dollars, twenty dollars—Tiffy, it all adds up. We really need to get into the habit of cutting back.'

All week she'd been trying so hard. She'd just wanted to reward herself with a little treat—dessert someplace inexpensive, holding hands across the table. Was that really going to break them?

He pulled her to him. 'I've got a better idea.' He handed her the TV remote. 'This doesn't cost a thing. I'm going to work on the Jeep, so the remote's all yours tonight. I bet one of your reality shows is on.' With that, he left her alone and unsatisfied.

She went through the next day at work with a smile pasted on her face, watching other women parade through the salon. No one paid by cheque or with cash. The whole world ran on credit. It was like being the only woman at a dance with no date.

She thought back to Black Friday, when she and Brian had their big fight. He'd insisted they get rid of the credit cards. Those cards were going to ruin their marriage. Well, now she had no credit cards, and she wasn't seeing much of an improvement in the marriage department.

By the time she left Salon H, she had a good head of angry steam propelling her out of the door, and the last thing she wanted to do was go home to Brian. She still had her tip money in her pocket. Suddenly she was possessed by a need to buy . . . something, anything. It took over, guiding the car towards the mall. Then it drove her from the mall parking lot into the nearest department store, where she found, miracle of miracles, the same shoes she'd got the week before and had to return. She had just enough money to buy them . . . if there was no sales tax. She frowned at the money on the counter.

'If you open up a credit-card account, you get ten per cent off,' said the clerk.

'I have an account,' Tiffany muttered. 'I don't have my card.'

'We can look up your card number,' the clerk said brightly.

Good idea. She'd only be spending a dollar more than what she already had sitting on the counter. 'OK,' said Tiffany.

On the way out of the store, she saw a clearance rack at the back corner of the Juniors department. She'd just take a minute and look. Oh, that top. It was only $8.99. She'd make that much in tips tomorrow. She marched to the service counter.

When she got home, she left her purchases in the trunk. Not that she had anything to hide, really. She'd only spent her own tip money. Well, today's and tomorrow's, but that was beside the point. The point was she was in control of her spending.

She went inside and found Brian in the kitchen, stuffing sandwiches and wine coolers into a grocery bag. 'What are you doing?'

'Getting ready to take you out to dinner,' he said.

She looked inside the grocery bag. In addition to sandwiches, he'd packed a couple of snack-sized packets of crisps and two bottles of her favourite coffee drink. And what was this? She pulled up a Hershey's chocolate bar and looked questioningly at him.

'I had a dollar in my wallet,' he said with a smile. He took the candy bar from her and dropped it back in the bag. 'You ready?'

'Where are we going?'

'Someplace romantic,' he assured her.

Someplace romantic. There was hope after all.

They climbed into the Jeep, and he drove her to the public park on the lake. Taking his bag of goodies and a blanket, he led her down to the far edge of the lake and spread out the blanket on the grass. 'I know it's not a restaurant,' he said, 'but will it do?'

It would more than do. This was a perfect diva-on-a-dime, romantic date. Why hadn't she thought of it? 'Yes,' she said, and put her arms around his neck and kissed him.

'I'm sorry I'm being a hard-ass,' he murmured, nuzzling her neck. 'I don't want you to be miserable, Tiffy. Sometimes I wish I was rich. Then you could buy all the bargains you want.'

She thought guiltily of the purchases hiding in her car trunk.

'I don't need to be rich,' she assured Brian, and kissed him, vowing to cancel her credit cards the next day. All she needed was to keep the empty spot filled. Not an easy task, for the empty spot inside of her was always crying for more. And what it wanted most she wasn't sure she'd ever be able to give it. 'Brian, I'll do better, I promise,' she said, her voice quavering.

'Me, too,' he said, and they kissed again.

Then they enjoyed their meal while watching the evening sunlight dance on the water. The sound of laughter drifted in to them from somewhere out on the lake, mixing with their own happiness. Now, this was cosy.

Tiffany had just finished her half of the chocolate bar and sighed happily when Brian cleared his throat. 'This probably isn't the best time to tell you this,' he said, 'but you need to know. Starting next Monday, I have to take two weeks off unpaid.'

'No pay?' she squeaked.

'I'm not the only one,' Brian said. 'We're all taking turns, hoping nobody else will have to get laid off.'

Two weeks with no pay. The shoes would have to go back. Again. She would have to do better. For real this time. She found herself wishing she had someone to help her, like an AA sponsor, or even a support group. Wait. She had one in her own back yard.

4

IT WAS JESS'S first day of flying solo, and she had three classes. She looked at the eight little girls and the one boy who was already all over the mat like an escaped slinky and thought, *I can handle this.*

If she couldn't, Brenda Bletznik would tell the whole neighbourhood. Why, oh why, thought Jess, did I get stuck with the daughter of the biggest mouth in Heart Lake in my class?

'All right. We have to stretch all our muscles really good so they'll be happy,' Jess said. Her muscles would probably never be happy again but, oh well.

The students looked at her eagerly and mimicked her every move. The parents smiled benignly. So far, so good.

'Now we're going to play follow the leader. Do what I do.' She demonstrated, showing off her new sashay skills. 'Can you do that? Follow me.'

Around the gym they went, Jess sashaying for all she was worth, arms held gracefully to the side like a ballerina. She checked over her shoulder. They were all following her like so many baby ducks. 'You're doing great,' she called. The children smiled.

And then something sneaked in front of her foot. Down she went like a whale doing a belly flop, her startled 'Oomph' ricocheting off the walls of the gym. All her students stopped in mid-sashay to stare. She clambered to her feet and turned to see what had caught her so unaware. The stupid practice balance beam—why hadn't she noticed someone had moved it?

'Are you all right?' called Brenda from the edge of the gym.

'I'm fine,' she replied with a game smile. It was a lie. Her ankle was on fire, and so was her toe, just like her face.

'We'd better move this balance beam a little bit.' If she wasn't in so much pain, she'd have kicked it. 'We don't want anyone else to trip, do we?' Not that anyone else would. She was the only klutz in the room. She heaved the beam out of the way. It fell with a satisfying *whump*. She returned to where her students stood gaping, limping as she went. *Ow, ow, ow.* Her ankle was already swelling.

'OK, everyone,' she said weakly, 'we're going to sit down and stretch for a minute.' And while her little dears stretched, she crawled to the phone and called Mary Lou. 'Can you come down here? I think I need help.'

She also needed Advil, ice, a doctor visit and an Ace bandage.

Warm air caressed Jess's face as she limped out of her front door on Friday to go meet with Rachel and Tiffany. It wasn't their usual craft night. This get-together was at Tiff's request.

It was a beautiful evening. The only thing marring it was Jess's uncertain future, she thought miserably as she made her way next door to Rachel's two-storey colonial. She diverted her eyes when she passed her red Volkswagen convertible, not wanting to see the For Sale sign in the window.

'You love that car. Are you sure?' Michael had asked her.

She'd steeled herself and said, 'Yes. We don't need the car payments.' They had Michael's car and the truck, which was free and clear. How many vehicles did two people need, anyway?

Her feet disappeared in Rachel's shaggy grass as she crossed the lawn. Rachel had trouble keeping up with the rest of the block when it came to yard maintenance. Of course, it was nothing compared to the house on the other side of Rachel, which had been in foreclosure. That was the neighbourhood eyesore—not good for property values.

A large grocery bag sat on Rachel's front porch with some kind of dirt-encrusted plant bulbs inside. Maybe Rachel was about to change her ways and get in touch with her inner gardener.

Jess knocked on the door and then let herself in. Rachel and Tiffany were already in the formal living room with glasses of iced tea.

'What happened to your foot?' asked Rachel.

'Occupational hazard,' said Jess. 'What's with the bag on the front porch?' she asked, accepting an iced tea from Rachel.

'It's rhubarb,' said Tiffany. 'Maude brought it to the salon today. We're supposed to split it three ways.'

'Never turn down free food. That's my new motto,' put in Rachel.

'Speaking of free things,' said Tiffany, 'that's actually why I wanted to meet tonight. I want us to start being a money group. I thought if we met every week and talked about what we were learning from all those books you got at the library, it would . . .' She stopped and gave a little shrug. 'I don't know. Keep us on track.'

'That might not be a bad idea,' Rachel mused.

'And maybe you guys can help me not spend money,' Tiffany said. She gnawed her lip, making Jess and Rachel exchange concerned glances. 'My *Diva on a Dime* book is great, but she's not exactly around when I'm haveing a money problem. I need something like AA that we could do here in our own neighbourhood. I mean, Rachel, you're going to have to be on a budget, and, Jess, if you don't move . . .'

'We'll be on the street,' Jess finished glumly. OK, that was overstating it. But it was going to be a challenge to pay the mortgage and the bills. 'Why, oh why, didn't we save more when we were making good money?' she lamented.

'The same reason I never squirrelled away a nest egg,' Rachel said, with a shrug. 'I thought I was doing fine.'

'It's not too late,' Tiffany said. 'We can help each other. We've got the books. How about instead of doing crafts once a month we meet once a week and work on ways to save money?'

'Design our own money class?' asked Rachel.

'And support group,' added Tiffany.

'All right,' Rachel said decisively. 'I don't think any of us is going to inherit a million dollars in the next few months, so we'd better do what we can with what we've got.'

'Since you're the teacher, you can lead it,' said Tiffany. 'OK?'

'Me? I teach grade-schoolers,' Rachel protested.

'Perfect,' said Tiff. 'That means you won't make it too hard.'

Rachel heaved a resigned sigh. 'OK. I'll see if I can pull something together for our first meeting.'

'Awesome!' cried Tiff happily.

The next Friday the three women reconvened at Rachel's house.

Jess's portion of the evening was fun as she had brought the ingredients for homemade bath salts, providing them with an inexpensive craft.

Rachel's contribution didn't go over quite as well. 'Your spending personality?' Jess's eyebrows rocketed up as she read the questionnaire Rachel handed her. 'I don't know if I want to know mine.'

Rachel sneaked a look at Tiffany. Tiff was curled up in an easy chair, twirling a lock of blonde hair, and scowling at the paper. 'You guys wanted to do this. Remember?'

'I didn't want to do *this*,' retorted Tiffany.

'Look, we've all got leaky financial boats. If we don't get a handle on why we spend, we're bound to keep springing leaks. We can start with me. I'm a guilt spender.'

'How do you know that?' asked Tiffany.

Rachel could feel her cheeks growing warm. 'Because that's what motivates where a lot of my money goes. Both Claire and David get an allowance, but every time they want money for something, I give it to them. I'm trying to buy my children's love.'

'They already love you,' Tiffany said.

Rachel found it suddenly hard to look at her friends. 'I know, but I want them to love me more than Aaron. Pretty sick, huh? I mean, he is their father. But somehow, it doesn't seem fair that he gets the same amount of love. So I've let myself get sucked into this bidding war that I can't possibly win.'

'Someday he'll get what he deserves,' Jess predicted.

'Meanwhile, he's Mr Popularity, and I'm Meanie Mom,' said Rachel. 'And I'm really going to be Meanie Mom when I break the news to them that we can't afford to go anywhere this summer.'

'We've got a great lake right here. Do you really need to go somewhere?' asked Jess. 'How about planning a staycation?'

'I know what the diva on a dime would do,' piped Tiffany. 'She'd make staying home like a camp and do beading and baking and fun stuff like that. I could come over and give free pedicures to Claire and her friends. We could have a girls' spa day.'

'I like it,' Rachel said with a nod. 'That takes care of Claire. Any suggestions on what I can do for David?'

'Let him camp out in a tent in the back yard, and he'll be happy,' Jess assured her. 'I'll throw in a few tennis lessons with Aunt Jess.'

Rachel found herself smiling. She could do this.

'Look at that,' Jess was saying, 'you've already saved a small fortune by not going on vacation.'

'I need to find a way to bring in more money though,' said Rachel. 'Maybe I can tutor.'

'You could do a get-ready-for-school programme in August,' suggested

Jess. 'I'd have been all over that like a rash when Mikey was little.'

Rachel nodded. 'I like it. OK, who wants to go next?'

'I'll go,' said Jess in a resigned tone.

As they talked about Jess's expenditures, it was easy to see Jess did a good job of rationalising whatever she spent.

'But I don't normally do that,' Jess excused herself. 'I mean the work wardrobe—I had to have that. And we can't go in and see Mike's mom and not take her out to dinner.'

'Why not?' asked Rachel. 'You could bring her something.'

'You know I don't cook,' Jess replied.

'The diva on a dime says you save a fortune by making food from scratch,' said Tiffany.

That went over like a failed soufflé.

'It's a great way to be creative,' said Rachel.

'You can't be creative in everything,' argued Jess.

'She's a rationaliser,' Tiffany said. 'Write that down.'

Jess frowned and wrote.

And then it was Tiffany's turn under the microscope. 'I already know,' she said in a small voice. 'I'm a retail-therapy shopper.'

With a little sob, she confessed her latest relapse. Soon she was spilling everything, from her other spending relapse to her concern that she couldn't give Brian the family they both wanted.

'Don't give up,' said Jess, handing her a tissue. 'Look at me. I had a miscarriage, but now I have two great kids.'

Tiffany nodded and smiled, trying to convey that she'd be fine.

Maybe they all would, because by the end of the evening Jess was smiling and Tiffany was looking determined. And Rachel was pumped. 'Here's to small changes,' she said.

'They'd better make a big difference fast,' added Jess grimly.

On Monday Rachel took Claire to Dr Rencher for a consultation and took her first step towards change. Braces were definitely in order. 'Then let's get started,' she said to him after they'd finished the consult. 'Bill Aaron. He's taking care of this.'

She left the office with a smile. Before yesterday she'd have sucked it up and paid her share. Not today. She had a new attitude.

And somewhere, a little gremlin was cowering.

Every Day, in Every Way,
We're Getting Better and Better

5

'IT'S GOING TO TAKE FOR EVER to pay off my credit cards,' Tiffany complained to Cara, the stylist on duty at the salon.

'So speed up the process,' said Cara. 'Girl, you got a fortune in clothes hanging in your closet. Sell 'em on eBay. You can make money doing that. My sister in California is.'

'What's she selling?' asked Tiffany.

'Stuff she finds at garage sales. Last year she got all kinds of cool junk: knockoff handbags, Gucci sandals.'

Tiffany's eyes bugged. 'Serious?'

'Oh, yeah.'

Gucci sandals at a garage sale—that was worth looking into.

'I'm thinking I might start an eBay business,' Tiffany said to Rachel later that day. 'Want to hit some garage sales this Saturday?'

Rachel nodded thoughtfully. 'You know, I haven't been to a garage sale in years. Sure, I'll ride shotgun.'

Tiffany proved to be a garage-sale power shopper. She had an eye for finding valuable trinkets, and she was fast. She found a Lenox figurine for five dollars and beat a senior citizen to a jazzy, pink rhinestone clock. Rachel felt the woman's scowl like a laser beam. Tiff was oblivious.

'Wow,' said Rachel, as they drove away. 'You don't mess around.'

'This is business,' said Tiffany. She tapped the pink clock. 'But I may keep this.' Rachel frowned at her, and she added, 'Or not.'

After returning from the garage sales, Rachel started on some much-needed house cleaning. She was washing windows when she heard a lawn mower fire up next door. It was a sound no one had heard over there for a long time, and she peered out of the family-room window for a closer view. Sure enough, someone was mowing the lawn. Whoa. That was some someone.

She squirted more glass cleaner and quickly rubbed the window for a clearer view.

Holy Danielle Steel, but he was gorgeous. She took in the slim hips encased in Levi's, the T-shirt stretched across broad pecs, and the arm muscles rippling under caramel-coloured skin, and swallowed hard. This man could be a cover model.

The sun was out, and the weather was perfect for weeding flowerbeds. Maybe she would just go out and pull a few weeds.

The man next door was now doing the side yard, giving her a clear view of raven-black hair and eyebrows, gorgeous brown eyes. And that strong-square jaw that practically screamed, 'Touch me.' Would he like a drink of water? Was he hungry? Was he married? She craned her neck, trying to zoom in on his ring finger.

'Mom, what are you doing?'

Rachel gave a start, and the bottle of window cleaner dropped from her weak hand. 'Claire.' She picked up the bottle.

Her daughter looked at her like she had slipped a cog.

'Did you need something?' Rachel asked.

'Can you take Bethany and me to a movie?'

Rachel turned her back on the view out of the window. 'Is your room clean?'

Claire nodded emphatically. 'Yes.'

'And you have money left from your allowance?'

Emphatic turned into hopeful. 'Could I have five dollars?'

'Sweetie, I can't keep bailing you out.'

Claire frowned. 'You don't give me enough allowance.'

Her daughter could find Rachel's guilt button blindfolded. She gave up. 'All right.' Still, nickelled-and-dimed-and-dollared to death—this was no way to save money. 'I tell you what,' Rachel added. 'I'll give you five dollars today, but that's the end of the gravy train. Starting next week, we'll sit down together and work out a budget for your allowance. And when the fun money is gone, it's gone. No more bailouts. I am not the government. Got it?'

Claire nodded. 'Got it.'

Of course, she probably didn't get it at all, Rachel thought as they walked to the car. How could she? She was only twelve.

Out of the corner of her eye, Rachel was aware of Señor Gorgeous mowing the lawn. He was probably married. Or gay. Because that was one of those stark realities of life every woman over twenty-five had to face. Good men didn't grow on trees. And they sure didn't show up next door, mowing the lawn.

Still, that didn't mean she couldn't be neighbourly. When she got home, she'd offer him a glass of water. She surreptitiously checked out his truck, looking for the name of the lawn guy. The truck was an older model, white and beat up. She didn't see a lot of equipment or yard refuse in the truck bed, but maybe this was his first job of the day.

Picking up Bethany took some time since her mom wanted to chitchat. And then there were the usual arrangements to be made regarding the rest of the girls' day. 'I can pick them up, and Claire's more than welcome to stay for dinner,' Bethany's mother offered.

David was already off at a friend's house and wouldn't be back until after dinner. Rachel would have the whole day to . . . weed.

'Can I?' Claire asked eagerly.

Rachel pretended to consider. 'I think we can make that. Thanks, Alice. Well, we'd better hurry. You don't want to miss the movie.'

She dropped the girls at the theatre. By the time she got home, the white truck was gone, and so was Señor Gorgeous.

With the temptation removed from her field of vision, her common sense returned. *You need a man like a diabetic needs a Twinkie.*

She sighed as the realisation hit her. Just because a woman developed a problem with sugar, it didn't mean she lost her taste for sweet things. It sure looked like Rachel hadn't.

You are pathetic, she told herself. Maybe she needed a little aversion therapy. She took a moment to revisit the pain Aaron had inflicted on her in the past year and a half.

What gardener?

Jess came home from her afternoon nail appointment—which was probably another spending leak, but Tiff needed the business—to the sound of angry male voices. *Oh, no.* In the kitchen, Michael and their son stood nose to nose, faces red, neck muscles bulging. In spite of the age difference, they looked so much alike it was scary. Same hunky profiles, same lanky build, same stubborn set to the jaw.

'Hey, if you don't want me here, I'm gone,' Mikey yelled.

'Fine. If you want to be a bum, go live like a bum.'

The anger in the room came at her heart like a knife. Michael and Mikey had had their father–son clashes, but never like this.

Mikey marched towards the kitchen door, but Jess blocked it. 'What are you two doing?'

'I'm out of here,' Mikey announced, and pushed past her. Behind his angry bravado, she could see her son was close to tears.

She shot a punitive glare at her husband and then chased after Mikey. He was already in the living room when she caught him by the arm. 'Mikey, honey, this is no way to settle things.'

'I'm done, Mom. I've been trying, but he doesn't believe me.'

She wasn't sure she did either, which made her feel ashamed of herself. 'He's just concerned.'

Mikey's eyes flashed. 'Yeah, I can see that. So what if I haven't had any interviews? I've been on the Net looking every day. I don't see him going on any interviews.'

Now Michael was in the living room, too. Mikey stiffened at the sight of him. Their son had always been a good kid. OK, more interested in playing computer games than doing homework. But he'd buckled down and finished college and got a job, and everything had been going so well. Until he lost the job.

Michael came up to their son and laid a hand on his shoulder. 'Son, I'm sorry I lost my temper with you.'

Mikey's lips clamped together. He managed a nod.

'I just need to know you're trying, that's all.'

'I *am*, Dad.' Mikey's voice broke. 'There's nothing out there.'

'You'll find something,' Jess assured her son.

He frowned and nodded. 'I gotta go.' He bent over and gave Jess a kiss on the cheek and then slipped out of the front door.

Jess staggered to the couch and fell on it. She frowned at Michael, who had taken the chair opposite her. 'What did he do, anyway?'

'Well, he finally got up at eleven. He came in at two a.m. last night, the same time he came in on Wednesday and Thursday night. How hard do you think he's working to find a job if he's out with his buddies all night and sleeping the day away?'

Michael's voice was going up in volume. 'Why are you yelling at me?' Jess protested.

He fell back against the chair cushions. 'Sorry. I don't mean to yell. Mike has got to get serious. All I want is for him to try a little harder. Why does he have to take that so personally?'

Jess shrugged. 'Because he's a man?' She came over and squeezed into the chair with Michael.

'That's exactly why I want him to set some goals,' Michael said sternly. 'He needs to log in as much time looking for a job as he would working a job. Now, are you going to tell him that or am I?'

'I'll take care of it,' she promised. She gave him a kiss.

He closed his eyes with a sigh.

'It'll work out,' she murmured. One way or another, she was going to make sure of it.

It took a couple of days of mulling for her to realise that her baby bird needed motivation. Michael was right. Mikey was having a hard time mastering the art of job-hunting. Maybe that was because he'd got his first job so easily. Michael had had a friend in HR who'd pulled a couple strings on Mikey's behalf. Now he was sitting under the employment tree, wondering why he couldn't reach any plum position. Someone was going to have to teach him the importance of finding a ladder and climbing up to get what he wanted.

On Monday Jess came home from hopping around on the mats in the gym to find her son raiding the fridge. 'I could use a sandwich,' she said, dumping her bag on the kitchen counter.

He nodded, and went to work building her a super turkey sandwich with everything from green peppers to avocado.

'You put together a mean sandwich,' she said with a smile. 'Maybe you should become a chef.'

He shook his head. 'I think you have to go to school for that.'

She took a bite. 'Good stuff. You know, I've been thinking.'

Mikey looked at her suspiciously.

'I think right now you are having a crisis.'

'Well, duh, Mom.' He poured himself a glass of milk.

'But, lucky for you, I have a solution to your crisis.'

'You found me a job?'

'Don't be sarcastic. And yes, I've found you an interim job.' She grabbed a piece of paper and started making a list.

'Where?'

'Here,' she said brightly.

'Here?'

'It's the pits having nothing to do,' Jess continued. 'You feel like you have no purpose. So, until you find something, you'll be working for me, Mommy Dearest.'

He didn't look at all thrilled with his new boss. 'Doing what?'

She shoved the paper at him. 'All kinds of things. Most people like a job with variety, so I'm going to make sure we vary your job description from week to week.'

He picked up the paper and looked at it. 'Clean garage.'

'Dad really doesn't have time. It's a mess.'

'Weed flowerbeds?' He looked slightly sick. 'Paint house? Mom, you expect me to do all this in one week?'

She took the list from his suddenly limp hand and examined it. 'OK, you can do the garage next week.'

'How much am I getting paid for all this?'

'Paid?' She looked at him as if he had spoken in a foreign language. 'You're getting free rent and all the food you can eat.'

He frowned. 'Funny, Mom.'

'Mikey, I'm not being funny,' she said. 'I understand that you're looking for a job, but until you find one, this will be a way for you to feel good about yourself and help us out, too. Since you're not working for someone else, you may as well work for me.'

'But you don't pay,' Mikey protested.

'Correction. I don't pay what you want. But until you find something, I'm the best game in town.' If that didn't motivate him to turn over every rock for a new game, nothing would. She picked up the plate with her sandwich. 'This sandwich is really good. I think I'll have you cook some meals for me, too.'

'I don't like to cook,' he protested.

'Me, either,' she said, and left her baby bird gaping in shock.

On Friday evening, Jess arrived at Rachel's house before Tiffany.

'So, where's Tiff? I thought she'd be here by now,' Jess said, handing over a bottle of white wine. 'I ran into her at Safeway, and she was all excited about some big surprise she'd bought for us.'

'Oh, no. She's spending money again?'

'In a way. She told me to bring three dollars to cover my share of whatever this is, and some gardening gloves. I left them on the porch along with a pair for you and a couple of spades.'

'Gee, thanks,' said Rachel. 'Whatever she got, it had better be edible.'

Jess pointed out of the living-room window. 'Speak of the devil.'

Rachel looked to see Tiffany coming up the walk, balancing a large cardboard container full of plants. Whatever was in the box was making it tippy.

'She's going to drop them,' said Jess, hurrying for the door.

They got to Tiffany just before she dumped the entire contents on the front walk. 'Thanks, guys,' she said. 'That was a close one.'

'Are those strawberries?' asked Rachel.

Tiffany nodded. 'Kathy at the Trellis gave me a great deal. We can put them in our flowerbeds along with the rhubarb.'

'Strawberry and rhubarb pie,' said Rachel, her taste buds thinking ahead. 'For that I'll garden. Let's get started.'

They had to pull a few weeds to make room for the new plants, but the evening sun was warm. The hum of a lawn mower drifted to them from down the street. It felt so idyllic.

'We'll have jam from these next summer,' Rachel predicted as they moved on to Jess's yard.

'Too bad it's too late for this year,' said Tiff.

'We can still pick berries,' said Rachel. 'My friend Elsa was just telling me that she's got tons of raspberries, more than she knows what to do with. I think they'll be ready soon.'

That made Tiff smile. 'So we will get jam this summer.'

'Tons,' said Rachel. 'After the raspberries the blackberries will be ripe. Then in September the huckleberries should be ready to pick. Green Mountain is only five minutes from here, and I hear there are tons of wild huckleberries there.' Green Mountain was the closest thing Heart Lake had to wilderness.

'I don't like going out in the woods,' Tiffany said.

'We should at least give it a try,' Rachel urged.

Jess shrugged. 'I'm all for stocking the pantry, especially now that I've got a live-in cook.' Tiffany stopped planting to stare at her, and Jess grinned and said, 'My son. He still doesn't have a job, so I've put him to work for me. Until he finds employment, he is my slave.'

Rachel high-fived her. 'I saw him painting the house today.'

'It's getting done slowly,' Jess said. 'He's been pretty busy sending out résumés all week.'

'Sounds like things are improving at your house,' said Rachel.

'They'd be improving more if my husband found a job,' Jess said. 'Sometimes I wonder if we should have said yes to Ohio.'

'Don't even wonder,' Rachel said sternly.

Jess sighed. 'If I was thirty, I'd start a band.'

'You still could,' said Rachel, but Jess shook her head. 'OK, this will do it for me. Let's plant the rest at Tiff's place.'

'You should help me with my eBay business,' said Tiffany as they crossed the street with the last of the strawberries. 'My clock went for fifty-one dollars. And the figurine for thirty-eight.'

'Wow,' said Rachel. 'I'm impressed.

'So is Brian,' said Tiffany.

'At this rate you'll have your charge cards paid off in no time,' Jess told her.

Tiffany nodded. 'Except when the money comes, I'm going to reinvest it in my business. I have to have things to sell.'

That was hard to argue with, so the friends moved on to Rachel. 'Claire and Bethany are so excited about Girl Camp,' she said once they'd settled back in her living room. 'We start right after the Fourth. I bet I can get them to help us pick raspberries. We can all learn how to make jam together.'

The phone rang, but Rachel ignored it. The people who called her most were right here with her, which meant it would be for Claire. Sure enough, she heard an excited squeal from her daughter.

A moment later, Claire was bounding into the living room, phone in hand. 'It's Daddy.'

Rachel took the phone. 'Hi, Aaron. What's up?'

'Well, we're making some vacation plans over here. My parents really want to see the kids.'

His parents lived in New York, glamour capital of the world. Rachel quickly gave herself a good mother speech. *The children need to see their grandparents, and you can't deprive them of time with their father.* Her competitive mother side chimed in. *He's doing it again. He's buying their affection, the bastard.*

'We thought while we're at it we might as well take a quick jaunt down to Disneyland.'

'Because it was right on the way? Please.' Girl Camp shrivelled and died under the shadow of Disneyland. She was aware of her daughter hovering, her face a study in excitement and worry. Of course Rachel had to say yes, but not before she got a few things off her chest. She got up and left the room, not wanting to spill her bitterness in front of her daughter.

'When are you planning to take this trip?' Rachel asked.

'Actually, I'd like to leave right before the Fourth.'

New York, Disneyland. He could afford expensive junkets, but he fought her tooth and nail over things like orthodontist bills.

'You are such an incredible bastard,' she hissed.

'Because I'm involved with my children?'

'Oh, don't pretend you don't know what I'm talking about. I'm barely scraping by here, and do you help me at all?'

'Yes,' he said. 'Who is footing the bill for the orthodontist? Cute move, by the way.'

'Oh, my heart is bleeding. Don't think I don't know what you're trying to do. You're trying to buy our children's affection. Fine time to be worrying about their affections, by the way, after you split up the family.'

'You're the one who wanted a divorce.'

'You're the one who had the affair and made me!'

'Rachel, we can't go back.'

She rubbed her aching forehead. He was right, much as she hated to admit it. 'OK. Just take them.'

'I can only be gone for two weeks, but my parents want them to stay for the whole month. They don't get to see them very often.'

'Fine.' Her former in-laws would spoil the kids even more than her ex. But they were still her children's grandparents.

'Until the end of the month then,' she said. 'I want them back in August though. And if you're going to California, you have to promise to give them a couple of days in San Francisco with my mom.' What the heck? She might as well work a deal.

'I don't know if there'll be time,' Aaron hedged.

'You make time, Aaron,' she growled.

He heaved a long-suffering sigh. 'All right.'

'Good. I'll tell Mom to expect you. Goodbye, Aaron.'

She came back to the living room to find Claire looking hopeful. 'Yes, you're going,' she said, and forced herself to smile.

Claire squealed and hugged her fiercely. 'Thank you. You're the best mom in the world.' She ran down the hall, squealing all the way. The price for being the best mom in the world kept going up.

6

THE FOURTH OF JULY weekend was garage-sale heaven, which made up for the week of hell Tiffany had endured with Brian being home and grumpy. She returned from her bargain safari laden with treasures to add to the piles of goodies she already had in the spare room that served as Brian's home office. Not only had she taken over his office, she'd pretty much taken over the dining room, too, using her glass-top dining-room table as a staging area where she took pictures of her goodies before putting them up for sale.

'Good God, did you hit every house in Heart Lake?' Brian complained as he helped her lug her finds into the house.

'Just about,' she said.

With raised eyebrows, he held up a Christmas plate. 'Who's going to buy this in July?'

She took it from him and set it back down on the table. 'No one, silly. But it will sell like crazy in November.'

'Speaking of selling, what's been happening to the money from the stuff you already sold? I thought that was going to pay down the credit cards.'

'I'm going to. But I have to build my business first.'

Brian looked at all the items spilled across the table. 'Uh, I think you've got enough to sell between this and all the junk in my office. There's barely room for me in there now.'

'It's not junk. And yes, once these go, I'm going to have a big, fat wad of money.'

Well, hopefully. Some of her items had been sitting around like eBay wallflowers, with no bids and no watchers. She wasn't going to tell Brian that, though. He'd say she was wasting money they didn't have and tell her to quit, and she had no intention of quitting. She got as big a buzz watching her bids go up as she got when she was bargain hunting. And, talk about bargains—she'd found some great things for herself on eBay. That probably had something to do with why she wasn't turning a profit more quickly. But she was saving a fortune staying out of the stores. Talk about will-power.

Brian shook his head. 'If you ask me, this looks like one more way to get deeper in debt. How much of the money you've made has gone to pay down those credit cards?'

'I'm getting them paid down,' she hedged.

He raised an eyebrow.

'I am!'

Brian just shook his head and walked away.

Claire and David were having a great time in California. They'd done Disneyland and now were seeing the sights in San Francisco. 'But they miss you,' Rachel's mother had assured her when Rachel called to check in on Tuesday.

After talking to her mother, Rachel went online to see if any teaching positions had appeared on the school district's website. No miracles there. Her job situation was disheartening.

She ventured a look out of her window, but there was no sign of her own personal Mario Lopez today. Sigh.

She'd seen him in the crowd at the lake when she went with Jess and Michael to watch the fireworks on the Fourth. He had stood talking with two other men and a couple of Latina women. Those women had been drop-dead beautiful, and she'd wondered if he was with one of them. He must have felt her gaze on him because he'd turned his head and looked right into her eyes.

She'd felt a Roman candle-sized zing. Embarrassed, she'd quickly found a new direction to look, but it had been impossible to stop from sneaking another peak when she thought he wasn't watching.

It had also been impossible to resist imagining them sitting together on a blanket, her tucked safely against him with his arms round her. That had been a nice fantasy, but it was time to come back to the real world. She went to her office to dig into her finance book and come up with ideas for how to save more money.

The more she worked, the more inspired she became. In fact, she became so inspired she decided to start a blog. Why not chronicle what was happening with her and Jess and Tiff? After an hour of fingers flying over the keyboard, she had her first entry on her new blog site, which she had titled 'Small Change, Big Difference'. *Feel free to join the Small Change Club*, she finished. *Let's start a movement.* She smiled.

On her way to the kitchen for a cup of coffee her eyes strayed to the window again. This time she was rewarded with a glimpse of a paint can and a fine male posterior wrapped up in denim going up a ladder. Señor Gorgeous was back. This would be a good day to weed. Did she have any cute weeding clothes?

Deciding to channel her inner Jess, she dug out a sleeveless red top and the shortest pair of shorts she could find. Sadly, they fell into the mom shorts category. She cuffed her shorts to show off some leg, applied some red lipstick, and stepped out of the door.

She could certainly be out here all day and never run out of things to do, she thought as she walked through her backyard. Her flower beds were a mess. Probably the only neighbourhood eyesore bigger than hers was the house next door, and that was quickly changing. First the lawn, now a fresh coat of paint in a new colour—somebody was clearly putting some money into that place.

She casually strolled round to the side of her house. The hunk was at the top of the ladder, swinging that paintbrush like he meant it. And he was gloriously shirtless.

He was much too busy to notice her, but he couldn't stay up there for ever. When he came down, she'd say a friendly hello. She knelt daintily in front of the side flowerbed—at an angle so she could keep sneaking peeks at those rippling back muscles.

You're being ridiculous, she scolded herself. What was she doing out here? She started back round the house.

'Hot day, isn't it?' called a voice.

She turned to see Señor Gorgeous stepping off the ladder.

Maybe she wasn't done gardening after all. 'It is,' she agreed. What the heck. 'Could I offer you a glass of water?'

One of those dark eyebrows rose cynically, making her wonder what she'd said wrong. 'Sure. Why not?'

She nodded and walked into the house. In the kitchen she filled a glass with ice and water and hurried outside. She held out the glass with a brain as blank as a new whiteboard.

'Thanks,' he said with a nod, and took it.

She watched as he tossed down half the contents. Even his throat was gorgeous. 'I live next door.' Had she just said that? Of all the inane . . . 'My name's Rachel.' She held out her hand.

'Chad Alvarez,' he said, taking it.

Her mouth suddenly felt dry. *Think of something to say!* 'It's nice to see this place getting fixed up. Do you know who bought it?'

'As a matter of fact, I do.'

'Do they have children?'

He shook his head. 'Afraid not. The owner's single.'

'Oh. Is he going to live in it?'

'He's going to rent it out. As soon as he finishes painting it.'

She nodded. As soon as he . . . 'He? You?'

His smile was mildly mocking. 'Yeah. He me.'

'I thought . . .' She stumbled to a stop.

The eyebrow went up again. 'That I was the hired help?' He finished off the water, then handed back the glass. 'Thanks for the drink.'

'I guess you didn't need it since you could get one anytime you want.'

'It was a nice thought.'

'I get those sometimes. When I bother to think.' She managed an embarrassed smile.

He smiled back. 'I appreciate the neighbourly gesture.'

She managed a one-shouldered shrug. 'What are neighbours for? I guess I'll get back to my weeding.' *And go swallow my tongue.*

'Weeding can be thirsty work,' he observed. 'Maybe I should bring you some lemonade later.'

'Lemonade definitely tops water,' she said.

He nodded. 'I'll be ready for a break after I finish this side of the house. You can tell me about the neighbourhood.'

She noticed he didn't say anything about telling him about herself. Maybe he figured he'd learned enough about her already. *Horny woman who hits on helpless manual labourers.* Pathetic.

But later, when they sat on her front porch, drinking lemonade, he did show an interest in her. 'So, you have children?'

'Two. They're with their father for a few weeks.' *And I'm all alone in this big, old house.* 'How about you? Oh, yeah. Single. No children. And you do your own painting?'

'I like to do my own maintenance work. It keeps me in shape.'

'And what beautiful shape you're in.' Oh, no. Had she really just said that out loud?

He chuckled. 'It's refreshing to meet a woman who says what she thinks.'

'What do you do besides make over houses?' she asked.

'Real estate.'

'So I guess you heard about this house at your real estate office.'

'Something like that,' he agreed.

He must have sunk his fortune into the place and was now trying to make a go of it. 'Kind of a gamble, isn't it?'

'Life's a gamble,' he said, and took a swig of lemonade.

'Well, I admire anyone who's out there trying,' Rachel said.

'What about you? Are you out there trying?'

'The best I can. I'm a teacher, learning how to live on next to nothing.'

'Yeah?' he prompted.

She leaned back on her elbows and told him about what she was doing with Jess and Tiffany, finishing with the blog she'd started.

'I admire a woman who's willing to work for what she wants. Some women would be out there looking for a rich man to take care of them.'

Rachel gave a snort. 'Like we have a lot of those in Heart Lake.'

'Wealth is overrated anyway,' Chad said.

'So I hear. But I'm coming to suspect that most of the people who say that sort of thing don't have to live on a budget.'

'Everyone lives on a budget, even rich people.'

'Define *live*.' She shook her head. 'Don't mind me. I'm just your typical bitter divorcée.'

He didn't say anything to that. Instead, he downed the last of his drink. 'Well, I'd better get back to my painting.'

'Thanks for the lemonade.'

'Sure,' he said. Then he turned and walked back to his house.

As she watched him go, she wished she'd asked if he had any more lemonade. Except now that he knew she was a bitter divorcée he probably wouldn't give her another drink even if she paid for it. *Way to impress a man, Rachel.* Oh, what did she care anyway?

She hauled herself inside—it was too hot to work outside any more—and started pulling together information for her next meeting with Jess and Tiff. That kept her busy for the next hour. Now what? Jess was back from her job at the gym. Maybe she wanted some company.

Chad was nowhere in sight when Rachel came out. He'd probably moved his ladder to another side of the house. That was just as well. Out of sight, out of mind.

He was so out of mind that the first thing she said when she stepped inside Jess's door was, 'I met the new neighbour, and he's a total hunk. He looks like Mario Lopez, only better.'

Jess's eyes got big. 'No way.'

'Way,' said Rachel, following her into the family room. 'His name is Chad Alvarez, and he bought the house as an investment.'

'Never mind that part. Is he single?'

'As a matter of fact, yes. But let me tell you, nothing's going to happen.' Rachel gave a rueful smile. 'I think I scared him away. First I mistook him for the gardener. Then I told him I was a bitter divorcée.'

'Wow, girl, you really know how to make an impression.'

'I don't want a man, anyway.'

'Correction. You don't want a man like Aaron,' Jess said. 'You can't lose your faith in people.'

'I haven't lost my faith in people, just men.'

'You haven't been divorced that long. Give yourself some time. Your mojo will come back,' Jess predicted. 'If you don't get out and live a little, you *will* become a bitter divorcée.'

With those pithy instructions, Jess sent Rachel back across the street to be available in case Mario Lopez knocked on her door.

Rachel watched from the living-room window as he loaded up his ladder and paint cans. Then she saw him walking across the lawn towards her front door. Her hormones rose from the dead.

The doorbell rang, and her heart went berserk. She forced herself to walk to the door. She took a deep breath and opened it.

'Hot day out,' he observed.

Obviously. He had a nice sheen going on that gorgeous caramel skin. 'It is,' Rachel agreed. 'Would you like a glass of water?'

He smiled, appreciating her humour. 'No, I was thinking more like a drink. If you don't have anything going on this evening.'

'I think I can fit you in.'

'How about at the lake?'

'They serve drinks at the lake?'

'I do. I thought you might like a picnic.'

Of course, the man was in hock up to his eyeballs. He wouldn't exactly be a big spender. But that was OK with Rachel. 'You know, that sounds like fun.'

'How about meeting at the public dock at six?' he suggested.

'I could do that.'

He smiled at her and left for his truck.

She let out a calming breath as she watched him walk away. A picnic at the lake with the most gorgeous man she'd ever met. She shut the door, ran to the phone, and called Jess. 'I've got a date.'

'All right! Way to work it,' Jess approved.

'What was I thinking? Do you know how long it's been since I've gone out with a man?'

'It'll all come back,' Jess assured her. 'Like riding a bicycle.'

Rachel tried not to think of all the times she'd fallen off her bike as a child. Well, too late now. She'd accepted, so she had to go. After all, she wanted to be on good terms with the new neighbour.

Very good terms, added her hormones.

7

TIFFANY WAS ON HER WAY home from the salon when the call came through. 'Rachel has a date,' said Jess, her voice urgent. 'With the gorgeous guy who bought the house next door.'

'Oh, no,' said Tiffany. 'She doesn't have anything to wear.'

'Tell me about it. We need to do a wardrobe consult.'

'Wardrobe consult? She needs a whole make-over. What time is her date?' asked Tiffany.

'In an hour.'

'Oh, my gosh! I'll be right there. Don't let her leave the house.'

Almost everything from Rachel's closet now lay on her bed. They were nice clothes, purchased back when she'd had some money to blow. Looking at them now, though, nothing seemed worthy of a date with a gorgeous man. She frowned at the sweater sets, slacks and jeans. The weather was too hot for jeans. It looked like the mom shorts were the best she could do.

Why the heck didn't she have hotter taste in clothes?

'I'm here,' Jess called from the foot of the stairs.

'Come on up,' Rachel called back.

Jess blew into the room, her head hardly visible behind a mountain of clothing that winked with sequins. 'Have no fear. Your personal wardrobe consultant is here to save the day.'

'You realise none of that is going to fit,' Rachel said.

'Hello,' called a new voice from downstairs.

'The rest of the make-over crew?' Rachel enquired.

'You need help,' Jess explained.

Now they could hear Tiffany running up the stairs. She burst breathlessly into the room and announced, 'I came as soon as I could.' She, too, had her arms full of clothes.

'Don't bother. Those are not going to fit either,' said Rachel.

'They might,' Tiffany said. She held out a pale blue camisole and a top to go over it. 'Here, try this.'

Rachel sighed, but obeyed. Tiffany and Jess studied her.

'I don't think that's your colour,' Tiffany said. She produced a black ribbed sleeveless top. 'Try this. I was going to sell it on eBay.'

Rachel put on the top.

Jess nodded approvingly. 'Now, that looks good. But what is she going to wear for shorts?' She held up the mom shorts Rachel had worn earlier. 'Is this the best you can do? My God, with legs like that, you're wearing things like this. You should be ashamed.'

'If my wardrobe is so bad, how come neither one of you said anything before now?' Rachel demanded.

'Duh,' said Tiffany. 'You didn't have a date with a hot guy.' She pulled a pair of shorts from her pile of clothes. 'Try these.'

'You're a petite. No way am I going to fit in those,' said Rachel.

'Just try them and see.'

Rachel struggled into the shorts. Of course, they were too small. 'My crotch is numb.'

Jess nodded approvingly. 'Tight shorts are a good look for you. You need to start showing off your assets.'

'My assets are about to split these shorts at the seams,' said Rachel.

'You look great,' Tiffany assured her.

'I can barely breathe,' Rachel said, and reached for her own shorts, making Tiffany shake her head in disgust.

Tiffany picked up a pair of Jess's black sequinned flip-flops and held them out. 'At least put these on.'

'They're going to be too small,' Rachel predicted, but she obliged.

Jess and Tiffany both checked out her feet. Both sighed.

'Told you,' muttered Rachel.

'Well, you can't wear those ugly sandals of yours,' Tiffany said. 'Jess's flip-flops will have to do until we can get you a consignment-shop make-over.'

That decided, they did a hair consult, refusing to let Rachel gather her hair in a ponytail. Then they made sure she put on gobs of mascara and lipstick and finally sent her out of the door.

'Have fun,' said Jess. 'And try to be a little mysterious. That's always good on a first date.'

'You so have to call us when you get back and tell us how it went,' Tiffany said.

'I will,' Rachel promised. Feeling like a high-school girl getting sent to the prom, she climbed into her minivan and left for the lake.

Chad was already waiting for her at the dock, holding a canvas grocery bag that bulged with goodies. He stood talking with the man who ran the boat rentals, a grizzled senior citizen wearing a baseball cap, plaid Bermuda shorts, and a Hawaiian print shirt. Chad was the picture of virility in his cut-off jeans and shirt.

'Hi,' he greeted her. 'How about a cruise?' He motioned to the row of swan-shaped paddle boats moored behind him.

'A cruise?' she repeated stupidly. Every time she looked at him her brain cells short-circuited. 'What girl doesn't like a cruise?'

'I guess we're good to go,' Chad said to the man. He walked to the nearest boat and deposited his bag of goodies, then climbed in after. The thing bounced in response like an oversized rubber duck.

It had taken Rachel most of her teen years to learn to manage her long legs. The little bobbing boat looked like a recipe for disaster. 'Where's the land version of this?'

He held out a hand to help her in. 'These are impossible to tip.'

She grabbed his hand and hopped into the boat. It rocked, and she lost her balance, tipping into her Sir Galahad and sending him backwards. They both landed on one of the turquoise plastic seats with an 'oomph', her stretched out on him like a clumsy lap dancer.

'Sorry,' she said, scrambling off, her face flaming.

'Don't be sorry on my account,' he said with a smile.

He started pedalling. She followed suit, and the little boat eased away from the dock, the paddles *clack-clack*ing as they went.

'Do you always take girls on a cruise on the first date?' Was this a date?

'Only the ones who I know will appreciate it.'

All right, it was a date. 'So, are you staying around here while you fix up the house?' she asked.

'I've got a friend with a place on the lake.'

Nice to have friends like that. 'When do you think I'll have some new renters next door?'

'Maybe by the end of summer. I'm going to spruce up the inside, and it will take time to find good renters. I'm pretty particular.'

'You've done this before?'

'A couple of times,' he said. Now they were out in the middle of the lake. Someone on the far end was water-skiing. He pointed to the skier. 'Do you do that?'

'Only when I have a death wish,' she said. 'We went to Lake Chelan a couple of summers ago. The kids and my husband—ex'—she corrected herself quickly—'did some water-skiing.'

'And you didn't?'

'It took a long time to get a licence to operate these things on the sidewalk,' she said, sticking out her legs. 'I wasn't sure how well they'd work on water.'

He gave them an admiring look. 'It would be a shame to damage something so fine. But you might be good at water-skiing.'

She could feel herself blushing like a kid at the compliment. 'Maybe. I've never broken anything though'—except her heart—'and I wouldn't want to start now.'

'Sometimes you have to take a risk. Otherwise you miss out.'

He stopped pedalling, so she did, too, and she watched as he picked up his canvas bag and pulled out a bottle of wine and two plastic glasses. 'I hope you like pinot grigio.'

'Love it,' she said, and held out the glasses so he could pour. Next came a baguette, cheese and grapes.

It was a veritable feast, but Rachel found she couldn't eat much. She had too many butterflies in her stomach. So she listened as Chad told her about growing up in eastern Washington, picking apples in the fall and cherries in the summer to pay for college.

'A degree in business, that's got to be good to have during hard economic times,' she said.

'I think the best thing to have during hard times is common sense, a good work ethic, and a certain amount of distrust.'

'Distrust?' Although Chad hadn't told her his age, he looked like he had a couple of years on her, which gave him plenty of time to develop a history and a wary attitude.

'If you don't protect what you have, you'll lose it,' he said.

She studied him. 'Isn't that a little cynical?'

'No, it's smart. Did you trust your husband?'

She took a healthy slug of wine before answering. 'Yes.'

He shrugged as if to say, 'See?'

'Not everyone is like my ex,' Rachel said.

'When it comes to money, most people are like your ex.'

'I take it you learned that from personal experience?'

'I have an ex, like you,' he admitted.

Hence the healthy sense of distrust. Had the ex taken him to the proverbial cleaners? Was that why they were in a paddle boat instead of in an expensive restaurant? Not that Rachel cared. A man who appreciated the simple things was more her style now.

'I suppose the only way to protect yourself from heartbreak is to become a hermit,' she mused.

'I don't think I'm ready to do that,' he said. 'Women are like fine wine. A man could live without them, but who wants to?' He smiled at her, making her heart do a complete flip, and they touched wineglasses.

'I don't want to be used,' she blurted. *Way to be mysterious.*

'Me, either,' he said. 'So it looks like we're on the same page.'

The longer Rachel and Chad sat in the paddle boat, the more perfect he became. They talked about movies. Of course, being male, he loved anything with action, but he also enjoyed films that were thoughtful and funny—just like she did. They talked about books. Chad enjoyed reading, and was a big fan of the classics.

The conversation flowed easily as they pedalled along. As they made their way back to the dock, he said, 'We need to have drinks again. Or maybe dinner.'

'I know the perfect place,' said Rachel.

'Yeah?'

'My house. Next time you work on your place, I'll feed you.'

'A home-cooked meal, that sounds good.'

And so, just like that, she had another date with a gorgeous man. She could hardly wait to tell Jess and Tiff.

A perfect man, a perfect date, a perfect day.

It would have remained so, too, if she hadn't decided to hop off the paddle boat and help moor the thing. Just when she was congratulating herself on her grace, one of her Cinderella-sized flip-flops did a slip-slop, and she lost her footing and went down into the water with an undignified screech that turned to 'urghlugggg' once she went below the surface.

She came up spluttering and barely able to see through a wall of wet hair. She made a clumsy grab for the two pairs of hands reaching for her and was caught and hauled back up to dry land.

'Well, there, missy, that was quite a feat,' said the same old man who had launched them.

Feat. Feet! Hers were now bare. 'My flip-flops!' Or, rather, Jess's.

There they went, slowly drifting away.

She'd barely spoken before Chad slipped into the water and swam for them with Olympic star grace. Meanwhile, she stood on the dock, shivering and feeling like the world's biggest dingbat.

She knew she was blushing from her neck to her forehead. She tried to ignore it as he gracefully pulled himself back up on the dock. The man looked good dry, but he looked incredible wet, with his hair and skin glistening. Rachel's blush got hotter when he took her ankle and lifted her foot.

She watched as he slipped a flip-flop back on her foot, praying all the time, *Please don't notice that my foot's too big.* Either her prayer worked, or Chad was very gallant. He kept his mouth shut.

'Thanks,' she murmured. 'I'm sorry you got wet.'

'It felt good,' he said.

Chad walked Rachel to her minivan and opened the door for her.

'Sorry you fell in. I hope that didn't ruin the day.'

'Impossible,' she said, her gaze drifting to his lips.

'Good.' Then, before she could say anything, he kissed her. She felt it from her lips to her toes and everywhere in between.

'Thank you,' she murmured, not sure which she was thanking him for, the boat ride or the kiss or for looking hot in wet clothes.

'I'll see you soon,' he said.

She nodded, trying to wipe the goofy smile off her face and look mysterious, even though, after falling in the lake, it was too late for that.

Mom was right. Whenever one door shut, another opened.

'Have you got your money?' Tiffany asked Rachel before they set out on their bargain shopping safari.

Rachel held up a twenty-dollar bill. 'I do.'

'Twenty dollars?' That was what Rachel was spending on a new single-and-ready-to-mingle wardrobe? Tiffany was good, but she wasn't that good.

'This is all I'm going to spend,' Rachel announced. 'Anyway, I am who I am, and anyone I date may as well know it up front.'

'Absolutely,' said Jess, 'but you can still be who you are and have some hotter clothes.' She linked arms with Rachel and led her out of the front door. Tiffany smiled and followed them out.

Bargain Boutique was a fairly new business, located in Valentine Square. Bonnie, who ran the consignment store, was a regular at Salon H. Tiffany had alerted her that they'd be arriving with a bargain make-over in tow. She'd described Rachel in detail, and now Bonnie stood ready with an assortment of clothes for Rachel to try.

'Just like at Nordstrom's,' Tiffany explained.

'Only more affordable,' added Bonnie.

Tiffany moved over to the clothes Bonnie had set aside and started sorting through them. She pulled out a knit navy top, paired it with a hot-pink sweater, then handed them to Rachel, along with a sleeveless black satin top. 'Here. Try these on.'

Rachel took the items and stepped into the dressing room.

Meanwhile, Bonnie held up a halter top with a floral pattern in varying shades of red. 'I thought this would look good on her, too.'

Tiffany checked the price. Seven dollars. 'Absolutely.'

'Oh, yeah,' agreed Jess. 'That goes in the keeper pile.'

Rachel stepped out of the dressing room to model the black top. Combined with her long, dark hair, it turned her into a goddess of sleek. She struck a pose. 'What do you guys think?'

'Perfect,' Tiffany approved. 'Add some silver jewellery and a pencil skirt, and it will be totally hot.'

'Or she could wear it with her jeans and cute shoes,' added Jess.

Rachel next modelled the navy top and pink sweater. 'They look great,' Tiffany approved.

'I'll take them.'

Tiffany took some white shorts over to her. 'Try these on. They're only five dollars.'

'Then we need to get her some decent sandals,' said Jess.

'I'm afraid I can't help you there,' said Bonnie.

'That's OK,' said Tiffany. 'There's a great discount shoe store over in the mall.'

Rachel and Jess looked at her like she'd fessed up to planning a bank robbery. 'I don't think the mall is a good idea,' said Rachel.

'It's OK. I can handle it.'

'So can I,' Rachel said. She snatched the shorts from Tiffany without even bothering to try them on and marched to the counter. 'I'll write a cheque for all this, then use my cash to buy sandals. Will you take a cheque?'

'Sure,' Bonnie said. 'By the way, Tiffany told me about how you're helping each other with saving money. I think it's great.'

'Well, we're trying,' said Rachel.

'Think of all the money we just saved,' Tiffany told her, feeling immensely pleased.

'I'm not sure about the mall,' Jess worried as they left Bargain Boutique.

'If I even touch anything, you guys pull me away,' said Tiffany.

'Gladly,' said Rachel. 'We don't want Brian to murder you. Which he'll probably do if you come home with anything more.'

Rachel's words jogged Tiffany's memory. She suddenly had a vision of a small pile of packages sitting on the porch. She'd bought a few little bargains on eBay. It was nothing much, but Brian might not understand if he saw them. She checked her watch. Could she make it to the shoe store and then home before Brian got there?

Jess was still putting on her seat belt when Tiffany roared off down the street. 'Whoa,' Jess protested. 'Where's the fire?'

Tiffany slowed down to a semi-reasonable speed.

The Shoe Bin was Tiffany's favourite discount shoe store. 'We'll find the best bargains here,' she said as they walked in.

Rachel got stalled in front of a display of flashy flip-flops. Tiffany pulled her away. 'Come on. They'll have those on the aisle.'

Jess caught up with them and was carrying a pair of delicate silver sandals. 'How about these?'

'They would go great with my silver bracelet,' said Rachel. She slipped on the sandals.

'Oh, yes,' approved Jess. 'Those with jeans and your new top and the silver bracelet, and you're lookin' like something.'

They did look great. 'Perfect,' Tiffany approved.

'See. You can wear fabulous shoes and still be you,' Jess teased as they moved to the cash register.

'Maybe there's more to me than I realised,' Rachel admitted.

Tiffany tried not to pace as the clerk rang up her friend's purchase. Maybe she could still beat Brian home.

No such luck. His Jeep was already parked in the driveway when she pulled in. Maybe the packages hadn't come. She didn't see any on the porch. She let out her breath. Saved.

'This was great,' Rachel said. 'I'm now a beauty on a budget.'

'You mean diva on a dime,' said Jess, grinning at Tiffany.

'That, too.' Rachel hugged them both. 'Thanks, you two.'

'No problem,' said Tiffany, who was breathing easier. Since her packages hadn't arrived, there would be no problem at home.

But there was a problem at home. She slipped inside the door to see a tiny tower of boxes on the entryway floor. Uh-oh.

She wanted to run away. Instead, she called, 'I'm home,' trying to sound normal. She got no answer. This was not good.

'Bri?' She went through the living room and into the kitchen. She found him under the sink, repairing the leak she'd been after him to fix for the last two weeks. 'Oh, you're fixing the sink. Thanks!' Brian was home and happily puttering. All was well.

But he didn't say anything.

She tried another conversation starter. 'We were giving Rachel a make-over at Bargain Boutique.'

He came out from under the sink and set his wrench on the counter. He kept his back to her as he dried his hands on a rag. 'And what did you buy there?'

His voice sounded like steel. She sat down. 'Nothing.'

'No money left?'

Now he turned and looked at her. Tiffany felt suddenly cold. 'I . . .'

'You. Yeah, that about sums it up, Tiff. It's all about you. That's who you were thinking about when you bought that crap in the hall. It sure wasn't us. It sure wasn't about helping us get out of debt.'

'Brian.' Again, she couldn't seem to get anything else out although her heart was crying, 'Please don't be mad. Please love me through this even though I know I don't deserve it.'

'I'm moving out.'

'What?' *Oh, please tell me I'm dreaming this.* 'Brian, no.'

'I think we need time apart. I just . . .' He shook his head.

'Just what?' She could barely get the words out.

'I can't watch you do this. It's like being married to an addict.'

'I'm working on this,' she said, her voice pleading.

He sighed. Then he took his wrench and started for the garage.

'Where are you going?' she protested.

'To put this away.'

'I mean after.'

'I don't know yet. I'll let you know.'

She followed him and stood in the doorway, watching as he hung his wrench back in its place on the garage wall. 'So you want a divorce?' She could barely get the words out.

'I don't know that either. I'll let you know,' he said. He looked at her sadly. 'God, Tiff. We used to be so happy. What happened?'

Before she could answer, he slipped past her and walked down the hall to their bedroom. A moment later he was back with a satchel in hand. 'Goodbye, Tiff,' he said, and then walked out of the door.

She suddenly couldn't get her breath. What had she done?

'You shouldn't have bought that stuff on eBay,' scolded her conscience as she stood in the doorway crying.

Too late. It wasn't like she could return it. But she could sell it. She didn't need that stuff anyway. She didn't need a lot of things.

One thing she did need was Brian, and there was only one way to get him back. She had to kick her shopping addiction once and for all. All those things she bought hadn't filled up the empty places anyway, so there was no point wasting any more money on them.

It's all about you. Was Brian right? Was it all about her?

She marched to the hall and scooped up all her packages. These were all going up for sale. Before the year was over, those charge cards would be paid off, and Brian would want to come back.

What if he didn't? She went cold at the very thought. He'll come back, she assured herself. And when he did, he'd find he'd returned to a new woman. She wanted the Tiffany she used to be, the woman who was always happy no matter what, the Tiffany who didn't hide things under the bed or lie to her husband.

She'd get her husband back and her life back, and most important of all, she'd get herself back.

After her fun shopping adventure, Rachel's solitary dinner felt anticlimactic. The novelty of having time to herself had worn off, and she felt the absence of her children like a gnawing toothache.

Rachel sighed. Both her children were growing up so fast. This month was a taste of loneliness to come. *So you'd better build a life for yourself*, she thought as she went to her computer to make a blog entry.

Blogging was a small building block, but it was something. Rachel was pleased that she was already getting comments. 'I love the idea of making small life changes,' wrote one woman. 'I'm going to check your blog every day for tips.'

'I'm going to make time to cook more meals from scratch,' wrote another visitor. 'That should save me a bundle.'

A third woman wrote, 'I kept thinking I needed to make a ton more money to fix my life, but you've got me thinking that what I really need to do is learn to manage what I already have.'

Rachel couldn't help but feel warmed by what she read. To actually see women responding was heady stuff indeed. Maybe she should post a picture of herself in her new bargain clothes.

She paired her new black top with some jeans and slipped on her hot sandals. She liked what she saw in the bedroom mirror. 'You diva on a dime, you,' she said to her reflection. She grabbed her digital camera and snapped a shot, then looked at the image on the screen. A shot of her taking a picture of herself looked goofy. She needed a photographer.

She called Jess. 'Are you guys still eating dinner?' she asked when Jess answered.

'No,' Jess said. 'What's up?'

'Well, I was wondering if I could get you to take a couple of pictures of me in my new bargain wardrobe. I want to put them up on my money blog.'

'I'll be right over,' said Jess.

A moment later she was walking through the front door.

'Look at you,' she approved, taking in Rachel's outfit. She crooned a line from 'You Sexy Thing'.

'Yes, I am, aren't I?' Rachel agreed, pleased with herself.

'We should take several shots,' said Jess. She looked critically at Rachel. 'And we should get Tiffany to come over and fix your hair. Brian's Jeep is gone, so that means she's home alone, and she hates being alone.'

'Good point,' said Rachel, and snagged the phone.

Tiff must have seen her name on the caller ID because she didn't bother with 'hello'. 'Brian's left me,' she wailed.

Rachel blinked. 'What?'

'He . . . he . . .' The sentence ended in sobs.

'Get yourself over here right now,' Rachel commanded. 'I'll break out the chocolate.'

'What's wrong?' Jess asked, as Rachel started for the kitchen.

'He left her, the bastard,' Rachel growled.

Tiffany was in the house now. They could hear her sobbing her way to the kitchen. Jess went to meet her and returned with her arm round Tiff's shoulder. Rachel stuffed a chocolate in her mouth, led her to the family room, and settled her on the sofa. 'What happened?'

Between crying and chewing, Tiffany wasn't able to answer.

'I'm sure he's not gone for good,' said Jess.

'Why did he leave?' Rachel asked.

Tiffany swallowed. 'He found my eBay stuff.'

Rachel was confused. 'The things you're selling?'

'Nooooo. The things I bought.'

Jess and Rachel exchanged looks.

'My life's a mess,' Tiffany sobbed. 'Brian hates me.'

'No, he doesn't,' said Jess. 'He'll be back. He probably needs to cool down. That's all.'

'You have got to get yourself under control,' said Rachel, and Jess shot her a look that said, *This is hardly the time for a lecture.*

But Tiffany didn't take offence. Instead, she sniffed and nodded. 'I know. I don't need all this stuff. I really don't. I just need Brian.' This started a fresh round of sobbing.

Rachel patted her arm. 'That's a real epiphany. Have another chocolate.' The phone rang, and she picked it up. The number on the screen wasn't one she recognised. 'Hello?' she said uncertainly.

'Hi,' said a deep voice on the other end of the line. 'It's Chad.'

Excitement swirled inside her. Tiffany was still sobbing, so she moved out to the patio.

'Is this a bad time?' he asked.

'I have a friend having a crisis, but we're dealing with it.'

'Well, I wondered if that dinner offer was still open. I'm coming over to the house to do some work tomorrow.'

'Tomorrow will be fine,' said Rachel. 'How about around six?'

'That suits me. See you then.'

Tomorrow. She had a date tomorrow.

By the time Rachel stepped back inside the house, Jess had managed to calm Tiffany down from sobs to sniffles. 'I can't blame Brian for leaving me,' Tiffany whimpered. 'I'd leave me, too.'

'It'll be OK, Tiff,' Rachel said, rubbing her shoulder.

Tiff stood. 'I'm going home. I need to finish listing my stuff. I'm going to make money and pay off those credit cards if it kills me. I'm going to prove to Brian that I can do more than spend money.'

Jess said to Rachel, 'I'll take your picture now. Then I'd better get back.' So the pity party broke up, and Jess returned home.

8

THE FOLLOWING MORNING, before going to work, Jess got on the computer and checked out several musicians' classified ads, just for the heck of it. It was a long shot, but she knew that if she didn't at least try she'd regret it. On one, she found an interesting ad. *Wanted: keyboard player for all-girl band. Classic rock/country. Must be able to sing lead and BGV's.* Background vocals? Yes! She loved singing harmony. *No drugs, no booze, just music*, the ad concluded. That worked fine for Jess. What she wasn't sure would work was her age.

What the heck. She had nothing to lose. Knowing it was a long shot, she sent off an email extolling her talent and then ran to get dressed for a day of hopping around on mats at the gym.

The thought of getting to be in a band again got her blood pumping. As she climbed into the truck, the possibility of getting to play to a crowd again took her mind off the sad fact that she was not in her little red VW any more.

Miracle of miracles, there was an email waiting for her when she arrived home. 'Yes, we're still looking for a keyboard player,' wrote Amy Burke. 'Our band is called The Red Hots. We're practising tomorrow night at seven if you want to come jam with us. Let's see how it works.' She gave her address, then added, 'Bring your keyboard.'

Jess suddenly felt sick. The Red Hots? She was more lukewarm. They'd take one look at her and laugh her out of the room. Her keyboard didn't look any better. It was an ancient Casio that had been hot stuff back when the pterodactyls flew. Did she want to show up for an audition with that thing in tow?

She chewed her lip. How fancy a keyboard did she need? It wasn't the instrument; it was the player. A good player could play anything. She'd make do with what she had, and if her equipment wasn't good enough, then this wasn't the band for her anyway.

Everything was ready for Rachel's dinner with Chad. The chicken had been marinating, and the barbecue was fired up. Her potato salad was done, and so was the tossed salad, and she had white wine cooling in the fridge. A freshly baked raspberry pie sat on the counter. The patio table looked pretty with her best dishes and flowers from Jess's garden.

She was wearing her new navy top with her new shorts and sandals, and Tiff would have been proud to see that she was wearing her hair down—no horsetail. The scene was set.

The doorbell rang, making her pulse jump. There he was. Good grief, she felt like she was fifteen again. She took a deep breath and hurried to the front door.

It was like opening the door on a work of art. In jeans and a simple tee, Chad Alvarez put Michelangelo's *David* to shame. A perfect body, a perfect face with the most mesmerising brown eyes she had ever seen, he looked too good to be true.

He held out a bottle of white wine. It wasn't the cheap brand she had chilling in the fridge. 'I hope this was a good guess.'

'Perfect,' she said, and took the bottle. 'Come on out to the kitchen. I was just about to put the chicken on the barbecue.'

'How about I put it on for you?' he offered.

'Great. Thanks.'

Chad slipped out onto the patio to man the barbecue, and Rachel opened the wine and put some Brie and crackers on the patio table. She handed him a glass, and he tipped it in her direction with a smile. 'Here's to a memorable evening.'

Her mind immediately played word association. Memorable? Kiss! Very good, said her hormones, and her heart rate jumped.

'You look nice, by the way,' he added.

She looked down at her hot self. 'I do, don't I? I found this outfit at Bargain Boutique.'

'You are a smart shopper,' he approved.

'I don't know about that,' she said, 'but a girl's got to do what a girl's got to do.' She shrugged. 'Sometimes I think it would be nice not to have to struggle with money so much.'

'Sometimes the struggling makes you appreciate it all the more when you get it,' he said, giving the chicken a turn.

'There is that.' She realised that, while her life was fast becoming an open book, she still didn't know much about him and what he did. 'So, do you struggle?'

He smiled. 'I work hard. Does that count?'

'I'd say so.' Having just invested in the house next door, his budget had to be tighter than hers. 'Kind of a tough market around here for selling real estate right now,' she observed.

'Things will turn around,' he predicted. 'They usually do if you wait long enough.'

She thought of her love life. 'I think you could be right.'

A few moments later, Chad judged the chicken ready to eat. She brought out a platter, and they set it on the table along with the rest of the food. He scored points by declaring her potato salad the best he'd ever eaten. And he earned her sympathy by admitting that he hadn't come off of the romantic battlefield unscarred. She'd already guessed as much on their date when he'd mentioned having an ex. He said he'd been single for several years.

'You never wanted to get back on the horse?' she asked.

'You get kicked hard enough, and it makes you think twice,' he admitted. 'It would take a very special woman.'

'Define *special*.'

'The right values, the right heart. I'm not in a hurry. Are you?'

After what she'd been through with Aaron? 'No.'

'But I'd be lying if I said I wasn't attracted to you and that I didn't want to take this relationship further.' He reached for the bottle of wine and poured more into her glass. 'How about you, Rachel? What do you want?'

She wanted her prince to come. She wanted to never get hurt again. She wanted to feel loved. She said, 'I want you to kiss me.'

Amy Burke, the leader of The Red Hots, had given Jess an address in the Shoreline area, which lay south of Heart Lake and north of Seattle. Jess had just loaded her keyboard in the back of the truck when Michael returned home from a late-afternoon interview.

'How did the interview go?'

'I've had better,' he confessed. 'I suspect they're going to hire from within.' He took in her tight jeans, ribbed black top and dangly earrings. 'Got a hot date?'

'Got a band audition.'

His brows drew together. 'Audition? When did this happen?'

'Well, I didn't want to tell you since I may not even be what they're looking for.'

'If you're not, they're nuts.'

She kissed him on the cheek. 'There's lasagne in the oven,' she told him. Then she kissed him one last time and got in behind the wheel. Maybe she wouldn't get the gig. Maybe they'd laugh her out of the room. She gripped the steering wheel and swallowed hard.

Jess was glad she'd allowed herself plenty of time to find where the band was practising since, even with the directions, she'd managed to get lost. But now she was standing with her trusty keyboard and amp at the front door of a split-level house in a middle-class neighbourhood. A boy's bicycle leaned against the garage, evidence that Amy Burke had at least one child. Jess rang the doorbell, and the chime started some sort of small dog yapping. Kids, dogs, and a messy front lawn—it reminded Jess of her own life a few years back.

'Killer, stop!' commanded a female voice. The front door opened wide, and there stood a pretty thirty-something blonde, holding a Chihuahua. 'You must be Jess.'

'That's me,' said Jess, trying to inject youth into her voice.

'I'm Amy. Come on in. Everyone else is down in the basement.'

Jess manoeuvred her equipment through the narrow landing and down the stairs. She wound up in a huge rec room that housed a battered pool table at one end and a band at the other. She quickly took in her possible future bandmates.

At the drums sat a skinny blonde who looked like she was barely into her twenties. The bass player stood chatting with her. She didn't look much older than the drummer. Jess took in the stylish clothes, maroon hair, the tattoo and the multiple ear piercings and suddenly felt old. These women were hip. They'd never want to play with her.

The bass player smiled at her. It was an open, friendly smile.

'Well, this is us,' said Amy. 'You obviously know who I am.' She motioned to the drummer. 'This is my baby sister, Kit Mason.'

The drummer saluted Jess with a twirl of her drumstick. 'Hi.'

'And I'm Melissa,' said the bass player.

'You don't even want to know her last name,' added Amy. 'Her husband's Czech, and none of us can pronounce it, not even her.' She motioned to a small cooler. 'If you get thirsty, we've got Diet Pepsi, Dr Pepper and Starbucks fraps. That's about as wild as we get. You saw the ad. We don't do drugs, and we don't drink when we're playing. Ever,' Amy added sternly.

'I'm cool with that,' Jess assured her.

Amy nodded. 'So, here's us in a nutshell. Melissa just had the big three-oh and a baby. Kit's not married, but she has a serious girlfriend. And me. I'm the fearless leader.'

'Bossy old bat,' added Melissa. 'We call her BOB for short.'

Amy pointed a disciplinary finger at her. 'Hey, I'm only five years older than you. Watch who you're calling old.'

If thirty-five was an old bat, Jess was the walking dead.

Amy went on. 'I've got two boys in grade school, so to keep sane, I do the band thing on weekends. We play a couple of clubs in Seattle. Mostly we do the animal clubs.'

Eagles, Elks and Lions—Jess had done her share of them, too. 'How did you all get together?' she asked.

'I started the band,' said Amy. 'I did time in Nashville trying to make it as a songwriter. I finally got tired of starving and came home. But I missed the music. Ya know?'

Boy, did she ever. Jess nodded.

'We met Melissa at Gig Land,' Amy continued. 'She was looking for a bass, and we were looking for a bass player.' She looked speculatively at Jess. 'You've had some experience, it sounds like.'

'About a million years ago,' Jess admitted. 'But I've missed the music, too. And my husband's been laid off, so I decided it was time to jump in again,' she finished, then worked up her nerve to add, 'One last time, before I'm too old.'

Amy gave a snort. 'Hey, look at Bonnie Raitt. You're never too old if you're good. So, let's see what you can do.'

With cheeks suddenly warm, Jess broke out her keyboard.

'Whoa, dude, that is a dino,' said Kit.

'It is,' Jess admitted. 'But I can still get some sound out of it.'

'Well, let's see,' said Amy, picking up her electric guitar. 'Know any Bangles?'

The eighties was Jess's prime time. 'Yeah,' she said with a confident smile.

They launched into 'Walk Like an Egyptian'.

'Not bad,' approved Amy when they'd come to an end.

Not bad? That had been a blast. Within a short period of time, they'd tried on everything from 'It's Raining Men' and 'Girls Just Want to Have Fun' to Carrie Underwood's 'Before He Cheats'.

'You're good,' said Melissa admiringly when they'd finished.

Amy said, 'You can play, girl, and you've got a nice voice. If you want to be a Red Hot, you're in. We've got a gig at a club downtown, and you can jump in as soon as you feel ready.'

Oh, yes, she wanted in. Jess left Amy's house buzzing.

Rachel and Tiffany were delighted when she told them that Friday evening as they met at Rachel's house to brainstorm cheap craft projects. 'We'll have to find a different time to meet since I'll be working Friday nights.'

'It's the end of an era,' said Rachel with a sigh.

'I suspect your Friday nights will be starting to fill up anyway,' teased Jess.

Rachel's self-satisfied smile said it all.

'Getting paid for something fun, that rocks,' said Tiffany.

'Getting paid for anything rocks,' said Jess. 'And speaking of money, how are your eBay bids doing?'

Tiffany beamed. 'I have bids on everything. So far, I'm over two hundred dollars, and my bids don't close until next week. As soon as the money clears, I'm writing a cheque to pay down my credit cards,' Tiffany said with a determined nod. 'Then, as soon as my credit cards are paid off, I'm getting a divorce.'

Oh, no, thought Jess. 'You don't want to rush into anything.'

'Believe me,' Rachel added, 'divorce is no fun.'

'Neither is being married to Brian,' Tiffany snapped.

'Maybe you guys should try counselling,' said Jess.

'We probably can't afford it,' Tiffany grumbled.

Rachel's phone rang, and Jess said, 'If that's a certain hunky Latino, tell him you're busy. And don't say it's us. It's good for him to think you're in high demand.'

Rachel wasn't much of a game player, but she did tell him she was busy.

'Then how about tomorrow night?' he asked. 'Dinner and dancing.'

'Dancing sounds great. If you want to come over, I can make dinner,' she offered.

'Are you thinking I can't afford a dinner out?' he teased.

'Yes,' she said truthfully.

He chuckled. 'Don't worry. I'll pick you up at six.'

'OK.'

'What have you got to wear?' Tiffany asked later as she and Jess and Rachel were poring over recipes for tea and coffee drinks.

Rachel felt mildly panicked. 'For going dancing? I don't know.'

'Let's go shopping in your closet,' suggested Tiffany. 'The diva on a dime says sometimes you already have great outfits. You just have to look at stuff with new eyes.'

'I don't think the diva on a dime has been in this closet,' Jess said, once they got there.

It was a little disheartening. Rachel's classic outfits were great for teaching, but they sure didn't say, 'Take me on the dance floor.'

'Look.' Tiffany pulled out the red floral halter top Rachel had got at the Bargain Boutique. 'How about wearing this and adding that beaded necklace you made last year, the one with the garnets? And you know, I've got the perfect skirt.'

'It'll be too short,' Rachel predicted.

'And the problem with that is?' Tiffany retorted, and disappeared. She was back five minutes later with a gauzy black skirt in hand. It was definitely short.

'And hot,' Jess assured her. 'You look great. Now you can go to the ball, Cinderella.'

Rachel had a hard time getting to sleep that night. *Cinderella*. Funny that Jess referred to the classic fairy tale. Were women hard-wired to want a happy ending, to long for a prince?

Chad Alvarez had the whole package: looks, charm, brains. She couldn't help wondering what she'd find when she unwrapped the package further. What kind of heart did he have? It wasn't too late to stop now, before she gave away any more of herself.

But by the time she sat in Chad's vintage Mustang, riding into the city, she'd lost her desire to get him out of her system. In fact, she was flying high. She had on a perfect dance ensemble thanks to her closet shopping expedition, she was out with a gorgeous man, and she felt sexy.

'You look amazing tonight,' Chad told her.

'Well, you look amazing every night,' she said.

He chuckled. 'I suspect you always say what's on your mind.'

'Your suspicions are correct. But you like that. Remember?'

He nodded. 'Yes, I do.' He smiled over at her. 'I haven't found anything I don't like about you.'

'Oh, keep looking. You will,' she said lightly.

They shot on down the freeway past Seattle, not exiting until they got south of it. In a little neighbourhood in a small town, they pulled up in front of a Mexican restaurant. 'They have the best food this side of eastern Washington here,' said Chad as they walked in.

Obviously. The place was packed.

But that didn't prevent the pretty Latina hostess from letting out a squeal at the sight of Chad and giving him a hug. '*¡Hermano!*'

Hermano. Brother? 'This is my sister, Maria,' Chad said. 'She and her husband own this place. Maria, this is Rachel.'

'*Bienvenida*,' said Maria.

'*Gracias*,' said Rachel. '*Agradable encontrarle*,' she added, hoping she was remembering her college Spanish correctly.

This made the woman's face light up. '*¿Usted habla español?*'

'*Poco*,' said Rachel. 'Very little.'

'Well, we are happy to have you here. Any friend of Chad's is welcome,' she added, giving her brother a look that Rachel didn't have trouble translating. Sis was obviously hoping her brother had found Miss Right.

Once they were seated and had ordered drinks, Rachel said, 'So you have family on this side of the mountains.'

'Only my sister and her husband. My parents and my little brother still live in Yakima.'

'She has a very traditional name. You don't. What's that about?' Rachel couldn't help asking.

Chad's easy smile tightened. 'It was my grandfather's name. My mother picked it in the hopes that it would make up for her marrying a Latino instead of a white guy.'

'Oh.' This was uncomfortable territory. 'Did it?'

'Nope. My dad had his own landscaping business, but in my grandfather's eyes he was always "the gardener".'

Rachel found her cheeks warming as she remembered that was exactly what she had thought Chad was when she first saw him.

He saw the blush and managed a half-bitter smile. 'Latino guy: gardener or illegal.' He shrugged. 'Stereotypes happen.'

Rachel sighed. 'Yes. You forgot another important one though.'

He cocked an eyebrow. 'Yeah?'

'Hot Latin lover.' She blushed as she said it.

He smiled. 'I like that one.'

'Me, too,' she said shyly.

Their waiter arrived with two margaritas in glasses big enough to swim in. 'My God,' said Rachel, looking at hers. 'If I drink all this, I'll be dancing on my lips. Are you trying to get me drunk so you can seduce me?' she teased.

'Do you think I need you drunk to do that?' he teased back.

There he sat, with those gorgeous brown eyes. 'Absolutely not.'

Later, as he moved her round the dance floor to the rhythms of a hot Latin band, teaching her how to salsa, her skin burning at the touch of his hand, she knew she was going to invest her whole heart in this man. She only hoped it turned out to be a safe investment.

Small Changes, Big Difference

9

THE SMALL CHANGE CLUB was now officially meeting on Saturday afternoons, and this Saturday the three friends were in Tiffany's kitchen, making jam from freshly picked raspberries.

Tiffany had assured herself several times that she was having a great day. It was actually her birthday. She was now twenty-five.

And separated from her husband and childless. Some happy birthday. She wanted her life back. She wanted Brian back, even though he obviously didn't want her. How pathetic was that!

She'd only heard from him once, and that had been a message he'd left on her voicemail telling her not to worry. He was taking care of paying the mortgage and utilities. There had been no call from him this morning.

Cara had a cake and balloons for her at the salon the day before, and she'd pretended to be happy, like she was doing now.

'I'm not sure this is saving us any money,' Jess observed, pulling the pot of bubbling berries, sugar and pectin from the burner. 'Jars and seals and sugar—jam doesn't cost that much at the store.'

'Of course we're saving money,' Rachel insisted. 'The berries were free. Remember? Plus we've got a start on Christmas.'

'I know my son will love getting a little basket of jams,' Jess retorted.

'Your mother-in-law will,' said Rachel. 'Speaking of sons, what's the latest with Mikey?'

Jess smiled. 'He seems more motivated now. He's actually going to some temp agencies on Monday. Hopefully, that will work better for him than it did for me.'

'With a degree in business, it should,' said Rachel. 'It looks like life is improving for all of us. I mean, financially,' she added, looking apologetically at Tiffany. 'And speaking of finances, how are your bids going?'

OK, here was something Tiffany didn't have to pretend to be happy about. 'Awesome. I made seven hundred dollars!'

'That is something to celebrate,' said Rachel. 'Speaking of celebrations, someone has a birthday today, and we have a cake from Sweet Somethings.'

'Your favourite,' added Jess as Rachel pulled out a pink cardboard cake box from the pantry. 'Lemon poppy seed.'

'Aw, you two are the best.' Everyone had remembered except Brian. Well, he probably just didn't care anymore. She blinked back tears, determined not to ruin her friends' sweet gesture.

Rachel lit the candles. 'Jess, you sing "Happy Birthday". I can't carry a tune.' Jess obliged, and Rachel added, 'Make a wish.'

Tiffany closed her eyes and wished for all her bills to be paid off. At least it was something she had a hope of making come true.

As soon as she'd blown out the candles, Jess said, 'And now, do you want to know what else we're doing to celebrate?'

'There's more?'

'We're going out tonight to hear Jess's band,' Rachel announced.

She wouldn't be alone on her birthday. 'Awesome.'

'Wear your dancing shoes,' said Jess as Rachel handed Tiffany a piece of cake.

Tiff took a bite of the cake. The lemon frosting melted in her mouth. Oh, yeah, this was going to be a good birthday after all.

'**W**hat are you doing right now?' Chad asked.

Rachel propped her cellphone between her ear and shoulder and walked to her closet to pull out her black top. 'I'm getting ready to go with Tiffany to hear my friend Jess play with her new band.'

'So, you'll be out clubbing with your girlfriends?'

'Yes, I will. And dancing and picking up men,' she teased.

'Picking up men, huh? Where is this club.'

She told him.

'I think I might have to show up to make sure no one comes along and steals your heart.'

'I'd love it if you came. I want you to meet my friends.'

'I'll see you later, then,' he said.

Sure enough, The Red Hots were finishing up their second set when Chad made his way between the tightly packed tables to where Rachel and Tiffany sat, nursing drinks. Actually, Rachel was nursing her drink. Tiff was already on her third.

He slipped into a chair next to Rachel and gave her a kiss, and Tiffany pointed at him.

'I thought this was going to be just the girls,' Tiff said to Rachel.

'I wanted to come by and meet Rachel's friends,' Chad said smoothly. 'Can you make me an honorary girl for the night?'

'I guess,' Tiff said grudgingly. 'It's my birthday,' she informed him. 'We're celebrating.'

Jess joined them now, eyes shining. 'OK, guys, what do you think?'

'You're great,' said Tiffany. 'An all-girl band, that's awesome. Who needs men?'

'She's having some problems with her husband,' Rachel explained to Chad. 'She's not usually like this.'

Jess turned her attention to Chad. 'I'm Rachel's neighbour, Jess Sharp.'

'I've heard a lot about you. Both of you,' Chad added.

'You'd better not break her heart,' warned Tiff. 'She already had one man do that, you know. You're all bastards.'

'That is an opinion not shared by everyone at this table,' said Jess. 'Don't let her have any more mudslides,' she said to Rachel.

'I don't want any more,' Tiffany retorted irritably.

Jess saw her bandmates starting for the stage. 'I guess I'd better get back to work,' she said. 'Thanks for coming, guys.'

A moment later the music started again with Jess singing Alicia Keys's 'Everything's Gonna Be Alright'.

'Want to dance?' Chad asked Rachel.

'Go ahead,' said Tiff, her voice dripping with resentment. 'Have fun.'

'This wasn't one of my better ideas,' Rachel said, once Chad had her in his arms. She looked over to their table. Tiffany was pouting now. Even pouting, she looked cute, and a guy in a baseball cap was already pulling up a chair next to her. 'She's not normally like this.'

'I understand hurt, don't worry.' He planted a kiss behind Rachel's ear, making her shiver.

She understood hurt, too. She didn't want to go there ever again. But where was this relationship taking her? Chad's arm skimmed her back, heating her skin. Surely, surely this was too right to go wrong.

Tiffany decided to stop being a pill. Better to have fun. She clapped and cheered for Jess. She ordered another drink. And she danced. And danced. And danced. 'You know,' she told her new number-one fan, taking his hat off and putting it on her head, 'tonight's my birthday, and I'm all alone.'

'Well, I can change that if you want.'

'I don't know what I want any more,' she muttered, punctuating her observation with a hiccup.

'Do you want another drink, birthday girl?'

'No, that's OK,' said Rachel, appearing out of nowhere. 'She's had enough to drink. It's time to go home.'

That was easy for Rachel, Tiffany thought as her friend hauled her off. Rachel had a home, with children. All Tiffany had was a house.

And it was dark and uninviting. No Jeep in the driveway, which meant she had no husband waiting to make up. She wished she'd remembered to leave a light on as she fumbled for the front hall light switch. There was something so creepy about an empty, dark house.

Suddenly she realised her house wasn't empty. A solitary figure was coming towards her in the dark. With a shriek, Tiffany grabbed the vase on the hall table. 'Get back!'

'It's me,' protested Brian.

Now that he was closer she could see that it was, indeed, him. She turned on the light and replaced the vase and let out her breath. 'I thought you were a burglar. What were you doing here in the dark? And where's the Jeep?' Maybe he'd thought sneaking into the house and scaring her to death would be cheaper than divorcing her.

'It broke down halfway here. I walked. I've just been sitting and thinking about what a jerk I've been.'

He walked here to get to her? Her heart melted. 'You did?'

'Aw, Tiff.' He pulled her to him and hugged her. 'I'm so sorry. God, I'm a bastard.'

His voice broke, and that was all it took for her to burst into tears. 'I thought you hated me.'

He picked her up and carried her to the couch, settling her on his lap. 'You should hate me. I'm the one who walked out.'

'I don't blame you for wanting to leave me. It's all my fault we're not pregnant. I can't do anything right. I can't even have a baby.' Saying it out loud ripped her heart in two.

'Tiffy, I don't blame you that we're not pregnant, and I want to be with you whether we have a baby or not.'

She started to cry again. 'I've been a terrible wife. I'm sorry I spent all that money. It's just that it . . . Somehow, finding bargains—it made me feel good about myself. For a while, anyway.'

He heaved a big sigh. 'We should have gone for counselling.'

'We couldn't afford it,' she said. Like they hadn't been able to afford fertility treatments. Except if she hadn't spent so much money, maybe they could have at least afforded counselling. What a mess she'd made of things. This thought put her in tears all over again.

'Don't cry,' urged Brian. 'Oh, baby, I'm so sorry.' He kissed her, moved her off his lap, then stood and held out his hand. 'Come on. Let's go to bed.'

Bed, with Brian. That was what she wanted.

The next morning they lay spooned together in bed, talking like they had when their life was problem-free.

'I'm sorry I wasn't there to celebrate your birthday,' he said.

'You're here now. That's all I care about,' Tiffany said.

'From now on, we need to remember we're in this for the long haul,' he said. 'We're a team. If you want to buy something—'

'I'm done buying things,' she said firmly, cutting him off.

'We still have to live. So if you want to buy something, we'll budget for it. We have to learn to stick to a budget, that's all.'

'And we have to be patient with each other,' she added.

'I can handle that if you can,' he agreed, wrapping an arm round her. 'I don't want to lose you.'

He'd already lost the old, money-wasting Tiffany. She was history now. The new and improved Tiffany was a keeper.

'**G**uess what I got,' Tiffany said as soon as Rachel and Jess walked through her front door. She had already happily announced to her friends that she and Brian were back together.

'Gee, let me think,' said Rachel. 'It's Saturday, and you've been hitting garage sales. Sooo, something to sell on eBay?'

'Actually, something for me,' said Tiffany. 'And Brian is OK with me keeping it cos he knows I'll save a fortune.'

Rachel and Jess exchanged concerned looks. This was the kind of reasoning that had got Tiff in trouble. She led them out to the kitchen. There, on the counter, sat an espresso maker.

'Ta-dah!' crowed Tiffany.

'That's a pretty big purchase,' Rachel observed.

Tiff frowned. 'I only paid twenty dollars, which is about the cost of five lattes. Not that I've been buying many,' she quickly added.

Jess's mouth dropped. 'You got an espresso maker for twenty dollars?'

Tiffany nodded eagerly. 'I've always wanted one. And the diva on a dime says this is the smart way to have lattes.' She held up a package of coffee. 'I got this on the way home. I'm going to make us mochas before we pick blackberries.'

Rachel spotted the bottle of coffee syrup. 'So you paid another eight for the coffee and probably another ten for the syrup.'

'It's still cheaper than going to The Coffee Stop all the time,' Tiffany insisted. 'Now, do you want a latte or not?'

'What the heck,' Rachel said with a shrug.

Tiffany opened the coffee. 'This is going to be so great, you guys,' she said. 'Just think, lattes every day for next to nothing.' They all stood watching the machine, like kids in an ice-cream shop, waiting for the server to hand them their cones.

She pushed a switch, and the machine came to life. Another minute and they were enjoying caramel mochas.

'You were right,' said Rachel. 'This is a great investment.'

'It's the only thing I've got in weeks,' Tiffany assured her.

'You're doing great,' said Jess, 'and we're proud of you. We're all doing great,' she added with a decisive nod.

'I'm feeling pretty pleased with us,' Rachel said with a smile. 'And just think, after today we'll have more jam for presents.'

'I'm keeping some of this batch for myself,' said Jess. 'Anything to help the grocery budget. I may even keep that blackberry liqueur we're going to make for myself, too. If Michael doesn't have a job by Christmas, I'll drink every drop.'

The party atmosphere fled the kitchen. Poor Jess. Heck, poor all of them, thought Rachel. The job offers hadn't exactly been rolling in for her, either, and Brian's job was still tottering on the edge of oblivion. 'He'll find something,' Rachel assured Jess.

Jess heaved a sigh. 'At least the temp agency is keeping Mikey busy. He and his friend Dan and another guy are going to get an apartment together in the city.'

'So life is good for the kids,' said Rachel.

'Thank heaven, because at the rate we're going, we may wind up having to move in with them.' Jess took her berry-picking bucket from the counter. 'Come on. Let's go scrounge up some free food.'

The three friends didn't have far to go thanks to a patch of berries at the far end of the development. After two hours of sweat, they had harvested a bumper crop. 'This should be enough to get half of Heart Lake bombed,' said Jess, as they walked home.

'We can freeze them and make the cordial in November,' said Rachel. 'I think the recipe said it needs six weeks to ferment.'

'I say we make some now and sample it,' said Jess with a grin.

'Good idea,' agreed Tiffany. 'Who knew it was so much work to save money? No wonder hardly anyone ever does.'

'But think of the fun we're having while we work,' Rachel reminded her.

Tiffany looked at her scratched hands. 'Yeah, fun.'

It was fun, Rachel wrote later in her blog, conveniently forgetting to mention the heat and the scratches from the stickers. *It's hard to describe how rewarding it feels to work together to help each other survive. This is what our grandmothers and great-grandmothers did when they canned together and had quilting bees. The work got done, and they kept their friendships strong.*

Rachel sat back to recheck her grammar and spelling. Good enough, she decided. Chad was taking her to his sister's restaurant for dinner and dancing. After that, she would change back from swinging single woman to mom. She could hardly wait to see her children, but she was going to miss the freedom she'd been enjoying. The irritants that were Aaron and Misty had been happily missing from her life, and she had lived in a romantic bubble. After tonight the bubble would probably burst, but, like Scarlett O'Hara, she'd think about that tomorrow.

Rachel's last ride in the bubble was perfect. Chad had arrived bearing a single red rose. Amazing how much the man could accomplish on little money. Chad's sister Maria had been delighted to see her again and kept them supplied with margaritas. And dancing with Chad had got Rachel hotter than a chilli pepper.

Remembering his kisses was enough to heat her up all over again as she drove to Sea-Tac Airport to fetch the children on Sunday.

Once she was at the luggage claim and saw them, all thoughts of romance were obliterated. Her babies were back!

David bounded up to her all smiles and energy. He'd grown at least an inch, she was sure of it. Even Claire was smiling. She had changed, too. Claire had a new haircut.

'Look at you,' said Rachel. 'Don't you look all New York?'

'Grandma bought me new clothes for school, too,' said Claire.

So much for getting a new haircut as part of Girl Camp. But, Rachel reminded herself, she should be happy her children had grandparents who could afford to spoil them.

'I'm starving,' announced David.

The stomach with legs had returned. Rachel tousled his hair. 'I figured you would be, which is why we're going to get hamburgers before we go home.'

'All right!' said David. Even Claire was still smiling.

All through the meal the children regaled her with tales of their adventures in New York. She listened and said all the right things, but her resentment grew. The children had spent a month living the high life thanks to Aaron and his parents. Now that they were back it was going to be burgers and budgets once more. It was unfair.

'Are we still doing Girl Camp?' Claire asked as the minivan sped down the freeway towards home.

'Do you still want to do it?' asked Rachel.

'Well, yeah,' said Claire in a voice that implied if her mother thought otherwise she was beyond stupid.

'Then we are,' said Rachel, and tried not to think about how pathetically her Girl Camp activities would stack up next to New York and Disneyland.

The following day, Girl Camp was in full swing, starting with Belgian waffles for breakfast and followed by egg yolk facials. Lunch was lemonade and egg salad sandwiches dressed up with fancy shapes prepared by Rachel and served by David, who agreed to be a waiter in exchange for his very own batch of peanut butter cookies. And in the afternoon Rachel taught them some salsa steps.

'Wow, Mom. When did you learn to salsa dance?' asked Claire.

'A friend taught me,' Rachel said with a smile.

'That was so fun,' Bethany enthused when her mother came to pick her up. 'What are we doing tomorrow?'

'Beading, and after lunch Tiffany's coming over to give you manicures and pedicures.'

'Wow,' breathed Bethany.

'You're setting the bar pretty high,' teased Bethany's mom.

No, setting the bar high was a month-long stay in New York, thought Rachel.

As the week rolled by, Claire and Bethany enthused over every activity she came up with for them. Of course, every day included some kind of girlie spa thing, and a craft of some sort. Three days Jess met them at the tennis courts as soon as she was done teaching gymnastics and gave both the girls and David tennis lessons. The highlight of the camp was on Friday. David, not wanting to dress up, ate early and escaped to shoot baskets while the girls enjoyed a gala dinner of hamburger stroganoff and biscuits that they had made themselves. They finished off with strawberries they had dipped in chocolate and sparkling cider served in Rachel's good champagne glasses.

'So, a toast,' Rachel proposed. 'To being a girl.'

'And to my mom,' added Claire. 'She's awesome.'

It was all Rachel could do not to cry as they all clinked glasses. She grabbed her camera and held it at arm's length, capturing the three smiling faces—two young, fresh, and hopeful, and one not so fresh, but hopeful all the same.

Dressed in fancy clothes they'd found at the Goodwill, the girls paraded to the living room to enjoy a teen chick flick. Rachel watched them with a smile. Girl Camp was a success. She'd expended little money, and what she had right now was priceless.

The movie was half over when Chad showed up at the front door, holding a pizza box. 'I was in the neighbourhood and thought I'd stop by and see how Girl Camp went.'

Rachel noticed that her son was already coming their way, the smell of pizza luring him like the Pied Piper's pipe. 'Hi,' he said.

'Hi,' said Chad, and introduced himself, offering a hand for David to shake, which, well-mannered child that he was, he did.

'What kind of pizza is that?' asked David.

'Four-cheese,' answered Chad.

'Awesome,' said David, following him into the house.

The girls weren't above taking a break from their movie to snag some pizza, so Rachel made introductions as they got glasses and plates from the cupboard. The girls wandered back to the family room to watch TV, and David joined them, sprawling on the floor.

'Would you like to go out on the patio?' Rachel suggested after she'd handed Chad a glass of lemonade.

'Sure,' he said, giving her an intimate smile.

As she followed him out, she heard Bethany ask Claire in a low voice, 'Is that like your mom's new boyfriend?'

'I guess,' said Claire.

'He's sooo cute.'

'He's OK.'

Rachel was happy to settle for OK. OK was a good place to begin. In fact, it was a perfect place since she had no idea what kind of ending her story was moving towards.

10

By MID-AUGUST Chad had found renters for his house, and Rachel had new neighbours. David was in heaven because he suddenly had two boys right next door who lived to shoot hoops.

There was no reason for Chad to stay in Heart Lake. 'I suppose you'll be moving on to build your real estate empire,' Rachel said when Chad called her later that week.

'Not yet. I've got the place on the lake for as long as I want.'

Ah, yes, the mysterious friend's house. Much as she and Chad had been hanging out together, he'd never taken her there.

Rachel imagined the place to be one of the little cabins left over from the days when the lake was an undiscovered summer getaway, nestled in among the trees, hiding from the finer homes built in the last fifteen years. Maybe his humble living quarters embarrassed him. Maybe he was embarrassed by his circumstances in general. All their dates had been fun yet inexpensive. Maybe she'd have to come right out and ask him about finances. He was always vague about his business, making it obvious that he didn't want to share. But times were tough for lots of people, and she didn't care how much money he made. She'd learned from Aaron that the size of a man's bank account was far less important than the size of his heart.

When he called to invite her family to the North County fair, she accepted, but said bluntly, 'Only if we pay our own way in.'

'Don't worry,' he assured her. 'I can afford it.'

'Can you?' she countered.

'If I couldn't, I wouldn't have asked you.'

She let him pay their way in, but once they hit the midway, she sent David and Claire to buy ride tickets with allowance money.

'Actually,' said Chad, 'I'm picking up the tab for the day.' He gave both kids a twenty-dollar bill.

'Cool,' said David.

'Thanks,' said Claire, smiling round her new braces.

Rachel didn't say anything. Instead, she stood bug-eyed while her children darted to the ticket booth.

Chad cocked an eyebrow. 'Why are you looking so surprised?'

'Because that's a lot of money.'

He smiled and put an arm round her. 'It's OK to splurge once in a while. And I figure since this is the first time I've gone out with you and your kids I should make a good impression.'

'In other words, buy their affection?' teased Rachel.

'Why not?'

'Because it's not necessary. You didn't need to buy mine.'

'That's one of the things I love about you,' he said, and gave her a kiss that sent her insides whirling. 'I suspect your kids are a harder sell,' he added. 'Come on. Let's get some tickets for us. I'm sure you want to ride the Ferris wheel.'

'And go through the fun house,' Rachel decided.

'And the roller coaster.'

'Not so much.'

He gave her a squeeze. 'It'll be OK. I'll hold on to you.'

She loved following Claire and David through the fun house, manoeuvring over shifting floors and standing next to Chad in front of mirrors that distorted their reflections. Riding the Ferris wheel felt like a scene from one of her romance novels as she felt herself whisked round, cuddled next to Chad. But as they sat behind Claire and David on the roller coaster, she experienced a very different feeling. 'I hate these things,' she muttered. Up and down, whipping round corners at breakneck speed, if something broke, if somehow the little train of cars disconnected from the track . . .

When the ride ended, she walked away on shaky legs.

'Let's go again,' said David, bouncing in front of her, grinning.

'I am never going on that thing again.'

'Aw, Mom. We still have tickets left,' David protested.

'How about we let them finish up, and I'll buy you a scone?' suggested Chad.

Much to her children's delight, she let him distract her with a simple cake wrapped round jam. She was so easy.

Later he bought her children hamburgers and cotton candy, and then he took them all to a concert featuring a popular country band. By the time they drove back to Heart Lake in his Mustang, it was dark. David was snoring in the back seat, Claire was texting, and Rachel was thinking how family-like this moment felt.

She could see this man as part of their family. Was that where they were going with this relationship? She hoped so.

'I'm going over to Sam's for a minute. He wants help timing his carburettor,' Brian said, giving Tiffany a kiss on the cheek.

'Have fun,' she said, logging onto her eBay account as he wandered off. She had things to do herself. Then she'd be off to Jess's house for her weekly finance pep talk. She could hardly wait to share how well her business was doing.

Up popped her list of current bids. Good. Everything was selling. Come fall, her first charge card would be paid off.

She was logging off when her phone rang. It was her mother, calling for her weekly check-in. Tiffany happily told her all about her latest money-making triumphs.

'Your father will be so pleased,' said Mom. 'Now I have some news for you. Cressie's pregnant.'

Her baby sister was pregnant? Cressie had only been married a year. How was that possible? 'Oh, wow. I'm happy for her,' said Tiffany. She was. She'd run right out and buy a present to prove it.

'It would be nice if you could call her. I think she was a little hesitant to tell you for fear of making you feel bad.'

'I can't feel bad that we're going to have a new baby in the family,' Tiffany said as much to herself as her mother.

'That's what I told Cressie.'

Tiffany felt like her throat was closing up, but she said, 'Tell her I'll have a baby shower for her.'

'You could tell her yourself,' suggested Mom.

'I will. But right now I have to go. I'm late for my money club.'

Tiffany managed to say the proper good-byes and I-love-you's, but by the time she hung up, she was close to hyperventilating. She'd be a supportive sister and a fab aunt. There was no reason to feel sorry for herself. She was happy for her sister. Happy.

'Where's Tiff?' asked Rachel as she and Jess settled on Jess's deck with their iced tea. 'I thought she'd be over here already.'

Jess checked the wall clock. Tiff was her usual fifteen minutes late. 'I'll call her.' The second Tiffany answered the phone Jess could tell she'd been crying. 'Oh, no. What's happened?'

'Everything's fine,' Tiffany insisted, her voice watery.

'I can tell. You'd better get over here right away.'

'Actually, I have to go run an errand.'

Jess covered the mouthpiece. 'She says she has to run an errand,' she reported to Rachel. 'She's been crying.'

'Keep her talking,' said Rachel, and took off.

'We could run errands with you,' Jess suggested.

'That's OK,' said Tiffany. 'I'll catch up with you next week.'

Jess was still scrambling around for a way to keep her talking when Tiffany hung up.

Tiffany had her bag and was at the door when Rachel walked through it..

'What's going on?' Rachel demanded. Her eyes narrowed at the sight of Tiffany's bag. 'Were you going shopping?'

'Just to get a baby present.' And . . . who knew what else? 'My sister's pregnant, and I'm so happy for her,' Tiff added, blinking furiously to keep back the tears.

'Come here, you,' Rachel said, and gathered Tiffany into a hug.

'I hate myself for being jealous,' Tiffany said. 'What kind of horrible woman gets jealous cos her own sister is pregnant?'

'You wouldn't be human if you weren't a little green-eyed,' Rachel assured her. 'Come on over to Jess's and have some iced tea.'

'I should get a present,' insisted Tiffany. She had to show Cressie how happy she was for her.

'Uh, no. Her baby's not due for months, right? So, come January we'll go to the children's department together and get something awesome on sale. OK?'

Tiffany took a deep breath. 'OK.'

'Now, do you need to call her?'

'I can't. I'll cry, and she'll think I'm not happy for her.'

'No, you won't,' Rachel said sternly. 'Because you're going to be thinking how much fun you're going to have spoiling your niece. Or nephew.'

Rachel looked her in the eye to see if she was getting through.

Tiffany nodded. She fetched the phone and dialled.

Her sister answered. 'Tiff, did Mommy tell you?'

'Yeah, she did. I'm so happy for you,' said Tiffany, and even as the words came out of her mouth, she realised she was.

'Did Mommy tell you I want you to be the baby's godmother?'

'A godmother?' Tiffany breathed.

'We had the ultrasound, and we think it might be a girl.'

'A girl.' Tiffany had always wanted a girl. 'Perfect.' She'd be the best godmother in the entire world.

'I'm so excited,' gushed Cressie.

'Me, too,' Tiffany said, assuring them both. 'I'm going to throw you an awesome baby shower. And names! I'll get you a baby name book. And I can help you set up a nursery.'

'You're the best sister ever. My child is going to be so lucky to have you for a godmother.'

They exchanged I-love-you's and I'll-call-you's, and then Tiffany hung up. 'Wow, I'm going to be a godmother,' she said to Rachel.

Rachel nodded solemnly. 'It's a huge honour.'

Tiffany nodded, internalising that. The main reason she'd wanted to be a mother was so she could have a child to love. She could give herself to her sister's baby. Cressie would share the love.

'You'll be a great godmother,' Rachel predicted. 'Come on. Let's go tell Jess the good news.'

Tiffany followed her friend out of the door, tossing her bag on a nearby chair as she left the house. She wouldn't be needing it.

'Back-to-school shopping season is almost here,' moaned Rachel, as the three women settled in for their weekly session.

'I thought Grandma had come through with the clothes,' said Jess.

'Only for Claire. I have David to outfit, plus school supplies.'

'I remember that,' said Jess. 'It adds up in a hurry.'

'At least I've got some kids lined up to tutor. That plus subbing should get me through for a while.'

'I bet Chad would help you if you really needed it,' said Tiffany.

'The king of the cheap date? I don't think so. Anyway, I wouldn't ask him. It wouldn't be right.'

'I don't see why not. After all, he did spend a fortune taking you guys to the fair,' argued Tiffany.

'And I suspect he paid for it big time.' Rachel shook her head. 'No, I'd rather depend on myself than a man, anyway.'

'Do you have any idea how much longer he's going to be hanging out at his friend's cabin?' Jess asked.

Good question. 'I don't know.'

'Do you think he doesn't have any other place to go?' asked Tiffany. 'I mean, maybe all he has is this rental house. Maybe he's barely making it.'

Hearing someone else voice her suspicion was a little unnerving. 'I don't know,' said Rachel.

'Did he ever tell you who he works for?' asked Jess.

'Well, no. But I never asked,' Rachel said. 'I know he goes to the city a lot.' She saw Tiffany and Jess exchange worried looks. 'He's not a scammer if that's what you're thinking.' He couldn't be. She'd met his sister, for crying out loud.

'It just seems odd that he's so secretive,' said Jess.

'Maybe he's really rich,' said Tiffany, 'and he doesn't want you to know cos he wants to be sure you like him for him.'

'A man who's kind, hot *and* rich? Do they ever make them that way?' asked Rachel.

'I wouldn't get your hopes up,' Jess agreed. 'He's probably just uncomfortable talking about money. A lot of people are.'

'Well, I guess when the time's right, he'll show me his balance sheet,' Rachel said with a shrug. 'Right now we're just dating.'

She wanted it to be more, but she wasn't going to push. She had plenty of other good things in her life to keep her busy.

As school approached, Rachel got busier, signing the kids up for activities, meeting the students she'd be tutoring, and blogging. Her site was starting to get a lot of hits, and she was learning that it took effort to find new information and money-management tips to post. But it made her feel good to know she was helping others.

'Who knows? Maybe you can find a way to make this pay,' said Jess when the subject of the blog came up again.

They were sitting on the public dock with a picnic, helping Rachel celebrate the first day of school and enjoying the unusually warm fall day.

'I don't know how I'd do that,' said Rachel.

Tiffany snapped her fingers. 'You could write a book! You're putting up all these tips and stuff. Turn 'em into a book.'

'I'm no expert.'

'I don't know that you have to be an expert,' Jess said.

Tiffany gave a lock of blonde hair a thoughtful twirl. 'You could talk about how we started our club and what we've learned so far and all the things we're doing to save money.'

'There are all kinds of online sites for self-publishing now,' Jess continued, warming to the subject.

'It's a thought,' said Rachel. 'Speaking of saving money, Chad and I were hiking on Green Mountain with the kids last weekend. The huckleberries are almost ready to pick.'

Tiffany stopped twirling her hair. 'Is that where the bears are?'

'Lions and tigers and bears. Oh, my!' teased Jess. 'I can go any day next week. I'm done at the gym, so my mornings are free. And my income's been slashed in half, so the more free food I get, the better.'

'Does Michael have any leads?' Tiffany asked.

Jess shook her head sadly. 'His severance money is disappearing, and our medical runs out at the end of the year. If only we'd had some savings. I tell you, sometimes I feel like a walking example of what not to do.'

'Things will turn around. You'll see,' Tiffany said.

Jess heaved a shaky sigh. 'Sorry. I guess it's all starting to get to me. Michael isn't sleeping well. He tosses and turns half the night.'

'I wish there was something we could do to help,' said Tiffany.

'Just being able to talk helps. Thanks for listening,' Jess said.

'Hey, you should put this in your book, too,' Tiffany said to Rachel. 'Having a money support group with your friends is about more than money. It's the only way to get through hard stuff.'

'That's for sure,' said Jess.

They were right, thought Rachel. Brainstorming ideas for making extra income, working together to save money, and encouraging each other hadn't necessarily kept the wolf from the door, but it was helping them all feel like they could face him if he got in.

'Speaking of doing things with friends,' said Jess, 'when do we want to go huckleberry-picking?'

Tiffany's smiled dropped. 'I need another muffin.'

'I don't know about this,' said Tiffany as Rachel pulled her minivan into the parking lot at the foot of Green Mountain on a Friday morning.

'No bears are going to get us,' Rachel assured her. 'Instead of thinking about bears, think about that wild huckleberry jam we're going to be making for our families and friends and the pies we'll get to eat. And think of the money we'll save.'

'If we live,' Tiffany muttered, but she grabbed her pail and the big Tupperware bowl Rachel had brought and got out of the van.

A large map mounted behind glass and posted under a rustic little cedar roof showed hikers where to find various trails. The women didn't have to follow the main trail very far before spotting the berry bushes. The things branched out on all sides.

'Wow,' breathed Jess, taking it all in. 'It's a berry gold mine. Free food, here I come.' And with that, she left the beaten trail and charged into the thick of the bushes. Rachel followed after.

Tiffany lingered on the trail and picked from a nearby bush.

'You have to blaze new trails to find the bushes that haven't been picked,' Rachel told her.

Tiffany took a tentative step.

'Oh, come on, will you?' Rachel said in disgust. 'Nothing's going to get you. Do you see any bears?'

'Of course not,' snapped Tiffany. 'They sneak up on you.'

'Get out here and quit being such a weenie.'

Tiffany scowled and marched through the underbrush to join them. 'OK, fine.' She started picking. Meanwhile, Jess had slowly wandered off. 'Where's Jess?' Tiff asked ten minutes later, panicked.

Rachel looked around and frowned. 'Jess!'

'Over here,' came Jess's voice. 'I've hit the mother lode.'

'Come on,' Rachel said, starting off in search of Jess.

'We're getting farther from the trail,' protested Tiffany.

'We won't lose it. All we have to do is retrace our steps.'

A second later Rachel heard an 'oomph' followed by the snapping of twigs. This was quickly followed by an emphatic 'damn!' She turned to see Tiffany picking herself up and looking like a thundercloud. 'What happened?' As if she couldn't tell.

'I tripped over a branch.' Tiffany picked up her pail, which was now empty. 'And I spilled my berries,' she groaned.

'Oh well. You didn't have that many anyway,' Rachel said. 'Come on, now. Try to make this fun, will you?'

'All right, all right.'

Now Jess was in sight. She held up her big soup pot and tipped it so Rachel could see. The pan was already a quarter filled.

'Wow, you've made great progress,' Rachel praised her.

'I'd made progress, too, till I fell,' Tiffany grumbled, grabbing a branch and pulling a handful of berries off of it.

'Listen,' said Rachel. 'You hear that?'

'What?' Tiffany looked over her shoulder.

'Voices,' teased Jess in sepulchral tones. 'We are not alone.'

'People are hiking up the trail,' said Rachel. 'See? You're not really in the wilds.'

'Wild enough,' grumbled Tiffany, but she gamely kept picking.

Oh well, thought Rachel, *we can't all be nature girls*.

But as Tiffany's pail began to fill with berries, she got more into the spirit of the outing. It was a perfect September day, and the morning sun fell warmly on Rachel's shoulders, lulling her into a sense of peacefulness. So what if she was on a shoestring budget? She was in love, her children were healthy, and she had her friends.

She was so busy musing that she didn't hear the crashing in the underbrush until Tiffany screeched.

'Bear!' cried Tiffany. She threw her pail over her shoulder and bolted, starting a female stampede.

She pushed into Jess, and Jess's big pot of berries went flying as well. Jess didn't stop to mourn. Her eyes were the size of CDs as Tiffany swept her forward. The two of them collided with Rachel, who was still taking in the whole drama—the screaming friends, the lost harvest, the black shape bounding towards them. Down they all went like the Three Stooges in drag.

Tiffany scrambled up and bolted off in a direction that Rachel was sure wouldn't lead them back to the trail. Jess hauled Rachel up and was ready to follow.

Too late. The animal was upon them. It burst forth from the underbrush, and Rachel's heart stopped. Jess let out a shriek.

And the big, slobbery black lab jumped up on Jess, ready to play, and knocked her back down on top of a huckleberry bush.

'Moose!' called a male voice.

'Moose,' muttered Rachel. 'That is not a bear.' She reached down and hauled Jess back to her feet.

'Oh my God,' panted Jess. 'I almost had a heart attack.'

Now two young guys wearing jeans and sweatshirts came running up. 'Sorry,' said the one wearing glasses. 'Did he scare you?'

'Well, our friend is still running,' said Jess.

The spectacled guy grabbed the dog by the collar and snapped a leash on it. 'Sorry. He saw a squirrel.'

After apologising again and helping the women find their now-empty pails, the invaders moved off, and Rachel and Jess went in search of Tiffany.

'Tiff! It wasn't a bear,' called Rachel.

'I don't care,' Tiffany's voice echoed back to them. 'I'm done.'

They exchanged glances. 'I guess we are, too,' Rachel said.

'Let's stay a little longer and see if we can recoup our losses,' Jess suggested. 'She'll wait at the van.'

Jess was right. It would be stupid to abort the mission simply because one of them was a wimp. 'Hey, Tiff, wait at the van,' Rachel called. 'We'll be there in a little bit.'

'Fine. Don't blame me if you get eaten,' Tiffany called back.

Jess rolled her eyes.

'I'm not sharing my berries with her,' Rachel said as they started picking again. 'She who doesn't work doesn't eat.'

'You're a mean one, Mrs Grinch,' crooned Jess.

'That's right, and proud of it,' Rachel said with a smile.

They picked on for another forty minutes with no sign of a bear. Or a dog. Or any human life. It was now afternoon, and Rachel realised she was beginning to overheat. 'We'd better head back,' she said. 'I want to make sure I'm home in time to beat the school bus.'

'I think we've got enough berries for a few gift jars anyway,' said Jess.

Rachel started in the direction of the trail.

'Wait a minute,' said Jess. 'Where are you going?'

'To the trail?'

'Well, it's not that way.' Jess pointed in a different direction. 'We need to go that way.'

'That's not going to take us there,' Rachel insisted. 'I'm positive.'

Jess shrugged. 'All right. Have it your way.'

'Trust me,' said Rachel. 'I know what I'm doing.' Twenty minutes later, she said, 'All right. We're lost.'

'Great,' said Jess irritably.

'I'm sorry,' Rachel said humbly. 'I don't know how I could have got turned round. What way do you think we should go?'

Jess looked around. 'Your guess is as good as mine.'

Rachel heaved a sigh. 'Let's try this way.'

Off they went. This way didn't work any better than that way had.

Rachel had to be home for her children. She checked her watch. At the rate she was going, she'd be lucky to get home in time to make dinner let alone be there for them when they got out of school. And she had a student coming for a tutoring session at five.

Another ten minutes of walking didn't bring them any closer.

'Now what?' Rachel asked Jess.

'Scream for help?'

Why hadn't she thought of that? 'Great idea.' Tiff was at the van. They could follow her voice and find their way back.

'Tiffany!' they both screamed.

No answer.

They looked at each other. Rachel saw her own panic reflected in Jess's eyes.

'Tiffany! Tiffany!'

Maybe a bear got her. 'Tiffany!' Rachel screeched.

Finally a faint voice echoed back. 'Rachel?'

'We're lost,' called Rachel. 'Keep hollering.'

They heard her again. 'Stay put. I'm coming in.'

Rachel collapsed on a stump and hugged her pot of berries. Jess fell onto another stump. They heard a crashing in the underbrush. Another moment and a black, four-legged form bounded into sight. Moose. A moment later the two college boys appeared, followed by Tiffany. Saved. They were saved!

'I brought help,' said Tiffany.

'Thank God,' said Jess. 'We've been wandering for hours. Why didn't you answer when we first called?' she demanded of Tiffany.

Tiffany blushed. 'Well, it was so nice and warm. I stretched out on the hood of a car and fell asleep. These guys actually heard you.' She smiled at one of the rescuers. 'Good thing they woke me up,' she added.

'We knew right where to find you,' said the one with glasses. 'Didn't we, Moose?'

The dog wagged its tail and barked.

'Just so you know how to get us out of here,' said Rachel.

'No prob,' said their bespectacled hero. 'Come on, Moose.' The dog bounded off into the huckleberry bushes, and the humans followed at a more sedate pace. Moose's daddy pointed to Jess's pot. 'That's a pretty good haul. What are you gonna do with all those?'

'Make jam,' said Jess. 'If you give me your address, I'll save a jar for you.'

'Sweet. My name's Ted, by the way. This is Mark.'

As they made their way to the parking lot, it became apparent that Tiffany had already pretty much shared their entire life stories.

'Your blog sounds awesome,' Ted said to Rachel. 'I'm gonna have my girlfriend check it out.'

It took them less than fifteen minutes to hike back to the parking lot. Rachel thanked their rescuers, and Ted and Jess exchanged information. 'Here's my number and my dad's,' he said to Jess. 'He's in HR at Microsoft. Have your son give him a call.'

'How cool is that?' crowed Tiffany as they waved goodbye to Ted and Mark.

'Very cool,' admitted Jess.

Even more cool, thought Rachel, was the fact that it looked like she'd make it home in time to meet her children off the bus.

'I can hardly wait to go home and drink a gallon of ice water,' said Jess once they were back in the minivan.

'I hope we're done picking berries for the year,' Tiffany said from the back seat.

Picking? Who had been doing most of the picking? In fact, who was responsible for the fact that they'd lost their first harvest and had to start picking again? Rachel was going to bean Tiff with her pot. She glared at Tiff's reflection in the rearview mirror.

'Don't do it,' said Jess, reading her mind. 'We have no place to hide the body.'

Tiffany looked from one to the other, perplexed. 'What?'

'Never mind. Just be glad we're letting you live another day,' said Rachel. But she'd be doing it without any of their precious huckleberries.

'Great last set,' Amy told the band as she unhooked herself from her guitar.

The party was over for another weekend, and the remaining hangers-on at the club where The Red Hots were playing were putting on their coats, ready to face the rainy fall night. Jess had forgotten how much she loved this life—the way the band fed off the crowd and then one another, the fun of watching people dance, the high of making harmonies. Too bad a girl couldn't really make a living doing this.

'We rocked this place,' agreed Kit. 'That piano lick you played on Amy's new song was dope,' she told Jess.

'Thanks,' Jess said with a smile.

'Are you coming to Denny's?' asked Amy.

'Not tonight. Some of us have a long commute, you know. Even going straight home, it'll be another hour before I'm in bed.'

Jess lowered her keyboard into its case. If she didn't get some sleep, she'd be a zombie on Sunday.

Jess got some sleep, but she was still a zombie on Sunday. She stumbled out of bed and made her way to the kitchen around ten, following the aroma of coffee like a bloodhound on the scent.

Michael was already up and parked at the kitchen table, checking out the newspaper want ads. 'How'd it go last night?' he asked.

'We rocked the house, of course,' she said, and poured a mug of caffeine. Strong, black coffee—the weekend warrior's friend.

He laid the paper on the table. 'What would you think about moving?'

She almost choked on her coffee. 'Ohio?'

He shook his head. 'Nope. That ship already sailed.'

'Then where?'

'My mom was hoping maybe we'd move in with her.'

Move to Seattle and live with her mother-in-law? Jess blinked. 'When did this happen?' Not that she had anything against her mother-in-law. Myra was great. But to up and leave their house and move back in with a parent at their age felt a little extreme.

'We were talking last night,' Michael said. 'The house and yard are getting to be too much for her.'

No surprise there. Michael's widowed mother suffered from arthritis, and wasn't in the best condition to maintain a two-storey, three-bedroom house with a good-sized yard.

It was hard for Jess to imagine herself living in that house on Magnolia with its decor that was caught in a time warp. Not that she had anything against pink bathrooms and powder-blue carpet and crystal chandeliers. They just weren't her. Of course, the idea of going bankrupt wasn't exactly appealing either.

'I know you don't want to move,' Michael said gently. 'But I don't know what the future holds. I'm thinking it might not be a bad idea to see if we can sell this place.'

'You could find a job tomorrow,' Jess protested.

'Jess, I don't know how long it will be before I get another job. I don't want to wait until we're broke to put a plan B in place.'

She willed her brain to think of the right thing to say. 'I hate that house.' This had not been the right thing to say. How had she let it slip out?

Michael's face fell, but he nodded gamely. 'Well, I wasn't sure how you'd feel.'

But he'd suspected. She laid a hand on his arm. 'I love your mom. You know that. But that's her home. It would never be mine.'

'She said you could redecorate.'

'That wouldn't be fair to her. She loves the place just like it is.'

Michael nodded and returned his gaze to the newspaper.

Michael didn't want to move any more than she did, she was sure of it. To suggest such a drastic measure, he had to be desperate.

Jess spent the next two days weighing her options. Which was better, being a bankrupt woman with a house in foreclosure or a noble daughter-in-law? When she looked at it that way, noble daughter-in-law suddenly didn't look so bad.

Once you say it, you can't take it back, she reminded herself. She thought of the fun times she'd had with Rachel and Tiffany and swallowed hard. Seattle wasn't all that far away. She could still come back to Heart Lake to visit.

'Let's put the house up for sale and see what happens,' she said.

That had been the right thing to say. Her husband smiled gratefully at her. 'I know you don't want to leave your friends.'

'It's not like I won't ever see them again,' she said, both to Michael and herself. 'We have to be responsible.'

On Monday night Laney Brown from Lakeside Realty came over to check out the house. Next thing Jess knew Laney had a six-month exclusive listing and was pounding a For Sale sign into their lawn. Laney had barely left when both Rachel and Tiffany were at the front door, wanting to know what was going on. Jess burst into tears, and they led her over to Rachel's house for a strong dose of chocolate.

Rachel was crying, too, before she even had the Hershey's Kisses out of hiding. 'I can't believe this. Where are you going?'

'To live with my mother-in-law.'

'Eeew,' said Tiffany, grabbing for the candy bag.

'It's OK.' Jess sniffed. 'I like my mother-in-law. But I hate her house, and I don't want to leave you guys.'

'At least you're only moving to Seattle,' said Tiffany. 'We'll still get together.'

'It won't be the same as having her next door,' said Rachel.

'I can still come up for our Saturday meetings.'

'And you haven't moved yet,' added Rachel.

'Maybe it won't sell,' said Tiffany hopefully. 'Except you need it to, don't you?'

'Yes, unless Michael miraculously gets a job.'

'Then let's hope for a miracle,' said Rachel.

A miracle happened all right. The house sold in two weeks.

They would have money in the bank. Plus Jess would be closer to most of the clubs where the band played. Why, then, did she want to cry? *You don't have to live there for ever*, she told herself. It would just feel like it.

'Tis the Season to Be Frugal

11

IT WAS THANKSGIVING WEEKEND, and the three friends had gathered at Rachel's house to start preparing their holiday gifts.

'Gosh, I miss this place,' Jess sighed as she stood at Rachel's sink, bottling the liqueur they'd made from the blackberries they'd picked over the summer. The women had been saving salad dressing bottles all fall and now a variety of sizes sat on the kitchen counter next to Jess, waiting to get filled with either berry syrup or liqueur.

'It's not the same without you,' said Tiffany, who was busy decorating their gift bottles. 'The new neighbours are so not fun.'

'Well, I have to use a pink bathroom,' said Jess.

'I think pink accessories are pretty,' said Tiffany.

'This isn't just accessories. Everything's pink: tiles, tub, shower curtain, even the toilet paper. It's like taking a bath inside a Pepto-Bismol bottle.'

'If I lived with my mother-in-law, I'd have to take Pepto-Bismol every day,' said Tiffany, wrinkling her nose.

'My mother-in-law is great, and she loves to cook, which is a good deal for me. The hardest part is Michael's not having found a job yet. Thank God at least Mikey is working full-time. Who knew getting lost in the woods would turn out to be such a good thing?'

'I wish you were going to be here for Christmas,' said Tiff. 'It's not gonna feel right without your Christmas open house.'

'I guess you'll have to carry on the tradition,' Jess told her. 'We'll come. Speaking of holidays,' she said, turning to Rachel, 'how was your Thanksgiving with Chad's sister and her family?'

Now, there was something nice to dwell on. 'Perfect.' Thinking back, the day was a swirl of laughter, music and spicy food. With the warm welcome, the games and the impromptu dancing, she had felt right at home. Surprisingly, so had her children.

'Christmas is coming. I bet you'll get a ring,' predicted Tiffany.

'If he can afford one,' teased Jess.

'He bought another rental house, so I guess business is picking up.'

'So, he's actually telling you something about his balance sheet? That's a good sign,' said Jess.

Everything about the life she was building with Chad was a good thing. She had yet to meet his parents, but she was sure that was coming soon.

'You know this is the first time in for ever that I haven't been at the mall doing the Thanksgiving weekend sales,' said Tiffany, putting ribbon round the last bottle of liqueur. 'I'm so proud of us.'

Jess smiled. 'Me, too. We're all doing what we have to do, and it's paying off. We just have to remember that this Christmas.'

'Anyway, Christmas isn't about stuff. It's about being with the people you care about and making memories,' said Tiff.

'So, we're going to have a nice, simple holiday this year and make lots of new memories,' Rachel concluded as she, Claire and David enjoyed a treat of Sunday-night popcorn.

Somehow, the atmosphere in Rachel's kitchen wasn't as glowing as it had been the day before with Jess and Tiffany.

'Does this mean we're not going to the *Nutcracker*?' asked Claire with a frown.

'I'm afraid not,' Rachel said. They'd made a tradition of going into the city and enjoying the Pacific Northwest Ballet's performance of the beloved masterpiece. 'I can't afford it this year.'

'But we always go,' Claire protested. 'It's so not fair.'

'I know,' Rachel agreed, nobly resisting the urge to remind her daughter that life wasn't fair.

'OK, fine,' Claire said in her best snotty voice. 'I didn't want to go anyway.' She shoved away from the table.

Rachel started to go after her daughter and then changed her mind. What was the point in chasing Claire to her room and promising something she couldn't afford to give?

There had to be some way she could take her daughter to the *Nutcracker*. She decided to poke around online. After a few minutes she'd found the perfect solution. Coeur de Danse, Heart Lake's dance studio, was putting it on, and for what they were charging, she could afford to do both the *Nutcracker* and the Christmas tea special that Sweet Somethings was running.

She left her computer in search of Claire.

Her knock on her daughter's door only brought a tearfully dramatic, 'I don't want to talk.'

'Not even if I told you I found a way for us to go to the *Nutcracker*?'

A moment later the door swung open. 'Really?'

'Almost really. I can take you to a local performance, and we can do Christmas tea at Sweet Somethings. Are you good with that?'

Claire's face lit up. 'Yesss!' She threw her arms round Rachel's neck and hugged her. 'Thanks, Mommy.'

'You're welcome,' Rachel said, hugging her back.

Claire pulled away and bit her lip. 'I'm sorry I wasn't very nice.'

Rachel raised her daughter's chin so they could look each other in the eye. 'You weren't, and I understand you were disappointed. But often we can't get what we want. I'm doing the best I can for all of us. I hope you know that.'

Claire nodded.

'Good.' Rachel hugged her again. 'We'll have a good time.'

'We will,' Claire agreed.

And they did. Claire loved the tea at Sweet Somethings, consuming every cookie on the three-tiered cookie plate, leaving it to Rachel to consume the cucumber tea sandwiches. The *Nutcracker* performance was amateur, but Claire didn't seem to care.

Later, Rachel wrote in her blog: *There are always frugal alternatives to favourite activities. You just have to look for them.*

Tiffany was literally dancing when she met Rachel and Jess at her front door. 'I paid off my first credit card!'

With squeals and laughter, the three women managed a group hug that turned Tiff's entryway into a mosh pit.

'Come on out to the kitchen,' said Tiff. 'Brian's got champagne.'

They found Brian standing at the counter, uncorking a bottle of modestly priced champagne. Nearby sat a plate of chocolate truffles. 'So how great is my girl?' he greeted Rachel and Jess.

'She rocks the house,' said Jess.

The champagne cork came out with a pop. 'I figured you deserve to celebrate,' Brian said, pouring champagne. 'I'm proud of you, Tiffy,' he said, and handed her a glass. She took it with pink cheeks, and he handed glasses to Rachel and Jess. 'A toast,' he said. 'To my wife, who's paid off a fortune and is priceless.'

'To Tiffany,' echoed Rachel and Jess.

'And to my friends, who helped me stay on track,' added Tiff. 'By this time next year the other one will be gone and we'll be debt free.'

'I guess it's not bad to have a card for emergencies,' said Jess.

'But Brian and I have decided it's better to have money in savings,' said Tiffany with the zealous enthusiasm of a new convert. 'That way we can earn interest instead of pay it.'

Rachel helped herself to a truffle. 'What I have in savings wouldn't earn me enough interest to buy one of these. But slow and steady wins the race. Hmmm. I think I'll put that in my book.'

'So, are you really gonna write one?' asked Tiff.

'Why not? Maybe I'll become the next Suze Orman.'

'Between Jess and her band and you and your book, one of you guys is bound to get famous,' Tiffany predicted.

'Never mind the fame. I'll take the money,' Rachel said.

Ten minutes later Brian took off for the gym, leaving the women to enjoy working on their latest craft. 'OK, I've got six garage sale teacups for our teacup candles,' said Rachel. 'Did you bring the votive candles?' she asked Jess.

Jess held up a little bag. 'Got 'em. And I brought my glue gun. Let's get to work while I'm still awake. I tell you, I can't stay up till two in the morning any more.'

'That's the price you pay for being a hot band chick,' Rachel said.

'Speaking of my band, who's going to come hear us play on New Year's Eve? I need to reserve space at the band table.'

'We are,' said Tiffany.

'Count me in, too,' said Rachel.

'And Chad?'

'Hopefully.' Who knew? He'd already warned her he'd be over at his parents' for Christmas.

She'd been disappointed when she learned Chad wouldn't be around. Secretly, she'd been hoping for a ring, which, of course, was utterly stupid since they'd only been seeing each other a few months.

Still, the night he came by the house before leaving town with a small gift box for her, she couldn't help thinking *ring*. Naturally, she had something for him, too—a bottle of her blackberry liqueur and a framed picture she'd taken of him when they'd gone mushrooming.

He seemed genuinely pleased. 'I like it.' He gave her a little squeeze. 'Open your present.'

She pulled off the wrapping paper and opened the box to find a pair of pink pearl earrings. 'They're beautiful,' she said.

'Do you like them?'

Of course, they were gorgeous. 'I love them.' *They're not a ring.*

And so what if they weren't? Did she need a ring to be happy? Did she need a man to be happy, for that matter? Really, she had to stop operating her life under the influence of romance novels. 'Thank you,' she murmured.

'And don't make any plans for New Year's Eve,' he added.

Because then she'd get a ring? Oh, stop, she told herself firmly. 'I already told Jess I'd come hear her band play. Want to join me?'

'OK, but how about dinner first?'

'I think I could swing it.'

He nodded, pleased. 'We'll make it a night to remember.'

What did that mean, dinner and a ring?

It means a new year, Rachel told herself firmly. And she was going to make it good no matter what happened on New Year's Eve.

The three friends had their own holiday celebration right before Christmas, a potluck lunch at Tiffany's house.

Gifts were bargain goodies selected with care. Jess was thrilled with the Cyndi Lauper poster Tiffany had picked up at a garage sale. 'Girls just wanna have fun, right?' said Tiffany.

'That's always been my motto,' said Jess, and hugged her. 'Thank you so much! Now, you two, open yours.'

They did and found twin pink glass piggy banks.

'This is so cute!' cried Tiff.

'Somehow, I thought it was fitting,' Jess said.

The fun gifts went on: a book Tiffany had found at a garage sale for Rachel on how to test her man's IQ, a flower ring made of sequins for Jess along with a children's cookbook Rachel had picked up at the Goodwill as well as a used book full of inexpensive crafts for Tiffany. The big present of the day was for Rachel from Jess and Tiffany.

Rachel pulled out the gift card for a haircut at Salon H and almost cried. 'Hey, we're supposed to exchange inexpensive presents.'

'I bartered with Cara,' Tiffany assured her. 'Anyway, we figured you needed a new look to go with your new man.'

'Speaking of your new man, did he give you anything for Christmas before vanishing to eastern Washington?' prompted Jess.

'Pearl earrings,' said Rachel.

'Can a ring be far behind?' Jess teased.

Rachel's shrug was nonchalant and, Jess suspected, totally fake. 'Who knows? Meanwhile, we're enjoying being together.'

OK, maybe Rachel was perfectly happy to drift along with no commitment. It wasn't Jess's idea of a wise way to run a relationship, but in light of past hurts she could understand the need to take their time. Love was such a gamble. Heck, life was a gamble.

Lately, it looked like Jess and Michael had gambled and lost. Reduced from never having to worry about money to living with her mother-in-law. Boy, had her fortunes changed in a hurry. But it was the season to be jolly, and that's what she was going to do.

When Mikey and Erica and her new husband arrived on Christmas Day, their arms filled with festively wrapped presents, Jess saw first-hand how rich she was. Her children loved her and were happy to be with her. They were all well and safe, and they were about to enjoy a holiday feast. Did it get any better than that?

She and Michael had warned the kids that this would be a budget Christmas, and they'd kept their word, limiting the presents to a gift card for each one tucked into a gift basket filled with their mother's homemade goodies.

'Wow, Mom. You really made all this?' asked Erica.

'Living proof that jam doesn't always come from the store.'

'I used to make my own jam,' put in Myra, managing a bit of motherly one-upsmanship. 'But I admit, I never tasted anything as good as that huckleberry jam you gave me,' she added, beaming at Jess.

OK, Myra might just live to see the new year.

'And so prettily wrapped. You always had a flair for that sort of thing,' Myra added, helping Jess remember why she did, indeed, love her mother-in-law.

Mikey gave his father a bottle of champagne. 'To celebrate when you get a job,' Mikey explained.

'Thanks, son,' Michael said. 'That was really thoughtful,' he added, and his voice broke. He got up and hugged his son.

Then Erica handed Jess a box. 'Here, Mom. Open this next. It's from Mikey and me.'

Jess opened the small chequebook-sized box and found, nestled inside some tissue paper, a gas card. She looked up, surprised.

'So you can go see your girlfriends at the lake,' Erica explained.

Jess burst into tears.

'Told you she'd love it,' Erica said to Mikey.

No, what she loved was her children.

The biggest present of all came inside an oversized Christmas card from Myra to Jess. Jess pulled out an estimate for a bathroom remodel from Seattle Bath. 'What?'

'All you have to do is pick the colours,' Myra said with a smile.

She'd said Jess could redecorate, but Jess had never believed she really meant it. Considering how much Myra loved her pink bathroom, this was the ultimate sacrifice. In addition to the card, Myra had written Jess a note on her favourite floral stationery.

Dear daughter,

I have always loved you, and you have always been a blessing. But never more so than these last few months. I can only imagine how hard it has been to leave the home you loved and move into another woman's house, but you did it without complaint. I can only hope that someday you get a daughter-in-law who is as good to you as you have been to me.

Jess was crying by the time she finished. It had been a miserable year with the money worries and having to leave her home. But it had also brought unexpected blessings, like an opportunity to live her rock chick dream and a chance to make precious memories with Myra. She hugged her mother-in-law and sent up a quick prayer of thanks for allowing her to become such a rich woman.

12

'DO YOU LIKE MY OUTFIT for New Year's Eve?' Tiffany asked, twirling in front of Brian.

He turned aside from his computer game to take in her backless black dress and silver heels with an appreciative eye. 'Oh, yeah.'

'Want to know where I got it?'

Wariness flitted across his face. 'I don't know. Do I?'

'Yes, you do. I went shopping in Cara's closet. And Cara's wearing my dress from last year. Am I good or what?'

'Yes, you are,' he agreed. 'Come here, you.' She came and perched on his lap. 'I like it even better when you're bad.'

She was just showing him how bad she could be when the phone rang.

'Let it ring,' said Brian, running a hand up her thigh.

'It might be important,' she insisted, and picked up.

'What is it?' demanded Brian, taking in her shocked expression.

Only the call of a lifetime.

You never told me where you were taking me for dinner,' Rachel said after Chad had got her settled into his vintage Mustang. She hoped she wasn't overdressed. She'd dug out some black velvet trousers she'd had for ever and teamed them up with her slinky black top and some rhinestone jewellery Jess had loaned her.

'I'm taking you someplace I hope you'll like,' he said. Instead of heading for the freeway, he turned the car towards Lake Way. 'I thought you might like to see my place,' he said.

'Oh, you mean where you've been staying.'

He gave her a cryptic smile and nodded.

As they drove, she could catch glimpses of the lake hidden among the trees. She'd often driven by the lake with a jealous eye, wishing she could live on it. Not likely, even if she had the money. Lakefront houses rarely came up for sale. Chad turned down a private gravel road, hidden among fir, alder and general forest tangle.

'Secluded,' Rachel observed.

He looked at her. 'Is that a good thing or a bad thing?'

'It depends on who your neighbours are, I guess.' She had liked her house, but she'd loved the camaraderie of the neighbourhood thanks to Tiff and Jess.

'I actually have nice neighbours,' Chad said, 'but I like the fact that we can't see into each other's places.'

'Oh, you get used to it,' said Rachel, thinking about all the fun she'd had running back and forth from her house to Jess's.

'You miss your next-door neighbour, huh?'

'There's an understatement,' said Rachel. The road ended, leaving them in front of a two-storey cedar home. She looked at Chad in surprise. 'This is your idea of a cabin?'

'It's only three bedrooms. But it's got a great deck.'

He took her in through the back door, and they passed through a combination mudroom-laundry room, then down a hall past a couple of doors which, she assumed, led to bedrooms. She caught a whiff of something spicy, probably their dinner, as she followed him through a den area complete with leather couch and chairs and a flat-panel TV. Then they were in a huge great room that housed a state-of-the-art kitchen, dining area and living room. Floor-to-ceiling windows framed a view of the lake. A fire burned in the woodstove in the corner of the room. The sofa and two chairs were sage microfibre, big and comfortable-looking.

'Wow,' Rachel breathed. 'Some cabin. I can't believe your friend has let you stay here so long.'

'We're tight,' said Chad, moving to where he had champagne chilling in an ice bucket next to the table, which was set for two.

Rachel followed him over, taking it all in as he opened the bottle and handed her a glass of champagne.

He touched his glass to Rachel's. 'Here's to the new year.'

'To the new year,' Rachel echoed, and they drank, watching each other over the rims of their glasses.

He took her hand and led her over to the couch. Once they were settled, he took the champagne glass from her hand and set it on the coffee table. Her heart began to flutter in anticipation.

'Rachel, I've got something I need to tell you.'

His serious tone of voice erased her happy glow.

'You need to know a few things about me.'

'What, you're a serial killer?' she joked.

He smiled and shook his head. 'I haven't been entirely honest with you, but before I shared more of my life, I wanted to be sure of what we were building together.'

'You're sure now?'

'I'm sure enough to tell you that this place doesn't belong to a friend,' he said. 'It belongs to me.'

How was that possible? He was broke. 'You?' she stammered.

'I was hoping you'd like it enough to want to move in.'

'Move in? With the kids?' she said stupidly.

'I figure you're a package deal,' he said with a smile. 'Do you think they'd like living on the lake?' Now he was reaching into the pocket of his jacket. Out came a little box.

This time she knew it wasn't earrings. Her shocked gaze flew from the box to his face.

He was looking at her with love and hope. He handed it to her, and she opened it with trembling hands.

There it was, the diamond ring she'd been dreaming of.

'Will you marry me?'

Say yes! 'There's still so much we don't know about each other. I thought you were poor, like me.'

He grazed her cheek with his fingers. 'I was, once.'

'So you own this house and . . . more?' This was too weird. The cheap dates, the secretiveness—it made no sense.

'Actually, I own several rentals. I'm far from poor, Rachel.'

She blinked. She was sitting on a couch with Prince Charming and staring at a gorgeous diamond. 'When you told me you were in real estate, I thought you meant you were a realtor, that you sold it.'

'I do. I buy, too.'

'Why didn't you tell me?'

'Did it matter? Did you need to know I was rich?'

He was rich. Tiffany's words from months ago popped into Rachel's mind. *Maybe he's really rich, and he doesn't want you to know cos he wants to be sure you like him for him.* Tiff had nailed it. 'I get it. We were doing a princess-and-the-pea-thing. You were testing me to see whether or not I'm a gold-digger.' Which meant he'd questioned her character. She went to stand in front of the window while excitement over Chad's proposal fought with her sense of outrage. 'I don't know what to say.'

He was behind her now, his hands on her shoulders. He turned her to face him. 'Come back to the couch. Let me tell you a story.'

She let him lead her back to the couch. She perched on the opposite end, facing him, and waited. There, between them, sat the ring, still in its box. It was silly to smart over the fact that he hadn't been more forthcoming with her. He'd been being cautious. So what? She'd felt cautious at first, too.

But she had told him everything about herself. And he hadn't trusted her. She frowned. 'So, once upon a time there was a young prince named Chad.'

'Who fell hard for a girl he met in college,' Chad finished. He suddenly became fascinated by the sight of the flames dancing behind the glass in the woodstove. 'He was quiet, a little shy. She was beautiful and had so much personality, so much life. Every day with her was like a party. He worked hard to give her everything she wanted.' Chad's expression turned sour. 'The harder he worked, the more she wanted, but he kept trying, thinking if he could become as rich as Bill Gates, then maybe she'd finally be happy.' Chad fell silent.

'And when he became as rich as Bill Gates?' Rachel prompted.

Chad turned and looked at Rachel now. 'I didn't. But I had a good chunk, and she took half when she left me for another man.'

His pain, so like hers, burned into Rachel's heart. 'I'm sorry,' she said softly.

Chad shrugged. 'I should have learned from that, but I didn't. Chita was the first; Monica was the second. We were together for almost eight years before it dawned on me that if I lost everything she'd be gone in a heartbeat. I haven't had a serious relationship since . . . until you.' Now his expression pleaded for Rachel's understanding. 'I had two strikes against me. I wanted to make sure that you wouldn't be the third. I wanted to find a woman who wants to be with me for what we can be together, not what we can buy together. I'm hoping I've found her.'

Rachel took the ring out of the box. She picked up his hand, turned it palm up, and dropped the ring in it. 'What do you think?' she asked, and held out her hand for him to slip the ring on her finger.

His smile split his face. 'I think I found her.'

And there, in the glow of the firelight, Rachel experienced a fairy-tale moment where she was kissed by her prince and offered the world. They finally came up for air, and drinking more champagne, they talked. And talked. And talked. When he finally remembered to offer her dinner, she found she didn't have much appetite. The only thing she was hungry for was Chad.

'Where's Rachel?' wondered Tiffany, looking around the club. Some revellers were dancing; others were sitting at tables, wearing funny hats. All were drinking. 'If she doesn't get here pretty soon, she's going to miss midnight.'

'And our big news,' Brian added, kissing Tiff's hand.

Jess and the band were on break, and she was sitting opposite them. 'Well, while we're waiting, I have some fun news,' Jess said. 'Guess where The Red Hots are playing in February.'

'Las Vegas,' joked Brian.

'Better,' said Jess. 'Heart Lake. So you guys can take turns putting me up on the weekends.'

'Oh, my gosh, that will be so fun,' said Tiffany.

'Hey, here comes Rachel with her boyfriend,' said Brian, pointing towards the door.

Rachel was wearing the same velvet trousers Jess had seen her in for the last three holidays, but she still looked elegant. In fact, she looked well beyond elegant. Rachel had the glow of a woman in love.

'What's that I see on her finger?' Tiff said, pointing. 'Oh, my gosh!' she cried, and jumped up from the table, ploughing her way through the crowd to hug Rachel.

'It looks like everyone has news tonight,' said Jess with a smile.

Sure enough, Rachel had a ring with a fat diamond to show off. Jess hugged Rachel and said how happy she was for her.

'Have you set a date?' asked Tiff after the men had been introduced and they were all seated at the table.

'We're thinking June.' Rachel smiled at Chad, and he smiled back.

'Let me do the music for the wedding,' Jess offered.

'We can do the flowers, too,' offered Tiff. 'And we can make the invitations ourselves. We'll do a diva-on-a-dime wedding.'

Rachel shot a look in Chad's direction, which Jess found hard to interpret. 'I don't think we want a big wedding.'

'Well, you still have to have flowers and music,' said Jess.

'And friends, which means you'll need invitations,' Tiffany said.

Rachel laughed. 'OK, you've convinced me. We'll do a diva-on-a-dime wedding. And I'll blog about it.'

'Just so you don't blog about the honeymoon,' said Chad as he signalled for the cocktail waitress.

'This calls for champagne,' said Brian as she arrived.

'I've got it,' Chad assured him, and ordered a bottle of champagne that Jess knew Brian sure couldn't afford. Big spender.

'While we're sharing good news, Brian and I have some,' said Tiffany. She was practically bouncing in her seat.

'You're having a baby,' guessed Jess.

Brian grinned, and Tiff nodded eagerly.

'Oh, Tiff, that's wonderful,' cried Rachel. 'When?'

'Next month.'

'Next . . . what?'

'We're adopting,' Brian explained. 'Tiff has an uncle who's a doctor. He has a patient about to give birth, and she's decided that she doesn't want to keep the baby. We're doing a private adoption.'

'My parents are helping us with the bill,' said Tiffany.

'So do you know if it's a boy or a girl?' asked Rachel.

'It's a girl,' said Tiffany. 'We're going to name her Grace.'

'I love that name,' said Rachel.

Tiffany smiled at Brian with tears in her eyes. He took her hand and held it. 'It seemed like the perfect name. Cos that's what I've been given a lot of lately, especially from my husband.'

The champagne arrived. Jess proposed a toast. 'To my friends, who are getting what they so richly deserve. Happy New Year.'

'Happy New Year,' everyone echoed.

It was midafternoon on January the 1st when Rachel's children came home from their sleepovers. She found herself more nervous than she'd ever been in her life as she set a plate of cookies on the kitchen table. Her engagement ring was burning a hole in her jeans. She hadn't had the courage to wear it. What she would do if her children didn't like the idea of her marrying Chad, she had no idea.

The doorbell rang, and she jumped. There's no reason to be nervous, she told herself as she let Chad in.

He smiled and gave her a fortifying kiss after he came through the front door. 'Where are the kids?'

'In their rooms, putting away their things. Claire, David,' she called. 'Come down here. We've got company.' She lowered her voice. 'I am terrified.'

'No need to be,' he said, and took her hand.

First they heard the thunder of feet on the stairs. Then Claire and David came into view.

'Oh, hi, Chad,' said Claire. Her tone of voice asked, *This is your idea of company?*

They'd done everything with him from mushroom-hunting to playing board games. He probably didn't qualify as company any more. Rachel hoped he qualified as family.

'Hey, Chad, wanna shoot hoops?' David asked eagerly.

'Maybe later,' Rachel said. 'Come out to the kitchen, you two. We need to talk about something.' The kids plopped down at the table, and Rachel got down glasses for milk to go with the cookies.

Claire eyed her mother. 'Is something going on?'

'You could say that,' said Rachel. How hard was it to come right out and say . . .

'Your mother and I are getting married,' said Chad, taking the whole decision of how to do this out of her hands.

David grinned and snatched a cookie. 'Cool.'

Claire looked at her mother, her eyes big. 'Really?'

'We want to,' said Rachel. 'Are you OK with that?'

Claire's brow furrowed. 'Um, where will we live?'

'How about on the lake?' said Chad.

Claire sat up instantly. 'On the lake? For real?'

'Awesome!' cried David. 'Do you have a boat? Can we water-ski?'

'Probably,' said Chad.

That clinched it. Rachel's offspring looked at each other like two lottery winners who couldn't believe their good fortune.

They weren't the only ones. Neither could their mother. 'Pinch me,' she said to Chad later that day, after he came in from playing basketball with David and the neighbours.

Chad looked appreciatively at her backside. 'I could do that.'

She slipped her arms round his neck. 'I never thought I'd fall in love again.' *I never thought anyone would want me.*

'That makes two of us,' he said, and kissed her.

'I still can't believe it,' Rachel said to Jess later that week as they talked on the phone. 'I feel like any minute now I'm going to wake up and be back in the real world of pinching pennies.'

'I guess you won't have to do that any more,' said Jess.

'Not so much, but Chad is definitely the millionaire next door, and I'll still be on a budget.'

'But a heck of a lot bigger one than you had before,' said Jess. 'And to think I was worried about him not having any money.'

'I'd marry him even if he didn't,' said Rachel.

'I know you would. Now, for the most important question: where are you going for your honeymoon?'

'We haven't decided, but it's looking like the Caribbean.'

Jess began to croon the Beach Boys' 'Kokomo'. 'Need someone to carry your suitcase? Oh, that's right. It's your honeymoon. Clothing optional. You may need to remind Tiff of that. She'll want to help you shop for an entire trousseau.'

'I have a feeling she's going to be too busy with her new baby to worry about my trousseau,' Rachel predicted.

Sure enough. Every time Rachel talked to Tiffany it was baby, baby, baby. Amazingly, Tiff hadn't gone overboard with spending though. She had found bargains on eBay to round out what her friends had given her at the baby shower Cara hosted at the salon.

'I can't believe it. Grace comes in two weeks,' said Tiff, as she showed Rachel the finished nursery. Of course, the pink room looked fit for a princess. Tiff's smile slipped a little. 'Do you think I'll make a good mother?' she asked in a small voice.

Rachel gave Tiff a hug, saying, 'Trust me. You'll be a great mother.'

Tiff sighed happily. 'Here I was so miserable last year, and now we're going to have a baby. Things sure can change in a hurry.'

They sure could. Rachel could hardly believe she wasn't dreaming. There was so much to decide and plan and do. And every day included Chad, which made every day wonderful.

January was coming to a close, and she was getting her teaching materials ready for an afternoon of tutoring when he stopped by. 'I know you're trying to get ready,' he said, 'but I wanted to drop off some papers for you.' He held out a fat, legal-sized envelope.

'Oh, what's this?' She opened it and slid out the papers.

'Just a formality,' he assured her. 'You don't have to sign it right now. Take your time. Read it over.'

She began to skim the first page. Phrases started jumping out at her. *Each party has separate property, the nature and extent of which is fully disclosed in the statements of assets and liabilities . . . Thereafter, each of the parties shall separately retain all rights in the property he or she now owns . . . each party hereby waives, releases and relinquishes any right, title or interest whatsoever . . .*

Rachel looked up, shocked. 'This is a prenup.'

Chad's dark skin couldn't hide the guilty flush. 'Yes, but like I said, it's only a formality.'

A cold chill swept over Rachel. 'No, it's more than that.'

He looked pained. 'Rachel, it's a safeguard, that's all. Please don't make this into more than it is.'

'I know exactly what this is. It's proof that you don't trust me.'

'Rachel,' he cajoled.

He moved to take her in his arms, but she backed away.

He looked pained. 'This has nothing to do with you. It's standard operating procedure when there's money involved. It's simply a legal document, like a marriage licence.'

'Not quite,' said Rachel. 'A marriage licence proves to the world that we're committed. This proves to the world that you don't trust me. I understand you've been hurt. But so have I. Remember?'

He threw up his hands. 'If you understand, why are you making a big deal out of this? If we're going to be together for the rest of our lives, what does it matter if you sign a simple document?'

'If we're going to be together for the rest of our lives, what does it matter if I don't?' she countered. 'I have to sign this for you to marry me, don't I?'

His hesitation gave Rachel her answer.

She could feel tears building up, but she kept her voice level. 'I guess we don't know each other as well as we thought, because if we did, you wouldn't be here with this. I loved you when I thought you had nothing.' Her voice broke.

'Rachel, don't.'

She longed to hear him say, 'Never mind. You're right; I'm being paranoid,' but the words didn't come.

She could feel her heart cracking. 'You may have a big bank account, but this is the only asset I have,' she said, putting a hand over her heart. 'I was willing to give it to you without any safeguards. I was willing to put everything I have on the line for this relationship. You're clearly not willing to do that.'

'That's not it at all,' he insisted. 'This is . . .'

'Insurance?' she finished for him. 'I guess in this day and age you need insurance. But I can't go there.' She pulled the ring from her finger and dropped it in the envelope, then pushed it at him, forcing him to take it. 'I'm sorry. I can't do this,' she managed.

The doorbell rang, and she opened the door to find her first student standing on the porch. Her storybook romance had just been destroyed, and now she had to go to work.

Good thing she hadn't quit her day job, such as it was, she thought bitterly. 'Goodbye, Chad,' she said.

'We'll talk later,' he insisted.

She shook her head. 'No, we won't.' What would be the point?

13

'WHERE'S CHAD?' David asked at dinner.

Rachel hadn't had time to process what had happened to her. How was she supposed to explain to her children? She took the coward's way out. 'He had some things to do.'

That satisfied David, but Claire was a little more observant. Taking in Rachel's red eyes, Claire asked, 'Did you guys have a fight?'

'No,' Rachel lied. 'Everything's fine.'

'Then where's your ring?'

The ring. Rachel stared at her bare finger. 'We've decided to wait a little.' Another lie.

David frowned. 'Does that mean we don't get to live at the lake?'

'That means I don't know,' Rachel said. After a reasonable interval, she'd tell the children that she'd changed her mind.

'Does that mean he's not even coming over?' David demanded.

'For the time being.'

David pushed his chair away from the table and stalked off.

'David!' Rachel called after him, her voice sharp.

'He's mad, Mom,' said Claire. 'He liked Chad.'

'Well, so did I,' Rachel snapped. Now Claire was looking hurt. 'I'm sorry,' Rachel said.

Claire got up, but instead of marching out of the kitchen like her brother, she came round to where Rachel sat and draped her arms round Rachel's neck. 'I'm sorry, Mommy,' she murmured. 'I bet you guys will make up.'

Rachel put on a brave front and gave her daughter's arm a pat and said, 'You never know.'

There was another lie. The chasm between Chad and her was too great to cross, and that horrible knowledge kept her crying into her pillow late into the night.

'**W**ell, good riddance, then,' said Jess, as the three friends sat in Tiffany's living room taking turns holding the baby.

Little Grace was perfect. With her blonde fuzz and rosebud lips, she promised to grow up to be as pretty as her mother. Who at the moment was wearing what all new mothers wore: dark circles under the eyes, neglected hair, and a towel draped over one shoulder. She gave Grace a kiss, and then took her to the nursery for her nap.

'I can't blame him for being leery,' Rachel said to Jess. 'Not after getting taken by two women.' She couldn't blame him, but she found she couldn't quite forgive him, either. He'd called twice since she returned his ring, but she'd refused to talk to him.

'Still, if you can't start out a marriage with trust, you're in trouble. I think that increases the odds that you'll fail,' said Jess.

'I don't have to worry about that now,' Rachel said bitterly. 'You know what's really bad? I still want him.'

Jess hugged her. 'I'm so sorry.'

Sorry didn't even begin to cover it, Rachel thought as the lump in her throat grew to unbearable proportions.

A moment later Tiff was at her other side, holding out a box of tissues. 'Things will work out. I know they will.'

'No, they won't.' Rachel glared at her friend to make sure Tiff got the message. *No false cheer wanted.* Tiffany pulled out a tissue and handed it over, and Rachel snatched it and blew her nose.

'You don't know that,' said Tiffany. 'If you guys really love each other, one of you will make the first move.'

'Then, it will have to be him,' said Rachel. 'I already passed his damned princess-and-the-pea test.'

Tiff's brows knitted. 'What test was that?'

'Loving him even when I thought he was poor. I mean, if that didn't prove I wasn't after his money, I don't know what would.'

'Signing the prenup,' said Tiff.

'Are you delirious? Why would I do that?'

'Cos you don't care about money and you love him,' said Tiff.

'You're right. I don't, and I do, and he should know that.'

'He probably does in his heart,' said Tiff. 'I guess he just wants reassurance. So, why not sign the stupid thing?'

'Why ask her to sign it in the first place?' argued Jess. 'If he trusts her, he shouldn't need her to sign a piece of paper.'

'But if she loves him, maybe she should be willing to prove it,' said Tiff. 'How bad do you want him?' she asked Rachel.

There was the most important question of all. Rachel thought about it long after she left Tiffany's house. She carried it round with her the next week as she filled in for sick teachers, tutored, did laundry, made meals and helped her children with their homework. What if she did sign that agreement? She didn't need his money.

But she did need his love. Ever since she'd given him back his ring, she had been walking round with a hole in her heart. Chad wasn't perfect, but he was as close as she'd ever come. If she wanted him, she was going to have to overlook his insecurity.

Valentine's Day was right round the corner by the time she finally went online. It didn't take her long to find some free prenup forms. She printed one out, filled in what she could, and signed it. Then she put it in a manila envelope along with an invitation to join her on that special day at The Last Resort to hear Jess's band play. As she left the post office to go sub at Heart Lake Elementary, she had a dark moment of doubt. What man would ask this sort of thing of a woman? What kind of love was so selfish?

She could only answer her questions with more questions. When a man asked this sort of thing, did he act because he was selfish or because he was wounded? And did she have it in her to heal him?

She hoped she did. In fact, she was sure she did.

Rachel hoped she would hear from Chad before Valentine's Day, that he'd rush over the minute he got the prenup and put the ring back on her finger. But he didn't rush over. And he didn't call.

As Valentine's Day drew nearer, she got more nervous, so nervous in fact that she actually finally went in to Salon H and had Cara cut and dye her hair. She even went to Bargain Boutique and bought a new dress: basic black, with beading. But still no word from Chad.

'You *are* coming to hear the band tomorrow, right?' Jess asked her the day before.

'I'm coming,' she said. It was her last hope. She had to be there.

Valentine's night she stood in front of her mirror, assessing herself. She half wished her kids were home to assure her that she did, indeed, look wonderful, but they were both at friends' houses. So that left only her.

'You look great,' she told herself. 'And you'll have fun tonight, no matter what.' Who was she kidding? If Chad ignored her invitation and didn't show, she was going to throw herself in the lake.

'Not funny,' she scolded her reflection. Then she grabbed her bag and left the house to meet her fate, whatever it might be.

The Last Resort was the closest thing Heart Lake had to a club, and it was hopping. The air was thick with the scent of every perfume and cologne known to man. Twenty- and thirty-somethings crowded along the bar, all dressed to kill, and couples and foursomes sat at the small tables, laughing and leaning in close, trying to talk over the band. The little dance floor was packed with Valentine lovers and The Red Hots were in great form. Jess looked like a superstar in her tight leather trousers and red sequinned top.

Rachel spotted Tiff and Brian and Michael holding down a table near the dance floor and wove her way through the crowd.

The music wound down as Rachel took her seat. 'Hi,' Tiff greeted her. 'I was beginning to think you'd never get here.'

Rachel checked her watch. 'It's only nine. The band just went on, didn't they?'

'Well, yeah,' Tiff admitted. 'But we can't stay all night.'

Brian smiled indulgently at her. 'The baby will be fine. She's with my mom.'

Rachel couldn't help smiling. She remembered those new-mother nerves. It had probably taken every ounce of Brian's persuasive power to get Tiff to come out.

Rachel looked around the room, but saw no sign of Chad. Disappointment settled over her like a cloak.

Now the cocktail waitress was at her side. 'Let me buy you a drink, Rachel,' Michael offered. 'What would you like?'

Arsenic, she thought, but she ordered a Chocolate Kiss martini.

Chocolate Kiss martinis were highly overrated. So were love songs, and it looked like the band was going to play every romantic rock song ever written.

The night would have been perfect if Rachel hadn't been alone, if she had hope that she wouldn't wind up alone for ever. But nothing was perfect. It had been almost forty-five minutes now, and there was still no sign of Chad. He obviously wasn't coming.

'I'm going to go, you guys,' she said to the others.

Tiffany looked panicked. 'No. You can't leave. We're . . . not done. Jess wants to join us when the band goes on break.'

'Don't go,' Michael added. 'Jess'll be disappointed if you don't stay long enough to say hi.'

Rachel resigned herself to her fate and took another sip of her martini. This had been such a stupid idea.

The band ended the song and launched into a new one. It took Rachel a minute to realise Jess was singing the old Beatles song 'Can't Buy Me Love'.

The song was half over when Rachel knew she had really had enough. In fact, if she stayed any longer, she was going to have a complete nervous breakdown. She'd call Jess tomorrow and tell her the band had been great. 'I really need to go,' she told Michael. 'Tell Jess I'm sorry. I don't feel good.' No lie. She was sick at heart. She picked up her bag.

Tiff grabbed her arm and looked at her with narrowed eyes. 'Don't. Leave.'

The song came to a screaming halt, and the crowd on the dance floor clapped and hooted. Jess spoke into the microphone. 'Happy Valentine's Day, Heart Lake.' More hooting and clapping.

Yeah, happy, thought Rachel. Here she sat pinned to her chair by someone who was supposed to be her good friend.

'We have someone tonight who has a special delivery to make and a special song request,' Jess continued. 'Where's Rachel Green?'

'Here,' called Tiffany, waving an arm while keeping one hand on Rachel.

Rachel felt a million eyes on her, and her face caught on fire. What was going on? She hadn't requested any song.

'OK,' said Jess. 'There she is. Go get her.'

And suddenly there came Chad, weaving his way among the tables to catcalls and clapping, a manila envelope in his hand. Rachel's heart went into overdrive.

He stopped in front of her and opened the envelope. Down drifted a shower of torn paper. He smiled down at her. 'You were right. We don't need this.' He pulled her engagement ring from his pocket and held it up questioningly.

Rachel could feel tears spilling from her eyes. She put a disbelieving hand to her mouth. Was this really happening?

'Take it,' called a female voice from the crowd.

Her heart was going to burst. She held out her hand, and he slipped the ring on her finger; then he pulled her to him and kissed her while it seemed like all of Heart Lake applauded their approval.

'OK, you two,' said Jess. 'This song's for you, so you'd better get out on the dance floor while there's still room.'

The band played Metallica's 'Nothing Else Matters', and Chad pulled Rachel to him. She was hardly aware of other couples drifting onto the dance floor to join them. 'I didn't hear from you. I thought . . .' she said.

'I was gone. I went to see my family and get my head screwed on straight. They can hardly wait to meet you, by the way."

So they were on again, just like that. 'Chad, are you sure?'

'I should be asking you that,' he said. 'I'm sorry I hurt you. I'm a fool. If I can't trust you then there's no one in this whole world I can trust. I love you.' And to prove it, he kissed her.

She kissed him back. God bless those romance writers.

The song ended, and the band went on break.

Tiffany was practically gloating when Rachel and Chad returned to the table. 'So, I guess you're staying after all?' she teased.

Chad squeezed Rachel's hand, and she smiled at him. 'Yes, I guess I am. And I suppose you were in on this,' she said to Tiff.

'I recruited their help,' Chad admitted.

Now Jess had joined them. 'It looks like we need to make a toast. Did you order the champagne?' she asked Michael.

Right on cue their cocktail waitress arrived with the glasses. After everyone had taken one, Michael raised his and said, 'To love.'

'And to second chances,' said Tiffany. 'Everybody needs one.'

'And to the third time,' said Chad. 'It really is the charm.'

Small Change, Big Difference

IT HAD BEEN NEARLY a year since Tiffany, Rachel and Jess altered their financial lifestyles. To celebrate, Jess had baked a cake. 'From scratch, no less,' she'd bragged. It was a little on the dry side, but Rachel and Tiffany had praised her for her efforts.

Now they sat at Rachel's kitchen table among bits of ribbon, stamping supplies and card stock, addressing the last of the homemade wedding invitations. This year a wedding, next year they'd be making invitations to celebrate a graduation. Jess was back in school finishing up her music degree.

Baby Grace sat on a blanket in the family room, laughing as Claire and her friend Bethany entertained her with the new toys Tiffany had snagged at a garage sale. Yells and hoots drifted in through the open kitchen window from outside, where Chad was playing half-court basketball with David and the neighbour boys.

'That's the last one,' said Jess, slipping an invitation into the envelope.

'It's funny, isn't it? Here you are marrying a millionaire, and we're sending out homemade invites,' Tiffany observed.

'That's how people with money keep their money,' said Jess. 'They're careful with it. And let me tell you, we've learned our lesson. The savings account is growing. Slowly,' she added, 'but slow is better than not at all. And if Michael's executive temp job turns into something full-time, we'll really be able to grow our rainy-day fund.'

'And maybe move back?' Tiff asked hopefully.

'I think I'm stuck in Seattle for a while,' said Jess. 'But at least I'm not stuck in a Pepto-Bismol bathroom. And I'm not worried about how we're going to make the mortgage payment.'

Tiffany shook her head. 'I can't believe how different my life is now from last year.'

'I need to do an anniversary blog post,' Rachel decided.

'And put it at the end of your book,' Jess advised.

Rachel grabbed a piece of paper and a pencil from her kitchen junk drawer. 'So, what do we want to say? Have you two got any great advice for my readers?'

'Just because you buy something on sale it doesn't mean you're saving money,' said Tiffany with a decisive nod. 'Oh, and things won't make you happy.'

Rachel smiled. 'I love that.' She looked expectantly at Jess. 'Got anything to add?'

'Budgets are our friends. And *save* is not a four-letter word.'

'How about you?' asked Tiff. 'What are you going to say?'

'You know, I'm going to have to think about that.'

Much later, after her friends had gone home and Chad and the kids were busy making his mother's recipe for enchiladas, Rachel sat at her computer, reading what she'd just written for her blog.

I've come to realise three important facts of life this year.
1. Cinderella can keep Prince Charming. A good man's love is all
any woman needs to make her feel like a princess.
2. The only person who can fix your life is you.
3. Small changes can make a big difference.

And that about summed it up.

Sheila Roberts

You write about what is near and dear to many women's hearts—family, friends and chocolate. Are these the most important things to you too?

Absolutely. And church. My faith is a big part of my life. And the people in my life are what make it wonderful. I think when a woman has good friends and close family she can face anything. Chocolate helps, too!

Small Change **highlights the global financial situation and its effect on everyday lives. Have you too made small changes to save money?**

For years. Most of my married life we lived on a very tight budget and I've come to learn that it's the small things that either do you in or help you. I firmly believe that you don't have to earn a large salary to live large. Helping women learn to live well and enjoy life on a budget is something I'm passionate about, and I can speak from experience since I've done it myself. Small changes really do add up to make a big difference.

What would your top tips on saving money be?

1. Budget. When you decide in advance where your money is going, you're mapping your way to financial success. It's hard to reach your financial goals without a plan. 2. Shop alone. Friends often encourage you to spend money you don't have on items you don't need. The exception to this rule would be to take along like-minded thrifty friends who will pull you away from temptation. 3. Find your financial Achilles heel

and protect it. We all have our weaknesses. Some of us spend out of guilt (I see a lot of working moms fall into this trap), some of us can't distinguish need from greed, others love to rationalise poor spending decisions. When you know your weakness you can take steps to change it.

Heart Lake is a fictional town but would you like to live there?

Definitely! There is something about that small town sense of community that can be hard to find in our busy, fast-paced lives. Heart Lake is actually a combination of the island town where we used to live and the little lake we live on now—both places I love, both with great people.

How do you relax?

I hang out with girlfriends or my hubby and play cards and games. In fact, as I answer these questions I'm anticipating the annual surprise birthday party I throw for myself every year, which will consist of playing lots of silly games and consuming cake and copious amounts of chocolate. I can hardly wait! When I'm not playing with my friends, I'm either out dancing with my long-suffering husband, reading, watching movies or writing songs with some of my music buddies. I love my life!

What keeps you awake at night?

Not much. I need my beauty sleep. Seriously, I try not to worry about anything. Worry never helps. Instead I try to focus on counting my blessings. And I take a good book to bed, manage to get in a few pages and then conk out.

Is there one special item you would save from a burning house?

The photo albums.

What's currently in your handbag?

Comb, lipstick, wallet, hanky, outdated grocery list, pens, business cards. I also carry a little booklet in there which I use to make notes, write down titles of books I want to read, or recipes, websites to check out, song titles, book ideas. You name it.

You used to play in a band. Did you sing or play an instrument?

I sang and played keyboards and had a great time.

Which song would be the soundtrack to your life?

Maybe *Fun, Fun, Fun* by the Beach Boys.

Is there one book that you would read over and over again?

Actually, if we're talking novels, several. One of my all-time favourites is *The Masqueraders* by Georgette Heyer. I also love Katherine Neville's *The Eight*, *The Count of Monte Cristo* by Alexandre Dumas and Jane Austen's *Pride and Prejudice* and . . . oh, that's right, I'm supposed to pick one. Seriously?

What's your top tip for life?

Be thankful.